I0644778

"We need more books like this from vital voices in culture like the brilliant Daniel Maritz and Hernu Maritz. A great story set within an exciting world that also honors God's story and plan."

—**Dallas Jenkins**, creator of *The Chosen*

"In *Lightborn: Dawn of Darkness*, Daniel Maritz and Hernu Maritz created more than just an engaging story—they revolutionized Christian media the way God intended. The story of Uldako effortlessly fills the reader's desire for adventure while still instilling within him or her a deep, powerful truth that points to our redemption in Jesus. The extreme care taken to craft a culturally, historically, and biblically accurate preflood world is unsurpassed in any modern novel. This story is safe to share with your family and friends who need to hear the gospel."

—**Joshua and Caleb Colson**, the *Bearded Bible Brothers*

"In their first book together, brothers Daniel Maritz and Hernu Maritz take the reader back to ancient Mesopotamia to the days before the Great Flood. The hero and his companions experience dramatic and spectacular adventures in an ancient landscape filled with strange and marvelous creatures. The authors succeed remarkably well in combining the biblical account of those early days with extrabiblical detail that brings the biblical narrative brilliantly to life. *Lightborn: Dawn of Darkness* is a gripping tale about personal and spiritual growth, great bravery, and enduring faith. Daniel and Hernu's captivating story makes for a great companion for all pilgrims on their way to the eternal city."

—**Willem McLoud**, PhD, scholar and author

LIGHTBORN™

Dawn of Darkness

Daniel Maritz & Hernu Maritz

HARVEST HOUSE PUBLISHERS
EUGENE, OREGON

Cover design by Tim Green, Tiny Giant Co.

Cover illustration by Kirk DouPonce, DogEared Design

Interior images © Tatyana Larina, sbayram / Getty Images

Map illustrations by Jason Edwards in collaboration with Harvest House Publishers

Interior design by KUHN Design Group

For bulk, special sales, or ministry purchases, please call 1-800-547-8979.
Email: CustomerService@hhpbooks.com

This logo is a federally registered trademark of the Hawkins Children's LLC. Harvest House Publishers, Inc., is the exclusive licensee of this trademark.

Lightborn: Dawn of Darkness

Published by Harvest House Publishers
Eugene, Oregon 97408
www.harvesthousepublishers.com

ISBN 978-0-7369-9469-9 (pbk)
ISBN 978-0-7369-9470-5 (eBook)
ISBN 978-0-7369-9588-7 (eAudio)

Library of Congress Control Number: 2026932601

Printed in the United States of America

26 27 28 29 30 31 32 33 34 / LB / 10 9 8 7 6 5 4 3 2 1

To our parents, Etienne and Trudie Maritz,
who raised us in the knowledge of God
with love, truth, and sincere faith.

To the Lord, who drew us out of darkness
and into His light, back to Himself.

And to all who seek the Light,
may He draw you close and lead you to walk
in the great story that He has written for you.

ACKNOWLEDGMENTS

A heartfelt thank-you to our God-given wives, Nikita and Theresa, whose support, sacrifice, and love carried us through the long nights of writing. Thank you for caring for our families and giving us the space to finish the first book of *Lightborn*. And thank you for still loving us even when we lived on coffee, forgot what day it was, and talked more about ancient stories and maps than real life.

To our brothers and sisters in Christ at DLM Christian Lifestyle and Ruach Entertainment, who supported us in more ways than we can list here.

A special thank-you to Jason Edwards, whose insight helped shape the novel in many ways, but also the future *Lightborn* game we hope to develop.

And finally, our deep gratitude to Harvest House Publishers for walking with us every step of this journey and helping us shape this story into an epic work that glorifies God.

AUTHORS' NOTE

The following tale draws on ancient Sumerian language and names. A glossary and character list are included at the back of the book for curious readers.

• • •

The events of this story are set in the world before the global flood, in a time when humanity did not yet possess the written Scriptures or the full revelation we have today. The people of that age interpreted what they witnessed through the limits of their understanding, shaped by what they saw, heard, and believed to be true. We don't fully know the extent to which God revealed certain truths to them.

Lightborn: Dawn of Darkness is a work of historical fiction inspired by the biblical account. While it seeks to remain faithful to Scripture, it includes content about imagined characters, dialogue, and events on which the Bible is silent. We also acknowledge there are different views about the identities of the Nephilim and the sons of God. Care has been taken not to alter or contradict what is written in God's Word, but to imagine how these events may have played out and been experienced by those who lived them. This is not Scripture. The Bible alone is the inspired and final authority, and readers are encouraged to test all things against it.

Eagle Kingdom
Mountain of Il
Great Abba-Lugal
Zagros Mountains
(E-šarra)
(Nippur)
(Kis)
(Shuruppak)
Zerach Fish-Camp
(Umma)
Tigris

(KI-EN-GI)
Jabal, Dumu of Lamech
(Bad-Tibira)
(Magan)
(Unugki)
Arad Mine
-Euphrates-
Good Farmlands
Jabal Arena
Narath
(Eridu)
Arad Camp
Tree Camp
Serpent Kingdom

Preface

In a time long forgotten, when the echoes of ancient tales still lingered, the world was a canvas painted with strange creatures—ancient dragons, humans whose lifespans stretched over many centuries, and flora that whispered secrets in the language of leaves. They found their existence under the light of day and the dark of night—a symbolic battleground depicting the true nature of this mysterious world, a perpetual struggle between the forces of light and darkness. Humans carved their existence amidst the harsh landscapes of primal beasts.

Survival safe camps unfolded as humanity learned to live protected among the Behemoth's roar and the Leviathan's dominance. Yet, the most dangerous creature in this age wasn't a dragon, but mankind itself. The real darkness lurked within the hearts of men.

In the primordial lineage, Adam and Eve, shaped from the dust and filled with the breath of *Il*, eked out a fragile existence. From their endurance, lineages flourished—building cities and villages in defiance of nature's ferocity.

Adam and Eve's lineage, marked by light and darkness, unfolded a saga of wanderers and cities across all the lands of the ancient world.

A great evil is about to descend upon humanity—fallen gods called the *anunnaki*, with a dark mission: to birth through females the *Ašag-dingir*, mighty beings that cast long shadows over the age. Alongside this, we embark on the odyssey of Uldako.

Born a slave, Uldako's journey begins in the depths of suffering and oppression, but his heart burns with an unyielding desire for freedom. Rescued by the descendants of Adam, Uldako's path intersects with ancient prophecies and celestial beings as he seeks to uncover deeper truths about life, his heritage, and the cosmic struggle between light and darkness. His quest will take him through treacherous landscapes, confrontations with monstrous creatures, and the battle against the inner darkness that threatens to consume mankind.

Along the way, unexpected companions will rise, some wild, some wise, and one whose presence will awaken a depth in Uldako he never knew he carried.

Join Uldako in this epic adventure, where the past and myth intertwine and the fate of humanity rests in the balance. This is a tale of courage, redemption, and the eternal fight against the shadows that seek to engulf the world.

1

Life

A forgotten age stirs beneath a silent sky…

Uldako looks up at the passing mist and finds solace in the tranquil display, a brief respite from the turmoil of his thoughts. "Strange how the sky can be so beautiful…on the day the *anunnaki*, if they even exist, choose to watch me die," he murmurs to himself, his voice barely audible in the vast expanse.

His moment of reflection is shattered by the piercing cry of a flying dragon, its presence a striking reminder of the harsh realities of existence.

Is this the sum of life? Uldako wonders. *Born to slavery, condemned to die, while this* ušum-mušen *feasts on my lifeless body?*

A drop of blood trickles into his eye, jolting Uldako back to the stark truth before him: Uldako, son of Deborah, teeters on life's brink in a world steeped in pain and suffering. Bound and starving beneath a desolate tree, he is confronted by his tormentors—three young slave masters of Magan's slave camp, their faces twisted with cruelty beyond measure.

A profound evil has ensnared the world, birthing a crucible teeming with wicked men and savage beasts. Yet even within the yoke of Magan's slave camp, Uldako has heard whispers—fragments of a time when peace embraced every heart. He has clung to those rumors like dying embers. Tales of noble warriors and defenders of the light have offered some solace, though Uldako often doubts such men have ever truly existed.

All twenty-five years of his life have been spent hewn into the dark veins of the earth, cutting stone and stoking fire, laboring beneath the lash. He has never set foot beyond the walls.

Until now.

Dragged outside, not for freedom but for execution. And still…the sky, the wind, the sheer vastness of it all, so much more than the scraps of stories he has hoarded in his mind.

"So this is the world," he whispers, eyes tracing the horizon. Despair grips Uldako as he yields to the cruelty of his tormentors. He knows all too well how this tale ends: Slaves live and slaves die for the pleasure of their masters. "They're going to gut me like an animal," he reflects, his mind a dark maelstrom of resignation. "No, not even like an animal. Worthless slaves like me are always discarded at the mines. Even a rat holds more value than I," he muses bitterly, his soul crushed under the weight of his grim reality.

Above, the sound of beating wings draws Uldako's attention to the dragon as it lands on top of an old tree, an indifferent spectator to the brutality below. The empty landscape bears witness to what Uldako is feeling in this moment—nothing. Uldako, with dulled eyes and a battered soul, closes his eyes to the searing light above, convinced there is no light left in his life.

The malicious laughter of his assailants mingles with the restless wind as one of them steps closer. Behind him, the one-eyed man growls, "Kill this thing. Prove you're a real man!" Another adds with a bark, "The *anunnaki* told your clan to thin the herd anyway."

A glimmer of relief fills Uldako. Finally, the end is here. Finally, the pain and torment will stop. He feels a strange solace, realizing that countless others will continue to endure the suffering for centuries, while his pain is about to end.

The third—youngest of the three, and son of Uldako's slave master—moves like a lion without a mane, eager to bare fangs he hasn't earned. His eyes fix a malevolent gaze upon Uldako, a sinister grin etched across his face as he leisurely approaches, reveling in his dark nature to consume another soul. "The cursed king is not even as cruel as I am. You will wish you were never born, slave!" he spews.

Uldako opens his eyes, and as they meet the gaze of his master's son, something shifts. The air tightens. In the distance, a divine figure appears—cloaked in pristine white, wrapped in a soft golden aura. Uldako's breath catches. He has never seen such a being.

Is that…a dingir*?* he wonders.

Suddenly, the hilt of the young slave master's blade crashes against Uldako's face. Blood oozes down from his brow, clouding his vision, yet he forces his eyes open. In a haze of disbelief and yearning, Uldako pushes past the searing pain, desperate to confirm the surreal vision of a god before him, to see if the rumors he once dismissed as mere myths could be true.

Maybe I'm starting to see things, he wonders, trying to rationalize. *Is this what happens when you're slipping out of this world?*

But then—there it is. A figure, cloaked in white, surrounded by light.

The being lingers only a moment before the glow vanishes, swallowed by the haze. In its place, the illusion of distant horses thunders toward him.

For a breathless instant, Uldako hovers between brutal reality and something else—something otherworldly. *What is happening?* Uldako wonders, his thoughts churning as he tries to make sense of it all. The glowing figure has vanished, yet in its place, horses appear—majestic and thundering across the plain. Then he hears it: the pounding of hooves, real and close.

Wait...those sisi *are real!*

They are the most majestic steeds he has ever seen, so unlike the overworked and malnourished ones from the slave camps. These are special bred horses of the finest quality. Their manes dance in the wind as they run toward Uldako, ridden by fierce warriors clad in colors and visages unknown to him.

Consumed by bloodlust, the young slave master remains oblivious to the approaching warriors behind him. With his sword poised at Uldako's throat, he spews venomous words. "No one cares about you, and no one will miss you if you die. You are nothing."

Blood drips down Uldako's neck as the blade grazes his skin. Uldako stares defiantly at his tormentor, anger kindling within him. Mere moments ago, he had resigned himself to death, but now a surge of life pulsates within him, urging him not to surrender.

A spear thuds into the tree beside the young slave master. Startled, the cruel men turn in surprise to discover an intimidating group of horsemen. They behold six riders who are led by a fierce warrior clad in rare armor of the highest quality. With a raspy voice, the leader commands, "Stop!"

The three slave masters, recognizing the impending threat, panic. The one with rotten teeth shrieks, "Run!" and the trio scatter like frightened mice.

The group of warriors approaches Uldako, moving with the coordinated confidence of a pack of timber wolves, led by their formidable alpha. They reach the tree and halt, and a strange quietness envelops the scene as if time itself has paused. Uldako looks at the warriors in awe, for he has never seen men like these before.

The leader—a battle-hardened warrior—exudes confidence, strength, and an air of mystery. Uldako estimates him to be around seven to eight hundred years old, the oldest man he has ever laid eyes upon. He had heard whispers of the ancients, but never knew they could live to be this old yet carry the strength of a young dragon. The warrior's presence radiates a timeless authority, and Uldako feels a surge of hope as he takes in the sight of these astonishing saviors.

With wild, snowy hair cascading over his broad shoulders and a dark brown leather band encircling his forehead, the leader stands as a figure of raw power and ancient wisdom. The armor he wears, unlike anything Uldako has ever seen, gleams with an otherworldly sheen. Recently, a blacksmith in the slave camp had spoken of crafting rare and magnificent armor, reserved for only the most skilled artisans—armor rumored to withstand even the ferocious bite of a dragon. Uldako has dismissed these tales until now.

Even from this distance, Uldako can see the intricate details of his shoulder armor, molded in the likeness of an eagle and the matching emblem adorning his breastplate. Uldako realizes the gravity of the situation. While some slave masters bear the mark of a serpent, this mysterious figure bears the symbol of something else, a clan or kingdom unknown to Uldako. The armor is not just worn for protection but as a statement of immense power and respect.

The finely chiseled muscles beneath his bronze and leather armor speak tales of countless battles, showcasing unyielding strength forged through relentless victories. The fur of a predator drapes over his shoulders, adding to his imposing figure, while his braided beard, woven with beads, gives him a timeless, almost mythical appearance. Uldako's eyes travel from the warrior's armor up to his ice-blue eyes, which feel like they are piercing right through Uldako's soul.

Raising his finely forged axe, the old warrior directs one of his men with a voice that resonates with an unwavering command, "Cut him loose!"

The man to his left swiftly dismounts and slices through Uldako's ropes effortlessly, a testament to the quality of their blades. Uldako, still in a state of shock and awe, realizes he is in the presence of a legend, a figure of immense power and mystery.

Freed from the tight bonds, Uldako draws a deep breath, meeting the eyes of the group's leader. A visceral power emanates from the ancient one, reducing Uldako to an ant in comparison. Summoning every ounce of courage, Uldako stammers, "Th…th…thank you."

The old warrior, regarding the young slave with curiosity and empathy says, "You are welcome, young one. I see you are a slave; from which clan did they take you?"

Uldako grapples with the unfamiliar question about his clan, a subject never raised before. Uncertain, he responds to the mighty warrior, "That I do not know. I was born a slave and have lived in the slave camp all my life."

The weight of Uldako's duties in the slave camp tugs at his thoughts. Out of habit, he mutters, "I have to get back to my slave pen. They will take my head if I do not go back."

The warrior scrutinizes Uldako, peering into his soul. "No, young one, you do not have to go back," he asserts.

Uldako, gripped by his lowly status, insists, "I have to. I am a slave. I have no choice."

The warrior grunts. "Look at me!"

But Uldako remains fixated on the ground, the embodiment of a soul broken by a lifetime of oppression.

The warrior's authoritative shout pierces the air, "I said look up. Look at me, boy!"

Reluctantly, Uldako lifts his head to meet him. "I freed your body from the tree, but your mind is still bound. Those bindings you must break yourself. You are free! You were created in the image of *Il*! No man or beast can bind your soul!"

Tears start to run down Uldako's face as he considers the warrior's empowering words. Something stirs within him—hope, perhaps? Uncertain, he queries the warrior, "I…I'm free?" The word feels foreign on his tongue.

He stares at the cut bindings, hardly daring to believe. His chest rises and falls, shallow. For a moment, no other words come.

At last he whispers, "You saved me." His eyes search the warrior's face, then fall again to the ground. "Good men…I thought none existed in this dark world." Another pause. He swallows hard, voice breaking. "Why me? Why save a lowly slave?"

The memories press in, heavy and dark. "I have been a slave all my life." He clenches his fists, then lets them drop. A faint, pained smile. "Only my *ama* ever showed me kindness."

A small grin creeps across the warrior's lips. "You are right, no one is truly good, but a few men still follow *Il*." He gestures to his warriors. "We, who know the way, are still trying to be good men. We understand the meaning of life, and together, we bring light into this dark world."

Hope and curiosity swell up within Uldako—an unfamiliar sentiment in a life defined by the shackles of slavery. His entire existence has been based on misery, condemned to toil and perish under the tyranny of evil men. The cruel men of Magan confine the slaves within the working camp, granting only a select few to do work outside the walls, but always under the control of a whip. When their work is done, they return to the camp and remain segregated even among their fellow slaves. They are seen as the bottom rung of society, easy to control as long as they are kept in the dark about the world outside the slave camp.

Observing and comparing these unknown warriors with the evil slave masters of Magan, Uldako senses an otherworldly aura—a difference that beckons him toward a newfound hope.

Uldako takes a bold step and unleashes a torrent of questions all at once. "All I have ever known is a life of servitude to the masters. What is the meaning of life? What should I do now? Where can I go? Do you have a safe place for me? Who is *Il*?"

The old warrior, eyes carrying a hint of sorrow, recognizes the vast unknown that engulfs the young man. Realizing the complexity of the answers, he replies, "So many questions, and so little time. Come with me, and all will be made clear."

A warm sensation courses through Uldako, a foreign feeling. Could this be joy? For the first time, someone extends a hand to help him. Yet, in this moment, Uldako's mind drifts to the one other soul who has ever shown him kindness—his mother.

"I want to...but, but I need to go and free my *ama* first. She is still suffering as a slave. I just...I cannot leave her like that. The things they do to her—can you help me to free her?" Uldako's plea carries the weight of a lifetime of anguish, a desperate cry for freedom not only for himself but also for his mother.

The sorrow that had lingered in the warrior's eyes now consumes them entirely. "Where is she kept?"

The question is akin to a dagger that pierces Uldako's heart. His eyes widen and he realizes he has no idea. They have been separated for a long time. She was there one day, and the next, taken away with five other slaves. Uldako, lost in his uncertainty, mumbles, "I don't...I don't know where she is, or even where to start looking."

A voice from the back interrupts, "Excuse me, great-grand *abba*, but if we want to make it to our destination before dark, we will need to hurry."

The urgency pulls the leader back to his mission. He turns to Uldako with a heavy gaze. "Forgive me, young one," he says softly. "I wish I could do more, but without knowing where she is, I cannot aid you." His voice falters for a moment then steadies. "I must reach my *abba*. He is not well. But we will pray that *Il* watches over you and gives you the strength to one day find and free your *ama* from her bonds."

As the warrior turns to leave, Uldako stands frozen, uncertain. Without warning, the man tosses a heavy bag toward him. "Take this!" he calls. "There's a waterskin and food. It's enough to keep you alive for a few days."

As Uldako struggles for a moment to lift the bag, he realizes the stark contrast between his strength and that of the older warrior. He ponders to himself, "Maybe, I am just weak, and this is the difference between slaves and normal men."

The warrior, understanding Uldako's inner turmoil regarding his mother, breaks the silence. "I have to go now!" Immediacy hangs in the air as he imparts a final piece of wisdom. "May *Il*, the Most High, reveal Himself to you and protect you!" The old warrior signals to his companions to turn their horses. At his command, the unified force thunders away.

Uldako stumbles forward, voice cracking with desperation. "Wait! Please... don't leave me! I can't survive alone! I know nothing of the world!"

His cry echoes into the wild, swallowed by the wind as the warriors ride on without a word, dust rising behind them like a hammer slamming shut the door of hope. But not all vanish. At the rear, the leader and his great-grandson pull their reins.

Their black horses rear high, hooves striking the air, lifting the warriors above the earth. From atop their steeds, they turn—eyes fixed on the trembling figure behind them.

In that suspended moment, Uldako stands alone between silence and possibility.

The elder warrior calls out, his voice thick and raspy, "Get on your feet. Survive. And come find me when you are ready."

His horse lands with a thunderous grace, hooves thudding against the earth, then pivots with a smooth, elegant turn. A breath later, he vanishes into the swirling dust, leaving Uldako alone with nothing but the echo of hope.

The great-grandson, less experienced in handling the horse, struggles to match the elegance of his forebearer. While this unfolds, Uldako, filled with dismay, stares blankly at the ground, unsure of what to do next. In a moment of realization, he shouts, "Wait! Who are you?"

The great elder is out of earshot. Behind, the young grandson, finally steadying his horse at the rear, calls back, "His name is Seth, and we are the *dumu* of light." With a firm nudge to the horse's flank, the young warrior urges the steed to dash back to the group, its hooves pounding the earth with tremendous speed.

As Uldako's eyes remain fixed on the disappearing warriors, a quiet breeze stirs the dust, and silence wraps around the land like a shroud. "What now?" he whispers to himself. For the first time in his life, he is truly alone—yet also, for the first time, he is free to choose his own path.

Without warning, the air ripples as though the sky itself is being torn open. The divine being Uldako glimpsed before now manifests again, but this time right beside him.

Uldako freezes.

The presence radiates an overwhelming strength—ancient, boundless, and utterly beyond words. It presses against his soul, not with violence, but with a might that humbles every breath.

Uldako's mind struggles to comprehend the scene unfolding before him. *Is this real? A vision perhaps? Or merely a dream, a fleeting escape from the grim reality of my suffering. Or perhaps I am already dead?*

Overwhelmed, Uldako falls to his knees, powerless. Then, a great voice like many waters speaks to him. "Uldako, you have been set free! Become stronger and find Seth. If you truly seek *Il* with all your heart, He will reveal Himself to you!"

Uldako, startled by the sudden voice that seems to echo from nowhere and everywhere at once, feels his heart lurch. "Who...who are you? A *dingir*? One of the *anunnaki*?" he manages to utter, his voice barely a whisper.

Uldako dares to glance up, and what he sees burns itself into his soul. The figure stands cloaked in a pure light, his eyes like blazing fire and hair white as wool. Uldako cannot hold the gaze; the very air around the being seems to tremble with power—a presence ancient and commanding yet surprisingly familiar.

Lowering his head and closing his eyes against the overwhelming light, he hears the voice respond, "I Am!" The voice is both thunder and whisper, echoing through Uldako's soul. The very air shimmers around him, pulsing with unseen power.

"Now rise and become what you were meant to be!"

Before Uldako can fully grasp the words, the figure disappears like mist swallowed by a strong gust. Silence settles over the air, leaving Uldako rooted in place, his breath taken by awe, his mind overwhelmed with disbelief.

After a few moments, he feels his strength not only returning but multiplying. He raises both hands before him, studying them intently. Slowly, his fingers curl into fists. A new expression, one never before seen in his gaze, begins to form.

For the first time in his life, Uldako wants to live!

The fire within him kindles into resolve. He will brave the perils of this world. He will find Seth. He will uncover the truth his soul aches for.

And above all, he will free his mother from the yoke of slavery.

Uldako rises slowly, a newfound power rushing through him as he grapples with the lingering shock of the spiritual encounter. Awe gives way to determination, driving him forward with an unyielding resolve to survive and grow stronger. Weighing his options, he considers whether to seek shelter for the night or return to the slave camp to find his mother—both paths fraught with challenges.

Just the thought of returning to the slave camp sends a cold shiver down Uldako's spine, but he knows it is the only way to learn where they took his mother. They alone know. But if he returns, they will seize him again. In his current state they would break him, and he would be powerless under their cruelty.

"I have to become stronger first," he mutters. "My body, my skills...and the ways of this world beyond walls. I must learn it all."

Uldako's gaze sweeps the wild around him. The dangers crowd his mind, and an unknown fear grips him. *I need to hide. I need to run!*

Then another thought comes to mind: *The water in the waterskin will only last me so long, and the sun is bearing down in full might. I will need to find another water source if I want to survive the next few days.*

A sudden, thunderous roar shatters his thoughts, and Uldako instinctively drops to the ground. Above, a brown dragon soars into view, its presence foreign and unsettling but not unlike the familiar horrors used to terrorize slaves in the camps, where the weakest were fed to such beasts. A cold terror claws at Uldako's heart as he realizes that in this open and unforgiving wilderness, he is but prey to any lurking beast.

A recollection strikes him; the slave masters mentioned a small lake nearby where one found a massive red crab. Joy rises within Uldako as he recalls the direction, pointed out by the leader during his captivity.

Walking around the tree, he spots their tracks, confirming the path. "There it is, so now looking back, it must be on my left." Bag slung over his shoulder, Uldako sets out, a mix of fear and excitement pulsing through him. The outside world, fraught with dangers, both human and bestial, unnerves him. Yet, after meeting Seth and the encounter with the spirit, a newfound eagerness to survive emerges.

With alert senses, he casts his eyes about, wary of lurking beasts. The harsh land offers little shelter, but Uldako presses on, determined to find a safe spot for the night. Scattered dry bushes dot the landscape, and the heat forces most animals into hiding. "The sweltering heat keeps most predators away, but it threatens to sap the life from even the hardiest of men," Uldako muses, beads of sweat dripping down his face.

But facing the jaws of a wild beast—or worse, an *ušumgal*—in these desolate lands? That's a fate far more harrowing. He shudders at the thought. *Yet, would being devoured offer a quicker end than wasting away from hunger and thirst? Oh, but what if they eat me slowly?* he wonders.

Uldako shakes his head, trying to shake off the gruesome imagery. Still, his thoughts persist. *I don't even know what kind of beasts are lurking out here. I'm pretty sure there are scarier things than the creatures I saw in the mines.*

Uldako's senses remain on high alert as he traverses the land. Without the protection of camp gates, he realizes he is fair game, defenseless without a weapon.

Every noise is unfamiliar, a cacophony that assaults his ears. He knows that while he's surrounded by these mysterious sounds, every one of them could be accompanied by death.

Each step into the unknown feels heavier than the last. The dry wind stings his face, and the sun beats down without mercy. The waterskin Seth gave him is precious now—without it, he wouldn't last long. But it's not thirst that tightens his chest. A distant, thunderous screech splits the silence like a blade. Uldako stills, breath held. Something massive is near. Hunting.

Uldako's heart races as he plunges to the ground, hoping the dragon does not see him. He becomes a silent observer to the awe-inspiring yet terrifying spectacle playing out before his eyes. The massive brown dragon, its scales glinting in the blazing desert sun, devours a deerlike creature with voracious appetite. A rush of emotions swirls within Uldako—wonder at the majestic beast's sheer power, terror at the prospect of being its prey, and a bone-deep fear that keeps him rooted in place. The dragon's every movement is a manifestation of its dominance over the land, and Uldako realizes that he is witnessing the raw, untamed force of nature.

"That deer could have been me! I didn't even notice the *mušmaḫḫu* until I heard the attack," he reflects. The air is thick with trepidation as Uldako, heart pounding, waits with bated breath for the dragon's feast to conclude. "I should be more careful," Uldako muses, as every crunch and snap of bone churns his stomach, amplifying the dread that moves through him.

A powerful roar announces the huge lizard's departure, and relief washes over Uldako. As the echoes of the beast fade into the distance, Uldako rises, his muscles protesting from the prolonged crouch. A sense of weakness permeates his limbs, a reminder of three days without having any sustenance, the life of a lowly slave. The relentless struggle of survival in this unforgiving world dawns on him, and with a deep breath, he readies himself for the journey ahead.

With a gnawing emptiness in his stomach, Uldako stumbles upon a small hill, crowned by a solitary tree that seems to cradle the promise of refuge. Intrigued, he approaches and delves into his bag. At first, he is careful of the unknown items, cautiously inspecting them one by one with curiosity. At last he learns what may be consumed, trying fruits and nuts of many shapes and colors, things he has never known before.

At first bite, his lips tremble. A golden fruit melts on his tongue—soft, sweet, and rich with a taste he cannot name. He stares at it in disbelief, overwhelmed by the pleasure of it. Then a handful of nuts, warm from the sun, crack beneath his teeth with a buttery crunch and such depth of flavor, it feels almost sacred.

Tears well, born of awe. "Is this what food was always meant to be?" he murmurs in shock.

His mind flashes back to memories of moldy roots and cracked grain, of licking grease from discarded bones, of swallowing ash-flavored gruel just to silence the ache in his belly. In the slave camp, meals were punishments disguised as sustenance. They were cold, sour, colorless things shoveled into bowls as if feeding livestock.

Amidst the bounty, Uldako's fingers brush against an unexpected find—a small bronze knife. Memories of the slave camp's crude forges flow through his mind. At Magan, some slaves mined copper and black rock; in rare veins, tin was found. Others melted the metals together, forging bronze—used to craft tools, weapons, and instruments of survival in that merciless place.

This recent discovery of forging tools and weaponry from bronze was said to trace its origins back to a man named Tubal-cain, the master forger and *dumu* of the one who ushered in the dark wisdom of weapon-making and the invention of slave camps. Uldako despises him with every fiber of his being, as all slaves do. Yet now, for the first time, he wields a bronze weapon of his own free will—to survive.

A rare smile creeps across Uldako's face as he removes the knife from the bag to take a closer look, whispering, "Well, aren't you something!" The finely crafted knife, a relic of skillful craftsmanship, is his newfound companion. Uldako makes a rough band from his torn garment, knots it twice around his waist, wraps a second strip beneath the hilt, and lashes the knife fast at his side.

Uldako strides confidently with his new knife, his bag slung over his shoulders.

But after only a few steps, his face contorts as he realizes he's in the middle of nowhere with an urgent situation brewing in his bowels. He scans the landscape frantically, searching for the perfect spot, knowing he is out of time. He decides to swiftly return to the tree. With a furrowed brow and drenched in sweat, he braces himself for what's about to happen under it.

His stomach rumbles ominously, protesting against the feast he indulged in earlier. Uldako's eyes flare with sudden realization—he's never eaten this much food before, let alone such a variety all at once. It seems that a lifetime of near starvation has left his body unprepared for this sudden abundance.

Unable to hold on any longer, Uldako sinks to the ground in defeat, tossing his clothes aside and letting nature take its course as he relieves himself. After what feels like an eternity, he finally emerges from his ordeal, slightly disheveled but feeling better.

Uldako picks himself up, slinging the bag over his shoulders once more. He climbs the ridge of the little hill, and as he crests the top, his eyes widen in disbelief. Spread out before him is an unrivaled sight: verdant trees, vibrant flowers, and a glistening lake nestled in the distance. Overwhelmed, he blinks, questioning the reality of this living vista. Tears well up as the pure beauty of nature pierces his heart.

A swell of emotions floods Uldako—an intense rage against the slave masters who kept him ignorant of such wonders and an unwavering determination to liberate his fellow captives. His vow echoes through the air. "I will end their tyranny and reveal this world to the oppressed. *Ama*, I will rescue you and share the beauty that has been denied to us!"

He takes a step forward, then another, each stride forging a path of resolve. For the first time, Uldako walks not as a slave but as a man on a quest to understand freedom, to rescue his mother, and to seek the answers his soul has long hungered for.

2

Resilience

Uldako approaches the enchanting lake and a symphony of birds above the trees welcomes him, each species contributing to a heartwarming melody. The abundance of colors and the diverse beauty of these feathered creatures astounds him, prompting him to ponder humanity's capacity for cruelty amidst such natural wonders. Yet, the idyllic scene is abruptly shattered by a sinister sound, plunging Uldako into cover behind a massive tree trunk.

His eyes flare with terror as a creature rises from the depths of the lake. Uldako's eyes widen and his jaw drops as he beholds a creature more extraordinary than his wildest dreams, a breathtaking dragon. Its presence is overwhelming and magnificent, far bigger than anything he has ever seen. His heart sinks at the realization that even the mere sight of such a being can render a man powerless. The mighty lizard emerges before him with a grandeur that defies description—its back adorned with shields, and its limbs resembling colossal tree trunks. Its very breath conjures forth flames and smoke, and the terror it exudes leaves Uldako frozen in time.

Terrified, he contemplates the futility of any weapon against this mighty being, knowing it would mock the feeble attempts to challenge its invincibility. It counts iron as straw, and bronze as rotten wood. The arrow cannot make it flee. For this dragon, sling-stones are counted as stubble, and it laughs at the rattle of spears.

The dragon's underparts are likened to sharp potsherds, and its movement transforms the earth beneath it. It spreads its body like a threshing sledge on the lake, making the deep boil like a pot. Behind, it leaves a shining wake; one would think the deep to be white-haired. On earth there is not its equal; it is a mighty creature without fear. Uldako's mind races with the realization that this creature must be the famous Leviathan of the deep, the sovereign ruler over all beings of pride.

As Uldako wrestles with the awe of encountering such a colossal entity, he slowly becomes aware of the dragon's departure. He glances at his humble bronze knife, contemplating its insignificance against the beast. Musing over his stroke of luck, he mutters to his weapon, "Aren't you glad the *mušmaḫḫu* didn't spot us? You would've been of no help at all." Filled with gratitude for his escape, Uldako resolves to find a secure spot for the night.

"I can't set up camp too close to the water; that *mušmaḫḫu* might return, along with other beasts seeking to quench their thirst. Yet, I can't venture too far into the open either. I'll need to explore the area to find the right spot." As Uldako walks away from the lake, the environment transforms into denser bushes, and a small hill with a cave catches his eye. Moving silently, wary of lurking beasts, he inspects the area. It's quiet, nothing in sight.

Uldako examines the cave's entrance, ideal for a barricade of branches to keep out potential threats. With just enough space for around six large humans to lie down, the cave becomes his improvised shelter. "This will be the first home for our new journey," Uldako declares, touching his small blade as if confiding in a companion.

Uldako quivers as he steps into the cave, the dampness clinging to his skin like a second layer of clothing. His eyes dart around, and all looks safe. After swiftly clearing the cave and meticulously padding the ground with leaves, Uldako plops down to test its comfort. "Ah, perfection!" he declares with a satisfied grin.

As he settles into his makeshift bed, a sense of relief washes over him like a warm cloak. But the peace is short-lived as movement catches his eye. Squinting into the dimness, he spots a large, hairy creature scuttling along the cave wall—a spider as big as his hand, its many legs twitching in unsettling harmony. Terror bolts through Uldako's spine as the beast turns and charges straight toward him. He yelps—an embarrassingly high-pitched squeal bursting from his throat. When clarity returns, he grabs a stick and flings the spider out of the cave with a shudder.

Uldako retreats to his heap of leaves, exhaling a sigh of pure relief as he sinks into its embrace. Gazing out of the cave's entrance, he witnesses the sun's descent and the encroaching darkness. Strange and unfamiliar sounds carried by the breeze fill the air.

Lying in silence, Uldako absorbs the melody of the night. "What a world this is; where do all these creatures come from? Who crafted it all?" he muses, his thoughts spiraling into the mysteries of the world. A realization dawns on him—predators could easily wander into the cave. Jolted by the thought, he jumps up and quickly sets to work, stacking sticks and branches to close off the entrance fully.

"Can't have dinner guests walking in uninvited," he mutters with a wry smile, amused by his own predicament.

With the cave entrance secure, he lies down again, his mind more at peace. His thoughts circle back to all the wonders of the outside world he is yet to explore. As he contemplates the origins and marvels of the world, Uldako's thoughts gradually segue into the realm of dreams.

He hears his mother's desperate cries. "Uldako! Help me!" The sound of a whip and the laughter of evil men follow. Uldako runs toward her, but the faster he tries to run, the slower his legs move, and he can't reach her in time. One of them approaches his mother with a whip, ready to strike. The impact rips Uldako from the nightmare back into reality.

Awake, he realizes it was just a dream, breathing heavily with both relief and anger. "I have no time to waste; I will save you, *Ama*! Oh *dingir-meš*, make me strong to bring her back," he prays to the gods.

Pushing away the branches from the cave entrance, he sees daylight has dawned. Uldako silently observes his surroundings, listening for potential dangers. After a few minutes, he steps out, lingers for a moment, takes a final look around, and heads toward the lake. His waterskin needs refilling.

As Uldako approaches the lake, a feeling of profound tranquility washes over him. His eyes settle on a gathering of formidable horned lizards. Their massive bodies are adorned with three imposing horns jutting from their heads, lending them an aura of strength and resilience. Despite their fearsome appearance, they exude an unexpected serenity as they leisurely sip water from the lake, showing no interest in the smaller, more vulnerable creatures nearby. As Uldako observes the creatures with caution, he carefully assesses whether they present any danger.

Gradually, he eases into a sense of reassurance as he discovers that they are only plant eaters and won't be eyeing him as a potential snack, posing no threat to him. Their peaceful demeanor and majestic presence captivate him, banishing any lingering apprehension. With newfound confidence, Uldako seizes the opportunity to approach the lake openly, intending to replenish his water supply without fear.

In the days that follow, his aim is simple—grow strong. But his struggle for survival intensifies as he scours the landscape for sustenance. He attempts to hunt for red crabs, but they remain just out of reach, deep beneath the water. *Maybe it's the time of year,* Uldako wonders to himself.

The sparse fruits on the trees offer little nourishment, often small and unripe. The memory of the meager provisions Seth had provided now feels like a distant luxury, leaving Uldako to contend with gnawing hunger and the looming specter of starvation.

With the fading light comes a new wave of threats. The wilderness comes alive with the sounds of moonlight predators, their haunting calls serving as a grim reminder of the dangers lurking in the darkness.

One evening, as night descends, sleep eludes Uldako, his restless mind haunted by memories of captivity and the brutal truth of his present circumstances. "At least I had gruel in the slave camp," he muses bitterly, his resolve wavering momentarily before steeling once more. "No, what am I thinking—I need to get stronger and learn how to survive on my own to free my *ama.* I'd sooner face death than be enslaved again."

Still, hunger begins to wear him down. His ribs have started to show, and his steps feel heavier each morning. He turns over stones in search of beetles and grubs, roasting them carefully over his small fire and forcing them down with a grimace. Though some tastes repulse him, he tells himself it is strength for the day, each bite a bitter offering to keep his body moving. He speaks less now, moves less, weighs the energy he needs for each task, conserving his strength. The wild is teaching him one brutal truth: Survival demands more than strength; it demands resolve.

With each passing day, exhaustion gnaws at Uldako's limbs, dragging him ever closer to the brink of despair. Yet, in the desolation, a glimmer of hope emerges one bleak morning as he approaches the lake. His weary eyes catch sight of a lone human figure near the water's shore.

Careful to keep himself hidden from the stranger's view, wariness tingles at the edges of Uldako's consciousness as he contemplates the mysterious presence. Is he a *lu-kur,* or could he be one of the three evil men in the service of Magan's slave masters returning to find red crabs? His instincts urge him to retreat into the safety of the surrounding foliage.

With caution as his guide, Uldako positions himself at a safe distance, observing the stranger with apprehension and cautious optimism. The distance between them is too great, and Uldako knows he must summon the courage to move closer for inspection.

As Uldako stealthily advances through the dense undergrowth, his heart pounds with a mixture of trepidation and curiosity. Each careful step brings him closer to the mysterious figure, his senses heightened in anticipation of what he might discover.

Navigating through the tangled foliage, he seeks to flank the man, his movements fluid and silent as he closes the distance between them. With each step, the stranger's features become clearer, revealing subtle details that stir intrigue and wariness within Uldako.

Uldako pauses to observe the man, shrouded in a dark cloak that conceals his face, giving him an air of mystery that even the deep night might envy. The figure, quietly fishing and tending to a small campfire where two fish sizzle, possesses a calm, untroubled demeanor. The mouthwatering scent of the fish reaches Uldako, and his stomach growls so loudly it's a wonder the fish don't leap off the fire.

To his surprise, the man speaks, his tone warm and unexpectedly light. "Ah! I see we've caught more than just fish today. We have a hungry *lu-kur*. Come, stranger, have something to eat!"

Taken aback, Uldako takes cover again, uncertain of what to do.

The man stands calmly by the lake, his voice steady and reassuring as he calls out, "You can come out if you mean no harm; I assure you that I won't hurt you."

Stunned, Uldako hesitates, torn between his instinct to distrust and his desperate need for nourishment. He has learned the hard way that trust can be dangerous, yet starvation looms over him like a shadow. Weighing his options, Uldako decides to test him. "Who are you, and why should I trust you?"

Without turning, the man responds in a calm, almost indifferent tone. "Just a traveler, on an errand. Passing through. I come in peace, that's all you need to know. Now, are you hungry or not?"

Uldako stammers, "I…I am not hungry!" But just as the words leave his mouth, his stomach betrays him with a loud, rumbling growl.

The man's lips curl into a knowing smile as he chuckles. "It seems your stomach has a different opinion!"

Clearly embarrassed, Uldako takes a deep breath and admits, "Maybe a little. How do I know I can trust you, *lu-kur*?"

The man turns at last, his eyes meeting Uldako's with quiet intensity. "If you don't take the chance, it seems hunger might do what your enemies have yet to accomplish. The choice is yours, but my offer remains."

Uldako scrutinizes the man from head to toe, searching for any signs of deceit or hidden weapons. The stranger's attire is unlike anything Uldako has ever seen, a hooded garment of deep charcoal and earthy brown, the colors blending effortlessly with the surrounding shadows of the forest. His face remains partially obscured by the hood, revealing only a glimpse of his features, yet Uldako senses something in the man's eyes, sharp, vigilant, and full of knowledge.

The cloak draped over the man's shoulders seems to catch even the slightest breeze, giving him an almost ethereal quality. His arms are bound in leather bracers, each adorned with intricate, timeworn patterns. Around his waist, a deep crimson sash is tied with purpose, its ends fluttering with the same quiet determination that seems to radiate from him. The cloak parts slightly at his legs, revealing a long, weather-worn tunic bound at the waist, the hem stained by dust and time. His feet are wrapped in rugged leather sandals, fastened with sinew, silent steps worn smooth by the journey of many suns.

The entire ensemble is worn yet functional, the attire of someone who has traveled far and seen much. Despite the battle-hardened appearance, there is a grace in the man's stance, a fluidity that suggests he could move like the wind itself, swift, unseen, and lethal. Uldako can't shake the feeling that this is no ordinary man but a being who moves effortlessly between the visible and unseen realms, carrying secrets untold.

Uldako has never encountered different clans of humans before, but he has heard whispers of strange shamans who commune with the gods. This man seems to fit those tales, cloaked in mystery, revealing nothing of his identity, and withholding even his name. The ease with which he offered food, coupled with his peaceful demeanor, is baffling to Uldako, a strangeness he can't quite grasp.

His mind races with the possibilities: Could this man be a shaman, a druid, or perhaps even a spirit? Struggling to contain his swirling thoughts, Uldako finds the question slipping from his lips. "Are you a shaman, a spirit…or what are you?" The words linger in the air, heavy with curiosity.

The man chuckles softly, the sound low and unthreatening. "A spirit? No. Just a traveler passing through." He pokes at the fire with a stick, sending a few sparks dancing into the air. "But I don't blame you for asking. Divine beings sometimes walk among men, disguised in human form, or so it is said."

He pauses, then glances at Uldako with a subtle smile. "Still, asking that question tells me something. You believe the *anunnaki* might be real, don't you? Do you believe in the *dingir-meš*?"

The question of the gods stops Uldako. His brow furrows. "I wasn't sure before, but recently I saw something…a divine being…that I can't explain."

The man bursts into laughter. "You've seen a *dingir*, a spirit?" he scoffs. "They don't just appear to mortals. Sounds like your eyes were playing tricks on you."

Uldako's jaw tightens. "I think I saw one of the *anunnaki* once from a distance, and another time, it even spoke with me."

The man chuckles again, shaking his head. "You think? It spoke with you? Ah, now I understand. You look half-starved and like you've been alone in the wild far too long. In your condition, people start seeing all kinds of things."

Annoyed and in no mood to argue, Uldako glares at him then lowers his gaze, silent.

The man tilts his head, watching him with quiet interest. Sensing the shift in the air, he gestures toward the fire and the sizzling fish beside it. "Come," he says gently. "Eat with me."

Uldako, still guarded, gives a slow, wary nod. He lowers himself to the ground a few paces away, close enough to converse yet far enough to flee if needed.

As they share the meal, the man's voice cuts through the crackle of the fire. "I apologize if I offended you. I didn't mean to mock you. I do believe in the spiritual realm. Two centuries is a long time to listen, to watch, to learn. Let me tell you what I've seen."

Uldako nods, emotions churning with anticipation. He tears off a piece of the strange red-scaled creature. The soft, flaky meat melts on his tongue, infused with smoky sweetness from the fire. A wave of warmth spreads through his chest, and his eyes widen. *So this is what fish tastes like.* His mind struggles to process the flavors, as if his senses have been awakened after a lifetime of slumber.

He hears the man's voice nearby, speaking calmly, but the words dissolve into the background. Uldako is lost in the experience, completely undone by the taste. Compared to the bitter scraps and gruel of the mines, this is something divine. This is food for the gods! For a moment, the world feels right, even beautiful.

Tears prick the corners of his eyes, not from sadness, but from the sheer overwhelming joy of the moment.

The man's voice becomes clearer again. Uldako blinks, refocusing. The fish is still warm in his hands, but now he listens.

"As I was saying," the man continues, his voice low and steady, "what many call *dingir* are actually spirits. They dwell in the unseen realm, which is why mortal men cannot perceive them unless they choose to reveal themselves. That is *what* they are. *Who* they are is another matter entirely."

He leans closer to the fire. "These spirits are known as the *dumu* of *Il*, the spiritual creations of the Most High. *Il* is the Creator of all living things, the one above all. In this region, and in the Land of Nod, He is now often called *An* and not *Il*. His *dumu*? In these lands, they're called the *anunnaki*."

The fire snaps, a log splits.

"But be careful," the man adds, eyes narrowing. "Not all of them are good!"

Uldako's eyes go wide. "So let me understand this—there are many *dingir-meš*, but they're all *dumu* of *Il*, the Most High. Why? Did He give birth to them or create them? And how do you know all this? What are you?"

The man studies Uldako quietly, a faint smile tugging at his lips. "You still don't believe I'm just a man, do you?" he says gently. "But I am flesh and bone, like you."

He pokes the fire thoughtfully. "Among the *anunnaki*, there are those who dwell in the heavens, beings of immense power and mystery. They are called the heavenly *anunnaki*. But not all who bear that name are the same. Some now walk the earth, earthly *anunnaki*, and they are…different."

His gaze lifts to the sky. "And then, there is one who stands apart from all of them, not merely one of the many lower created *dumu*, but the only true begotten *Dumu* of *Il*. He was not created. He has always existed with *Il*. His name is *Il-Il*."

The man pauses, giving Uldako a moment to absorb his words. Uldako feels overwhelmed, like a fish out of water, as he struggles to gather his thoughts. After a moment, he finally speaks. "I don't know what to make of these beings, but I know this: I was a slave, one breath from death, when a figure, something like a spirit, appeared just as a powerful ancient warrior saved me. That same being came again and gave me the strength to live. I've known nothing but bondage and darkness since I was born. Why would the divine rescue someone like me…a slave?"

The man looks at him with quiet compassion. "You are no longer a slave," he says gently. "You've clearly endured much, so take a breath. Tell me, now that you've tasted freedom, what will you do with it?"

Uldako gazes up at the rustling treetops, as if seeking answers in the dance of leaves. "First, I only want to save my *ama* and bring justice upon the evil slave masters."

The man pauses then offers a quiet truth. "I know the weight of suffering. But now, you stand at the edge of something greater. Pain can forge purpose. And within uncertainty lies the power to become more than you ever imagined."

Uldako shifts then finally says, "But even with this new freedom, something aches inside me. A sense of loss clings to me. Those men—no, not men, but monsters. I long to make them feel the agony they gave my *ama* and me. But how? I'm only one man. I am weak...and with each day that passes, my *ama* still endures their cruelty."

The traveler's words bring calm and clarity. "A tooth for a tooth, blood for blood. If this is how evil is repaid, then how are you better than them? Let me ask you this: Do you think you need to focus on them or on your *ama*?"

Uldako's eyes are drawn to the shimmering water before him, and with determination, he declares, "My *ama*! I need to free her, but I also need justice. However, I am not sure what I can do."

The traveler nods slowly, his expression one of quiet understanding. "I don't believe you will free anyone in the state you're in. You will have to learn how to take care of yourself first, how to forage, make food, and how to gather supplies for a journey. You'll need tools and possibly weapons for such a task."

The traveler exhales thoughtfully, his gaze steady. "Whatever path you choose, remember this: No one knows what they're capable of until they try. Don't give up. When strength returns to your limbs and resolve fills your heart, the way will become clear. Do not chase the days ahead. One can plan wisely, but live the one before you since each day carries its own weight."

Uldako, grappling with doubt, questions, "What if I cannot save her?"

The traveler looks at him, sensing the lie of worthlessness taking root deep within Uldako's inner man. "Your body is free, but your mind is still in shackles because of fear. Only when you cast off the burden of fear will you taste true freedom. And from that freedom, you'll have the power to shatter the bonds of others. Become the light that darkness cannot silence."

Unaccustomed to such wisdom and encouragement, Uldako feels a new warmth stirring in his heart, a feeling both strange and comforting. He decides to press further, hoping to learn more about the mysterious man. "What should I call you?" he asks.

"Call me *dusa*," the man replies, his voice carrying a quiet, elusive weight.

Uldako frowns slightly, puzzled by the cryptic title. Why would he hide his true name? Why simply "friend"? But sensing the man's guardedness, he chooses not to press further.

As time passes and they finish the simple meal, their conversation drifts from deeper things to the practical. The man teaches Uldako a few basic lessons about survival, how to recognize safe plants, which berries to avoid, and a particular herb that, when crushed and pressed into wounds, draws out infection and speeds healing.

After a thoughtful pause, the man adds, "Our talk has been meaningful, but time slips quickly, and I must continue on my path."

Uldako quickly speaks up. "Before you go, could you teach me how to catch those fish?"

The man pauses, noting the desperation in Uldako's voice, then gives a small nod. "Rise. I'll show you the way of the fisherman—simple, quiet, and enough to keep you alive."

From a pouch at his side, the man pulls a coiled cord of finely twisted plant fiber and a small, sharpened bone hook. With practiced ease, he threads a piece of fish gut onto the hook and hands the line to Uldako.

"Find deep water where the surface stirs. Cast it gently. Then wait. When you feel the pull, don't hesitate. Set the hook quickly by snapping the line tight."

Uldako kneels beside the stream, clutching the cord. He watches the rippling surface, breath held in quiet anticipation. Moments pass. Then, a sharp tug. He yanks the line, arms straining.

"I got it!" he cries, eyes wide. "Look!"

But when he turns, the man is gone.

Stunned, Uldako pulls in the fish while he scans the trees, the rocks, the shadows. Nothing. No footprints. No sound. Only the hush of the forest and the murmur of the stream.

His gaze drops to the fish thrashing in his grip, nearly the length of his forearm, its scales glinting with bronze and red flecks in the fading light.

"What kind of fish are you?" he whispers.

He kneels by the fire and begins to prepare it, his hands still trembling. As the aroma of roasting meat fills the air, he breathes in deeply, savoring the warmth in his belly and the memory of a stranger who vanished like smoke, leaving behind more than just survival.

After a while, he can no longer resist. He cautiously removes the fish from the fire, the skin perfectly crisped. The fish's tender, flaky flesh melts in his mouth, an explosion of delicate sweetness that spreads from his mouth to his little toes.

As he savors each bite, Uldako glances at his knife and speaks to it like an old friend. "I'll call you Haber," he murmurs, holding it up with a faint smirk. "You're the only one I can talk to now."

The silence left by the stranger's absence weighs on him. Talking to the blade feels oddly comforting.

"So, Haber, what now? He was right…I need to get stronger. There's fresh water here, plenty of fish. Maybe I'll stay for a while."

His gaze sharpens. "But the slave masters know this place. They'll come back for those big red crabs." He tightens his grip on the knife. "Maybe this is my trial. I'll wait. Grow stronger. And when they return, I'll be ready. I'll make one talk. I'll find out where they took my *ama*."

As Uldako ponders the looming threat of the slave masters, he makes his way back to the cave, his temporary refuge.

He lengthens his stride, imagining the rescue—the shock in his mother's blue eyes, surprise breaking into gladness. He can almost hear her saying, *I always knew you could become great if you could only escape the yoke of slavery, my little* ugubi. He never truly knew what an *ugubi* was—only that his mother said it was a small forest creature with bright eyes, a long tail, and quick hands, clever enough to survive anywhere. The word lived in her mouth like a smile, playful and warm of affection whenever she spoke it.

He stops. A sudden longing for his mother overcomes him—her dark, wavy hair, the way she looked at him. She alone had given him the will to endure life as a lowly slave. The masters had noticed her beauty as well, but he refuses to follow that thought. He steadies himself, shakes the shadows from his mind, and turns back to the task at hand: securing safety for the night.

But the moment he steps inside the cave, something hairy and fast darts across his foot. He freezes then leaps back with a gasp. A spider, massive, with legs like twigs and eyes like polished beads, scrambles into the shadows.

"By the stars!" Uldako blurts, shaking his leg as if it's cursed. "How are you that big? What did you eat to get this size—other cave squatters?"

He exhales sharply, eyeing the dark corners of the cave with suspicion. "Perfect. Just perfect. Freed from bondage, nearly eaten by dragons, and now I'm sharing my new home with venomous hairballs on legs."

Just as he settles down, slightly irritated by the hairy residents of the cave, a rogue droplet from the cave ceiling lands squarely on his face, prompting another startled leap to his feet. "That is it! I have had it with this cave!" Uldako grumbles, swatting at the offending droplet. "First spiders, now water attacks? What is next, a host of biting ants?"

Wiping his face and shaking his head, he continues, "It is high time I took matters into my own hands and built a shelter, a place of my own." As he steps out of the damp cave and surveys his surroundings, Uldako whispers to himself, "I need to find a safer, more secure area, a place where my new house won't be seen while I wait for the slavers. I also need it to be safe from the creatures that prowl in the night." A wry grin tugs at his lips. "Preferably one without spiders or surprise waterfalls."

As he searches for the prime spot to build his new shelter, Uldako reflects on the words of Seth and the stranger. The idea of getting stronger resonates with him, not just physically but mentally. "Strength is more than a strong arm; it is resilience, resourcefulness," he murmurs to himself, a surge of determination rising within him.

Uldako knows that if he's to survive this wild world, he must adapt. The cave offers shelter for now, but it's no way to live. His eyes drop to his hands, rough and calloused. Clenching them into fists, he mutters, "I need to build my own shelter, with these hands."

After some searching, Uldako finds the perfect spot—tucked between towering trees with trunks like walls, hidden from wandering eyes. "This is it, Haber. Our new home." With his blade in hand, he sets off to gather branches, leaves, and whatever else he can use to craft a shelter.

As the sun moves from east to west, the construction of the shelter becomes a ritual of self-discovery. Uldako learns to tie knots and weave branches together, turning the natural elements into a fortress of his own making. With each knot secured, he envisions breaking free from the yoke of his past, symbolically intertwining his fate with the home he is building.

As night falls, Uldako sits by a small fire near the cave, gazing into the flames. The shelter is only just begun, a small start in his hands, the rest lying in the days ahead. Haber, now positioned at his side, seems to whisper encouragement. The warm fire symbolizes a glimmer of hope in the darkness that has defined Uldako's life. Just like the previous night, the distant hoots of unknown creatures echo through the night.

Uldako, utterly alone in the wilderness, contemplates the unknown journey ahead. He looks up at the bright stars—distant gods in his eyes—and murmurs, "Those must be the *anunnaki* watching over me, protecting me. The *mušmaḫḫu* hasn't returned to the lake, and no great beast has come to drink or devour."

He glances down at his knife. "Haber, we're still alive. We know how to catch fish now, and we are surviving on our own." He marvels at the thought, a mix of pride and disbelief in his voice. The serenity of the night contrasts sharply with the chaos of his past, offering a moment of peace. The flickering flames and the vast, starlit sky serve as silent witnesses to his resilience and the promise of a new dawn.

With the taste of freedom still fresh on his lips, he embarks on the path of self-discovery, guided by the flickering flames and the unwavering determination within.

A few days pass as Uldako regains his strength while he continues to build his new shelter and keeps an eye out for the slavers who might come for the crabs.

One night beneath the veil of darkness, Uldako sits alone, just inside the cave's entrance, wrapped in silence. The shadows press close, and his heart aches with longing for his *ama*. With none to speak to but the stars and the faithful blade beside him, he gently touches the hilt and whispers, "You know, Haber…" A pause. His voice falters with sorrow. "In a world drowned in darkness, my *ama* was my only light."

He blinks away the water gathering in his eyes. Thoughts of his *ama*, the suffering she endures beneath cruel hands, press heavily against his heart. Memories blur with imagined horrors that may even now be unfolding. "She deserves so much more," he whispers, the words heavy with sorrow. "They've trampled her body ever since I can remember, yet her soul has never broken, not once. There's a fire in her, Haber—a strength carved deep into her being. Deeper than pain. Stronger than fear."

As his words fade into the silence of the night, a memory stirs, a glimpse into warmer times, when her gentle hands brushed his hair, her voice soft amidst the turmoil outside. *There, rest your eyes*, she'd say, pulling him closer in their little corner in the hut. *My little* ugubi, she teased, her voice laced with warmth. *I'm not a little* ugubi*! I'm Uldako!* he would always protest with a pout.

How he longs to hear those warm soft words from her now. "My little *ugubi*," he murmurs softly to himself.

Tears trace a silent path down his cheeks, a trace of the ache of longing that grips his heart, compounded by the weight of guilt for his perceived inadequacy in freeing her. Uldako hits his fist on the ground. "If only I were stronger." Resolve hardens in Uldako; sorrow yields to a fixed purpose as he vows to muster every ounce of strength to rescue his beloved mother.

As night descends, it covers the cave in darkness. Uldako drifts into a troubled slumber, only to find himself in a haunting dream.

In the otherworldly realm of his subconscious, a colossal red eye of an ancient serpent looms before him, its imposing presence casting a shadow of fear upon Uldako's soul. As he turns to face the evil eye, its unearthly ancient serpent form becomes visible around it, radiating with an aura of dark power. Its sinister stare fixates on Uldako.

Slowly, two more eyes open beneath the first, set wide on either side of the serpent's massive head, until three blazing eyes regard Uldako as one. The creature's eyes, glowing with an unholy darkness, seem to penetrate his very being, as if attempting to plant seeds of shadow within his mind. Uldako's body is consumed by a fiery sensation, an intensity of hatred and evil unlike anything he has ever experienced, even far worse than being in the clutches of Magan's merciless slave masters.

Despite his terror, Uldako finds himself paralyzed, unable to break free from the wyrm's hypnotic hold. Behind the great creature of old are smaller dragons and serpents, each with different colors and powers awaiting their orders. With each step the creature takes, Uldako feels the crushing force of impending doom pressing down upon him, a chilling reminder of the monster's intent: to devour him whole.

In an instant, the serpent halts its advance; its head turns to the side as he inspects Uldako with disdain. Uldako feels the scornful thoughts echo in his mind. *You insignificant human! You are not worthy of my attention*, before vanishing into the ether. With the departure of the malevolent presence, Uldako finds himself released from its suffocating grip, gasping for air as he awakens from the torment of his nightmares.

His body is drenched in sweat, chest heaving, heart pounding like a war drum against his rib cage. Uldako stares into the darkness, his breath shallow. "What form of darkness was that…the very heart of evil itself?" The vision still clings to him like a shroud. But slowly, reality seeps in. It was only a dream—terrifying, vivid—but a dream, nonetheless.

He draws a long breath, steadying his trembling hands.

"It was just a dream. Calm yourself, Uldako."

He whispers it again, not to believe it but to bury the dread still coiling in his gut. The shadows cling a moment longer—then slowly, like mist retreating before the sun, they begin to lift. He closes his eyes, breathes in the cold air, and lets the silence steady him.

The fear does not vanish, but he rises anyway.

He steps beyond the mouth of the cave with eyes set, jaw clenched, and ready to face the savage dawn and continue shaping his shelter in the merciless wild.

3

Survival

The new shelter is rough, damp, and crooked, but after days of hacking, stacking, and scraping, Uldako steps back and allows himself a rare smile. He wipes the sweat from his brow and inspects his work—a hollow in the wilderness, shaped by grit and stubborn hands.

"It's not perfect," he mutters, "but it stands, and it's mine." He turns to Haber, sprawled beside the fire pit, and lifts a hand like a showman unveiling treasure.

"Welcome," he proclaims, "to our grand home."

He gestures to a mossy patch of earth. "Here is a resting place fit for a *lugal*, soft if you squint." Then to a crooked line of stones. "And this, of course, is the sitting area. Finest rock seats in all the wildlands." A dry chuckle slips from his lips.

"We've got everything—walls that don't fall, a roof that mostly holds, and a fireplace that smokes just enough to keep the bugs in fear."

He looks down at Haber. "What do you think? Too grand?"

Uldako glances at the shelter then back at Haber, and after a moment of silence, he continues, "Ah, you don't have to say anything; it's perfect!" The humble abode, crafted with his own hands, stands as proof of his unyielding resolve. The sleeping place is simple yet gives ease; by the hearth, a log for sitting keeps one warm through the cold nights.

As he walks through the small space, Uldako's heart swells with a sense of accomplishment. He realizes that this modest shelter, built from the sweat of his brow, represents more than just a refuge. It symbolizes hope and a new beginning.

He steps outside and looks at the beautiful nature around him. "Now I just need to make this wilderness my home as well, instead of fearing it. When the slavers return for the crabs, they'll be in my world!"

• • •

Many days pass…

Uldako immerses himself deeply into the mysteries of the wilderness, gradually transforming into a keen student of nature. Each day he watches the forest's elusive dwellers, especially the deer, learning how they feed, how they move, and where they vanish. Every discovery draws him deeper into the wild and further from the life he once knew.

He sharpens his skill at catching fish by the lake and develops a keen eye for spotting the red crabs hidden beneath stones and reeds. Not only does he uncover their hiding spots, but he also devises simple but effective traps from wood and reeds to catch them. Each trap is the result of careful thought and trial, a sign of his growing mastery over the land around him. With each successful find, Uldako feels a swell of triumph, a hidden facet of his character coming to light, honed by necessity and relentless determination.

Among the rugged terrain, Uldako stumbles upon special rocks that seem impervious to the relentless passage of time. These ancient stones, weathered but unyielding, become his lifeline. From them, he painstakingly forges tools of survival—an unbreakable stone spearhead and a fearsome axe. These creations, though far from the quality of bronze and iron, speak volumes of his adaptability.

As a slave, Uldako acquired rudimentary knowledge of crafting tools and weaponry. Now, in the wilderness, he is perfecting these skills. With newfound resilience, Uldako transitions from a mere slave to a survivor, and then from a survivor to a relentless hunter. His body, once frail from labor and hunger, grows lean and strong. Chasing deer through forests and over stone hardens his legs; climbing trees, hauling wood, and carving tools shape his arms and shoulders. His breath no longer fails him on long treks. The wild is reshaping him—training not only his body but also his mind, teaching him endurance, focus, and discipline.

With nature as his tutor, Uldako teaches himself to create clothing and armor. Using the hides from his hunts, he begins the slow, meticulous process of crafting. He scrapes the skins clean with sharpened stone and stretches them over branches to dry in the sun. Smoke from his fires helps cure the leather, while river stones soften it. He cuts and shapes each piece with care, binding them with sinew and plant fiber. Over time, he fashions a rough tunic, sandals, and layered armor lined with fur to guard against the cold.

The hides he wears are more than protection—they are symbols of transformation, shaped not by a master's hand but by his own. They mark the shedding of his old self and the forging of someone new.

• • •

Twenty more days pass…

Uldako now moves through the wild with quiet confidence, his spear and axe slung across his back like old companions. The steady rhythm of hunting deer and smaller beasts has hardened his body and sharpened his mind, but it is no longer enough. He hungers for a greater trial—one that will test his next transition, from hunter to warrior. The time draws near to face the slave overseers, to find and free his mother. But before that day comes, he must know his own strength. And deeper into the forest, he knows of a predator worthy of such a test.

The time for that trial has come. But before Uldako can face the beast, he must learn its ways. He must track its movements, study its habits, and uncover its strengths and weaknesses. He must prepare for the battle to come, to become a warrior. If he can claim victory over this beast, he can beat a slaver. He can save his mother.

Each morning, he ventures into the deep woods, moving through stone and shadow with instinctual ease. What once felt foreign now answers to him. He reads the land as a tablet, not of clay but of earth—claw marks on bark, disturbed soil, bent reeds. Each sign builds the image he needs.

With quiet resolve, he hunts not only for food but also for understanding. The forest no longer intimidates him; it listens when he moves, parts when he passes. His senses, sharpened by solitude, catch even the subtlest cues. This is no reckless charge—Uldako stalks the predator as a student preparing for war. The thrill of the chase drums in his chest, mingled with fear, but his steps remain steady. He will not face the slave masters untested.

Lately, he has found signs near his shelter—scattered bones, clawed stones, half-eaten stores. The creature is not just a distant menace; it has become a thief, a tormentor. It prowls his camp while he's away, and with every missing scrap of food, Uldako's patience thins. These raids strike not only at his body but also at his pride. He cannot allow it to continue. To transition from hunter to warrior, he must confront this dangerous beast once and for all. He must prove to himself that he is no longer the one being hunted.

Today, Uldako is finally on the hunt. He scours the land, his senses sharp, tracking the creature. He has glimpsed them before—massive, brown-furred beasts with daggerlike teeth. Each encounter is a dance with fear, his instincts screaming retreat. And who wouldn't flee when faced with claws that could gut a man in one swipe and jaws strong enough to tear through flesh and bone—perhaps even the scales of smaller dragons now circling the lake?

For reasons unknown, several dragon breeds have appeared near the water's edge in recent days. Uldako watches them from a distance, studying their ways. Some sleek and serpentine, others squat and armored, with thick, rounded skulls they use to bludgeon their prey. He knows he is not ready to face such monsters. Not yet.

But watching them has lit a fire within. Determined to grow stronger, Uldako has thrown himself into training—refined his armor, sharpened his weapons, and struck at an improvised dummy carved from a thick tree trunk. Day after day, sweat and pain shape his body. Strength returns to his limbs. Agility sharpens. Now, at last, he feels ready to test the warrior he is becoming.

Uldako knows the beast's habits, its pace, its weaknesses. Moving like a shadow, he slips through the wilderness—sometimes along the forest floor, sometimes weaving through the canopy of trees above. Each step is silent, each movement precise, shaped by weeks of hard training. He pauses often, ears tuned to the whispers of the wild, alert to the rustle of leaves or the distant snap of twigs. His deep knowledge of the forest and its creatures guides him now, allowing him to stalk unseen, draw close, and strike with sudden, lethal force.

Then he hears it—a sharp crack echoing through the forest, wood splintering under great weight. Uldako freezes. Eyes narrowed, he scans the area, senses straining for movement, sound, scent. Through the underbrush, it appears: a massive, fur-covered beast, unaware it's being watched.

"We've found it, Haber," Uldako whispers.

Without hesitation, he lowers into a crouch and readies his spear. His breath slows. Every step forward is silent, deliberate. In his mind, he begins to plan the encounter—tracking the angles, the distance, the creature's blind spots.

For a moment, it feels like any other hunt. But then it strikes him—this isn't just about survival.

This is the trial.

This is the fight.

He tells himself again, "If I can claim victory over this beast, I can beat a slaver. I can save my *ama*."

Moving with practiced stealth, Uldako circles downwind, keeping the trees between himself and the beast. His heart quickens, each step thrumming with anticipation. Drawing closer, he slips behind a massive trunk and crouches low, watching.

The creature towers ahead—massive, thick with muscle, its sheer size enough to freeze a lesser man. Every movement ripples with power. Uldako stares, both awed and wary. There's a savage beauty in its form, something ancient and untamed. Fear gnaws at him, but so does fascination. He should feel only danger, yet something about the beast draws him in, even as every instinct urges restraint.

Sweat beads on Uldako's brow as a long-buried terror claws its way to the surface. His eyes stay fixed on the beast, but doubt flickers—brief, unwanted. *Can I truly do this?* It is twice his height and many times his weight.

A sudden cry slices through the stillness. A bird—sharp-voiced and shrill—erupts from the tree above.

Uldako flinches, cursing himself as the beast turns. "I didn't see the *šeg-mušen*...foolish mistake," he mutters inwardly, breath catching. But there's no time to linger in regret. With a thunderous roar, the creature rears up onto its hind legs—massive, towering, and fully aware. The hunter is now the hunted.

Uldako, resolute, takes swift action, aiming his spear at the beast's heart as it rears up, poised for an attack. Hands shaking but with practiced precision, he hurls the spear with all his might, a decisive move in the unfolding duel between man and beast. Only it is not as accurate as Uldako intends.

The spear's impact catches the beast off guard but enrages it further, as the blow seems to have missed its heart by the width of a thumb. Uldako, recognizing his second mistake, swiftly retrieves his axe from behind his back. He understands the peril of the encounter—one wrong move and his life ends here. Faced with a superior opponent in terms of sheer strength, Uldako reminds himself that patience and precise timing are needed—no room for another mistake. No more chances.

The enraged beast easily wrenches the spear free and charges at Uldako with a bone-chilling roar. Seeking cover behind the tree trunk, Uldako narrowly evades the razor-sharp claws that swipe through the air, a hair's breadth from his head. As the beast attempts to maneuver around the tree, Uldako seizes his moment. With a sharp strike to the beast's neck, blood gushes out, and Uldako adeptly retreats around the other side of the protective barrier of the enormous trunk.

The beast, now visibly weakened, struggles against its injuries. Uldako, drawing from his observations of these hairy beasts fighting against dragons, understands the heightened danger posed by an injured opponent. Despite the beast's diminished state, Uldako remains vigilant, knowing that wounded creatures can be unpredictable and therefore even more daunting adversaries.

Uldako inhales deeply, centering himself in the midst of the intense confrontation. His focus narrows, fixating solely on the formidable opponent before him. As the wounded beast attempts to maneuver around the tree trunk, Uldako, barely within its line of sight, strategically circles the tree. Patiently, he allows time to exacerbate the effects of the beast's injuries, leveraging the advantage provided by its diminishing strength.

As Uldako paces, a sound to his right distracts him, drawing his attention to a furry cub unmistakably calling out for its mother. In that moment of distraction, the wounded beast seizes the opportunity and lunges toward Uldako. Reacting with swift agility, Uldako leaps to the side, executing a roll on the ground to mitigate the impact. Despite narrowly avoiding a fatal encounter, the beast managed to slash Uldako's shoulder, his hide-armor taking the majority of the damage, but blood still wells from the gash beneath.

Quickly regaining his footing, Uldako squares to meet the charge. The close call sharpens his focus. As the beast crashes in, he slips to the side as the sweep of its claws whispers past his ribs. In the same heartbeat he answers, thrusting into the same weak notch at the base of its neck he marked before. The axe bites deep as Uldako puts all his weight behind it. With a final, resonant roar, the mighty beast shudders, staggers, and falls heavily onto the forest floor.

The previously hushed woods now echo with the lively chorus of chirping birds, and in the distance, the little cub's plaintive cries become more audible. Though Uldako notices the beast lying helpless on the ground, still clinging to life, his compassion for animals prevents him from allowing unnecessary suffering. Determined to grant an immediate end to the creature's pain, he approaches and delivers the decisive blow.

As life fades from the once-mighty animal, a wave of emotions rushes over Uldako. Remorse grips him as the cub—small, wide-eyed, and trembling—emerges, nudging its mother's lifeless form with a sorrowful cry. Uldako's breath catches. His grip on the spear loosens.

"I...I didn't know," he whispers. "I didn't know she had a cub."

As the cub's cries rise, so does Uldako's resolve. A line has been drawn in his heart. Never again will he take life for training or pride. From now on, he will only kill if survival demands it.

A deep sorrow settles over Uldako as he steps closer to the cub. He studies its trembling form then lowers to one knee. "I killed your *ama*, who fought to protect you," he says softly. "In her place, I will protect you."

The vow settles in his chest like stone as he rises to cut what he needs from the defeated beast—fur, meat, sinew—and folds it neatly into the hide. Binding it tight, he slings the bundle over his back. Then, without a word, he gently lifts the cub from the forest floor. It doesn't resist. Cradled in his arms, the small creature breathes softly as Uldako looks into its eyes.

Although the victory is bittersweet, Uldako is bolstered by this triumph. He returns home, his stride surer than before. Each step resonates with a determination to improve, to rectify the crucial errors that nearly proved fatal in the encounter with the predator. The forest, once a realm of potential peril, now serves as a backdrop to Uldako's vow: "No more unnecessary kills and no more missteps when I am forced to fight for survival, Haber! We cannot afford to make any mistakes, or we won't live long enough to save my *ama*."

As the pulse of battle fades, pain flares in Uldako's shoulder. Each step sends a dull throb through his body, worsened by the weight of the cub in his arms and the bundle of fur and meat slung across his back. But through the ache, one memory surfaces—the stranger's voice. Among the lessons he shared, one stood out: A certain plant, when crushed and pressed into wounds, can quicken healing.

He recalls the man's words: *Uldako, look for a plant with thick, spear-like green leaves growing in a tight circle close to the ground. The surface feels rough, but inside is a clear gel that oozes when cut. It is soothing, powerful, and known to heal most wounds. It thrives in dry places, stubborn and strong—just like those who survive out here.*

With the sting of the fresh cut on his shoulder pulsing as a constant reminder of the battle, Uldako knows he must find the healing plant. As he moves through familiar terrain, his eyes search the underbrush for the clustered green leaves he's seen in this area before.

"I wonder…did the *lu-kur* somehow know this would happen? Maybe he's not even human." The question lingers like a shadow in his mind.

As time crawls by, the pain in his shoulder worsens, and there is still no sign of the plant. Just as Uldako loses hope of finding it, a flicker of vibrant green catches his eye—a hopeful sight. Closing the distance, he confirms his discovery with a triumphant nod. "Yes, it is you!" Uldako promptly harvests a portion, securing the precious find.

Returning to his humble abode, he gently places the cub within and tends to his own wound. With meticulous care, he cleanses the injury with water before slicing a leaf from the newfound plant. As the vibrant green yields its healing nectar, Uldako massages the soothing balm into his wound.

Casting a glance toward the cub, who remains fixated on him, Uldako begins to reflect. "Your *ama* nearly claimed me, little one. This wound will remain a sign of my survival, but it is also proof of her love for trying to protect you."

The cub, blissfully unaware of the weight that hangs in the air, stumbles over on clumsy legs and bumps into Uldako's feet. It lets out a soft, snorting grunt, then flops onto its back with all four paws in the air, squirming like a pup. A moment later, it rolls over and begins tugging playfully at the strap of Uldako's sandal with tiny, determined teeth.

Uldako blinks, confused by the creature's bold affection. "What are you doing?" he mutters, more curious than scolding.

But the cub continues—pawing, chirping, letting out tiny squeaks that seem too small for its frame. And then something stirs in Uldako. A crack in the shield. A sound escapes his chest—rough at first, like a cough. But it grows, unbidden, into something deeper.

He's laughing.

For what feels like the first time in his life, he is laughing. And it feels like something long buried is breathing again.

Contemplating a name for his new companion, Uldako glances down at the cub nestled beside him and speaks softly to Haber, his silent companion.

"Hmmm...what shall we call him? Maybe Spot, for the mark above his eye?" He pauses then shakes his head. "No, that lacks strength."

The cub lets out a tiny snort and flops across Uldako's lap like a clumsy rock.

"How about *Dugud*?" he chuckles. "You're heavier than you look."

Another paw swipe, followed by a sneeze.

"Not *Gu* either...even if you nibble everything. You might be a great fighter and protector like your *ama*!" Then, without warning, the meaning behind his own words clicks into place. He smiles, the name settling in his heart like a promise when he looks at his new friend.

"You are Šarru...my new *dusa*."

Lifting the cub gently, he adds with a grin, "We'll be good *dusa-meš*, Šarru. I might even train you to hunt with me, once I've healed."

In the dappled light of the forest, Uldako and Šarru forge a bond as strong as the ancient oaks themselves. At first, Uldako's attempts to train the young cub are met with playful resistance. Šarru pounces on anything that moves, including Uldako's own toes, mistaking them for prey. With patience and persistence, however, Uldako begins to instill in Šarru the skills necessary for survival.

Their training sessions often begin at dawn, when the forest is alive with birdsong and the rustle of undergrowth. Uldako leads Šarru through the dense foliage, teaching him to move silently and melt into the shadows, blending seamlessly with their surroundings. "Patience, Šarru," Uldako whispers, as the cub's enthusiasm often threatens to give them away.

As they venture deeper into the forest, Uldako points out the signs of potential prey—a rustle in the bushes, the flicker of movement in the branches above. With a nod from Uldako, Šarru crouches low, his eyes fixed on the target, muscles tense with anticipation.

Their first attempts at hunting are comically clumsy. Šarru bounds after a squirrel, only to end up tangled in the branches of a nearby tree, while Uldako chases after him, laughing at the sight of his enthusiastic but inept new friend. "You will get the hang of it, Šarru," Uldako reassures him, his voice filled with affection.

Gradually, Šarru begins to hone his instincts, learning to track the movements of their prey with uncanny precision. With Uldako's guidance, he develops a keen eye for spotting hidden creatures and a quick, silent approach that leaves their targets with little chance of escape.

Their partnership flourishes as they hone their skills together, each learning from the other in a dance as old as time itself. And as the sun dips below the horizon, Uldako and Šarru return to their shelter, their bellies full and their hearts lighter from the bond they share.

• • •

Many days pass…

Uldako, now fully healed, emerges transformed. He's clad in improved armor—stitched from rawhide and fur, trophies of recent victorious hunts. Seated in a hand-carved wooden chair beside a murmuring fire, with Šarru resting at his side, he no longer resembles the frail slave he once was.

The tattered rags of his past are gone. In their place: a fox fur cloak draped over his shoulders, his hair grown long and braided, his beard thick and proud. The body, once weak and starved, has been forged by suffering and honed through relentless training. Every sinew speaks of strength earned, not given.

Uldako is no longer just surviving—he is becoming a force to be reckoned with.

His brown eyes, now sharper and more focused than ever, lock onto the fire as he contemplates his next move. He needs to rethink his strategy to find his mother.

Beside him, Šarru—now larger and stronger from weeks of shared hunts—lies curled between him and the fire, breathing slow and steady, content in the quiet. Uldako, however, remains alert, caught between the stillness of the moment and the reckoning he knows is coming.

But waiting wears on him. "I thought at least one of the slavers would've shown up by now to get some crabs."

Uldako, agitated, stands up and bursts out the door. He paces outside, pondering his options under the vast canopy of stars. "I can't sit here and wait forever while my *ama* suffers; I need to do something now." Looking at the myriad of stars, he shouts, "Where are you *dingir-meš*? Is this what you allow to happen? My *ama* is suffering! Where are you *Il-Il, An, Il,* or whatever people call you?"

Sensing Uldako's restlessness, Šarru rises and nudges him gently, offering silent support. Uldako glances down at his companion, then speaks aloud, his voice low and firm.

"You know, Šarru, I was planning to ambush those men. The ones who tried to kill me under the tree. One of them mentioned catching the big red crabs at the lake."

He pauses, eyes hardening. "I was going to take two of them out. Leave the last alive—just long enough to tell me where my *ama* is."

Uldako's gaze shifts to the stars, as if receiving guidance from them. "I think I have a better plan. We'll scout the slave camp, just like we've done with the beasts of the forest. Learn their habits. Watch their routines." He leans forward, eyes burning with intent. "If they want to behave like beasts, we will track them as beasts! Then we strike. We take one alive to tell us where my *ama* is."

He glances at Šarru and grins. "Tomorrow, we hunt a different kind of prey."

Šarru's mane bristles; he rumbles once and sits at Uldako's heel. The two stride back into the shelter, ready to embrace the dark and rest for the challenges awaiting them at dawn. Uldako lets his eyes fall shut in the silence of the night.

From the dark—a crack. Not the heavy snap of hooves or paws, but a sharp give, as if weight searched for a quiet place and failed.

Uldako's eyes open wide. He holds his breath and looks at Šarru to confirm his instincts.

Šarru lifts his head, ears forward, drawing the air in small pulls. A low line of sound hums in his chest and Uldako knows…

Outside, the bark of a tree rasps once, as if something has brushed it—skin or cloth. Then stillness, the length of a held breath.

Uldako grabs his axe and bursts out the door.

4

Stranger

Axe in hand, Uldako moves swiftly, every sense alert. That sound—it wasn't a normal animal. Too light for a beast, too quiet for wind. Something, or someone, is out there.

The silence thickens, broken only by the low whisper of wind through the trees. His eyes sweep the dark, searching for movement.

Then—a flicker behind a tree. An arm.

"I see you, *lu-kur*," Uldako calls, his voice low but edged with warning. "Who are you?"

Under the silvery glow of the moon, a figure materializes, diminutive in stature with ears that taper to points and eyes reminiscent of serpents, framed by a prominent scar etched above his right eye. Peering cautiously from behind the shelter of a tree, Šarru, the guardian, issues a guttural warning.

Uldako, caught off guard, recalls hushed tales in the slave camp of diminutive beings—dwarfs or pygmies—whispers that spoke of their role as shamans in the outside world. Others insisted they were a group belonging to the enigmatic gods, newly arriving in this realm. Rumors also hinted that some of these entities imparted knowledge to Cain and his sons, especially Tubal-cain, revealing the secret arts of crafting advanced tools and weaponry. Yet before now, Uldako had never encountered such a being and was not one to believe in stories created from people's imaginations.

Gathering his resolve, Uldako demands, "Who are you?"

The dwarf steps forward slowly, raising his hands high in a sign of peace.

Uldako nods but keeps his grip firm. "If you come in peace, we won't kill you. But if you lie, we'll end you slowly."

The stranger—barely half Uldako's height—draws closer, his yellow eyes locking with Uldako's piercing gaze. "I'm just a hungry traveler," he says, voice low, "seeking grace after a long journey. I lost my wife to a monstrous *mušmaḫḫu*."

If the dwarf's wife was truly eaten by a dragon, the man must be in sore grief, yet whether he speaks the truth is another matter. Uldako's eyes study him carefully. The man is shorter and far hairier than any human he's known. He wears a worn traveling cloak and carries a small bag. His weathered face and sunken eyes suggest an age far beyond Uldako's, perhaps over three centuries.

The dwarf's eyes look sincere, but Uldako is unsure as he remembers the traveler's words of warning, "Be wary, for not all *anunnaki* are pure anymore." Uldako knows that the same counts for humans and probably these pygmies too. At this moment, Uldako is unsure if this dwarf is just a normal short man from another clan or if he is another "special" being.

He decides to maintain caution as both can be dangerous from his limited experience. "Stay there, do not move a foot! I ask you again, who are you, and why are you here?" The exchange reveals Uldako's transformation from his once lowly status of slave to warrior, vulnerability to assertiveness.

The pygmy, seemingly harmless, pleads for mercy, sharing the tale of the recent loss of his wife to the dragon. Uldako, empathetic yet cautious, proposes an agreement. "I'm sorry for your loss," he replies, his voice firm but not unkind. "I won't offer you shelter, but I'll prepare some food, on one condition."

It appears as if the old pygmy's eyes light up with hope as he agrees to any condition. "You can sit down and share a meal with me outside the shelter, but do not touch anything that is mine. I will not allow you to enter my door or come near me," Uldako strictly warns, pointing his axe at the dwarf.

"As you say, I won't dare touch a thing," the dwarf replies quickly.

Uldako, still on guard, gestures to a spot near the fire with his axe. "Then sit there, but I'll warn you again. Touch anything, and my *dusa's* teeth will be the last thing you see." He points to his furry friend, Šarru.

Šarru rises slightly, eyes locked on the stranger. A low growl rumbles from his throat, leaving no doubt that he doesn't trust him either.

The dwarf's eyes widen in astonishment as he takes in the sight of Šarru. "That's an *uḫuš-gal*! I never imagined such a beast could be tamed."

Uldako absorbs the term, realizing for the first time that Šarru is no ordinary beast but one of the great cave bears.

Šarru growls loudly, clearly offended by the suggestion of being tamed.

A grin tugs at the corners of Uldako's mouth, as pride glints in his eyes. "Easy, boy," he says, steadying the bear with a hand. "Let's give him a chance. But if he tries anything, you have my permission."

As the old pygmy settles by the fire, Uldako studies him in silence. The flicker of flame dances in the dwarf's strange yellow eyes, and the pointed ears and heavy brow only deepen the mystery. Uldako has lived most of his life in slavery, starved of truth as much as freedom. The wild taught him how to survive but not why the world is the way it is. Ever since the fisherman passed through and opened a crack in the walls of his understanding, Uldako has hungered for more.

Who are these beings? Do others like him exist? What do they know that he doesn't? This strange traveler might be annoying, but he's also a gateway—perhaps—to knowledge long denied. And Uldako has no intention of remaining ignorant any longer.

As they feast on a meal of succulent crabs, the dwarf is the first to break the silence and tactfully probes, "So, why are you here? Do you dwell in solitude in this wilderness?"

Uldako faces a pivotal choice—to unveil the raw truth or spin a web of tales. The memory of Seth's bravery floods his thoughts, guiding him toward transparency. "I walk the path to free my captive *ama*, ensnared by wicked slave masters," he says, voice tight. After a breath, he adds, "And then I will go on a quest to seek a man of great importance."

The pygmy nods slowly. "Ah…but if you succeed in freeing your *ama*, do you have a safe camp—your own people—to bring her back to?"

Caught off guard, Uldako shoots him a skeptical glance. "That's none of your concern."

The traveler chuckles softly, as if amused by some ancient truth. "Forgive me, I mean no offense. But this looks like your only home, and from the signs, you've been here for some time. Perhaps you've been lucky so far, but luck won't shield you forever. Safety is woven into the life of every clan that sets a proper camp—watch-fires, warding thorns, a sentry at dusk. This wisdom stretches back to the great city Enoch, first of all cities, which still stands in the Land of Nod. Yet you walk alone, without a haven."

He pauses, watching Uldako carefully, then adds, "This shelter in the wild has no walls, no guards, no tribe. You won't last long like this, my *dusa*. You need a safe camp."

Angered by his own ignorance, Uldako snaps, "First, we're not *dusa-meš*. And second…" A breath passes and Uldako realizes there may be wisdom in the visitor's opinion. "Well, yes, perhaps you're right." Then, quieter, more curious, he adds, "Safe camps? Cities like Enoch? I never knew such places existed. You're right, I have no refuge to protect my *ama*. I was a slave until a fierce warrior intervened. His name was Seth. He broke my yoke."

The dwarf's brow furrows, his expression darkening with sudden seriousness. "Seth, you say?" His voice lowers, reverent now. "Then you may be walking the path of fate. You remember what I told you about my wife? A few sunsets ago, the man who pulled me from the jaws of the *mušmaḫḫu* that devoured my beloved, the ancient war-chief who stood against the beast with no fear, the man whose armor bore the mark of the eagle—his warriors called him Seth!"

Uldako leaps to his feet. "That is him! Seth! Did he say where he was heading?"

The old traveler's face lights up with a knowing smile. "No, but let me etch the last place I saw him onto your map."

Uldako squints, a perplexed frown forming. "Map?" he mumbles.

Ignoring Uldako's confusion, the pygmy continues. "Just be cautious, because I think Seth and his men worship a fallen spirit and—"

Uldako, overwhelmed by the unfamiliar concept, finally snaps. "What is a map?"

The pygmy freezes. "You do not know what a map is? Did you grow up under a rock?"

Uldako lowers his gaze, annoyance and shame warring in him. "Of a sort. I lived in a slave camp all my life…until recently. I know nothing of the outside world."

The dwarf tilts his head with raised brows. "All this time! What a miserable life…a slave."

Uldako meets the pygmy's yellow eyes, speechless, sensing a quiet arrogance behind the dwarf's gaze—as if he were studying Uldako as a lesser creature.

The pygmy blinks, realizing Uldako has glimpsed his true thoughts, and quickly looks away.

Uldako holds his tongue, choosing silence over offense to preserve their fragile rapport and the chance to receive more information.

The pygmy gestures and makes an offer. "Do you have fine clay in the area to shape a cuneiform tablet—or perhaps a piece of leather or hide I can use to sketch a simple map?"

Uldako nods and returns with a hide from a recent hunt. As night deepens, the dwarf sketches a rough map with a charred stick, while Uldako clings to every word, drawn into a world of hidden knowledge beneath the star-crowded sky. Even though he cannot read, he quickly understands the drawings of hills and valleys, predator-haunted zones, and most important of all—the last place Seth was seen.

As the night deepens, Uldako, sensing the encroaching darkness, looks at the dwarf with genuine gratitude. "You have shared much knowledge with me. Thank you."

The dwarf, basking in self-satisfaction, leans forward. "You know, perhaps finding Seth before freeing your *ama* is a wise move. A man like Seth likely has a safe camp. Staying there would be safer. It would be tragic to rescue your *ama* only to face peril in this unforgiving world without a safe haven."

Though reluctant to accept it, Uldako acknowledges the dwarf's wisdom. "I don't know, perhaps I should find Seth first—or I could build a safer refuge of my own. I need time to think." He looks to the stars, as if searching for wisdom from the gods. "I'll decide in the morning."

The fire flickers, casting shifting shadows across their faces as they continue speaking. Uldako ponders the crossroads ahead, unsure of the path fate has placed before him. Overwhelmed by the flood of newly gained knowledge, doubt creeps in like a quiet shadow. Suspicion stirs toward the dwarf's tales and the hidden motives behind them, yet Uldako hides his thoughts, pretending to believe and hang on every word the dwarf utters.

Unexpectedly, exhaustion slips over them, and the old traveler glances around, acknowledging the enveloping darkness around him. "Would you mind if I stay here for the night? It is already too late and dangerous for me to continue my journey. Going out into the dark night is as good as walking into death itself."

Uldako, torn between caution and gratitude, reflects in silence. The pygmy shared valuable knowledge, yet they've only met today, and Uldako does not trust him. Still, the dwarf looks weak and poses no real threat, especially now that Uldako has the strength to face even fearsome bears.

Seth once rescued him without knowing his name, and he would likely help this pygmy too. Remembering that kindness, Uldako finds it hard to turn the dwarf away.

"Why not," he finally concedes.

The older dwarf offers a warm smile. "Thank you, young one. Now, if I may ask—where might I rest my weary head?"

Uldako opens the door to his humble abode. "Come in, but don't touch anything. I will make some space for you next to the fireplace." Together with Šarru, the three retire inside for the night.

As weariness tightens its grip, Uldako struggles to stay alert, unwilling to lower his guard around the pygmy he still does not trust. The dwarf appears to be fast asleep. As an unnatural exhaustion overtakes Uldako and Šarru, they slowly surrender to its pull. In that hazy space between waking and sleep, Uldako imagines he sees a faint smile touch the dwarf's lips—a quiet, hidden gesture as the darkness of slumber swallows him whole.

Abruptly, Uldako is in the haunting walls of the slave camp. The slave overseer's grip on his hair, the screams, the accusations are all too vivid. "You're worthless…good for nothing," echoes in his mind. "I told you there is not enough food, now you dare ask for your *ama?* I will beat you into submission!" The whip with hooked lashes descends on his back with a force that sends shockwaves through his body.

He jerks awake. It isn't a whip at all but Šarru's big paw on his shoulders, trying to rouse him. He turns to the bear as the dream fades. "Ah…again. Another dark dream! Thanks for waking me, Šarru."

Uldako scans the vacant house, a realization settling in—the dwarf is gone. He jumps up, rushes to the door, and finds nothing but the sound of restless leaves dancing in the wind. A profound sense of loneliness engulfs Uldako. He looks at his faithful companion, Šarru, still at his side, and mutters, "I guess, it is just you and me again."

As Uldako surveys the now-empty house, another revelation hits him—not only is the dwarf gone, but Uldako's belongings have vanished too. Fury clenches Uldako's jaw. "That devious…" Anger simmers within him, an unsettling reminder that trust is a luxury he cannot afford.

The thief, cunningly disguised as a weak and helpless wanderer, has snatched away most of Uldako's vital possessions—food, armor, tools. His rage intensifies, boiling over, especially as he realizes his special knife, Haber, is also among the stolen goods.

The door swings open, and Uldako unleashes a guttural scream into the daylight, a proclamation of his wrath. "You thief! May the *anunnaki* send a real *mušmaḫḫu* to eat you whole this time!" The echo of his voice fades, leaving only the vast forest as his witness to the betrayal.

A sudden shift in the air grips Uldako's senses as a radiant being takes form before him. The sheer force of its presence drives him to his knees. As the radiant spirit casts its eyes upon him, Uldako feels the fury within him dissipate, replaced by an overwhelming sense of reverence and wonder. Uldako kneels, not from fear but from a deep, unspoken reverence. Its appearance is as rapid and striking as lightning, its robes a pristine white akin to freshly fallen snow. Vast and overwhelming power radiates from the figure, yet its aura carries a gentle calm.

Uldako feels infinitesimal in the presence of the spirit, as insignificant as an ant beneath its gaze. Overwhelmed by a feeling of unworthiness, he hesitates to meet the being's eyes. Gathering his courage, Uldako slowly lifts his head until his eyes lock with the spirit's own piercing stare.

His eyes seem to bore into Uldako's soul as it speaks, its voice resonating with a divine authority. "Inherent darkness dwells within every soul, even within you as you felt wrath toward the fallen spirit who deceived you," the being intones. "The question now stands, Uldako: How will you live out your temporary life on earth? Will you succumb to the shadows, or will you seek the light?"

As the spirit's words take hold, Uldako, grasping the truth behind his doubts, asks, "What kind of *dingir* are you, and what do you mean by *fallen spirit*?"

The being steps forward, dimming his celestial radiance just enough to make himself clearer. "Understand this first: I am no *dingir* but an emissary of light—a messenger of *Il*." He pauses, allowing Uldako a moment to absorb the weight of his words before continuing.

"Second, understand this: The world has shifted irrevocably. A number of *Il*'s created *dumu-nita-meš* rose in rebellion. Their leader was a prideful cherub spirit, Hêlêl. Among men he is also called the lord of the earth—*Enki*, in your tongue. He is one of the mightiest spirits *Il* ever formed. We witnessed his fall, as he was cast down from heaven like lightning. Now he roams the earth with his legions of fallen spirits, bent on devouring humanity. Some of his followers have recently overstepped the boundaries set for this world."

Stunned, Uldako inquires, "Earthly boundaries?"

With a heavy heart, the spirit explains, "After their defeat, the fallen spirits were spared death but banished to the earth by *Il's* grace. Boundaries were set for them, laws they cannot transgress while on earth. Without these constraints, they would have wrought untold destruction upon humanity, sparing no one from their wicked deeds. Instead, they became Watchers of the earth. But some of these fallen spirits—the *anunnaki* of the earthly realm, as some humans in these lands call them—have recently exceeded their authority. They entered your dimension, taking the daughters of men to create things that are unimaginable, the shining ones...something the world has not witnessed before."

Uldako's thoughts race as he tries to make sense of it all. "This is overwhelming," he admits. "Much of it is beyond my grasp, and I am not sure why you are telling me all this. Are you here because of the pygmy? Was he a—"

The spirit nods. "He was possessed by one of the *anunnaki*, a shaman type. You piqued his interest because *Il* helped you survive."

Curious, Uldako asks, "You mean a fallen spirit is inside that dwarf? Why did he appear to me, a lowly slave?"

The spirit reveals, "Yes. Fallen spirits can possess someone if they have been given access to do so. As I am a *dumu* of the light, so he is a *dumu* of darkness. He is only interested in fulfilling his *abba*'s desires—the *abba* of darkness and of all those who practice lawlessness."

A deep furrow etches across Uldako's brow as he grapples to discern the identity of this father of darkness. Yet, before he can delve deeper into his thoughts, the spirit interjects.

"He sought to divert you from your destined path with tales and misdirection. He lied about meeting Seth, and the location on the map he provided to you will bring you close to death, which is his desire. His intention was to lead you to the Jabal clan, whom he knows might attempt to kill you."

The truth strikes Uldako like a breaking wave. "So what should I do?" he exclaims.

A look of quiet confidence settles on the spirit's gaze as he continues, "*Il*, who knows the future, permits this, for even in adversity, He can bring forth good from all things. He has sent me to warn you of this truth."

Determined, Uldako questions, "I don't understand. Does that mean I should still go?"

The spirit assures with unwavering confidence, "Yes. Fear not, but understand the world has changed. Men have started worshipping these rebellious spirits of *Il*, the Most High, as *dingir-meš*, altering the course of everything."

Uldako leans forward, brow furrowed. "Why give me this message?" he asks softly. "I'm no one."

But no answer comes.

With those words, the spirit vanishes into the unseen, leaving Uldako stunned beneath the weight of revelation. Time blurs. He does not move. He barely breathes. He sits in the same place, frozen in shock, trying to comprehend all he has just seen and heard. The sun creeps slowly across the sky—a full hand's breadth—while his thoughts swirl like dust in a rising wind.

His mind shifts at last to the theft of all he had gathered. Darkness creeps in. But then, from deep within, a spark of resolve stirs. He will not be broken.

As he walks beneath the vast sky and the silent trees, he reflects. The world he had clung to these past months—soil, bark, stone—was only one layer of existence. Beneath the visible realm, an unseen realm moves, like wind lifting birds higher without a wingbeat—unseen yet undeniable. For the first time, Uldako feels small, not from weakness but from awe. A quiet reverence grows within him for the vast, living tapestry in which he now knows he walks.

Šarru, the faithful bear, senses the emotional turmoil within Uldako and moves closer, standing by his side and offering a comforting touch. Uldako looks down at his loyal friend with affection. "Evil exists in this world, Šarru, but so does good," he murmurs softly.

Though uncertainty lingers in Uldako's heart, gratitude wells up within him for Seth's inexplicable rescue and the messenger of *Il's* timely appearance. Despite the setback, Uldako's resolve remains unshaken.

"Staying here and doing nothing is not going to help my *ama*," he declares firmly. "Perhaps the slave masters will never come for the crabs. I crafted tools with these hands to survive, and I will do it again. I will overcome every challenge to save my *ama* and find Seth. I'll be strong to rescue the weak!"

With fire igniting within his eyes, Uldako sets out to craft new tools, his hands moving with an almost innate precision, a dance of craftsmanship honed by survival. His body moves as if it has a mind of its own, while his own mind is occupied by something else. "I wonder why these diving beings would appear to me, a nobody, a mere slave," he whispers to himself.

His movements are fluid, as if the act of crafting tools has become second nature to him. A sense of urgency propels him forward. "Šarru, it is time for a new challenge," Uldako declares, his voice brimming with purpose.

"I can't save my *ama* until we have a safe camp. Seth might aid us with that, but we also need stronger weapons for our journey to find him. Weapons so formidable they'll carve the way for the battle to save my *ama*. I'm forging two one-handed stone axes and a spear like nothing you've ever seen before. And together, we're going to train tirelessly until the weapons become an extension of my very being!"

The fire in Uldako's eyes blazes with more than just determination; it mirrors a steadfast commitment to surpass his own limits. With unwavering resolve, he embarks on the creation of his most formidable weapons yet, toiling late into the night.

Every strike, every carving is driven by an unshakable belief: These weapons will be needed. Battles are coming.

5

Outside-In

Uldako rises with the first light of dawn, the morning chill clinging to his skin as he finishes his preparations. He had labored deep into the night, forging weapons with purpose—tools not just to survive but also to aid him on his quest to find Seth. His pack, carefully loaded with provisions and his newly forged arsenal, lays by the door.

With a final check of his equipment, Uldako steps out, the weight of his resolve as tangible as the pack on his shoulders. His first destination is the traps he's set around the lake, a routine check that today holds the promise of securing food for his journey.

Uldako ventures out to inspect the traps, granting Šarru a well-deserved slumber. The past few days have been a flurry of activity, and Šarru has admirably matched Uldako's pace. However, the journey ahead demands ample rest, and Uldako knows Šarru must gather his strength for the trials ahead.

The forest is waking, a chorus of sounds filling the air, masking Uldako's silent footsteps as he makes his way through the dense foliage. As he approaches, the lake unfolds like a tranquil tapestry, mirroring the hues of the waking sky, its surface serene and undisturbed.

It's a delightful season, marked by the subtle shift in nature's rhythm, heralding the arrival of a new beginning. Along the tranquil shores of the lake, signs of life stir with the changing seasons, occasionally revealing glimpses of scuttling crabs along the water's edge.

Uldako approaches with practiced stealth, his eyes scanning the surroundings for any sign of danger. Then he sees him—a lone figure by the water's edge. A slaver, unmistakable by the tools on his belt. A hunter of flesh. A predator of men. He stands at the water's edge, focused intently on the crabs that now skitter along the shore. In recent weeks, the weather has shifted, driving the crabs out from deeper waters for reasons unknown to Uldako.

Uldako can't believe his luck. After months of waiting for any of the three young men in the service of Magan's slave masters to approach the lake, why now, just as he is about to depart? It seems almost too convenient. Taking in the scene, Uldako observes the man's relaxed posture, a rare moment of vulnerability. This could be his best opportunity yet to strike, perhaps his only chance.

The slaver, oblivious to Uldako's presence, goes about his work, completely unaware of the danger closing in behind him. Uldako moves in, silent as a shadow, until he's within striking range. With the precision of a predator, he bursts from concealment—swift and soundless as he closes in.

But just as Uldako attacks, the slaver lunges sideways to snatch a crab, causing Uldako's strike to glance off his shoulder instead of taking him down.

Uldako stumbles forward from the missed blow, momentum throwing him off balance. He crashes into the man just enough to knock the crab from his grasp. It sails through the air and plops into the mud with a wet splatter. The slaver trips and goes down hard—face-first—right into the muck.

For a breath, everything pauses.

Uldako scrambles upright, readying himself. The slaver lifts his head slowly, blinking as mud drips down his face. He wipes his eyes with the back of his hand and stares at Uldako in stunned disbelief, as if trying to decide whether he's been attacked or just part of some absurd accident.

Then, as if the moment cracks in two, their instincts take over, and the fight begins.

The struggle erupts into fierce combat, Uldako's surprise assault turning into a desperate grapple for survival. The slaver, caught off guard, counters with wild strength, his shouts ripping through the stillness of the lake. It becomes a battle of wills, a primal dance between predators locked in a fight for dominance.

But the slaver's cries serve as a summons to those nearby, and soon Uldako finds himself surrounded. Slave hunters emerge from the woods like specters of vengeance. Outnumbered and outflanked, Uldako fights with the primal fury of a cornered beast, his newly forged weapons tested in the crucible of combat. Yet for every taskmaster he repels, more pour from the forest shadows—a relentless tide of malice and fury.

The truth hits Uldako—this is not a battle he can win. Hands close around him, dragging him into the swarm. Then comes the sound, cold laughter echoing across the lake. He doesn't recognize the men from whom the laughter emanates from, but the tone is all too familiar—mocking, condescending, more chilling than the morning air. Bound and beaten, Uldako's thoughts spiral in a whirl of rage, despair, and wrath.

As day fully breaks, gentle light spreads over the lake that was tranquil only moments ago, now marred by the morning's violence. Uldako lies on the ground, his body bound in fresh bindings. Pain pulses through him, each movement a reminder of the brutal fight. He grimaces, aching in every limb, certain some of his ribs are broken.

After their taunts, mockery, and cruel laughter over the "abnormal crab" they'd caught—Uldako himself—the slavers returned to the water, now focused on catching actual crabs. The joke still hangs in the air, but Uldako is not laughing.

As time passes and morning light filters through the dense canopy, slow-moving shadows drift across Uldako's prone form. His heart wrestles with the harsh reality of captivity. Lying on the cold ground, he feels the pull of twisted cords digging into his flesh—a cruel reminder of freedom lost.

The bitter taste of defeat mingles with echoes of past enslavement. Once again, he faces the haunting specter of his darkest days. But deep within, a fierce resolve rises. He refuses to surrender. His soul remains unyielding, despite the bindings. The memory of freedom—the wind on his skin, the gift of choice, the untrodden paths ahead—ignites his determination.

With every breath, he reaffirms his vow: "I will not endure the yoke of slavery again. My freedom is a prize worth any sacrifice."

Uldako contemplates calling out to Šarru for aid; perhaps his voice would carry to the shelter where the bear still slumbers. But he hesitates. If Šarru comes running into the lake clearing, the slavers would see him from afar and swarm him. They far outnumber him, and Uldako, bound and helpless, could do nothing to protect his friend. The thought twists like a knife. No, he cannot risk it. Escaping the restraints becomes imperative, a fleeting window of opportunity before he's ensnared by enclosures and reinforced guards.

In a moment of distraction as the slavers focus on their pursuit of luminescent crabs, Uldako seizes the chance to free himself. With steady hands, he loosens the rope securing him to the tree, his movements calculated and deliberate. Every sinew of his body taut with anticipation, he prepares to make his escape, his senses sharp and attuned to the slightest movement of the evil slave masters.

Fear tightens its grip around his throat, his heart thundering in his chest, yet Uldako refuses to succumb to the specter of enslavement once more. *Rise up! Swiftly! Run!* His internal command echoes like a clarion call, urging him forward with a fierce determination.

However, the taskmasters are vigilant, their cruelty rivaled only by their watchful eyes. Uldako's attempt at freedom is short-lived—he is caught mid-motion. The punishment that follows is swift and merciless. Blow after blow rains down, each strike blurring the world around him, until pain fills his vision and darkness closes in.

• • •

Time slips away…

When Uldako's consciousness returns, he is enveloped in darkness. It takes a moment for him to realize it is night. The throbbing pain coursing through his body serves as a harsh reminder of his failed escape attempt. Disoriented, he finds himself within the cramped confines of a small cage, its dimensions barely accommodating his frame. The air is thick with the stench of sweat and despair.

Confusion gives way to a crushing realization, and with it comes a surge of anguish. He is caged again, trapped like an animal. The truth hits him like a wave, heavy and suffocating. "No!" The word tears from his heart, not just spoken but shouted—a raw cry of fury and denial. It echoes through the silence, clashing against the wooden walls of his new prison.

"Shush! Be quiet, or you'll bring them down on all of us!" The urgent, hissed warning comes from a neighboring cage, thick with fear.

Uldako's breath comes heavy, his eyes searching the shadows until they land on a figure nearby. In the dim light, little can be seen, yet the man's trembling voice lays bare the dread that hangs over them.

"Where…where are we?" Uldako asks with a dry and cracked voice.

"Narath," the man whispers with a tone of resignation. "The slave market. A place no one wants to end up…and from which no one escapes."

"A slave market?" Uldako echoes, shock reverberating in his voice. Uldako's heart sinks further, the weight of his yoke becoming all too literal. He tries to process the information, to find a glimmer of hope, but the darkness seems to swallow it whole. Fear rises within him, a primal urge to flee igniting every nerve. His fingers claw at the bars, but to no avail. He thrashes against his restraints, the rustling of the cage echoing his desperation.

He stops, realizing it won't help. In the dim light, he searches for the figure again in the direction where the voice came from.

"Have you seen any way out? Any weakness in their guard?" Uldako asks, voice low but urgent. Each word comes with a wince, his body still aching from the beating.

The man in the next cage lets out a dry, bitter chuckle. "If there was a way out, do you think I'd still be here?" His skepticism is palpable, a defense mechanism honed by disappointment and despair.

Uldako stares into the dark, the cold truth pressing down on him like a heavy cloak that increases with weight as time passes. "I was free. I will be free again," he murmurs—not to the man but to himself. A quiet vow in the silence, a spark of defiance refusing to submit to the yoke of slavery again.

Silence settles between them, thick and suffocating in the cramped confines of their cages. Around them, Uldako hears the soft rustling of more slaves shifting in the dark, the sound of quiet despair woven into the night like a heavy shroud.

"What's your name?" The question breaks the stillness again, the man's voice carrying a faint flicker of curiosity beneath the weight of resignation.

Uldako hesitates, then replies, "Uldako, *dumu* of Deborah. You?"

"Jem, *dumu* of…I don't know," comes the answer, plain and resigned. A simple exchange of names—but here, in the pit of captivity, it is an act of defiance—a quiet stand against being reduced to mere flesh and labor.

The conversation stalls as footsteps approach, the sound of the guards' sandals against the hardened ground a grim reminder of their dire predicament. Uldako and Jem fall silent, each retreating into their own thoughts, their brief connection severed by the reality of their bondage.

As the guards' presence fades, Uldako lies in the eerie stillness, refusing to surrender to despair. Somehow, Jem's bitter skepticism has only sharpened his resolve. "I will find a way out! For myself, and for anyone who dares to hope," he vows. The road ahead will be perilous, shrouded in danger and uncertainty, but Uldako knows the first step toward freedom is believing it to be possible.

As Jem sits in contemplative silence, thoughts of the newcomer, Uldako, fill his mind. It has been many moons since he has encountered such resolve and strength in another slave. "It's a tragic reality," he murmurs, "that even the strongest souls eventually break beneath the yoke of slavery."

He pauses, the burden of decades carved into his weary eyes. "But perhaps," he adds, his eyes drifting to where Uldako lies, "this one is different. There is something in the young man's eyes—not just anger, but fire, unbroken and fierce. A will that hasn't dimmed."

That dark of night lingers on, heavy and unbroken—until, without warning, it gives way to morning.

Uldako's awakening is abrupt, a jarring shift from the murky depths of unconsciousness, or was it sleep? For a moment, he lies disoriented, the line between the two blurred by exhaustion and pain, his constant companions. He can't tell if he truly rested or if his body had simply surrendered to the dark.

Then comes the sharp clamor of slave overseers' voices, tearing through the fragile silence of dawn and shattering any illusion of peace. Uldako's eyes snap open, and with them, the grim clarity of his captivity returns. In the light of early morning, he can now see what the darkness had masked—the cages, crudely fashioned from thick, gnarled wood. A telling detail, revealing both the ingenuity of his captors and their utter disregard for the lives they hold.

Uldako looks at his surroundings—the early sun, a gentle orb of warmth, casts long shadows upon the earth below. Around the cages, the ground is packed and unyielding, worn down by the weight of countless steps—tracks from those who roam free and those who languish in bindings.

Surrounding him, ranks upon ranks of similar wooden enclosures confine others like him, each one a grim reminder of the cruelty they endure. These figures, gaunt and hollow-eyed, their bodies mere shadows of their former selves, gaze out from their confines with a visible sense of despair.

The encampment resembles an open-air dungeon, providing no refuge from nature's fury, only subjecting its inhabitants to the unrelenting gaze of the sun during the day and the aloofness of the stars at night. Guards circle the perimeter, vigilant for the slightest hint of rebellion, their hands poised near their waists, where lashes and other implements of punishment dangle ominously from their belts.

The cages stand within an open-air enclosure, ringed by thick thorny branches and strong wooden poles. Two gated entrances mark the boundaries. One remains slightly open, watched closely by a sharp-eyed guard. Through it, Uldako catches glimpses of another fenced area—the place where the guards seem to come from—though his view is limited by his position in the cage.

The second gate, a massive door that remains tightly shut, is located on the opposite side of the enclosure. This gate seems to lead to the outside world, as Uldako sees treetops beyond it, hinting at the freedom that lies just out of reach.

As time crawls on, the slave traders begin their selection process, choosing who will be put on display for the day's buyers and who will be consigned to labor. Uldako watches as some of his fellow captives are pulled from their cages, inspected with a callousness that reduces them to mere commodities. Those deemed fit for sale are led away through the open gate to the adjacent encampment, where they will be displayed like livestock, their humanity stripped away in the pursuit of profit.

But when a slave trader stops at Uldako's cage, he takes one look at the bruises, dried blood, and defiant stare, and scoffs. "Too wild…too damaged," he mutters to a guard. "No buyer wants a beast that bites back. Send him to labor, but break what's left of him first."

Uldako is herded alongside others deemed unfit for the market—toward the outskirts of the camp, where the day's grueling work awaits. Not punishment but a calculated step in the process of breaking souls.

As Uldako is forced into the line of laborers, his mind races. The wooden bars of his cage, the crude fences enclosing them, the cold division between those paraded for sale and those sent to break under toil—every detail etches itself into his memory, a fragment of the larger puzzle. This is no random cruelty; it is a system designed for evil. And within him, the fire to escape this system, and to reclaim the freedom that was stolen, burns fiercer than ever.

He looks at the faces around him, noticing a stark absence of the resolve he feels burning within himself. Instead, he sees a sea of hopeless faces, eyes that have long since stopped dreaming of hope. These are not the faces of potential allies, ready to rise at the first sign of rebellion, but of fellow prisoners beaten down by the relentless grind of captivity. Their expressions speak of a resignation to their fate, a surrender to the darkness that envelops their existence. Despite this, Uldako's determination does not waver. If anything, it solidifies.

As they are herded toward the labor grounds, Uldako studies the rope binding his wrists. It isn't merely a tool of restraint—it's a statement, a cruel symbol of control over every breath and movement. His eyes follow the coarse fibers until they meet another pair of bound hands. He is tied to a stranger, another soul fated to share in the toil and humiliation of the day.

The man beside him is of a sturdy build, his physique bearing the marks of hard labor but also the signs of malnutrition that plague them all. His features are rugged, weathered by the sun and the harshness of their reality. His clothing is tattered and threadbare, offering scant protection against the elements. Despite his apparent strength, there is an undeniable weariness in his posture, a physical manifestation of the years spent in captivity.

A sudden cry snaps Uldako's attention forward. Just beyond the line of workers, a group of new slaves—young, trembling, and freshly captured—are being dragged toward a raised platform where flames roar beneath a bed of glowing bronze rods. One by one, they are forced to their knees, heads bowed low in enforced submission, the backs of their necks exposed.

The overseers show no urgency, only a cold efficiency. They aren't branding shoulders or arms where flesh is thick and survival more certain. No, this is deliberate cruelty. The back of the neck is a sensitive, vulnerable place. Close to the spine. Close to the skull. Close enough to paralyze, disfigure, or even kill if the rod burns too deep. That is the point; the message is clear. They own your very life.

Uldako's chest tightens as the first red-hot brand is pressed into a young slave's neck. A guttural scream tears through the air, raw and piercing. The scent of burning flesh rises like smoke from a cursed altar. The young man's legs buckle, and he collapses, unconscious before they even finish the mark.

Another tries to resist—twisting, pleading—but the guard slams her down and sears the mark into her skin. She doesn't pass out. She just shakes, violently, as the symbol blisters across her neck—𒀴𒈲—*arad-muš*, slave of the serpent.

The overseers laugh out loud, their hearts hardened by wicked joy.

Uldako's hand instinctively rises to his own neck, fingertips brushing the old scar hidden beneath grime and sweat. They branded him the same way when he was just a child—too young to understand what it meant but old enough to remember the pain.

This is no mere label of ownership. It is a brand of worthlessness, a permanent declaration that they are subhuman—marked for life beneath the serpent clans, the bloodline of the cursed king, Cain. No matter how many times a slave is sold, traded, or captured anew, the brand remains. It ties them all to the same system of control. And perhaps one day, that shared pain will bind them in brotherhood.

But there is cold logic in the cruelty. A mark on the neck is hard to hide. It makes escape nearly impossible. Any stranger can spot it at a glance. The brand isn't just punishment; it is a proclamation. A curse. A reminder.

Uldako looks away as another slave screams and drops to the dirt. The sun continues to move in the sky, the fire crackles on, indifferent. The guards don't even flinch.

But in Uldako's heart, something else begins to burn, clearly visible in his eyes as he forces himself to look back at the new slaves being marked.

"This cursed mark," he whispers, "is meant to break us. But one day, it will bind us in rebellion."

Moments later, the line of slaves is driven toward the outskirts of the camp, where the day's labor awaits among the looming trees. The task set for the day involves wood harvesting, drawing them to the forest's edge where the promise of freedom lies close yet impossibly far.

The tools provided are rudimentary yet surprisingly efficient—axes and cutting knives fashioned from a type of stone that Uldako has not encountered before. These are sharper than any he has managed to craft by the lake, and he is surprised by how much of a difference the type of stone can make. However, he knows it is still no match for the metal he has recently learned to smelt at the mines.

As the labor begins, Uldako grits his teeth with each swing of the axe, pain lancing through his battered frame. His wounds throb and burn, yet he refuses to slow. He does not want to draw attention that might endanger the others. He turns to the man at his side, their movements bound together.

"I am Uldako, *dumu* of Deborah," he says, breaking the silence between them when the moment feels safe.

The man tied to Uldako casts a fleeting glance at him, a moment of hesitation flickering in his eyes before he responds. "Tarn, *dumu* of…it doesn't really matter," he says with a resigned tone.

Uldako senses the burden of despair in the man's words and chooses to continue their labor in silence, for now.

Their toil in the forest unfolds to the rhythmic cadence of axes meeting wood. As time passes, Uldako notices that the sound of axes provides a suitable cover for hushed conversations. Seizing a fleeting moment of solitude amidst the distraction of the guards, he directs his question to Tarn, his voice barely rising above the din of their labor.

"How did you come to be here, Tarn?" Uldako's voice is low and gentle, meant only for Tarn amidst the dull rhythm of axes and groans.

Tarn hesitates, his axe midair. For a moment, he seems unsure, weighing the risk of honesty. But with the guards distracted, he finally speaks. "I was a trader. I was returning home from a nearby village, a path I'd taken countless times. But on that last journey, they ambushed me. It's been three years." Tarn's voice falters then steadies. "Three years since I last saw the faces of my family."

Uldako pauses in his work, the weight of Tarn's story settling heavily upon him. "Your family?" he prompts gently, encouraging Tarn to continue.

Tarn nods slowly, a faraway look in his eyes. "Yes, I have a wife and three small *dumu*," he says, his gaze drifting as if seeing them in the clearing ahead. "They're still out there, waiting…probably still hoping I'll walk through the door any day now." He pauses, a quiet breath escaping. "My other *dumu* are older, finding their own way in the world."

There is pride in his voice, pride for the strong, self-reliant souls he has raised, though sorrow lingers just beneath it, like a shadow he can't shake.

"The little ones," Tarn continues, "they're still too young to understand why their *abba* hasn't come home yet. And my wife..." He trails off, the pain of separation evident as a tear rolls down his face.

Uldako listens intently, Tarn's tale resonating deeply with his own sense of loss and yearning for freedom. The details of Tarn's life —his family, his unexpected capture, and the life he was torn away from—reveals the man beside him not merely as a fellow captive, but as a father, a husband, someone who has known love, responsibility, and freedom.

Tarn's narrative serves as a stark reminder of the fragile thread that tethers some slaves to their past lives, now as distant as the freedom they yearn for. Unlike Tarn, many slaves have never known life outside the walls of slavery; it is their only reality. Despite its brevity, their conversation forges a connection between them, a shared understanding of the high stakes they face.

As the sun traces its arc across the sky, measuring the passage of time with the subtle shift of shadows, Uldako feels a kinship with Tarn deepen. In the rhythmic dance of daylight, spanning the width of four hands, he senses within Tarn a kindred spirit. Like him, Tarn harbors a flicker of hope for freedom, albeit faint and fragile. Tarn's previous life, outside the walls of slavery, is also a reminder to Uldako that their current state is not their natural condition. They are more than the sum of their labor and suffering.

As they toil side by side, Uldako cautiously broaches the subject of escape to Tarn. "Have you ever thought about escaping?" Uldako whispers.

Tarn tilts his head to Uldako. "Escape? And what then? The slave masters don't just punish the one who tries to flee; they make an example of us all. It's a heavy price to pay."

Uldako absorbs this revelation, the implications of Tarn's words pressing heavily on him. The notion that an individual's attempt at freedom could bring suffering upon others is a tactic designed to quash any thoughts of rebellion, to maintain control through fear and collective punishment.

"What are you two doing?" a guard barks. Uldako tenses, bracing for harsh reprimand, believing their quiet exchange has drawn unwanted attention. But it isn't Tarn and himself the guard berates. Another slave has collapsed from exhaustion, a short distance away.

The guard's wrath falls upon the man already lying on the ground, his blows landing with savage intent. But the fury does not end there. The man's partner, still tethered to him, is yanked down as well—caught in the cruel logic of shared punishment. The overseers close in, and their ire is swift and merciless, a bitter reminder that in this place, one laborer's failure is every slave's burden.

Uldako and Tarn can only watch in silent horror as the two are beaten, not for any act of defiance but simply for one's inability to withstand the grueling labor any longer.

This moment illuminates a grim reality for Uldako: The physical restraints that bind them are just one aspect of their captivity. The true power of their captors lies in the psychological bonds they wield with precision—the fear of collective punishment, the constant threat of violence for any perceived weakness, and the relentless pressure to endure beyond one's limits. It is a strategy designed to break souls as much as bodies, to foster a sense of isolation among the captives despite their physical proximity.

Uldako feels a surge of anger at the injustice, a sentiment mirrored in Tarn's grim expression. This moment of cruelty further bonds the two captives.

Uldako's recent taste of freedom has heightened his awareness of the injustices around him. When he was a slave before, he had been numbed to the cruelty, his heart dulled by constant oppression. Now, with a new perspective, he can sense the insidious ways their captors maintain control, and this awareness strengthens his determination to fight for true freedom.

As the day drags on, heavy with the weight of the recent incident, Uldako's thoughts churn. He begins to grasp that their bondage is multifaceted, that their struggle is as much against the mental constraints imposed upon them as it is against the physical ones. This begins to reshape his understanding of what it will take to truly be free.

As evening approaches and they are marched back to their cages, Uldako's mind burns with a new awareness. True freedom, he realizes, isn't just about escaping—it is about the ones still left behind. The incident in the forest, that brief moment of shared pain and helplessness as he watched fellow slaves beaten, has planted something deeper in him: the first root of empathy, and the beginning of a purpose beyond himself.

As they trudge back to their confines, the day's exhaustion does little to dim Uldako's resolve. That night, lying on the cold, unforgiving ground of his cage, he stares into the fading light, his mind churning with thoughts and possibilities.

In the stillness, with only the soft rustling of sleeping bodies around him, Uldako reflects on his own transformation, his recent physical freedom that sets him apart, and the awakening of his will. For the first time, he has carved his own path, made his own choices. And with that freedom comes a deeper truth: Physical escape isn't enough. If his people are ever to be truly free, they will need to awaken—to rise not just from their cages, but from the bindings within.

The memory of his own awakening—from numb acceptance to defiant hope—casts Uldako into bittersweet reflection. He knows too well the abyss of despair that captivity carves into the soul, a darkness so deep it swallows the will to dream. He had once stood in that same pit, unable to imagine any path out. And now, seeing that same emptiness in the eyes of those around him fills him with sorrow.

Yet, beneath that sorrow, a fierce determination stirs. He has tasted freedom—if only briefly—and it has changed him. He has stepped from shadow into possibility. Memories of Šarru surge within him: the first time he laughed, the perils they faced together, the bond that grew between them. Despite the dangers, his time in the wild has been the most alive he has ever felt.

This experience of freedom has gifted him with a newfound clarity of purpose and an unwavering belief in the possibility of liberation—not just for himself, but for his mother and all others ensnared by the bonds of slavery.

But as he considers the path forward, a sobering truth presses in. He has clawed his way out of the pit—but can the others do the same? Their souls have been ground down over years, some over lifetimes. The restraints that hold their minds have been forged not of rope or metal, but of resignation. And those are often the hardest to break.

"Perhaps I must escape alone." The realization settles over Uldako like ash. The sorrow of it stings, because he knows the darkness that holds them. He has lived in it. And though a fire now burns within him, he can't assume he can spark the same flame in those too long beaten, too long afraid.

He can't count on the others to escape. Uldako realizes with a heavy heart that if he flees alone, the others will surely face harsh punishment. But for his mother's sake, he knows he has no other choice. The path he must tread requires a solitary resolve, a singular focus that might not allow for the weight of additional lives dependent on his success. The thought of leaving behind those who are his brethren in suffering pains him. Uldako's escape, when it comes, will be a lone endeavor—a silent, stealthy attempt to slip through the shadows and find his way back to the freedom that had once been his, however fleeting.

"First, I will escape…and find Seth," Uldako resolves, his jaw set with quiet fire. "Then I will free my *ama*, whether he helps or not." His fingers curl into fists as the force of his vow settles deep within him. "But that won't be the end."

He looks toward the sleeping captives around him, their faces hollowed by suffering. A new desire stirs in his chest, one he has not expected. "One day, when I'm stronger, when I've grown more in mind and in might, I will come back here and find other slave camps. I will not just free one, but many. I will lead them all out of darkness, into the light of freedom!"

As the silence of night begins to envelop the slave market, a gnawing hunger claws at Uldako's insides, a clear reminder that he hasn't eaten all day. The realization prompts him to look around at his fellow captives. Their faces, illuminated by the dimming light, reveal the harsh truth of their existence—they, too, are victims of deliberate malnourishment, a strategy employed by their captors to keep them weak and compliant.

The sight of so many gaunt figures, their bodies little more than clothed skeletons, underscores the severity of their situation. Uldako understands it is a tactic of control, as effective as the ropes that bind them and the walls that confine them. In their weakened state, escape seems an unattainable dream, a cruel mirage in the desert of their captivity.

This revelation hits Uldako with the force of a physical blow. The urgency of his situation becomes painfully clear. If he remains in captivity much longer, he too will be reduced to a mere shadow of himself, a living skeleton devoid of the strength to pursue freedom. The thought of succumbing to such a fate, of his body and soul being eroded by starvation and despair, only feeds the fire within him more.

He has to escape soon, before the relentless toll of hunger and malnourishment claims whatever strength he has left. The understanding that his window of opportunity is narrowing with each passing day lends a new desperation to his plans. Uldako understands that his fight for freedom is not just against the physical fetters and psychological warfare of his captors, but also against the creeping, insidious threat of starvation that seeks to sap him of his vitality.

6

Leverage

Uldako shifts his attention to the cage around him again. It looks rough, but it is stronger than it seems—thick ropes knotted tight around the beams holding everything together. He has tugged at them many times, but they barely move. Not enough to make a way out.

The lock is worse—hidden just out of reach, cleverly built so no slave can open it. Uldako squints in the low light, trying to see its shape. He studies the cages nearby, watching for a clue. How did the guards open them? If he wants to escape, he has to know every detail. But with darkness pressing in and his limbs bound by the cramped space, even that small hope feels far away.

He will have to wait—observe, endure, and choose his moment carefully.

The following day brings no respite for Uldako, only a continuation of the grueling cycle of labor that defines existence within the slave market. This time, he finds himself bound not to Tarn but to a youthful woman whose frailty is masked by a veneer of determined silence. She neither seeks nor offers conversation; her eyes are firmly fixed on the ground before her. It is as if the very act of acknowledgment will consume the scant energy she preserves for the day's toil—or worse, garner her the attention from the cruel guards.

Her pace is slower, just enough to go unnoticed by the guards. It isn't weakness, Uldako realizes, but a skill learned through long suffering. Every step measured, saving strength, keeping her from collapsing. It speaks of someone who has endured much…and learned how to survive.

Uldako observes her and recognizes in her silent fortitude a different kind of strength. Her way of navigating the brutal world of the slave market—through quiet resistance and a calculated conservation of energy—is a stark contrast to his own, yet it commands his respect.

The air rings with the barking orders of the taskmasters. "Move faster!" "No slacking!" Their voices cut through the clamor of labor like whips. Every few moments, the shouts are broken by violence—a sudden blow, a scream, a body hitting the ground. One captive stumbles, too weak to stay upright, and is beaten without mercy. The message is clear: Weakness, real or imagined, means pain.

Uldako and the woman toil on, her silence a stark contrast to the chaos around them.

Despite the ever-present threat of violence, she maintains her steady pace. As the shadows lengthen and the day's labor draws to a close, Uldako and the young woman, along with the rest of the laboring slaves, are herded back toward the slave market. The journey back is marked not by conversations or exchanges of defiance, but by a heavy silence, a collective exhaustion that seems to weigh down every step. The woman's pace, consistent and calculated throughout the day, now mirrors the resigned steps of those around her, each footfall an echo of the day's toil and the singular goal of survival.

As they press onward, moving in unison toward their pens, a significant detail seizes Uldako's attention. Some slaves are already securely locked in their cages, a scene that unfolded before the laborers' return. This discrepancy in timing offers Uldako a crucial observation opportunity he did not have before—how exactly the taskmasters secure the cages.

In the dwindling light, Uldako strains to watch as a guard methodically locks a newly returned captive into a neighboring cage. The mechanism, though rudimentary, is right on top of the cage, effectively out of view and reach from the one inside. The guard uses a wooden lever, inserting then rotating it to engage a locking bar that slides into place. The simplicity of the action belies the ingenuity of the design, ensuring that without the correct leverage or tool, the lock remains inaccessible to the efforts of those it imprisons.

This observation, though brief, is imprinted in Uldako's mind. A revelation dawns on him that the key to unlocking the cages lies not in brute force but in understanding the mechanism's design and exploiting its few vulnerabilities. The locking process, executed with such casual efficiency by the guard, now appears to Uldako as a challenge to be deciphered, a puzzle that, once solved, could lead to freedom.

That evening, as Uldako lies in the confines of his cage and the day's final rays of light fade into darkness, his mind teems with possibilities. He mulls over the locking design, envisioning its components and pondering how he might replicate the guard's action from within his confines. It is now clear to him that any hope of escape will require careful planning, observation, and perhaps crafting a tool that can manipulate the lock from the inside.

As night deepens, Uldako's thoughts turn to his only true companion—Šarru. Worry gnaws at him. "I hope he hasn't wandered off, thinking I've left him behind," he mutters. The thought strikes deep, stirring something fierce inside him. With each passing moment, his resolve to escape burns hotter.

As dawn breaks, casting a soft glow over the market, the day starts as all days do in this place of despair. Each morning unfolds with the same grim ritual, a predictable routine akin to the rising sun, yet no less distressing with its unyielding repetition. The guards move methodically through the rows of pens, their eyes evaluating each captive with a cold, calculating gaze. "This one looks hearty," one taskmaster remarks casually, as if discussing livestock rather than human lives.

"And that one; she's got fire," another adds, indicating a woman whose resilience is evident even in her silence.

"And that one's wounds are healing well," another adds, pointing to a figure whose recent injuries seem to have diminished, making him a more appealing product for the day's market.

Today, for the first time, Uldako finds himself the subject of their scrutiny. "See here," a guard says, pausing in front of Uldako's cage. "This one looks strong and his swelling's gone down. He'll fetch a good price." The others nod in agreement, their decision made with a few blunt words exchanged over his head.

Realization dawns on Uldako—he is being chosen for sale on this day, and a tide of emotion builds within him. On one hand, it is a departure from the exhausting labor that marks his daily existence; on the other, it underscores his status as a commodity to be traded.

To his surprise, he is pulled from his cage, subjected to a brisk washing that is more about product presentation than personal cleanliness, and given a small portion of gruel—the first sustenance he has seen since he got here.

Then he is escorted through the open gate to the section where the marketable slaves are assembled. Uldako's mind sharpens with a flurry of thoughts as the unexpected change in his routine offers a rare opportunity. It allows him to observe the market more closely—to study the patterns and behaviors that have always eluded him from the confines of his cage or the labor grounds.

The market sprawls larger than the area where slaves are kept overnight. In the center, cages stand prominently, showcasing slaves for sale. Surrounding this presentation area are hovels, likely housing the guards who monitor and secure the market. The towering walls encircling the market seem insurmountable, adding to the feeling of confinement. Notably, a massive locked gate with two guards stationed on elevated platforms looms at the entrance, vigilant for any prospective buyers or threats.

Despite the fear and uncertainty that cloud his thoughts, Uldako clings to the hope that this day, with its new vantage point, might offer him the insight he needs to plan his escape. The selection process, before only observed from a distance, is now his reality, and he is determined to use it to his advantage.

As the day wears on, Uldako remains on display with the others, eyes sharp, senses strained. Buyers move through the market like vultures circling the weak, their eyes cold and calculating. Each one brings a flash of hope—or fear. Could this be when his fate will shift? Or just another step deeper into misery?

He never knew people could trade, buy, or sell things...let alone *other humans*. The idea feels unreal, twisted. He wonders how and what they trade—how worth is measured. Is it with metal? Stones? Secrets? But deals are done behind closed doors, in a separate corner of a hovel, far from the sight of the branded.

Yet, as time crawls by, the market sees little activity. Only two buyers show significant interest, one interested in a young male and another merchant whose gaze lingers not on Uldako but on the selection of females presented for sale.

The buyer voices his interest in three women, his sickening grin betraying more than words ever could. The transaction proceeds with the brisk efficiency characteristic of the slave market—swift, impersonal, and devoid of ceremony. The women, each with fear and resignation in their eyes, are led away to an uncertain future.

Uldako remains a silent observer to the fates being altered before him. The thought that he could have just as easily been taken sends a chill through him, but what weighs heavier is the cruel fate of the three women.

As the day in the slave market comes to an end, the air shifts—from anxious tension to quiet resignation. Those who have been on display, including Uldako, are herded back to their cages, their brief time under the gaze of buyers fading with the sun. The return to captivity is done with cold efficiency, just another part of the routine. Another day has passed, and they remain nothing more than property in the eyes of their captors.

Not long after the market falls silent, a different kind of procession begins. The labor slaves—those sent out under the cruel eyes of the taskmasters—begin to return. Their bodies sag with exhaustion, their faces hollow from the day's relentless toil. The contrast between their weary return and the earlier relocation of the unsold slaves underscores the dual aspects of their captivity: the physical toll of labor and the psychological weight of being traded.

It is then that Uldako notices the clear division within the ranks of their captors. The group that manages the sales, presenting and bargaining over the lives of slaves, is distinct from those who oversee the daily labor. This observation reveals an organized structure among the slave overseers, a division of responsibilities that allow the operation to run effectively.

The team responsible for sales focuses on maximizing profit, assessing each slave for their marketability, and ensuring they are presented in a manner that will attract buyers. Conversely, the group tasked with managing the laborers is indifferent to individual value, concerned only with extracting as much work as possible from each captive.

The clear division of roles within the slavers' operation strikes Uldako as important. For the first time, he begins to see how the system works—how each part serves the whole. Understanding this structure gives him a new perspective... and possibly, a way out. If there are different ranks and factions among the overseers, then there might also be weaknesses—gaps he can use to his advantage.

Uldako leans back in his cage, watching the laborers return one by one, broken and silent. They are locked away again, just like him. As night creeps in, he wonders when food will come—if it comes at all.

Then, footsteps. Three guards approach his cage.

One of them raises his chin toward Uldako in a gesture and mutters, "This one's got some meat on him."

Uldako stiffens, a cold wave running through him.

Another guard grins. "Yeah, he'll do nicely. Let's get him ready for dinner."

No... they're not serious! Surely they wouldn't eat another human... would they? Uldako's thoughts spiral as the guards yank him from the cage, slam him facedown, and bind his hands. Terror floods through him. They drag him toward the main part of the slave market, out of sight from the others.

As they move, Uldako hears their laughter, dark and cruel, speaking of the amusements that await them. He tries to make sense of their words, but dread tightens in his chest. They are heading toward the display area. Straining against the ropes, Uldako lifts his head, just enough to glimpse more guards gathering ahead.

Without notice, they drop him to the ground like a sack of stone.

"Here's our pick," says one of the guards who dragged him in.

"Wait! No new ones," another guard objects, stepping forward.

"He's not new! Been here more than two days," the other guard defends.

The slavers, amused by the prospect of pitting two slaves against each other for sport, exchange nods and grins. Bets are quickly placed among them, with some form of crude tokens of value changing hands as they size up the fighters.

Uldako glances around, seeing he's standing in some kind of makeshift arena. Dust hangs in the air, swirling in the torchlight. Across from him stands a hulking figure—broad, scarred, and silent. Sinewy muscles twitch beneath torn rags, and a grim focus hardens the man's face as he waits for the signal to begin.

For a heartbeat, Uldako's mind drifts back to the years he spent beaten into submission. He was never allowed to raise a fist in anger, only to cower or be crushed. But now he has tasted freedom, however fleeting. And with that taste comes a spark, a question burning in his chest: If he doesn't fight back, he'll only be beaten worse—or starved, or left to rot. This is his test, his chance to discover whether he can defend himself at all.

In the other slave's gaze, Uldako sees no hatred—only exhaustion and the instinct to survive. Both of them know what this is. Only one will walk away; the other—pain and possibly even death.

With a guttural command from an overseer, the fight begins. Uldako hesitates for a moment, then braces himself as his opponent charges with primal fury. The clash of their bodies echoes through the arena, each strike pounding with the weight of their captivity and the raw will to survive.

Despite Uldako's agile attempts to evade and counter, his opponent's relentless onslaught soon gains the upper hand. The gap in strength and experience becomes clear as Uldako struggles to defend himself against the barrage of blows. The crowd, wild with bloodlust, cheers and jeers with every hit, indifferent to the pain unfolding before them.

In a final, crushing moment, Uldako takes a well-placed blow that sends him sprawling to the ground, the air ripped from his lungs. Pain floods his chest as dust swirls around him. Defeat settles over him—bitter and suffocating—blending with the sting of failure and the cold truth of the slave market's nature.

He lies there, gasping for breath, the sky above him spinning. Dust clings to the sweat on his face. Voices blur. Pain throbs through his ribs, his limbs heavy, his will shattered.

Then—rough hands seize him. He doesn't resist. There's nothing left to fight with. The guards drag him from the arena like discarded meat, ignoring the bruises, the blood, the defeat.

His cage yawns open like a waiting tomb. They hurl him in without a word. The bars slam shut.

The cold grip of captivity wraps around him again. His body aches, blood crusting along fresh wounds, breath shallow from the fight. He lies still, staring at the stars above.

At least I'm not dead... not yet. The words echo in his mind like a bitter comfort.

To the slavers, the match was for nothing other than sport. But to Uldako, it's a cruel reminder of the world he's trapped in—a place where strength decides worth and survival demands more than fists.

Darkness creeps in, slow and suffocating, the pull of unconsciousness. His body shuts down. His mind fades.

In the days that follow, Uldako's life sinks into a grim routine. Some days he's dragged to the logging site, where the work is brutal and unending. The forest is thick and dim, the air heavy with pine, sweat, and strain. Every swing of the axe sends fire through his muscles. He dreams of escape, but the pain always pulls him back.

The slavers watch without pity, shouting orders, counting loads, and driving the slaves with chilling precision. To them, suffering is normal. To Uldako, it is a prison of flesh and fear.

On rare occasions, Uldako finds himself among the slaves displayed for potential buyers. Standing in the glaring sun, he feels like a mere commodity, appraised and prodded by prospective masters. The marketplace buzzes with activity, with merchants haggling and overseers barking orders. Uldako observes the ebb and flow of this cruel commerce, noting the patterns and routines that might someday offer him a chance at freedom.

Night brings its own torment. Uldako is sometimes forced to fight other slaves for the amusement of the guards. The matches are savage—desperation clashing with fear—while the overseers place bets like it's sport. Though he lacks formal training, his time surviving in the wild has honed his instincts. He now fights like a cornered beast, driven by the hope that each blow might turn the tide. He's seen slaves fall and never rise again, yet somehow, he still breathes. With every fight, his skills sharpen. In the dim torchlight, the crowd's howls echo through the arena—cruel, unrelenting, and hungry for blood.

Amidst the grinding cycle of toil and pain, Uldako begins reaching out to the other slaves—trying to spark even a faint ember of hope. In stolen moments of rest, he speaks softly with them, sharing stories of what was and what might yet be. These hushed exchanges, fleeting as they are, kindle fragile bonds between kindred souls. He sees it in some of their eyes—a flicker of strength, the birth of quiet camaraderie.

Yet not all welcome it. Some turn away, preferring numbness over a hope that might only be crushed again by the slave masters' cruelty. Uldako understands this. He too has tasted despair. He does not blame them, for some wounds are too deep to risk reopening.

As Uldako observes the daily routines unfolding within the slave market, a discernible pattern begins to emerge, drawing his keen attention. Every few days, a procession of new slaves is ushered into the camp, while others are led away, either traded or transferred to distant camps. This orchestrated routine hints at a well-coordinated communication network between the various slave camps, suggesting a larger, more intricate organization at play.

Within the confines of the camp walls, the slaves designated for sale are systematically extracted from their cages at dawn, their separation from those assigned to labor not merely a logistical necessity but a calculated stratagem. It becomes evident to Uldako that this early removal is intended to present potential buyers with only the freshest and most presentable captives, thus maximizing their market value.

In the afternoon, as the sun begins its descent, these same slaves destined for sale are the first to be escorted to their cages, well before the laborers make their weary way back from the day's grueling work. This staggered schedule, Uldako notes, ensures that the two groups remain distinct, their paths rarely crossing.

One morning, as the light of dawn pierces the gloom of the slave market, a ripple of expectation passes among the slave guards, not for any event that would change the fates of Uldako or his fellow captives, but for the arrival of a special and loyal buyer known for preferring only young females. This preference dictates the day's selections, leaving Uldako among those not chosen for sale. Instead, he is assigned to labor, the arduous task of woodcutting again—a critical activity for the market's maintenance and trade.

Uldako finds himself paired with a different person for the day's work, someone whose presence evokes a strange sense of familiarity. It isn't until they are both led to the area designated for logging, away from the immediate confines of the market, that Uldako's suspicion grows. The way this man moves and the outline of his profile in the morning light stirs memories of a conversation held in the shadows of Uldako's first night in captivity.

Seizing a moment when the guards' attention is diverted, Uldako leans in and whispers, "Are you Jem?" The response is a quiet affirmation, bridging their past whispered exchange to their present circumstance.

Amidst the relentless toil of timber harvesting, under the oppressive watch of the guards, Uldako wonders if the desire for freedom burns within Jem as well. If it does, he must find out how fierce that desire truly is, and whether it can be kindled into an alliance. Words between them are risky, each utterance a potential invitation for punishment.

A shift in the guards' focus provides an opening. Uldako moves closer to Jem, his voice barely more than a breath against the backdrop of their grim surroundings. "We weren't born to be caged or to die under the yoke of slavery."

Uldako meets Jem's eyes and feels a mix of relief and hope. The spark of determination is still there, shining faintly beneath the weariness.

"There's a whole world beyond these trees, waiting for us." Uldako's voice is filled with steady conviction.

Jem, casting a cautious glance around them, speaks low. "Uldako, hope is a dangerous thing for men like us. I've witnessed too many crushed for daring to dream. And as for freedom? It's but a fleeting illusion, snuffed out by the guards quicker than a flame in the wind." His words carry skepticism, a test of Uldako's resolve.

Jem's words strike Uldako like a physical blow, the harsh reality of a man both strong and broken by the unyielding grip of captivity. Here stands a soul resigned to the fate of a slave, a fate Uldako is desperate to challenge.

"But isn't it worth trying? To taste freedom, even if it's just for a fleeting moment before we face our end?"

Jem shakes his head. "Uldako, it's noble to dream, and I admire the fire in you. But we must be realistic. The chances of escape are slim at best. Clinging to dreams of freedom only makes our yoke heavier," he explains as his eyes return to the work before him. "Survival is our sole concern now. Anything beyond invites only more suffering."

Their conversation is cut short as the guards draw near. Uldako returns to his work, his heart heavy with Jem's resignation yet not entirely swayed. The dream of freedom, of a life beyond the confines of the slave market, burns fiercely within him and he refuses to relinquish.

As the day's toil finally comes to an end, Uldako and the other slaves are herded back to the slave market, their bodies weary from the relentless labor and their stomachs gnawing with hunger. The journey back is a silent march of exhaustion, each step heavier than the last.

Just before the guard locks Uldako in his cage, another calls out, "What's for dinner?" Seizing the moment of distraction, Uldako leans forward to study the locking mechanism. He observes the way the guard secures the latch, a simple yet effectively designed bolt that slides into place with a finality that speaks of long nights to come. This moment of observation is pivotal; Uldako etches to memory the precise manner in which the latch operates, understanding that this knowledge could be the key to his escape.

Once locked inside, the guards distribute their meager sustenance to a select few—gruel carelessly dumped onto the ground of their cages. Uldako looks down at the pitiful serving, the realization dawning on him with stark clarity: He needs to act, and soon. The gruel, barely enough to sustain him, is a grim indicator of his dwindling strength over the last few days, a countdown marking the time he has left to enact his escape before weakness can seal his fate.

Eating with a resolve hardened by his circumstances, Uldako understands the urgency of his situation. The observations made earlier—how his cage is locked, the guards' routines, the layout of the slave market—these are the pieces of a puzzle he has now solved.

I will need to escape in the deep of night, when most guards are asleep.

Unfortunately, he understands that escape is a solitary endeavor. There seems no feasible way to free the others, and remaining in this place is simply not an option.

That night, beneath the cloak of darkness, Uldako sets to work with renewed purpose. His observations from earlier in the day, the locking mechanism of his cage, now guide his actions. The piece of rope, seemingly innocuous, that holds part of the wooden structure of his cage together, becomes the focus of his attention.

Carefully, with movements as silent as the night, Uldako begins to work the rope loose. His fingers, though tired and worn from the day's labor, move with a precision driven by the urgency of his situation. He needs a tool, and this rope, integrated into the very structure meant to confine him, offers a glimmer of hope.

After painstaking efforts, he succeeds in loosening a length of rope sufficient for his needs. Crafting it into a crude lasso, he devises a bold yet straightforward strategy: loop the rope around the latch from the outside, pull it open, and manipulate a part of the latch arm from within to unlock the cage.

The risk of discovery is high, and Uldako knows that if he's caught, the consequences will be severe. Yet, the prospect of continued captivity, of surrendering to a fate he cannot accept, spurs him on. He works quietly, pausing at every sound, every shift in the air that suggests he might not be alone.

The air is thick with tension as Uldako positions himself at the most advantageous point within his cage, his movements deliberate and silent. With a practiced flick, born of countless rehearsals in his mind, he tosses the loop of rope toward the latch. The first attempt misses, and the rope falls limply against the cage. Heart pounding, he retrieves it quickly, mindful of the noise, and tries again.

On his fifth attempt, the loop catches the latch. Holding his breath, Uldako pulls gently, feeling the latch begin to slide. A wave of exhilaration fills him, mixed with disbelief at the simplicity of the act. The truth that the guards have indeed underestimated the ingenuity and resolve of a desperate man spurs him on.

Uldako pulls the mechanism with the rope from the outside while pushing against part of the lock mechanism from the inside. It takes a few tense moments to maneuver it correctly, but then, with a push that seems to gather all his hopes and fears into a single motion, the door creaks open.

Uldako pauses, expecting an alarm to sound, for the night to erupt into chaos. But there is nothing—only the steady breaths of his fellow captives and the distant, unsuspecting murmurs of the guards. The shock that he has successfully opened his cage without detection is both thrilling and terrifying.

He knows this is just the beginning. Freedom lies beyond the confines of the slave market, through the dark woods and into territories unknown. The risks are immense, the journey fraught with peril, but the alternative is a return to slavery, to a life of servitude and despair.

With a steady breath, Uldako steps out of his cage, the rope still clutched in his hand. The night ahead stretches before him like a perilous path, each footfall a gamble in a deadly game of stealth and survival. But the thought of the open sky—of a world beyond cages, with Šarru by his side—fills him with immense courage.

With his heart pounding in the silence of the night, Uldako moves like a shadow, each step measured with care to avoid the slightest sound. He slips through the open gate between the pens and the larger market, past a guard slumped over in sleep. The pens behind him already feel like a distant world as he creeps along the dim, winding paths of the slave market. His eyes adjust to the gloom, scanning ahead for the dark outline of the camp's gates—the final barrier between him and the freedom he longs for.

The camp's perimeter is fortified with towering palisade walls, constructed from vertical half-logs sharpened at their peaks, standing shoulder to shoulder in a formidable barrier. Along the inner side of these walls, wooden walkways—simple yet functional—provide elevated patrol routes for the guards, allowing them to survey the surrounding terrain and respond swiftly to any threats.

As Uldako approaches the main gate, the danger sharpens. Two guards stand watch atop the walkway, another stands guard at the gate below, their presence an impossible obstacle to a direct escape. The gates themselves, large and cumbersome, will take too long to open quietly and without drawing attention. Uldako's mind races, calculating risks and possibilities in the span of heartbeats.

Circling wide, he searches for another way out, his body coiled with tension, ready to vanish at the first sign of movement. The market is a twisting maze of shadows and half-formed shapes, a terrain he knows well—but tonight it feels different. Tonight, he sees it through the eyes of a fugitive. His path skirts the outer edge of the camp, where the guards' torches grow dim and the wild darkness of the world returns.

And then—near disaster. One careless step. A sharp rock bites into his foot, and a curse escapes his lips before he can stop it. He freezes. A guard stirs. The sound—barely more than a breath—hangs in the air like a warning.

Heart drumming against his rib cage, Uldako dives into a nearby hovel—a crude shelter or storage space dug somewhat into the earth, concealed by the night. His relief is short-lived. In the pitch darkness, his foot connects gently with something unexpectedly soft and warm—a sleeping taskmaster. The sudden movement beneath him ignites a surge of terror and a rush of fire through his veins. Fear is etched across his face as his eyes widen and he struggles to steady his breath.

"Who's there?" The slaver's voice, groggy and disoriented, escalates quickly into alertness as Uldako tries to silence him, a struggle ensnaring them both in a desperate fight for survival. Uldako, driven by instinct and the overwhelming desire for freedom, fights to keep the man quiet, aware that any noise could doom his escape.

The scuffle is brutal but silent—a clash of shadows in the cramped darkness of the hovel. Driven by fear and grim resolve, Uldako fights not just to stay quiet, but to survive. One hand clamps over the man's mouth as they struggle, limbs locked in desperate motion. The taskmaster, stunned at first, recovers quickly. He is no easy foe—his own instinct to live burns strong. But the arena taught Uldako well: end the fight quickly, before the enemy can gather strength or even think. His body moves before his mind commands it—guided by instinct, memory, and the will to overcome.

In the terrifying closeness of the struggle, with one hand still clamped over the taskmaster's mouth, Uldako's free hand finds his neck. He hits hard. The body goes limp. Silence falls, thick and unnatural. As the stillness takes hold, the weight of what he has done presses in on him—Uldako has killed the taskmaster in self-defense. The weight of his action, the finality of it, leaves him momentarily paralyzed, a mix of shock and disbelief coursing through him. This taskmaster has caused countless slaves to suffer, but to take another human's life feels unnatural and evil to Uldako as he gazes at the lifeless body in shock. He has always been surrounded by violence and death. He is used to it, but this is the first time he has taken a life by his own hands.

As he regains his thoughts, the fear that the commotion has alerted others surges anew. But the silence that follows is unbroken, save for the heavy breaths that heave from Uldako's chest. It dawns on him then—the guard he has been hiding from outside is not the threat; the true danger was the one he had unwittingly stumbled upon in the dark.

The realization brings a rush of emotions—relief that no alarm was raised, shock at the death he caused, and a sharp awareness of how fragile his escape truly is. Uldako stands at a crossroads. His path to freedom is no longer just a flight from bondage—it now carries the weight of what he has done. It pushes him into a darkness he has never walked before, both in the world and within himself.

In the silence that follows, Uldako wrestles with his next options. The night around him feels heavier, the darkness more oppressive. Uldako's mind whirls as he crouches in the darkness of the hovel. Dread claws at his thoughts. Staying here is not an option. They will find him and they'll see what he has done. His heart pounds in his chest, a maelstrom of fear, regret, and an overwhelming urge to survive.

7

Recurrence

In the midst of his turmoil, Uldako's eyes land on a surprising discovery within the hovel—a small cache of food. Seizing it instinctively, driven more by survival than reason, he clutches the unexpected find of dried meat and fruits. The sustenance, a tangible piece of survival, briefly anchors him amidst the tumult of his emotions.

As he regains composure, he cautiously peers out of the hut toward the gate to see if maybe the two guards have left, or maybe he could distract them. Yet now, to his dismay, there are six of them engaged in some form of hand game where they show different signs. Uldako has seen this game before at the slave camp where he grew up, though he never understood it. Escaping through there seems an impossible task at this moment.

I need to act swiftly; the sun will soon rise, and I'll be discovered with the lifeless guard, but there's no other immediate exit. What can I do?

He watches them, eyes narrowing, mind sharpening. The way out is blocked, and there's nowhere to run. Then, a revelation strikes him: Escape is imperative, but for now, disappearance is his only advantage. He must go to the one place they wouldn't think to search for him—at least not immediately. His cage.

With a stealth born of necessity, Uldako slips from the hovel, the market around him eerily quiet, save for the occasional shift and murmur. Each step is measured, a delicate balance between haste and caution as he navigates the familiar yet perilous path back to his enclosure.

Moving stealthily through the open gate toward the pen with the guards still fast asleep, Uldako catches the attention of several other slaves. Their eyes widen in the dim light, registering shock as they struggle to comprehend what they are witnessing, their gazes fill with flickering questions. Realizing he has taken too much food in his panicked state, Uldako makes a swift decision. Tossing portions of his stolen bounty to the other captives, he shares his unintended fortune, a silent plea for their silence and complicity.

Finally, he reaches his own cage. With a look that encompasses both the freedom he has nearly grasped and the complex web of consequences his actions have woven, Uldako reenters the confines of his imprisonment. The irony of seeking refuge in the very place he has fought so desperately to escape is not lost on him, but the pressing need for concealment overshadows all else.

His heart, still racing from the fight and the stealthy return to his cage, now hammers with a new urgency. He needs to secure the latch, to make it appear as though he has never left, to blend back into the ranks of the enslaved without drawing the suspicion of the guards.

In the dim light, Uldako examines the latch mechanism closely, his fingers tracing the contours of the bolt he manipulated earlier with the rope. The catch rope, his tool of liberation, now serves a new purpose—to pull the latch shut in a mimicry of being locked from the outside.

With meticulous care, Uldako loops the rope around the latch, each movement deliberate and silent. With a gentle tug, he guides the bolt into place, the sound of it thudding shut echoing in the stillness—a clear reminder of the danger surrounding him. The finality of the click, as the latch settles into its locked position, brings both relief and a foreboding sense of the uncertainty that lies ahead.

In the tense moments following his return to the cage, Uldako is acutely aware of the fragility of his circumstances. Dawn creeps closer, ready to expose his deeds under its first light. His gaze locks onto the rope, eyes wide. The fear that the guards might come bursting in at any moment drives him to act with urgent resolve.

The rope, his temporary tool for attempted freedom, now needs to vanish back into its original setting, melding indistinctly with the rest of the cage's structure. Returning it to where he had initially found it, Uldako works rapidly to integrate the rope back into the fabric of the cage. His fingers, adept from the night's earlier efforts, move quickly, weaving the rope among the existing strands and wooden beams. This is no time for precision or careful craftsmanship; his goal is to make the rope look as if it has never been disturbed, to ensure that no guard will cast a second glance its way.

As he finishes, the rope once again appears to be just another part of the cage, indistinguishable from the rest. Uldako takes a brief moment to survey his work, ensuring there are no obvious signs of tampering.

Heart still quivering from the night's exertions of his hurried efforts, Uldako barely allows himself a moment to catch his breath. He positions himself in the cage as though disturbed from sleep, trying to present an image of innocence and weariness, hoping to eliminate any suspicion that might arise.

In this moment of forced calm, as he seeks to steady himself and quiet the turmoil of his thoughts, Uldako becomes acutely aware of the eyes upon him. The other slaves, shrouded in the semi-darkness of the approaching dawn, watch him. Once potential allies in silent suffering, now their eyes bore into him with cold judgment. They have all witnessed his futile attempt at escape, and in their eyes, his actions are not those of a hero but a harbinger of heightened danger for them all.

This is a community where survival depends on keeping one's head down, and Uldako's defiance has unwittingly drawn a dangerous light on them all. Their glares are a silent indictment, a unified message that his reckless pursuit of freedom has breached the unspoken contract of mutual invisibility that has kept them all safe.

Those who received pieces of food from Uldako act with swift discretion, consuming the evidence of his generosity with hurried, furtive bites. They understand the stakes as well as he does; the nourishment, a fleeting gift in their world of scarcity, now represents a risk to them all. In a silent pact of unity, they share what they can with others, ensuring that no trace of the food remains.

This act of communal concealment is an embodiment of their unspoken bond, a mutual understanding that survival in the slave market is a shared endeavor. The wait for the guards to make their morning rounds is agonizing, each breath stretched thin by anticipation and fear. Uldako remains acutely alert to every sound, every footstep that approaches, ready to adopt the guise of just another slave, worn from the day's labor and oblivious to the night's shadows.

In the end, the immediate burst of activity he had feared does not come. Dawn breaks over the slave market with its usual, oppressive routine. Uldako's quick actions might have bought him another day, another chance to plan and dream of freedom, even as the weight of what has transpired—and what he has done—settles heavily upon his shoulders.

The guards arrive with their usual demeanor, showing no sign that anything is amiss. *They must have found his body by now. Why don't they question the slaves?* Uldako's mind spins as they let him out of the cage with the others.

Today, however, marks a change in Uldako's immediate fate: He is among those chosen for the slave market's trade. As he and the other chosen slaves are led toward the display cages, a palpable tension hangs in the air, each step a reminder of the peril awaiting them.

The morning procession halts abruptly as an overseer rushes toward the guards watching over Uldako and the other slaves. His eyes are wide and breathless, his voice tight with urgency.

"They found Goran dead in his bed," he blurts, the words slicing through the dull routine like a sharpened axe. Shock ripples through the guards, cracking their usual mask of indifference for a fleeting moment.

The immediate concern turns to the possibility of an escaped slave, a direct threat to their control and order. "Any slaves missing?" one of the leading slave masters demands, his eyes sweeping over Uldako and the others.

After a quick look, the reply comes, "No, all accounted for; they were all here at the morning distribution." The guards, visibly unsettled by the news of Goran's death, are instructed to return the slaves to their usual quarters. The group is hastily disbanded, the guards called away by the slave master of the camp to investigate the murder and to decide on the next steps.

Uldako, amidst the confusion and sudden shift in plans, feels a cold shiver run down his spine. Though the oppressors did not yet link the incident to him, the discovery of Goran's body means that the moment of reckoning creeps closer. The precarious balance he maintained is now at risk of crumbling under the weight of suspicion and potential retribution.

As Uldako is led back to the relative safety of his regular enclosure, he thinks about the possible implications of Goran's death being discovered. The market, already a place of despair and suffering, will tighten its grip in the wake of this violence. Security will be heightened, the guards more vigilant and cruel, the space for Uldako to maneuver ever shrinking.

In the safety of his cage, he understands that his situation has become more dangerous than ever. The need for caution, for a well-thought-out plan, has never been more critical. As the market reels from the shock of the murder, Uldako knows that every action, every decision, will now be under scrutiny.

Uldako feels the pressure as many eyes are upon him. The other slaves, their expressions filled with fear, awe, and unspoken understanding, know what has transpired. Yet, within this silent acknowledgment, there is an agreement: No words will be spoken, no accusations made. The seriousness of the situation is understood by all; if it becomes known that a slave has killed an overseer, the retribution will be swift and merciless. The customary response to such an act of defiance is brutal—the execution of many slaves to quell any hint of rebellion and to serve as a grim reminder of the power the masters hold over life and death.

Yet, as Uldako lies there, contemplating the possible outcomes, he can't help but wonder about the likelihood of the masters resorting to such extreme measures. The slave market is different from that of normal slave owners; would they really risk losing many of their "stock" over the actions of one slave? The trade of slavery, grim as it is, suggests they might not. However, the uncertainty of this assumption does little to ease his mind.

In the stillness of the cage, Uldako wrestles with the consequences of his actions. The possibility that his bid for freedom might inadvertently lead to a harsh crackdown on his fellow captives presses heavily on him. Yet, there is no turning back. The deed is done, and all he can do now is navigate the treacherous path ahead with as much caution and foresight as possible.

As two hand movements of the sun pass, the slave market reluctantly resumes its oppressive routine. Slave masters reappear, orchestrating the grim spectacle of showcasing slaves for trade once more. Among them, taskmasters congregate to select the day's workforce from the remaining captives.

Uldako stands within a display cage once again, a mere property for potential buyers to scrutinize. While he awaits the uncertain outcome of being on display, Uldako's attention is drawn to a hushed conversation among the guards nearby. They are discussing the murder of the guard, Goran, in tones laced with suspicion and unease. It is clear from their words that they suspect foul play within their own ranks, a twist Uldako didn't anticipate.

"All the slaves were locked up, so it could have been any of us, really," one guard mutters, his voice barely audible.

"Who'd have the most to gain from Goran's death?" asks another, their speculation weaving a complex web of mistrust among them.

This revelation offers Uldako a sliver of hope amidst his dire situation. The guards' assumption that one of their own is responsible for Goran's death significantly diverts suspicion away from the slaves. Uldako listens intently, absorbing every word while keeping his expression neutral, aware that any change in his demeanor could betray his keen interest in the conversation.

Their deliberation over motives and opportunities hints at deep-seated rivalries and grievances within the ranks of the overseers, a dynamic Uldako had been previously unaware of. The guards' focus on identifying a culprit among themselves presents an unexpected advantage, buying Uldako precious time.

As the guards continue to speculate, their theories growing more elaborate and distracted from the reality of the situation, Uldako can't help but feel a grim satisfaction. The chaos and confusion his actions have sown among the slavers is unintentional but welcome. However, he remains acutely aware that this respite could be fleeting. Any new evidence or shift in the guards' suspicions could easily place him and the other slaves back in jeopardy.

For now, though, Uldako uses this opportunity to observe the market's dynamics more closely, searching for any advantage or insight that might aid in his continued quest for freedom. The guards' internal discord is a reminder of the complexities of human relationships and power structures, even among those who uphold the brutal institution of slavery.

As Uldako waits in his display cage, a woman approaches the trading grounds, flanked by several figures who seem to be her family or close kin. Their arrival breaks the dull rhythm of the day, casting a new shadow of possibility over the captives lined up for barter.

The slave traders, quick to sense an opportunity, begin parading their human wares with cold efficiency. "This one's strong—fit for any hard labor," one of them says, gesturing lazily at a male slave with a flick of his hand.

The woman steps closer to inspect the man. "We need someone useful—not just for lifting stones," she replies, her tone detached, like she's shopping for animals, not humans.

Her companions chime in, their conversation weaving around the slaves like an impersonal breeze. "Remember, we need someone who can last. The last one barely made it through the season," another voice adds, a hint of annoyance threading through the words.

As their bartering continues, it becomes clear they come from a large settlement—a city called Larak. The name stirs something in Uldako. His world has been small, confined to cages and camps, but every passing mention of distant places feeds the fire inside him. The more he hears, the more he longs to be free…to see what lies beyond the walls.

At one point, their attention shifts toward Uldako, their eyes appraising him as a potential candidate. "What about this one? Seems strong enough, and he has an intelligent look to him," the woman muses. "But maybe he has a bit too much fire in his eyes. I need a slave whose soul is utterly broken."

After a brief discussion and further consideration, they opt for other slaves, dismissing Uldako with a casual indifference that stings less than he expected.

As the sun dips below the horizon, and shadows lengthen across the slave market, Uldako returns to his cage, his mind actively churning over the day's revelations. Realizing that the simmering distrust among the guards—intensified by the recent murder—could be exploited, Uldako begins formulating a plan. His strategy is bold and requires meticulous execution. By sowing further discord among the guards, he could create an opportunity for escape.

In the quiet depths of the early night, as the slave quarters envelop in a tense silence, Uldako discerns the unease and the expectant glances from his fellow captives. They are aware, to varying degrees, of his involvement in the recent disturbances among the guards. This truth serves as a dual-edged sword, kindling hope in some while instilling fear in others.

Sensing the anticipation, Uldako knows that the moment has arrived to address them, to lay out his plan not just as a path to freedom but as a way to rally them together.

"Listen, all of you! I'm escaping this place. Alone or together. You choose!" Uldako begins in a low but bold whisper.

"Hush! The guards will punish us," a voice says, speaking sharply from a nearby cage.

Uldako turns to the speaker, unfazed. Whether the command came from resentment or fear, he neither knows nor cares. "If you had been watching your masters," he replies quietly, "you would know they are now out of earshot, eating and drinking before they take their posts for the night. But how can you see anything while you are blinded by fear? You've seen what I can do. The guards are already turning on each other. We can use their distrust against them." He pauses, locking eyes with as many as he can, measuring their will to fight or follow.

"What exactly are you proposing?" whispers a woman whose strength has waned from countless hardships. Her once sturdy frame has grown gaunt and frail, with sunken cheeks and blue hollow eyes that still glimmer with a hint of defiance. Strands of her thin, matted hair frame a face etched with lines of suffering, and her hands, though trembling, clench into determined fists. Her voice carries the depth of her enduring fire.

Uldako leans in, his voice steady. "I plan to stir the pot," he explains. "Tonight, I'll begin by moving small things—items that won't be missed immediately but will seed doubt when found where they shouldn't be. These subtle disruptions will escalate their mistrust, possibly leading to infighting. Some might even abandon their posts or injure each other in disputes."

He looks into the eyes of his fellow captives, seeing both fear and flickering hope.

"When they are weakened by their own chaos and their numbers dwindle or a fight breaks out, that's our moment. We must be ready to seize it, to break free, no matter what." He takes a deep breath, pausing to see their reactions. "And when they're busy accusing each other, that's when we make our move," Uldako continues, a strategic gleam in his eyes. "But this isn't just about escape. It's about survival. If they discover one of us was behind Goran's death, they might take revenge on all of us."

The woman nods slowly, understanding the stakes. "And what if you're caught?" she asks, voicing the fear that hangs over them all like a shroud.

"I won't be," Uldako assures her, though he knows the risks are high. "But I will need your aid. Not just to stay silent, but to be ready. When the opportunity comes, we must all be prepared to act quickly as one."

The group trades glances, a tense silence stretching between them. At last, a young man with sharp brown eyes and short, spiked hair leans forward and grips the frame of his cage tightly as he breaks the silence.

"I am Haron, son of Rhakuf. I'll stand with you," he says—his voice quiet, but firm. "Better to risk everything for freedom than to rot here waiting for death." He pauses, casting a glance at the older woman, who had spoken earlier. "Join us, Mara," he urges, his gaze earnest. Then, turning to the others, he continues, "If we unite our efforts, we might just attain the freedom we've long yearned for. The time has come! Now or never!"

Haron's words seem to ignite a spark of courage in the others. One by one, they nod, each silently pledging their support.

Uldako is overwhelmed with gratitude and a sense of responsibility toward these courageous slaves who stepped forward. "Thank you," he says sincerely. "Keep your eyes sharp and your hearts ready. Ignite that ember of hope within each of you into a blazing fire that will engulf all obstacles on our path to freedom! We're not just fighting to escape this place; we're fighting for the right to live as free men and women out there in the world. We must remain united. Together, we are formidable, but if we are divided or hesitant, we will falter."

Uldako's words resonate with hope and practicality, rallying many of the slaves to his cause. They understand that this isn't a rash breakout but a calculated series of actions that will unfold over time, increasing their chances of success. This renewed feeling of purpose fills them with cautious optimism, though some remain understandably wary, their spirits dampened by the harshness of their bonds.

Uldako respects those who are concerned but remains undeterred, his resolve fortified by the necessity of his plan. As he lies in his cage that night, he is not just a captive but a strategist, setting the wheels of his plan in motion. The coming nights will see him implementing the first phase, testing the waters of his strategy and adapting as necessary.

The air in the slave market is still, but beneath that calm, tension builds—tension that Uldako hopes will one day drive them all toward freedom. The path is fraught with risks, but the promise of freedom, for himself and any who dare join him, spurs him onward. This is the beginning of a delicate dance of deception and strategy, one that Uldako is prepared to lead.

As dusk turns to deep night, sleep eludes Uldako. His mind races with the enormity of his plan. His body remains still, but within, anticipation rages. The quiet murmur of the other slaves settling down does little to calm his nerves. Tonight, his actions could set the stage for everything that follows, not just for him but for all those counting on him. Every breath he takes feels like a countdown to the moment when everything could change.

Uldako revisits his earlier plans, refining them into a bolder, more daring strategy. Previously, his primary concern was escaping before malnutrition weakened him beyond hope. Now, there is an added layer: He needs to ensure that everyone has enough strength to make a break for it when the opportunity arises. Stealing extra food from the guards' stockpile becomes crucial. Bolstering the spirit and strength of his fellow captives could provide the vital spark needed for the impending escape. This is no longer just about his own survival; it's about igniting a collective rebellion that could shatter their bondage for good.

Uldako plans to wait until the dead of night when most of the camp will be asleep, relying on the guards' exhaustion after a day of heightened suspicion. The timing has to be perfect. Too early, and too many eyes will still be open; too late, and dawn might catch him in the act. As the night deepens, each moment seems to stretch into an eternity.

"It's time," Uldako whispers to himself. He knows the risks are greater tonight. The guards will likely be on high alert given the recent tension and suspicions among them. Every sound seems amplified in the silence, every shadow a potential threat.

Carefully, Uldako begins to work on the rope that he had manipulated before, his fingers skilled and silent. He needs to ensure it will hold when he uses it to unlatch the cage once more. As he loosens the rope, he keeps one eye on the guards' station, noting the shifts in their movements and the timing of their patrols. Every detail is critical. The night air is thick with anticipation, but Uldako's mind is focused, his resolve unshakable.

As he continues to work the rope, an escalating sense of dread grips Uldako. What if his plan fails? Earlier, he spoke with conviction, trying to instill optimism and unity among the other slaves. But now, alone with his thoughts, the dread of potential failure looms large. Will they see him as a fool, blinded by dreams of freedom and oblivious to the danger he puts them all in?

His heart races, pounding so loudly he fears it might betray him. Each beat echoes his doubts, yet he forces his trembling hands to keep moving, knowing that hesitation now could mean the end of their only chance for escape.

A subtle vibration tingles through the ground beneath him. Uldako freezes, wondering if he imagined it. But then, it happens again—a slight shudder, like the impact of a heavy object being dropped. He holds his breath, straining his senses. The sounds are faint, likely unnoticeable under normal circumstances, but in the dead quiet of the night, they are unmistakable.

His mind is filled with possibilities. Are the slavers building something this late into the night? It feels as though large logs or heavy trunks are being systematically dropped somewhere within the camp. The vibrations grow stronger, more frequent, each thud sending a ripple through the soil that reaches his cage, stirring the dust around him.

The pattern of thuds grows louder, faster—each strike pulsing with urgency, maybe even desperation. Uldako frowns, confused. Why would such work happen in secret, and without slaves? What else could make such a sound?

Then it comes—a scream. Wild and piercing, it tears through the still darkness. It isn't from pain or the clash of battle—it's something deeper. A cry born of raw, instinctive terror. The echo lingers in the air, pressing in from all sides, thick with dread.

Almost immediately, shouts erupt from near the main gate. A guard's voice, sharp and commanding, barks orders into the darkness, though his words are muffled and distant.

The camp, previously steeped in an uneasy silence, now buzzes with chaotic commotion that fills Uldako with unease. His mind churns with confusion as he tries to piece together what's happening, frustrated by the barrier that blocks his view of the main market area. The wall, thick and unyielding, stands between him and the source of the chaos, leaving him to guess at the dangers unfolding beyond it. His nerves tingle with fear, urging him for action.

Amidst the growing disarray and the sounds of guards scrambling to positions, another sound emerges—a deep, resonating roar that vibrates through the air, primal and powerful.

8

Flight

It's a sound so foreign, so fearsome, it seems not to belong to the world Uldako knows. The roar reverberates like a mountain cracking from within—a terrifying bellow that seems to speak of ancient, untamed forces unleashed.

"What was that?" His eyes widen with dread. *What kind of beast or wrath has fallen on the taskmasters?* he wonders.

In an instant, all his careful plans, every strategy and flicker of hope for a silent, calculated escape, teeters on the edge. Shadows stretch and voices rise. The camp is unraveling, and something ancient and terrible has come knocking.

The once peaceful night erupts into chaos as screams, yells, and roars fill the air, blending into a cacophony of terror. Guards leap to their feet, sprinting toward the source of the commotion. It sounds as though a massive beast is trying to break through the main gates. Wasting no time, Uldako swiftly unlocks his cage, his hands moving deftly in the darkness.

As he flings open the cage door, a massive crash reverberates through the camp—it sounds like the beast finally breached the gates. For a fleeting moment, Uldako feels a rush of grim satisfaction. The slavers, who had seemed so monstrous just moments ago, are now facing a real monster. Amidst the din of chaos, with the sounds of screams and the clamor of disarray surrounding him, Uldako knows this is their moment.

"Now is the time," he shouts to his fellow captives. "We need to get out of here—escape or get eaten!"

Although part of him wonders if the slave overseers, with their spears and coordinated efforts, might eventually subdue the creature, Uldako is not willing to wait and find out. This disturbance is the perfect catalyst to spur the slaves into action. Wasting no time, Uldako moves quickly along the row of cages, unlocking each one.

"Help me open the others!" he urges those he's freed. "We move together!"

As the slaves spill out of their cages, they begin to assist one another, some unlocking more cages, while others help the injured or weaker slaves to their feet. Uldako directs them toward the smaller gate that leads to the lumber area. The layout of this area is familiar to many, and it offers the best chance of slipping away unnoticed into the forest beyond.

"Stay quiet, and keep moving," Uldako instructs in a hushed whisper amidst the chaos. The risk of encountering guards remains, and caution is essential, even in their desperate bid for freedom.

The group moves as one, a sudden unity forged among the slaves. They navigate the familiar paths toward the workers' gate, supporting each other and moving with a purpose ignited by the promise of freedom and the immediate threat of the monstrous roars that continue to shake the night. With every step, their resolve hardens, the terror behind them serving as a reminder of the peril they face and the urgency of their escape.

As they reach the camp gate, the group finds it expectedly unguarded, just as Uldako had hoped. Seizing the moment, they quickly swing it open, and for the first time in their lives, they step out by their own free will—not to perform the grueling work that has been their daily torment, not burdened by exhaustion and the dread of beatings, but with the exhilarating prospect of freedom before them. The night air feels different on their faces, filled with the scent of liberation and the promise of a new beginning.

They move swiftly through the woodworking area, a place familiar from days spent felling trees under the harsh watchful eyes of their captors. Now, they traverse it in a rush of desperation. The once oppressive surroundings feel like an ally in their escape, each step taking them further from their bonds.

As they press on, the forest grows denser, the shadows of towering trees enveloping them like a protective cloak. The foliage provides cover, guiding them away from their past lives and into the embrace of freedom. Behind them, tumult engulfs the camp, the screams and the deep terrifying roars of the beast echoing through the night. Yet, ahead lies the unknown—vast and uncharted.

Their pace quickens as the urgency of escape ignites their movements. Branches snap underfoot, leaves rustle around them, and the cool night air fills their lungs as they run deeper into the forest. Uldako's goal is clear: put as much distance as possible between themselves and the slave camp. As he glances at the faces of his fellow escapees, he sees the same fire of determination burning in their eyes. They are driven by the awakening awareness of what freedom might truly mean.

As the night deepens, the group of escaped slaves pushes forward relentlessly, navigating the dense forest with grit and focus. The distant sounds of chaos—screams and roars—has long since faded, yet they continue as if propelled by some unseen force, an invisible taskmaster driving them onward with an invisible whip.

The terrain is unforgiving; trees emerge like silent sentinels, thorns and branches reach out to snag their ragged garments and tear at their skin, but they do not slow. They move under a haze of desperation and resolve, helping one another over fallen logs, supporting those who stumble, all in a profound silence that speaks volumes of their shared ordeal.

After much time has passed, the first faint light of dawn begins to sneak through the canopy of trees, and the world around them gradually comes into view. The sun rises as it does every day, indifferent to the turmoil that has unfolded under the cover of darkness. Its light seems almost surreal, a stark contrast to the darkness they felt while imprisoned.

Gradually, the pace of their flight begins to slow. Realization sets in, tugging their minds like a weight. They are running relentlessly, they are still malnourished, their bodies pushed to the limit.

As dawn breaks more fully, they start collecting themselves, their composure returning in the face of the new day's light. Slowing their pace, they finally look at one another, taking in the toll of their escape on each other's faces.

"Is everyone okay?" Jem's voice breaks the silence, his tone as much for his own reassurance as for others'. It is a moment for them to pause and take stock of their reality.

"Let's rest a short while," someone suggests, and no one argues as they walk through a relatively clear area where they can sit without the underbrush pricking at them. Dropping to the ground, they each feel the weight of their freedom and the physical demands of their flight.

"We need to make a plan," another voice chimes in. "Where are we going?" The question hangs in the air, heavy with implications. They are free, yes, but what does freedom mean in this vast, unfamiliar wilderness?

The group huddles together, their breaths coming in ragged gasps. Uldako knows they have little time to rest. They need to decide their next move quickly.

"What's the plan?" Jem asks, looking around at the group. His voice is calm, but his eyes betray his concern.

"We can't linger here," Uldako says, shaking his head. "The slavers might regroup and hunt us down. We have two options: split up to evade capture or stick together and find a safe place to regain our strength. If we stay here, they will find us."

A heavy silence settles over the group as they weigh their options. Fear of recapture is written plainly on every face, yet no one dares to speak.

At last, a woman breaks the silence. "They've faced beasts like that before." Her voice is calm but firm. "They know how to repel it—and they've likely already done so. They'll be coming after us soon."

Worried glances pass between the others, uncertainty carved into their features. Most have never known the freedom to choose—only the harsh orders of their slave masters. An older man speaks up, voice rough and trembling. "Zara, your calm has always steadied me. But seeing your eyes now fills me with dread."

"Then we don't have much time," Uldako says, rising to his feet. "I have a small camp not far from here. It's hidden, with some supplies. It's our best shot."

Tarn nods. "We've got no better option," he says, glancing around. "We need to move—and fast."

Reluctantly, the others agree. The fear of being hunted again gnaws at them, but the hope of shelter—however small—is enough to drive their feet forward.

"We need to cover our tracks," Tarn adds, stepping ahead. "Uldako, take the lead and the rest of us will follow you in a line."

During the trek, Tarn moves with practiced skill, brushing out footprints, guiding them over thick tree roots and patches of stone where their steps won't show. He orders two young men to guard the rear, teaching them how to scatter tracks when they see any left behind.

Uldako observes Tarn's adeptness in forging a path while concealing their tracks. "You're quite skilled at this." Admiration is evident in his tone.

Tarn glances at him, a look of shame crossing his face. He hesitates for a moment before speaking. "A few days ago, I told you I was a trader," he begins, his voice barely above a whisper. "I talked about my family, about how I used to travel and make deals. But there's more to it than that. I wasn't just any trader." He pauses, his eyes avoiding Uldako's. "I was a slave trader," he admits, the words laden with regret. "It's something I'm deeply ashamed of."

Uldako is taken aback by Tarn's revelation but decides to mask his true feelings for the moment. Questions still burn in his mind, yet he sees the weight in Tarn's eyes—the pain, the guilt, the silent battle of a man wrestling with his past.

"Well," Uldako says, giving a firm nod, "your skills are helping now. What matters is what you do from here."

Tarn gathers the courage to meet Uldako's gaze, a mix of gratitude and determination etched on his face. "Now you know who I am. There are no more dark secrets," he vows. "I want to help us all make it through this. Maybe it's my chance to make amends for the wretched things I've done."

The group continues moving, but Uldako can't shake the feeling that they are being followed. He keeps glancing over his shoulder, expecting to see the guards emerging from the trees at any moment.

After the sun has climbed several fingers across the sky, they see a spot to rest up the hill. Exhausted and malnourished, their bodies have been pushed to the limit.

They climb up to higher terrain, and Uldako signals for the group to stop. As they sit down to catch their breath, he looks down into the valley below. His heart sinks at what his eyes are telling him, as if he is trapped in a nightmare. He sees the taskmasters far in the distance, moving steadily in their direction.

"They're coming," he says quietly, a chill of fear running through him. "They are somehow following us."

A murmur of fear and uncertainty spreads through the group. Some voices tremble with the suggestion of surrender, while others whisper the desperate urge to keep running. "We can't run forever; we are too weak!" one of the men says, his voice laced with exhaustion. "They'll catch up to us sooner or later."

Tarn steps forward, his face set with grim purpose. "He's right. We can't keep running. But we can use this terrain to our advantage. We can lay an ambush. I've done it before."

The group looks at Tarn, a mixture of hope and skepticism in their eyes. "How?" Zara asks, her voice tinged with doubt.

Tarn meets her gaze evenly. "Trust me, I know what I'm doing. We'll use the terrain to our advantage and catch them off guard by setting traps."

Uldako nods in agreement. "Tarn's right. That is our only choice. We'll stay here, set up our defenses, and arm ourselves. We need to make the most of what we have."

"Then let the *dingir-meš* protect us!" Zara chimes in, her eyes burning with resolve. "We'll fight for our freedom. We won't go back; we will be free, in life or in death."

"Yes, we will. We'll fight, and we will survive, or we will die as free men and women!" Uldako agrees, feeling a renewed fire of purpose.

The group springs into action, their fear gradually replaced by determination. They gather branches, vines, and stones to create makeshift traps and weapons. Tarn guides them to identify the best spots to set the traps and plan the ambush.

As they work toward one goal, Uldako feels a growing bond of camaraderie among the group. They are no longer just a collection of captives; they are a united force, bound together by their shared struggle for freedom. The slavers might be coming, but they are no longer defenseless captives. They are prepared to defend their newfound freedom with their lives.

As the sun begins to rise higher in the sky, Uldako and the others finish their preparations and take their positions. The peaceful night had erupted into chaos and left them with fear of the unknown, but now, in the light of day, they are ready to face their fate. With Uldako and Tarn leading the freed slaves, they have a chance—a chance to finally be free once and for all.

As the sun slips past the span of a hand, they wait with bated breath, the tension palpable in the air. The distant sounds of the slavers moving through the forest grow closer, but they stand ready. Each member of the group hides among the trees and underbrush, their hearts pounding in unison as they ready themselves for what is to come.

In the intense silence, every rustle of leaves, every snap of a twig sets their nerves on edge. But they hold their ground, ready to fight for their freedom.

Finally, the slavers appear—a small group moving swiftly through the forest, their eyes scanning the surroundings for any sign of their prey. They are heavily armed, their faces set in grim resolve.

Uldako's heart pounds in his chest as he watches them approach. He signals to the others, and they ready their weapons—makeshift spears, rocks, anything they could find.

As the oppressors move closer, they trigger the first trap—a hidden hole covered with leaves and branches. One of the slave overseers falls in with a cry, and the others leap into action, their attention focused on rescuing their comrade.

"Now!" Uldako shouts, and the group launches their attack. They emerge from their hiding places, throwing rocks and jabbing with their spears. The overseers are taken by surprise, their formation breaking as they try to fend off the sudden assault. The battle is fierce and chaotic.

Uldako fights with everything he has, his movements driven by desperation. He can see his comrades fighting just as fiercely, their faces set in grim resolve.

Despite their initial success, the overseers are skilled fighters, and the tide of the battle begins to turn. Uldako knows they can't hold out forever. They are too weakened, malnourished, tired. They need to end this quickly.

"Focus on their leader!" he shouts, pointing to the man who seems to be directing the slavers. If they can take him out, the rest might scatter.

The group rallies, their attacks becoming more coordinated. They press forward, driving the slavers back. Uldako fights his way to the leader, their eyes locking in a moment of mutual recognition.

With a fierce cry, Uldako lunges, spear aimed at the leader's chest. The man blocks it, swinging his sword in a sharp arc—but Uldako ducks just in time as the blade slices the air above him. A sudden rush of focus and clarity floods him. The world slows. Sound fades. All he sees is the enemy drawing back his sword for another strike.

But he's too slow.

Uldako sweeps the man's legs out from under him. The slave master crashes to the forest floor, and in one clean motion, Uldako drives the spear through his chest. The man gasps once, eyes wide in disbelief—then lies still.

The remaining slavers hesitate, their courage shaken.

"Now! Drive them back!" Uldako shouts, pulling out and hurling his bloodied spear into another slaver as the rest stare in shock.

With a final surge of strength, the group drives the overseers back, forcing them to retreat in disarray. The last few are quickly surrounded, and the captives finish them off with unrelenting resolve. For every slave, this is the moment they've waited for. After years of pain and suffering, they finally strike back—against the ones who beat them, branded them, and killed their kin.

Zara plunges a sword into the chest of the final slaver, her face streaked with tears. All the torment, all the buried screams of her years in bondage, erupt in that single blow.

Then, at last, the forest falls still. The echoes of battle fade, and silence takes hold once more.

Uldako's breath comes in ragged bursts as he surveys the scene. His gaze falls on the still forms of two fallen comrades among the bruised and bloodied survivors. Weariness marks every face, yet something wild glimmers in their eyes, something impossible—they are free.

The aftermath hums with the memory of violence, but beneath it stirs a deeper truth: the fetters are broken. Their freedom is real, and it floods their chests like fire and wind—unbelievable yet undeniable.

For a moment, the forest floor feels hallowed. In this quiet, stained ground, hope—fragile but fierce—begins to rise.

Uldako's emotions erupt in a loud roar, a primal release of everything pent up inside him. One by one, the others join in, their voices merging into a triumphant chorus. Some cry, tears streaming down their faces, others collapsing to the ground, overwhelmed, while a few laugh out loud, a sound that has been absent for far too long.

"We did it!" Zara's voice trembles with shock and relief.

Uldako lets a weary smile spread across his face. "We did," he says softly. "But two gave their lives so that we may be free. Their sacrifice will not be in vain."

Jem steps forward. "Indeed. We will never forget this day. We can rest here for the night, but come dawn, we need to move to a safer location."

Uldako glances at Tarn and looks back at Jem. "A good plan. We are too weak to continue our journey now. I advise you all to use this time to tend to your wounds and to get some rest. Also, try to find some food nearby. Scavenge what you can from the slavers."

Zara steps forward with a desperate look in her eyes. "What are we going to do with the bodies of Mara and Haron?" she asks with tears still lingering on her cheeks. "We cannot just leave them here."

Uldako stands frozen, uncertain of what to do or say. He has never faced a moment like this before, and the uncertainty gnaws at him. A young man with deep brown eyes steps forward, his voice cold and practical. "Why not leave them here? They're dead."

Jem's brow furrows in response, his face reflecting clear disapproval. "Here in the South and in the East, they may abandon their dead without a second thought, but it is not right. We should honor them, give them a proper farewell. I say we burn their bodies, let the flames carry their souls away." He turns to Uldako, searching his face for agreement. After a pause, Uldako gives a slow nod.

As they turn to ready the fire, Jem looks at the dead slave masters and speaks again. "And the slavers? We should burn them on a separate pyre. They were evil, but they are still human."

"They are not. They are monsters. Let them rot!" Zara bursts out.

"Uldako?" Jem presses.

Hearing Jem's words, Uldako realizes how numb he has become to death and violence after so many summers as a slave. Yet recently, he caught a glimpse of light in this dark world—the words and actions of Seth and his warriors.

But now with more blood on his hands, he knows he must be careful not to slip further into darkness. His soul battles within. *It should not be this easy to kill. I cannot become like the slave masters. But Zara is right; they deserve to rot after everything they've done.*

Yet another thought burns within him as the traveler's words echo in his mind from long ago: *A tooth for a tooth, blood for blood. If this is how evil is repaid, then how are you any better than them?*

Uldako stares down at his hands, the blood dark against his skin. The weight of it settles in his chest. "I must try to kindle the light within me," he tells his heart.

He looks at the slavers, torn between justice and mercy. The battle within him grows stronger with each breath. *What would Seth do?*

It is Tarn that comes to Uldako's rescue. "We don't have the strength to burn all of them. It will take too much effort to gather all the wood required to burn so many. We are too weak and barely hanging on ourselves. Let's only take care of Mara and Haron and rest."

Jem reluctantly agrees. "I guess you're right."

With quiet resolve, they set to work, gathering wood and building a pyre. The silence that follows is thick, broken only by the crackling of the flames as they consume the bodies. Each slave stands motionless, the fire's glow reflecting in their eyes, a grave reminder of how close they have come to death themselves. They understand the cost of their freedom and the risk they have taken to escape the cruelty of their masters.

After a time, Uldako turns away from the flickering flames, his voice steady as he begins to delegate tasks to the group, guiding them back to the work that still lies ahead.

The group moves carefully, helping one another, tending wounds, and searching the area for anything edible. The gatherers return with a few small pieces of dried meat from the slavers, insects, worms, and bitter green leaves—meager scraps, yet to the starving, it feels like a feast. For the first time, they eat by their own choice.

"We'll need water soon," someone murmurs, scanning the dry terrain.

"We'll find some tomorrow," Uldako says with quiet certainty.

As night falls, exhaustion takes over, and the group quickly falls asleep under the dark canopy of the forest. Uldako, Tarn, and Jem take turns standing guard, vigilant against any unwelcome visitors, whether man or beast.

When dawn breaks, the group stirs from their rest, ready to face the challenges of a new day. They gather their belongings and set off once more, hearts lifted by their hard-won victory over the slavers. They know the journey ahead will be grueling with their weakened, malnourished bodies, but they have proven that they can fight back and win.

As they set out, Zara walks beside Uldako and asks, "How far is your shelter?"

"Not far," he replies. "Three hands to the sun, and we'll be there."

He spots the distant hills rising ahead—the ones he remembers well. Their shape stirs confidence within him. "My camp is near those hills in the distance."

Tarn guides their movements once more, meticulously masking their trail. Uldako knows that without Tarn's expertise, the slave overseers would have found them much sooner and held the upper hand. They move through the forest with a heightened sense of urgency, fully aware that the remaining slavers could still be in pursuit when they find out what happened to the others.

After what feels like an eternity, Uldako finally declares, "We're here! The lake is just ahead."

As they break through the dense forest, a vast, glistening lake stretches before them—fresh water, clear and still. A young man bolts toward it, but Uldako catches his arm, eyes searching the area for danger.

Only when he gives the signal does the group erupt in joy, rushing forward to drink. Laughter and gasps of relief fill the air as they drop to their knees and taste freedom in the water.

"My shelter is just up ahead," Uldako says as he wipes the water off his mouth while looking for any signs of Šarru. He can't help but wonder what has happened to his friend since his capture. While there are many dangers in the wild, Šarru can certainly fend for himself. Yet, would the bear have any reason to stay in this place?

Uldako leads the group to his hidden refuge that he crafted—it isn't much, but it will offer shelter and protection from the elements for some of the escaped slaves. The space is small, but he figures some of the wounded can sleep inside while the others rest outside.

As they get closer, Uldako rushes ahead to check the shelter for Šarru, but his face falls—there's no sign of him. Pushing down his concern, he shifts his focus to the supplies. To his relief, some dried food still remains. It isn't much, but at this moment, it's a lifeline.

His stone tools and weapons are also untouched—a small but crucial arsenal. Just seeing them again strengthens his resolve.

Stepping out of the shelter, Uldako calls to the group, "Come—let's share what little food we have."

As they gather around, a cautious optimism begins to replace their exhaustion. The simple act of sharing a meal brings a fleeting sense of normalcy and camaraderie. Uldako scans the surrounding area, his thoughts drifting to his loyal companion, Šarru. The bear's absence weighs heavily on him. The presence of Šarru would not only bolster their spirits but also provide invaluable support in the challenges that lay ahead.

Before emotion can overtake him, Uldako forces himself to focus on the present. He turns his attention to the weary faces around him—each one marked by suffering, each one carrying silent scars.

Beneath the ancient trees, they eat, rest, and tend to their wounds, finding a brief shelter in this hidden refuge. As they share the last of Uldako's hidden supplies, the truth settles over them like a low, creeping fog. They are free—but their freedom is fragile, uncertain, and shadowed by the threat of pursuit.

The slave masters will not give up easily. Ruthless and unrelenting, they thrive on control and coin. When they learn that the first search party has failed, they will send more—driven by a cold resolve to reclaim what they believe is theirs.

Yet, amidst the looming threat, there is a glimmer of hope. The dense forest and their carefully covered tracks offer a sanctuary, at least for now. They are a good distance from the slave camp, making immediate discovery unlikely.

Just as an uneasy calm begins to settle over the group, a rustling in the underbrush shatters the silence. Hearts race and muscles tense, ready for another confrontation. But then, out of the darkness, comes a familiar, comforting sound—a low, rumbling growl.

Uldako's heart skips a beat as he knows what is about to happen, but his new friends do not!

A large shape emerges from the shadows, and there, standing before them, is a terrifying great bear. Instantly, the group of former slaves erupts into chaos. Screams pierce the air as everyone scrambles to cram into the tiny shelter at once, arms and legs flailing as they push and struggle to flee from the approaching beast.

The scene is pure pandemonium, with elbows jabbing and feet stomping in a desperate bid to squeeze into the small space. Someone shouts, "Every man for himself!" while another gets wedged sideways in the doorway, legs kicking helplessly.

Meanwhile, Šarru, completely unfazed, ambles up to Uldako and nuzzles him with affection. Uldako bursts into laughter, wrapping his arms around the bear with a joy he can't contain.

"Šarru! I'm so glad you're still here," he says, a tear slipping down his cheek as he realizes just how much this bond means to him.

The bear lets out a cheerful grunt—blissfully unaware of the terror he's caused.

Seeing Uldako's reaction, the group slowly realizes there's no danger. They emerge from their shelter pile-up, looking sheepish and disheveled. Laughter bubbles up as the tension dissolves, everyone now chuckling at the absurdity of the situation.

Uldako, still grinning, introduces his friend. "Everyone, meet Šarru—my loyal *dusa* and protector. No need to worry; he's on our side."

The group relaxes, relief and wonder mingling as they watch the great bear settle beside them. The creature's unexpected calm turns their tense day into a moment of shared warmth and laughter—the first of many as they begin their new path to freedom.

They had feared an enemy, but instead, they found a new ally. The group watches in awe and disbelief as Uldako reunites with Šarru. The bear, sensing the group's exhaustion and fear, seems to understand. Šarru stays close, providing a sense of security and warmth with his presence.

After a brief rest, Uldako stands and signals to some of the group. "Let's gather more food before the sun sets," he suggests. Together, they venture out, collecting supplies, including the plentiful crabs they spotted earlier. The sight of Šarru, now a reassuring guardian, fills them with renewed hope and confidence.

After the search for food, they gather to eat and rest together. Though weariness clings to them, a quiet hope begins to take root. They start sharing stories, voices soft but steady, and in those small moments, new bonds begin to form.

Settling in for the night, Uldako feels profound gratitude. They have survived another day and found a safe place to rest. Tomorrow will bring new challenges, but for now, they are together, and they are free.

The night passes with an unusual calm. The presence of Šarru seems to ward off any other dangers. The group sleeps in shifts, keeping watch and tending to their wounds.

Morning arrives slowly, the first light of dawn filtering through the dense canopy of trees. One by one the group stirs, stretching their sore limbs and preparing for the day. As they sit in the clearing, Uldako gathers the group around the campfire, his face solemn but determined.

"I need to set out on a quest soon. I need to find a man named Seth and gather more information about the location of my *ama*," he begins, his voice steady. "You're free to stay here—the slave overseers might not come looking for you in this area."

One of them raises a concern. "But Uldako, if you lived here, does that mean you were captured here? Could the slave traders know this place?"

Uldako nods slowly. "You're right. Slave hunters caught me at the lake and sold me to the slave camp. Even some of the slave masters from my old camp—Magan—know about the lake. But not the shelter. They don't know about this hideout and wouldn't come looking for slaves here, but they might pass through to catch crabs or refill their waterskins. So wc still need to stay alert."

As Uldako meets the uncertain gazes of the freed slaves, he reassures them, "I will remain here with you for a couple of days to gather my strength before embarking on my quest." The relief is clearly visible among them as they express their gratitude for Uldako's extended presence, feeling safer in his and Šarru's company.

Over the next few days, Uldako becomes a pillar of strength for the group, guiding them through the intricacies of survival with unwavering resolve in the area he knows so well.

As they toil together, forging makeshift tools and gathering provisions, a sense of unity begins to take root among them. Šarru, the steadfast bear, becomes not just a guardian but a companion to all, his presence lending an air of reassurance to their makeshift camp.

Amidst the tasks and quiet preparations, an unspoken truth settles over them all: Their time together is short. A few express a desire to follow Uldako into the unknown, but he gently refuses. His path is uncertain, and he knows he can't offer them a future—at least not yet. They'll be safer with Jem, who speaks of a hidden camp beyond the reach of the slavers.

Most agree to go with Jem. Some of the older ones—those not born in captivity—long to return to the homes they once knew. Each person carries their own uncertainty about what lies ahead. Yet in the silence between them, there is comfort. They've endured together, and the bond forged in pain and survival now steadies their steps, even as they prepare to part ways.

On that final night, as they gather around the crackling flames, their stories intertwine like tendrils of smoke rising into the night sky. Laughter mingles with tales of triumph and loss, weaving a tapestry of memories that will sustain them in the days to come.

With the first light of dawn painting the horizon, Uldako rises from his place by the fire, his gaze lingering on each member of the group as he realizes they are all preparing to leave. "Looks like the time has come," he addresses them as he prepares his goodbyes.

Jem steps forward. "We've decided to leave this place the same time you do. I will take most of them under my wing and go to the safe village I know."

Uldako nods with a smile. "Well then, they are all in good hands!"

Once the final preparations are done, Uldako turns to the group, locking eyes with each one. A tightness rises in his chest, and he struggles to hold back the tears. They've become more than survivors—they've become family. He sees the same emotion mirrored in their eyes.

"Stay safe," he says, his voice thick with feeling. "And remember, you are free!"

They nod in silent understanding, their expressions full of gratitude and determination. Then, with overwhelming emotion, one of them exclaims, "Thank you for saving my life. I will spread the word of Uldako, *dumu* of Deborah!"

Echoing sentiments follow, each member expressing their heartfelt appreciation. In Uldako, they have discovered more than a leader; he is a symbol of hope, a guiding light in their world of darkness. Though his physical presence will soon depart, his legacy will endure, a light of strength to navigate the challenges that await them.

With a final farewell, Uldako and Šarru set out into the unknown, their steps echoing the rhythm of their collective journey. And as they disappear into the depths of the forest, the rest of the group sets out on their own journey, their hearts lifted by the knowledge that they have faced the darkness together and emerged stronger, united in their quest for freedom.

9

Jabal

Uldako sets out, journeying west—toward the region where the safe camp of Eridu is said to stand. Though Eridu is not his destination, the worn map in his hand marks a smaller, lesser-known camp called Jabal, nestled somewhere between that city and his shelter.

With Šarru at his side, Uldako moves cautiously, venturing further than ever before. The dense forests begin to thin, giving way to open terrain—rolling hills and wide skies stretching above him. The wind carries unfamiliar scents. Every shadow, every whisper of movement, draws his eye. He walks not just through land, but also through mystery.

The world begins to change.

He passes through lands teeming with life—creatures both strange and wondrous, unlike any he has seen. Towering herbivores move in slow herds, while scaled predators stalk the brush with primal grace. Peculiar beasts with twisted horns and luminous eyes peer through the undergrowth, vanishing before he can blink.

It feels like stepping into a forgotten age, a living tapestry woven from the breath of creation itself. And through it all, Uldako presses on—alert, awed, and unshaken—toward the place marked only by a name and hope.

Among the creatures, a marvel catches his eye—a flightless bird with a regal bearing, adorned in plumage of every hue imaginable. Its powerful legs propel it forward with an effortless grace, each step leaving a delicate imprint upon the earth. Uldako marvels at the bird's intricate feathers, which shimmer like a cascade of precious jewels in the dappled sunlight.

Nearby, a creature of intriguing demeanor ambles along, its form cloaked in a sturdy shell that gleams with an otherworldly sheen. With each deliberate movement, it seems to carry the weight of ancient wisdom upon its back, its eyes peering out from beneath its protective armor with a tranquil gaze that speaks of a life lived in harmony with the rhythms of the natural world.

Amidst the verdant expanse, Uldako's eyes are drawn to a herd of deer, their graceful forms adorned with ethereal white spots that seem to glow with an inner light. As they move with a fluid elegance through the foliage, their presence evokes a sense of purity and innocence that stirs something deep within Uldako's soul. He watches in awe as they dance under the emerald canopy, their movements a mesmerizing display of beauty and grace.

And then, soaring high above, Uldako catches sight of a group of creatures that seem to defy the very laws of existence—dragons with wingspans that stretch wide, like dark shadows cast against the sunlit misty clouds. They command the air with effortless grace, their slender bodies adorned with sleek, streamlined features, perfectly adapted for soaring through the heavens.

Their long, toothless jaws open and close in silent anticipation, scouring the landscape below for signs of small prey. Their keen eyes are set deep within their sockets as their wings beat with a thunderous rhythm that echoes across the land.

Uldako's heart races at the sight of all these different and unique beings, their presence igniting a fire within him that burns with the intensity of a thousand suns. Tears start to flow as he realizes how he has been kept all these years from the beauty that is in the world.

With each new encounter, Uldako feels himself drawn deeper into the heart of the wilderness, his soul soaring on wings of wonder and awe. The world around him teems with life in all its myriad forms, each creature a vision of infinite creativity. And as he walks in the splendor of the wild, Uldako knows that he has embarked upon a journey unlike any other, one filled with mystery, adventure, and the boundless natural beauty of the earth.

Uldako's attention is seized by movement beneath a tree. A formidable creature, its eyes fixated on him with an unwelcoming intensity, disrupts the tranquil journey. Robust and muscular, its coat ranges from red to dark brown, with a majestic mane encircling its head and neck. Keen amber eyes convey a blend of power and elegance. Šarru growls in unease, prompting Uldako to calm him with a gentle command.

Uncertain of the beast's intentions, Uldako adopts a cautious stance, analyzing every nuance of its behavior. The predator, its eyes betraying a hunger for flesh, reveals sharp claws and teeth in a fearsome display. A resonant roar echoes through the land, encapsulating the mystique of this awe-inspiring creature.

The beast advances, locking eyes with Uldako, who senses the imperative need to stand unwavering in the face of this display of strength.

Aware that Šarru could offer assistance, Uldako still questions if they can overcome the beast, realizing the magnitude of the adversary. This is a primal standoff, where any sign of weakness might be his last. The beast's deliberate approach, the intensity of its gaze, and the resounding growl all hint at a formidable opponent, leaving Uldako grappling with the reality of his predicament.

After a tense moment of stillness, the beast gives a thundering roar, showing its deadly teeth as a warning, but to Uldako's astonishment, Šarru swiftly rises onto his hind legs and releases a resounding roar, a challenging echo to the adversary. In this unexpected display, Uldako realizes the true stature his loyal companion has attained, standing taller than ever.

The beast, momentarily taken aback by this unforeseen transformation in both behavior and size, retreats slowly, retaining a regal demeanor but conceding its position as the sovereign of the jungle. The unexpected alliance of man and beast, now standing side by side, marks a surreal victory, leaving Uldako in awe of the newfound strength and unity between him and his friend.

After the harrowing encounter, Uldako breathes a sigh of relief, patting Šarru on the head then embracing the bear with gratitude. "You surely saved us there, Šarru," exclaims Uldako.

In response, Šarru acknowledges the praise with a subtle growl, a gentle rumble echoing his appreciation.

As hunger and thirst grip Uldako, he finds a secure spot between two gigantic boulders, and the two companions sit down to share a meal of fish. While they share the food, Uldako becomes more aware of the profound connection he has developed with Šarru. He contemplates the depth of his affection for this beast, reflecting on the bear's intellect, emotions, and distinct personality.

As Uldako's gaze shifts from Šarru to the drifting mist above, the passage of time becomes palpable, each passing moment a reminder of his mother's perilous existence in slavery. "We have to move," Uldako declares, rising from the ground. "My *ama* could die at any moment while we waste time."

With renewed focus, Uldako and Šarru press onward in their quest. Eventually, they reach the marked location on Uldako's makeshift map—a nomad camp named Jabal.

Concealing Šarru and himself behind bushes, Uldako surveys the camp, realizing it is no ordinary settlement. This camp boasts small animal skin houses anchored to the ground with ropes—a sight entirely foreign to him. He can't help but admire the ingenuity and skill of whoever conceived such a design. These shelters are cleverly constructed for mobility, capable of being relocated from one place to another with ease.

The safe camp is surrounded by a fence resembling the one from the slave camp Uldako was used to, yet with a notable distinction—people move freely through the gate. The camp appears substantial, accommodating around six hundred people all working together with one mind.

After meticulously observing the nomadic safe camp for an extended period, Uldako decides to move closer to search for a way through the gate, hoping to unravel the mystery of Seth's whereabouts. Turning to Šarru, he instructs, "Wait here."

With a disapproving yet obedient growl, Šarru settles back, allowing Uldako to flank the entrance gate and stealthily approach the road where arriving travelers pass. Patiently, he waits for the opportune moment and seamlessly falls in line behind the last man, who remains oblivious to his presence.

As Uldako approaches the gate, snippets of conversations among the men reveal the significance of a man also named Jabal, the leader of this place. Voices murmur about the prospect of purchasing livestock and finding beautiful women. A man of apparent importance steps forward, with his hand on his sword. "You!" he bellows, reprimanding another. "If you even touch one of our women, I will put my *ur-bar-ra* on you!"

The young man appears to hold a position among the gate guards. Though not towering or imposing in stature, there is an air of authority about him. He is clad in thick, weathered animal hide, fashioned into what resembles combat armor, suggesting a readiness for confrontation. Across his back rests a formidable weapon, crafted from the bones of a massive creature. Its blade, sharp on one end, hints at its potential lethality, while its size demands the use of both hands for wielding.

Walking alongside the guard, tethered to his waist by a sturdy rope, is a formidable hairy beast with large teeth. *This man referred to this beast as an* ur-bar-ra, Uldako reflects as he learns the existence of another animal. The beast reminds Uldako of Šarru as it moves in tandem with its human counterpart, almost like a living extension of the guard himself.

Within the line of people approaching the gate, whispers identify this man as being Jabal, suggesting divine origins with the blood of the dragon. The man previously reprimanded by Jabal apologizes profusely, avoiding eye contact.

Uldako edges closer to the gate, the scene within becoming increasingly discernible, but a sharp command slices through the air, halting him in his tracks.

"Stop right there, *lu-kur*!" The man identified earlier by some as Jabal fixates his gaze on Uldako. "Your armor is different from the people around these parts of the land. Who are you, and what do you want from the Jabal clan?"

Uldako, quick on his feet, retorts, "You have a keen eye, my *dusa*. I've journeyed from afar, drawn by tales of the magnificent livestock available here. I seek only peaceful trade, Jabal."

Laughter erupts among the men as they turn their questioning gazes toward the guard, one of them jesting, "Jabal, indeed! Hahaha!"

It is then that Uldako realizes his error, having mistakenly believed the whispers and assuming that the apparent leader of the guard was named Jabal.

The leader, flattered and puffed up, clarifies that he is not Jabal, merely the leader of the guard. Uldako responds with feigned innocence. "My mistake. But as you noticed, I clearly see you as a great man!"

The captain of the guard, pleased with the flattery, continues in conversation with Uldako. Meanwhile, Uldako catches a glimpse inside the gate and notices men constructing a substantial project in the distance.

Expressing genuine fascination for the architectural marvels, Uldako's curiosity about the ongoing project piques. The guard leader, now warming up to Uldako's interest, divulges the purpose behind the construction—a grand ritualistic chamber for a newly worshipped god called *Ninurta*.

"Truly? Is he one of the *anunnaki*?" Uldako's eyes squint with intrigue.

The guard, clearly enthralled by the topic, continues. "Indeed! *Ninurta* is the new *dingir* of war, hunting, and a few other things. He is our warrior *dingir*, associated with all heroic feats."

Uldako, eager to improve his relationship with the guard who clearly reveres this god, says, "That is magnificent! Tell me, where does this new *dingir* come from?"

The guard takes a step forward, pride evident in his voice. "Some *anunnaki* recently descended to these lands. There have been many sightings here in the South and in the East, the Land of Nod. We have been favored by *anunnaki—Ninurta, Utu, Inanna, Ninhursag, Nanna, Ningal, Nisabba, Geshtinanna*, and many others! Some of them have even singled out the Jabal clan for their divine attention."

Uldako nods curiously, as if he and the guard are like-minded, prompting him to continue. "Their leader speaks directly to Jabal, bestowing upon him otherworldly knowledge and igniting a surge in our skills—from crafting intricate tents to breeding superior livestock and constructing magnificent edifices."

With a feigned air of excitement and interest, Uldako leans forward, his eyes wide with enthusiasm. "Incredible! Your clan must be great for this leader of the divine to deem your people worthy. What is his name?"

The guard nods enthusiastically. "Yes, indeed. The leader of the *anunnaki* should not be named carelessly. We worship him mostly through the other *anunnaki*. Like I said, that structure over there that we are erecting is a temple dedicated to *Ninurta*."

Uldako ponders inwardly. Ninurta*...and a stronger, mysterious* dingir *ranking above him and the other* anunnaki*—that must be* Enki.

These gods evoke a mix of discomfort and curiosity within Uldako. Yet, he has little opportunity to dwell on them as the guard proceeds, describing the altars in intricate detail.

"Altars are rising everywhere." The man's voice fills with reverence. "Each one built with care, shaped by divine instruction, aligned perfectly with the stars. Most will be used for sacred rituals—especially the great ziggurat in Eridu." He pauses then adds with a trace of awe, "Our humble altar is nothing compared to the great temple they're building in Eridu. It's being raised for the new *dingir* of the earth."

Uldako's jaw tightens. *A new god?* He has no idea who the man is speaking of, but he leans in, playing the fool.

"Truly? The *anunnaki* have come down to help us?" he says, feigning wonder. "That's incredible."

The captain's brow furrows. "Why don't you already know this? Where've you been lately—stuck in a cave?"

The rest of the guards roar with laughter, savoring the moment. "Everyone knows it. People across these lands have seen the *dumu-meš* of *An* walking among them. The *anunnaki* are with us, and the news is spreading far and wide."

He lowers his voice, glancing around cautiously before whispering, almost reverently, "*Enki* is the new lord of the earth."

Then, resuming his normal tone, he adds, "He has declared that his seed—the blood of the dragon—will be established among our clans. We have been chosen!"

Uldako understands the delicate balance of his words, opting to steer the conversation away from potentially dangerous topics. "Yes, indeed," he continues. "I've been out in the wilderness for quite some time, unaware of these momentous events. But I've also heard whispers of something else, or someone unusual, traveling through this area."

The captain's curiosity is evident as he leans in closer, eager for more details. "Care to enlighten me?"

Uldako hesitates, weighing the risk of revealing too much. However, the possibility of gaining information about Seth outweighs his hesitation. "Well," Uldako begins cautiously, "there have been rumors circulating about a special elder, a formidable warrior named Seth. He is adorned in magnificent armor bearing the symbol of an eagle's head. It's said he travels with six mighty warriors, exuding an air of confidence and power. Have you perhaps heard anything about such travelers passing through here?"

The air thickens with tension as the captain advances, his demeanor taking on a more ominous tone. As he draws nearer, Uldako catches sight of the emblem emblazoned on his armor—a dragon, a stark contrast to the eagle symbolizing Seth's allegiance. Uldako recognizes the significance of this rivalry, the age-old enmity between the eagle and the serpent, now intensified by opposing deities. Uldako understands the dangerous balance of his situation and the need for caution in his words and actions.

Uldako's surprise is notable as the guard leader unexpectedly proposes a deal. "I think…" The man's voice trails off momentarily as he appraises Uldako with a calculating gaze, before firmly asserting, "I know who you are referring to, but—" There's a sense of reciprocity in the air, a mutual understanding that hangs between them. The guard leader leans in slightly, his tone carrying a hint of intrigue as he continues, "Do something for me, and I will tell you what I know."

Uldako feels the sudden shift in the guard captain's demeanor, like the twist of a gust changing its course. Trust becomes a scarce commodity in this moment, but facing the reality that this guard holds the door to information about Seth, Uldako grits his teeth and plays along.

"What do you need?" Uldako's tone is a delicate dance between caution and compliance.

The captain gestures toward the cages, home to captive coyotes, wolves, and huge eagles, awaiting their next meal. Their once wild eyes now hold a subdued glimmer, a stark contrast to the fiery spirit Uldako remembers from untamed animals in the wilderness. "Our companions here," the captain explains, a sly glint in his eye, "require sustenance to maintain their strength. Bring me food to feed them. Do this for me, and I shall offer you the information you seek. That's the way things work here in Jabal—nothing is freely given."

Uldako, skeptical yet realizing the fragility of his situation, reluctantly replies,

"I'll be back." The weight of uncertainty falls upon him as he wonders whether this gesture of goodwill will truly pave the way to the information he seeks.

Returning to Šarru, the duo embarks on a hunt. Uldako spotted deer and other small game earlier on their way to Jabal's camp, and he instinctively knows the perfect direction to pursue. Šarru's body brims with anticipation, sensing the thrill of the imminent hunt. It doesn't take long for them to discover a deer, perfectly sized to transport back to Jabal's camp.

Moving downwind, Uldako readies his spear, silently narrowing the distance between them, and skillfully launches it directly into the deer's heart. As they approach, Uldako takes a moment to appreciate the majestic beauty of their prey. It's a magnificent creature, boasting a slender and graceful build, with a shoulder-height stature. Its coat showcases a vibrant reddish-brown hue, complemented by a pristine white underbelly and throat. The most striking features are its lyre-shaped horns, spiraling upward with elegant ridges. Expressive eyes, beneath delicate, pointed ears, hold a sharp, watchful focus. A dark, horizontal stripe along its flank adds a contrasting touch to its overall appearance.

Šarru is poised to feast on the deer, but Uldako intervenes, halting his companion's advance. "No, Šarru, this one is not for us," he declares. Unpacking his bag, he retrieves the last piece of dried fish, tossing it to Šarru. The bear catches it midair, a display of contentment. He clearly loves fish!

Uldako leaves Šarru to hide in the bush and strides back to the captain of the guard, effortlessly hoisting the deer off his shoulders. With a determined gaze, he declares, "Here you go. Now, tell me about Seth."

The captain, looking at Uldako and the deer with a mixture of surprise and approval, acknowledges, "Well, you're certainly a skilled hunter to bring back such a prize in so little time. I'll give you that." However, the captain's demeanor takes a turn as he suggests, "But wouldn't you want me to teach you the art of taming animals like these? Imagine having loyal companions that can fight alongside you during your perilous journeys. What do you say?"

Uldako dismisses the man's offer with a firm, "No thank you. I already know how to tame a beast. Now, share the information about Seth."

The captain, undeterred, swiftly devises another strategy to withhold the details. "Alright, how about this," he proposes. "I'll disclose the whereabouts of Seth, *dumu* of Adam, the first *En-Lugal*, but only if you can best me in a duel. And, if you manage to defeat me, I'll not only reveal where he is heading but also teach you the art of crafting a tent."

The thought intrigues Uldako, but he is not exactly sure what the last reward entails, mumbling out loud, "What is a tent?"

Laughter erupts from the guards, and Uldako feels a pang of embarrassment for his lack of knowledge yet again. The man looks down at Uldako, condescendingly remarking, "Under what rock did you grow up? These shelters inside the camp, fashioned from skins and rope, are what we call tents."

Uldako recognizes the significance of mastering this skill, understanding that these meticulously crafted tents could be invaluable on his journey. Determined, he declares, "I accept those terms. Let the duel begin."

The guards gesture toward the heart of the camp, guiding Uldako alongside the captain to the dueling pit. As they approach, the guards begin to chant, "Fight, fight, fight." The other men and women in the camp rush toward them as they hear the chants, now forming a crowd and joining the guards in their chanting. The clamor intensifies as people gather from all directions, drawn to the spectacle. Uldako realizes this is a customary and cherished event for them.

Ascending toward the pit, he notices the circular space filled with black sand, surrounded by boulders sculpted into makeshift seats for the eager spectators. Across from him, a majestic reddish tent stands out, surpassing all others in craftsmanship. The intricate patterns woven into its fabric are a showcase of their mastery of the tent-making craft.

Abruptly, the chanting ceases, giving way to the emergence of a formidable figure from the tent. Commanding respect with his presence, the man appears older than most, though not as old as Seth. A subtle resemblance flickers between them—similar eye shape and nose. Yet, Seth's eyes hold a tranquility that eludes this man, who exudes a different aura, not of authority but of intense wickedness.

Cloaked in black attire of unparalleled craftsmanship, and bearing subtle horns that hint at a darker nature, the man emerges as a figure of imposing elegance. A scar etched on his left cheek adds to his rugged allure. The crowd falls into respectful silence, anticipating his words with bated breath. Leaning toward Uldako, the captain of the guard imparts with reverence, "Behold, the true Jabal, *dumu* of Lamech and Adah and scion of Cain, the marked one."

Uldako's shock is tangible as he responds, "Cain?"

The guard's pride is evident as he confirms, "Yes, Cain—the firstborn of Adam, the inaugural human sage."

Jabal's voice rings out with exhilaration. "We've got ourselves a challenger, a wildling, by the looks of him."

Laughter ripples through the crowd, an overt insult aimed at Uldako. Undeterred, Uldako, fired up by his purpose, steps forward and declares, "I am no wildling! I am Uldako, *dumu* of Deborah."

A ripple of confusion surges through the crowd, their murmurs tinged with curiosity and unease. One man leans forward, his voice cutting through the rising noise. "A woman?"

Another quickly interjects, "Why does he name his *ama* and not his *abba*?"

A third voice, weighed with suspicion and the gravity of tradition, declares, "Lineages are always traced through the *abba*, not the *ama*, but it seems like this is not the case wherever this *lu-kur* is from."

Another chimes in, "I've never heard of such a custom in all my days. Only a weak man would do that!"

Without missing a beat, Jabal swiftly retorts, "There you have it, Uldako, *dumu* of some lowly woman, challenging our second-best warrior, Hubara, *dumu* of Gruskar, the captain of the guard, to the death!"

In a state of shock, Uldako exclaims, "No, I only agreed to a normal duel, not a battle to the death!" The crowd erupts in laughter once again, and Uldako realizes the cruel trick these dishonorable people play on unsuspecting challengers—luring them into a duel, only to force a fight to the death against the reigning champion within the inner camp.

Jabal continues, "Hubara! What is the reason or bargain struck for this duel?"

Hubara steps forward, "I gain nothing, but the pleasure of my weapon cutting through this lowlife and using his body to train the *ur-bar-ras* to hunt for human flesh. However, I vowed to teach him the art of tentmaking and—"

Jabal calls for silence, "I have heard enough. There is no need to entertain what he would gain if he wins, for such an outcome is impossible. Let us proceed and conclude this duel swiftly!"

Stepping back from the captain, Uldako's heart races amidst the cacophony of voices and the ominous chants for his demise. It's a haunting reminder of the dehumanizing treatment he endured under the evil slave masters. "Calm down," he whispers to himself, drawing on the lessons learned from surviving in the wild and fighting in the slave market.

The clamor gradually fades into the background as Uldako regains composure, his mind sharpening its focus. A resolute calm takes hold as he assesses the situation—the guard is larger but slower due to heavy armor. Just as with a bear, Uldako knows speed will be his ally.

Turning around, the guard pivots like a colossal beast, fixing his gaze upon Uldako. In his eyes, Uldako is nothing more than a mere rat, a plaything much like the countless others who have faced him in this very pit before Uldako. Jabal's commanding voice pierces the air. "Begin!"

10

Warrior

Uldako stands amidst the raucous clamor of the crowd, their bloodthirsty cries echoing through the pit like a chorus of evil spirits. The spectators, their eyes glinting with savage excitement, are hungry for spectacle, for the spectacle of death. They bellow for his demise, their fervor roused by a dark thirst for bloodshed, their cheers a symphony of malevolence.

Even in this sea of hostility, Uldako holds himself firm. His heart churns with fear, anger, and defiance, but he draws in a slow breath, forcing the unruly emotions within to still, anchoring his heart against the chaos rising around him. With every beat of his heart, he sets his spirit firm against the looming threat, knowing that in this pit, survival is not promised. And so, with spear in hand and determination in his eyes, he braces himself for the imminent clash.

Uldako draws his spear in one fluid motion, calling upon the lessons carved into him by the wild—the memory of the cave bear rising sharp and clear, for Hubara's towering form stirs that same primal awareness. Uldako has fought many before in the pits of the slave camp, but those were weak and desperate slaves like himself, not warriors as big as this champion. Hubara stands before him brimming with strength and life, wrapped in hardened hide and bone, wielding a great blade nearly as tall as Uldako himself. Patiently, he awaits the opportune moment to strike.

As Hubara strides toward him with heavy, deliberate steps, he jeers, "You know, I liked you at first…until you spoke the name of Seth."

With the mention of Seth, Hubara unexpectedly lunges forward, wielding his colossal double-handed bone sword with formidable might. Caught off guard, Uldako narrowly evades the strike by quickly leaping to the left, executing a roll on the ground to absorb the impact, and swiftly rising back to his feet using the momentum to his advantage.

Uldako's senses sharpen like an eagle's, locked onto Hubara. Every twitch of muscle, every shift in stance might reveal the path of the next strike. He reads the tension like a hunter, knowing that even the smallest motion could mean survival or defeat.

Then, unexpectedly, Hubara steps back, raising both arms with a roar to the wild crowd. They explode with cheers, fists pounding the air as they chant his name, "Hubara! Hubara! Hubara!"

Uldako realizes that this is the ultimate test, a crucible to hone his combat skills if he hopes to confront the oppressive slave masters. An opportunity arises as the champion turns, distracted by a captivating woman stepping from Jabal's tent. With his attention wavering, Uldako recognizes his moment to strike. Without a moment's hesitation, he launches his spear with all the force and precision he can muster, aiming true at his distracted adversary.

The crowd falls silent as Hubara turns, fury burning in his eyes. The spear has struck—but only shallowly. It juts from a thick cuirass of layered hide and bone, the point buried no more than a finger's depth. Hubara shifted at the last instant, the toughened armor absorbing the blow and turning what should have been a killing strike into little more than a wound. Uldako sees it plainly now: Weapons of stone will not break men easily who wear the hides of monsters and the bones of their kills.

Hubara seizes the spear with a single hand, extracting it from the wound. Blood trickles down the armor as he hurls the spear back toward Uldako's head.

Uldako easily slips aside, the weapon cutting through the air where he stood a heartbeat before. Uldako sees it as a display of the champion's resilience—an attempt to convey that the spear had little effect on Hubara. Unsheathing both axes discreetly from behind his back, Uldako maneuvers cautiously around Hubara.

The crowd, reigniting their fervor, clamors for blood. Unfazed by the spectators' underestimation, Uldako remains focused on the champion, searching for any vulnerabilities. Amidst the crowd's renewed cheers, Jabal's voice rises, "It seems this wildling is not as feeble as we presumed. Perhaps we are to witness a remarkable battle!"

Hubara, his face contorted with rage, charges toward Uldako like a savage beast unleashed, his eyes burning with an insatiable hunger for dominance.

Uldako's senses are heightened as he anticipates the impending clash. There is nowhere to run, and as courage fills Uldako's heart like never before, he decides to make a stand. As Hubara's ferocious blows crash toward him, Uldako moves with the swift, instinctive grace of a seasoned hunter, slipping past each strike. With each swing of Hubara's massive bone blade, the air tightens with tension, and the clash of bone against stone echoes through the arena like the cracking of heavy branches.

Uldako's confidence begins to rise. Blow after blow, he evades each strike—barely at first, then with growing ease. He realizes something: He isn't being hit. He can clearly see Hubara's movements, and they seem to slow with each passing moment. The attacks that once felt overwhelming now seem slowed, their intent plain to him.

He bides his time, waiting for the right moment.

Then, with breathtaking precision, his stone axe intercepts Hubara's weapon mid-swing. The impact sends a jolt through Uldako's arms—but he doesn't falter. In one swift, fluid motion, he counters with a crushing strike of his own. The blow lands firmly in his opponent's side, striking through the thinner part of the armor and driving Hubara back with a sharp cry of pain.

Caught off guard by the sudden reversal, Hubara staggers, his wounded side a clear sign of Uldako's skill. As he recoils from the strike, his focus momentarily shifts, allowing Uldako to seize the opportunity. With a fierce rush of instinct, Uldako launches himself into the air, a whirlwind of motion and intent.

In that fleeting moment, time seems to stand still as Uldako's axe connects with Hubara's neck with a resounding impact. The arena falls silent as Hubara, the second strongest champion of the mighty Jabal clan, crumples to the ground like a colossal tree felled in the forest.

Breathless, Uldako takes a step back, his chest heaving with exertion. In the hush that follows the battle, the full meaning of what he has done comes upon him. For the first time, he has emerged victorious in combat against a real warrior, and not just any warrior—a champion. Uldako, shaped by his dark upbringing and the relentless emotional abuse inflicted by the slave masters, had never once considered himself capable of achieving such a triumph. He stands more shocked than those around him.

The once-rousing crowd now hovers in stunned silence. Their esteemed captain lies defeated on the arena floor, vanquished by a stranger, someone who appears to be a wildling armed only with stone weapons.

A guard breaks the silence, bellowing for Uldako's demise and charging toward him. Uldako swiftly readies his axes, prepared to fend off those now thirsting for his blood. Amidst the chaos, a commanding voice pierces the air. "Stop!"

The authoritative command freezes everyone in their tracks. It's Jabal, now approaching Uldako with a curious expression. "Well, I must say, that was unexpected! The only other person to have ever defeated Hubara was me, the reigning champion of the pit. Somehow Hubara survived our duel, and I allowed him to face new challengers. They have to defeat him first to even stand a chance against me. But you, Uldako, you're different."

Jabal paces around Uldako, his eyes piercing and calculating. Uldako feels the man's scrutiny upon him, sensing the underlying threat in his words. With newfound boldness after his victory over Hubara, Uldako declares, "The terms were clear: If I bested your champion in an honest duel, I would be instructed in the craft of tent-making and provided the whereabouts of the old warrior who passed through here—Seth by name. That is what I demand.'"

Jabal retorts sharply, "Seth? Demand? Who do you think you are to demand anything from me? I only halted the guards from ending your life because I respect your strength. Tell me this, and I will decide your fate." With narrowed eyes, Jabal steps closer, his gaze running over Uldako from head to toe. "Who are you truly, and where did you acquire the prowess to fight with such incredible speed and agility? Did you learn it from the clans of Etana, those carrying the emblem of the eagle?"

Uldako meets Jabal's eyes without flinching. "Etana?" he echoes. He knows nothing of this figure but is all too aware that Seth carries the emblem of the eagle—a symbol that could call doom upon him among these people.

With a steady breath, he continues, "I don't belong to any clan. But I've crossed paths with those who wear its sign. I was forged in the fires of slavery, here in the South."

He pulls back his armor, revealing the seared brand of *arad-muš* behind his neck that was burned deep into his skin as a youth.

Gasps erupt. Whispers ripple through the crowd like a sudden wind. Some take a step back. Others stare, wide-eyed, as if seeing him for the first time. A few cover their mouths, stunned that a slave—marked and discarded—could defeat the great Hubara.

"Seth shattered my yoke of slavery," Uldako declares, his voice rising with fire. "And now, I must find him to aid me with…something."

Jabal, intrigued by the inner strength of Uldako, steps even closer. "Interesting. What is that?" he inquires with a low voice, his eyes probing Uldako for truth.

Hesitant to reveal too much, Uldako utters cautiously, "Something that could help my *ama*."

"Your *ama*...Deborah, as you mentioned earlier. I see now who and what you are! What a fool! You are from no clan, just a slave on his own, a little boy trying to help his *ama*," Jabal remarks, his respect for Uldako visibly diminishing.

Undeterred, Uldako declares, "Well, this slave just defeated your second-best warrior."

Jabal exhales sharply, frustration plain on his face. "You're right," he admits with reluctant respect. "That's the only reason I'm offering you two choices: First—join our clan and fight as one of my warriors. Or, take your belongings, and go chase after your precious *ama* on that fool's errand of yours. The decision is yours."

"I will take the latter," Uldako says, jaw tightening. "But I still deserve to know where Seth is."

Jabal snaps, "You're testing my patience! That was your deal with Hubara, and he's in no position to fulfill his end of the bargain anymore, now is he?"

Uldako feels the sting of Jabal's words, realizing the truth in them despite the injustice he feels. It was a cunning trap, a bargain that would never have granted him the prize. But then, as if struck by a sudden thought, Jabal's demeanor shifts, a calculating glint in his eyes. "However, upon reflection, I might be persuaded to strike a new deal with you."

Uldako sighs, acknowledging that he has no choice but to hear Jabal's proposition. "What is it?" he asks wearily.

"Strike a pact with me on this, and the secrets of tentmaking and the whereabouts of Seth shall still be unveiled to you," Jabal proposes with an air of mystery.

Uldako folds his arms, his eyes narrowing with suspicion. "And what do you expect in return?" he asks, wary of hidden motives.

"Now, listen closely." Jabal's face hardens. "I need you to undertake a crucial task in safeguarding our tribe and livestock. All was well until a great *úr-maḫ* appeared without warning a few days ago. It has slain some of our people and our animals as well."

Uldako's brow furrows. "What is an *úr-maḫ*?"

Jabal's face contorts with a mix of shock and laughter. "Your tale of growing up in a slave camp must be true if you're unfamiliar with this beast. Well, this particular cave *úr-maḫ* is a dangerous animal, capable of swiftly cutting down any man, but fear not—you have already proven your skills. Bring me its head, and our deal stands."

Uldako nods once. "Very well, but give me more details about the beast—its appearance and whereabouts."

Jabal grins while gesturing. "Walk with me to the gate, and I'll explain." The dispersing crowd leaves them as Jabal divulges the creature's characteristics and location.

As Uldako starts on his way through the gate, a guard questions Jabal, "You are sending him on a death sentence, aren't you?"

Jabal looks at the guard. "You are correct in discerning my intention, but he did manage to surprise me once. Whatever the outcome, we stand to gain. If he succumbs, well, good riddance, as he killed our champion. However, if, by some twist of fate, the *anunnaki* favor him to defeat the *úr-maḫ*, then we'll be free of the beast that has been feasting on our livestock!"

Still within sight of Jabal, Uldako strides forward and signals for his trusted bear companion, Šarru, hidden in the bushes, to join him. The bear runs to meet his friend, closing the gap with surprising speed.

A shrill cry pierces the air from the camp as the guards see the great bear charging toward Uldako. "An *uḫuš-gal*! Watch out!"

Uldako glances over his shoulder at the guards, a mischievous grin spreading across his face. With a dramatic flair, he turns back, axes at the ready, pretending to brace for a fierce battle with the ferocious bear. But just as Šarru looms closer, Uldako tosses his weapons aside and opens his arms wide, welcoming the bear into a warm embrace.

The guards stand frozen, their jaws hanging in disbelief at the unexpected turn of events. Uldako breaks into a grin, his eyes sparkling with amusement. "Did you see their faces, Šarru? Absolutely priceless!" he chuckles, giving the bear a hearty pat.

With a wink to his furry friend, they continue on their journey, leaving the bewildered guards and Jabal behind in their wake, murmuring in astonishment at the unprecedented sight of a human embracing a bear with such ease.

As the sun moves across the sky, marking the passage of two hands, Uldako arrives at the location marked by the heightened activity of the cave lion. He scrutinizes the surroundings, searching for signs—tracks, broken branches, or the remnants of a recent kill. Uldako senses the heightened tension in the air as Šarru's fur bristles, a clear sign of danger.

The rush of excitement courses through Uldako's veins, a stark contrast to the fear that would have gripped him just two summers ago. The transformation from a fearful slave to a warrior is evident in his newfound anticipation of the challenge ahead.

As he follows a fresh set of tracks in the sand, possibly belonging to the elusive cave lion, Uldako signals to Šarru, who keenly detects the trail as well. The duo navigate the wilderness with a fluid grace, moving seamlessly through the landscape. The surroundings open up, revealing scattered trees on a hill and a dark cave in the distance. An unspoken tension fills the air, as if nature itself anticipates the impending confrontation.

"This area is definitely its home," Uldako muses to himself.

A sudden rustle explodes to their left, causing both Uldako and Šarru to snap to attention. Šarru's hair stands on end, and a low growl rumbles from the depths of his throat. Uldako, spear in hand, moves with feline grace, advancing toward the source of the disturbance alongside his vigilant companion.

In the eerie stillness that follows, a deceptive calm settles over the area, as if nature is holding its breath. The tranquility shatters as a small rabbit bolts from the underbrush, startling both Uldako and Šarru. Surprise flickers across their faces, only to be replaced by something far more primal. Before the rabbit's escape has even faded into the silence, the true threat reveals itself, a beast with a blur of feral power, lunging toward them with deadly intent.

Uldako, with only a brief moment to react, pivots just in time to witness the colossal predator hurtling toward him. In a swift, instinctive move, he drops to the ground as the beast soars over him, narrowly avoiding a perilously close encounter.

The creature pivots with immense speed, its movements as erratic and deadly as the shifting sands, aiming to strike Uldako while he struggles to regain his footing. Just as the fatal blow seems inevitable, Šarru jumps into action, launching a ferocious assault from the side. Teeth and claws tear into the lion's flank, leaving deep, bloody furrows.

Fired up by the desperate need to protect his friend, Uldako moves to his feet, knowing he cannot let Šarru face this colossal threat alone. With practiced precision, he drives his spear into the lion's side, blood pouring from the wound. Despite the injury, the beast remains standing, its eyes burning with rage as it swipes at Uldako, the strike missing his face by a hair's breadth.

Seizing the momentary diversion created by Uldako, Šarru unleashes his might. His claws, as formidable as his teeth, tear into the lion's side with potent force. The seamless coordination between Uldako and Šarru speaks volumes about their deep bond and the extensive training they've undergone together while hunting near the lake.

As the lion redirects its attention to Šarru, Uldako, with an astonishing display of speed, unsheathes his two axes from behind his back. In a whirlwind of blows, he rains down a torrent of strikes upon the mighty beast. Overwhelmed and succumbing to its injuries, the creature collapses to the ground.

Breathless and victorious, Uldako drops to his knees, hands pressed to the earth in a moment of exhaustion and triumph. The lion's blood is splattered across his face and body, visceral marks of the battle just won.

Šarru, recognizing the shared achievement, approaches with a low growl and nudges Uldako's side, silently acknowledging their victory.

As Uldako gets his breath back, he studies the cave lion, admitting it is a powerful and majestic predator. It boasts a robust and muscular build, characterized by a sleek, tan-colored fur coat with faint stripes that aid its camouflage in this natural environment. No wonder he hides so well in the wilderness. Its long, slender body once stood at an impressive height, and its broad head features prominent, rounded ears. Its tail is long and thick, and its limbs end in massive retractable claws.

With a glimmer of recognition crossing his features, Uldako's gaze shifts to his companion. "Šarru, this creature before us is akin to the one you drove off during our journey to Jabal's camp. Now we know it is called an *úr-maḫ*." To Uldako, the cave lion embodies strength, stealth, and a silent prowess, symbolizing its role as an apex predator, adaptable to diverse landscapes.

As Šarru approaches to inspect the fallen beast, Uldako expresses his gratitude. "Once again, my *dusa*, I owe you my life. Without your aid, I would not have triumphed over this formidable foe. Now it will not hunt down any of the tribe members or their animals. Let us claim its head as a trophy, a step closer to uncovering the whereabouts of Seth and securing the freedom of my *ama*."

They return to the Jabal camp, and as they get closer to the gate, the guards' eyes widen in disbelief, their jaws dropping in astonishment. "Y...you're still alive?" one stammers before correcting himself, "I mean, you did it!"

Uldako, realizing it was a death sentence, is unaffected by the shock of the guard and commands, "Summon Jabal, now."

To the guards, Uldako now appears as an imposing figure, a warrior of immense prowess, standing tall with the severed lion's head in one hand and the mighty bear, Šarru, by his side. Blood streaks down his face and body, a badge of his recent triumph. The guard, visibly intimidated, nods to a subordinate, who swiftly departs to summon Jabal.

After an agonizingly tense wait, Jabal arrives. His eyes widen in shock as they fall upon the grisly trophy. "The *anunnaki* must favor you," he mutters, his voice a mix of awe and begrudging respect. The sheer disbelief and reluctant admiration in his tone underscore the gravity of Uldako's achievement, leaving an indelible impression on all who witness the scene.

Uldako, his patience wearing thin, firmly presents the cave lion's head and demands the promised information about Seth.

Jabal, seemingly indifferent to his own promises, approaches Uldako with an air of arrogance, locking eyes with him. "You think I care about empty vows? I don't, but your tenacity intrigues me," he remarks, his tone laced with disdain. "There's something about you, a touch of divine protection perhaps."

Jabal pauses for a moment before relenting. "Fine, I'll share the last known location of Seth by marking it on your map. But the secrets of crafting a tent, a skill bestowed upon me and my family by the divine Watchers, remain our cherished knowledge."

Uldako approaches, handing over his rudimentary map to Jabal. The clan leader scrutinizes the simple sketch, disdain evident on his face. "A map with only a few locations hardly qualifies as a map," he scoffs, tossing it back. Summoning a guard, Jabal instructs him to fetch a proper map.

As the new map is unfurled, Uldako stares in awe at its detail—camps, hills, and rivers all marked with deliberate care. The scope is staggering.

Jabal catches his expression and grins smugly. "Impressive, isn't it? A true map, crafted by the Jabal clan. We added all the major landmarks, including important big camps. See here, Enoch, Göbekli, Sippar, Shuruppak, the ancient Nippur, Eridu, and others."

He taps a marked region. "My scouts last saw Seth near here. But tread carefully when you find his people."

Uldako frowns, his voice low. "Why?"

Jabal's eyes narrow. "Why? Because Seth still follows the old *ways*." He leans closer, his voice sharp with conviction. "But *Enki* has brought us new *anunnaki*, ones who've given us wisdom, secret knowledge, and freedom. We can improve ourselves—think, act, choose! Seth and his kind resist that. They reject the *dingir-meš* who empower us. So tell me! Why should we bow to their rules when we are becoming more than human?"

Jabal takes a moment to try to discern Uldako's thoughts and continues, "Verily, they harbor envy for our strides in the mystic arts and perhaps fear the waning of their dominion over us and the rest of the land. I do not know which *dingir* you invoke, Uldako, but choose wisely, for the consequences are yours to bear."

Sensing a deeper layer beneath Jabal's fervor, Uldako presses, "And what do they command you to do?"

Jabal looks away, jaw tightening. "They say there is only one *dingir*," he mutters. "They boast of their so-called morals and values, as if they are above us. But it's their laws that bind them—binds they willingly wear."

His voice grows sharper. "They condemn us for seeking freedom. For choosing our own path. For raiding the weak. For offering sacrifices to the *anunnaki*. Etana—the fool *lugal*—calls us evil for eliminating threats to our progress. But we follow new *dingir-meš* now. Stronger *dingir-meš*. And we will crush anyone who stands in our way."

Uldako, sensing the depths of Jabal's arrogant ignorance in the tangled web of beliefs and power struggles, feels an urgency to distance himself from the conversation. Though he acknowledges his own limited understanding of these intricate matters, he knows his true priority lies elsewhere—time is fleeting, and his quest to reunite with his mother presses on.

Turning to Jabal with quiet resolve, Uldako states, "Every man has his own determining free will, treading his own path, shaped by his perceptions of the truth. What may be virtuous for one could be deemed wicked by another, inevitably leading to strife. My path leads me to seek the truth that does not bend with the hearts and desires of men—and to find Seth and free my *ama* from real bindings made by mankind. And for that, I bid you farewell."

Jabal, amused by Uldako's unconventional demeanor, grins and utters, "You're an enigmatic one, indeed, and you've added a spark to my day. May the newfound *anunnaki* guide your way."

Uldako strides purposefully toward the marked destination on the map, relief washing over him. He exhales a heavy sigh, knowing he has navigated the treacherous waters of the Jabal clan unscathed. With Šarru faithfully by his side, he can now cast aside the facade of strength that was a necessary shield against the malevolent men of Jabal, who would wield death swiftly if they sensed even a hint of weakness.

As he looks at the expansive sky, each passing cloud assumes a unique form, captivating him with the mesmerizing hues of blue that fill him with calm. The road ahead unfolds, transitioning from open fields to a denser forest, characterized by towering trees surpassing any he has encountered before.

As his eyes drink in the extraordinary landscape before him, a cascade of thoughts surges through Uldako's mind. "How do people remain blinded by darkness when such beauty envelops them? What happened to mankind to be this evil, and where do we really come from?" Uldako pauses, his gaze falling to his hands as he murmurs, "What is the purpose of life, and what is truth?"

It's as though time itself holds its breath, a profound stillness enveloping Uldako as he, for the first time ever, directs his focus to the most important questions of the world. Questions that drive him to seek the answers to the truth of life itself. A whisper echoes in his inner man, urging, *Seek Seth to find the answers.*

Uldako's thoughts sharpen as he steps toward towering trees, their shadows stretching like fingers from another world. It feels as though he's crossing a threshold into a realm of hidden truths—a place where the seen and unseen worlds collide. This forest, untamed and full of secrets, mirrors the uncertainty within him. With each step, the revelations about the gods and the unseen forces shaping mankind loom larger in his mind. The air thickens with possibility, and as the forest swallows him, Uldako knows that the answers he seeks may lie beyond these ancient trees, intertwined with the mysteries of Seth and the truth of life.

11

Watchers

Isn't this place intriguing, Šarru?" Uldako murmurs as they cautiously navigate the dense forest. The air vibrates with a symphony of unfamiliar scents and sounds, overwhelming Uldako's senses.

Šarru, ever curious, seems to revel in the exploration of this uncharted territory. Yet, amidst the allure of the unknown, a noticeable aura of mystery and peril lurks in the shadows. With hunger gnawing at his belly and fatigue creeping into his bones, Uldako decides it's time to rest beneath the canopy of colossal trees and drink from his waterskin.

"Strange creatures indeed," Uldako muses aloud as he observes a small, elongated creature with hundreds of legs skittering over his foot. "What manner of creature are you?" he wonders, eyeing the tiny black scales covering its body and the multitude of legs propelling it forward. With caution etched in his movements, Uldako refrains from touching the creature, opting instead to delicately nudge it away with a nearby branch.

"Did you see that, Šarru?" he exclaims, a breath of wonder lacing his words as the creature curls into a protective ball in response to the disturbance. "Out here, it seems survival is the great equalizer, regardless of size or stature."

Uldako's gaze instinctively drifts upward, as is his habit to look at the sky, only to be met with a dense canopy of treetops, veiling the blue sky from his view. With a curiosity fueled by the unfamiliar surroundings, Uldako examines the diverse flora surrounding him, contemplating the possibility of constructing a home under towering trees such as these, perhaps even within their lofty branches. He wonders how these ancient trees rose to such height. Maybe this area receives more mist, giving an increased amount of water to them.

However, his reverie is abruptly shattered by an unfamiliar noise, reminiscent of the occasional grunt emitted by Šarru in his sleep, yet distinctly different, louder, more raucous. Uldako's eyes narrow, his hunter instincts sharpening as he scans the area for the source of the disturbance with Šarru at his side, equally vigilant.

A dark brown creature darts from one bush to another, igniting Uldako's primal instincts with thoughts of sustenance. Without hesitation, Uldako and Šarru spring into action, hot on the trail of their elusive prey.

"Get him, Šarru!" Uldako exclaims, urging his companion forward as they execute a coordinated hunt. Šarru's relentless pursuit drives the prey to maneuver erratically, attempting to evade the looming threat behind it. However, its evasive maneuvers play into Uldako's strategy, affording him the opportunity to flank the creature.

As the animal comes into view, Uldako vaults over a small bush, spear poised midair, and hurls it toward the target. With unerring accuracy, the spear finds its mark, knocking the creature off balance as Šarru closes in with lethal precision, ending the chase with a swift bite to the neck. It is over.

"Good work, Šarru! Let's have some lunch," Uldako praises, gratitude evident in his tone.

Crouching beside the fallen creature, he assesses it with a mixture of curiosity and respect for the untamed essence of the natural world it embodies. The animal's fur, though similar to Šarru's, is less abundant, hinting at its rugged existence in the wild. Its robust, four-legged frame displays strength, complemented by a coarse, earth-toned exterior that blends seamlessly with its surroundings. Despite its formidable appearance, there's a certain grace in its movements, a harmonious balance of power and agility. The prominent snout and tusks further attest to its primal nature, reflecting an innate sense of strength and resilience.

Uldako hoists the beast onto his shoulder, then he gives his instinctual scan of the surroundings to confirm no immediate threats. However, a peculiar sight in the distance catches his attention, drawing his focus away.

"What is that, Šarru?" he whispers to his companion, his voice tinged with awe and disbelief as he puts the tusked animal on the ground again in order to have a better look. At first glance, he mistakes the creature's neck for a colossal tree, but as it moves, Uldako's astonishment grows.

It's a creature as tall as the tallest tree, moving with an otherworldly elegance and grace. Sensing the enormity of the situation, Uldako crouches once more, recognizing his vulnerability in the presence of such a majestic being.

With Šarru by his side, he cautiously takes cover behind a nearby tree, their eyes fixed on the awe-inspiring creature before them.

Sparked by intense curiosity, Uldako inches forward, seeking any available cover to observe the creature more closely. As he reaches a vantage point, his breath catches in his throat. "This is the largest we've ever seen," he murmurs in amazement.

"Šarru, look. It's eating plants. That means it might not want to eat you," Uldako whispers with a hint of jest.

Šarru gives Uldako a deeply offended glance, prompting a defensive response. "Hey, don't give me that look!" Šarru continues to stare at the dragon without fear, indicating to Uldako that he is not easily intimidated.

"You're staring down a *mušmaḫḫu*, Šarru. A huge *mušmaḫḫu*!" Uldako says.

Šarru gives a low growl, showing he has no fear.

Uldako grins and says, "Yes, I know, you're a force to be reckoned with. You terrify an *úr-maḫ* and you're stronger than an ox, but let's be real here—facing off against that colossal *mušmaḫḫu*? That's a whole other story, my *dusa*."

Šarru lets out another growl, clearly unimpressed with the comparison. Uldako chuckles, patting Šarru's massive shoulder. "Oh, come on, don't be so grumpy! Just think of it as a really big lizard that happens to level trees and can eat things bigger than us."

Šarru huffs, as if rolling his eyes, and finally gives a begrudging nod, still clearly unhappy with the situation but resigned to following Uldako's lead. "That's the spirit," Uldako says with a chuckle. "Now let's just hope it sticks to its plants."

As they continue to watch, Uldako notices smaller animals moving around and beneath the dragon's massive form. "Ah, they're there for protection," he realizes, piecing together the relationship between the massive dragon and the smaller creatures. "The *mušmaḫḫu* isn't interested in hunting them; it's focused solely on vegetation."

Despite what it usually feeds on, Uldako acknowledges the dragon's potential to defend itself against any potential threats. After observing the beast's behavior for some time, a daring curiosity compels Uldako to take a chance and approach closer, eager to learn more about this magnificent behemoth.

With calculated precision, Uldako adopts the guise of a grazing animal, inching his way closer to the colossal dragon. Šarru stays put and watches Uldako with a mixture of curiosity and confusion as his behavior diverges from the norm.

The other creatures in the vicinity first appear unconcerned by his presence, but then all eyes are on him as the dragon fixes its gaze upon Uldako, scrutinizing his every movement. Aware of the delicate balance, Uldako suppresses any hint of aggression, opting instead to mimic the harmless behavior of a grazing plant eater. As the tension eases, Uldako spits out the greens in his mouth when the dragon looks away and subtly increases the distance between himself and the dragon, feigning calm on all fours.

Satisfied, the dragon resumes its meal, leisurely consuming leaves from the lofty treetops with its elongated neck, oblivious to the observer below. Uldako takes advantage of the moment to study the magnificent creature, absorbing every detail with captivated attention.

As he beholds the colossal dragon, he is overwhelmed by its sheer size. The dragon's towering presence commands reverence, casting a shadow that dwarfs even the brilliance of the sun. Its elongated neck reaches skyward, crowned with a diminutive head that seems inconsequential compared to its massive form. The dragon carries an aura of formidable strength, evident in the robust muscles that ripple beneath its skin. It eats leaves and grass like a deer, but it has immense strength in its loins and power in the muscles of his belly. He makes his long tail stiff like a cedar tree; the sinews of his thighs are knit together. His bones are like tubes of bronze, his limbs like great bars of iron.

The ground trembles slightly with each step, emphasizing the dragon's dominance in the natural order. Uldako's heart quickens its pace as the creature turns and unexpectedly moves closer to him.

Accustomed to many of the creatures of the wild, Uldako is awestruck by the behemoth's majestic movements, which belie its immense size with a surprising grace. Its presence radiates a timeless aura. "Surely this is the *lugal* of all animals," Uldako ponders with fear as it moves closer.

As the behemoth draws near, Uldako freezes, willing himself to become stone, tree, moss—anything other than a man about to be stepped on. The ground trembles with every step; leaves shiver; small stones hop. A shadow swallows him whole as the creature passes directly overhead, its belly a moving cliff that blocks out the sun.

Uldako does not breathe.

He does not blink.

He becomes a very dedicated patch of dirt.

The beast keeps walking, utterly uninterested.

One of the creature's massive legs rises—blotting out the sky above him—and hangs there for a terrible, eternal moment.

Please choose anywhere else. Anywhere. Anywhere but here, he pleads inside his own skull, eyes wide and unmoving.

The enormous foot settles down just beside him, close enough that he feels the ground pulse beneath his cheek.

Only when the last tremor fades does he finally exhale, thin and shaky. "Thank the stars, I am not a footprint."

Returning to Šarru's side, Uldako casts one last glance at the awe-inspiring dragon, overwhelmed by a profound sense of respect and admiration. "Šarru, if such magnificent beings exist in this world, imagine the boundless power of the *dingir* who created them. Perhaps the *Dingir* Most High created it—and all of us," Uldako muses, his imagination ignited by the spectacle.

Then, another notion crosses his mind. "Oh, just imagine what it would feel like to ride that behemoth, soaring high above the world, untouchable by any danger below!" Šarru responds with a disapproving growl as he walks away. Uldako looks at him, puzzled, and remarks, "What's wrong with dreaming a little, eh?"

He glances one last time at the dragon and back to Šarru, speaking softly, "We are often ignorant of what we do not know, but the truth, once revealed, has the power to change everything." Emotion wells up within Uldako as he reflects on the plight of the slaves, deprived of the wonders and beauty that surround them. Tears stream down his face as he slings the robust beast, with tusks and a peculiar snout, over his shoulder again. With a heavy heart, Uldako searches for a suitable spot where he and Šarru can share a quiet lunch together.

After a hearty meal, Uldako's strength is replenished, infusing him with renewed vigor as he presses onward, confident that he's nearing the location of Seth. As time drags on, Uldako senses their proximity. "Šarru, we're close now. Stay vigilant," he murmurs.

Šarru responds with a low growl, silently affirming his readiness. With heightened senses, Šarru sniffs the air to detect any unusual scents. After a few steps, he halts in his tracks, his nostrils flaring as he senses something amiss.

Uldako's grip tightens on his spear, a silent acknowledgment that danger may be lurking nearby. His senses sharpen, attuned to a faint but distinct sound echoing through the forest. "Šarru, do you hear that?" he whispers, his voice barely above a breath.

The bear steps forward, nostrils flaring again as he catches the scent carried by the breeze. Uldako inches closer, the mysterious cacophony growing louder, its unfamiliar blend of noises stirring something deep within him. It's a symphony of sounds, unlike any he's encountered in his life. "This sound is not from animals, but of humans," Uldako murmurs to himself, his excitement clearly visible.

As they press onward, the source of the intriguing sounds gradually reveals itself. "Up there in the distance, Šarru! It looks like people living in the trees." Uldako points with his finger as his other hand tightens the grip on his spear. They cautiously approach, blending seamlessly into the cover of the surrounding foliage.

When they finally reach the area, Uldako's eyes widen at the sight above—an elaborate network of treehouses woven into the high branches, each one crafted with care and purpose. But before he can study them further, something below draws his attention.

From the shadowed undergrowth, a woman steps into view. Her presence is like mist in moonlight—soft, striking, and almost unreal against the towering trees behind her. She moves with quiet grace toward the largest treehouse and disappears behind its massive trunk.

Uldako stands enthralled. In all his twenty-five years, he has never seen beauty like hers.

He waits in breathless anticipation, hoping for another glimpse of her, but she remains concealed from view. A voice drifts down from the treetops, blending with the rustle of leaves and the distant melody. Uldako strains to listen, realizing the woman must have ascended the tree. Noting that the massive trunk serves as the entry point to the treehouses above, Uldako proceeds with caution, flanking the area as he approaches.

His senses are on high alert as he strategizes his approach to the dwellings above. With the agility of a predator, he stealthily navigates the forest floor, his eyes darting for any signs of movement. Yet, to his surprise, the ground below remains eerily still, hinting that the inhabitants are all aloft, engaged in some unseen event.

Undeterred, Uldako fixates on the towering trunk serving as the gateway to the elevated abodes. With a mix of determination and curiosity, he approaches, noting the sturdy ropes coiled around the trunk as lifelines. As he begins his ascent, each calculated movement propels him closer to the secrets hidden above. Thoughts of the advantage of such lofty dwellings swirl in his mind, igniting his resolve to uncover the truth behind the inhabitants and hopefully enlist their aid in his quest to find Seth.

Uldako cautiously emerges, his head just high enough to take a peek into the elevated platform, his gaze sweeping across the intricate network of interconnected treehouses. Each structure, breathtaking in its craftsmanship, stands as tribute to the skill and ingenuity of its creators. As he surveys the sprawling settlement from his vantage point, Uldako estimates its capacity to house scores of individuals, with room for further expansion.

With a silent nod to Šarru below, signaling him to remain concealed, Uldako moves onto the wooden floor with the grace of a stalking lion. His movements are deliberate, his senses keenly attuned to any signs of danger. Approaching the largest treehouse, where the lively sounds emanate, Uldako pauses at the threshold, his curiosity piqued. With a steady hand, he pushes the door slightly open to take a look inside, eager to uncover the mysteries that lie within.

As Uldako looks through the gap of the door, he stands bewildered, his eyes locked upon the surreal scene before him, a spectacle that challenges his understanding of the world. The haunting melody swirling around him beckons him closer, enticing him to abandon caution and immerse himself in its embrace.

Yet, before he can heed its call, a sound of movement from behind snaps him back to reality. Uldako whirls around to find the woman he had spotted earlier, now standing before him, her beauty magnified by proximity. Her ebony locks cascade around her shoulders, framing a smile that radiates warmth and assurance. "Well, don't just stand there and spy on us, go inside," she urges, her tone inviting yet firm.

Caught in an ocean of conflicting emotions, Uldako grapples with uncertainty. Doubt and suspicion race through his mind like wild stallions, questioning the motives behind the woman's sudden hospitality, yet there is some strange power pulling him to her.

She's the most beautiful woman I've ever seen, he muses inwardly, *but can I truly trust her? What if this is a trap?* Uldako struggles to formulate a response, as he inexplicably finds his thoughts scattered in the presence of the woman.

Sensing his inner turmoil, the woman extends a hand in an inviting gesture. "Come on. I'll accompany you," she reassures him.

Uldako feels compelled to follow, his thoughts swirling like leaves in a gust. *Why do I feel so powerless in her presence? Her voice is a soothing balm to my skeptical thoughts, yet it's also the reason she might be dangerous.*

With little time to dwell on his reservations, Uldako finds himself drawn forward by an irresistible force. His senses are ablaze with wonder and trepidation as he steps into the cavernous chamber that is brimming with mystery and intrigue. Uldako stands frozen, overwhelmed by the surreal sight unfolding before him. Women of boundless beauty move gracefully about the chamber, their movements fluid and mesmerizing. Some bow reverently, while others manipulate strange instruments that emit the enchanting sounds that had drawn him here. Their voices, rich and melodious, weave together in a harmonious chorus.

As Uldako struggles to comprehend the scene before him, the woman beside him leans in, her gaze curious. "Do you like the music?" Her voice is gentle yet insistent.

Uldako is stunned. The music, unlike anything he has ever known, washes over him like a warm blanket—beautiful, mysterious, and powerful. It steals his breath, leaving him unable to speak. But before he can gather his thoughts, another voice cuts through the chamber—a voice firm and commanding, impossible to ignore.

At a distance, he sees a group of women kneeling before a towering figure cloaked in authority. With arms lifted in reverence, they begin to sing together, their voices rising in a chorus of worship.

Uldako turns to the enigmatic figure, who emanates an air of majesty and power. It is evident that these women worship him as a deity, their devotion visible in every gesture and word.

Uldako's bewilderment deepens as one of the women shouts, "Shamsiel, *dumu* of *Utu*! Great *dingir* of light, love, and music! We praise you, O great one!"

However, the woman beside Uldako catches his attention with a similar expression of discontent. Puzzled, he wonders why she appears displeased amidst the fervent devotion.

As Uldako surveys the scene, one thing is certain—there is no peace within him.

The man standing at the center appears human, extremely striking in appearance, but the air around him tells another story. Uldako senses the weight of concealed power, and he knows—just as everyone else seems to know—that this is no ordinary man. He is probably a spirit...one that has taken on human form.

As Uldako glances at the woman beside him again, he notices that the distrust evident in her expression grows. With a newfound urgency to get out of this place sooner to find Seth, Uldako turns to the woman, summoning his courage with a deep breath, and softly asks, "Excuse me, what is this place?"

She regards him cautiously and gestures for him to follow her, leading him away from prying ears. With a disappointed sigh, she begins, "You seem like a reasonable man, so I'll tell you the truth. We are a new offshoot, once part of the Jubal clan, dedicated to the craft of music. Perhaps you've heard of us?"

Uldako, still clueless about the regional clans, shrugs. "Not really. I've only heard of a *Jabal* clan—which sounds suspiciously like *Jubal*, so I'm not sure if someone was just bad at pronunciation." He leans in. "I'm looking for a man named Seth. Older, strong, had six warriors with him. And he carried a special eagle—"

Before he can finish, the woman gasps and cuts him off. "Yes! I remember him! An elder with an eagle emblem—I will never forget such a magnificent man!" Her eyes widen. "His presence…oh, it was something else. So dignified. And handsome—*very* handsome for someone probably over seven hundred years old. I've never seen such deep, thoughtful eyes in my life. Moved like a man half his age. Honestly, if I had been just a few centuries older—"

Uldako lifts a hand, exasperated. "Alright, alright! I get it—Seth is impressive. But did he say where he was going? Did you actually speak to him, or were you too busy swooning?"

With a frown etched on her brow, she halts his barrage of questions. "Hold on. One question at a time. I will tell you what I know, but first, will you help me with this…situation here?" She nods toward the women worshipping Shamsiel, her eyes revealing a sense of urgency.

Perplexed, Uldako inquires, "What?"

Leaning closer, the woman whispers, "My *dusa-meš* here believe this Shamsiel, as some call him, is one of the new *dingir-meš*. They think his *abba* is *Utu*, the *dingir* of the sun, justice, and light. But I know the truth about him."

Uldako's interest is piqued. "And what truth is that?"

Lowering her voice, the woman leans in. "He and his so-called *abba* are part of the *anunnaki*, as some are calling them now." Her tone shifts—half awed, half disturbed. "But this one…this being…he's something else entirely." She swallows. "A Watcher from realms unseen—trying to breed with human women."

Uldako blinks, stunned. His instincts scream caution, but his face remains calm. He nods slightly, masking his unease with forced curiosity. "A Watcher? And what exactly do you mean by breed?"

With a stern look, the woman explains, "I believe these Watchers came to earth pretending to be heavenly *dingir-meš* and now seek to sire earthly *dingir-meš* with human women."

Uldako opens his mouth then closes it. "I…don't even know what to say." He pauses, then asks, "How do you know all this?"

She steps closer, her voice dropping to a near-whisper. "I overheard them—Shamsiel and another voice, not seen but felt. They spoke of the *Dingir* Most High, of them being cast down. There was rebellion—led by something ancient…

dark. The name was *Enki*. And he spoke of others—*Azazel* and *Shemihaza*—with sinister plans. I think they were sent by him."

Uldako's thoughts race. His voice comes low. "I've heard similar stories like that…about spirits—some good, some evil. But I—"

Impatience laces her voice as she cuts him off. "Look, we can stand here all day and talk, but we need to help these women now! So, will you aid me or not?"

Uldako senses the woman's desperation and sees an opportunity for a better deal. He blurts out, "If I help you, I need the location of Seth, and one of those instruments that make that beautiful noise—deal?" His words have barely left his tongue when he's struck by them, feeling a pang of shame wash over him. *That's exactly what I despised in the men back at Jabal, always seeking their own gain, never lending a hand without expecting something in return. This isn't who I am.* The memory of Seth flashes through Uldako's mind as he looks down at the ground, a reminder of selflessness in all situations, even in the face of danger. Yet here he stands becoming what he hates.

The woman puts her hand on his shoulder and says, "*Lu-kur*, if you aid me, I will tell you about the old warrior, and as a bonus, I'll teach you how to play music!"

Uldako, grappling with conflicting emotions, reluctantly agrees. "Thank you, but just the information regarding Seth will be enough," he utters.

He stands there waiting in complete silence, expecting her to give a plan of action to help the women. But she does nothing. She just smiles at him. Warm. Patient. Still smiling.

Uldako shifts his weight. Nods. Waits. The silence stretches.

She stares back at him, nods in return. Still smiling.

"So…" he says slowly, gesturing vaguely toward the worshippers, "what exactly am I supposed to do?"

The woman blinks, confused. "What do you mean?"

"I mean, what's the plan?" he says, motioning between them. "You know—the 'help your *dusa-meš*' part?"

She blinks again. "I don't have a plan. No, I was hoping you would have one!"

Uldako's eyes widen. "Me? Why me? You're the one who dragged me into this situation."

She shrugs with a half-smile. "Well, you look brave."

He straightens instinctively, caught off guard. "Brave?" he repeats, voice cracking slightly. He clears his throat. "I mean—of course. Yes. I am. Very brave."

She raises an eyebrow, clearly amused.

Uldako tries to recover. "I just thought...since you were already here, maybe you had, you know, some sort of secret plan or idea of what to do?"

She chuckles softly.

He sighs. "Great. So neither of us has a plan."

Then, her eyes brighten. "Wait! I did hear something once. From travelers out of the North. They said evil fears one name above all others: the *Dingir* Most High. The One who made them. In these parts, He is also known as *An*."

Uldako's posture shifts. He speaks more softly. "I've heard another name... *Il*. Maybe, just maybe *Il* is the true *Dingir*, the Most High of all that exists. And maybe even these Watchers tremble at His name."

The woman regards Uldako with raised eyebrows, her confusion evident. "Maybe, but how is that going to help us here and now?"

Uldako's eyes light up with sudden realization. "I'm going to try something," he declares with newfound resolve.

Sensing the gravity of the situation, the woman whispers a warning. "Be careful! These beings are powerful. They can kill you!"

But Uldako's determination is unwavering. "It might kill me," he acknowledges, "but I need to find Seth no matter what. Stand back!"

As Uldako steps closer to the fallen spirit cloaked in human form, he feels the air grow heavier, charged with something unnatural. The Watcher is stunning—almost too perfect to be real. His hair gleams like polished obsidian under the soft light, his eyes shimmer with an unnatural depth that seems to pull at the soul, and his form is statuesque—taller than any man Uldako has ever seen, carved with inhuman symmetry and strength.

Even from a distance, Uldako can sense the strange allure radiating from him—the same spellbinding presence that has entranced the women. The closer he gets, the more it clings to him like mist. A twinge of insecurity creeps in, unbidden. For a moment, Uldako feels small, flawed, and painfully human.

Scraping together the courage needed, he steps forward and speaks with determination. "Shamsiel! Reveal the truth of your identity!"

The spirit fixes his gaze on Uldako, his eyes ablaze with dark fury. "Silence, you insignificant pest! Begone!"

Despite the tremble in his legs, Uldako stands firm, sensing the immense power emanating from Shamsiel. Yet, he speaks courageously. "I know who the true *Dingir* is, the Creator of the heavens and earth, the Almighty." The words come, even as doubt lingers within him. "All authority and power belong to *Il*!"

Shamsiel recoils with a piercing shriek. "No!" he cries. "You dare not utter that name in my presence!" His visage begins to warp, subtle changes manifesting in his face and hands, hinting at his true form. His eyes turn to crimson red while his fingers transform into claws.

As the conversation unfolds, Shamsiel's appearance undergoes a slow and sinister transformation, each alteration revealing more about his malevolent nature. "Who are you?" Shamsiel demands through gritted teeth, his voice laced with malice, his question more of a threat than a query.

With confident strides, Uldako steps forward, his voice ringing out with authority. "I come to you in the name of *Il*, the Most High! Hear my—"

His words are cut short as Shamsiel's demeanor shifts at the mention of the name *Il*, revealing his true malevolent nature fully. Rising to his feet, Shamsiel towers over Uldako, exuding a substantial aura of power. "*Il*, I know, but who are you? You are nothing and wield no power over me!"

Fear grips Uldako, his resolve faltering as he takes a step back, pleading, "Wait! Wait!" Uldako staggers backward, his body lurching as he collapses to the ground, his hand raised in a plea for mercy. In a swift blur, the fallen spirit advances toward him, closing the distance with dreaded speed. "*Il*, help me!"

Suddenly, a radiant figure bursts into view, pure light wrapped in flame. The air ripples with power as he descends like a bolt from heaven. Wings spread wide, his very presence banishes the darkness from the chamber. In one fluid motion, he seizes the Watcher by the throat, his fiery sword burning with holy fury.

"Fallen one!" the spirit thunders, his voice shaking the very walls. "I rebuke you in the name of *Il*, the Most High! Begone from this place!"

Shamsiel shrieks—a sound not of this world—as his form contorts and vanishes in a hiss of smoke and flame.

The radiant being turns, his face flashing like lightning as his piercing gaze meets Uldako's for a single heartbeat—deep, knowing, eternal. And then…he is gone.

Silence crashes down like a wave.

The chamber, once full of music and reverence, is now hollow and still. A strange, weighty stillness settles in the air, thick with awe and fear.

Uldako and the woman remain frozen, wide-eyed and breathless. Even the other women, once lost in worship, stand motionless—shocked, as if they've just awoken from a dream.

Then, one voice pierces the silence, trembling and raw: "He was an evil *dingir*! Did you see Shamsiel's face?"

Like a hive suddenly disturbed, the chamber erupts in a flurry of voices.

Questions, disbelief, cries of shame and relief all rise at once as the women try to piece together what just happened—what they had almost become a part of.

And through it all, Uldako remains still, heart pounding, soul burning with something new.

Clarity.

12

Defeat

The woman steps closer, her eyes wide with wonder and fear. "You would've died if not for that spirit of light," she whispers. "We've seen the truth, haven't we? The *anunnaki*—they're not what they claim to be. They're dark spirits, leading us astray."

Uldako stands silent, breathing shallow, hands trembling. The memory of divine light and shadow still burns in his mind. "I am powerless," he murmurs. "*Il*...He must be more than I imagined."

They both turn, gazing back toward the place where the spiritual clash unfolded. The air still shimmers faintly, as if heaven and earth have only just separated.

"I've never seen anything like that," the woman says, her voice unsteady. "Two opposing forces, like fire and ice. Something is happening in the unseen realm." She turns to Uldako and taps his shoulder, trying to jolt him from his trance. "Have you seen anything like that before?"

Uldako blinks, slowly returning to himself. "Yes," he says. "I wondered why it appeared to me, but now I think I know. Something is stirring. The spirits no longer stay hidden. I think there's a war unfolding—and it's breaking into our world more and more."

He draws a long breath, his voice low. "And if these fallen ones pose as *dingir-meš*, then how many more walk among us? How many shadows whisper lies with divine tongues?" He looks toward the sky. "And how many true *dingir* are there—like *Il*?"

The woman nods slowly, her expression thoughtful. "I've heard rumors that many in the kingdom of Etana believe in only one true *Dingir*. They call him *Il*, the Most High, like you said. But lately, in these parts—and in the Land of

Nod—people have started calling the *Dingir* Most High *An*. Some even say that *Il* revealed His true name to the line of Cain as *An*."

She glances back toward the place where the spirit appeared. "But after what we just saw, I doubt that. The one who helped us calls him *Il*."

Uldako nods, his brow furrowed. "Amidst the flood of voices and conflicting beliefs, finding the truth becomes a daunting task."

The woman paces slowly near the wooden beams, her fingers trailing along the carved wall as her thoughts spill out. "Maybe they're one and the same, or maybe there's more to it. What if there are multiple high *dingir-meš*, and *Il* is only one of them? Perhaps *An* is another high *dingir* and even answers to *Il*, who sits above them all. I mean, who created *An*? And who created *Il*?"

Uldako turns to her, locking eyes. "That kind of thinking never ends," he says firmly. "You'll keep asking: Who created the *dingir* who created *Il*, and who created the one before that…and the one before that?" He draws a steady breath. "But it makes no sense. Somewhere, there must be a beginning. A self-existing *Dingir* Most High—one who has always been. Who created all, yet was never created. A being beyond comprehension. The true origin of all things."

The woman's eyes widen as she absorbs the profound revelation. The wisdom of Uldako's words seems to hang in the air, filling the silence with an almost tangible sense of understanding. The idea of an eternal, self-existing God reshapes her perception of the divine and the world around her.

Uldako takes a deep breath, gathering his thoughts, and continues, "I am not sure of many things, but I am starting to believe that *Il* must be good. He has helped me a few times, and for someone like Seth to worship Him, He must be good! I must find Seth and uncover the truth for myself."

The woman smiles warmly, facing Uldako squarely. "Well, I promised to divulge Seth's whereabouts if you aided me, and you have. Thank you, *lu-kur*."

Uldako modestly shrugs, humbled by the woman's gratitude. "I merely played a small part. It was the spirit who saved us all." Realizing he hasn't introduced himself, he adds, "I am Uldako, *dumu-nita* of Deborah."

The woman bows her head slightly. "Pleased to meet you, Uldako. I am Ishara, *dumu-munus* of Beniah."

Uldako, still feeling a twinge of awkwardness, manages a shy smile. "Nice to meet you." He then hands her his map, asking, "So, Ishara, *dumu* of Beniah, would you be so kind as to tell me the whereabouts of Seth?"

Ishara studies the map, her eyes scanning the intricate lines with quiet admiration. "Remarkable craftsmanship," she murmurs. "Let me mark where I believe Seth was headed."

She carefully marks a point then adds, "He may already have moved on. And venturing further into the jungle alone now would be dangerous."

She glances at Uldako with a soft smile. "Stay the night. I'll teach you what I know—about singing and the language of instruments. You'll need more than a sword where you're going."

Uldako hesitates, considering the implications of accepting Ishara's offer. "I fear the music played here may be tainted by evil, and I'm not sure if—"

Ishara interrupts, her tone gentle yet firm. "There's nothing inherently wrong with music itself; it's all in how it's used. In our case, we'll use it for good."

Uldako nods thoughtfully. "True…" Then his eyes widen. "Šarru!" he exclaims, straightening.

Ishara blinks, caught off guard. "What? Who's Šarru?"

Uldako turns toward the direction of the door. "I nearly forgot—he's still waiting beneath the treehouses."

"Who is he?" she asks, following him as they step through the door.

"I can't leave him out there all night," Uldako says, scanning the darkening forest below. "Not in these wilds."

She crosses her arms, brow raised. "Uldako, who exactly are we talking about?"

Uldako grins, his eyes sparkling with fondness. "Šarru? He's an *uḫuš*—my closest companion since he was a cub."

Ishara's eyes widen when she hears he is a bear, mischief dancing in her gaze. "An *uḫuš*, huh? My father's also an *uḫuš* of a man, big and strong!"

Uldako stifles a laugh, shaking his head. "No, no. I mean an actual *uḫuš*! You know, fur, paws, growls—my companion is a real *uḫuš*!"

She stares at him, blinking once. "You travel with a *real uḫuš*?"

He nods. "He's loyal. And smarter than most men I've met."

Ishara stops mid-step, tilting her head. "And you want to bring him up *here*? Into a tree village filled with people who like having faces?"

Uldako raises both hands, placating. "He's calm. He won't harm anyone unless threatened."

Ishara lets out a slow breath, clearly weighing her options. "You're full of surprises, Uldako. But an *uḫuš*? By the stones of the earth…" She shakes her head. "Fine—but *you* are responsible for him. If he so much as sniffs at someone the wrong way, he's going back down."

She turns reluctantly toward the edge of the platform. "Follow me. I'll show you the tree lift. Just make sure he doesn't see me as a snack."

Arriving at the tree lift—a contraption of ropes and a large wheel—Uldako marvels at its ingenuity. "What a remarkable invention! This is how you survive here, far above the dangers below."

As they descend, Ishara freezes at the sight waiting below.

Šarru.

The massive cave bear, broader than any she's ever seen, stands beneath the trees. His amber eyes gleam in the half-light, tracking every movement as they descend. With each movement downward, the wood beneath the lift creaks.

Ishara stiffens. "That's not a normal *uḫuš*."

Uldako grins. "He's an *uḫuš-gal*."

Her eyes widen. "You're serious? A real *uḫuš-gal*? I thought they were just creatures of legend!"

The platform reaches the ground, and Uldako gestures for Šarru to step on.

Šarru moves with slow, theatrical weight, parting his jaws just enough to make her heart stop.

Ishara stumbles back instinctively, hands half-raised.

Then the giant beast snorts…and lowers his head, gently brushing it against her thigh like an affectionate pup.

She blinks, stunned.

Uldako laughs. "That's his idea of a joke—terrifying first impressions."

Ishara shoots him a glare, though a smile breaks through. She slowly reaches out, fingers threading into Šarru's thick fur. "You're awful," she mutters. "And so is your *uḫuš-gal*."

Šarru huffs, clearly pleased with himself, and drops down beside her like a mountain of warm fur and muscle.

As they ascend, Uldako senses Šarru's tension and gently strokes his thick fur. "Easy now, Šarru…easy, my *dusa*." The great bear shifts uneasily, glancing down at the rising height, muscles tight. But as Uldako continues to murmur calm reassurance, Šarru settles, holding still until the platform reaches the top and he can step off safely.

That night, Uldako and Šarru join Ishara and her friends, sharing a hearty meal, exchanging tales of bravery and adventure, and immersing themselves in the art of crafting and playing musical instruments—particularly the lyre and the flute, which they also call the pipe. To Uldako's surprise, Ishara begins to add words to the sounds of the instruments. Her voice, rich and melodious, fills the night air with a playful touch of jest.

I once met a warrior, who roamed where few dare go,
Crossing peaks and valleys where cold winds blow.
With a fierce *uḫuš* steady at his side,
He walks the wilds with a watchful stride.

Oh, have you heard of Uldako, the *lugal* of the wild?
Eyes like dusk, with a spirit fierce and styled.
Alone in the forests, with his bear he does tread,
In search of truth where others have fled.

I once met a warrior, with axe and spear in hand,
Still learning the truth of where he stands.
He fights to free those bound by lies,
And questions the powers that darken the skies.

Oh, have you heard of Uldako, brave and unknown?
His path is his own, though he walks it alone.
He stood face-to-face with a spirit's might,
And called on *Il* to pierce the night.

I once met a warrior above the treetops green—
Oh, what a tale…what a day it has been!

Uldako feels his face heat up with embarrassment as Ishara's song places all the praise on him—something he's never experienced before. The unfamiliar attention unsettles him, but at the same time, he's captivated by the beauty and power of her voice. Each note weaves a mesmerizing harmony around the gathered crowd, drawing everyone into its grasp. As Ishara finishes, the crowd erupts in applause and cheers, but Uldako remains frozen, staring at her in awe. He's never heard anything so beautiful in his life, and the surge of emotions overwhelms him.

Ishara notices Uldako out of the corner of her eye. Nothing in his face is guarded; his thoughts lie open, plain to see. It disarms her. Most men wear masks. This one wears nothing but his soul. He is unknown, rough, and strange—but in that moment, something stirs in her heart. A recognition. A pull she can't quite name.

Initially she wasn't quite sure about him. She thinks back to earlier in the day when they met, before she knew anything about him. She first noticed

Uldako watching through the door of the tree-shelter and studied him from afar. A stranger. Alone. She did not know his intention, and caution rose in her. Yet she also remembered her prayer—for a helper.

She formed her plan swiftly: Draw him inside, among others, where she could watch him safely and learn who he truly was.

Silent as a shadow, she moved in behind him to urge him to enter the shelter, and that decision led to where they are now.

As the night deepens, she knows that he was the one she prayed for. When the music and gathering finally come to a close, Ishara leads Uldako and Šarru to a sheltered place to rest. For the first time, Uldako feels truly safe as he lies in the shelter high above the ground in the treetops. He hadn't realized how exhausted he is—both mentally and physically—for as soon as he lies down, he slips into a deep, restful sleep.

As the sun rises on a new day, Uldako awakens to a breathtaking spectacle. The sky is painted in a palette of soft hues—delicate pinks, warm oranges, and gentle purples—blending seamlessly into the deep blue of the receding night. Golden rays of sunlight filter through the leaves, casting a warm, ethereal glow over the treetops and illuminating the intricate patterns of the treehouses.

The air is fresh and filled with the sounds of birds greeting the morning, their songs intertwining with the gentle rustle of leaves in the breeze. Uldako's mind buzzes with the melodies and craftsmanship he encountered the previous night. Despite his new, humble skills in music and instrument-making, he feels a deep determination to hone them as he ventures forth, inspired by the beauty and tranquility of the dawn.

The sky begins to pale as Uldako readies his pack in silence, careful not to wake the others. The village still sleeps, wrapped in the hush of dawn. Only the wind moves, whispering through the leaves as he and Šarru step toward the edge of the platform, eager to continue their quest.

Then, a voice breaks through the morning stillness—familiar and urgent. "Uldako! Wait!"

He turns, startled.

Ishara bursts from the shadows of the hut, hair tousled from sleep, eyes wide with determination. Her feet are bare against the wood as she rushes toward him, breathless. "Wait, please!"

Caught off guard by her sudden appearance, Uldako halts in his tracks, turning to face her with a sheepish grin. "Oh, sorry, I didn't want to wake you," he stammers, feeling a pang of guilt for his abrupt departure.

Ishara's frown melts into a smile as she steps closer, her eyes bright with quiet resolve. "It's all right. But *dusa-meš* don't slip away without saying goodbye, do they? We're not *lu-kur-meš* anymore. We're *dusa-meš* now, aren't we?" she says gently, catching Uldako off guard with her honesty.

Feeling their bond set, Uldako bows his head. "We are," he says, warmth rising in his chest.

But then comes the unexpected twist. Ishara, with sudden boldness, declares, "Then I'm coming with you!"

Uldako stares, speechless, as she strides past him without hesitation—her resolve clear, her mind already made.

"You'll need me to show you where Seth is," she says, chin lifted. "So I'm coming with you—no matter what you say!"

He glances at Šarru, who lets out a low grunt and nudges Ishara's hand as if in agreement.

Uldako studies her—the fire in her eyes, the steadiness in her voice. And for a moment, something stirs in him. Respect…maybe even something more.

"Well," he says, a slow smile forming. "I suppose an extra hand—and someone who can turn fear into courage with a song—might come in handy. So, if you're truly set on joining us two humble travelers, then come along."

Ishara's shout of pure contentment pierces the air. "Yes! Okay, just give me some time to collect my things. I will need my harp, definitely more clothes, and then some pottery…" Ishara continues to talk out loud as she walks off to collect her belongings.

As the moment arrives to collect her belongings, Uldako stands in disbelief at the sheer mountain of bags before him. "Uh, we can't possibly carry all of this," he mutters, eyeing the assortment of containers with growing trepidation. His gaze falls on a stack of pottery and a collection of cuneiform tablets. Shaking his head, he adds with a frown, "The pottery stays—and all those cuneiform tablets too. We won't need them."

Ishara, undeterred by his concerns, brushes off his protests with a wave of her hand. "Nonsense, we can manage," she insists.

Uldako strides forward, his tone firm and decisive. "I don't think so," he interjects, his gaze steady. "We don't want to be overburdened with too many bags if a beast decides to attack us, do we?" He gestures pointedly to the overstuffed packs. "Just take your flute, harp, and a change of clothes. As for the food, we'll only need a little. Šarru and I can handle the hunting as we go."

Ishara hesitates, torn between her desire to hold on to her belongings and

Uldako's practical reasoning. Sensing her internal struggle, Uldako nudges her gently. "I know these things are precious to you, and you can come back for them—they'll still be here, safe. But I'd rather have you alive without them than risk losing you because you're carrying too much."

Reluctantly, Ishara relents with a sigh. "Fine," she acquiesces, her tone bordering on frustration. With a flicker of annoyance, she gathers only the essentials, leaving behind the excess baggage.

Some of her clan awakens and come to say their goodbyes after hearing of her plans. They stand together for a long moment, saying little. One by one, hands clasp, foreheads touch in farewell, and voices soften. A few tears are brushed away quickly, hidden behind small smiles. No grand speeches, only quiet words of gratitude and promises to remember. Then Ishara turns to the lift with Uldako and Šarru.

Together, the trio descends from the treehouses, and as they set foot on solid ground, a sense of anticipation fills the air, mingled with the uncertainty of what lies ahead. With determination in their hearts and the promise of adventure beckoning, they embark on their new journey to find Seth.

Over time, Uldako, accompanied by his fierce yet affectionate bear companion Šarru and the enchanting Ishara, journey northwest in search of Seth. They sleep under the stars, take shelter in caves, and perch high in the branches of towering trees, their bond growing stronger with each passing moment. To his surprise, Uldako finds himself drawn to Ishara in ways he hadn't anticipated, a feeling stirring within him that's both unfamiliar and intriguing.

Their path leads them through a verdant landscape unlike any Uldako has seen before. The terrain unfolds with scattered cone-shaped trees, vibrant flora in a kaleidoscope of hues, and an array of curious wildlife thriving amidst the lush surroundings.

One evening as dusk approaches, Uldako observes the changing sky, noting the gathering mist. "Looks like we might get a bit wet," he remarks, casting a glance toward Ishara.

Her eyes lift to the horizon. "I think I've spotted a suitable campsite up ahead." She points toward a sheltered spot beneath a hill, and they make their way toward it.

Soon they settle near their newly kindled fire, the land now thicker with mist. A sudden surge of wind roars through the treetops, making the branches sway and groan like great beasts stirring in their sleep. Uldako jumps to his feet, heart hammering at the deep, rolling sound that seems to howl from everywhere at once.

Ishara bursts into laughter, eyes bright with delight. "Oh, that was priceless! You should've seen your face!" she teases. "Startled by a breath of the world itself, are we?"

Uldako's cheeks warm. "I wasn't startled," he insists, struggling for composure. "I was...merely attentive."

Her grin says she believes none of it.

As her laughter fades, a cool wave of mist moves through the clearing, curling low along the ground. Šarru snorts, roused by the shifting air, and pads over to Uldako's side. The great bear settles against him with a slow, heavy exhale.

Without thinking, Uldako rests a hand in Šarru's fur.

No words are spoken.

Uldako looks up at the waters above. He has always felt drawn to water for reasons he cannot name. Perhaps it is the peace it brings to his inner man. Tonight his thoughts return to it more deeply than ever before. *Where does it come from?*

He knows there is water beneath their feet, and there are the waters above that rest beyond the sky. He does not understand how they were set apart, only that they are. At times, the high waters seem to stir and shift with living color, especially on still nights when mist rises from the ground and the air calms down. The earth around them quiets as the mist settles. Warmth lingers across the clearing, and a simple peace rests there.

Uldako rests against Šarru's great side, the two of them watching the heavens. Evening deepens like dye spreading through clear water, the sky shifting from soft rose to violet to a deep blue that feels close, as though it could be touched. High above, long veils of light move in slow folds, green and gold flowing through them like drifting rivers in the sky.

The glow settles softly across the trees, along the leaves, and across the ground itself, and everything seems to share in it. Šarru releases a slow breath and becomes still. Uldako lifts his hand toward the moving light.

Ishara whispers, "Only a mighty *dingir* could shape beauty that rests so softly on the world." Uldako agrees. The colors rise and fall above them, and the world rests open beneath that great and gentle expanse. Ishara's gaze flickers between Uldako and Šarru, a gentle observer of their silent bond, before she succumbs to sleep.

As the lights continue to drift across the sky, Uldako remains awake, his thoughts moving with them. Is this the work of the Most High, casting colors from the heights? Or perhaps it is simply the world breathing, old and alive and beyond all knowing.

He shifts uncomfortably, unfamiliar with the unknown wonders. Earlier, Ishara had placed a covering gently across his shoulders—finely woven, soft as animal fur but patterned with strands of flax and palm. "It's called a blanket," she'd whispered with a smile. "It's for warmth, not armor."

He didn't know how to respond, only nodded, unsure if he deserved such a gift. Now, beneath its unfamiliar comfort, he tosses and turns, unable to silence his mind. Only when the sky begins to pale and the colors retreat does weariness finally overtake him, and he drifts into a restless sleep—wrapped in something far stranger than the waters above: kindness.

The next morning, as the sun climbs higher in the sky, Uldako is jolted awake by a sensation on his face—a wet, slobbery greeting from Šarru. The bear's rough tongue drags across his face with unfiltered affection.

With a groan, Uldako pushes him away, scowling through sleep-blurred eyes. "Alright, alright, I'm up," he mutters, rubbing his face with both hands.

He sits up slowly, the pull of exhaustion still lingering, and glances around the shelter. But to his surprise, Ishara is nowhere in sight.

Uldako's heart skips a beat as wild urgency grips him—where could Ishara have disappeared to? Frantically, he calls out her name, his voice echoing through the still morning air. "Ishara! Ishara?"

"Above you." Her response drifts down to him, guiding his gaze upward to where she stands atop the hill. "I'm up here," she calls down, excitement evident in her tone.

Uldako's curiosity stirs, and he quickly climbs the slope to join her, his brows rising at the sight before him.

"Look!" Ishara shouts with wonder. "Look at all these mushrooms!"

Spread out before them is a sprawling field of fungi, their delicate caps glistening with dew under the morning light. Uldako slows, taking in the strange, beautiful sight.

"And the best part? They're not poisonous. We can eat them!"

Uldako's skepticism is plain. "How can you be sure?"

Ishara smiles, warm and confident. "My *ama* taught me. She knew every plant and mushroom in the wild. These"—she crouches to pick one gently—"are safe. I've eaten them since I was young."

Uldako studies her face, then the mushrooms. Slowly, he nods, the tension in his shoulders easing. Whether a gift from the mist or the gods, he accepts the unexpected bounty.

As they begin to gather the mushrooms, Ishara's voice rises in song—soft at first, then full and bright, wrapping the morning in melody. The forest listens. So does Uldako.

Oh, listen close to stories of yore,
Ah-ah-hah-ah-aha!
Of *Il*, the eagle, sovereign and sure,
Ah-ah-hah-ah-aha!
The dragon's breath, a rebel's might,
In heavens high, a fearsome fight,
Spirits clashed in celestial roar,
As the dragon fell to earth's floor.
Oh, heed the call of legends untold,
Ah-ah-hah-ah-aha!
Il's grandeur shines bright and bold,
Ah-ah-hah-ah-aha!
Two bloodlines of earth, entwined in fate's dance,
In serpent's whisper, and eagle's glance,
Their ancient feud, a tale to be sung,
From the dawn of time, till the setting sun.
Oh, heed the call of legends untold,
Ah-ah-hah-ah-aha!
Il's grandeur shines bright and bold,
Ah-ah-hah-ah-aha!
In earth's embrace, their powers entwine,
Serpent's cunning, eagle's divine,
In cosmic duels, they clash and fight,
In shadows deep, and in dawning light.
Oh, heed the call of legends untold,
Ah-ah-hah-ah-aha!
Il's grandeur shines bright and bold,
Ah-ah-hah-ah-aha!
So listen now to tales of yore,
Ah-ah-hah-ah-aha!
Il's legacy, forevermore,
Ah-ah-hah-ah-aha!

For a moment, Uldako forgets everything else. His chest rises, breath shallow, as a strange warmth fills him—weightless, unearned, but real.

"This," he murmurs, barely audible, "this is the happiest I've ever been."

He watches Ishara and Šarru, the two souls who've carved out a space in his world. Something stirs behind his eyes…too much to name.

But when Ishara looks up, meeting his eyes, he quickly turns away, pretending to focus on his work. He can't let her see it, not yet. Not the true feelings hidden beneath his quiet resolve.

Ishara's song fades into the quiet, the final note settling softly, like a fading ember. Moved by the hush that follows, Uldako speaks.

"You have an incredible gift," he says softly. "That song…it's beautiful. What does it mean, and where did you learn it?"

Ishara looks up, her eyes distant, as if searching the sky for something long forgotten. "My great-great *ama* used to sing it to me when I was little," she murmurs. "But beyond that, I don't know. I'm not even sure it means anything. Maybe it's just something my tribe made up long ago, like we often do today." She pauses, her voice quiet as her brow tightens. "But that is the name you used for the Most High…so maybe it carries truth from ancient days. I just never gave it much thought. It does feel older than memory."

As Ishara bends down to gather more mushrooms, she shares an intriguing piece of knowledge with Uldako, her voice low with intrigue. "Did you know some clans forbid certain mushrooms? They're said to unlock a spiritual journey—guiding the soul up the mysterious world tree, allowing one to commune with the *dingir-meš* above." Her words linger in the air, like a whisper of ancient knowledge wrapped in mystery.

Uldako's expression shifts to one of surprise. "That seems strange!"

Ishara meets his look with a playful glint in her eyes. "Indeed, the world is brimming with curious tales and wonders to discover. Some are mere fanciful stories spun for simple pleasure, but others may hold a kernel of truth. As for mushrooms, I know of potent varieties that can sway the mind. They say shamans use them in rituals—to try to reach the spiritual heavens above." Ishara's voice lowers slightly. "There are whispers…that long ago, in the garden of Eden, there was a very special kind of tree. And *An*—though now I think we know His true name is *Il*—declared its fruit forbidden. Some say it wasn't a fruit at all but a kind of mushroom."

She shrugs, a faint smile tugging at her lips. "No one in my clan really knows for sure. Some from the kingdom of Etana say it was a fragrant tree, beyond all scents of the earth. Its leaves and blossoms were exceedingly beautiful, and its fruit resembled clusters of grapes. Maybe it's true. Or maybe it's just one of those old stories meant to sound wise around the campfire."

Confused, Uldako furrows his brow. "Why would *Il* forbid anyone from eating such a thing? And this isn't the first time you've mentioned the kingdom of Etana. What is it? Where is it exactly?"

Ishara straightens, her expression shifting. "Well, to be clear, it wasn't exactly a fruit. The old word just meant *produce*—something that grows. As for why it was forbidden—like I said, I don't really know. No one in my clan really does. It's one of those old tales—maybe true, maybe not."

She glances at him then looks away. "As for Etana…it's strange you've never heard of it. Everyone I know has at least heard whispers. We're told not to ask questions. Just that it's dangerous—dark, forbidden."

Her voice drops to a hush. "But after what happened in the treehouse—when that spirit of light called upon *Il*, not *An*—I can't stop thinking about it. What if everything our leaders told us was wrong? What if the kingdom of Etana isn't the threat they claim—but a threat to their lies?"

A long silence follows. Uldako steps forward and slowly unbinds the fur and hide across his shoulders. "I've never heard of Etana because I wasn't raised in a village or by a clan."

Ishara turns, curious.

Uldako steps closer, his voice low. "I was born in a slave camp. My *ama* was taken there, while I was in her belly. I came into the world behind the kennels—in the filth."

He looks up, his tone sharpening. "They had a system. Let the strongest babes live, brand them young, and raise them like livestock. It was easier than acquiring new slaves—and more effective. They shaped how we thought…what we believed we were. We weren't human. We were investments."

For the first time, Uldako shares the full truth. He pulls aside the fur from around his neck, revealing the scar on the back. "*Arad-muš*. It means slave of the serpent. They gave me this before I could speak. To mark me as property. But somehow I was freed, thanks to Seth."

As the words leave his lips, Ishara's eyes glisten, her chest rising with a quiet, trembling breath. With a sudden sob, she steps forward and throws her arms open, rushing toward him.

Instinctively, Uldako jumps back, startled by the unexpected movement. Ishara, now visibly embarrassed and shocked by his reaction, freezes in place.

Still reeling from the encounter, Uldako is left speechless, unsure of what she had just tried to do. Their eyes lock, tension hanging between them. Finally, Ishara breaks the uncomfortable silence, her voice soft and apologetic. "I just wanted to give you a hug…after hearing everything you've been through, but if you—"

Before she can finish, Uldako interrupts, his brow furrowed in confusion. "What is a hug?"

Ishara blinks, caught off guard. "You mean you've never had one? Not even once in your life?"

He does not answer, knowing she talks more to herself than to him.

Her voice softens with emotion. "A hug is…it's similar to what I've seen you do with *Šarru*—when you rest your forehead against his, or when he leans into you. It's a way humans offer comfort. To show someone they're not alone. That they matter. It's hard to describe, but it's warmth, from one soul to another."

Uldako lowers his gaze, the truth settling over him like a shadow. "They always kept us apart," he murmurs. "My *ama* was the only one. But after the weaning age, they forbade physical contact."

His hand drifts instinctively to the scar on his neck. "Apart from my *ama* when I was very young, I've never been touched without pain. Not once. *Šarru*… he's the only one I've ever allowed near me."

Ishara stares at him, breath caught in her throat. She sees it now—how he's trying to make sense of something foreign, something he's never been allowed to feel. Her eyes well, and tears slip down her cheeks in silence.

"I can't even imagine," she whispers. "To go your whole life without comfort, without anyone holding you close…that's not living."

Uldako lowers his gaze, something hollow flickering in his expression. Ishara immediately winces at her words.

"I'm sorry," she says quickly, stepping forward. "I didn't mean to offend you, Uldako. Truly. May I…may I show you?"

He stiffens. A knot coils in his stomach. But when he lifts his eyes and meets hers—so open, so steady—something inside him loosens. He swallows hard.

"Well, uh…okay," he says quietly. "Show me what a hug is."

Ishara moves slowly, reverently, as if approaching a wounded animal. Her hands hover over his shoulders, giving him space to pull away.

"This is what you call a hug," she whispers.

She wraps her arms around him—lightly, warmly. No pain. No fear. Just human closeness.

And in that moment, brief and trembling, Uldako feels a rise of emotion he cannot name. Discomfort, yes. But beneath it, something deeper stirs, fragile and real.

As Ishara slowly steps back, her eyes still brimming with compassion, she says softly, "Your past is dark, but you can forge new memories now. Let's begin there."

A gentle smile touches her lips, not out of pity but hope. With a graceful turn, she moves toward the nearby undergrowth, stooping to gather a few more mushrooms for their meal.

Uldako watches her go, his chest tight. The echo of her touch still lingers on his skin, and something in him feels exposed, vulnerable in a way that unsettles him.

He clears his throat, his voice a little too sharp, a little too quick. "Ishara, I'll see if I can find us some meat."

She pauses, glancing over her shoulder. "Don't take too long," she says, a thread of concern woven through her voice. "And be careful."

Uldako looks to Šarru, and the great bear meets his eyes. Uldako gives a soft, chest-deep *hrrk*—the call they learned together while hunting. Šarru rises and falls into step beside him, steady and sure, as they disappear into the trees.

Uldako doesn't look back.

As he ventures into the wilderness, thoughts of Ishara's hug and the words about Etana's kingdom linger in his mind, but for now, they must wait. After a while of tracking and hunting, Uldako and Šarru return triumphantly, bearing two small animals whose species remains a mystery to them.

With a sense of accomplishment, Uldako lifts the creatures aloft and presents them to Ishara. "Look what we got!" he exclaims proudly.

Ishara's eyes light up with approval as she inspects the catch. "Well done! Those are hares, similar to another animal called rabbits. You can tell by their larger size, longer legs, and those enormous ears. Hares live alone or in pairs in above-ground nests, while rabbits cozy up in groups of fifteen or twenty in underground warrens." She flashes him a playful grin. "These will go perfectly with the mushrooms. Let's get that fire going!"

Uldako turns to Šarru with a smirk, muttering under his breath, "So now we know what they are—hares, not rabbits. Guess we're learning something new every day, old *dusa*."

As the trio resumes their journey after breakfast, Ishara's voice carries a note of caution as she addresses Uldako. "We're nearing a dangerous city. Eridu lies ahead, and it's a place fraught with danger. The inhabitants are known for their wickedness, and I've heard rumors of a new temple where dark rituals take place."

Uldako's senses sharpen at Ishara's grave tone. "Yes, I have heard from the Jabal clan that they are building an enormous ziggurat. But tell me, what distinguishes a city from a safe camp?" he asks.

By now, Uldako's questions—common knowledge to most—no longer surprise her. Walking alongside him, she gently rests a hand on his shoulder and begins to explain. "Think of a safe camp like a small village. But as it grows larger, with more people and resources, it becomes a city. And cities often have rulers called *lugals*—leaders who oversee everything and ensure order."

"So, who was responsible for building Eridu?" he asks, intrigued.

Ishara looks skyward, pondering. "Hmm…I'm not entirely certain. Eridu has stood for a few hundred years, growing in size over time. Some attribute its construction to a figure also renowned for founding many cities in the Land of Nod to the East—Cain."

Uldako recognizes the name but decides not to interrupt her.

"The first city he established was Enoch, named after his *dumu* Enoch. But beyond that, my knowledge is limited. The East and a part of the South is the domain of Cain's descendants, but many offshoot branches of their family moved south. Even our clan, Jubal, is part of their family tree, or so the elders say. I never truly cared about such matters, as I always only wanted to focus on and improve my musical skills."

While Uldako, Šarru, and Ishara navigate the far outskirts of Eridu, they remain cautious, avoiding any direct paths that might draw unwanted attention. Their conversations drift through various topics, expanding Uldako's understanding of the world beyond his past. The group deliberately stays well beyond the city's reach, knowing full well the dangers that lurk within—the men of Eridu are known for their cruelty, and crossing into their territory would invite trouble. Skirting the city's shadow, they move northward, their route winding through hidden trails.

After traveling for two hand movements of the sun, northwest of Eridu, an abrupt shift in the atmosphere brings them to a halt. The uneasy stillness around them feels unnatural, as though the very land is whispering a warning of new dangers ahead. Uldako's instincts stir, telling him that peace is fleeting in this unfamiliar territory.

Advancing through a cluster of trees, their progress is interrupted by distant fearful screams piercing the air.

"Those sound like the cries of *dumu-meš*!" Ishara says, her pace quickening.

With stealthy precision, she advances, darting from one tree to the next for cover, with Uldako and Šarru trailing closely behind.

The dense canopy of trees parts, revealing a vast, boundless expanse of grasslands dotted with scattered marshes stretching to the horizon. Towering blades of grass sway gently in the breeze, whispering the ancient secrets of the land. Here and there, solitary poplar and tamarisk trees stand like silent sentinels, their sparse branches offering patches of shade from the relentless heat, as if guarding the serene, endless plain.

Uldako stands transfixed for a breath, as if ensnared by an enchantment, beholding the breathtaking view unfolding before him. Clusters of shrubs and low bushes dot the landscape with patches of green amidst a sea of gold. Above, the sky stretches out endlessly, a vast canvas of blue interrupted only by a billowing mist that drifts lazily across the heavens.

A jolt brings Uldako back from his trance as in an instant, three children dash past him, their screams carrying through the trees as they flee. They vanish from sight as swiftly as they appeared, leaving Uldako, Šarru, and Ishara momentarily dumbfounded, their minds echoing with the same incredulous question: *Did that just happen?*

Then, as if to confirm their worst fears, a horde of diminutive dragons, no taller than one's knee, charges past them in hot pursuit of the children. Their guttural growls, though faint, make Uldako's skin tighten as he watches in stunned silence, realizing the imminent danger that looms over the helpless youngsters.

With no time to think, Uldako launches into motion—his body a blur of instinct and purpose. Šarru runs behind him, claws tearing the earth. Ishara, startled at first, shakes off the shock and sprints after them.

"Be careful!" she cries. "They may be small, but together, they're deadly!"

Uldako's muscles coil and release like a sabertooth cat, his speed honed by survival and hunting in the wild with Šarru over many moons. As the pack of small dragons surges toward their prey, Uldako's axes flash—twin arcs of sharp stone guided by fury and precision.

One of the creatures lunges at a child who has tripped.

Uldako doesn't hesitate. With a brutal downswing, he buries an axe in the beast's neck, knocking it aside before it can strike. The child scrambles away, wide-eyed and gasping, saved by the smallest margin.

All the dragons begin to turn their attention to Uldako, who killed one of their own. Uldako's blade finds its mark once more, severing another's head in one swift motion.

In the midst of the chaos, Uldako stands resolute, even as the odds are stacking against him. With each swing of an axe, he faces the onslaught head-on, meeting the ferocity of the dragons with his own unyielding strength.

Šarru leaps into the fray without hesitation, an expression of their unbreakable bond. Uldako's heart swells with pride at the sight of Šarru fearlessly defending him by defeating one of the dragons that almost bit his right leg.

As the battle rages on, Ishara arrives on the scene and observes the battle from a distance with bated breath, her heart gripped with fear for Uldako's safety. She knows even if she attempts to aid them, the numbers of the lizards are too many, and it is likely they will all perish. She scrabbles to find a branch or stick, something she can use to help. Her voice carries across the battlefield, a desperate plea for caution in the face of overwhelming danger. With each passing moment, the situation grows more dire, the relentless assault of the dragons taking its toll on Uldako's battered form.

Despite his valiant efforts, Uldako and Šarru find themselves outnumbered, the relentless onslaught of the dragons wearing him down with each passing moment. Uldako slices and slices, but it feels like there is no end to these lizards.

Suddenly he feels pain on his left shin—one of them got him good. Uldako slices with all his might and the dragon falls lifeless on the ground, but then another attacks his right leg. Uldako's movements grow sluggish, each breath coming harder, his limbs heavy from the long struggle and the amount of wounds that pile up. His strength is failing. Pain beats through him like a second heartbeat. Yet even as his body falters, he does not yield. He forces himself to stand, refusing to surrender to despair.

With his last reserves of strength, Uldako fights on, his will unbroken despite the overwhelming odds. They press in from behind and below, from every side at once.

He turns—and terror seizes his chest. His beloved friend is pinned beneath the dragons' relentless assault, locked in a desperate struggle for breath.

"Fight, Šarru!" Uldako's voice is hoarse with exhaustion, his own strength waning as he succumbs to a barrage of wounds and blood loss. Barely able to remain standing, he endures the biting agony, his body awash in blood and weariness.

As Uldako feels the cold embrace of impending death, a surge of defiance rises within him. *This cannot be the final day of my life*, he thinks to himself, refusing to accept defeat in the face of darkness. Uldako's strength wanes at a dangerous rate, while the world around him blurs into a cacophony of screams and chaos.

Ishara charges into the fray with a large piece of wood. Her cries pierce through the haze as Uldako struggles to remain upright, his vision dimming with each passing moment. Then, a glimmer of hope emerges as he catches the distant sounds of more men rushing to his aid. The ground rushes up to meet him as consciousness slips away, enveloping him in complete darkness.

13

Farming

Uldako's mind drifts off into darkness, besieged by haunting flashes of his past: the relentless cruelty of his life as a slave, the frantic image of his mother, slaves crying out moments before they are tortured, all their voices echoing in despair. In the midst of these tormenting visions, he hears his mother's piercing screams calling out to him, "Uldako! Help!"

Uldako jerks awake, his scream tearing through the silence of the room. He exhales sharply, the weight of his nightmare still clinging to him like a heavy shroud. As his vision clears, the dull ache of his wounds flares into sharp focus. "Ugh," he grunts, his voice low and strained, each throb in his body a reminder of the brutal attack he endured. Pain gnaws at him, relentless and unyielding, settling deep into his bones.

Gathering himself, Uldako looks up and finds a formidable figure standing at the end of the bed, his gaze shrewd and guarded, a blade held firmly in his grasp. The man exudes strength and resilience, his physique akin to that of a powerful bull. Deep, serious brown eyes peer out from beneath thick, furrowed eyebrows that arch upward at the edges. His bald head contrasts with a voluminous rough white beard, reminiscent of a lion's mane. His weathered hands bear the marks of hard labor and the passage of time, and his attire, rugged yet practical, consists of a camel-colored undergarment overlaid with a sturdy light brown vest and trousers.

The man steps forward slowly, his gaze full of suspicion as he points the tip of his sword at Uldako's throat. "How do you know Seth?" he demands.

Uldako, feeling disoriented and unsure of his surroundings, replies cautiously, "W…what do you mean? And where are Šarru and Ishara?"

The man presses the tip of the sword a bit harder against Uldako's throat, his tone growing more urgent. "You have been screaming Seth's name while dreaming. I can clearly see that you are not from the northern kingdom, so I ask you one last time, *lu-kur*, how do you know Seth?"

A sudden movement at the door catches Uldako's eyes; the little children he saved peek into the room. The tension in the air shifts as the man's gaze follows Uldako's, his expression softening momentarily before hardening once more.

Uldako's heart swells with relief as he sees the joyful faces of the children he rescued, their wide eyes brimming with curiosity and compassion. One of them, unable to bear the tension any longer, speaks up with trembling words, "Don't kill him, *Abba*. He saved us!"

The man issues a stern warning to all his children standing at the door, instructing them to step away from the door and allow the adults to converse. With downcast expressions, the children reluctantly comply, retreating from the doorway.

Uldako now knows who has kept him alive, and he is grateful. "Allow me a moment to tell you who I am. I am Uldako, *dumu-nita* of Deborah. I assure you I am a peaceful man, who once was enslaved by the cruel slave masters of Magan. I seek Seth, for he rescued me from the clutches of death and bondage. Our conversation was cut short, and he bid me to seek him when the time is right."

The man maintains his stance, the tip of his blade still poised dangerously close to Uldako's throat. His gaze pierces into Uldako's eyes, probing for the truth. "Trust is scarce these days. Why should I trust you, *lu-kur*?" he challenges.

Uldako lets out a weary sigh, feeling the weight of his words. "I saved your *dumu-meš*," he begins, his voice steady despite the circumstances. "I could have ignored their pleas for aid, but I chose to help them, and now I am gravely wounded and at your mercy. I pose no threat to you in this condition."

The man's voice carries a hint of reluctance as he acknowledges, "You're here because my men saved you and brought you here. My wife tended to your wounds. Had you not saved our little ones from those wretched dragons, our discussion would have taken a far darker turn, if you catch my meaning. But despite this, I still need assurance that you're trustworthy. My family's safety comes first, as I'm sure you can understand."

Uldako remains still, his jaw tightening as he weighs his next words. His voice, when it comes, is quiet but resolute. "I understand what it means to protect family," he says. "I only have one left—my *ama*. She's still under the yoke of slavery." He pauses, glancing at the man's blade, then at his eyes, judging. "I heard Seth might be able to help me and my *ama*, or at least guide me. That's why I've been searching. Not for power or favor, just a way forward." Uldako lowers his gaze slightly, the weariness in his voice more than just physical. "But I won't say more than that. Not until I know if I can trust you, or not."

The man eases his grip on his sword, a glimmer of consideration in his eyes as he perceives Uldako's heart. "If your good intentions toward Seth are genuine," he says cautiously, "perhaps I'll permit you to recuperate here. But make no mistake—if you step out of line, I won't hesitate to deal with you."

Uldako nods in gratitude, his eyes sincere as he extends his hand in friendship. "Thank you for your hospitality and for saving me," he says warmly, his voice filled with genuine appreciation. "Now that you know my name, may I know yours?" Uldako asks politely, eager to build more trust.

The man, seemingly more at ease with Uldako's presence after hearing his explanation, steps back and introduces himself. "My name is Mahalalel, *dumu* of Kenan," he reveals with a hint of pride. "I brought you to our safe camp, or shall I say small farming village. You are in my home right now."

Uldako listens intently, absorbing the information. "I am honored to meet you and express my gratitude to your wife for her aid," he says respectfully.

Mahalalel acknowledges the sentiment with a quiet nod, revealing himself to be a man of few words. Uldako presses on, his concern evident. "How much time has passed since my arrival? And what of Šarru and Ishara?" he presses.

Mahalalel looks out the window, his expression contemplative as he appears to tally the passing days. "It has been seven days now," he reveals.

Shock crashes through Uldako. "No! It can't be that long!" he gasps, disbelief and urgency flooding his voice. He flings aside the blanket and lurches forward, driven first by a single thought—his mother is still in binds. "I can't waste any more time!"

But the moment he moves, pain surges through him like fire, buckling his limbs and clouding his vision.

Mahalalel reacts at once, stepping in to steady him and ease him back onto the bed. "Your wounds are far from healed," he says firmly. "You need rest, whether you like it or not."

Uldako exhales a heavy, bitter breath, his eyes burning with frustration. "Fine. But tell me—what of Šarru and Ishara? They were with me when the little dragons attacked."

Mahalalel lifts his hand in a calming gesture. "Šarru's resting in the next room. His wounds were severe, but he's healing—slowly. When we found you,

I nearly had him speared, thinking he was some wild beast. It took Ishara yelling at me for a full minute before I realized he wasn't trying to eat anyone."

Uldako's face hardens. "He's more than a beast. He's like a *dumu-nita* to me," he replies with protective pride in his voice. "But where's Ishara?"

Mahalalel exhales through his nose, eyes widening slightly. "Ah, Ishara." He chuckles under his breath. "She nearly tore down the walls, that's where. Feisty doesn't even begin to describe her. I questioned her just like I did you, and she answered with fire. Maybe too much fire. I've had no peace since."

He rubs the side of his head and adds with a sigh, "I locked her in the spare room when we first brought you here—just to be safe until you woke up. Since then, she's been shouting through the door like a hawk with a bone stuck in its throat."

Uldako's eyes fly open. "That does not sound like Ishara at all—wait! You what?" he blurts, staring at him like he's gone mad.

Mahalalel's face hardens. "I had no choice. My first duty is to protect my family—and this land has grown darker with each passing season. Men have become beasts. You wouldn't believe the things I've seen, especially these days."

Uldako nods slowly. "I understand. It spreads like dark fire," he mutters. "And I was raised in the center of it—believing that was the world. That cruelty was normal." His eyes narrow, voice low. "Pain shaped most of my life. After my *ama*, Seth was the first man who treated me like a human."

He takes a breath, steadies himself, then meets Mahalalel's eyes. "But now that you know I can be trusted, surely you can release Ishara?"

Mahalalel gives a firm nod. "Very well." He turns and strides down the hall, passing his wife who tends a bubbling pot of vegetable soup. Her long braids fall neatly over her shoulders, framing a face softened by hazel eyes that shine with quiet warmth. Though slender, there's a quiet resilience in the way she moves—graceful, composed, and capable. She wears a flowing linen robe, light brown in hue, simple yet dignified, reflecting a life marked by humility and strength.

As Mahalalel passes, her voice rises in a gentle whisper. "Husband, why didn't you tell him about Seth?"

Mahalalel's footsteps slow as he meets her gaze. His eyes are steady, but his voice is low. "Talita, I do not trust him fully. In times like these, trust is a costly thing we cannot afford. We must watch them carefully—before we say anything about our bloodline."

Talita's eyes reflect understanding and quiet sorrow. She shakes her head gently. "I know, Husband, but ever since we left the lands of the far north and came south for better farming soil, something in you has changed. You've grown hard. Suspicion clings to you like dust. I understand the dangers here—evil spreads faster than weeds—but we cannot let it choke out who we are. Let time test their hearts. Not fear."

Mahalalel grunts, silent but thoughtful, and with a final glance at his wife, he continues toward Ishara's room.

Ishara stands by the narrow window, letting the soft breeze brush against her face as if it might carry some comfort. Her thoughts whirl with worry—about Uldako, about what lies ahead. "Please let him be alright," she murmurs. She turns away, her pacing slow but restless, each step heavy with unease.

Finally, she sinks to her knees beside the bed, her heart heavy with fear. "*Dingir-meš*," she pleads in desperation, using the plural form for *gods*, "listen to me!" Her expression darkens into a frown, her gaze dropping to the ground as she contemplates silently.

"No, that's not right. I don't want those fallen spirits to also hear me." Taking a deep breath, she continues, "*Il* Most High, if you hear my voice, please help me. Please help me and Uldako! Please save his life!"

As Ishara sits and prays for aid in the quiet of the day, there is a sudden knock on the door. The unexpected bang startles her, and she jumps to her feet and shouts, "Please open the door. You can trust us, because I—" Ishara calls out, but before she can finish, to her surprise the door swings open to reveal Mahalalel, his sword in hand.

"Uldako is awake. I will take you to him if you behave," he declares firmly, his tone brooking no argument.

"Oh, praise the *dingir-meš*—I mean, praise *Il*, he is awake! Please, take me to him." Relief floods her voice.

Uldako lies still, his body aching, his thoughts full of frustration. *Why now? I just started to make progress. My* ama *still suffers in fetters, and I can't even stand to help her*. His fists clench at the helplessness gnawing at him.

Then—voices. Footsteps. Ishara appears in the doorway. Without hesitation, she rushes to his side and wraps him in a tight embrace. "I've been so worried! I'm so glad you're awake," she breathes, her voice thick with relief.

Uldako winces as pain flares through his body. "I'm glad you're safe too," he says, voice strained, "but your hug—it hurts!"

Ishara quickly steps back, her face flushed with concern. "Oh! I'm sorry—I didn't mean to! I'm just so relieved you're awake."

Before the moment can stretch further, Mahalalel steps into view, still guarded but more composed. "You both look like you could use some fresh air," he says. "If you want, my men can help you outside."

Uldako nods appreciatively. "Some fresh air will do us good!"

Mahalalel gives a curt nod in response before calling for his men, who promptly assist Uldako in making his way outside.

As Uldako and Ishara step outside, they are greeted by a breathtaking sight that leaves Uldako speechless. Visibly awestruck, he stutters in disbelief, "What do you call this?"

Ishara, noticing Uldako's astonishment, explains, "This is a field of crops—food that is grown." She realizes that Uldako has never seen such cultivated land and probably is unaware that it is possible. Even Ishara, who is familiar with working the ground, is taken aback by the sheer size of the fields sprawled before them.

Uldako's eyes drink in the sight, disbelief washing over him. "Large fields of food, how is it possible? I have always struggled to survive through hunting, fishing, and foraging," he murmurs in disbelief, watching as men and women diligently tend to the crops. "I had no idea this could be done!"

Mahalalel, observing the fields with a sense of pride, explains, "My family and I are what you call workers of the ground. We cultivate the bountiful produce of the earth for sustenance."

Uldako's gaze shifts to Mahalalel, his curiosity piqued. "So you don't hunt or kill animals for food?"

Mahalalel's expression twists with disdain. "No. *Il* set the seeds and fruits for eating, and we keep the creatures under our hand, not under our teeth. We use animals for tending, offering, and for skins and hair, for cord and thread, for tools of horn and bone, and for barter. When it comes to eating, my family subsists solely on fruits, vegetables, nuts, grains, and whatever the earth provides. Long ago, it was much easier to work the ground, but now it is cursed and brings forth thorns and thistles."

Uldako's eyes widen in realization. "I never knew!"

Ishara moves closer to Uldako, a gentle smile gracing her lips.

Mahalalel turns to Uldako, his tone steady. "If you head north and northwest from here, you'll reach the kingdom of the eagle. It is known in these parts as the kingdom of Etana, named after its current ruler, *En-Lugal* Etana. Most people there still live on plants alone. Over many generations, they have learned to tend the earth and cultivate a great variety of nourishing and flavorful foods.

Uldako is still taken aback by the revelation. "All my life," he murmurs, "I thought there was no other way. I've hunted for food. I did it because I had to. To survive." He pauses, his voice heavy. "But no one ever told me there was another way to create your own continuous supply of food." He looks up at Mahalalel, a flicker of shame in his expression. "I want to try it—this way of living to work the ground. But tell me, how do you manage it in a world like this? The earth is cursed, full of thorns, crawling with beasts and wicked men. How do you protect it—and your people?"

Mahalalel places a steady hand on Uldako's shoulder. "I've lived long enough to know trust is a fragile thing. I can't speak freely about our safe camp…or Seth, my great—"

The moment the words leave his mouth, he stops, realizing he's said too much.

Uldako blinks, stunned. "Seth is your great *abba*?"

Mahalalel's jaw tightens. He exhales sharply, clearly irritated with himself. "Forget I said that. Look, I don't know you well enough, and I can't afford to be careless—not when the lives of my family and everyone here depend on it."

He takes a step back, the edge in his voice giving way to something more restrained. "But you did save my *dumu-meš*," he concedes. "That counts for something. Once you're strong enough to stand on your own, I'll show you how to work the land. Consider it repayment. But don't expect more."

Uldako, still reeling, stares at him. "But I need to know Seth's—"

Mahalalel's hand shoots up. "Enough," he snaps, regret flashing in his eyes. "I shouldn't have mentioned that." He exhales, rubbing the bridge of his nose. "Look, I don't know what's in your heart, and I'm not about to gamble the safety of everyone here on a *lu-kur*. I've buried too many *dusa-meš* who trusted the wrong man. So no—Seth, my lineage, our camp—we won't speak of it again."

Before the silence can stretch too long, a voice cuts through the tension from behind.

"Oh, Mahalalel," the woman says with a sigh, her tone both warm and scolding, "must you always be so stubbornly inhospitable? Can't you discern that they mean us no harm?"

Uldako turns to locate the source of the voice and finds himself facing a woman of striking beauty, with an air of wisdom that belies her age—around four hundred years, much like Mahalalel.

"This is my wife, Talita," he introduces her with a gesture. After the introductions, Uldako and Ishara extend their gratitude to Mahalalel and Talita for their hospitality, expressing their eagerness to learn the skill of working the ground.

As many days trickle away, marked by tireless learning and the cultivation of newfound skills, a transformation takes root.

Uldako and Šarru's wounds fully mend, their strength restored to its former vigor. Alongside Ishara and Šarru, Uldako stands poised to resume their quest to locate Seth. Emboldened by their grasp of plant-craft, they ready themselves to journey forth, armed not just with determination, but also with some fruits of their labor.

Just as Uldako and his companions are preparing to depart, Mahalalel approaches, a rare warmth softening his weathered features.

"Uldako," he begins, his voice steady, "these past days have revealed much. You've shown yourself to be a man of courage and honor. In you, I've remembered something I had nearly forgotten—something my *abba* once taught me, and his before him: The way to overcome darkness is not with more darkness, but with light. Fear had begun to take root within me, and I allowed it to twist my judgment. But you"—he pauses, studying Uldako—"you reminded me that not all *lu-kur-meš* are to be feared. That even in the fiercest lands, *Il* may still raise up a man of goodness. I never thought one from the southern clans—known for blood and cruelty—would be the one to save my *dumu-meš*, let alone soften my heart."

With a sincere smile, Mahalalel extends his hand, offering a gesture of friendship and sealing a bond forged through time and the sweat of their brows.

Uldako steps closer to Mahalalel, a mix of appreciation and surprise clear in his eyes as he addresses him directly. "It was you who helped us, Mahalalel. I owe you a great debt. And I won't forget your words of overcoming darkness with light."

Mahalalel, too proud to linger on the matter, simply grunts in approval, his gaze shifting to the ground. The tension between the two men lingers, but Ishara quickly fills the silence.

"Well, we're all packed and ready to go, but, Uldako, I'm not sure Seth will still be in the same place. It's been many days since we last heard of his location. Do you still want to go there, or should we consider other options?"

Talita looks at Mahalalel, nudging him gently with her shoulder and raising her chin in the direction of Uldako. She whispers, "Tell them."

Mahalalel nods slowly, then turns to Uldako with a look that carries generations of memory. "I've already told you, I am of Seth's bloodline. And the last message we received came from those close to him: Seth was traveling to be with Adam, who has fallen gravely ill."

He pauses, the weight of the moment thickening his voice. "Adam—the first of us. The breath of *Il* still lingers in his frame. If Seth has gone to him, it is no small matter. They were last seen along the Euphrates, between Nippur and the reedlands to the east, where thick groves grow and travelers speak of an ancient plain some call Isin."

Talita, standing beside Mahalalel, rests a gentle hand on his arm before offering her guidance. Her voice is warm yet firm with wisdom. "If you cannot find him along the Euphrates River, go to Nippur. The elders there descend from Seth's line. Just tell them we have sent you."

Uldako hesitates. "But how will they know they can trust me?"

Talita's eyes narrow slightly, as if recalling something old and sacred. "We have a secret word of trust we use in such moments."

Uldako straightens with growing anticipation, knowing he is about to learn some long-hidden word spoken only by the line of Adam. A phrase whispered through generations, sealed with fire and light. He imagines it will be a sound that can shake the trees or summon heavenly beings. A word carved into forgotten stone, guarded by dragons, or passed only through blood.

Talita leans in, her voice low and solemn. "The secret word of trust is—*The dung beetle is watching.*"

There is silence. The letdown is palpable.

Uldako stares at her, mouth slightly open. "That's…not a word. That's a sentence." His voice cracks. "Is that a joke or a proverb?"

Talita nods without blinking. "Yes."

Šarru snorts beside him. Ishara covers her mouth, clearly fighting a smile. Talita adjusts the satchel over Uldako's shoulder like nothing strange has just been said then turns calmly to rejoin Mahalalel, the faintest grin curling her lips.

Uldako remains frozen. This was not the ancient password of power he had envisioned. He had braced himself for the roar of the heavens, a flash of light, or something. Instead, he got a warning about a beetle with opinions.

He looks at Šarru. "You understood that, right?"

The bear offers no answer.

Uldako glances at Ishara then back at the grinning faces of Talita and Mahalalel. A strange moment indeed. One that makes no sense. And yet, deep down, he senses it was crafted to be exactly that way.

So all he says is, "Okay."

He adjusts the strap across his chest, exhales, and nods respectfully. "Thank you. Though it's not much to go on, we'll do our best to find Seth." With those final words, Uldako looks at Talita and sees a tear slip down her cheek. She brushes it away at once, as if hoping no one will notice. Something painful tightens in his chest. Their time together has ended, and the reality of it weighs on him more than he expected.

Talita and Mahalalel have come to matter to him, as he and Ishara have to them. He feels it now in the quiet between them, in what goes unsaid. He has never known bonds like this before, not with others beyond his mother. To care and to be cared for in return is strange to him—and the thought of leaving stirs an ache he does not know how to name.

He looks at the ground, unwilling to let the feeling show. Their journey calls, and he clings to it as an excuse.

Ishara sees through Uldako at once. He has never stood in a moment like this and is not used to farewells. She knows he is trying to outrun it. Before he can turn away, she steps forward and takes Talita's hands in hers, thanking her for all they have done for them.

Few words follow. The pause stretches. Uldako shifts where he stands, his jaw tightening, his gaze fixed anywhere but on them. At last he speaks, low and restrained. "Yes, thank you." Then he steps back from the group, slow and careful, as though he does not trust himself to linger.

When the moment becomes too unbearable for him, Uldako turns to Ishara and Šarru. "Let's head in the direction of the river. This way!"

Uldako strides off with confidence, his eyes fixed on the horizon. Ishara clears her throat, trying to suppress a grin. "Um, Uldako, it's the other way."

Uldako stops mid-step, turns slowly, and rubs the back of his neck. "Right, of course. I was just, uh…testing your sense of direction," he mutters, flashing a sheepish grin before moving toward the correct path.

Ishara struggles to contain herself. "You were walking to the river, but it was the wrong one. We don't want to go toward the Tigris but to the great Euphrates."

Mahalalel and Talita chuckle as they exchange a knowing glance, both amused by the interaction. "Be careful!" they call after the departing trio.

Šarru seems elated, pressing against Uldako with a low, eager rumble as they proceed toward the Euphrates.

Ishara walks beside him and says, "The Euphrates is a mighty river, sustaining the lives of many who dwell along its banks," she begins. "But it also poses dangers, as we cannot predict what or who we might encounter. Therefore, I propose we follow the river but maintain a safe distance."

Uldako gives a single nod, impressed by Ishara's reasoning. "You make a valid point," he concedes.

The trio press on, measuring their progress by the sun's position in the sky with their hands. After two hands' worth of travel to the sun, Uldako catches sight of a small, secure camp on the horizon. He comes to an abrupt stop, his attention immediately drawn to the unique settlement ahead.

Sensing his hesitation, Ishara asks, "What is it?"

Uldako remains transfixed, his thoughts racing. "There's a safe camp ahead," he murmurs. "It would be better to avoid it and stick to our path along the river. But what if they have information about Seth? If we bypass them without speaking to anyone, our chances of finding him are slim."

Ishara looks at the camp then back at Uldako, her expression grave. "You might be right, but," she acknowledges solemnly, "we must proceed with utmost caution. I know little about this region, and I've heard tales of camps that sacrifice strangers to the *anunnaki*."

She locks eyes with Uldako, her voice low but urgent. "Promise me you'll protect me. And that we'll move with caution. The world grows darker by the day, and danger no longer waits on the roads—it hunts."

Uldako rests a steady hand on her shoulder. "I swear I'll protect you with everything I have. No matter what comes."

A flicker of color rises in Ishara's cheeks. She looks away, flustered, her lips curving with something between relief and something else she doesn't yet name. "That's all I needed to hear," she murmurs, almost too softly to catch. Then, with a small breath, "Now let's go."

Uldako strides purposefully toward the direction of the encampment, his eyes narrowing as he points to a small, grassy hill nearby. "We shall position ourselves atop that rise, where the earth's curve provides both cover and sight. Let us take some time to observe and scout our surroundings. Patience and vigilance will guide our next steps."

They cautiously ascend the hill, staying vigilant. Scattered bushes and sporadic trees dot the landscape, offering limited concealment. They navigate carefully to a denser area, settling down to observe the camp from a safe distance. From their vantage point, they can see a few guards patrolling the perimeter and the activity at the camp's entrance. Ishara urges them to watch for any distinguishing symbols to identify the tribe.

Uldako surveys the area but sees nothing, only to be startled by a voice behind them.

"Spying on our camp, are we?"

14

Kingdoms

Uldako's blood runs cold at the words spoken behind them, instantly recognizing they've been caught in the act. Šarru's muscles coil with aggression, but a reassuring touch from Uldako calms the bear. "Easy, Šarru," he whispers steadily despite the tension as he turns to face their adversaries.

Uldako takes note of their attire—leather armor with animal-hide pauldrons—and their formidable but similar spears. The sides of their heads are shaved, adorned with intricate black markings unfamiliar to Uldako. However, it's the emblem engraved upon their chests that truly captures his attention: serpents entwined with a female humanoid figure designed into some sort of a tree, each detail meticulously crafted. It's a symbol both mysterious and foreboding, hinting at deeper secrets yet to be uncovered.

Uldako senses the weight of the situation, recognizing these men as guards from the nearby camp. Uncertainty clouds his thoughts as he weighs their options. Meanwhile, Ishara observes Uldako's hesitation and swiftly interjects, her voice steady and friendly. "Ah, greetings," she begins, her tone disarmingly casual. "We mean no harm, just travelers curious about your camp."

As Ishara's diplomatic words fade into the tense silence, the air grows thick with hostility. The leader steps forward, spear leveled at her chest, his movements slow and deliberate—a predator circling prey. Šarru releases a deep, guttural growl that stops the man in his tracks, the sound low and primal, a clear warning.

"I'll be the judge of that," the man replies coldly, his eyes never leaving them. "I am Zarathos, commander of the outer guard. And by crossing into our territory unannounced, you've made yourselves a threat."

Uldako moves to stand, his mouth opening to protest, but he doesn't make it far. A brutal strike lands across his face before a word escapes, sending him crashing back to his knees. Blood pools at the edge of his lip.

The guard who struck him sneers, clearly enjoying the moment. "Sit down. Be quiet. Speak only when you're told."

Zarathos's gaze lingers on Ishara, his eyes narrowing as a cruel smile tugs at his lips. "You're a strange little group," he murmurs, turning back to Uldako, his tone laced with quiet menace. "The *uḫuš-gal* is impressive—more so that you've managed to tame it. But let me make your situation clear." He steps closer, his voice lowering but sharpening like a blade. "You've wandered into our domain, and here, we hold all the power."

His eyes drift back to Ishara, lingering far too long. "And you travel with a rare beauty…too rare to be left unspoken for."

Uldako seethes with rage, his words laced with barely contained fury. "Don't even think about it," he growls, his tone so sharp it catches even Ishara off guard. He adds coldly, "Because I'll make sure you regret it." Despite the threat, the trio laughs mockingly—clear proof they underestimate him.

However, Zarathos's demeanor shifts abruptly from mirth to something much darker. He strides purposefully toward Ishara, his expression now one of sinister intent. "Take these two away and dispose of them," he commands coldly, his gaze fixed on Ishara, "while I have a little chat with this exquisite creature."

Just as Uldako braces for a strike, Ishara moves first—swift as a hawk. She draws a hidden knife from her boot and slashes Zarathos's throat while his eyes are on the other guards. Blood pours as he drops his spear, clutching his neck in fear. But Ishara doesn't hesitate—she seizes the opening and unleashes a rapid flurry of precise strikes to his chest.

Uldako and Šarru charge at the two stunned guards, seizing the moment of chaos. With great speed and brutal precision, Uldako swings his axe, driving it into one guard's chest and sending him crashing to the ground. At the same instant, Šarru lunges at the second man, who tries to flee, but the massive bear reaches him, ending his life with a fatal blow.

As the dust settles, the trio stand together, their adrenaline-fueled victory tinged with the gravity of their actions. Breaking the tense silence, Uldako turns to Ishara, his expression filled with relief and admiration. "That was too close for comfort," he says, his voice still edged with the weight of what just happened.

For a moment, neither of them speaks. The heaviness lingers then slowly begins to lift.

Uldako looks at Ishara as realization dawns on him. "I had no idea you were such a skilled fighter."

She meets his gaze with a mischievous twinkle in her eyes. "Well, you never bothered to ask," she quips, a playful smile dancing on her lips.

Uldako can only stare at her in astonishment, momentarily speechless at her unexpected revelation. "Here I was thinking I needed to protect you on our journey."

Ishara's eyes hint at playfulness, "Well, what woman doesn't appreciate a man who's willing to lay down his life for her?"

Uldako, still unfamiliar with the nuances of flirtation, simply looks at her in silence, unsure of how to respond.

Recognizing the urgency of their situation, Ishara says, "I think we have to move away from this camp and continue our journey, Uldako. These are evil people, and they won't answer our questions regarding Seth even if they do know something."

Uldako grasps the weight of her words and nods without hesitation. "You're right. We can't afford to linger in a place like this," he says, voice steady. With renewed urgency, they resume their journey toward the river.

As they approach, the silhouette of distant mountains against the horizon comes into view, with a vivid blue streak of water cutting through the landscape. Uldako's eyes widen with excitement at the sight, prompting a flurry of questions directed at Ishara. "Is that the Euphrates? It is magnificent! Have you ever seen a river before? I haven't! That blue line there is the river, right?"

A glint of affection twinkles in Ishara's eyes as she observes Uldako and teases him gently, "Has anyone ever told you that you speak a lot when you get excited about something?"

Uldako's cheeks flush with embarrassment as he casts his gaze downward, but Ishara's warmth persists. "Yes, of course I have seen a river before," she continues. "But this river is special. It's the mighty Euphrates, teeming with abundant fish and life-giving water that sustains the world around it."

Uldako quickly suggests, "Then this is indeed a special moment! Let's find a secure spot to replenish our waterskins before we proceed. Then as we continue our journey, we'll maintain a safe distance from the river, ensuring we can still trace its course as we search for Seth."

Ishara's gaze flickers with understanding, aware that their waterskins are already half full. Yet, she discerns Uldako's eagerness to get a closer look at the river. "Of course," she assents with a nod, concealing her amusement at his enthusiasm.

The trio quickens their pace as they advance toward the riverbank, their senses alert for any potential threats lurking in the area. Ishara's keen eye spots a secluded spot nestled among towering trees, providing easy access to the river. "There," she points, her hand indicating the chosen spot.

Uldako's face lights up with anticipation at the sight. "Looks good to me," he exclaims eagerly. Drawing closer, they move with deliberate silence and stealth, mindful of the frequent visitors, both human and beast, to the water's edge.

With confidence Uldako steps closer to the water and declares, "It's safe."

A collective breath escapes them like a quiet exhale from the trees. They ease their shoulders and draw near the riverbank, the soft sound of rushing water soothing their nerves. Uldako kneels, mesmerized by the crystal currents and the shimmer of fish darting beneath the surface.

"I wonder what kind of fish swim down there," he muses aloud, eyes narrowing thoughtfully. "And more importantly, what do they taste like?"

Ishara laughs, caught off guard. "Do you even know how to fish?"

Uldako straightens proudly. "Of course! I love it. The scenery you enjoy while waiting with a line in the water, the silence before the bite, the sudden tension, setting the hook, the fight, and then the taste—yum."

She laughs harder, shaking her head.

Still smiling, she glances out over the water. "It really is beautiful. There's something about water—it quiets the world and stirs the soul. The color, the gentle sound of its flow, and the vibrant wildlife surrounding it all contribute to a sense of inner peace and tranquility."

As Ishara engages Uldako in conversation, Šarru eagerly quenches his thirst, lapping up water after their arduous trek under the scorching sun. Just as Uldako finishes refilling his waterskin, a ripple in the water near Ishara catches his eye. He wipes the sweat from his brow to get a clearer view, and there it is again—something lurking beneath the surface.

"Ishara, get back!" Uldako warns urgently. Ishara follows his gaze and spots the creature emerging from the depths. With a leap, she retreats to Uldako's side as the dragon prowls the shallows, its predatory instincts on full display.

Uldako watches in awe as the creature reveals itself—a majestic elongated beast with a sinuous body clad in rugged, armored scales. Its formidable head, adorned with rows of razor-sharp teeth, gazes menacingly from above the waterline. With each stealthy movement, propelled by its muscular tail, it commands the water with surprising swiftness—a true apex predator lurking in the shadows, ready to pounce on unsuspecting prey.

As the dragon slinks back into the depths of the Euphrates, its failed attempt at stealth leaves ripples in its wake. Uldako's voice, barely more than a whisper, breaks the eerie silence. "What was that?"

Ishara, still catching her breath from the near-miss, stares at the spot where the creature slipped back beneath the current. Her eyes remain fixed, haunted by what she saw—or what nearly saw her.

"The river *ušumgal*," she whispers, the name falling from her lips like a curse.

Uldako turns to her, frowning. "What does that mean?"

She blinks, breaking from her trance, and locks eyes with him, urgency hardening her voice. "If it's what I think it is—a serpent-spirit of the deep. I'm not certain, but I know this: It hunts both beast and man."

Her words hang in the air like the stench of old fear. Uldako glances at the water's surface—once serene, now shrouded in unseen menace. The beauty of the river feels thinner somehow, as if behind its shimmer lurks ancient hunger.

Šarru presses gently against Uldako's hand—just once. A silent nudge. A reminder. *We must move.*

Uldako looks at Ishara, his expression set, jaw tight with resolve. "Let's find Seth," he says, "before the next shadow finds us first."

With renewed purpose, the trio press on, trailing the river from a safe distance, their eyes scanning the landscape in a relentless quest for any clue that might unveil Seth's whereabouts.

Their journey unfolds amidst a mesmerizing tapestry of wildlife, each creature a reflection of the earth's boundless wonders. Among them, a magnificent sight catches their eye: a colossal deer, larger and more majestic than any Uldako has ever beheld. This noble beast stands regally; its towering frame supported by graceful, elongated limbs. Its most remarkable feature, however, lies atop its head: a pair of grand spiral horns, adorned with intricate twists and turns that speak of age and wisdom. Clad in a coat of resplendent brown, adorned with subtle stripes and spots, the long-horned grazer blends seamlessly into its verdant surroundings. With every fluid movement, it radiates an otherworldly grace, its hooves rhythmically echoing the chant of *kudu, kudu, kudu* as it gracefully traverses its domain.

In the midst of peril and uncertainty, the world still unfurls its wonders in breathtaking splendor, the embodiment of nature's resilience and majesty. Every moment is a revelation, a symphony of sights, sounds, scents, and sensations that stir the soul. Uldako, though overwhelmed by the sheer magnitude of it all, conceals his tears and emotions from Ishara, a silent guardian over his own vulnerability.

As he gazes upon the awe-inspiring spectacle before him, his thoughts drift to his mother, confined to a world devoid of such marvels. "*Ama*," he murmurs wistfully, "if only you could witness the beauty that surrounds us."

Ishara's voice jolts Uldako back to the present, her words pointing out a big trail snaking away from the riverbank. "Do you see it?" she asks, her eyes fixed on the distant path.

Uldako's keen eyes trace the human-made brown streak etched into the landscape.

Ishara warns, "We must tread carefully." Her caution is unmistakable, her words laden with the weight of potential danger lurking beyond the horizon. "Different clans use those created paths to move between big camps."

Uldako says nothing, but the firm nod he gives says enough. His resolve mirrors hers. With growing urgency, they move—quiet at first, then quicker, weaving through brush and under branch, feet whispering over roots and leaves. The landscape blurs around them in green and gold as they start to discern the distant murmur of life.

Before long, they slow, instincts sharpening. The terrain slopes gently, the foliage thickens, and they duck low into the shadows of a thicket. From behind the cover of wild bushes and gnarled limbs, they find their perch.

Below, the road uncoils like a big serpent through the trees.

Travelers move along it—figures cloaked in dust and sun, carts creaking, beasts plodding. Words drift to them on the breeze, fragments of conversation and laughter mingled with the soft rhythm of footfalls. Stories pass between strangers like wind-borne seeds, unaware of the hidden eyes watching from the undergrowth.

Ishara's hushed voice carries a sense of urgency as she and Uldako observe the bustling activity from the safety of the shadows. "It seems these people move about freely, unencumbered by fear," she remarks quietly. Uldako, sensing the significance of their surroundings, turns to Ishara with a furrowed brow. She explains, "This must be the beginning of Etana's realm." Her tone is laced with mystery.

Uldako's curiosity awakens, and he leans in closer. "I need to know more about Etana's kingdom before we continue into this land," he whispers.

Ishara tilts her head to him, her eyes filled with wonder and awe. "Then listen carefully," she begins. "Those of us from the East and the South are mostly kept in the dark about the northern kingdom. Most of our leaders are descendants of Cain or controlled by him and his *dumu-meš*. Like most leaders, they dictate what we believe about the world. So most of Etana's domain, to the north and northwest, remains shrouded in mystery, shielded from our understanding by our leaders and forces beyond our control."

Ishara pauses, then a glint of fascination dances in her eyes as she continues, "However, intriguing whispers of the northern kingdom manage to seep through the cracks from time to time."

As Ishara's words linger in the air, something stirs in Uldako—curiosity flaring like a spark catching dry tinder. He leans in without realizing it, eyes locked on hers, drawn in by the weight of her voice.

"Tell me more," he breathes, the words almost reverent. "How was the kingdom created?"

Ishara's eyes gleam with the treasure of ancient secrets. "Legend speaks of a mysterious kingdom that ruled the whole world, its origins lost to time," she tells him, her voice soft. "In our lands, the kingdom of the Northwest is said to be the oldest of all realms, tracing its lineage back to a man named Adam—or *Adapa*, as some call him. Mahalalel mentioned him as Adam. According to the oldest tales, Adam and his *dumu-meš* once were guardians of peace and justice, appointed as judges over all the peoples of earth. Some even whisper that it was Adam who first founded a sacred city where Eridu now stands—before it was razed by the *dumu-nita* of Cain and rebuilt in their own twisted image.

"In time, Adam led his people north and west, and as his years lengthened, his *dumu-nita* began to take up his mantle. Now, in our day, it has passed all the way down to Etana. And the name Etana itself, as you may know, means *he who ascends*. And so, Etana really did ascend to the title of *lugal*, ruler of the North. The prophets and sages claim that Etana was anointed as *lugal* by *Il* Himself."

Uldako's mind buzzes with the weight of this newfound knowledge, his thoughts racing like a river unleashed from its banks. "Who, precisely, are these people, and how far back do they trace their lineage?"

Ishara's voice wavers with uncertainty. "I believe they are among the first families—ancient ones—elders of a line that seeded the nations, not just here but across the whole earth. Yet so much is lost...buried beneath the silence of passing ages," she murmurs, her eyes distant with the haze of half-remembered stories.

"Some say the world is immeasurably old; others claim it is scarcely a thousand years. My oldest elders speak of a time when Adam and his kin ruled all the realms, guiding the world with justice and peace. But that age has vanished, like mist before the rising sun."

Uldako strains to imagine a world shaped by peace and light—a world untouched by the cruelty, hatred, and sorrow that carved his youth into scars. The thought feels distant, almost forbidden. He studies Ishara with quiet wonder as she continues.

"Yet our rulers dismiss such stories as childish fantasy, urging us to forget the past and live only in the present," Ishara says with frustration. "Lately, they've turned their praise toward the so-called divine gifts taught by the *anunnaki*—those same beings you and I know to be nothing more than fallen Watchers."

A faint smile tugs at the corner of her lips as her tone shifts. "Though to call them Watchers isn't quite right anymore. That title belonged to them when they merely observed us from the unseen realm. The ones who step into our world—like Shamsiel—have crossed that line. They're no longer just Watchers. They should plainly be called for what they are—evil spirits."

A flame of curiosity rises in Uldako's chest. "Imagine if we could uncover the truth ourselves. We've seen the evil spirits, but there are good ones too. Who's to say some haven't given some humans gifts—real ones—meant to be used for good? To stand against the corrupt powers the fallen ones brought to mankind."

His words linger, heavy with hope and uncertainty. After a moment, he glances back at Ishara, the question forming softly. "Tell me, what is the northern kingdom like now?"

Ishara speaks softly, as if sharing secrets carried on the wind. "I don't know much, only scattered whispers. Some are dark, others ridiculous—but a few sound like truth, even if they're rare. I hold on to those. They say the kingdom of the North is like no other—a realm of justice untouched by the decay we see here. You may have noticed the eagle—same as the one worn by Seth. That's their symbol."

Her eyes drift, uncertain but longing. "They say that under Etana's rule, peace still breathes and honor has not withered. His people live without the bindings of slavery, without fear. In the North, they say slavery is forbidden, injustice hunted down without mercy. But I've never seen it with my own eyes. All I know is that those who rule there do so with a different kind of power—one that flows from grace, not cruelty. Respect and order reign supreme, for they follow the commandments of *Il* and His word."

Uldako's brow furrows in contemplation. "Two kingdoms, each tethered to divergent *dingir-meš*, their paths veering farther apart with each passing day," he muses, his voice heavy with concern. "The prospect of war looms like a shadow over our land, fueled by the clash of beliefs and the thirst for power. It's a conflict that threatens to consume us all."

Ishara's deep blue eyes are ablaze with determination. "But let us not surrender to despair. These are but tales spun from the whispers of time, and truth eludes us until we seek it out ourselves. Let us continue on this journey, Uldako, and unravel the mysteries ourselves!"

Uldako's face lights up with a rare smile as his eyes meet Ishara's, her presence always a light of warmth and hope in times of uncertainty. "Absolutely," he affirms.

Observing the steady stream of passersby on the road, Uldako suggests, "Shall we take the opportunity to engage with those who seem trustworthy?"

Ishara scans the crowd, her eyes settling on a lone woman emerging from the riverbank, balancing a woven basket heavy with fish. "There," she whispers. "A woman with a fish basket—looks harmless enough. Now we don't want to startle—"

"Did you say fish?" Uldako blurts as he cuts her off and is already on his feet.

Before Ishara can utter another word, he's off like a lightning bolt, eyes locked on the glistening catch as if it were treasure from the gods. Ishara sighs, exchanges a glance with Šarru, and the two hurry after him in resigned silence.

As the trio steps into view, the woman looks up—only to see a wild-eyed young man charging toward her with the goofy intensity of a long-lost lover. Her brows lift in alarm. Then her gaze shifts.

Šarru barrels out of the shadows behind him.

The woman doesn't wait for clarification. She lets out a scream worthy of a hunting horn. "An *uḫuš-gal*! Run!"

She flees in a panic, nearly bowling over a pair of onlookers who scatter in opposite directions, shouting.

Uldako skids to a halt. "Wait—what?"

Everyone stands frozen in the aftermath, the man-made path now half-empty.

Ishara folds her arms, giving Uldako and Šarru a slow, withering look. "Of course they'd run."

Šarru grunts. Uldako shrugs.

She shakes her head and turns back toward the shadows. "Come. Next time, we do it my way."

Hastily retreating to the concealment of the shadows, they wait, watching for the next passerby. When a diminutive figure clad in simple plant fiber attire comes into view, devoid of any visible weapons, Uldako and Ishara exchange glances before cautiously stepping forward while directing Šarru to remain hidden. Concealing their apprehension with feigned conversation, they stand casually near the path as the man draws near. Seizing the moment as he passes them, Ishara addresses the man, her tone polite yet inquisitive.

"Excuse me, could you perhaps tell us where this road leads?"

The man hesitates, keeping a cautious distance from the pair who clearly don't belong to the region. "You've been walking on a road you don't know? You do realize you've entered the realm of Enoch? Or Etana, as some of you *lu-kur-meš* from distant lands might call him."

Uldako and Ishara exchange a sharp glance—startled by the name Enoch yet lit with hope that they've finally arrived.

Sensing their reaction and growing uneasy, the man shifts his weight and quickly adds, "You do know this is where peace reigns…among men and women? We do not want troublemakers." His voice wavers, a blend of uncertainty and discomfort.

Ishara offers a reassuring nod, her demeanor warm and friendly, nudging Uldako subtly to soften his expression. With a concerted effort, Uldako manages an awkward smile, his features relaxing into a more amiable countenance. "Indeed, we've journeyed from afar, hopeful to find ourselves in a land blessed by peace," he replies, his voice earnest yet tinged with uncertainty.

The man, still wary of the strangers before him, proceeds cautiously. "Well, the path west leads to the river," he gestures toward the worn trail, "where you can find the ferryman. Pay him, and he'll take you across, opening the way to other kingdoms. But beware, it's a dangerously long journey through dry, arid lands once you're across. Alternatively, heading east," he points in the opposite direction, "will take you to the neutral city of Umma, part of the Kingdom of Enoch, *dumu* of Jared."

In a rush, the man mutters, "I have to go now—may *Il* be with you!" Without waiting for a response, he strides off toward Umma, throwing cautious glances over his shoulder at the strangers he left behind.

"Thank you, sir!" Uldako calls after him, his voice echoing with genuine gratitude.

Ishara nudges him gently, a smile dancing in her eyes as she looks at him, filled with the excitement of their journey. "We've truly arrived in the kingdom of Etana, just as I said!" she exclaims, her voice bubbling with joy.

"Yes, you were right, as always." Uldako shares her smile, but it fades into a thoughtful frown. "But that means we've already missed Seth. We walked along the river for a long time and saw no sign of him."

Ishara nods, one brow raises as she thinks aloud. "We could go to Nippur, like Talita advised, but that journey would take even longer than Umma. We might as well try the city first—maybe someone there has seen him. This is the kingdom of the North, after all. Surely someone knows his name."

Uldako nods in agreement. "It sounds like a good plan. And honestly, I'm curious to see what a city in Etana's kingdom looks like."

"All right!" Ishara cheers, throwing her hands in the air. "Umma, here we come!"

The trio press onward, their steps light with anticipation as they follow the winding path toward the distant city. Excitement hums beneath their skin, each heartbeat echoing with the hope of what lies ahead.

And then, far beyond the golden plain, Umma comes into view, a glimmering silhouette beneath the sun, rising like a dream from the horizon. Its distant towers shimmer in the heat, a manifestation of mankind's ambition. Ishara lets out a joyful cry that breaks the stillness.

Uldako looks at the city in awe, a sense of wonder filling his chest, but alongside it, a quiet curiosity stirs. So much is unknown. So much yet to uncover.

15

Trust

As the sun climbs higher in the sky, they reach the crest of a hill overlooking the plain—and there, stretched before them in staggering detail, stands the city of Umma.

Uldako has no words.

Up close, the city is even more magnificent than he could have imagined. Massive walls glint in the morning light like polished bronze, encircling towers and spires that pierce the heavens. The structures rise from the ground like something out of the old legends—bold, defiant, eternal.

He stands in silence, awe coursing through him. This is no ordinary city. It is a monument to forgotten power—a cradle of secrets waiting to be stirred.

Ishara steps beside him, her voice soft with wonder. "I've seen my share of villages, but never anything like this." Her eyes scan the skyline. "Tower upon tower of sunbaked mudbrick rising from the dust…a living city that stretches farther than the eye can follow."

Before them looms an immense wall, wide as a river and higher than a cedar—unlike anything they have ever seen.

Ascending the hill, glimpses of the city beyond the gates come into view. At its heart stands a towering temple, its grandeur unmistakable, even from a distance. Around it, the labyrinthine streets pulse with life, lined with countless shelters and bustling marketplaces where merchants ply their trades.

Laughter echoes through the narrow alleys as children play, their joy reaching even the surrounding hills. Above, the sky extends endlessly, mirroring the sprawl of the city below. This is Umma—a jewel of civilization.

Hearts brimming with joy and excitement, they hasten toward the colossal entrance gate, a behemoth of timber standing sentinel, flanked by guards bedecked in meticulously crafted leather armor. Each guard brandishes a sword and shield, emblazoned with the proud emblem of a lion. Beyond the gate rises a towering ziggurat in the distance, its majestic silhouette piercing the sky and commanding the attention of all who behold it. Along the city walls, vigilant sentries stand watch, clad in the same supple leather armor, armed with bows and arrows poised for any threat.

Before the imposing city gates, a queue of eager individuals stretches out, patiently awaiting inspection by the vigilant guards. Each person undergoes meticulous scrutiny, ensuring the safety of Umma's denizens. Those deemed harmless are granted entry with a nod from the guards.

After observing the scene and catching fragments of whispered conversations, Ishara leans in and speaks low. "Umma seems to pride itself on being a neutral ground—welcoming travelers from all regions, as long as they pledge to keep the peace."

She looks at a nearby banner. "Though it's tied to the northern kingdom, the city flies a lion emblem, not the eagle. Perhaps to mark its role as a place apart—a refuge where trade and discourse thrive, and rival factions are bound by law to leave their quarrels at the gate."

She casts a sharp look his way, realizing he hasn't heard a word—completely lost in the splendor of the city and its towering guardians. With a playful tug at his arm, she pulls him back and whispers, "Are you listening to me?"

Startled, Uldako blinks and stumbles a step. "Sorry, Ishara. I am overwhelmed," he says with a sheepish grin.

"Lost in the sights and sounds of Umma, huh?" Ishara teases, a mischievous glint in her eye. "You better not start daydreaming about joining their guard or something."

Uldako chuckles, shaking his head. "No worries, I promise to keep my feet on the ground...most of the time."

As they approach the gate, the clamor of the city intensifies, engulfing Uldako in a wave of unfamiliar sensations. Not accustomed to the flurry of activity surrounding him, he feels a rising tension within.

Sensing his unease, Ishara gently clasps his arm, her touch a soothing balm against his angst.

In that instant, a wave of warmth sweeps through him, anchoring his scattered thoughts. Her hand—gentle, steady—finds his for the first time, and the angst within him stills.

Her touch...so gentle, he thinks, stunned by how something so small can silence the roar of a city that moments ago had consumed every corner of his mind. The towering walls, the crowds, the sheer scale of Umma—all of it fades, as if her hand alone holds him above the chaos.

With each step forward, his thoughts no longer chase the marvels around him. They return instead to the softness of her fingers, to the calm she brings.

A sudden voice jolts Uldako back to the present, and he finds himself face-to-face with the gate guard. "I asked, how did you tame that animal, and is he dangerous?" the guard repeats, eyeing Šarru with suspicion.

Uldako meets the guard squarely. "This is Šarru," he responds firmly, gesturing toward the bear at his side. "He's been with me since he was a cub. He is not a threat unless someone tries to hurt us."

The guard captain narrows his eyes at Šarru then shifts his visage to Uldako with a skeptical grunt. After a moment, he turns to a jittery junior guard and commands, "Go check the beast."

The poor man pales. "Me?"

"Yes, you."

Muttering a desperate prayer under his breath—"Don't eat me, please don't eat me…"—the guard tiptoes toward Šarru like a man approaching the jaws of death. Sweat glistens on his brow, his legs trembling with every step.

Uldako watches, barely containing a grin. He knows exactly what's coming.

As the guard gets too close, Šarru lets out a deep, rumbling growl and flashes his teeth with dramatic flair.

The guard yelps, flails backward, and lands flat on his backside with a thud. His helmet clatters off and rolls away in shame.

Uldako bursts into laughter and pats Šarru on the side. "Good boy," he says, stepping forward and nudging the bear's massive head playfully toward the terrified man. Šarru responds with a soft huff and a friendly nudge, as if to say *just kidding.*

The other guards roar with laughter, pointing at their fallen comrade now frozen between humiliation and gratitude that he's still alive.

The guard leader's hearty laughter rings through the air as he jests, "Looks like you got a bit more than you bargained for, eh?" he chuckles, glancing at the flustered guard. "But enough of this," he adds, clearing his throat. "There's a long line of travelers waiting, so let's wrap this up. Your *uḫuš* seems to have some manners. The rule is that animals need to be leashed—though I doubt a leash would stop that beast if it really wanted to attack someone, but nonetheless put one on him." Seeing Uldako's confused look, he raises a brow. "What?

Don't tell me you've never heard of a leash? So—who are you two, and where do you come from?"

Ishara responds with grace, explaining, "We are peaceful travelers from distant lands, drawn to the splendor of Umma."

A warm smile spreads across the guard's face as he looks into Ishara's beautiful deep blue eyes and replies, "Ah, well, visitors are always welcome here, especially ones as lovely as yourself. Just a small formality then," he adds with a playful wink. "You'll promise to keep the peace within our city, won't you?"

Uldako, feeling a growing unease at the guard's overly familiar demeanor toward Ishara, steps forward and interjects firmly, "Rest assured, we seek no trouble."

The guard's gaze settles on Uldako, his expression hardening. "Good to hear," his voice is edged with warning. "We follow a strict law here—tooth for a tooth. You cause harm, it comes back to you. Start trouble, and you'll answer for it. Understand?" He holds Uldako's eyes for a beat then adds flatly, "That means if you start a fight and someone ends up dead—even by accident—you'll be put to death. Got it?"

Ishara steps forward, attempting to ease the tension. "Yes, of course, and may I ask," she continues, "have you seen a man named Seth pass through here?"

The guard shakes his head. "I haven't seen the great elder in quite some time. You might find someone in town who can provide more information." He gestures for them to proceed.

Ishara smiles warmly, glad to hear Seth's name spoken with respect. Not wanting to delay the line or draw attention, she steps forward—only to be stopped by another guard.

"Here is a leash for you," he says, holding out a thick strap for Šarru.

Uldako hesitates, and Šarru grumbles, clearly displeased. But Ishara's firm look says enough. With a sigh, they relent.

As Uldako fastens it, memories stir—bindings, commands, and the sting of captivity. He hates the feeling, but he understands.

With the leash secured, the trio pass through the gate, stepping into the vibrant city, ready to uncover its secrets.

Uldako's senses are immediately overwhelmed by the vibrant scene unfolding before him. Travelers, bearing tales from distant lands, mingle effortlessly with the locals, creating a rich tapestry of cultures. The air is heavy with the aroma of exotic spices, and the chorus of voices fills every corner.

Everywhere he looks, there's a kaleidoscope of sights and sounds, each vying for his attention. His visage flits from the bustling market stalls, offering exotic foods he's never seen, to the artisans crafting intricate wares right before his eyes. The air is alive with the melodic strains of music drifting from a distant structure above.

Following Uldako's eyes, Ishara points out the towering building. "It is called an inn, Uldako," she explains. "A place to eat, enjoy music, and find a bed for the night."

Both awe and uncertainty flickers in his eyes. "I never knew a place like that existed or that a city like this existed for that matter…" He trails off, momentarily lost in thought before continuing, "These people are safe and protected. I never knew people could live like this."

Ishara's eyes meet his with quiet understanding, sensing the weight behind his expression. "Yes," she says gently, her voice steady with reassurance. "And this is the kind of place where you and your *ama* could live in safety, if such shelter were freely given."

Uldako's smile carries a hint of gratitude—grateful not just for her words, but for the way she sees him. Even without knowing his mother, Ishara's care feels real, and that means more than he can say.

"Right, let's get to it!" Ishara interjects with purpose, her tone firm yet determined. She turns to Uldako, her eyes alight with a plan unfolding. "How about you search through all the merchants here and inquire about Seth and his whereabouts?"

Uldako's brow furrows slightly as he processes her proposal. "What about you?" There's a hint of concern lacing his voice.

Ishara's gaze drifts toward the inn, her mind already set on her next move. "I'll check with the innkeeper," she replies confidently.

Uldako shifts uneasily, his discomfort evident. "I don't like the idea of splitting up."

"You're eager to find Seth, aren't you?" Ishara says, her voice calm and sure. She points toward the bustling inn. "This is the fastest way—and it's safe. You don't need to worry."

Ishara moves toward the inn with steady purpose, casting a quick glance back at Uldako, urging him to trust her.

"Let's meet back at the gate in one hand of the sun!" he calls out.

She gives a firm nod without breaking stride.

As Ishara glides into the inn, the atmosphere hits her like a wave—thick with scent, sound, and movement. The air is warm and alive, crackling with voices, clinking mugs, and the earthy smell of spiced food and sweat. Her sharp eyes sweep the room with practiced ease, absorbing every detail.

The inn is no modest tavern. It's a sprawling stone-and-clay structure built around a central hearth, its high ceiling upheld by thick wooden beams carved with swirling patterns of falling stars, wild beasts, and strange runes that glow faintly in the lamplight. One phrase etched across the main beam catches her attention: *The stars walk among us.* Her gaze lingers, a flicker of thought stirring behind her eyes.

The walls are draped with animal hides and sun-faded banners from distant lands, each telling silent tales of battles, hunts, and vanished homes. Resin torches flicker in carved alcoves, casting shadows that dance across the packed earthen floor. Toward the back, a raised limestone platform offers a view over the crowd—likely used for storytelling or song, though now cluttered with resting travelers and quiet negotiations.

At the tables, a motley crowd feasts and drinks—some slumped in laughter, their voices booming off the walls, others locked in hushed conversation. It is a place alive with stories and secrets.

Among the guests, Ishara notes a mysterious lone traveler, his presence a stark contrast to the jovial atmosphere surrounding them. His identity is concealed beneath a hooded cloak and beautifully crafted armor. Ishara's gaze falls upon a woman serving food and drinks, accompanied by a formidable bodyguard whose imposing stature commands respect. His arms crossed, he surveys the room with a watchful eye, a silent sentinel amidst the cheerful chaos.

But it is the lady behind the table serving drinks who captures Ishara's focus, her poised demeanor hinting at a wealth of knowledge about the inn and its patrons.

As Ishara weaves through the lively crowd, prepared to engage with the innkeeper, her presence turns heads. She is graceful, composed, and clearly out of place among the rowdy patrons. A drunken man staggers to his feet in her path. His tunic is stained, his braided beard tangled with crumbs, and the stench of wine clings to him like a second skin.

"Well, well, look what we've got here, lads. Hallo, lovely!" he slurs, earning a round of crude laughter from his table.

Ishara halts, her eyes narrowing with disgust. Without hesitation, she shoves him back with a firm hand to the chest. "Don't even think of it!" she snaps.

Undeterred, the man persists, his drunken swagger turning aggressive as he grabs Ishara's arm. "Come on now, don't think you are better than—" he slurs, his words cut off as Ishara stops him mid-sentence with a hard slap to the face, the sound reverberating through the room.

Just as tensions escalate, a towering figure emerges from the shadows, the imposing guard stepping in to enforce order. With a single motion, he effortlessly lifts the unruly patron off the ground with sheer strength, swiftly escorting him out of the inn with a firm hand.

Ishara's gaze lingers on the guard, noting his strength and decisive action with a silent nod of gratitude. "Thank you," she acknowledges, her words conveying her appreciation as the guard returns to his post, a reassuring presence amidst the chaos of the inn.

As Ishara nears the counter, her eyes quickly take in the woman behind it—weathered skin, a short braid draped neatly over one shoulder, and warm brown eyes surrounded by freckles that hint at years under the sun.

"Hi, may I speak to the innkeeper?" Ishara asks politely.

The woman offers a small, knowing smile. "You already are, dear."

Ishara returns the woman's smile, her eyes drifting over the inn's well-worn walls and flickering lights. "You've built something special here," she says warmly. "I imagine you've met all kinds of people."

The innkeeper chuckles as she wipes down the table with practiced ease. "Oh, you wouldn't believe half of it," she says, her voice thick with stories unsaid.

Ishara smiles, a soft chuckle escaping her lips. "Well, I'm looking for someone rather unique. A legendary warrior named Seth, from the—" Ishara begins, but the innkeeper cuts her off with a raised hand.

"Let me stop you right there, my dear," she says sharply. "I don't know where you're from, but in this town, names like that aren't tossed around lightly—especially not his."

Her warm tone fades, replaced by a piercing gaze. "Umma may seem safe, but beneath the surface, trust is a rare thing. This city's neutrality draws more than just traders. Spies from every kingdom walk these streets, sniffing for secrets. Ask the wrong question to the wrong person, and you might find yourself with more trouble than answers."

Ishara's eyes narrow slightly, caught off guard. "Well, I'm not a spy, and—" she starts, but the innkeeper stills, her hand frozen mid-wipe on the table.

"But how would I know that?" the woman cuts in. She straightens and meets Ishara squarely. "Let me be plain. In this town, information has a price. Just asking about someone like Seth could put a mark on your back."

Her words settle like stone. "Every step you take here is watched. Every word weighed. Be cautious, my dear. This city smiles on the outside, but not all smiles are friendly."

Ishara pauses, her eyes scanning the room. She catches the subtle glances—curious, cautious, some suspicious. The weight of it presses in, but she turns back to the innkeeper with resolve. "I promise you, I'm just a traveler. I've no kingdom to call home anymore," she says. "So tell me—how can I earn your trust?"

The innkeeper studies her in silence, then gives a slow nod. "Listen," she says, her tone softening. "I'll tell you something most wouldn't—especially to a *lu-kur* like you. Trust here isn't given. It's earned. Slowly."

She looks toward a quiet corner. "You see that man over there? His name is Rafk." She speaks with a somber edge now, her voice dipping into memory. "Rafk was a quiet man. A retired guard from the North—kept to himself, never looking for trouble. But trouble doesn't always wait for an invitation." She casts a glance toward the man in the corner. "Five men came in one night—loud, drunk, and dangerous. They shattered stalls, overturned tables, and started swinging before anyone could stop them. Rafk stepped in to shield a vendor, nothing more. But when the city guard arrived, fear turned the truth upside down. No one dared accuse the real offenders. They pointed at Rafk instead."

Her jaw tightens. "He had already been beaten within an inch of his life. So he couldn't speak to tell his side of the story, barely moved. And no one stood for him. None but me."

She pauses, drawing a breath that's steadier than her eyes. "Most thought he wouldn't survive, and I made a choice. I nursed him through moons of silence, of pain. Cleaned wounds that wouldn't close. Fed a man too broken to eat. And slowly, trust grew between us—not just the kind spoken, but the kind proven."

Her eyes return to Ishara, now sharper. "But you…you're an outsider. A *lu-kur.* No one here knows what brought you or whom you serve." She folds her arms, her voice steady. "You want answers? Then live among us. Earn the right to be believed. Work. Listen. Let your actions speak first."

She leans in slightly, voice dropping to a near whisper. "This city may lift up *Il's* name, but don't let that fool you. Many here only worship power. Most are mere visitors, and even the locals show a lack of genuine worship, which has led to the erosion of good values and morals. Without honoring the divine order *Il* represents, many here live in deceit and corruption."

Ishara nods slowly. "I see," she says quietly. "Let me chew a bit on your words."

She turns from the innkeeper, her eyes searching the room. Her thoughts churn with doubt. If trust must be earned, then how can she trust this woman who hasn't earned hers?

She studies the crowd—merchants, drinkers, wanderers—until her gaze settles once more on the quiet figure in the corner. Still, watchful, unmoved.

Something about him draws her in—a presence unlike the rest.

With quiet resolve, she steps toward him.

With a spark of determination, Ishara strides forward and takes the seat across from the enigmatic stranger. "Hi, *lu-kur*," she says with a warm smile.

The man lifts his eyes to meet hers, a flicker of curiosity dancing behind a guarded expression. He glances around at the onlookers now watching them, then leans back with a dry smirk.

"Well now, you've certainly made a scene—and dragged me right into it. How thoughtful of you." His voice is laced with sarcasm and just enough amusement to keep her guessing.

Outside the bustling inn, the world hums to a quieter rhythm. Uldako stands beside Šarru, his towering companion casting a broad shadow across the sunlit street. He studies the bear's calm, watchful eyes, and a silent understanding passes between them—one forged through trials, not words.

"Looks like it's just the two of us again," he murmurs, a faint smile touching his lips.

He rests a hand on Šarru's thick fur, the familiar feel grounding him. Then, without hesitation, they step into the heart of the marketplace—a maze of voices, color, and motion. Together, they move with quiet purpose, the search for answers guiding each step through the crowd.

Uldako finds amusement in the varied reactions of the people as they catch sight of Šarru, their expressions a blend of wonder and trepidation.

They begin at the food stalls, where the air is rich with the scent of baked grains, dried fruits, and simmering roots. Uldako asks his questions in hushed tones between passing faces and patient vendors, but each response is the same—polite but unhelpful.

Undeterred, he and Šarru press on toward the artisans—potters, weavers, and blacksmiths—hoping for a thread of truth to follow. Yet the name of Seth stirs no recognition, only puzzled glances and quiet apologies.

Frustration simmers beneath Uldako's calm, his hope thinning with each step. Finally, he stops and raises his voice above the bustle of the square.

"Does anyone know Seth, the *dumu* of Adam?"

For a moment, only the rhythm of the market answers him—until a clear voice breaks through.

"Hey! You there—come closer!"

Uldako turns sharply. A young blacksmith steps from his forge, his face streaked with soot, the firelight behind him painting his frame in flickers of gold and shadow. He raises a darkened hand. "I know the *dumu-munus* of Adam. I know Seth."

Uldako's brow lifts, skeptical. "You mean his *dumu-nita*? He's a male, not female."

The young man's smile falters. "Ah—yes, yes! Just a slip of the tongue," he laughs awkwardly, waving off the mistake. "Too much heat and hammering—melts the mind!"

Uldako steps closer, voice firm. "Who are you, and where did you see him?"

The man straightens, his tone shifting to calculated charm. "Name's Deceiv. From the Tubal-Cain clan." His eyes glint with something more than pride—something guarded. "Tell you what: You do me a favor, and I'll take you straight to Seth."

Uldako's posture stiffens. "What kind of favor?"

Deceiv grins, wide and arrogant. "Simple. I'm not just any smith—I'm the best in the city. Maybe the best in the land. I work with bronze. Real bronze. None of that soft copper that's only fit for cups and trinkets."

He gestures to his workbench with a theatrical flourish. "But I've hit a snag. A massive order, due tomorrow…and no assistant."

Uldako narrows his eyes. "You talk in circles. Speak plainly."

Deceiv lowers his voice, glancing around. "Fine. My assistant's gone. I need help forging. That's it."

Uldako hesitates, unsure whether he can trust the man, even though he would be capable of aiding him. In the slave camp, he mostly worked in the mines, but at times he had to assist the forge master. It taught him just enough to know his way around a forge. He is far from a master, but he does know the basics.

"Alright," he says at last. "I'll help—but only with a few tools. And in return, you give me Seth's location. Deal?"

Deceiv's fist hits his own chest. "Deal."

Uldako mimics Deceiv's action, his clenched fist hitting his chest twice.

Then Deceiv's grin tightens. "One small issue. I'm out of copper."

Uldako scowls. "And that's my problem, why? You know bronze needs both copper and tin."

Deceiv's eyes widen. "How do you know that?"

Uldako doesn't answer.

"The knowledge to craft tools of bronze and now iron is closely guarded," Deceiv mutters, almost to himself. "Passed only to us by—" He suddenly clamps a hand over his mouth, eyes darting around the street. Then, "In this city of spies, loose tongues bleed gold and blood."

Uldako studies him, but his face reveals nothing more. He'd heard the whispers back in the slave camp—that the secrets of bronze were not found by men, but taught by the gods in the South.

"I'm from the South," Uldako says at last. "And I learned recently. That's all you need to know."

Deceiv recovers quickly, a sly smile creeping across his lips. He thinks Uldako knows the truth—and maybe shares in it.

Uldako folds his arms. "I don't have time to wait for your copper. If it helps, I'll work with another material."

Deceiv's face darkens. "That won't do. This is a custom job."

He gestures to a battered pickaxe near the wall. "Take that. There's a copper deposit nearby, hidden. I'll mark it for you. Do this—and you get your answers."

Uldako steps back, jaw clenched. "And you expect me to find copper by nightfall? That could take a lot of time."

Deceiv shrugs. "Then I guess you'll never find Seth."

A long breath escapes Uldako. Everything in him resists trusting this man, but he's running out of options.

"Fine," he says. "Mark it."

Deceiv eagerly leans over Uldako's map, drawing the location with precision. Uldako watches him closely, suspicion deepening with every stroke of the charcoal.

With the deed done, Uldako folds the map and turns toward the city gate, steps measured, thoughts racing, already calculating the next steps of their journey.

However, he stops short, casting a glance at Šarru, whose silent gaze meets his own. "We should find Ishara first," he says aloud, uncertainty threading his voice. "Maybe she's uncovered something—and we won't have to dig through half the earth to get what we need."

16

Foundling

Back inside the inn, Ishara presses on in her search for truth, seated across from the stranger cloaked in quiet intrigue. The room buzzes with voices and clattering mugs, but her attention never wavers. Leaning in with a curious smile, she says, "You're not like the others here. So tell me—who are you, and where do you come from?"

The man returns her smile, his expression enigmatic. "My name is Unknown, and my country is No Country," he replies cryptically.

Ishara pauses, weighing his reply, then continues, "I noticed you eyeing the soup those men were eating earlier. Seems to me you might need a meal yourself. Are you hungry?"

Caught off guard, the man shifts in his seat. "Umm, no, I—" he begins, but Ishara is already rising.

"I'll be right back," she says, seeing straight through his weak protest. Without another word, she strides toward the bar.

"Could I trade this for a bowl of soup?" she asks, producing a small precious stone from her pouch.

The bartender's eyes widen for a moment before she quickly nods. "Of course," she says, accepting the stone and passing over a steaming bowl.

After a short wait, Ishara returns and sets the bowl gently in front of him. The man hesitates, glancing at her, then at the steam curling from the soup. His fingers brush the edge of the bowl, and for a moment, he just sits there—silent, as if unsure he deserves it.

Then, slowly, he begins to eat.

Each spoonful seems to chip away at the wall around his heart, the warmth of the meal softening his guarded posture.

"Thank you," he murmurs at last, not meeting her eyes—his voice quiet.

Ishara takes a moment then leans in with a determined expression. "Well, if you truly want to thank me, I need some information," she asserts.

The man looks up at her with curiosity. "What do you need?" he responds cautiously.

Ishara's smile widens. "All I am searching for is a great old warrior, an elder named Seth, *dumu* of Adam."

"What do you want with such an important man?" His curiosity shows.

Ishara senses the need for caution and decides to withhold unnecessary details. "He saved my *dusa's* life, and we want to repay that debt," she says succinctly.

The mysterious man nods knowingly as he looks around him. "That name is well known around here, though most will act as if they've never heard it," he whispers with caution. "He's one of the founders and leaders of the northern kingdom. Speaking his name too freely in this neutral city can be risky—you never know who might be listening."

After glancing around, as if ensuring their privacy, he leans in closer. "I haven't seen him recently. You might have better luck up north, where more of his kin are known to dwell. Go to the city of Nippur."

Ishara exhales, the strain of travel and urgency pressing on her shoulders. "I've heard of Nippur. But it is far, and time isn't something we have in abundance. Are you sure you do not know where he is?"

The man straightens, his voice steady. "You have my word. I follow *Il*! I speak no lies. Unlike most in this city, I don't trade in deception."

Still unsure but sensing his sincerity, Ishara offers a polite, "Thank you," and begins to rise.

But before she can turn to leave, the man adds quickly, "The innkeeper might know more. She's been looking for someone to entertain her guests. If you can sing, it might be worth your while."

A glint of amusement sparks in Ishara's eyes. She nods to the man then approaches the innkeeper with renewed hope.

"I hear you're looking for a singer," she says with confidence. "Let me show you what I can do—then we'll talk."

Without waiting for permission, Ishara lifts her voice in song, and the chatter of the inn begins to fade, heads turning as her melody fills the room.

La la la laa-lila
In a world of darkness, we're born

Where hearts bleed and souls mourn
Lost in a labyrinth of pain
Where hope is a fragile flame
Oh, tell me where is the love?
We have learned from *Il* above!
Oh, tell me where is the love?
We have learned from *Il* above!
Can't you feel the weight of despair?
Crushing souls, it's everywhere
Beneath the masks, the smiles we wear
Lies a sea of tears, a silent prayer
Oh, where has love fled from sight?
Lost in the darkness, out of light
In a world where dreams decay
We seek the dawn of a brighter day
Let the melody of our sorrow rise
As we reach for love beyond the skies
In every tear, in every plea
Lies the hope for a love that's free
Oh, where is the love we've known?
In the hearts that ache and groan
In the hearts that ache and groan

As Ishara's final notes fade, a profound stillness settles over the room. The crowd remains frozen, caught in the wake of her voice—each soul gripped by the raw truth woven into her song. Her melody speaks to hidden sorrows, to longings buried beneath silence, and for a breathless moment, the inn seems to forget its own noise.

When Ishara returns to the innkeeper's side, she is met with wide eyes and wordless awe. The woman stares at her as if seeing something sacred—never before has she heard a voice so beautiful nor a song that reached so deep into the human heart.

Ishara tilts her head toward her. "So, what do you think?"

The innkeeper's posture and voice become warm and open. "Forgive me for not introducing myself earlier," she says gently. "I am Trude, *dumu* of Herkmhanus. And you, my dear, are welcome here anytime to sing for—"

Before she can finish, Ishara interrupts, "In exchange for information about Seth?"

Trude hesitates, torn between caution and the allure of Ishara's talent. Then recognizing the value Ishara's voice could bring to her inn, she relents. "Grace us with your song for seven days, and I will share what I know. Deal?"

Ishara's shock is clear. "Seven days!" she exclaims incredulously. Ishara turns and heads for the door, ignoring Trude's attempts to negotiate.

"Ok, five days—my final offer!" Trude calls after her, adjusting her proposal in a last-ditch effort to strike a bargain. But Ishara's resolve remains unyielding as she slams the door behind her.

As Ishara steps outside of the inn, she spots Uldako waving down below, Šarru at his side—but his face is clouded with disappointment. "Judging by that look," she mutters under her breath, "he didn't find Seth either."

She quickens her pace, her stride full of restless energy. As soon as she reaches them, both she and Uldako speak at once.

"Did you find anything?"

They exchange a knowing glance, the warmth between them unspoken. Uldako gestures for Ishara to speak first.

"No. These people are too guarded," she says with a sigh. "I'm not even sure they know anything. Maybe if we stayed longer, we'd get something out of them, but I think we're better off heading to Nippur. At least there, we know someone will have the truth. It seems Seth never entered this city—if anything, he may have only passed by. What about you two? Did you uncover anything?"

Uldako casts a tired look at Šarru, then begins to explain. As he recounts the encounter with the blacksmith from the Tubal-Cain clan and his shady proposition, Ishara listens intently, her brow furrowing. The deeper Uldako goes, the more his frustration shows, his voice tightening as he speaks of copper, forged deals, and the man's strange tone.

As Ishara listens, she knows that every further day in their search is another day Uldako's mother must endure slavery. She sees that awareness growing in Uldako's eyes, tightening him little by little. She isn't sure how much longer he can hold himself together.

Out of nowhere, a small figure emerges from the edge of the crowd—a boy, no older than eight or nine summers, moving with the quiet caution of someone used to being overlooked. His tunic hangs in tatters, barely holding together at the seams, and his face is streaked with dust and dried sweat. Wild strands of hair jut out in all directions, and his skin, darkened by sun and wind, bears the grime of many days without rest or shelter. He walks barefoot yet with a practiced ease, weaving through the crowd like a shadow that belongs nowhere.

"Excuse me, sir," he says timidly, his voice nearly drowned by the city's noise.

Uldako, already tense from his dealings with the blacksmith, doesn't even glance down. "Not now," he snaps sharply.

The boy recoils slightly but doesn't retreat. He lifts a small hand and gently tugs at Uldako's sleeve—hesitant yet determined.

Ishara notices him, her heart softening. But Uldako continues speaking, brushing the child's presence aside as he vents his doubts.

The boy speaks again, more urgently this time, though his tone remains humble. "But I have something to tell you."

Ishara hears the strain in his words—the kind that only comes from a child who has learned far too early not to expect kindness. His clothes are faded and threadbare, his body thin, but his eyes—dark brown and framed by long lashes—hold a quiet strength. Despite everything, they don't beg. They don't plead. They simply wait.

Just as he opens his mouth to speak again, Uldako snaps louder, "I said not now—go away!"

Uldako's outburst startles Ishara. She steps in without hesitation, placing a calming hand on his arm and gently guiding him aside. "Uldako," she says with a firm tone, "what's gotten into you?"

He mutters something under his breath, but she doesn't wait for an answer. Turning to the boy, she lowers herself slightly, meeting him at eye level. Her expression softens, and her voice follows suit, full of warmth. "I'm sorry for that," she says gently, casting Uldako a reproachful glance. "He didn't mean to be unkind. Tell me, what is it you wanted to say, little one?"

The boy swallows hard, summoning his courage. "I know the man you're looking for," he says. "His great *dumu*—Kenan—passed through here a few moons ago. I'm certain it was him because…"

Uldako's jaw tightens. The boy's words—so familiar, so carefully timed—hit a nerve. He doesn't mean to speak, but the words escape anyway.

"Let me guess," he mutters. "You want something first…before you tell us more?" His voice is low, strained—not angry, but weary. "People don't help for nothing. Not in this world."

The moment hangs heavy. His eyes flick to the dirt, as if ashamed of how deeply he believes it. Years of fetters, lies, and broken trust echo behind his words.

Ishara's sharp gaze pierces through him, her voice carrying a stern reprimand. "This is not like you! Why are you snapping at him? Let the boy speak, Uldako." She brooks no argument.

Uldako bows his head in acknowledgment, realizing the gravity of his outburst. With a sense of contrition, he listens as the boy, emboldened by Ishara's reassurance, continues. "I don't want anything. Kenan helped me once, so I want to return the favor."

The boy hesitates, his small hands fidgeting at his sides. His uncertain eyes shift between Uldako and Ishara, searching their faces for a moment. Then, with surprising steadiness, he speaks.

"Before I tell you more, I need to know you mean no harm to him—or to those with him." His voice is soft, but there's a quiet strength behind it. "I have to be sure."

Ishara meets his earnest gaze with a warm, reassuring smile. "You're right to be careful," she says gently. "So let me tell you why we're looking for him."

With calm patience, she begins to recount their journey—speaking not in grand tales but in steady truths. She tells of the miles they've walked beneath scorching suns and starlit skies, of the dangers faced along the way, and of the pain that clings to Uldako like a shadow. She speaks of the mother he longs to free and the weight of a past that still bruises his every step.

There is no pride in her voice, only firm conviction. And when she speaks of Seth, her tone shifts—filled with a reverence that silences doubt. Their search, she makes clear, is not for power or glory, but for healing, for hope, and for the truth.

As Ishara speaks, something shifts in the boy's visage. A flicker of understanding sparks in his eyes, growing brighter with every word. "Ah, I see now," he murmurs. "You really are good people."

Ishara's smile deepens, touched by his sincerity. "We try to be," she says gently. "So please, tell us what you know."

The boy draws a steadying breath, summoning his thoughts. "That great man…Kenan," he begins slowly. "I think he was not just a powerful warrior but some kind of high-ranking *šanga* or something. He spoke of things—spiritual things—I had never even imagined."

His voice wavers as emotion creeps in. "The people with him…they listened like every word mattered. They showed him such respect. And he gave me food."

He pauses, tears welling up in his eyes. "I looked at him, wondering why someone like that would even notice someone like me. And then he said…" His throat tightens. He lowers his face, struggling to steady himself as the memory rises. "He said, 'One should always try to do to others what you want them to do to you.'" A solemn hush falls over Uldako and Ishara as the depth of those words sinks in.

The boy continues, "It was as if he could see into my thoughts, and so I want to return the favor," the boy concludes, fixing Uldako with a steadfast gaze.

Uldako's heart softens as he looks at the boy—seeing, in that small frame and dirt-streaked face, a reflection of his own past: the hunger, the silence, the ache of being unseen. Something shifts in him.

With humble resolve, he steps forward and kneels, bringing himself level with the boy. He rests a gentle hand on the child's shoulder, his voice low and steady. "I'm sorry for judging you unfairly," he says. "Truly."

His eyes search the boy's, and the remorse in them is real. "I see now that your intention is pure. And if Kenan is half the man you say he is, then he may truly be Seth's great *dumu*. Please—go on."

Beside them, Ishara gives a small nod of approval, her expression warm. No words are needed. Uldako feels the fullness of her trust and draws strength from it, the barrier between him and the boy dissolving with each breath.

The little boy, now more at ease, continues his story with a heavy heart. "Kenan was the first person who ever treated me with real respect…not even my parents did. I felt as if he looked at me—not for what I was but for what I could be—and he showed me kindness."

He swallows, blinking back the memory. "When my people were attacked in our village, Kenan and the men who followed him fought off the raiders, but it was too late for the lives already lost. All of them…except me. My whole family was killed."

Uldako's heart aches for the boy, feeling the weight he must carry in such a small frame. He longs to offer comfort, to ease even a sliver of that pain—because he knows too well the silence that follows loss, the hollow ache it leaves behind. But for now, all he can do is listen and try to understand the world this child has endured.

After taking a deep breath, the boy continues, "Kenan brought me to this city and left me with a woman who looked after kids like me—ones with no one left. She said she would take care of us, and she did, but only for a little while."

He pauses, his voice trembling. "She passed away unexpectedly soon after Kenan left. After that, it was just us again. Just the orphans, alone."

He wipes at his face with the back of his hand, blinking through tears. "But Kenan did everything he could for me before he left. He was good. Really good. And I just want to do something right. For him. For his family."

Ishara places a gentle hand on the boy's back, her touch offering quiet comfort until his tears begin to fade.

Moved by the boy's words, Uldako's words are full of compassion. "I know your pain," he says softly. "When I was a slave, I was treated worse than an insect, bound, beaten, and left to starve. There were days I thought hope itself had forgotten me. I never knew an *abba's* love either…just hunger and suffering."

His lips form a gentle smile as he looks into the boy's eyes. "But I found a way forward. And you will too. This darkness—it's not the end. Not for me or for you."

The boy's eyes brighten, a flicker of hope dancing where sorrow once lingered. Uldako's words seem to settle something inside him—like a seed beginning to grow.

Ishara turns to him with curiosity. "Thank you for being so open with us," she says with warmth. "Do you think you could tell us more—about how you came to know where Seth might be? Anything you remember could help us."

The boy nods eagerly, his eyes lighting with the memory. "Back then, Kenan always let me eat with him when we made camp on the road to Umma. Every night, while the fire burned low, I'd listen while he and the others talked. They said they'd be visiting someone named Seth in just two full moons."

Uldako leans in, unable to hide the sudden spark in his voice. "Where?" he asks quickly. "Where were they planning to meet him?"

"I'm not entirely sure, but I do know where Kenan was headed next, and that might lead you to Seth," the boy says with excitement.

Uldako glances between Ishara and the boy, a faint hope stirring in his eyes. "Could you show me on the map?" he asks, holding it out.

The boy steps closer, tracing his finger across it before tapping firmly. "Here."

Ishara leans in for a closer look. "That's on the road to Nippur," she says with rising excitement.

Uldako's eyes meet hers, and for the first time in days, a grin tugs at his face. "Finally—a possible lead."

Then he turns to the boy, his smile softening. "Let me apologize to you, again. Earlier, I let my past and my sorrow speak for me. That blacksmith reminded me of people I've known—people who've hurt me. But that's no excuse. You didn't deserve that."

The boy gives a small, forgiving smile. "It's alright," he says simply.

But then his eyes widen. "Oh! I nearly forgot! I overheard something else. That blacksmith, Deceiv! He lied to you. I saw someone bring copper to his forge two days ago. He just made up that story to use you. I don't think he knows anything about Seth."

Uldako's face flushes red with anger as he turns and begins to stride toward the blacksmith, muttering under his breath, "That deceitful…"

Ishara intervenes, placing a firm hand on Uldako's arm to hold him back. "No, we can't afford to cause trouble in this city. Let's ignore it and focus on our mission," she urges.

"But he blatantly—"

Ishara interrupts sharply, snapping Uldako's attention back to the urgency of their quest. "Remember what Mahalalel told you—overcome evil with good. Every moment we waste here is another moment your *ama* remains in slavery. We must go."

A quiet calm settles over Uldako as Ishara's wisdom sinks in. "You're right," he says softly. "Let's move on."

But as he turns, his eyes land on the boy—still standing there, alone, uncertain. Something tugs at him. In that small, motionless figure, he sees the shadow of himself again: abandoned, forgotten, left to survive in a world that doesn't care.

Uldako pauses, then turns back. His voice softens. "What's your name, little one?"

The boy looks up and answers with surprising pride, "My name is Kunai—but you can call me Kun."

Uldako smiles at the confidence in his voice. "Nice to meet you, Kun. Tell me, do you have any special skills or know any crafts?"

Kunai thinks for a moment, then answers with quiet pride. "My parents kept sheep. Their wool kept us warm, and we drank their milk. I helped watch them every day, back when our people were still together. We had a safe camp until the evil men came and…" His voice trails off.

Ishara watches Uldako carefully as the boy speaks. She sees the look in his eyes and gives a small, knowing nod.

Uldako steps closer, his voice warm. "Then how about this—join me, Ishara, and Šarru on our journey. Help me find Seth, and later, when we find a safe camp, maybe I'll get us some sheep. You can tend them for me." He offers a soft smile. "You'll have food for your belly, a sword to keep you safe, and a place to rest your head. What do you say?"

Kunai's eyes go wide, his mouth falling open. "What? Really?" he gasps. "I can't even remember the last time I had a full meal—or a real place to sleep!" He breaks into a grin. "Yes, I'll join you!"

But before Uldako can respond, Kunai's attention shifts to Šarru. His voice rises with excitement. "Can I touch him?"

Šarru steps forward with surprising gentleness, sensing the boy's awe. Kunai reaches out and runs his fingers through the thick fur, his smile stretching from ear to ear as pure wonder fills his face.

"I am surprised you are not afraid of him," Uldako says.

Kunai looks up at him, eyes bright. "Afraid? No. He is why I followed you the moment you came into the city." He reaches up and scratches behind Šarru's ear, speaking with simple certainty. "I knew he was a good *uḫuš-gal*. A strong one but with a kind heart."

Šarru lets out a deep, rolling rumble of pleasure as the boy's fingers move through his fur. A small, soft laugh escapes Kunai—light, almost shy. "He likes me," he says, as if that explains everything.

Ishara smiles warmly at the boy. "Come on then, Kun," she says with a playful tone. "Just don't expect a proper bed—it'll be a blanket beneath the stars each night."

Kunai walks with a burst of liveliness as they head toward the city gate. His words come in a rush. "Does this mean we're *dusa-meš* now? I've never really had a *dusa*. Well…I had one. Her name was Puchy. She was a frog. But she ran away. So, where are we going? What tribe are you from, Ishara? Where are we going after we find Seth? Do they have *uḫuš* there too?"

Uldako laughs under his breath. "You're not going to talk this much the whole journey, are you?"

But Kunai keeps chattering ahead of them, undeterred, as if he's been waiting his whole life to speak without fear.

Uldako leans closer to Ishara, a mischievous glint in his eye. "You'll explain later what a sheep and a frog are, won't you?" he whispers.

Ishara stifles a laugh and nods.

As the sun dips lower in the sky, the four head north—an orphan, a warrior, a traveling songstress, and a silent guardian with paws like rolling boulders. The road ahead is long and uncertain, but for the first time in a while, their steps feel lighter.

Together, they walk toward the path that only they can tread and toward whatever mysteries await.

17

Slaves

With the day's long journey behind them, bathed in the warm glow of their crackling campfire, Uldako, Ishara, Šarru, and young Kunai gather together under a vast canopy of stars. Uldako leans in closer to the flickering flames, the map in his hands tracing their path through the wilderness. "It's going to take us a while to get there," he murmurs, glancing at Ishara for confirmation.

She nods thoughtfully, her head turning toward the darkness beyond their camp. "Yes, but our first order of business tomorrow will be at the river. Our water won't last much longer."

Uldako glances at Kunai, who sleeps soundly beside the fire—his small body is curled beneath a coarse blanket, the same one Uldako has used in nights past. Now it's wrapped around the boy, tucked with care. Uldako sits nearby, exposed to the chill, the cold pressing into his back as he leans into the warmth of the flames.

Ishara watches him for a moment. Then, without a word, she pulls a worn cloth from her side and tosses it toward him. Uldako catches it midair and drapes it around his shoulders, a quiet smirk playing at the edge of his lips.

Their eyes meet. No thanks are spoken, but the gratitude is there, glowing in the firelight.

He looks at Kunai. "It's a cruel fate," he murmurs. "To leave *dumu-meš* without parents…to tear their lives apart as if they mattered not."

His words rise into the sky, where ancient lights gleam high above—silent, eternal, and watching.

Uldako speaks slowly, "You know, Ishara, I used to believe those stars were divine beings—silent watchers scattered across the sky. When my body was covered in bruises from the slave overseers, I would lie awake beneath them, wondering how they could bear to watch and do nothing—how they allowed so much evil to walk freely in the world." His voice is rough with old hurt. "Did you ever think about things like that?"

Ishara shifts closer to Uldako, her voice low and steady in the quiet. "I have," she says. "Especially after meeting you. Even if they are *dingir-meš*, we can't always blame them for what we humans do to each other, can we?"

A crease forms between Uldako's eyes, a new thought stirring in him. He has never seen it that way. "You're right," he says, a heavy breath escaping. "But I didn't do anything wrong, and still, I was born a slave. How is that fair?"

Ishara's eyes narrow as if peering into the far currents of time. "The past is a river that has already flowed, Uldako. No hand, no power, can turn it back. But now, this moment is like clay in your hands. And the future still waits to be shaped by your choices."

Her voice softens, almost trembling, as if the words rise from a place deep within. She blinks, startled by the words coming from her lips. "Evil breeds more evil. If you don't let go of your pain and anger, they'll bind you to the past. They're a poison, creeping through you, eating away all the good inside."

Uldako's face darkens, doubt flickering in his eyes as he wrestles with Ishara's words. "I hear what you're saying, Ishara, but how can I just let go?" His voice roughens. "They should suffer like I suffered. Like my *ama* still suffers..." The anger rises in him, trembling on every word.

Ishara draws a slow breath, hearing the burden behind Uldako's words. "Pain is part of life when every soul has the freedom to choose their actions," she says softly. "Pain can be good or bad. Maybe that's the test—to see how we walk through good and evil. And if we choose what's right, maybe one day we'll stand among the stars."

Uldako's brow furrows. "What do you mean? Explain it plainly."

She turns to him, steady. "Think about it. If you hadn't been a slave, Seth might never have found you. You wouldn't have gone looking for him. And if you hadn't, you wouldn't have met me, or Šarru, or Kun."

Uldako stares at the fire, the thought settling in. "I guess that is true," he mutters.

Ishara continues with a thoughtful look. "Even the situation with that fallen spirit, Shamsiel, brought me and you together," she adds, a hint of wonder in her voice. "Not that bad things are good, but through them good revelations might come forth." She thinks for a moment then realizes something else. "Maybe *Il* does intervene at times, like the good spirit who saved us in that moment, but our free will was intact."

Uldako raises a brow, trying to grasp the concept. "You are right. Free will in a world of good and evil..." he says with curiosity.

Ishara looks up at the stars. "Maybe *Il's* thoughts are much higher than ours," she says softly, "like the stars above—far beyond our reach and understanding."

She pauses, thinking carefully. "I've thought about this for a long time. I believe the Most High has the power to wipe out all evil with a single breath. But if He did, He would take away the freedom He gave mankind and rule like a tyrant. I believe He gave us the gift of choice—to choose and then to walk in the light or the darkness. Unfortunately, some, like the slave masters, choose the darkness, and their choices bring more pain and suffering into the world."

She pauses, her expression thoughtful. "Didn't you say that divine beings appeared out of nowhere to guide you? Doesn't that suggest that *Il* does intervene at crucial moments in time, but with our free will intact? Did He at any time force you to do anything?"

Uldako's gaze meets Ishara's, a dawning realization flickering in his eyes. "I...no, He didn't..." he murmurs, the pieces of the big puzzle slowly falling into place.

Ishara's eyes shine with a clear light as she speaks, her voice calm and steady. "The more I think about it, if we can see and hate the darkness in the world, doesn't that mean there must also be good? Evil cannot exist without something good to stand against it. And if we can recognize the darkness, shouldn't it awaken a deep hunger in us to seek the light—to chase after what is good with all our strength?" Her words linger in the air, full of quiet certainty.

She pauses, as if hearing her own thoughts for the first time. "I'm just speaking from the heart now, but it makes sense to me. When I look at your life, Uldako, I see how facing evil made you start to run toward the light and the truth it brings. Maybe the pain we suffer is a sign that something is broken in us humans and in this world...and that's why we long for a cure."

A deep silence falls between them, stirring something inside Uldako. "So if *Il* is truly the *Dingir* Most High," Ishara goes on, "maybe the reason evil exists is because He gave His created beings the free will to choose to do evil. It doesn't mean He approves of it, but He might allow it so that we can truly have a choice. And even then, He can still turn it into something good. I believe *Il* might want us to choose the light with our own free heart."

Uldako listens intently as he learns Ishara's perspective. It's as if a veil is being lifted, revealing a new understanding of the world around him.

Uldako watches with wonder as a bright light streaks across the sky, like a flame thrown from the hand of the Most High. He points up quickly. "Look at that!" he says.

Ishara lets out a small laugh. "That's wondrous! It's like *Il* is showing us that He hears us speaking about Him!"

Uldako smiles faintly, his eyes full of awe as he watches the wandering light fade into the darkness. After a moment of quiet, he looks at Ishara and speaks in a soft voice, "I don't understand it all, but I've learned something from you tonight. And I'm glad I met you, Ishara."

A gentle breeze stirs the leaves around them, as if the night itself is listening. Uldako feels a quiet pull toward Ishara, their bond hanging like a thread between them. Slowly, without thinking, they begin to draw closer, guided by the path they have walked together and the trust growing between them.

Then, like a flame snuffed by wind, the moment shatters.

The quiet night breaks apart with the sound of rushing footsteps and loud shouts. Before Uldako and Ishara can move, a pack of armed men bursts from the shadows, catching them by surprise.

Uldako's instincts take over, and he dives for one of his axes, but seven men close in around him. Meanwhile, Kunai is grabbed by rough hands, and Ishara struggles as three men hold her.

In the middle of the chaos, Šarru wakes with a roar and leaps into the fight, his instincts driving him to protect his friends. With a savage snarl, he sinks his teeth into the shoulder of one attacker, tearing him away. But their leader moves fast. He grabs Ishara from behind and presses a blade against her throat.

Ishara freezes, her heart pounding, the sharp edge biting cold against her skin.

The man, his voice sharp with authority, shouts at Uldako and Šarru. "Stop! It's over!" he barks, tightening his hold on Ishara and pressing the blade harder against her throat. "Stand down, or I'll cut her throat," he growls, his words like a blade against Uldako's heart.

Uldako stiffens, his mind racing. He throws a quick glance at Šarru, who snarls but holds back, waiting for Uldako's command.

"Šarru, stay!" Uldako calls out, forcing the words through gritted teeth as he fights the urge to strike. One wrong move, and Ishara will die before his eyes. "Don't do it! Please, don't!" he pleads with the man. "Tell me, what do you want?"

Uldako realizes that this man is not a usual raider. He carries an aura of intimidating authority and confidence. His armor, meticulously forged and exquisitely adorned, sets him apart as a figure of considerable power. Crafted from gleaming bronze and iron, the armor is etched with intricate patterns, all converging toward a menacing serpent emblem emblazoned on his chest. Each piece of his attire speaks of wealth and status, from the finely wrought swords at his side to the impeccably crafted dragon on his left pauldron.

Despite his imposing presence, there is an unsettling darkness that surrounds him. His hair, a tangle of jet-black locks, frames a face marked by a sharp jawline and piercing eyes. His beard, trimmed to precision, adds to an air of calculated menace. Uldako notes the curious mismatch of his eyes: one a piercing blue, the other a deep dark brown, a rare and unsettling sight.

The man holds the blade steady against Ishara's throat, his every move calm and precise, the mark of long years of training and command. Something about him stirs an old memory in Uldako—he looks strikingly like Jabal, the leader who once watched him fight the champion, Hubara. But this man seems a little older, harder.

Every small movement from the man carries a sharp threat, and a hard tension runs through Uldako as the blade presses against Ishara's neck. When he looks into the man's eyes, he knows at once that this is someone who would kill without hesitation.

The man glares at Uldako with contempt and barks his orders. "We want everything! Drop your axes and step back," he commands with a heavy and dark authority.

Uldako lowers his weapons and tosses them to the ground, stepping back as ordered.

Helpless, he watches as the raiders swarm their camp like vultures, ripping through their supplies with brutal speed. His thoughts scatter and reform, trying to find a way to turn the tide, but every thought feels useless against so many enemies. He is outnumbered, outmatched, and one wrong move could cost Ishara and Kunai's life.

With a grim sense of finality, the raiders finish their plundering, satisfied with their spoils. One of them, his voice full of triumph, calls out, "I think we've got everything, Lamech!"

Uldako's eyes widen, and his jaw tightens in shock. That name, he has heard it before.

Hubara's words come rushing back to him: *Behold, the true Jabal, dumu of Lamech and Adah, and scion of Cain the marked one.*

And now he understands why this man's face stirred something in his memory. Others might share the name, but not the blood.

The face, the bearing, the cold authority—there is no doubt.

This man is the *abba* of Jabal.

Uldako's jaw clenches as he locks eyes with Lamech, seething with silent fury. "So your name is Lamech," he murmurs to himself, a vow of retribution forming in his mind. But before he can act, Lamech's chilling threat pierces the tense air.

"We're taking this fine woman of yours—and the little pest." Lamech's voice is thick with malice. "And if you so much as twitch or try to follow, they'll be dead before you can blink."

Uldako's muscles tighten with rage as he glares at him. "Kun is not a little pest," he growls through gritted teeth. "If you harm them—"

Lamech cuts him off with a harsh laugh, his voice full of cruel pride. "What will you do, little gnat?" he sneers. "You are nothing but dust beneath my feet. I have power beyond anything you can imagine. I will kill any man for attempting to wound me. Believe me, I am more wicked than even Cain himself!"

With a cruel smile, Lamech gives a sharp nod to his men to move to Uldako before turning to him, his voice low and full of venom. "Remember this," he sneers, "if Cain's revenge is sevenfold, then mine is seventy-sevenfold. I do not spare you out of mercy—I leave you breathing so you can live with the shame of losing those you loved by my hand."

As the menacing henchmen approach, Šarru emits a low warning growl, poised to defend his master. However, Uldako's firm command settles the tension, coaxing the loyal bear to stand down. With a reluctant nod, Šarru retreats slightly, his muscles tense with restrained aggression.

The assailant gestures for Uldako to distance himself from Šarru, and as he complies, a sudden, brutal blow crashes against Uldako's skull, sending him crashing to the ground. Uldako fights to stay conscious, his vision blurring as he struggles to focus. Through the haze, he sees Šarru's instinctive lunge toward the attacker, only to withdraw at Ishara's urgent plea echoing in his ears.

"Stand down, Šarru! Go hide!" Ishara's voice rings out, a desperate plea to stop the knife from cutting her throat. With a low growl, the bear obeys, his whole body trembling with anger he cannot release.

Uldako lies on the ground as screams cut through the chaos—Kunai and Ishara are being dragged away. The world spins around him, and before he can rise, the darkness closes in. His strength fades, and he slips into blackness.

• • •

Kunai is ripped from Ishara's side, and a wave of dread crashes over him, sinking deep into his chest. Memories of loss and fear flood his young heart.

Why does this keep happening? Why do the people I love always get taken by evil men? The ache inside him swells, raw and unbearable. "Maybe it's my fault," he whispers. "Maybe I'm no good…bad luck."

In a surge of defiance, Kunai summons every ounce of courage within him, lashing out against the man who holds him captive. But his efforts are futile against the brute strength of his captor, who merely scoffs at his feeble resistance.

Kunai struggles against his restraints, his small body shaking with fear and regret. *If only I were stronger*, he thinks bitterly. *I could have protected them.*

As he fights back tears, Ishara watches him, her heart tightening. She sees the fear written across his young face as he is hoisted roughly onto the shoulder of one of the raiders.

Her mind steadies. To lose her wits now would undo everything. She forces herself to stay calm, knowing that a clear head is their only hope. "Don't worry, Kun," she calls out gently. "We'll find a way out of this."

Kunai hears her words but doubt gnaws at his heart.

My parents said the same thing, he thinks bitterly, *and look where they are now.* His hope slips further away with each passing moment.

Ishara looks at the land around her, studying every detail to keep her sense of direction. They crossed the Euphrates River and have been dragged for hours across rough land and rolling hills. Now, in the distance, she sees the faint glow of a safe camp flickering against the night.

As they get closer, her heart sinks.

"No," she tells herself, bitter realization settling in. "It's not a safe camp…it's a slave camp." The weight of their situation presses hard on her, but she forces herself to stay alert.

Far behind, where the clash had ended, Uldako stirs. Slowly, his senses crawl back to him. A warm, familiar weight presses against his side—Šarru, licking his face with worried whines. With a groan, Uldako pushes himself up, the pounding in his head a painful reminder of the blow he took.

Surveying their surroundings with urgency, his eyes sweep the area, scouring the ground for clues that might lead them to rescue Ishara and Kunai. He speaks to Šarru, his voice tinged with concern and determination. "Šarru, show me where they went," he says, his words carrying a weight of resolve. Then Uldako gives the chest-deep *hrrk*—the call to action.

Šarru leaps into motion, his nose to the ground as he sniffs the air. For a moment, it feels just like the old days—tracking prey side by side. But this time, what they hunt is far more precious, and the cost of failure far greater.

"Šarru, they chose the wrong random travelers," Uldako says steady and fierce. "They woke the beasts within us, and now they will feel the fury of the wild."

Together, they stride forward and move with a quiet strength, their resolve unshakable as they set out on the hunt.

They track the men to the river, but Uldako finds no more signs. He exchanges a knowing look with Šarru, who seems to agree.

"Looks like they crossed to the other side," Uldako mutters with frustration.

Šarru sniffs the air, standing close, his body tense and alert.

"We don't have much choice," Uldako's says, eyes fixed on the dark water. "Šarru, stay sharp for the *ušumgal*, or any river serpents, like the one that nearly attacked Ishara. They could be lurking below. But we can't let that stop us, can we, old *dusa*?"

The duo surveys the river, studying the best place to cross while the sun rises. The area is strikingly still as they look for any hidden threats.

"It looks safe enough. The water is shallower here," he says, pointing to where the tracks vanish into the river. "That's our way across. We move together, quickly as one, Šarru! And let's make a lot of noise! It might scare off anything hiding beneath the surface if it thinks we are huge predators crossing the river."

They carefully move into the cool, clear water, the gentle flow brushing against their legs—a soft contrast to the urgency burning in their hearts. To Uldako's surprise, the riverbed is not as deep as he feared. He can even see the outline of his feet through the shimmering surface as the sun climbs higher into the sky. "It's not so bad, Šarru. Not as cold as I thought," Uldako says with relief slipping into his voice.

As they reach the middle of the river, Uldako catches movement far to their left. A large creature stirs beneath the surface. It notices them but shows no sign of moving closer. Still, Uldako watches it carefully, every muscle ready in case it changes its mind.

The creature rises slowly from the river, like a colossal boulder stirred to life. Its sleek, black hide gleams under the sun, with water streaming off its back in a bright cascade.

Just beneath the surface, small, round eyes—like twin moons—watch the world with a calm, steady gaze. Though it moves with a quiet grace, an overwhelming sense of power radiates from its massive form. Without warning, it arches its head back, opening a wide, gaping mouth lined with rows of brutal teeth—a clear reminder of the ancient dangers lurking in these waters.

Uldako's pulse quickens as more of them rise from the river. They are huge, thick-bodied beasts with hide like river-worn stone, water sliding off their backs in dark sheets. Others push through the brush along the bank, heavy steps crushing reeds as they wade in to join the rest. Uldako recognizes the danger—they seem to be slow on land but deadly strong in the water, and even more so in numbers.

With a sharp gesture, he urges Šarru to move faster. They press on, moving quickly through the shallows, Uldako stealing cautious glances at the beasts. Thinking ahead to how long this journey might stretch, Uldako can't shake the worry over their missing waterskins, stolen by the raiders. They have no way of knowing when they will find water again.

He cups his hands and drinks deeply, the cool river soothing his dry throat. Beside him, Šarru lowers his heavy head and laps up the water, both of them drinking what they can as they push forward, knowing they might not get another chance.

Reaching the far bank of the river, Uldako and Šarru stay sharp, their senses tuned to any danger that might be near. The land ahead looks empty, with no immediate threats in sight.

Turning to the sandy shore, Uldako carefully searches for tracks but finds none. Beside him, Šarru sniffs the breeze, his body tensing. A low growl rumbles from his throat—he smells something that Uldako cannot yet see.

Uldako gently pats Šarru's massive head, his voice filled with admiration. "Well done, my *dusa*. Lead on. *Hrrk*!"

With Šarru guiding the way, they continue their steady journey southward along the riverbank, the rhythmic sound of flowing water a constant companion. But then, without warning, Šarru halts, his nose twitching as he catches something new on the breeze. His ears perk, muscles tensing with purpose. A low, rumbling growl escapes his throat, signaling the discovery of something amiss.

Without hesitation, the bear veers sharply from their path, moving away from the river and into the wilderness. Uldako, trusting in his friend's instincts, follows closely, his steps quickening as he senses a new urgency in the air.

As they climb the hill beside the river, Uldako's sharp eyes catch signs that others might miss. Faint footprints and broken twigs, hidden to a casual glance, stand out clearly to him, guiding their path forward with silent clues left by those they chase. With a satisfied grin, Uldako kneels beside Šarru, both of them studying the tracks.

"Šarru, it's them!" he says. "Look at the spacing and the depth—they weren't moving too fast."

His eyes lift to the horizon, and a new fire rises in his voice. "We still have a chance to catch them." Without wasting a moment, the two set off, following the trail that will lead them back to their friends.

A great fish-eagle wheels overhead, its cry cutting clean through the sky. Uldako glances up, remembering how Ishara once spoke of them. Her clan says these birds carry an ancient memory in their wings—that long ago, one of their kind served as a spirit on the high places, guarding the secrets of the first righteous men. Some began to call it the great *anzu*, the shadow of the lion-eagle who once stood between heaven and earth.

A wave of longing rises in Uldako, a deep ache for Ishara's presence. But even as his heart pulls toward the past, his senses stay sharp to the land around him. The lush greenery fades, giving way to dry, cracked ground dotted with thorny bushes and rolling hills that block his view.

With every climb, Uldako moves carefully, wary of what dangers might wait beyond each ridge. As Uldako climbs another hill, a strange sight catches his eye to the right—a gathering of giant birds, taller than any he has ever seen. They stand on the earth as high as two men, moving with slow, regal steps across the open land.

"Magnificent creatures," Uldako murmurs to himself, slowing his pace slightly to watch them.

Their long, powerful legs carry their massive bodies with ease, and their feathers shimmer in the sunlight—earthy browns and grays woven with flashes of bright color. Against the dry hills and open sky, they look like living banners, a breathtaking vision stitched into the world itself.

Their heads are crowned with massive beaks, and their large, sharp eyes gaze out from beneath heavy brow ridges. There is a wild, majestic beauty to them—a living reminder of how rich and fierce life is in this world. Watching their heavy bodies stride across the land with slow, stately steps, Uldako wonders silently why they do not fly.

Perhaps they cannot. Or perhaps, he thinks, they no longer need to. Uldako presses on, leaving the great birds behind.

The sun creeps higher in the sky, and the light grows hotter on his back. His legs ache from the long journey, but a new strength rises in him, driven by the need to save his friends. Through the noise in his mind, Kunai's face returns to him—so young, so innocent and full of trust.

Why couldn't I protect him like I promised? The question burns deep inside him. He clenches his fists and pushes the pain aside. A steady fire stirs within him. *I cannot change what is done. But I will keep my word. I will save them both!*

As Uldako and Šarru cross the rise of another low hill, their chests tighten at the sight. Ahead, the raiders move steadily toward a rugged mountain that looms in the distance. Uldako leans in close to Šarru, his voice a low whisper. "There they are, Šarru. Let's follow carefully."

They move fast across the open land, closing the distance between themselves and the raiders. Uldako's thoughts twist and knot inside him. He knows he has been running on raw emotion, not strategy. Then Lamech's warning returns to him, cold and sharp: *If you so much as twitch or try to follow, they'll be dead before you can blink.*

Uldako turns to his friend. "How are we going to save them, Šarru? We need to think this through," Uldako murmurs, his mind whirling with strategies.

"If I confront them head-on, I might catch a few off-guard, but the rest will retaliate, and I'll be overwhelmed. I am also unarmed as they took my weapons!" He casts a glance at Šarru, who grunts in response, a silent reminder of past lessons learned the hard way.

Drawing closer to Šarru, Uldako speaks in a hushed tone. "Your *ama* taught me the importance of planning, Šarru. Every move must be calculated, every action deliberate, because one mistake can be the end of you." With new focus, he slows his pace, trailing the raiders from a safe distance.

Then, like a spark catching dry grass, an idea forms in Uldako's mind. "That's it, Šarru," he whispers, low but eager. "We wait for the right moment. When they least expect it, we strike."

His eyes gleam with new determination as he shapes the plan in his mind. "When they make camp for the night, we take them one by one while they sleep—or we slip in and free Ishara and Kunai before they know we are there."

As they crest yet another hill, Uldako's carefully laid plans crumble before his eyes. In the distance lies a safe camp, and a sinking feeling settles in Uldako's gut—this must be the safe haven the raiders are heading toward. Halting in their tracks, Uldako and Šarru crouch low, observing the movements of the raiders as they draw closer to the camp.

The camp sits tucked inside a natural basin, shielded by low hills and a great mountain rising behind it. From a distance, it stays hidden from any wandering eyes. It is not large, but as Uldako studies it, a chill runs through him.

"It looks like my old slave camp, Šarru," he mutters. "But this one seems newer. It also looks like a mining camp."

His heart sinks as he takes in the grim scene—low fences, only a handful of guards, and broken figures in torn clothing, their thin bodies bent under the weight of hard labor and hunger.

Anger flares within Uldako as he watches the raiders approach the gate. At the forefront stands a guard, blowing a horn that signals their arrival. The camp guards regard Lamech with deference as they all cheer him in. He strides confidently into the camp, flanked by two new captives—Uldako's friends.

• • •

Ishara's eyes widen in horror as she is forcefully pushed into the slave camp, her gaze sweeping over the grim surroundings in search of any advantage. With each step, she takes mental notes of the camp's layout, committing it to memory for a future escape plan with Kunai.

As they're dragged deeper into the camp, Ishara's keen observation reveals crucial details: There is a single entrance guarded by only two guards, while the rest of the guards are dispersed throughout the area, most of them overseeing the enslaved workers.

Counting the guards silently, Ishara tallies up their numbers, estimating around ten within the camp itself, in addition to the two stationed at the gate. With the arrival of Lamech's group, their combined forces would swell to around twenty, presenting a formidable obstacle to their escape. Ishara's heart aches at the sight of the broken slaves, their battered bodies marked by endless cruelty.

Anger rises within her, stirred by the injustice unfolding before her eyes. Ishara's voice cuts through the air like a blade, her words sharp with contempt as she faces the cruelty of their captors. "You are filth! Humans should not be treated like this!" Ishara shouts, her heart gripped by the suffering around her.

Some of the guards laugh and turn away, seeing her as nothing more than another slave, beneath their notice.

"Be silent, or I will tear out your tongue!" Lamech's voice cracks through the air like a whip, forcing the moment into stillness. But Ishara does not flinch. She meets his glare with steady, burning eyes.

The guards seize Ishara and drag her across the camp, but she does not resist. She knows there is no victory in fighting now. As they pull her forward, her tear-filled eyes sweep over the other slaves—thin, pale faces, hollow and drained of hope.

The guards shove her hard toward a thorn cage at the edge of the camp, the cruel branches reaching like claws to trap her inside. As Ishara sits in the thorn cage, she watches the other slaves and feels a deep shock—she has never seen humans so broken.

The despair carved into their faces tells a grim story, a dark shadow of the vibrant souls they once were. Young and old alike toil under the hard eyes of their oppressors, digging rare rocks from the cruel, stubborn earth.

Ishara's heart aches as she watches their suffering, each bent body a silent cry against the cruelty of their masters. She counts around forty slaves among them, each face a living wound, a bitter reminder of all that has been stolen from them.

Kunai's young eyes, still filled with the world's harshness, are now forced to face the depths of human cruelty even more. He stares at the grim scene before him—the slave camp heavy with misery, the broken souls trapped within it—and the sight crushes his tender heart. Tears spill down his cheeks, silent proof of the pain gripping him inside.

The guards shove Kunai toward a small cage woven from thorn branches, his small hands bound tightly behind his back. With rough hands, he is thrown into the cramped space, the jagged thorns tearing at his skin with every small movement. As Ishara steadies herself within her own cage, her heart sinks as she looks at Kunai. The cruel design of the cage leaves no room for comfort, no hope of escape. It is made to break the body—and the soul.

With no choice but to wait, Ishara clings to the faint hope of escape and the desperate thought that Uldako might still be alive. Worry gnaws at her mind, a fear she cannot shake. She whispers to herself, "I hope he's okay."

To her surprise, it is Kunai who speaks light into the darkness. "*Il* is our only hope," he says quietly.

Ishara knows he is right, even if he means it with a heavy heart. She remembers her last talk with Uldako—about pain, about why suffering fills this broken world—and she decides to give Kunai what she herself needs. Smiling gently through her sorrow, she leans closer to him.

"You are right, Kun," she says softly. "Let's not lose hope. Stay strong."

Her voice wraps around him like a blanket of warmth, even as her own heart trembles with fear she dares not show.

Hidden behind a low ridge, Uldako watches the despicable scene below. The sight of the slave camp—its cruel cages, its broken souls—twists his heart with grief and helplessness. The thought of Ishara and Kunai trapped inside that place burns like a blade in his chest.

He pulls back from the edge and paces, back and forth, the dry earth kicking up beneath his feet. Doubt and fear churn inside him. With each step, the silence of the God he had started to believe in feels heavier, colder.

"*Il*, where are you?" Uldako whispers. "Spirits of light? Did you guide me through fire and blood only to abandon me now?" His voice breaks in the emptiness, but no answer comes—only the low sigh of the wind, carrying his words into the endless sky.

Uldako lowers his head and mutters to the dirt at his feet, "Just as I thought… nothing. I thought you were a good God."

18

Freedom

The silence from above is deafening.

Uldako crouches behind the ridge, his hands curled into the dust, his heart pounding against a cage of doubt. The distant clang of iron, the crack of whips, and the muffled cries of the slave camp gnaw at his soul. Ishara. Kunai. He sees them in his mind's eye—trapped, alone—and the weight of his helplessness threatens to crush him.

"*Il*, where are you?" he mutters again, voice hoarse, barely more than breath. But the heavens give no answer.

A low huff draws him back to the present. Šarru nudges him gently with his snout, warm breath brushing against Uldako's face. The great bear doesn't speak yet says everything. *You are not alone.*

Uldako blinks hard. His fingers unclench. The trembling stills. He reaches out, resting his hand on the thick fur of Šarru's neck. The beast leans into the touch with a low rumble of comfort, as if anchoring his friend to the earth.

"I'm sorry," Uldako whispers. "I almost lost myself." For a moment, there is stillness—no whips, no bonds, just two souls in the wild.

Then, quietly, Uldako breathes, "Do you remember what Ishara said, Šarru?" His voice steadies as he meets and holds eyes with the bear. "She said pain might be a path. That even suffering can lead to something greater."

He rises slowly, a steady fire growing in his chest. "Maybe this is another trial—a test not just of strength, but of who we choose to become." The darkness hasn't lifted, but he no longer faces it alone. "We need to think," he says, brushing dust from his knees. "They haven't broken us yet."

With fresh resolve, Uldako pushes aside despair and focuses on what must be done. He glances at Šarru and speaks with quiet purpose. "Let's circle around and scout the camp."

The two move like shadows, careful and quiet, skirting the edges of the terrain as they gather what they can. Step by step, they climb the rocky slope behind the camp until they reach a narrow ridge high above. There, hidden by stone and scrub, Uldako and Šarru lie in silence—watching.

From their elevated vantage point, Uldako surveys the rugged beauty of the arid landscape spread out before them. The camp, nestled in isolation, appears formidable from afar, its defenses seemingly impregnable. Every movement below is measured, every weakness marked. Then something strange catches his attention.

Off to the far right of the camp, he spots a group of those same giant birds they saw earlier, nearly twenty of them, penned in together. As the taskmaster tosses feed toward the birds, Uldako leans in and murmurs, "They're feeding them. What would they use those flightless birds for, I wonder." His eyes shift beyond the pen and his breath catches.

There, locked in cages near the camp's edge, are Ishara and Kunai. Relief floods his chest. They're alive. But the feeling is short-lived, replaced at once by urgency.

Turning to Šarru, Uldako speaks in a low, firm voice. "We've checked every part of this perimeter—no weak spots in the fence, and no way to climb it without being seen. No one comes or goes. And with dusk closing in, our time is running out. The guards—there are too many to fight head-on."

As the sun sinks low, Uldako's mind races, each idea rising then falling apart under the weight of risk. The camp is sealed tight, its defenses unyielding. But then, something else catches his eye.

A guard steps out alone through the gate to relieve himself. After some time, his comrade steps out, wandering to that same spot for relief. A flicker of hope sparks in Uldako's chest.

He leans toward Šarru, voice low but alive with urgency. "This just might work…yes, it just might."

Rising quickly, he glances at the dimming sky. "Come. Let's circle around—closer to the gate—while there's still enough light to move."

With swift and silent steps, they navigate the terrain, their movements enveloped in secrecy. Uldako finds a concealed vantage point near the gate, his gaze fixated on their target with unwavering focus. He murmurs to Šarru in a hushed tone, "There are only two guards at the gate. But earlier, I noticed something—they take turns stepping away to relieve themselves. Always to the same spot. Alone."

His eyes narrow, voice dropping even lower. "When one of them leaves again, that's our chance. He'll be alone, exposed. And with nightfall creeping in, the darkness will cover our approach."

Uldako's voice, low and steady, carries the weight of a plan born from desperation and resolve. "We wait until one of the guards strays too far from the other," he says, eyes locked on the gate. "I'll move fast—take him down, strip his armor, and put it on myself. Then I'll return to the gate, acting like I'm the guard."

He glances at Šarru, his tone sharpening. "Once I'm close enough to the other guard, I'll finish him quickly and quietly."

He pauses, his gaze narrowing with purpose. "With both guards gone and me disguised in one of their uniforms, I'll walk straight into the camp. No one will suspect a thing. That's how I'll get to Ishara and Kun—hidden in plain sight."

As the sun dips below the horizon, enveloping the landscape in shadow, Uldako and Šarru inch closer to the spot where the guards typically wander to relieve themselves. Concealed behind the ridge of a hill, they maintain a vigilant watch over the gate, their movements as silent as the night itself. Torches within the camp cast a flickering glow, revealing glimpses of the surroundings.

In the stillness of the evening, a new thought stirs in Uldako's mind. *What if I free the other slaves, like I did at the slave market?* He considers the idea, wondering if their numbers could be turned against the guards.

But doubt creeps in. He remembers how long it took to rally the others last time—how broken they were, not just in body but in mind. These slaves might be even worse off, and to them, he would be just another stranger.

Too risky, he thinks. *Too uncertain.*

Then a sharp pull tugs at his mind—his true goal: Ishara and Kunai.

He clenches his jaw. As much as he longs to help the others, he cannot risk it—not now. With a heavy heart, he pushes the thought aside and forces himself to focus. But deep inside, the weight of it lingers. His heart doesn't want to let them go.

After a patient vigil, Uldako stealthily surveys the camp once more. It seems that the majority of the guards have retired for the night, leaving only a handful of sentries on watch duty. Three are positioned strategically within the camp, spaced out to monitor the slaves, while two stand sentinel at the gate. The remaining guards are sound asleep, their vigilance momentarily relaxed, presenting an opportunity for infiltration.

"Now's our chance, Šarru," Uldako whispers. "We just need one of them to answer the call of the bushes."

Time crawls by until one of the guards mutters something to his companion and steps away from the gate, muttering about needing a moment of privacy. Uldako stiffens, eyes narrowing. The moment has come. With only a stone gripped tightly in his hand, he lowers himself and begins to creep forward, guided by the moonlight.

The guard veers slightly off the path, turning his back as he lifts his tunic. Like a shadow in motion, Uldako closes in—silent, fast, precise.

One clean strike to the base of the skull, and the man drops without a sound.

"Forgive me," Uldako murmurs as he begins stripping the guard's tunic, leather harness, and helmet. "Not the most honorable thing to happen to a man, nor is it a good place to fall down."

He slips into the rough garments quickly, fastening what he can and pulling the helmet low. In the dark, it will be enough.

As Uldako adjusts the final piece—a head covering crafted with care—he marvels at its usefulness. "Why didn't I think of making something like this before? It shields from the sun and the dust storms," he reflects, noting its blend of protection and disguise.

With the guard's sword and shield in hand, his eyes catch the serpent emblem etched into the metal.

"No surprise there," he mutters.

He looks himself over in the dim moonlight, seeking reassurance from his furry friend. "How do I look Šarru, my old *dusa*?" Uldako asks, seeking quiet reassurance. As he runs a hand over the armor, he notes its fine craftmanship—thick, hardened leather, cleverly stitched and layered into a sturdy, flexible covering.

The armor comprises several components meticulously tailored for both mobility and defense. A sturdy chest piece, secured with leather straps at the sides, serves as the focal point, safeguarding vital organs while permitting agile movement of the arms and torso. Overlapping shoulder guards, adorned with intricate detailing, offer additional protection to the upper arms and shoulders, their design curved to deflect potential blows. These shoulder guards are intended to be affixed to the chest piece with durable leather straps, ensuring a snug fit and maximum protection in battle.

The arm bracers encase the forearms in sturdy protection, consisting of thick leather bands wrapped securely around the lower arms and fastened with laces. These bracers offer defense against slashes and strikes without compromising the wearer's agility and mobility in battle. Similarly, the leg guards are crafted in the same fashion as the arm bracers, enveloping the lower legs in durable leather armor. Secured with robust straps, they shield against attacks targeting the thighs and shins. The armor bears the scars of old battles—its surface scratched and worn, each mark a silent story of conflict.

With a firm glance, Uldako signals Šarru to stay hidden and keep watch from a safe distance. The sight of a bear would ruin everything. Heart drumming, he steps toward the gate, fully aware that even the slightest mistake could alert the remaining guard and destroy any chance of rescue. Each step draws him closer to the slave camp, a place he never thought he'd enter again.

As he approaches, the remaining guard at the gate shoots him a questioning look, his expression a mixture of concern and suspicion. "What took you so long?" he demands. "You can't afford to take risks like this, especially with Lamech inspecting us. We should be the finest of his new slave camps. He'll kill us both if we're not at our posts."

Uldako knows that speaking might betray his voice and ruin the disguise. Thinking fast, he clutches his throat and begins coughing, loud, hoarse, and unrelenting.

The nearby guard frowns. "What's wrong with you? You sound terrible," he mutters, then turns back to his post.

Uldako coughs harder, staggering slightly, drawing the guard's eyes again.

In that moment, close enough now, he strikes. One sharp blow drops the man before he can react.

Wasting no time, Uldako hauls the limp body over his shoulder and hides it in a thick patch of brush, safely out of sight. He moves quickly toward the cage where Ishara and Kunai are held, every sense alert for danger.

Two guards stand nearby. Uldako narrows his eyes—he knows they must be dealt with, or the rescue will fail before it begins. As he draws closer, Uldako is surprised to find one of the guards dozing atop a large wooden drum. Seizing the chance, he slips past the sleeping man without a sound and creeps toward the second guard, who stands near a broad wooden shelter.

Circling quietly along the edge of the structure, Uldako halts as low voices drift out from within. Women speak of gods and *Ašag-dingir*, stirring his curiosity. But then a name cuts through the murmurs like a blade: Jabal.

His heart skips. He leans in, pulse quickening. He learns from their conversation that one of them is Jabal's *ama*, so she must be the wife of Lamech! His thoughts race with the implications.

Before Uldako can fully process the shock, a harsh voice tears through the stillness of night, cold, commanding, unmistakable, and directed at the women he overheard.

"Adah, enough of your prattle with Zillah! The night is long, and I grow sick of my wives' voices clinging to the air like flies. Hold your tongues, both of you!"

Uldako's fists clench at the sound of Lamech's voice, but he forces himself to stay calm. One wrong move, and the entire rescue could fall apart. *Two wives*, he thinks, unsettled. *I've never heard of a man with two wives.* He shoves the thought aside. Now isn't the time for questions.

Peering around the corner of the shelter, he studies the layout. The remaining guard leans against the far wall, just out of reach. Too far.

Uldako knows the disguise won't hold up under close inspection, especially if he's forced to speak. He watches…waits…and then, a plan begins to form. He picks up a small stone and tosses it toward the nearest shelter beside him. The soft clatter draws the guard's attention.

He takes the bait.

As the man steps forward to investigate, Uldako strikes, and one swift blow to the head kills him without a sound. Quickly, he catches the guard midair and drags the limp body behind the structure and out of sight. His heart pounds, but the plan holds. With the path clear, he moves toward the cages with silent urgency.

"Uldako," Kunai whispers softly, filled with quiet hope.

Ishara's eyes shine with relief as she sees him approaching. She quickly hushes Kunai's excited whisper, fully aware that silence is their only chance for escape.

Uldako nods, offering a silent promise. Without hesitation, he slices through the bindings of the cage and pulls Ishara and Kunai into a firm embrace. "I'm sorry I couldn't stop them," he murmurs. "But I'm here now—and we don't have long."

As he prepares to move, Ishara gently grabs his arm, her expression tense. "We can't leave the slaves," she whispers, barely audible. "Uldako, you know their pain. You lived it. Please, we have to try."

Uldako hesitates, his mind racing with the risks of involving more people in their escape. "Your safety comes first." His voice is tight with concern. "We can't risk alerting the guards and endangering everyone's lives."

But Ishara's resolve is unshakable. "Why are our lives more important than theirs?" she presses firmly. "I won't leave unless we help them too."

Uldako meets her gaze, startled by the strength in her words. Deep down, he knows she's right. He looks to Kunai, who gives a silent, steady nod.

With a reluctant sigh, Uldako gives in. "So stubborn," he mutters—though a trace of admiration creeps into his voice. "Fine. But we move carefully. Stay close and follow my lead."

Taking a deep breath, Uldako scans the area, searching for a plan...then it hits him. He turns to Ishara and Kunai with renewed focus, assigning roles with confidence. He hands Ishara a sword, trusting her skill with the blade, then he kneels beside Kunai.

"Stay quiet, no matter what," he says firmly. "When we reach the slaves, free them quietly."

He stands and looks at them both with an intense gaze. "Then we strike as one! All the overseers must be taken down at the exact same time. There's no time for hesitation."

Ishara questions the need for violence, but Uldako knows the brutal truth. His mind flashes back to the slave market...the desperate escape...the overseers who hunted them like animals. Only two slaves fell that day, but this time, without a good plan, far more could die.

"We can't afford to leave them alive," he says grimly. "If we don't act now, they'll hunt us down by sunrise—and what comes next will be worse than fetters. Better never to escape at all than to try and fail."

Ishara sees the weight in Uldako's words—truth forged through experience—and nods. With resolve burning in their hearts, Uldako, Ishara, and Kunai move into the shadows to free the slaves and face their captors, knowing their actions will decide not only their own fate, but the fate of every soul they hope to save.

Uldako leads Ishara and Kunai swiftly through the shadows, their footsteps swallowed by the night. But a heavy thought weighs on his heart. This won't be as simple as Ishara believes. These people are not just weak; they are shattered. Their will has been buried under years of cruel slavery. To free them, they'll need more than unlocked cages. They'll need to believe they still have something left worth fighting for. Some may be too broken to try. Others might cry out in fear and bring the guards down on them all. This rescue cannot fail. If it does, they won't get another chance.

As they near the slave cages, Uldako's thoughts are cut short as he spots a guard. With a sharp hand signal, he halts Ishara and Kunai. Then, moving with precision, he slips behind the guard and knocks him out in one swift strike.

But just as they begin freeing the captives, one of the slaves stirs and opens his mouth to speak.

Uldako moves fast. He crouches beside the man, cutting his bonds while pressing a finger to his lips. "Quiet," he whispers urgently. "We're here to free you—but you must not make a sound."

The slave nods, wide-eyed.

Another slave started, "No, you can't, I'll call the masters! You'll—"

Uldako cuts him off mid-sentence and shows him the blade. "If they wake now, they will kill us all…that means you too."

Ishara and Kunai join Uldako, moving silently from cage to cage, their hands swift and careful in the dark. With many of the captives now freed, Uldako steps forward and addresses the startled group in a hushed, steady voice. There's urgency in his tone, but it's quiet and measured.

"Listen carefully," he whispers, his eyes looking at the weary faces around him. "I've known the sting of slavery, but I have also tasted freedom."

Noticing a few skeptical stares, he reaches up and pulls aside the leather strap of his armor, exposing the scarred slave mark burned into the back of his neck—*arad-muš*, slave of the serpent.

The captives gasp softly. Eyes widen as they see the truth—he is one of them. A slave who escaped and returned as a warrior.

Uldako straightens, his voice steady and resolute. "That same freedom is within your reach, tonight."

He pauses, letting the silence speak for him. "We must move together. You have a choice: remain here and die like an animal, slowly under the lash, or rise, risk everything, and run. Even if we fall, better to die as free men and women than live as slaves."

He leans in slightly. "I have done it before. Trust me. Follow me. And together, we take back our freedom."

An elder steps forward, his face worn by years of toil. "For once," he says, "I would like to taste freedom. I will follow your lead, young one." His words, shaped by suffering and wisdom, carry weight—and they stir the hearts of those around him.

One by one, others begin to nod slowly, their quiet murmurs of agreement rippling through the night like a silent oath. With a shared resolve, they move to free the last remaining captives, spreading hope like a spark in the darkness.

Ishara's senses sharpen at the sound of movement behind her. Spinning around, she finds herself face-to-face with a towering guard—recently awakened, eyes bleary as he stumbles forward. Uldako looks up at them and freezes. It's the guard he thought was still snoring on the large wooden drum.

"What's going on?" the man growls, his voice thick with sleep but edged with suspicion.

Before the guard can act, Ishara's instincts kick in. With a swift, practiced motion, she wields the sword Uldako entrusted to her, slicing through the air with deadly precision. The guard's startled cry is muffled as he clutches at his throat, crimson blood spurting from the gash inflicted by Ishara's blade. Sensing the imminent threat, Ishara moves swiftly, driving the sword through the guard's chest with unyielding determination.

As the guard crumples to the ground, his body convulsing in its final moments, Ishara acts swiftly to cushion his fall, ensuring that the impact is as quiet as possible to avoid alerting the other guards. With a mixture of relief, she meets Uldako's eyes, silently reaffirming their shared commitment to see their goal through to the end.

With a profound sense of admiration, Uldako silently acknowledges Ishara's bravery. *What an incredible woman,* he reflects with awe.

In the blink of an eye, all the slaves are freed from their binds, their eyes reflecting a combination of both fear and hope. Uldako wastes no time in rallying them.

"Quickly, arm yourselves with whatever you can find—pickaxes, tools, rocks, anything that can be used as a weapon," Uldako urges. But to his surprise, no one moves. They stand frozen, staring at him like statues. Sensing their fear, he meets their eyes and speaks with quiet urgency. "Running isn't an option. When dawn breaks, they'll come for you, and what follows will be worse than anything you've endured. You all know this!" They recognize the truth of his words.

Drawing from his own past, Uldako offers a spark of light in their darkness. "I once stood where you are now, bound in fetters. But someone showed me the way to freedom—and now, I offer you the same chance."

Taking a deep breath, he continues with conviction, "A wise man once told me that man is made in the image of *Il*, the God Most High. No man, no beast, can bind a soul." He looks into the eyes of the weary, the scarred, the broken. "You are already free. But you must believe it."

His voice sharpens, filled with fire. "Tonight, we fight. Not just for ourselves, but for every soul still living beneath the whip. Believe in our freedom, believe in each other, and together, we shall defy the whip and the rod. If you cannot find the strength within yourselves, then find it in me—for I stand as proof of the power of resilience and defiance."

With those words, something shifts. A light kindles in the eyes of the captives—first in one, then in another. Shoulders straighten. Heads lift. What was once only fear begins to harden into courage. They look at Uldako not as a stranger but as a brother, one who has walked through dark fire and returned to lead them out.

Murmurs of resolve spread quietly through the group as each slave finds, in that moment, the will to rise and reclaim what was stolen from them.

Ishara's heart swells with quiet awe for the man she has come to trust. Uldako, once a slave like the rest, now stands tall—a living banner of strength, a guide for those stumbling in darkness.

Moved by his words, the slaves begin to rally. One by one, they seize whatever tools, sticks, or sharpened stones they can find. Uldako moves among them, forming small groups, assigning roles, preparing them for what's to come.

Then, they wait.

The air grows heavy, charged with unspoken tension and rising courage. It is the stillness before the earth quakes. Each heart beats like a drum, counting down to the moment when the yoke of oppression will break…or blood will be spilled.

Uldako positions slaves at the entrance of each shelter where guards are likely sleeping, all waiting in silence for the signal. The plan is simple but critical: strike at the exact same moment, so no guard is roused by the cries of another. He surveys the camp one last time, eyes scanning every shadow. Then, with a silent prayer to *Il* for strength, Uldako raises his hand.

The uprising begins.

Chaos erupts. Screams tear through the stillness, weapons scrape against bone, and bodies clash in the dark. Uldako bursts into one of the shelters, swiftly cutting down two slavers still tangled in sleep. Without pause, he rushes back outside to gauge the battle.

All around him, the camp is ablaze with motion. Many slaves have struck true—but others are locked in brutal struggle, their cries for freedom swallowed by the roar of combat.

Uldako rushes to aid an older slave woman, but to his surprise, she cuts down her enemy with a single, clean strike. Before the body even hits the ground, his eyes catch movement ahead—a guard savagely beating several slaves in quick succession. Without hesitation, Uldako charges forward, ready to intervene.

But just as he's about to reach the fray, a blur of fur and fury flashes past him. Šarru barrels into the guard with devastating force, his massive claws slamming the man to the ground.

The threat ends in an instant, silenced by the bear's raw power.

Uldako shares a quick, knowing glance with Šarru—a silent recognition of the bond between them. The bear had waited patiently beyond the camp, choosing the perfect moment to strike. Without a word, the two move together, rejoining the fight.

Uldako finds his next target, every step sure and deliberate. But the way he fights now—it's different. No longer born by fear or desperation, his movements carry new purpose. This strength doesn't come from the instinct to survive; it comes from love.

His strikes are faster, more precise. His focus is sharper. He flows through the battle like a man awakened, fighting not for himself but for others. For those he cannot bear to lose.

Not far off, Ishara shields Kunai, guiding him behind a nearby shelter for cover. But safety is fleeting.

A guard lunges from the dark, seizing her arm and yanking her toward him, a sword gleaming in his other hand. Reacting swiftly, Ishara uses the guard's momentum to her advantage, swiftly maneuvering behind him. With a decisive thrust, she drives the sword through the guard's back, piercing through his chest. As the guard collapses to the ground, Ishara kneels beside Kunai, offering reassurance. "You're safe now, Kun. We're safe."

A voice cuts through the din—cold, commanding, unmistakable. Lamech.

Uldako hears it and his heart sinks. His eyes dart through the battlefield—until they land on the horror. Four slaves lie still, cut down where they stood, their blood staining the earth beneath Lamech's feet.

Jaw clenched, Uldako surges forward, weaving through the fray. He snatches up a fallen soldier's sword, his grip tightening with grim resolve. As Uldako closes in, Lamech surveys the battle, his eyes darting from one fallen guard to the next. The ground is littered with bodies—his warriors struck down before they could even rise. The attack had come like a thief in the night, and now, despite his command, the outcome is clear.

A flicker of disbelief twists across his face, soon hardening into a scowl of fury.

Then he sees him—Uldako, driving through the turmoil with fire in his eyes. And in that moment, Lamech understands—this is the man behind it all. The one he left unconscious when he took the woman and the boy. The ambush, the unity, the fearless charge. With a ragged cry, he bellows, "Adah! Zillah! To me! We flee!"

Uldako quickens his pace, determined to cut them off, but a towering guard lurches into his path, eyes burning with fury, sword swinging down like a falling cedar. Uldako dives aside just in time, the blade carving the air where his body had been. He rolls to his feet and lunges, striking hard, but the guard parries with ease, knocking him back with brute strength.

Weapons clash in a deadly rhythm as the two circle each other, blow for blow.

Uldako realizes his haste to reach Lamech is causing him to lose focus. He grips the sword with determination as his focus sharpens. Every movement is calculated, every breath drawn with purpose.

He sees it now—this man is more than muscle. He's trained. Dangerous. So Uldako waits, watching for the opening that will come.

Amidst the battle, Uldako's eyes flicker to Lamech's fleeing figure, a surge of righteous fury coursing through him.

With a calculated move, Uldako parries the guard's assault then swiftly drives his forehead into the man's face, disorienting his opponent. Seizing the opening, he thrusts his sword through the guard's heart, ending the threat with decisive finality as he pushes the enemy to the ground.

Uldako rises slowly to his feet, his chest heaving with exertion. His gaze locks onto Lamech and his wives, fleeing into the distance atop their massive flightless birds. A rush of frustration floods through him. "Swords and axes," he mutters under his breath.

Ishara and Kunai step closer. "Should we go after them?" There is concern in Ishara's voice.

"We'll never catch them now," Uldako growls through clenched teeth, his fury plain on his face as he sees the birds run off into the distance with remarkable speed.

As the clamor of battle fades and the dust begins to settle, Uldako surveys the aftermath. Lifeless bodies lie scattered—mostly fallen guards. He counts twelve slaves among the dead.

With a heavy sigh, he lifts his face to the sky, watching moonlight dance across the drifting clouds. For a moment, he stands still in the quiet, blood streaked across his brow, his resolve unshaken.

He then feels a gentle hand on his back, followed by Ishara's voice, bright with joy.

"We did it, Uldako. We actually did it."

She steps in front of him, her deep blue eyes alight with triumph. As he turns to her, a wave of emotion floods him. For the first time, justice and peace settle in his chest. He looks at the slaves around him, and he sees the change in their eyes too. The weight of their victory is real and undeniable, and it settles over all of them like dawn breaking after a long, starless night.

Memories flood in: pain, bindings, the echo of laughter from cruel mouths. Uldako remembers the days when he was told he was nothing, just a number, a tool, an animal meant to be broken. But now, standing amidst the ruin of his captors, he knows the truth.

He is not less than human. He never was.

He fought back, and he won.

Tears spill freely down his cheeks as he draws Ishara into his arms, clinging to her like an anchor in the tide of emotion. No words come; they aren't needed. The warmth of her embrace says everything words cannot.

Kunai rushes in, throwing his arms around them both. "You kept your word! Please, teach me to fight like you. You're strong!"

Uldako smiles through the tears, resting a hand on the boy's head, a quiet, steady affirmation.

A voice rises behind them, shaky, full of wonder. "You saved us…thank you. Thank you!" Uldako turns toward the sound, and his jaw goes slack.

19

Seed

As Uldako turns, he beholds the survivors—around twenty-eight souls, their faces streaked with tears, their bodies draped in blood-stained rags. Many do not speak, but they do not need to. Their grief, their awe, their quiet hope is written on every face, every trembling breath. And Uldako feels it all.

He knows that pain. He remembers the weight he carried when Seth first freed him from the burden of slavery. And now, he sees that same weight beginning to lift from them. He was alone, but they have each other.

They stand together in silence, arms around one another, drawing strength from shared suffering and hard-won freedom. He knows well what they need most at this moment.

Uldako steps forward, his voice rising with quiet conviction. "Today, you've shown the world that you are more than slaves. You are men and women, created in the image of *Il.* Go now—and never again bow to the yoke of slavery. You are free!"

He pauses, eyes moving from the faces around him to the bodies that lie still on the bloodstained ground. His jaw tightens. His voice wavers. "Live for those who fell to give you this chance."

A young man steps forward—freckles scattered across his face, dark brown eyes wide with wonder. He looks no older than sixteen. "What is your name?" he asks eagerly.

Uldako gives a small smile. "I am Uldako, *dumu* of Deborah."

The boy's face brightens, he brings his fist to his chest, and he lifts his voice in a chant. "Uldako! Uldako!" Others join in, one by one, until the camp echoes with the sound.

Ishara stands nearby, her hand resting gently on Uldako's shoulder. She says nothing, but her presence steadies him. The warmth of her touch grounds him amidst the rising chant. Uldako lowers his gaze, a flush creeping across his face. He has never cared for praise—never sought it. But he understands this is not about him. It is about them. About hope rising from ashes. About voices learning to speak again after years of silence. They need to give thanks, to name the one who helped break their bonds. So he says nothing. He lets their voices rise and does not turn away.

But as the chant swells louder, Uldako finally lifts a hand, calling for quiet. The crowd falls still. "It wasn't I who saved you," he says firmly. "It was your courage—your strength together—that broke the yoke of slavery. This victory is yours."

His words settle among them like a blessing. Freed men and women glance at one another, eyes glistening, lips trembling with the beginnings of real smiles.

Then a voice breaks the silence. "What do we do now?"

The question hangs in the still air. All eyes turn toward Uldako—some with fear, others with hope. Even Ishara and Kunai are watching him.

The question settles in his chest like a stone. It awakens memories he thought buried—of wandering in confusion after his own fetters were broken. He remembers the fear, the questions, the silence that followed his freedom. It feels as if his younger self has just spoken through one of them.

He draws a slow breath and steps forward. "You cannot stay here," he says. "Lamech may return with more men and greater wrath. Gather what you can and return to your people, your villages. But be watchful. The world beyond these hills is no gentler. Danger hides in every shadow, just as it did behind these walls."

The same young man who first asked for Uldako's name steps forward again, hope and worry mingling on his face. "Some of us have lost our villages. Can we come with you?"

Uldako meets his gaze with a sorrowful look before answering. "It is better for you to join together and seek those among you who still know a home. Do not follow me—I cannot bear that burden now. I am setting out on an important quest, and the road ahead is dangerous and uncertain. This is my path, and you each will have your own to walk."

Disappointment passes over the young man's face, but before he can speak, an older man steps forward. His long brown beard is streaked with gray, and his green eyes hold the calm of long years—nearly five hundred of them.

"If any of you are without kin or a safe place," he says with a steady and kind voice, "or if the weight of slavery still clings to your bones, I welcome you to my camp. My family has held it for a very long time. You will find shelter there—and a chance to begin again among *dusa-meš*."

A murmur stirs the crowd, and one of the freed men raises a hand. "Where is your camp?" he asks.

The man answers with calm assurance, "It lies one day's journey to the northeast, beyond the river. The eagle emblem marks our camp—and our devotion is to *Il* Most High and His *dumu*, *Il-Il*, as it was in the beginning."

The name *Il-Il* lingers in Uldako's mind. Many questions arise, but he buries them for now. This is not the time.

Uldako lets out a quiet chuckle, easing the tension. "Well then, what are you waiting for? Lamech and his men won't stay gone for long. Take what you can and begin your new lives. We must all be far from this place before they return."

With a sense of purpose, the freed slaves move through the camp, searching for anything of use. They gather food, water, tools—whatever they can carry. Some claim the very weapons and armor once used to beat them down, now turning them into symbols of freedom. Drawn by curiosity, Uldako walks toward Lamech's dwelling, with Ishara and Kunai close behind.

Ishara stands frozen in the doorway, blocking the entrance. Her eyes dart around the inside of the shelter, stunned into silence by what she sees. Behind her, Kunai hops up, trying to see past her shoulder.

"Well? Are you going in?" he asks, trying to peek past her.

She blinks and steps aside. "Yes, go on," she says.

As the three of them enter, they are met with a startling contrast to the rest of the slave camp. The structure is filled with riches—fine cloaks, polished weapons, and stores of rare foods. Ishara lets out a quiet whistle. "Now this is what I call a treasure."

Uldako moves slowly through the dwelling, and his eyes go wide as he takes in the carefully arranged goods. Everything here speaks of power—of luxury taken by force. Nearby, shelves and woven baskets overflow with vibrant fruits and strange nuts, unlike any he has ever seen. He hesitates, unsure what to make of them. Ishara steps up beside him and begins naming them quietly, her voice steady with the ease of one who has wandered far and seen much.

Among the riches lie lavish garments once worn by Lamech's wives, and beside them, a bronze breastplate gleams on a wooden stand—flawless in design, likely forged by a master smith. Ishara, ever curious, wanders to a corner clearly reserved for the women. Her eyes scan the shelves until something unusual catches her attention.

"You won't believe this, Uldako. Come here—quick!" she calls, half-laughing already.

Uldako steps over, only to stagger back as he spots a man staring at him from the polished bronze object in her hands. Instinct kicks in—his muscles tense, ready to fight. Ishara nearly drops the item, laughing so hard she has to brace herself against the wall.

Kunai peeks around her side, grinning from ear to ear. "I saw one of those at the market in Umma," he says between giggles. "But none as big as this one! People said it showed secrets...or souls trapped inside!"

Still frowning, Uldako shakes his head. "But how can a man's face be trapped inside it? Who is that strange man? Some kind of sorcerer?"

Ishara loses control again, laughter spilling out in waves. Kunai collapses onto a fur mat, wheezing with amusement.

Red-faced, Uldako glares at them, then turns away with a huff and walks toward an armor stand he spotted earlier, muttering to himself.

Wiping tears from her eyes, Ishara finally manages to call after him, "That was you, Uldako. The man in the bronze—it's your reflection!"

He stops mid-step and turns slowly, walking back with cautious wonder. Taking the polished disc into his hands, he stares into it. His demeanor is full of curiosity and wonder.

"I've only seen myself in the blurry reflection of water," he says softly. "But this is clear. Is this truly me?" His fingers brush his beard. "Look how long my hair has grown...and my eyes—dark brown. Huh. I take back what I said about that man. He's not strange—he's rather noble. Handsome, even."

Kunai and Ishara burst into laughter once more, relishing in Uldako's embarrassment as his cheeks flush crimson while he scrutinizes his reflection in the mirror.

Ishara steps closer, her eyes bright with wonder. "I've never seen a *zabbaršu* this fine before," she says. "Polished bronze, so flawless it looks like it holds a piece of the heavens."

She leans in beside Uldako, their shoulders lightly touching as they gaze into the mirrored surface. In the play of light and shadow, their faces appear side by side, sharp and clear. Uldako's breath catches. He's never seen the two of them together like this.

He shifts, uncertain. The clarity unsettles him, yet with Ishara so near, her presence warm against his, he finds himself enjoying the moment.

Every line and contour of their faces is revealed in startling detail. It feels like uncovering a secret that was always there, waiting.

But as the silence stretches, a quiet unease stirs within him. The closeness, the clarity—it's almost too much. He lowers his gaze and carefully places the mirror in Ishara's hands. "You keep it," he says in a hushed voice. "There's something unsettling about staring at myself for too long."

Then he turns toward the bronze armor once more, drawn back to its weight and purpose.

Meanwhile, Kunai eagerly bounces beside Ishara, pleading, "Let me see, let me see, please!" Ishara lowers the *zabbaršu* and reassures him, "Look, you're a handsome boy, Kun!" Kunai grins as he beholds his reflection, remarking, "Not bad, huh?"

Uldako meticulously scrutinizes the bronze armor laid out before him, each detail captivating his attention. Light dances across its surface—hammered smooth, then etched with patterns so precise they seem carved by the gods. No common smith forged this. Every curve, every joint, every engraved line speaks of mastery far beyond anything he has seen. It is the finest armor he has ever laid eyes on.

At its heart gleams the emblem of a dragon—its wings spread, its fangs bared in silent defiance. The beast is worked in blackened bronze against the brighter metal, coiled as if to strike. The plates interlock like dragon scales, shaped to turn blades and bend arrows.

Curious, Uldako lifts the cuirass and attempts to wear it, but the armor is far too large. Its heavy weight pulls at his shoulders, and the breastplate hangs loose around his frame. With a grunt, he sets it aside and returns to the comfort of his leather guard, lighter and better suited to his movement.

Behind him, Kunai plays with the mirror, making faces in the polished bronze while Ishara shakes her head, smiling faintly.

Uldako stands, brushing dust from his hands. "We must move quickly," he says. "Lamech may return—and not alone."

Ishara nods and swiftly gathers precious items into a bag found in the room, including some of the discarded clothing belonging to Lamech's wives. Among the attire lies a set of worn thick leather armor, evidence of a woman who did not shy away from combat.

Uldako's gaze lands on a finely crafted leather bag resting near the back wall—sturdy, well-stitched, and perfect for the road ahead. He slings it over his shoulder and begins filling it with fruits and nuts, their colors rich and inviting. The sweet scent tempts him, and he gives in, sampling a few.

Juice bursts across his tongue—sweet, ripe, unlike anything he's tasted. Each bite leaves him blinking in surprise.

"Leave some for the journey," Ishara chides gently, stepping beside him. Her voice is firm, but her smile softens the warning.

As Uldako digs deeper into the pile, his fingers brush against something cool and smooth. He pulls out a long knife, its blade well-balanced, the hilt wrapped in dark cord. It stirs a memory—a distant echo of the crude blade he once called Haber, back in darker days when he had no one.

He turns and kneels before Kunai, holding out the blade. "Take it," he says. "Carry it with care and wisdom."

Kunai accepts it with big eyes, gripping the hilt with both hands. For a heartbeat, he says nothing. He just nods, his expression filled with quiet resolve. Uldako watches him with quiet pride, knowing the boy is no longer alone—and neither is he.

As Uldako rises, Kunai beams. "Thank you! I'll treasure it. Wait…does this mean you'll teach me to fight?" he asks with excitement.

Uldako, mindful of the dangers that lie ahead, urges restraint. "We'll have time for that later. Patience," he advises, his tone tinged with caution.

Uldako glances around as he remembers his two stone axes. They were taken from him when Lamech and his men seized Ishara and Kunai, leaving him unconscious in the dirt. Everything they carried was brought here. The axes must be somewhere in the camp, but time is slipping away, and by now, one of the freed slaves has likely claimed them as their own.

He lets the thought go.

Instead, his eyes fall upon a two-handed bronze sword near the wall. It must be Lamech's weapon, sheathed in a richly carved scabbard. Uldako lifts it, testing the weight. The balance is excellent. The grip feels made for his hands.

With a sense of rising strength, he straps the sword across his back. The shift from stone to bronze feels like a step into something greater.

"This will serve me well." There's a quiet satisfaction in his voice.

Meanwhile, Ishara seizes the opportunity to don the leather armor she had spotted earlier. With a playful smile, she shoos Uldako and Kunai away, craving a moment of privacy to change. "Out you go, boys. I need a moment to myself," she announces with faint humor.

As Uldako moves toward the doorway, he stops as his eyes catch something. On a nearby table, something glitters in the low light—small, colorful stones, smooth and shining like drops of frozen fire. He steps closer, puzzled. He remembers seeing slavers accept these in trade, but he never knew their worth.

"What are these?" he asks curiously. "They look valuable."

Kunai trots over, peering at the stones with excitement. "Ooooh! Shiny! Now this is real treasure!" he exclaims. "They're not metal. They're special stones," he says. "People use them to buy stuff from traders. My *abba* used to trade sheep for things like grain or knives, but now everyone wants these shiny rocks instead."

Uldako lets out a quiet laugh and scoops the stones into his bag. "I guess it's easier to carry for trade. Well then, we'll be taking these."

As they step outside, the morning light greets them, and so does Šarru, towering and silent, waiting like a guardian at the edge of the clearing.

A few of the freed slaves who walk past them nod in silent gratitude as they begin their new lives. But his gaze shifts to a nearby couple locked in a tense exchange. Their voices are hushed but sharp.

"I'm telling you the truth," the woman insists, her eyes wide with fear. "That's what I heard. Lamech said it himself…we're all in danger."

She glances around then leans in closer. "Listen to me, Xavier. They are creating something. Beings called the *Ašag-dingir*."

The name strikes Uldako. He has heard it once before, and now his curiosity stirs like fire in dry grass. He calls out to the woman.

"Wait. What is the *Ašag-dingir*?" he asks, stepping toward them.

Xavier gives Uldako a quick glance and shrugs. "Ignore my sister. She chases stories and repeats rumors. There is no truth to any of it."

The woman spins toward Uldako, her voice sharp. "I am not making it up."

Uldako steps closer, eyes locked on hers. "Then tell me what you know," he says. "Even if it is only a whisper."

The woman takes a deep breath, her eyes fixed on Uldako. "I served as Lamech's personal slave," she begins. "I tended to his shelter, his clothes, and those of his wives."

Uldako inclines his head, urging her on. "Yes, and?"

She hesitates, then continues. "About a week ago, I overheard Lamech speaking with another man. What was his name? Ida? Ina? No…Irad. That was it. Irad was much older than Lamech. I'd say four, maybe five hundred years. And Lamech spoke to him with respect, almost like a servant to a master."

Uldako's interest sharpens. "Could this Irad be a relative? But more importantly, what did they speak of that troubles you so much?"

The woman's voice trembles as she responds, "They were speaking of the secret arts they've been learning from the *dingir-meš*, a small group of *anunnaki* who descended to earth." She hesitates, then continues. "It seems that Enoch the Terrible, the *dumu* of Cain, not Enoch the Good, who is the *dumu* of Jared, led them down from Mount Senir to dwell among Cain's descendants. Enoch the Terrible is now their high shaman, teaching them forbidden knowledge brought from the heavens."

Uldako's eyes widen as the woman continues, her voice urgent. "These *dingir-meš* are sharing strange powers—sorcery and other hidden arts. I saw Irad show Lamech how his staff could turn into a serpent. I swear I'm not lying. Please believe me."

Her brother rolls his eyes. "Of course no one's going to believe that."

Uldako lifts a hand calmly. "It's all right. Even if it sounds unbelievable, it's still worth hearing. And if there's even a chance it's true, don't you think your sister deserves to be heard?"

Encouraged, the woman steps forward. "Thank you. There's more. Besides sorcery, I heard them speak of the way of the stars—by divination—and advanced crafts like stone-working and metalwork. They're learning how to build stronger fortresses and forge weapons like nothing I've ever seen. They've started mining camps across the land, gathering rare materials for their tools and armor."

She hesitates, her voice dropping. "That is why they need more slaves. I think they're preparing for something. Something big and dark."

Uldako's hand drifts to the hilt of his new bronze sword, unease rising in his chest as he wonders where the weapon truly came from. His gaze returns to the woman, and a flicker of alarm passes through his eyes.

"I've seen the serpent clans," he says quietly. "Their hatred burns deep, especially for those who still honor *Il*. Are you saying they intend to rise against the northern kingdom?"

The woman answers, "I am not sure what to think, but I overheard them boasting about the newfound power they've gained and how it would aid their plans."

Still uncertain, Uldako leans in. "I see, but tell me more about this power."

The woman steps even closer, her voice low and steady. "They spoke of many being trained in these new arts and crafts. Some study the stars, not just to mark the seasons or planting times, but to glimpse what lies ahead. They believe the stars will reveal when the chosen one will come. Others delve deeper into sorcery, becoming shamans like the pygmies. Some train in survival, alchemy, or in forging stronger tools. All of it, they say, comes from the Watchers, a small group from the new fallen *dingir-meš* they not only worship but who now walk among them."

Still trying to piece it all together, Uldako narrows his eyes. "I don't understand half of what you're saying, but tell me this. How does it all connect to the *Ašag-dingir*? What is *Ašag-dingir*?"

The woman's voice is tense but steady. "Yes, yes, I'm getting to that. The *anunnaki*—those who've joined with the clans of Cain—are planning to take human women as wives. They're creating something new…a powerful race called the *Ašag-dingir*. The word *ašag* points to a supernatural force, but not a pure one. It's tied to evil spirits, to sickness, to chaos. And *dingir*, as you know, means *divine being*. They will be *dumu* born of divine blood mixed with corruption."

She pauses, probing Uldako's eyes before she continues. "The plan is that these *dumu* will rise as legends. Some will be giants and warlords, others gifted with shamanic power or unearthly strength. They'll be worshipped as kings and as *dingir-meš*. And if the serpent clans unite behind them, they'll spread their dark religion across the earth—by force."

Uldako staggers back a step, his breath caught in his throat. His eyes search hers, hoping for a trace of doubt. "No," he says softly. "That can't be true." But even as he speaks, the unease in his gut tells him otherwise.

The woman's brother casts Uldako a doubtful look and mutters, "See? My sister is always telling strange stories." He turns to her, already walking away. "Come, Imani. Enough."

Imani lowers her eyes, stung by his dismissal. But Uldako watches her face closely—her belief is real.

"Wait," he says urgently. "Did they say anything else? About when these *Ašag-dingir* would be created?"

Imani lifts her gaze to Uldako and exhales slowly. "I'm not sure when. They said a small group had already begun something, but there was much more! Some of it I didn't hear clearly." She furrows her brow, reaching into memory. "The older man, Irad, spoke of a prophecy. Something about specific bloodlines… names I cannot recall and the coming of a dark prince…important cities…"

She pauses, eyes filling with dread. "They spoke even more about harrowing things. There was a sacred ritual tied to it, a time when the stars will align. They called it the Rite of Celestial Conception. Royal blood is involved. A *lugal* or high priestess would be joined to a *dingir*, and through that union, a *dumu* would be born. Not just any *dumu*—the Dragonborn. The one meant to destroy the seed of the woman."

Uldako feels a shiver of uncertainty ripple through him as he murmurs to himself, "The Dragonborn."

Imani's eyes lock onto Uldako's, her voice unsteady as she speaks. "They say he is the chosen one—born from the seed of the dragon. A vessel for the spirit of *Enki* himself, reborn. To them, he is the new *dingir* of the earth."

She pauses, gauging Uldako's reaction, then presses on, the words spilling like a warning. "When he comes of age, they will give him full dominion—to rule the world and shape it in their image. He'll enforce their worship, their laws, their new order."

"Imani, enough!" her brother snaps, stepping forward with a scowl. "Stop feeding him these lies—these absurd and twisted tales."

Uldako stands speechless, the burden of Imani's words anchoring his thoughts. His thoughts whirl, struggling to make sense of it all. *Too detailed to be fantasy… but could any of it truly be real?* The question claws at him.

Just then, Ishara steps out of the shelter, draped in fresh garments, her face glowing with joy—completely unaware of the tension she's walked into. "Well? How do I look?" she asks, her voice bright with expectation.

Neither Uldako nor Kunai answer. Both remain frozen as they continue to look at Imani, the shadows of her tale still lingering. Ishara pauses, sensing the tension, her smile faltering. "What did I walk into?" she asks, eyes now fixed on Uldako's troubled face.

Before he can speak, Xavier sharply pulls Imani away, muttering that her words are madness. Ishara watches them, her brow furrowing, then turns back to Uldako, searching his face for answers.

As Uldako lifts his eyes to Ishara, the world seems to hold its breath. For a moment, all else fades. She stands in the sunlight, her new armor gleaming—a perfect blend of strength and grace. The dark leather hugs her form like it was shaped by the gods themselves, its surface smooth but scarred with the beauty of experience.

He stares, unable to speak, breath caught in his throat. "You look…uh… good," he finally says, though the words feel far too small.

He looks at the new bow cradled in her hands—elegant, lethal. The wood is polished to a mirror-like sheen, its sinew string catching the light like a strand of gold. Bone and horn reinforce the limbs, etched with intricate designs that shimmer with craftsmanship. Yet it is not the weapon that holds him—it is her. Fierce. Radiant. Unshakable.

Ishara walks past Uldako, Kunai, and Šarru with a mischievous glint in her eye. "Well, you can fill me in on what just happened while we're on the road," she suggests with a playful tone.

With Kunai and Šarru quietly by his side, Uldako remains motionless, still held by the force of Ishara's presence. She pauses mid-step, glances over her shoulder, and flashes a playful smile. "Well? Are you three planning to stand there all day, or shall we move?"

Her voice, light and teasing, cuts through the lingering tension like sunlight through mist. Then, without waiting for an answer, she turns and strides ahead.

Uldako, Kunai, and Šarru exchange glances and fall in step behind her.

As they approach the camp gate, Ishara shouts, "Wait! How silly of us! Let's use those majestic *gudmušen* to hasten our journey!"

Uldako's expression shifts to one of concern as he recalls how Lamech and his wives fled mounted on those very birds. "Ride thee *gudmušen*?" he says with worry evident in his eyes. "There's no way I'm getting on one!"

Moments later, Uldako finds himself perched atop one of the towering birds, its feathered body standing as tall as a man, its elongated neck and head extending the height of two. Glancing back at Ishara and Kunai, who are also mounted on their own feathered steeds, Uldako mutters, "I can't believe I let you talk me into this!"

With mischief sparkling in her eyes, Ishara warns, "Hold on tight!"

Uldako's fear intensifies as he anticipates Ishara's next move. In the blink of an eye, she delivers a swift slap to the bird's rear, propelling them forward with Uldako screaming and clinging desperately as the bird races across the terrain with incredible speed. Ishara and Kunai burst into laughter, their joy echoing through the air as they follow Uldako with Šarru racing beside them.

Kunai is thoroughly enjoying himself, shouting, "Heeehaaa! This is so much fun!" Ignoring Uldako's protests along the way, Ishara and Kunai press onward in their quest to find Seth.

Gradually, Uldako adjusts to the ride, finding his balance and easing into the experience. Catching Ishara's look, he senses her silent affirmation, *I told you riding these birds was a good idea.*

Finally, Uldako admits, "I suppose it wasn't such a terrible idea after all. We're making good time and conserving strength. These birds are surprisingly swift!"

Riding abreast with Ishara and Kunai, they soar forward, Šarru now leading the way. The ground rushes beneath them as Uldako lifts his eyes to the sky, where a fish-eagle circles again with a sharp cry. His mind stays fixed on Imani's words. The wind on his face does little to still the turmoil within. If what she said is true, the world is closer to breaking than he feared.

Ahead, the river glimmers like a silver thread cutting through the land. He tightens his grip on the bird, urgency rising with every beat of the *gudmušen's* stride.

Beside him, Ishara glances over and lifts a hand to the sun, measuring its slow descent. Nearly two hands have passed since they left the camp. She turns to him, voice calm but firm. "You've been silent this whole ride. What did that woman say to trouble you so deeply?"

Uldako draws a slow breath and begins to recount what Imani told him. As he speaks, Ishara listens in silence, her expression darkening with every word.

Before he finishes, Kunai leans forward. "I believe her," he says firmly. "It fits everything you two have told me. All of it."

Uldako and Ishara exchange a glance—quiet, but filled with shared resolve.

"We'll know more when we find Seth," Uldako says. "But we can't afford to waste another day."

Ishara looks ahead and says, "Then let's move. We cross the river and keep heading north—just like we planned, before the raiders."

As the river comes into view, the three riders slow their pace. One by one, they dismount, leaving the *gudmušen* to graze at the edge. With quiet determination, they step into the shallows and begin the next stretch of the journey on foot.

• • •

Two days pass…

The group of four emerges into a vast new land—an endless sea of golden grass swaying beneath the breath of the wind. The sky above stretches wide and unbroken, and the plains roll out before them like the edge of the world.

As they press forward, the beauty around them seems almost surreal, but Uldako's mind drifts—drawn back to the shadows of memory. His mother's face. Imani's words. The uncertain path ahead.

Kunai's voice breaks through, his thoughts like a hammer. "There it is!"

He points ahead, eyes shining with wonder. On the horizon stands a lone hill, and atop it, a towering tree rises like a spear into the sky, its silhouette visible from afar.

"Kenan spoke of this place," Kunai breathes. "A single tree, alone on a hill. That's the mark. We found it."

The others follow his gaze, and a wave of hope breaks over them. Without a word, Uldako, Ishara, Kunai, and Šarru break into a run, racing toward the hill and whatever waits beyond.

20

Fragments

Uldako reaches the hill's summit ahead of the others. He slows, looking at the horizon, eyes searching for any sign of movement—any trace of Kenan or his companions. The wind pulls at his hair as the golden grasses rustle below, but the land ahead offers no clear answer.

Ishara steps up beside him, her breath unsteady. "Anything?"

He shakes his head. "Not yet," he murmurs, though a hint of doubt creeps into his voice. The hope of finding Kenan, the one who might lead them to Seth, fades in his chest.

The wind whispers through the open field, and for a moment, Uldako stands beneath the great sky, unsure which direction to search further.

Kunai's voice calls out from the far side of the hill, sharp with urgency. "Over here! There are signs—someone camped here recently. Come look!"

Uldako turns to Ishara, and she nods. Together they descend the slope, their footsteps quickening with renewed purpose.

At the bottom, they find Kunai crouched beside a cold fire ring. Uldako studies the trampled grass, the disturbed earth. "There were men here," he says. "Three to five. They didn't stay long."

Kunai exclaims with excitement, "This is definitely the spot, but it seems they've moved on."

Ishara narrows her eyes. "Which way did they go? Uldako, you're skilled at tracking, right?"

Uldako glances at Šarru, who sniffs the air and sets off in a northeast direction. "It seems Šarru has already picked up their trail," he confirms.

The group follows Šarru's nose, and soon Kunai calls out as they reach the ridge of the hill. "Look, there's a camp just ahead, near a big lake! Perhaps

Kenan and the others are there, or the people in the camp may have seen where Kenan went."

As Uldako narrows his eyes toward the camp in the distance, a faint, chilling sound reaches his ears.

"Wait...do you hear that?" he mutters.

The wind carries it again—piercing, unmistakable.

"Screams."

Ishara and Kunai freeze beside him, faces tightening as the cries rise louder, sharper. Then Uldako spots the flicker of chaos below—movement, flames, fleeing figures.

"They're under attack," he says grimly. "Raiders."

No more words are needed. Uldako launches forward without hesitation. Šarru bolts beside him, muscles surging beneath thick fur.

Ishara draws her bow in stride, calling out as she passes Kunai, "Stay here, Kun!"

Then she vanishes into the charge.

As Uldako approaches, the screams grow louder. He takes in the scene before him: Approximately ten raiders, clad in leather armor and wielding a mix of wooden clubs, swords, spears with ivory tips, and stone axes, are assaulting the helpless inhabitants of the camp. Some women and children attempt to flee for safety, while others are forcibly dragged from their homes, with the raiders mercilessly slaughtering those who resist.

Approaching stealthily, Uldako recognizes the advantage of surprise; the attackers remain unaware of their presence. Uldako sees a raider dragging a woman from her shelter, her child crying out, "*Ama*! *Ama*!"

The scene before him pulls at memories deep within. In the child's desperate face, Uldako sees his own reflection. Not as he is now, but as he once was—small, frightened, and powerless in the slave camp. As the boy's mother is torn away, her screams blur into another voice, another moment. For an instant, she is no longer a stranger. She becomes his own mother, dragged from him all over again.

Something breaks inside him. The fire within overwhelms him, white-hot and uncontrollable. Rage coils in his chest, pressing against his ribs, demanding release.

Nearby, a man, likely her husband, stands his ground, armed only with a farmer's oxgoad and no armor to protect him. Uldako rushes forward, heart pounding, knowing he won't reach them in time. The raider sneers, effortlessly swinging his club in a brutal arc, delivering a crushing blow that sends the man crashing to the ground. The woman lets out a heart-piercing scream. She snatches up a stick from the ground and charges the raider. The raider strikes her down as well, laughing with open malice. The child watches, shock and confusion in his eyes, tears streaming down his cheeks.

Just as Uldako draws closer, reaching for his new two-handed sword strapped to his back, another raider emerges from the shelter, reveling in the chaos they've wrought. Uldako's fury ignites at the sight of the man's callous enjoyment of their heinous deeds. As the raider catches sight of Uldako, it's too late; a spray of blood erupts from his chest as Uldako's bronze sword cleaves through him.

Simultaneously, the other man shifts his attention toward the commotion, but before he can react, Šarru lunges at him. With the uproar of battle and the villagers' screams drowning out other sounds, some raiders remain oblivious to the unfolding events.

A younger woman breaks through the chaos, rushing toward the boy from the opposite side. In the way she wraps her arms around him without hesitation, Uldako understands at once—it is the boy's sister.

There is nothing more he can do for them. Not now. Others are already dying. He turns to her sharply, pointing to the boy, his voice low but unyielding. "Take him. Get him to safety. Now."

Uldako and Šarru synchronize their movements seamlessly, their eyes locked on their respective targets, aiming to dispatch the enemy swiftly and silently.

Uldako charges toward the next closest shelter where a raider stands unaware, his back turned to Uldako. In one fluid motion, Uldako drives his bronze blade through the raider's back. The tip bursts from his chest in a spray of blood.

The man lets out a strangled scream before crumpling to the ground. Around him, heads snap in Uldako's direction. The chaos pauses for half a heartbeat—then several raiders turn, eyes locking on the new threat.

Three of them charge at him, but Uldako meets the first head-on, their swords clashing in a fierce duel. As the second raider approaches, Šarru intervenes, catching the woman off guard with a ferocious attack. Despite her attempt to flee, Šarru's relentless assault brings her crashing to the ground.

Meanwhile, Uldako engages in combat with the raider who wields a wooden shield and a sword made from a combination of materials: a stone blade set into a bone handle. Though skilled, the raider is no match for Uldako, who gains the upper hand by shattering the blade with a decisive blow from his sword.

Before Uldako's fight can conclude, the arrival of the third raider disrupts the fray, threatening to tip the scales of battle. With quick thinking, the man whose blade lies broken seizes a spear, joining forces with his companion to face Uldako in a desperate bid for victory.

Attempting to fend off both adversaries at the same time, Uldako maneuvers skillfully, parrying their strikes and evading blows. In a crucial moment, an arrow pierces the chest of one of the raiders. Uldako recognizes Ishara's timely intervention, expressing his gratitude with a shout.

Seizing the opportunity, Uldako deftly evades a powerful blow from the remaining raider, swiftly sidesteps, and delivers a crushing overhead strike. Despite the man's attempt to defend with his shield, Uldako's force shatters the wooden barrier and delivers a fatal blow, sending the assailant to his demise.

Uldako and Šarru surge forward with savage speed, a sudden gust of motion and fury. Blood streaks Uldako's face, his eyes wild, his expression that of a beast loose for the kill. He spots another raider and charges with a raw, guttural roar—more animal than man.

The raider stumbles back in horror, eyes darting to the lifeless bodies scattered behind Uldako. He sees the blood, the madness, the fury—and it breaks him.

Fear overtakes reason.

"Run!" he screams, spinning to flee, voice cracking as he calls for his allies to run.

The four remaining raiders watch in stunned disbelief as Uldako and Šarru swiftly dispatch the fleeing raider, crashing him to the ground in an instant. In a moment of shock, another enemy is struck by an arrow, collapsing as his companions turn to flee in terror.

Despite their efforts, Uldako and Šarru find themselves unable to catch the fleeing marauders, their energy depleted from the intense battle. Halting their pursuit, Uldako delivers a menacing warning to the retreating foes, declaring, "If you ever come back here, my sword will be the last thing you see!"

Šarru adds to the intimidation, unleashing a fierce growl and asserting his dominance.

Even with the exhaustion of battle, Uldako can't help but admire Šarru's growth and strength as he acknowledges his loyal friend with pride. With the immediate threat quelled, they make their way back to the camp, where Ishara is already tending to the wounded, the echoes of their victory still reverberating in the air.

An older man, his four hundred years etched in the wisdom of his dark brown eyes, strides toward Uldako with a commanding presence. His dark black hair cascades over his shoulders, framing a long, bushy beard that speaks of age and authority. "I am the *lugal* of this clan," he declares. "May I know your name, young one?"

Uldako nods respectfully. "I am Uldako, *dumu* of Deborah. Who are you?"

The man steps even closer, peering deeply into Uldako's eyes. "Why did you help us? What do you seek from us? Will you enslave us as those raiders intended?"

Taken aback by the old man's cold suspicion, Uldako answers with quiet force, "No. Never. I was once a slave myself, until a man freed me. I could never bring that same torment upon another soul."

He pauses, watching the man's face for a flicker of belief. But the eyes that stare back are hard as stone.

Without another word, Uldako turns and lifts his hair, revealing the scarred brand at the base of his neck. "The mark of *arad-muš* is burned into me. It is not a tale; it is truth. That is why I fight—to break the yoke wherever it is laid on others. To free the enslaved, so they can choose their own path."

The words fall from his mouth with more weight than he expects. For a moment, he feels them settle deep in his chest.

It is no longer just something he says. It is who he is.

The man steps back, his eyes scrutinizing Uldako from head to toe. "In this wicked world, we're not accustomed to encountering goodness anymore. However, for now, I'll extend my trust to you, considering we owe you our lives, *lukur*. I am Raiyan, *dumu-nita* of Zerach."

A small smile graces Uldako's lips as he responds, "Great to meet you. So tell me, Raiyan, what exactly happened here?"

Raiyan gestures toward the camp behind him and explains, "Witness for yourself. This is a humble fishing settlement. We fashion fish traps and rely on the catch for food, and we trade or sell for precious stones. We are, in essence, fishermen. These raiders hail from an unknown barbarian clan and were tasked with seizing control of the entire camp. I overheard one of them mentioning their growing numbers and the need for more provisions."

Ishara and Kunai step closer to join the conversation, accompanied by a few others from the camp. Uldako turns to Raiyan, his expression serious. "I see. They seemed like quite a dangerous bunch. Much like the evil clans from the South."

Raiyan nods, his expression grave. "Indeed, they are from the serpent clans, and we've long been aware of their penchant for raiding and pillaging, but it appears they've now encroached upon the kingdom of Enoch. Hence, the recent surge in rumors of raids on neighboring villages. Today, regrettably, we bore witness to that harsh reality firsthand."

His tone carries the weight of sorrow and frustration. "They sought to enslave us and, in the process, claimed the lives of five of our kin."

Ishara glances at Raiyan, then at the circle of weary faces gathered around them. Bloodied, bruised, but alive. Her own face carries both compassion and resolve. "Then I'm thankful we arrived when we did, before more lives were taken."

Raiyan's eyes, still shadowed with grief, soften slightly as he meets her gaze. "We owe you both our lives," he says, voice low but sincere. "We are a quiet folk. Not warriors. Not like these cursed offspring of Cain who attacked us. We want no part in their darkness."

He pauses, glancing toward the scorched shelters and the wounded villagers nearby. "The northern kingdom has its flaws—yes, even among the *dumu* of light, there are those who wander. But never have we seen such cruelty here. Not like this."

As he speaks, Ishara kneels beside a red-haired woman clutching a wounded leg. Gently, she presses cloth to the injury, her voice steady. "The line of Cain—the Cainites—has always carried rebellion in their blood. But lately, Uldako and I have seen it growing, spreading like a sickness across the land."

Uldako nods grimly, stepping closer. His voice carries the weight of experience. "Every time I cross paths with them, I see it more clearly. That line is rotting from within."

Ishara glances at Raiyan again, then at the villagers gathered behind him. Her brow furrows with thought. "In my homeland, we heard whispers. Stories of Cain, the figurehead of the serpent, or dragon lineage as some call it, reigning over much of the East and the South. But in my homeland, we keep to ourselves, and I'm unfamiliar with the full tale."

She looks around the camp. "Do any of you know where Cain truly came from?"

Raiyan offers his insight, "I don't claim to have all the answers, but from what I understand, long ago, Cain lived in the Northwest with his kin before eventually traveling eastward, where he founded several cities."

Uldako looks at the elder with intrigue and says, "Please, tell us more."

Unexpectedly, a woman of around a hundred years breaks the silence with a sharp voice, "Few here dare to speak the name of Cain, let alone utter it freely."

Another man nearby adds, "Indeed, his name is believed to carry a curse!"

Stepping forward, Ishara queries, "What curse?"

Raiyan, the elder, silences the murmurs of the crowd with a commanding gesture. "Let's not fall prey to the superstitions spread by the uninformed," he admonishes, his stern gaze sweeping over the gathering. "There are many tales about Cain, but only a few hold any truth. What I can tell you is this: Some know him as Kish, the unkillable. The legend I've heard goes like this:

"In the ancient days, *Il* Most High, now called *An* by those in the east, marked Cain after he murdered his brother Abel. *An* spoke to Cain, saying, 'Now you are under a curse and driven from the ground, which opened its mouth to receive your brother's blood from your hand. When you work the ground, it will no longer yield its crops for you. You will be a restless wanderer on the earth.'

"Cain lamented, 'My punishment is more than I can bear. Today you are driving me from the land, and I will be hidden from your presence; I will be a restless wanderer on the earth, and whoever finds me will kill me.' Righteous *Il*, in His mercy, responded, 'Not so; if anyone kills Cain, he will suffer vengeance seven times over.' Then the Lord put a mark on Cain so that no one who found him would kill him."

Uldako stares at Raiyan, his thoughts churning, unsure what to make of the tale. But before he can speak, Kunai breaks the silence.

"What is this mark?" he asks with eagerness.

Raiyan's gaze settles on him, steady and unreadable. "None of us have ever seen Cain, lad. The mark is still a mystery."

Kunai lowers his eyes, the answer leaving a quiet disappointment in its wake.

Turning to Uldako, Raiyan inquires, "But tell me, what brings you all to our corner of the world? Where do you hail from?"

Before Uldako can respond, Ishara interjects, "We seek a legendary warrior named Seth or a man named Kenan who passed by here recently."

Raiyan gives a slow nod. "I know of whom you speak. Yes, Seth is the younger *šeš* of Cain."

Uldako and Ishara exchange stunned glances, both momentarily at a loss for words, learning they are brothers. Seeing their confusion, Raiyan tilts his head slightly. "Ah, I see. You're not familiar with the ancient bloodlines."

Before either can reply, a younger man, no more than forty, chimes in with a dismissive laugh. "Raiyan, the young ones these days don't care for old stories. We live in the now. Enjoy life—that's what matters!"

Uldako turns to him, his voice calm but firm. "Perhaps that is our problem. We humans are so engrossed in the present, consumed by our own desires, that we overlook the truth—the very essence that grants us comprehension and, consequently, fosters peace and purpose in our lives. Without truth, existence lacks significance."

His words fall over the group like a quiet wind. Ishara and several others glance at him, surprised by the sudden weight of wisdom in his voice. Even Uldako seems caught off guard by what he's just said.

The younger man lowers his gaze, shaken into silence.

Turning back to Raiyan, Uldako steps forward, his brow furrowed with urgency. "Tell me, how can Seth be Cain's brother? It makes no sense. Cain is the very image of corruption, but Seth—I've met him. I've seen the goodness in him with my own eyes!"

An elder emerges from one of the nearby shelters with a cough, commanding the attention of the entire assembly. Uldako sees the significance of this man from the reverent hush that falls over the crowd and the respectful demeanor exhibited toward him.

"Great-grand *abba*, you should rest," Raiyan says gently, stepping forward to steady the old man. The elder's frailty is plain, his form bent, his steps slow, his age etched deep into his face. Turning to the others, Raiyan adds with respect, "This is my great-grand *abba*, Zerach, the former leader of our fishing village."

Uldako and Ishara offer quiet greetings as another villager brings forth a wooden chair. Zerach lowers himself into it with care then lifts his gaze to the gathering, his voice raspy but sharp. "I've heard your words," he says. "And it grieves me to see how lost the younger ones have become."

He turns his eyes toward Uldako. "You spoke truly, *lu-kur*. This is why many are drifting from *Il*. Not out of rebellion alone, but ignorance. They no longer know the ancient truths." His eyes, weathered and piercing, sweep the group. "Let me remind you."

Though his body shows signs of decline, Uldako senses a strength in him still, something deeper than flesh. The man must be well over five hundred years old, though some strange illness has clearly worn him down.

Zerach clears his throat, his voice low and steady, wrapped in reverence. "Cain and his siblings were born to Adam and his wife, Eve." Zerach looks to the horizon, as if looking beyond the present. "Their names are not just carved in memory, but they echo across generations, enduring like stone."

A hush settles over the group as the elder continues, his eyes shimmering with the gravity of what he's about to share. "I once stood before Seth, *dumu* of Adam, a man shaped by faith and strength. And I met Enoch, the blessed one. The man who walks with *Il*."

Zerach's expression shifts, his gaze darkening as he recounts, "Conversely, I also crossed paths with Cain, the one destined for darkness. Those encounters from my youth are etched deep within me, their memories as vivid as the day they occurred."

Uldako's curiosity swells as he says in awe, "Please, go on!"

Zerach nods, affirming, "They are an old family, some say they are the first human family, others say there were humans before them. Personally, I do not know, but I do know that this family changed everything. Adam and Eve changed the world forever." With a sweeping gesture encompassing the assembled people, he adds, "From them, all of us trace our lineage."

Uldako, his impatience evident, interjects, "But where did they come from?"

Zerach takes a slow breath before continuing. "Most people today—especially those of Cain's line—do not know the whole account. Cain's *dumu* shares only what he chooses, shaping the memory of their elders to serve his own design.

"The truth is, Cain was the firstborn of Adam—whom some call Adama or Adapa—and was raised alongside his younger brother, Abel. But Cain's path darkened when he killed Abel, an act that led to his banishment from their ancestral homeland as punishment.

"In time, Cain founded his own lineage, building a city he named Enoch, after his first-born *dumu*. Despite his rebellious nature, Cain's descendants thrived, producing many descendants. They established powerful clans, and it's said they built over sixty fortified cities, spreading their influence across the land."

He pauses, allowing his words to sink in before continuing. "Meanwhile, Cain's parents, Adam and Eve, had many more *dumu-meš* in the Northwest—potentially around fifty in total. After Cain and Abel, they brought Seth into the world, whose lineage we honor as the men and women of righteousness—the *dumu* of light!"

Uldako is stunned, grappling with the revelation that the man who rescued him, Seth, is the third son of Adam.

Ishara poses a question, "But where did Adam and Eve come from?

Zerach looks at her with warmth in his eyes and begins, "I am not sure, but some tales unfold with *Il* crafting the first humans in His own likeness. The *dumu* of light say that *Il* is righteous and holy, yet He embodies love as well. Nevertheless, there are those, even among the realms of Etana in the North, who have grown callous in spirit."

The elder turns to the ground, regret etched on his face. "I must confess, I, too, have succumbed to growing cold, and now, on my deathbed, I rue it. I ought to have guided this community more effectively and shared the truth of *Il* with all of you! Yet, much like many in this present age, I prioritized my earthly desires. Regrettably, now most of the younger generation follows suit."

Uldako interjects abruptly, "But Seth and his descendants remain faithful, correct?"

"You speak truly, young one," the elder says with a knowing smile. "Seth and his line still honor *Il*, urging the rest of us not to forget His ways. Especially Enoch, the revered *En-Lugal*, known in the South as Etana. He walks closer to *Il* than most dare dream. His name carries weight both in heaven and on earth."

Uldako tries to grasp it all, the gravity of ancient names and unseen histories pressing down like heavy fog. He isn't sure what to believe...not yet.

But Zerach isn't finished. His voice hardens with sorrow. "When Cain was cast out, *Il's* word was fulfilled. Even now, Cain wanders cursed, unable to draw fruit from the soil, his hands rejected by the earth itself. *Il* has turned the harvest away from him."

Kunai's eyes open wide with excitement. "So you saw the mark of Cain? What is it?"

The elder raises a hand calmly, offering Kunai a gentle glance. "In time, young one. But remember, there is a difference between the curse and the mark. *Il* first declared Cain cursed from the ground. He said the soil would no longer yield its strength to him. That was the curse. Only afterward did *Il* set a mark upon him, so that no one would dare kill him."

He pauses to take a breath, his gaze turning distant. "Perhaps that curse played some part in his path. Cut off from the land's bounty, Cain became a wanderer, and in time, a marauder, taking what he desired. His descendants have followed suit, repeating the sins of their *abba*."

The elder's voice softens. "As I said, he wandered far, founding cities, raising clans. And no one laid a hand on him. They still honor him as their great *abba*, for he carries the mark *Il* placed on him."

Uldako stands silent, the depth of truth pressing into him like stone. He draws in a slow breath, then mutters, "Why does no one speak of these things? Why..." He trails off, his gaze falling to the ground.

Ishara picks up on Uldako's unspoken thoughts, adding, "Indeed, because humanity is more fixated on fulfilling their immediate desires than focusing on the truths of life. I wonder why we humans are like this?"

Amidst the circle of elders and mature men and women, Kunai raises his hand—not with the naivety of a child, but with the quiet boldness of one who knows he belongs in this sacred exchange. Though smaller in stature, he stands with purpose, his voice calm and sincere. "But why did you say Cain built a city in the name of his *dumu* Enoch, when Enoch belongs to Seth's family line?"

He glances from face to face, then adds with steady conviction, "And you still haven't told us what the mark of Cain is."

Zerach chuckles softly. "Ah, an insightful question, young one. A person can indeed be known by many names. Cain, for example, has a *dumu-nita* named Enoch, but he is also referred to as Uanna—just as Cain is known as Kish. However, the Enoch you're thinking of is from the fifth generation of Seth's line. His *abba's* name, if memory serves me, is Jared."

Uldako regards the man with a probing look and asks, "How do you come by all this knowledge?"

Zerach lowers his gaze to his weathered hands, a look of humility softening his features. "We elders have learned these stories from our ancestors, passed down through the generations—many of whom still live among us. Even now, my great *abba* is alive. Some elders, especially those in the far North, still cling to the full truth. But the further east and south you go, many, like us, hold on to mere fragments of that knowledge. And as time flows, those fragments slip through our fingers like sand, growing fewer with each passing generation, or even worse, those fragments are twisted.

"Sadly, most people today care little for truth. With time, much has changed. We see it all around us—thievery, violence, even murder, right here in our own lands. It's the nature of mankind. Look at us now—it was never like this when I was a young lad."

Uldako senses the anguish in the man's eyes and asks, "Why do you think the world is so steeped in evil? How did it all start?"

Zerach fixes Uldako with a penetrating gaze and begins, "Allow me to share what I do know, and all of you gathered here should heed my words. In my youth, I paid little attention to such matters, but in my twilight years, I've come to see the folly of my ignorance. So, I implore you, listen closely to my tale and glean from it what you will."

The people around them step closer, and more join as they are waved closer to hear the words of the elder.

Zerach takes a deep breath and says, "As a young lad, I was fortunate to come of age under the peaceful rule of Adam and his *dumu* Seth after him. Our home was a land where reverence for *Il* permeated every aspect of life. Our guiding principle, the cornerstone of our society, was simple yet profound: Worship *Il* and treat others as you would wish to be treated."

Zerach draws a long breath, his eyes distant, as though gazing through the veil of time. "I once stood among the crowd when Enoch ascended to kingship, taking the mantle from his *abba*, Jared, who was appointed *En-Lugal* by *Il* Himself. Enoch is the seventh *En-Lugal* from Adam, but he is more than a king. He is a *šanga*, a high priest or prophet who communes with the Most High.

"When Enoch spoke at the ascension of the *En-Lugal,* he spoke of an era when peace blanketed the earth, before the darkness he called *sin* descended upon humanity. It crept like a shadow into the hearts of mankind, severing their bond with *Il.* But the Most High did not just forsake humanity. He..."

Zerach coughs and a hush descends over the gathering as they all wait with bated breath for truth to be revealed.

Kunai can't contain his curiosity, "What? Tell us?"

The wind quiets. Even the birds seem to hold their breath. Then—without warning—a sharp hiss cuts through the silence.

An arrow whistles from the trees behind Zerach, fast and silent as a serpent's strike. It strikes Zerach in the back.

He gasps—once—his breath stolen by the blow. The shaft punches through his chest. For a heartbeat, he remains upright, eyes wide, lips trembling with unspoken words. Then his body crumples.

Gasps erupt from the crowd. Shock ripples through them. The elder's chair topples as Uldako lunges forward—but it's too late. Zerach lies still.

His last words, heavy with truth, fall upon the living like prophecy.

21

Water

For a heartbeat, the world stops.

Then Uldako explodes into motion.

A quake of emotion stirs behind his eyes.

The elder lies dead, his final words still echoing in the silence. Not from age or time but from a coward's arrow. Cut down mid-truth.

Uldako's hands clench around his sword hilt.

He looks where the arrow came from, and there they are, shadowy figures pouring toward them. The same raiders who once fled…now returned, and they've brought others. Twenty men, maybe more. Spears. Axes. Cruel eyes glinting with hate.

The camp erupts in disorder as more arrows fly. Children scream. Elders scramble for cover. Despair creeps like smoke, but Uldako stands tall.

"Hear me! Gather yourselves and think! Today, we fight for our lives! Follow my lead and we will survive!" His voice cracks like stone splitting. He scans the enemy, fast, calculating. There's no time for fear.

"Ishara!" he points to a low shelter behind them. "That roof! Now! Take the high ground! Shoot at will!"

She's already moving, bow in hand.

"Šarru, to me! *Hrrk*!" he commands, as the great bear growls and bounds to his side, fangs bared. Uldako draws his blade.

Turning to the men, he directs them to seize sturdy wooden planks used for fish butchering, and then to form a defensive line with him. With a firm voice, Uldako instructs those too young or unable to wield a blade to flee in the opposite direction and hide. To Uldako's surprise, the able women of the village join the battle as if they are used to it.

The clan swiftly assumes their positions in a half-moon formation as instructed by Uldako. He continues to issue directives, emphasizing the importance of unity in combat. Meanwhile, Ishara has ascended to the roof of the house behind them, unleashing a barrage of arrows upon the advancing raiders.

"As the enemy draws close, we'll brace for their initial assault by forming our shields into a unified defense," Uldako instructs those beside him.

He turns to a few nearby men, each gripping their fear but standing strong. "You three," he calls out, voice sharp, "gather spears from the raiders we felled earlier. Take position right behind us and await my signal."

They nod, urgency in their eyes.

He steps closer, his tone firm but focused. "When they charge, we'll hold the front with shields. Your task is to strike through the gaps. Attack like vipers, fast, hard, and without hesitation. Wait for my command. And when it comes, drive your spears like your kin's lives depend on it, because they do."

He meets their eyes one by one. "Stand your ground. Be swift. Be unbreakable. Today, you fight for your homes, for your people, and for the breath in your lungs!"

He steps and turns to look at the whole group. "We will not let evil triumph today!" Uldako's voice booms, rallying the morale of the clan, who echoes his fervent cry.

As the raiders breach the camp gate and charge toward them, Ishara's arrows find their marks, felling three men. With seventeen foes remaining, Uldako notes a weakness in the enemy ranks as they continue to approach.

"It appears they lack a clear plan of action, which points to weak or no leadership within their group. They think you are an easy target, just a normal fishing village! Their actions lack structure and cohesion. Some rush ahead while others lag behind, exposing their vulnerability. We can claim victory! Shields together!"

Two young raiders reach the shields and strike, but to no avail. Uldako, sensing their failed attempt, shouts with authority, "Spears, now!" The three men he directed earlier thrust and find their targets, felling the raiders.

"Fifteen left! Keep it up and they won't break through; it's working!" Uldako shouts, while Ishara's arrow finds its mark.

"Fourteen!" she shouts.

Impressed by Ishara's deadly precision, a brief smile flickers across Uldako's face as he glances her way. But there's no time to waste, as another wave surges forward, nine raiders crashing into the shield wall with brutal force.

A hulking raider swings a massive axe with a savage roar. The blow splinters part of a shield and carves deep into the defender's shoulder, dropping him to one knee.

"Protect the right flank!" Uldako shouts. "Middle! Thrust now!"

The defenders obey. Spears drive forward through the narrow gaps. Two raiders drop with gurgling cries. A third staggers back, blood pouring from a wound in his gut.

"Twelve still left!" Uldako shouts through the chaos like a hammer.

"Ten!" Ishara shouts back as her arrows claim two more targets.

An arrow whizzes past Ishara's head, causing her to quickly locate the source. She spots the man who targeted the elder earlier, his bow poised for another deadly shot.

Uldako, sensing the same imminent danger, looks at Šarru and gestures urgently toward the enemy. "*Hrrk*!" he commands.

Šarru tears past the shield wall, his massive form moving with startling speed. Raiders stumble back in disbelief, too slow to react as the great bear barrels through them, eyes locked on the enemy.

Ishara ducks as another arrow whistles past her cheek. She turns in time to witness the beast's charge. Awe flashes in her eyes as Šarru moves like no creature his size should.

The archer sees him, but it is too late.

With a savage lunge, Šarru slams into the man, knocking him flat. The bow clatters to the earth, the arrow never loosed. Claws dig in and the struggle ends before it can begin.

"Thank you, Šarru!" Ishara calls with relief and pride. The beast lifts his head, bloodied and unbowed, the threat silenced.

As the rest of the raiders clash against the shield wall, Uldako catches sight of two peeling away, circling toward Ishara's position on the roof. "Ishara, two on your left!" he calls out.

Without missing a beat, Ishara looses an arrow into the first man's chest, sending him tumbling off the slope. But before she can knock another, the second raider scrambles up and charges toward her, axe raised high.

Realizing she does not have enough time, Ishara backs away slowly, eyes wide, and raises her hands. "Please, I surrender! You can take me captive, just don't hurt me," she pleads, her voice trembling just enough to sound convincing.

The raider hesitates, grinning with sick satisfaction as he approaches. "Smart girl," he sneers, lowering his guard.

But Ishara is no victim.

In a flash, her hand whips behind her back, retrieving a hidden dagger. Before the raider can blink, the blade flies, burying itself deep in his throat. His smirk fades in an instant, and he collapses over the edge with a choking gasp.

Ishara spins around, eyes scanning the field. "Eight left!" she shouts clear and strong.

Uldako acknowledges Ishara's count with a sharp nod, a flicker of relief passing through him. But it's short-lived.

To his right, the line is buckling.

One of the raiders, the massive one wielding the two-handed axe, strikes again with brutal force. The heavy blade crashes through a defender's shield and buries itself in his chest. The man cries out and falls backward, leaving a gap in the formation.

The raider snarls and steps forward, circling around the exposed edge of the shield wall, raising his axe for the final blow on the fallen villager.

Uldako's gaze snaps to Šarru, who is just returning from his last kill. "Šarru!" Uldako roars as he points to the enemy.

In a blur of muscle and rage, the great bear lunges. The raider barely notices in time. Šarru slams into him with crushing weight, driving him to the earth. He tries to keep the beast's jaws at bay with his bare hands, but a heartbeat later, Šarru's teeth clamp down on the raider's throat, silencing him forever.

"Seven!" Uldako bellows.

The sheer ferocity of the beast stuns the attackers in the middle ranks, and Uldako wastes no time. "Left and middle, thrust now!"

Spears shoot forward through the shield wall's narrow gaps. One raider crumples with a cry.

"Six!" Uldako shouts. "You brought this on yourselves, you cowards!"

Another raider stumbles back, clutching his side as blood pours between his fingers. He does not fall, but his wound is grave. He looks around, his eyes wild with fear as reality sets in. Blood streams down his arm. Realizing the tide has turned, he staggers backward and shouts, "Run!"

Great fear ripples through the enemy ranks. The raiders break, fleeing in all directions.

But Ishara is ready.

She looses two arrows in quick succession, and both find their marks. Two men collapse mid-sprint.

"Four!" she calls out, already reaching for another arrow.

Uldako and Šarru are in motion. The bear barrels ahead like a living boulder, slamming into one raider with devastating force. Uldako's sword cleaves another down with a single, brutal strike.

The final two raiders don't make it far.

The villagers swarm them, dragging them to the ground. No mercy is shown, only justice, swift and burning, delivered by those left grieving.

The battle is won. Peace slowly returns.

When the chaos subsides, Raiyan and a few others embark on the task of locating their family members who had sought refuge in hiding. Quiet calls echo through the broken camp as some survivors emerge from the shadows, clinging to one another in relief or mourning.

Meanwhile, Uldako, Ishara, Kunai, and Šarru return to where the elder fell. Their eyes fall on Zerach, who is now lying lifeless amidst the aftermath of the raid. Ishara steals a glance at Uldako, observing the depth of sorrow etched upon his features as he looks upon the old man's still form.

Beside them, Kunai's shoulders tremble. His eyes brim with tears as he looks down at the fallen elder who had spoken with such wisdom, only to be taken in an instant.

Ishara wraps her arms around him, holding him close. "It's alright," she whispers, her voice tender and sure. "Sometimes the ones who walk ahead of us in life must take their rest before us. But they remind us of what matters, of the time we still have with each other."

Kunai nods slowly, pressing his face into her side.

Uldako's eyes linger on Zerach's still face. He says nothing. The silence stretches, deep, reverent, and full of things that cannot be spoken aloud. The wind stirs gently through the grass, and for a moment, time itself seems to hold its breath.

At last, he turns to Ishara, his eyes distant, his voice low. "What is a man's life?" he murmurs, each word pulled from the weight in his chest. "And what worth lies in chasing pleasures or hoarding possessions, when in the end, all of it slips through our fingers?"

He pauses, searching the sky as if the answer might be shown there. "One enters this world with nothing and leaves it the same way. So what is the point of it all?" His voice fades into the wind, heavy with reflection.

Ishara watches him quietly, her expression soft but unknowable.

Before she can answer, footsteps approach from behind and a calm voice breaks through the reverie. "I've been wondering the same," a man says warmly, his steps slow with weariness. He bears the look of one who has claimed victory in battle, yet he still fights the pain of grief within. "I am Thokar, *dumu* of Raiyan."

Thokar's eyes drift to Zerach's body, then to the scattered villagers, some tending wounds, others digging shallow graves. "Death is a cruel teacher," he murmurs. "But look around, Uldako. All these lives are still breathing because of you. We mourn, yes, but we must also live. And right now, that means standing with those who remain."

Uldako gives a slow nod, his gaze heavy with thought.

Thokar places a hand over his heart. "We have little to give. But would you stay, just a while longer, and eat with us? No one here has tasted a single bite today, and grief is heavier on an empty stomach." He glances around at the pale faces, the hollow eyes. "Everyone's shaken. And food alone won't heal that, but sharing a meal might remind us that we're still here. Still alive."

Uldako looks up.

Thokar meets his eyes with a tired but genuine smile. "Most of our supplies were taken or burned. But if your strength allows, we can pull fresh fish from the lake. Enough for us, and enough for your journey ahead."

Uldako glances around at the villagers again, some still tending wounds, others mending broken shelters, their faces etched with weariness. He opens his mouth, his tone hesitant. "I'm grateful for the offer, but perhaps it's better I stay and help. There's much to do."

Thokar steps forward, his voice filled with caring, "They'll manage, for now. What they'll truly need before the day's end is food, and I can't catch enough to feed the whole camp alone."

He searches Uldako's heart, eyes narrowing with quiet understanding. "I can see it in your eyes—you've suffered loss before, like all of us in this cruel world. Come. Let this moment be more than duty. Out there, on the open water, beneath the wide sky…something settles. The mind slows. The ache quiets. It brings healing in ways words cannot."

A faint smile touches his lips, though his tone shifts with strength. "But it's not all stillness. Beneath that calm surface, giants await—fish with bronze-scaled backs and teeth like carved bone. We face them from slender boats with barbed spears. One moment it's peace; the next, it's chaos. A different kind of battle—one that demands focus, strength, and instinct."

He gestures to the shimmering lake beyond the trees. "And the reward? Enough food to feed the whole camp. A feast worthy for a *lugal*."

Uldako notices Thokar's genuine attempt to lighten the heavy atmosphere and appreciates it, even if he can see intense pain behind those eyes. This is a man who thinks of others more than himself.

Just then, Ishara's stomach rumbles. She nudges Uldako with a sly grin, her eyes bright despite the weariness clinging to her. "Go. We're all hungry. Kun and I will help the others here. You've earned a little calm and maybe a little peace on the lake. Moments like these make life worth living. Take them when you can."

A reluctant smile forms on Uldako's face. "Well," he says with a chuckle, "how can I refuse a test of strength with bronze-scaled monsters?"

Thokar's face lights up. "Then it's settled! And while we fish, I'll share stories, rivers that run through jungle temples, sea beasts that shattered boats in a single strike, fish with eyes like moons. You'll not regret it."

Uldako raises an eyebrow. "Sounds like you've got a thousand tales, but let's start with one: how to find a fish with a spear without losing it."

Thokar smiles and claps him on the shoulder. "A fine place to begin. Come then! Let's fill these bellies before the stars find us. Follow me to the boat!"

As Uldako and Thokar make their way to the boat, Ishara turns to Kunai with a determined look. "Alright, Kun, while we wait for them, let's lend a hand in repairing the camp. If we help the villagers restore it, we can also inquire about Seth while we're at it."

Kunai nods in agreement, and the two of them begin aiding and engaging with the villagers.

Meanwhile, Uldako and his newfound fishing mentor approach the boat. As Uldako eyes the small boat, his jaw drops slightly, and he can't help but remark, "Are we supposed to fit in that tiny thing?" He gestures toward the compact dugout boat, which seems barely spacious enough for two people.

Thokar responds with a touch of pride and jest, "Indeed, my *dusa*! Don't tell me a mighty warrior like yourself is afraid of a little water?"

Uldako approaches the dugout cautiously, inspecting it with a mixture of apprehension and curiosity. "Well, I've never been on a dugout tree trunk like this before," he admits, his tone hesitant. "It's not that I'm scared, exactly…just cautious," he explains, though his nervous expression and the beads of sweat forming on his forehead betray his true feelings.

Thokar, stepping confidently onto the little boat, reassures him, "Trust me! This dugout is safe. Look!"

Uldako takes one step back when he sees it move from side to side. "I am not so sure about this," he admits.

"Ah, Uldako, fear not! This boat may seem small, but it's a mighty vessel, crafted by these hands of mine from the heart of a towering cedar tree. I chose the strongest, straightest trunk, and with patience and skill, I hollowed it out to create this beauty. Look at its sleek lines, its smooth surface—proof of its strength and stability. I've tested it myself on the waters many times, and it rides steady, like a leaf on a gentle breeze. Trust in its craftsmanship, trust in its strength. Step aboard, and let's go fishing!"

Uldako gathers his courage and steps into the boat. His legs tremble under the unfamiliar motion, causing him to plop down onto the boat floor.

Thokar's hearty laughter fills the air at the sight, and he reassures Uldako, saying, "No need to fret, my *dusa*. It's a common mishap for first-timers. Now, let me teach you the art of rowing." Thokar patiently imparts the essentials of boat handling and spearfishing to Uldako as they venture further into the depths of the lake.

On land, another woman approaches Ishara and Kunai, seeking their help, "Would you be so kind as to lend your aid in repairing the gate? Without it protecting us, the threats from beasts and man remain very real."

Ishara gladly accepts the task, and as they diligently work on the gate, the woman notices the snake emblem adorning Ishara's armor. Curious, she questions, "Why bear the serpent emblem if you and Uldako clearly reject their wicked ways?"

Ishara pauses her work, considering the question, then recounts the emblem's origin and its significance. Ishara explains how she found the armor, and concluding, she reflects, "I believe it will be wise to erase the emblem. I wouldn't want misunderstandings as we journey on. Yet, for protection, I must keep wearing it until I secure more suitable armor."

The woman's eyes widen with revelation. "Oh, my *dumu-munus* is a skilled blacksmith, trained recently by a wanderer. Not just any wanderer, but an elder with centuries of wisdom! I'm certain she can help!"

Ishara's face lights up with excitement. "Oh, that would be wonderful!"

The woman clasps Ishara's hands warmly. "It's the least we can do after you saved our entire village. I'll introduce you to her once we're finished here. Her name is Kesia, and my name is Ketzariah."

Back on the water, Uldako prepares himself to catch his first fish of the lake. With a fishing spear in hand and a rope attached to it, he searches the water intently. "Impressive job with those five fish, Thokar. Now, let's see if I can catch at least one!"

Thokar points toward movement in the water. "It's the great one! To your right, Uldako!"

Uldako's eyes follow Thokar's gesture, and he shivers as he beholds a fish as large as the boat itself. "Oh my! Bows and arrows! Shields and axes! It's enormous! What is it?" he exclaims.

Thokar's eyes lock onto the fish, studying its every movement. "I just call it *the great one* or *the big one*. I have only seen it once, when I was younger. Never again, until today!" he says with a grin, rising swiftly to his feet. "Stay focused before it slips away! Look! It's turning around, coming right at you!"

As Uldako wobbles to his feet in the dugout, his arms flail slightly as he tries to steady himself. His heart races, not just from excitement but from the sheer ridiculousness of what he's about to attempt. *Thokar's right*, he thinks, eyeing the fish that seems more like a monster than a meal. *This is the big one, and if I don't focus, I'll either lose it or end up being the one caught!* He glances at the enormous creature with fear. *That thing could either feed the entire camp or just have me for lunch!*

With a steady hand, Uldako readies his spear, his eyes hawk-still on the fish as he waits for the perfect moment. As the creature draws near, Thokar's voice cuts through the tension, urging him into action. "Now is your chance!"

With his will fixed like iron, Uldako propels himself forward, unleashing the spear with all the strength he can muster. The weapon finds its mark, piercing the water with deadly accuracy. But just as victory seems within reach, the fish retaliates with a surge of unimaginable strength, wrenching the rope with a force that nearly topples Uldako from the boat.

As he tumbles backward, the urgency in Thokar's voice cuts through the chaos. "Uldako, the rope!" he shouts, his words a lifeline in the tumultuous sea of battle.

With fire coursing through his veins, Uldako jumps into action, his movements borne by instinct and survival. His fingers close around the rope, each fiber thrumming with the raw power of the creature below. With each tug, the fish tests his resolve, challenging him to match its strength with his own. But Uldako refuses to yield, his grip firm as he braces himself against the ceaseless pull of the deep.

Thokar assesses the situation quickly. "The fish wasn't hit in a vital spot," he shouts, his tone grave. "Uldako, now you have a fight on your hands. He is fast!"

Confusion clouds Uldako's expression as he turns to Thokar. "Fight? What do you mean exactly?"

Thokar's eyes twinkle with amusement as he responds, "Don't you feel the fight in the rope? That power? It's now you against him, and victory is anyone's to claim!"

Uldako's heart pounds with excitement as the fish surges forward, pulling the dugout along with it. Gripping the rope tightly, Uldako braces himself against the unyielding force of the creature beneath the surface. With each surge, Uldako's determination grows stronger.

"The only way you can claim victory is if you tire him out. It is not about strength but skill! Relax your grip!" Thokar shouts with excitement.

The fish dashes forward with even greater force, causing the thin rope to strain dangerously. Uldako grits his teeth, his knuckles white as he clings to the rope. "It's going to break," he shouts over the rush of water.

Thokar watches the tension with a keen eye, his voice calm amidst the chaos. "Remember what I told you," he calls out, his words cutting through the roar of the waves as the boat is pulled along by the fish. "Relax your grip! When the fish pulls hard, give it more rope to lessen the tension. As soon as it slows, draw it in and keep the line tight at all times!"

Uldako's heart races as he tries to follow Thokar's instructions, his focus intense. With each surge of the fish's power, he releases more rope, allowing it to swim away. As the fish's strength wanes, he begins to pull it in, little by little.

Thokar's voice rings out with pride as Uldako begins to master the art of the struggle. "Now you're getting the hang of it, Uldako," he declares proudly.

The relentless tug-of-war between man and beast unfolds across the vast expanse of the lake. The fish pulls the boat in every direction imaginable, its immense strength testing Uldako and Thokar to their limits. With each powerful surge, Thokar deftly maneuvers the boat, guiding it through the tumultuous waters.

Their voices echo across the lake as the struggle with the mighty fish drags on, their determination unwavering despite the creature's evasive dance. Time seems to blur as the fish darts and twists, just beyond reach. Though sweat drips and his muscles cramp, Uldako grins and calls out, "I'm naming this fish Kaskal!"

Thokar gives him a puzzled glance. "Kaskal? What does that mean?"

Uldako chuckles, wiping his brow. "I don't know! But doesn't it sound like a creature so mighty it refuses to be caught?"

Thokar laughs softly, shaking his head. "A fish with a name as elusive as its nature—seems fitting."

Uldako grins. "Indeed! I think it's earned it."

Finally, after what feels like an eternity, the fish begins to tire, its movements growing sluggish as it nears the boat. The fish's broad, muscular tail sweeps back and forth with a powerful rhythm, while its sharp fins slice through the water like blades. With a swift and practiced motion, Thokar plunges his knife into the fish's head, bringing an end to the great battle.

"We got it, Uldako! Well done!" Thokar exclaims, a grin of victory spreading across his face.

Uldako, breathless from the intense battle, offers his gratitude. "Thank you, but it was you who made all this possible," he says humbly.

While Thokar secures the fish to the boat, Uldako takes a moment to admire their hard-won prize, marveling at the sheer size and beauty of the magnificent catch. He is struck by its imposing presence as the fish looms large, its sleek, silver scales shimmering in the sunlight like polished armor, with hints of iridescence reflecting hues of azure and emerald. Its massive form undulates gracefully beneath the surface, powerful muscles used to propel it through the water with effortless ease. Kaskal exudes an air of primal strength and majesty, a silent emblem of the untamed beauty of the natural world. Uldako can't help but feel a sense of reverence and wonder in the presence of such a magnificent creature.

After Thokar finishes securing the colossal fish to the boat, he sits back to catch his breath and looks at their surroundings.

"Uldako," Thokar begins, eyes taking in the beauty of the lake all around them. "Ever since I was a young boy, I have never handled sorrow well—losing those I love, and worse, watching others carry that loss. I flee to the wild places, to the water for peace and clarity. Thank you for coming with me. Now we can go to those who bear that grief, put food in their hands, and, by doing so, if only a little, lighten the weight they carry."

Uldako meets his eyes and simply inclines his head in a slow, measured acknowledgment. No other words are needed.

As they begin their journey back home, the weight of the catch dragging behind them, Uldako can't shake off the reality of what just happened. He turns to Thokar, his voice tinged with wonder. "Ishara and Kunai won't believe this!"

Thokar's eyes sparkle with shared excitement. "Your joy over this experience is evident, my *dusa*. It seems you've caught more than just a fish today! Consider the fishing spear a token of this unforgettable adventure, and may it serve as a reminder of the thrill that awaits you on your next hunt."

Uldako's gratitude swells as he accepts the gift, his heart warm from this unexpected gesture. "No one has ever given me anything before, except Seth. Thank you, Thokar. This means a lot to me."

Back on solid ground, Ishara and Kunai stand, surveying their handiwork alongside Ketzariah, the grateful woman they are aiding in fortifying the gate.

"Thank you both so much for your invaluable assistance!" she exclaims, her eyes shining with gratitude. "Now, allow me to go and introduce you to my *dumu-munus*, Kesia. She really is a remarkable armor crafter, truly gifted!"

With eager anticipation, they follow Ketzariah through the bustling camp, her words creating a vivid painting of her daughter's talents, just like most mothers do.

As they stroll, Ishara's attention is diverted by Uldako's arrival back on shore, but a curious sight distracts her: a woman, her gaze fixed intently on Uldako as she moves toward him, scrutinizing him from head to toe.

Kunai's excited shout about their return goes unnoticed by Ishara, her curiosity piqued by the stranger's unusual behavior. She watches the woman with an eagle eye for any signs of danger. The woman has long brown hair, braided intricately on the sides, framing her piercing hazel eyes. Her face is striking, with high cheekbones and a strong, angular jaw that conveys both strength and grace. Her brows are thick and expressive, drawn together in focus. Her overall visage is one of rugged beauty, reflecting both her resilience and purpose-driven lifestyle.

Her clothes are unlike anything Ishara has ever seen, a masterful blend of armor and clothing, meticulously crafted for both comfort and protection. Her outfit features reinforced leather with bone and stone studs, designed to allow ease of movement while providing substantial defense. The unique style whispers proof of the skills of the blacksmith who crafted it and carries both practicality and an undeniable warrior's elegance, evoking the strength and presence of a formidable warrior.

"Who is she? What is she up to?" Ishara muses under her breath, her instincts on high alert.

Uldako steps onto the shore, a feeling of unease washing over him as a woman, dressed in unique attire, approaches with an intense gaze fixed upon him. "Can I help you?" Uldako inquires with uncertainty.

The woman remains silent, circling Uldako with an almost unnerving scrutiny. Increasingly uncomfortable, Uldako attempts to break the silence. "Is something the matter? Hello? Excuse me?" he stammers, growing more perplexed by the woman's peculiar behavior.

The woman breaks her silence as her hazel eyes shift from his clothing to meet Uldako's gaze. "Oh! Don't worry," she reassures him, "I'm just studying your armor and weapons."

Just then, Ketzariah's voice interrupts, "Oh, my *dumu-munus* is already talking to Uldako. Let's join them."

Ishara feels a slight sense of relief, recognizing that the enigmatic woman is indeed Kesia. However, she remains wary of Kesia's piercing eyes as they scrutinize Uldako, prompting Ishara to step closer.

As Ishara moves to stand next to Uldako, Kesia's attention turns to her, and she inspects Ishara in the same scrutinizing manner as she did Uldako. Ishara begins to feel uncomfortable under the intensity of Kesia's gaze. However, to her surprise, Kesia remarks, "I think both of you could do with an upgrade to your armor. The person who crafted these is not gifted at all."

Uldako responds with a jest, "Oh, really? Because I actually crafted these myself." He watches her reaction, a mischievous grin forming on his lips.

Kesia's expression changes as she realizes her blunder in insulting Uldako's crafting skills. "Oh…apologies! I—"

Ishara interjects, "He's jesting. We took these from evil men we bested in battle, and their armor far surpassed our own. I think it's crafted impeccably."

Uldako adds, "Indeed, my armor is lightweight, granting me ample mobility. And this two-handed sword I wield is truly exceptional!"

Kesia scrutinizes their armor and weapons closely again in silence before continuing, "Fine, you got me! If I must be honest, Ishara, your armor is remarkable. I'm not certain I could improve upon it, and the same goes for your bow. However, Uldako, I can certainly craft something superior to the guard-type armor you currently wear. As for the great sword you wield, that's a different matter entirely. I've never seen a better-crafted bronze sword in my life, even if bronze tools are a new craft. They are extremely rare."

Uldako and Ishara share a puzzled look, uncertain how to respond. However, Kesia breaks the silence, her tone earnest. "Honestly, I've heard about your quest to find Seth and to find a safe camp. My failed attempt was to convince you to allow me to join you. My most valuable skill is metalsmithing, and I want to lend you my skills in crafting top-quality armor and weapons."

Kesia takes a step closer. "I've been confined to this small fishing village, but my true passion lies in metalsmithing. I want to learn from all the great smiths in the world and see how they work differently with metal in other places. I aspire to become the finest smith in the world, and I believe that journeying with you may help me achieve that. That is, of course, if you will have me?"

Uldako, taken aback, responds, "You want to join us? But you barely know anything about us or what our journey entails."

Kesia steps forward again, but with more confidence. "I've seen firsthand how you selflessly aided our village against the raiders, without seeking anything in return. I believe you're good-hearted people, and if you're going to help others on your travels, you'll need all the help you can get. Your journey to find Seth, and a good safe camp, will bring me closer to my goal, and that's all I need to know!"

Uldako looks at Ishara and Kunai for their opinions. After both nod in agreement, he looks back at Kesia. "In that case, you're welcome to join us! With more people like you, we might even establish our own safe camp in the future."

Ketzariah moves closer to her daughter, her eyes brimming with pride, but also with sorrow. "It will be sad to see you go," she murmurs, her voice thick with emotion. "The last of my twenty-two *dumu* leaving the nest. But I know you've been waiting for an opportunity like this for a very long time, Kesia."

She turns her focus toward Uldako and Ishara, her expression softening with hope. "And I believe with all my heart that you will be in very good hands."

Kesia's expression fills with gratitude as she looks at her mother. "Thank you, *Ama*," she says warmly. Turning to Uldako with a spark of curiosity in her eyes, she asks, "So, when do we embark on this journey, and where are we headed first?"

Ishara's voice resonates with determination. "Our quest is to find a man named Kenan, who can guide us to another man called Seth. Kenan passed through these lands recently. Earlier today, we discovered their tracks on the nearby hill. It was from that vantage point that we saw the raiders attacking your safe camp."

Kesia's eyes widen with recognition. "If that is the case, then I believe I know exactly of whom you speak."

Uldako shares quick glances with Ishara and Kunai before he leans in with eager anticipation. "Please tell us!"

Reflecting on her recent encounters, Kesia continues, "A few moons ago, we were blessed to see a special traveler pass through our village. He taught me the new art of crafting tools with iron, a skill I've been honing ever since. But alas, our supply of iron ran dry a while after he departed. Undeterred, I've been scouring the surrounding areas daily, hoping to stumble upon more. It was during one of these expeditions, as I traversed the nearby mountain, that I encountered an even more remarkable sight.

"Another special traveler! He was an elder with blue eyes, one of the ancients. A great warrior stood before me, unlike any I had ever encountered, exuding an aura of commanding respect. His armor was a marvel, a masterpiece unlike anything I had ever seen. Immaculately crafted, it was adorned with intricate details that spoke of both artistry and power. The shoulder piece was fashioned in the likeness of a majestic eagle's head, its beak outstretched as if issuing a rallying cry, capturing the essence of both ferocity and grace. Each element of his attire told a story of battles fought and victories earned, leaving me in great awe!"

Uldako's eyes widen with joy, excitement swelling within him. "That's not Kenan! That sounds like Seth! The man I've been searching for! Where did you see him?"

Kesia replies, "On the hill, but they left a few moons ago. I'm not certain of their current whereabouts, but we can ask my *dusa* Ruk. He saw them last."

Uldako, perplexed, asks, "Who is Ruk?"

Kesia explains, "He is my trusted companion who always accompanies me on my quests, like my search for iron. The wild beyond the gates of a safe camp can be dangerous, as you know. When we encountered Seth and his group, I went back to camp to return with food from the village. However, I was delayed in preparing the fish, and by the time I got back, Ruk informed me they had to leave in haste."

Uldako impatiently asks, "Where is Ruk?"

Kesia gestures behind Uldako. "He's right there, busy fileting the fish you caught."

As Ishara and Kun turn around, their jaws drop at the sight of the massive catch and Kunai shouts, "Whaaaat? That's the biggest fish I've ever seen! I think I'll stick to dry land from now on if those beasts are lurking beneath the surface."

Laughter ripples through the group as they approach Ruk. Uldako is mesmerized by the fluid grace with which Ruk expertly filets the fish, his hands moving with a precision borne of countless moons of practice. They are weathered and calloused, which points to a life of toil and dedication. Ruk stands compact and powerful, every muscle honed from many summers of hard work. His stature is modest but his presence commands attention, emanating an aura of quiet strength.

Ruk's head is cleanly shaven, save for a single thick braid trailing down his back. His eyes, a piercing shade of light blue, reflect a lifetime of experiences and hardships. His skin bears the marks of sun and wind, which come from countless time spent under the open sky. Despite the toll of time, there is a spark of vitality in his gaze, hinting at the indomitable spirit that resides within him.

Recognition dawns on Uldako as he realizes that Ruk is one of the men who bravely fought off the raiders, wielding a spear with precision and skill as the enemy tried to breach the shield wall.

Kesia's voice cuts through his thoughts, drawing his attention back to the present moment. "Ruk's not only a master butcher," she remarks with a hint of pride, her words tinged with admiration for her companion's skill. "He'll turn these fish into the finest delicacies you've ever tasted."

Her confidence in Ruk's cooking abilities is evident, and Uldako can't help but feel great anticipation at the prospect of enjoying the fruits of Ruk's labor.

Thokar interjects, "I've already asked Ruk to filet the fish and prepare it so we can celebrate our victory together with a feast tonight!"

Ketzariah chimes in, "Thank you, Thokar. We will celebrate our victory and honor those who gave their blood to achieve it. This evening we will give thanks and remember all the time we were given with those who were lost to us today. That is our way!"

Ketzariah turns to Ishara, "You, Uldako and Kunai should join us and rest for the night, safely within our walls. It's too late, too dangerous to continue your journey now."

Ishara nods, saying, "We accept the offer. Thank you kindly."

Uldako and Kunai echo her sentiment before Kesia redirects their attention to her friend. "Ruk, do you remember the man with the eagle armor from a few weeks ago?"

Ruk tosses the fish head into a nearby wooden bucket; it lands with a wet thud. He looks up. "Oh, you mean Seth! Of course, who could forget a man like that!"

Uldako and Ishara exchange surprised glances at the mention of Seth's name, but before they can respond, Kesia interjects, "How do you know his name?"

Ruk's smile broadens. "He told me."

Uldako asks urgently, "Ruk, do you remember where Seth and his men were headed?"

Ruk's brow furrows in concentration as he sees the desperation in Uldako's eyes and those around him. He also senses the heaviness in the air, especially after what they all experienced today, and he makes a small attempt to lighten it or, at the very least, to distract them for a moment. "Apologies, I can't seem to recall the exact destination," he admits, observing their reactions closely.

Uldako and Ishara exchange disappointed looks, while Kunai laments, "So, how do we find him now? It seems hopeless."

Suddenly, Ruk bursts into laughter, leaving everyone confused by his amusement in such a serious moment.

Kesia, breaking the tension with a smile, accuses her friend playfully, "You little liar. You do know where they went, don't you?"

Everyone holds their breath as Ruk finally confesses, "I can create a map on cuneiform for you, or if you already have a leather map, I can pinpoint their exact location, or at least where Seth mentioned he was heading." Uldako eagerly hands over his map, stepping closer to see where the location will be marked.

As Ruk marks the spot, he compliments the map. "Impressive map you have here. It seems more advanced than any other I have seen! Now, if I read the map correctly, Seth mentioned he was headed toward his *abba*'s home but had to make a detour to this low mountainous area here. When we were waiting for Kesia, one of his scouts returned and told him there were not only rumors but possible signs of new unknown settlers that have moved in, coinciding with a rise in raids in the region, so tread carefully if you decide to go there, because the tales about these people are unbelievable."

Uldako's eyes fill with concern. "What exactly do you mean?" he asks.

Ruk casts a wary glance around, ensuring no unwelcome ears are listening. Leaning in closer, his voice drops to a hushed, somber tone. "Seth whispered ominous tales of a savage clan living on the fringes of our world, behaving as feral beasts. They stalk the shadows, hunting humans as meat with the cold precision of predators."

Gasping in shock, Kesia scolds, "Surely you jest." Her voice is laced with disbelief. "Such horrors couldn't possibly occur in our northern lands."

Ketzariah calms her daughter. "My *dumu*, in this ever-changing world, nothing seems beyond possibility. Just today, Zerach shared dark tales with our guests, stories that mirror the creeping shadows closing in on us. Today, we've felt the bitter sting of malevolence firsthand, the greed and cruelty of men driven by their lust for power and wealth."

She pauses, drawing a deep breath as the weight of her words settles. "How much longer can we endure before we confront the harsh truths that lie before us? The land around is changing, darkness is spreading. Truth itself never changes; it is our flawed perceptions of truth that shift and blur. The more we turn away from reality, the more dangerous it may become for those who walk in blurred vision. Those who do not walk in the truth will without a doubt stumble in the dark. Our stumble today could have killed all of us if Uldako and his *dusa-meš* had not come to our aid! We have heard the rumors of raiders increasing in the North, yet we have not taken action to improve our camp's defenses because we did not believe it!"

A hushed silence falls upon the group until the distant voice of Raiyan slices through the tension. "We found them! The last remaining few of our clan who fled the battle earlier to hide for safety! Everyone is safe."

The group turns to witness the heartwarming scene as family members embrace, their reunion a sign of hope in the midst of turmoil. Life will go on. Uldako's heart softens as he looks at the touching sight, a pang of longing for his own mother stirring within him. In a quiet whisper, he vows, "Hold on, *Ama*. I will find you. I will save you."

As the evening progresses, the air resonates with the harmonious blend of Ishara's melodic tunes and the joyous laughter of the gathering. The aroma of fresh fish hangs in the air, and Ishara's fingers dance upon the strings of her lyre, weaving a tapestry of sound that captivates all who listen. With each verse, their spirits soar higher, their hearts uplifted by Ishara's enchanting voice. As she concludes her final song, applause erupts, echoing through the night.

The fervent cries of the people fill the air, their voices rising in unison: "We want more! We want more!"

Ishara, overcome with bashfulness, hesitates. "I'm sorry, but I don't know any other songs."

Yet, to her surprise, Uldako says eagerly, "Why not try improvising something?"

Ishara regards him with disbelief as he joins the crowd, but then a flicker of inspiration ignites within her. "Well, I have been working on something, though it's not quite finished," she admits hesitantly.

Encouraged by the supportive cheers of the crowd, she relents, "Alright, alright, but please don't laugh at me. Here we go. I call this 'Quest for Truth.'"

Taking her place beside the lyre, Ishara begins to play, her fingers dancing gracefully over the strings, while the entire camp gathers around, hanging on her every word.

In a world where shadows linger,
And uncertainty is a constant singer,
I walk the path of the unknown,
Seeking truths that lie alone.
On this quest for truth, I tread,
Through the darkness, I'm led,

With courage as my guiding light,
I'll conquer fears, take flight.
Through far lands, I roam,
In search of answers, I'll find home,
Though dangers lurk at every turn,
I'll rise above, my spirit won't burn.
On this quest for truth, I tread,
Through the darkness, I'm led,
With courage as my guiding light,
I'll conquer fears, take flight.
In the midst of darkness, I'll stand tall,
Against adversity, I'll heed the call,
For within me burns a fire bright,
To seek the truth, to fight the night.
On this quest for truth, I tread,
Through the darkness, I'm led,
With courage as my guiding light,
I'll conquer fears, take flight.
Though shadows may obscure my view,
I'll press on, steadfast and true,
For in the quest for truth, I'll find,
The light that guides both heart and mind.

As Ishara sings the final notes, a serene silence descends upon the camp, enveloping them in its tranquil embrace. Every eye is fixed on Ishara in reverent awe, as if holding their breath, afraid to disrupt the enchanting stillness that surrounds them.

Uldako's heart swells with an inexplicable emotion, a stirring deep within him that defies description. He looks at Ishara, captivated by her presence, feeling a connection that transcends mere words.

22

Tragedy

With the first rays of dawn filtering through the shelter, Uldako's eyes flicker open, brimming with anticipation for the journey ahead. As Ishara and Kunai still slumber, Uldako finds himself restless, unable to contain his eagerness. He rises, drawn outside by the allure of the morning sun revealing a mysterious mist over the land.

Šarru, ever faithful, senses Uldako's restlessness and joins him, his presence a comforting reassurance. Together, they step outside the shelter and stand in silent admiration of the misty morning, watching as the sun emerges on the horizon, a daily miracle that never fails to captivate Uldako's wonder.

With a gentle stroke of his hand against Šarru's fur, Uldako greets him. "Good morning, my old *dusa*." Šarru responds with a contented growl, pressing closer to Uldako's side, a silent affirmation of their unique and unbreakable bond.

As the sun ascends, its rays gently caress Uldako's chilled skin, infusing him with warmth. Lost in the splendor of the powerful sun, he contemplates the origins of this daily spectacle, pondering the significance it holds for countless souls who worship it as a deity. In this moment, the sun emerges as the epitome of beauty and power, illuminating the world with its radiant glow.

As the mist slowly dissipates under the sun's ascent, Uldako's thoughts turn inward, a silent plea directed toward the divine. "*Il*, if you can hear me," he whispers, his voice carried by the morning air, "guide me to Seth as soon as possible, not only for my *ama's* sake, but also that he may bring illumination to my darkened path, just like the sun brings light after the dark of night."

While in deep thought, Uldako feels Ishara's gentle touch on his shoulder, her presence comforting as they both gaze at the rising sun, a symbol of hope and promise. "Good morning," he greets her, a smile tugging at his lips. Ishara returns the sentiment, her eyes reflecting the morning's beauty.

Turning to her, Uldako's resolve shines through. "Let's wake Kun and embark on our journey to seek Seth."

Mid-conversation, they are surprised by the approach of Ruk and Kesia, both armed and ready for travel. Uldako's eyes widen in astonishment. "Ruk, are you joining us too?"

Ruk's grin is infectious as he replies, "Absolutely! Kesia and I are inseparable; we've been *dusa-meš* since birth. She would be lost without me."

Kesia lands a playful punch on Ruk's shoulder, teasingly retorting, "I think it's the other way around!" Uldako and Ishara share amused glances as they observe the banter.

Ishara chuckles and adds, "You're more than welcome to come along!" Uldako nods. "With that settled, we can be on our way as soon as Kun joins us. I'll go get him, and we will meet you at the gate."

The moment they return, the group of six steps cautiously through the camp gate, their eyes scanning the surroundings for any signs of danger. "It looks clear," Uldako declares.

After journeying for what feels like three hand spans of the sun's arc, Uldako pauses to consult the map alongside Ruk. "According to this, we should reach our destination in about two days. Does that seem accurate to you, Ruk?" Ruk looks at Uldako then scrutinizes the map once more and nods in agreement.

As they venture forth, the landscape unfurls like ancient clay tablets, revealing a rich tapestry of magnificent beings. Among the creatures, herds of horses gallop across the plains, their flowing manes billowing in the wind as they run. Uldako marvels at the sight of these majestic creatures. Standing about eight feet tall at the shoulder, the horses have muscular builds with sturdy legs, capable of carrying heavy loads and people over long distances if tamed.

Most of the horses boast coats of shimmering silver-gray, their powerful legs built for endurance. Their eyes hold an intelligent, almost ethereal glint. These ancient steeds, revered by the people, are not merely a means of transport but symbols of strength and resilience, embodying the spirit of the land and its untamed beauty.

As they cross a patch of trees, Uldako spots small, furry, humanlike animals eating fruits high in the trees, making strange noises. Ishara notices Uldako's questioning gaze as he looks at the animals who now also inspect him in return.

"Those are called *ugubi*. They are the type of animals that—"

"*Ugubi*!" Uldako blurts out, cutting her off.

Ishara startles, eyes wide.

"Oh—apologies," he says quickly, realizing her surprise. "It's just…my *ama* used to call me her little *ugubi*. But this is the first time I've ever seen a real one!"

A faint smile returns to Ishara's lips. "Well, they look a lot like us, don't they? Hands and feet with five fingers—it is also said they are intelligent."

As they continue, they see the great kings of the wild, the towering *gu-us*, its long neck reaching high into the sky as it grazes on the leaves of ancient trees. Its immense body, covered in pebbled skin, moves with a slow, deliberate grace. This ancient giant, towering above the horses, is a living monument to the awe-inspiring diversity of life that thrives in these primeval lands.

Movement catches Ishara's eyes as she points and says, "Look!"

Packs of agile *uridim* dart through the underbrush. Uldako enjoys the sight as he looks at their sleek, muscular forms blending seamlessly with the surrounding foliage. Their mottled fur of deep browns and tawny golds provides perfect camouflage, while sharp, intelligent eyes gleam with a predatory glint. Distinctive dark stripes run along their backs, and their pointed ears swivel to catch the slightest sound. Long, bushy tails aid in balance as they leap over obstacles with effortless grace. Communicating through low growls and yips, they move as a single, shadowy unit, embodying the wild, untamed spirit of the forest.

Kesia shouts to the right, "Look at that! In the distance, a massive *u-muš-da-gur*!"

The beautiful creature that roams the plains is like none other with its three formidable horns, two long ones above its eyes and a shorter one on its nose. A broad, bony frill extends from the back of its skull, adding to its imposing appearance as it grazes peacefully.

Then, Uldako catches sight of a fearsome dragon, its powerful jaws lined with sharp teeth like whetted knives, surveying its domain with undisputed dominance. The creature towers over the landscape, its massive frame supported by two powerful, muscular legs that shake the ground with each step. Its tiny forelimbs contrast sharply with its enormous head. The eyes of the *mušmaḫḫu*, cold and calculating, scan the surroundings, missing nothing. As it moves, small, peaceful, and beautiful creatures, with bodies the size of a man's hand and adorned with huge wings patterned in vibrant colors, flit around, disturbed from their habitat by the beast's presence.

The group of six remain vigilant as they press forward on their journey. After two hands to the sun have passed, Uldako stops in his tracks, his breath taken away by the sight before him. He points, "What magnificent animals are those? The huge beasts with two massive horns near their mouths, big ears, and a long thick tail in the front with a smaller one in the back?"

Ishara's eyes follow his gaze. "Oh! Those are herds of mighty *gud.sag.ga* roaming the grasslands. Their horned tusks show their strength and resilience, and their shaggy coats provide insulation against the cold. But never get too close to them; many have met their end trying."

Ruk adds with a nod, "Indeed, the only way to bring one down is with a large group of warriors, surrounding it and hurling spears from all sides. Their tusks can pierce through any man standing in their way. Every hunt almost guarantees the death of one or more hunters. Yet, the prize is worth the risk. Their fur can be used for so many things, and recently, people have started crafting tools from their tusks. Even jewelry!"

The group marvels at the majestic creatures, understanding the immense challenge and reward they represent for many. Yet Uldako respects these animals and simply enjoys their unique beauty and grace as they walk around them safely from a distance.

As they continue their journey, Uldako marvels at the wonders of the unexplored world, each sighting filling him with a profound sense of awe and reverence for the natural world and the mysteries it holds. As they continue their trek, his thoughts drift to the future.

I wonder what Seth will say when he sees me now, a warrior surrounded by great dusa-meš, he muses inwardly, glancing at his companions. *I hope he will allow us to stay at his safe camp with* Ama, *at least until I have learned all I need to know from him. Seth can teach me so much, not only about the truths of the natural world but also the spiritual forces that influence it. He might also know how to run a safe camp effectively, and perhaps even enhance my fighting skills. And then, when I am prepared to establish my own safe camp with my own family…*

A realization strikes Uldako mid-thought. "Oh, but to have a family, I will need a wife first," he whispers aloud without realizing it, his words hanging in the air like a quiet confession.

Fortunately, no one hears him. As his eyes shift to Ishara, he is captivated by her presence, but his own doubts assail him. *You were a slave, a nobody. Why would someone as great and beautiful as her, with the voice of a spirit, ever consider becoming your wife?*

Uldako grunts in disagreement with himself, his inner turmoil evident. *I am not a slave anymore, and all men are equal under* Il… The clash of conflicting thoughts echoes within him, as two opposing forces battle for dominance and truth in his mind.

"I am hungry!" Kunai's voice cracks the silence after a long hush. The others exchange knowing glances, realizing it's time to seek shelter and prepare a meal.

Ruk gestures toward a rocky area atop a hill adorned with massive boulders. "That might be a suitable spot. What do you all think?" They nod in agreement and make their way toward the rocky outcrop.

Upon reaching the location, Uldako takes charge, as is his custom. "I believe it would be best if Ishara and I work on gathering some large branches to erect a protective barrier against any potential threats," he suggests. "Meanwhile, the three of you can gather wood and get a fire going, while Šarru keeps guard. What do you think?"

Uldako notices a shift in Ruk's demeanor, a subtle resistance to being directed. Despite a glint of arrogance in Ruk's eyes, he chooses to suppress any objections and simply mutters, "Sure."

The hint of defiance in Ruk does not go unnoticed by Uldako, a reflection of the innate rebelliousness ingrained in human nature, but he opts to avoid confrontation. "I appreciate that," he responds calmly. "If any of you have any better ideas, I am open to give an ear!" They all seem content and start working on creating a shelter for the night.

As they part ways to complete their tasks, Uldako finds himself alone with Ishara. He confides in her, "I have a strange feeling about this area, especially after seeing the variety of creatures through our trek today. We need to be cautious of potential predators that might lurk in the moonlight."

Ishara picks up another big branch while saying, "Perhaps it's best if we keep watch throughout the night in shifts."

Uldako smiles at her suggestion. "Yes, that sounds like a prudent plan."

Uldako and Ishara swiftly construct a makeshift fence using wood and big rocks. By the time they finish, a warm fire crackles in the shelter's center. Ruk positions himself near the entrance, a choice the others respect. However, Uldako notices that Ruk frequently turns his back to the opening of the fence. Concerned, he says, "Ruk, just be cautious if you turn your back to the opening behind you, because—"

Ruk snaps, "You are not my *abba*, we are of similar age, and I know what I am doing."

Ishara, Kesia, and Kunai look at Uldako and Ruk with concerned eyes, witnessing Ruk's worsening attitude.

Just as Uldako is about to respond, Ishara interjects, "How about we all just eat and get something inside our stomachs? We might be a bit tense after the long day's walk with little to eat."

Seated around the fire, the group retrieves food from their bags. Among their provisions are snacks gifted by the fishermen's village. Uldako's eyes light up as he exclaims, "Oh, this will be delightful! Dried fish, bread, and berries. A feast fit for courageous adventurers."

As they dine, Uldako generously shares a fish with Šarru while addressing the group. "I'll take the first watch after dinner so you all can rest, but we'll rotate shifts every three hands' movement of the moon, if some of you would like to help."

Ruk, agitated by the directive, blurts out without restraint, "Who appointed you as our taskmaster?"

All eyes turn to him, and Kesia nudges him, whispering, "What's gotten into you?"

Ishara steps in to defend Uldako, knowing that Ruk's words cuts deep for Uldako, who carries the pain of being a slave. "Actually, it was my suggestion. Uldako is always receptive to input."

Uldako understands the importance of settling this issue right now at the start of their journey as he fixes Ruk with a firm stare and responds, "I am open to better ideas, but I will not allow any ill will in this group. I understand the journey today might have been long for you, but that doesn't justify speaking so rudely. If this is your demeanor after only the first day, I don't see you going the full distance. You chose to accompany us on my personal quest to find Seth. If you're unwilling to abide by my leadership, you're free to depart."

He pauses, carefully observing Ruk's reaction, then continues, "However, I am committed to leading this journey to its end. This mission is mine, as my *ama's* life depends on it, and I will ensure it is carried out with peace and harmony within our group. I will not tolerate any disruptions to the unity and love we have fostered."

Ruk is taken aback by Uldako's rational words, realizing his mistake as he sees their disappointed reactions. "I apologize," he admits.

Kesia interjects, sensing Ruk's reluctance to elaborate. "Ruk may not voice it himself, but I will in his place. This will be a long journey, and more understanding might bring wisdom in how we form bonds. Ruk struggles with authority figures due to his upbringing with his *abba*."

Ruk, clearly annoyed with Kesia talking openly about his personal issues, avoids eye contact and just stares into the flames of the fire.

Observing their reluctance to open up, Uldako attempts to foster trust. "It's alright," he reassures. "As long as we understand each other and remain unified on this journey, treating one another with respect. We all carry our own burdens. My *abba* is a mystery to me as I have never known him, and my *ama* is enslaved as we speak. Kun witnessed his parents' slaughter alongside the rest of his village. Ishara lived among *dusa-meš* deceived into worshipping a fallen spirit as a *dingir*. Each of us has a story, but now we're weaving a new tale together, and it's imperative we focus on that."

The group nods in agreement as Ishara chimes in, "Well, I can't wait for tomorrow. If we walk fast enough, we might be able to reach—"

Her words are ripped from the air as a sudden blur of movement explodes behind Ruk. In an instant, a creature lunges out of the shadows, its claws tearing into his flesh with sickening speed. Ruk's screams die in his throat as the beast's jagged teeth sink deep, locking him in its deadly grip. With terrifying strength, it begins to drag him away from the shelter, the ground beneath him streaked with blood as his body is pulled into the encroaching darkness.

Reacting swiftly, Uldako and Ishara, armed with their weapons, move into action to fend off the beast.

Meanwhile, Kunai and Kesia, horrified by the sudden attack, recoil and scream in shock as they watch the unfolding struggle.

First to react, Šarru leaps and strikes the predator, loosing a primeval roar that shakes the very ground, louder than any Uldako has ever heard from his guardian. For one heartbeat, Uldako is glad that such power stands at his side, not before him.

As Uldako charges toward the chaos, his eyes catch movement in the shadows. There are more beasts, lurking behind the first attacker, their eyes gleaming with hunger as they creep closer. His heart pounds. "Ishara!" he shouts, voice tight with urgency. "Light the torch, now! It's the only way to drive them back!"

Ishara promptly ignites the torch and tosses it to Uldako, who catches it deftly in midair. Meanwhile, Ishara readies her bow, poised for an opportune moment to strike.

Brandishing the torch high and wide, Uldako creates a ring of fire, causing the beasts to hesitate, their fear evident. The flickering light also aids Ishara's aim as she waits for the perfect shot. The blazing torch in Uldako's hand illuminates the darkness, revealing their adversaries in stark detail.

These predators are cunning hunters that have mastered the art of teamwork. Their bodies are robust and powerful, crafted for agility and strength. But what truly sets them apart are their elongated upper canines, curved like lethal ivory blades protruding menacingly from their jaws. Cloaked in thick fur, they move with grace and precision, their senses finely tuned for the hunt. Their eyes gleam with a primal ferocity, evoking both awe and fear in equal measure.

Šarru's initial attack weakens the beast, but with swift action, the predator retaliates, sinking its teeth into Šarru's upper leg.

Despite the pain, Šarru pulls away and readies for another strike, but the beast dodges and leaps onto him from the side, claws and teeth tearing into Šarru's back. With a resounding roar, Šarru grapples with the predator, his agony evident.

Caught up fending off the other predators, Uldako is unable to come to Šarru's aid immediately, but upon hearing his roar, he knows the situation is dire and shouts encouragement, "Šarru, focus! Strike now!"

Hearing Uldako's voice jolts Šarru, helping him push through the pain and focus on dislodging the enemy from his back. With a mighty effort, Šarru throws the predator to the ground, leveraging his size advantage.

He seizes the upper hand by clamping his jaws onto the predator's pelt, but the creature swiftly wriggles free and attempts to regain its position behind Šarru, aiming to leap onto his back once more.

Anticipating the move, Ishara seizes her opportunity as the beast lunges at Šarru again. With unwavering precision, her arrow slices through the air, finding its mark in the creature's chest.

Roaring in agony, the beast momentarily falters, allowing Šarru to use the opportunity to deliver the final, fatal blow by sinking his teeth into the predator's neck with unyielding force. It is the first time Uldako has seen this level of anger in the great bear.

The other predators begin to retreat, intimidated by Šarru's triumph and the flickering flames of the fire.

Uldako casts a brief glance toward Ruk as he drives the torch into the earth at the shelter's entrance. The look lingers a heartbeat too long before he turns away and fixes his attention on Šarru.

"Are you alright? Let me have a look." Concern is etched in his voice. As he inspects Šarru's wounds, Uldako's heart sinks at the sight of the deep gashes.

Guiding Šarru back to the warmth of the fire, they settle beside it, Šarru's movements now marked by a noticeable limp. With practiced haste, Uldako retrieves healing herbs from his bag, a precaution he now takes everywhere. Tenderly applying the herbs to Šarru's wounds, Uldako murmurs, "You'll be alright, Šarru. Hang in there. You fought bravely and emerged victorious."

As Ishara beholds Šarru's wounds, tears cascade down her cheeks, though she maintains a stoic facade.

A piercing scream echoes behind her, wrenching her focus away. Whirling around, Ishara's gaze falls upon Kesia sitting next to Ruk, who lies motionless on the ground. "I am so sorry," Ishara whispers, her heart sinking at the sight.

"No!" Kesia cries out, her voice trembling with desperation. "This cannot be happening! Open your eyes, Ruk. Please, open your eyes. Don't leave me!"

Ishara slowly approaches, her heart heavy as she confirms the grim reality. "He's gone, Kesia. I'm so sorry," she murmurs softly. "It was just too fast. He was already gone when we reached him and the beast."

After Uldako finishes tending to Šarru's wounds, he turns his attention to Kesia, recognizing that words alone offer little solace in such moments of profound grief. Instead, he chooses to sit beside her, offering silent support and comfort in her time of need.

As Uldako shares Kesia's pain and observes Šarru's injured form, he reflects without realizing he is thinking out loud. "This tragedy could have been prevented with better preparation and leadership," he acknowledges. He scrutinizes his actions, grappling with the weight of responsibility. "I should have insisted Ruk sit where he could see the shelter's opening as I felt in my gut. My hesitation cost him his life. It's all my fault…even Šarru's injuries."

Kesia snaps back quickly. "No. It's all my fault. He came with us because of me."

Ishara's voice cuts through the tension, her words carrying a reassuring clarity. "It's no one's fault," she insists firmly. "Ruk made his own choice to join us on our journey, and it was his choice to sit there. This is the risk we face in the wild. Uldako, it's not your fault, and Kesia, it's not your fault either. Ruk made his decision, and that is the end of that."

Uldako offers Kesia a reassuring gaze, his hand resting gently on her shoulder. "She's right, Kesia. This isn't your fault."

"These things just happen to good and bad people," Kunai says quietly, his expression flat in that terrible way of a child who has already grieved far too much.

After a few moments of solemn silence, Uldako rises, determined to prevent such a tragedy from recurring. He stokes the fire, casting its glow wider, then lights two additional torches to fortify the entrance against potential threats throughout the night. Settling by the fire, Uldako positions himself beside Šarru, offering comfort with a reassuring touch on the bear's fur, his eyes fixed on the shelter's entrance, vigilant and protective. Kunai silently takes a seat next to Uldako, moving his hand gently through Šarru's fur in an attempt to ease the pain.

Sensing Kesia's need for solitude, Ishara joins them, quietly taking her place beside Uldako. Leaning closer, she whispers, "How will we proceed with Šarru in this condition, and what should we do about Ruk's remains?" As Uldako's eyes meet Ishara's, she senses the weight of his inner turmoil, a wound that runs deeper than any physical injury.

After a moment of silence, he speaks in a hushed tone, "I don't know. We're on the verge...just one more day's journey, and then this happened." He falls silent, lost in thought, then steadies himself. "Brooding won't help! Let's consider our options tonight, keeping a close eye on Šarru," Uldako suggests. "Sleep will evade me once more, so I'll remain vigilant to ensure our safety. Perhaps you should rest."

Ishara's eyes soften with understanding. "If you don't mind, I'll stand watch with you," she replies. "Sleep eludes me as well."

Throughout the night, they sit in quiet vigil, their minds consumed by contemplation and concern. The darkness feels endless, pressing heavily upon them. Just when it seems the night will never end, the first faint glimmers of dawn begin to pierce the horizon. The darkness starts to yield to the light, bringing with it a sense of renewal and hope. As the sun rises, Uldako stands, his mind clear and resolute, ready to lead them forward with a firm plan for their next steps.

23

Hope

Ishara's eyes flutter open, greeted by the soft light of dawn gently illuminating the shelter. She realizes she has drifted into sleep, the weight of exhaustion lifting as a new day begins. Uldako's voice breaks the morning silence, drawing her attention.

"Good morning," he says, his tone resolute and filled with purpose.

Ishara responds with only a soft smile, knowing he has a plan of action. Uldako waits for her to sit up straight then quickly begins to outline his thoughts. "I've devised a plan. We need to act swiftly and decisively if we're to ensure our safety and reach Seth."

"Go on," Ishara encourages, brushing her hair back as she prepares for the day ahead. Her eyes lock onto Uldako's, filled with trust and anticipation.

"Initially, I considered constructing a makeshift bed from wood for Šarru, which we could drag to Seth, but it's too risky. He's too heavy, and it would take too much time. Moreover, if we encounter other beasts on our journey, they could easily target him in his weakened state."

Ishara nods as she continues to listen to Uldako. "I could return to the fishing village to seek aid, but that will take over two days to get there and two more to get back here. Šarru does not have that much time. Our best option is for me to leave you here to protect Šarru, Kun, and Kesia, while I press on quickly to reach Seth's location. I'll seek their aid to ensure Šarru can be helped. I won't leave him behind."

Ishara empathizes with the profound bond between Uldako and Šarru, and as they both regard the injured bear, it becomes apparent that his condition hasn't improved despite the passing night. "I share your reluctance to abandon him," Ishara admits softly, her gaze lingering on Šarru's weakened form. "Even with the best care, his chances are slim…"

Uldako's response is stoic, his eyes dropping to the ground as if unable to face the grim reality. "Let us do what we can," he finally utters. "If I travel alone and swiftly, I will reach Seth's location by midday, bringing aid back before nightfall. The elder has immense wisdom, and if anyone can help Šarru, it is him."

Ishara nods, but her concern extends beyond their immediate predicament. She gestures discreetly toward Kesia, who has succumbed to sleep beside Ruk's lifeless form. "I will do my best to protect them, but what of Ruk's remains?" Ishara queries, her voice tinged with concern. "We cannot simply leave him here."

Uldako looks at Kesia next to Ruk's body. "Yes, immediate action is necessary for him and for her," he affirms.

Ishara meets his gaze, understanding dawning in her eyes. "You mean to bury him now?" she queries gently.

Uldako nods once more, his expression resolute.

"Yes," Ishara agrees softly. "Let me wake Kesia and Kun to explain our intentions."

While Ishara attends to them, offering solace amidst tears and sorrow, Uldako busies himself with preparations for the burial and the impending journey. Hearing the grief of Kesia is too much for him to bear, and he tries to avoid it by keeping his hands busy. With his gear in order, he steps outside the shelter, his senses alert for any lurking dangers.

He advances to a suitable spot beneath the sheltering embrace of a nearby tree. Retrieving a big flat rock, he begins to dig, the earth yielding reluctantly to his efforts until he has excavated a fitting resting place for Ruk.

Returning to the shelter, Uldako is met with Kesia's tear-filled gaze, her eyes reflecting profound sorrow. Moved by her pain, Uldako approaches gently, his voice filled with empathy. "I am so sorry, Kesia," he murmurs, his words heavy with understanding. "But we must bury him now. We cannot leave him in this state. You know that."

Kesia's nod is a silent agreement, and she steps aside as Uldako lifts Ruk's lifeless form with care. Together, they lay him to rest, the earth embracing him in its final interment. As Uldako places the last stone over Ruk's face, Kesia's grief spills over, tears flowing freely in her uncontrollable sorrow as the earth takes him fully.

Ishara draws closer to Uldako, her voice carryings a note of uncertainty. "We must bring closure to this, but I have no words," she admits, her gaze reflecting her inner turmoil.

Meeting her eyes with understanding, Uldako nods in acknowledgment. "Neither have I," he confides softly. "But I'll try to find the right words while you offer comfort to Kesia." With Ishara's arms enfolding Kesia in solace, Uldako steps forward with Kunai at his side, grappling with the weight of the moment.

"In the face of death's finality," he begins, his voice tinged with solemnity, "we stand here, humbled by the honor of knowing Ruk. He was a great man who gave up his own life at the fishing camp to aid us on our quest. His presence will be sorely missed." Words faltering, Uldako retreats, finding solace in the silent embrace as he joins Ishara in comforting Kesia.

After a moment of stillness, Uldako quietly encourages Ishara and Kesia to return to the shelter and rest. As they turn, Uldako's gaze drifts to the slain beast, the one that had taken Ruk's life. Its massive form lies twisted near the edge of the clearing, jaws agape, its long canines catching the morning light. The head is striking, beautiful in its savagery, regal even in death.

Without a word, Uldako strides to the creature, raises his sword, and with a single, fluid motion, severs the skull from its spine. Kesia gasps softly at the suddenness of it. Uldako lifts the head by the base, blood still fresh on the bone, and turns to her.

"Can you fashion this onto a pauldron?" he asks, his voice low. "I want this skull molded into my armor to serve as a reminder that I must face my enemies with wisdom and force, before another *dusa* is taken from me."

Kesia looks at the skull, then into Uldako's eyes. There is no anger in him, only grief and resolve, like fire beneath still water. Her tears begin to fall again, but now with reverence. She nods, her voice lost but her answer clear.

As he prepares to depart, Ishara rushes forward, enveloping him in a tight embrace. "Please hurry, but be safe. I couldn't bear losing you too."

Meeting her eyes, Uldako offers a reassuring smile. "I'll be back before you realize I'm gone." Ishara surprises him, pressing her lips against his cheek. Startled by the unexpected gesture, Uldako's mind races with conflicting emotions. Unsure of how to respond, he takes a step back, momentarily speechless.

"Go," Ishara murmurs softly, breaking the tension, prompting Uldako to turn and embark on his journey. "You don't have time to waste!"

Uldako nods resolutely with a final glance to her and the others. Kunai shouts, "I won't leave Šarru's side! Uldako touches a clenched fist to his chest in silent thanks, then turns and strides toward Seth. Moving swiftly but silently, he remains vigilant, his senses attuned to any sign of danger as he navigates the terrain with agility and speed. Carrying only the essentials—food, water, and his trusty weapons—he travels light, allowing for swift progress.

As he presses on, the rugged hills gradually yield to a vast expanse of mountains looming in the distance. Consulting the map, Uldako deduces that this prominent peak marks the region that Seth had been journeying toward.

In this new terrain, a diverse array of life unfolds before Uldako's eyes. The haunting cries of golden eagles pierce the sky, while peculiar ground-dwelling creatures burrow among the rocky crevices for refuge. Majestic deer, their horns seemingly crafted for the ascent, traverse the steep cliffs effortlessly. Yet, despite the captivating surroundings, Uldako finds his attention drawn inward, consumed by weighty reflections.

Contemplating the nature of perception, Uldako realizes the power of controlling one's thoughts to discern truth impartially. He grapples with questions that gnaw at the soul, pondering the fate of those lost to death—the fallen Ruk, the victims of his own hand, and the countless souls murdered in the slave camps. Growing up in the Southeast as a slave, he has seen much death and it came to feel ordinary. Lately, though, it grips him more, tugging at his heart.

At the fishing village, he realized it even more. Since then he's felt an even deeper ache, not only for the loved ones lost but also for having taken an enemy's life. "A life ends in a heartbeat, but why do humans kill each other? Such a thing should not feel normal. Why could I not see this before? Now Ruk's life has also come to an end, or is it only his body that has ended? I can't believe this is all there is to life. If man is born only to die, what is the point? There must be more!" Uldako muses, grappling with the meaning of life as he continues to run silently across the land.

As he spots the dry bones of a deer, Uldako recalls the taskmasters' talk of the realm of the dead as they passed him in camp carrying their kill. He had dared to look, and they saw and struck him, for a slave was never to meet a taskmaster's gaze. He had not cared then, but now their words echo: *Death sends the soul below, to the underworld, the realm of the dead.* Whether it exists, he cannot say. "Seth might know," Uldako whispers, forcing his focus back to the present.

Uldako arrives at the foot of the mountain and begins searching for tracks at the designated location on his map. Soon, he spots it: a human trail ascending the mountain. The number corresponds with the men who were with Seth so long ago. Proceeding cautiously with hope, he follows the path, his senses heightened. A familiar scent fills the air, the unmistakable aroma of a campfire, prompting him to halt, his body poised for action. As distant voices drift on the breeze, Uldako hunkers down, ears alert to every word exchanged.

Strategically positioning himself amidst the foliage, Uldako eavesdrops on the conversation, gauging their number and intent. With cautious determination, he inches closer, each movement deliberate and calculated. Concealed behind a dense thicket, he steals a glance, heart pounding with anticipation.

What he beholds stirs a long-dormant ember within him, a feeling in his inner man, returned after such a long time—that feeling he first experienced when meeting Seth. The feeling of true hope!

Uldako slowly whispers to himself, "Can this be real?"

Five figures encircle the low fire, their silhouettes illuminated by the dancing flames. It is midday, but there are low clouds drifting over the mountain, casting a cold and misty veil over the surroundings. Uldako attempts a closer look, searching for the visage of Seth, but finds it absent. Instead, he identifies the features of the other men one by one. As recognition dawns upon him more and more, Uldako realizes the reality of the moment: These are indeed the noble warriors who rode at Seth's side so many moons ago and who came to Uldako's rescue.

Overwhelmed with emotion, Uldako rushes toward the five men gathered around the fire, but abruptly halts as a sword is brandished at his neck by a man he never noticed. "Who are you, and what do you seek?" demands a voice in a cold and commanding whisper.

Uldako freezes, meeting the intense gaze of the sword bearer, while the others are still casually sitting around the fire as if they all expected this to happen. The man before him is striking. His long, thick hair, braided on one side, cascades down his back, while his long black beard frames a chiseled jaw. Dark brown eyes, set beneath intense, thick eyebrows, and a scar that cuts through one eye hint at countless battles fought. Another scar on his neck further marks him as a seasoned warrior. He stands slightly taller than Uldako, his strong, lean muscles exuding both strength and agility. His armor, an impressive blend of rare, high-quality leather and bronze, gleams in the firelight. The bronze sword he wields is exceptionally sharp and clean, a witness to his skill and meticulous nature.

The tension hangs thick in the air until the man's expression shifts. Recognition dawns in his eyes, and he lowers his weapon with a grin. "Hold on, I know you," the man declares loudly.

At the sound of the man's voice, all eyes around the fire pivot toward Uldako.

Observing their demeanor, Uldako sees how their curiosity turns to familiarity and an absence of hostility. Then, one of the figures by the fire calls out, "Tiras, who's that you've got there?"

The man beside Uldako responds, "We've crossed paths before. Don't you remember him?"

Stepping forward, Tiras addresses Uldako directly, his tone softening with a hint of admiration. "You're the slave we rescued beneath that tree, are you not? I would have never thought we'd cross paths here. Come, sit with us by the fire."

Uldako settles into his place among the formidable and esteemed warriors of light, feeling diminutive compared to their grandeur. He speaks, his voice carrying a tone of reverence, "Yes, I am indeed the slave you saved so many moons ago, and I am deeply thankful!"

As the youngest man among them speaks, Uldako recognizes him as the one who long ago referred to Seth as his great-grand *abba*. "Yes, now I remember him as well," the young man affirms. "He also sought our aid for his *ama*."

Another man seated to Uldako's right chimes in, "Lamech speaks truth! Although you do look very different now. Back then you were a reed in the wind, but now you look like an oak. I blinked twice to be sure."

Lamech jests, "Of course I speak truth. My memory is sharper than my blade, unlike yours!"

Uldako's gaze shifts to Lamech as they continue to talk, taking in his youthful appearance. Lamech has blond hair that catches the firelight, framing a clean-shaven face. His green eyes are bright and observant, carrying an air of wisdom beyond his years, but perhaps a pinch of arrogance as well. His leather armor, expertly crafted, bears the emblem of an eagle, a symbol pointing to *Il* and the heavenly realm. Inscriptions dedicated to *Il* are etched into the leather, suggesting both devotion and craftsmanship. The intricate details and the care put into the armor hint at his important lineage and the reverence he holds for his heritage.

However, the name "Lamech" reverberates in Uldako's mind, stirring up memories of the sinister Lamech he encountered before. The young man notices the change in Uldako's expression and asks, "Is something troubling you, Uldako?"

Uldako responds, "Umm, no, I...I encountered another man named Lamech during my travels, but he was exceedingly wicked!"

Their faces turn to shock, and Tiras is the first to respond. "I am surprised you met him and still walk free! You are referring to Lamech, the *dumu-nita* of Methushael from the line of Cain. His dark deeds are becoming infamous, even more than some of his father's." He then gestures toward Lamech, clarifying, "This Lamech here is the *dumu-nita* of Methuselah."

Uldako turns his eyes slowly from Tiras to Lamech. "I see. I also recall from our first encounter that you mentioned Seth as being your great *abba*. Is that correct, Lamech?"

Lamech draws a deep breath and begins, "Indeed, let me explain. My *abba* is Methuselah, his *abba* is Enoch the blessed one, or as some of the Cainites from the east may call him, Etana. His *abba* is Jared, and his *abba* is Mahalalel, followed by—"

Uldako interrupts as the name rings a bell. "Mahalalel! I have met him and his wife Talita. They have huge crop fields!"

Lamech smiles warmly and continues, "Ah, yes, he moved far away with his family toward the South a very long time ago as crops usually grow better in the South than in the North. We seldom see them now. But let me continue. Mahalalel's *abba* is Kenan, then Enosh, and then Seth. Notably, Seth's *abba* is the renowned Adam, who brought peace and order to our land a long time ago. He is the great *abba* of us all!"

Uldako's eyes widen in astonishment. "Wow, that's quite a lineage. I imagine many branches extend from such a family tree. I don't even know who my *abba* is. I have no family beyond my *ama* and my new *dusa-meš*, who've become like family.

"That's also why I'm here now. I need your assistance at once. Where is Seth? My companions are in peril, and one of them is gravely wounded!"

Tiras stands tall, his gaze fixed on Uldako as he speaks. "Seth ventured higher up the mountain to commune with *Il*. We cautioned against it, for tales circulate of formidable men dwelling in these peaks, rumored to do unthinkable evil things. This very concern led us to halt our journey here. But he said *Il* wanted him to go and pray, so we await his return."

Uldako, urgency and desperation etched into his features, asks, "When will he return?"

Tiras, sensing the gravity of the situation, speaks gravely, "We are uncertain. Meanwhile, how may we aid you?"

Uldako, overcome with desperation, begins to speak rapidly and indistinctly until Tiras interjects. "Slow down. Articulate clearly, or we will comprehend nothing you say!"

Taking a deep breath, Uldako begins, "Last night, my companions and I were attacked by a pack of beasts with large upper teeth protruding from their jaws. Cloaked in thick fur, they moved with an uncanny grace and precision."

One of the men interjects, "That must be *zu-gal*!"

Uldako presses on, urgency sharpening his voice. "One of these beasts slew one of my companions and gravely wounded another, who now lies in desperate need of aid. I knew we were close to your location, so I left them there to seek help. Two women are now protecting the injured and a little boy, and they await my return. Please, you must help us. If we depart right now, we can reach them before nightfall. Should we delay, they may face another assault tonight."

Tiras seizes his sword, declaring, "Why tarry when two women are in danger? Let us set forth."

Lamech, rising with him, echoes, "You've heard the *šeš* of Seth. Let us proceed!"

As they gather their belongings, Uldako is stunned to learn that Tiras is Seth's brother. What astonishes him even more is their unwavering resolve to aid Uldako's friends without hesitation. Tears well in his eyes as he watches in awe as these men swiftly prepare their armor and weapons for the journey, their determination clearly visible and inspiring. As Uldako studies them closely; he knows that these men are on a different level. They are proof that there is still good in the world. *They are the light bearers!* he reflects inwardly.

After a brief moment, Tiras turns to Lamech and commands, "Remain here for Seth's return. But we cannot risk any harm befalling you in his absence, so kill the fire and hide until his return. He should be back soon."

Lamech protests, but the five warriors adamantly forbid him from joining their quest.

Moments later, Uldako sets out with the five esteemed warriors, feeling overwhelmed by the honor of their company, a swell of pride engulfing him.

As they approach the crest of another hill, the foremost man named Jano motions for the group to take cover, swiftly followed by Uldako. Their synchronicity hints at years of combat experience.

Jano's dark-brown hair is pulled back into twin braids, neat and oiled. His brown eagle eyes are keen and measuring, taking the measure of wind, ground, and men alike.

His armor is a masterwork: supple, earth-dark leather paneled for silent movement, edged in wolf-fur to break shape and sound. Across the breast rests the mark of the eagle, wings hammered in low relief and stitched with sinew so it gleams without clatter. No loose tassel, no careless ring, every piece is purposed for quiet speed.

Two iron swords ride his back, narrow-bladed and balanced for quick work, their edges drawn thin for cut and thrust. A clever harness is laced into the cuirass itself, an X of hide and hidden bronze toggles. This is marvelously designed so he can draw either blade over the shoulder in one smooth motion and reseat it without fumbling. Even at rest, he looks ready to move: weight on the balls of his feet, breath steady, gaze fixed—an eagle's focus in a man's face.

Jano points ahead. "Five men," he whispers low, "dragging two captives by their hair."

Tiras joins him, noting, "Could be those rumored raiders, known to prey on travelers."

Intrigued, Uldako edges closer, observing the scene below. The figures, larger and more robust than typical humans, boast broad shoulders and abundant body hair. Clad in scant animal hides around the waist, they show no signs of armor. With them, they drag two figures, a man and a woman, limp and likely unconscious.

Tiras signals with a hand gesture, and the five men charge forward with the silence of shadows, akin to stealthy predators. Uldako, a few heartbeats later, realizes what is going on and joins the action, failing to match their pace.

When they converge on the scene, Tiras lunges at one of the men in silence, pressing his sword against the man's throat. Simultaneously, the other four assail the remaining enemies with deadly precision.

Amidst the chaos, two of the enemies try to resist, but it is too late. The swift blades of Seth's men silence them, leaving crimson trails in their wake before a sound leaves them.

Uldako reflects inwardly, *Their prowess exceeds mine by far. My eyes could barely follow their movements!*

Tiras sternly addresses the three remaining men, "Who are you, and why have you taken them?" He gestures toward the male and female bodies they were dragging.

Uldako approaches to inspect the bodies and realizes they are already lifeless. The man held at sword point by Tiras responds callously, "We take them because we can."

Uldako's gaze narrows in disbelief as he observes human bite marks on the woman's leg, prompting him to question, "Why are these marks on her leg?"

Another of the hairy men retorts, "Isn't it obvious? We were a bit famished after traveling all this way."

Uldako's shock deepens as he realizes the man is serious and the rumors were indeed true. With composed demeanor, Tiras questions, "*Il* will surely punish you for such wickedness. Why commit such an evil act?"

One of the hairy men responds, "Our clan keeps its own ways, and this is none of your concern."

With immense speed, Jano drives a hard blow into his belly, knocking the breath from him. While the man wheezes, Jano draws the sword from his back and steps in close. "Answer the question," he says, low, "or it gets worse. I can be slow about it."

The man raises a hand as his breath returns. "We hail from distant lands where famine plagues our people. Factions emerged, warring over resources, and our shamans decreed that the victorious may consume the defeated as an offering to our war *dingir*. This tradition dates back to our forebears' time, and today it remains our means of survival. It is our way."

Uldako's anger boils over, and he bellows, "That is not 'your way.' It is the way of evil spirits pretending to be *dingir* causing you to kill your own kinsmen! And now you've brought your wicked practices to this tranquil land!"

Another of the intruders interjects defiantly, "In nature, the strong beasts prey on the weak, consuming their kill for sustenance. Those defeated in battle are feeble and deserve their fate!"

Tiras and Seth's companions are appalled, but Jano is the first to retort, "You are no beasts. You are humans. How dare you devour another human, created in the image of *Il*!"

As Jano grapples with the emotional weight of the revelation, the hairy captive beneath his blade seizes the opportunity to break free, shoving him aside and bolting. In a flurry of panic, the remaining two flesh-eaters also attempt to flee, sparking a chaotic scuffle that ends swiftly as Seth's men dispatch them to the ground.

With speed, Uldako moves to pursue the remaining captive who is fleeing.

24

Prophecy

Uldako barely moves two steps before Jano intervenes, cautioning, "Leave him! We can't afford to chase him. Our priority is to reach your *dusameš* before sunset. Time is of the essence."

Uldako acknowledges Jano's wisdom, his mind racing with the possibility of his friends not only encountering beasts, but also some of these flesh-eating humans who are walking around. Tiras and the others swiftly give the bodies to the earth, and death's weight settles on Uldako's heart again, the inner pain growing, not only for these hairy men, but also for those they took in such an evil way. As soon as they are done, they press on with urgency toward Uldako's friends.

An eagle cries powerfully in the sky, its call echoing through the rocks, snapping Ishara back to the reality of the world around her. With Kesia and Kunai by her side, she tends to Šarru, offering comfort and care as he struggles to recover. Ishara's thoughts had been on Uldako, reminiscing on their journey together and worrying about his safety.

She looks toward the setting sun, realizing that time is slipping away. As dusk approaches, worry gnaws at her, contemplating the dangers that lurk in the night if Uldako doesn't return in time.

Kesia, seemingly attuned to Ishara's thoughts, says, "Do you think he's safe?"

Ishara meets her concerned face. "I believe Uldako will do everything he can to get back here before sunset. Let's hope that *Il* will protect him."

Kesia's attention shifts to Šarru as she gently tends to him, running her fingers through his fur. "At least Šarru is not getting much worse, which is a good thing."

Ishara smiles warmly. "Yes, hopefully with proper care, he will be showing signs of recovery soon." Turning to the bear, who stirs slightly with a subdued growl, Ishara encourages, "You're a fighter, Šarru. Don't give up!"

Kunai has moved to the dim corner of the shelter, his gaze fixed on Šarru, who is in clear pain. Silence has cloaked Kunai, a silence born of despair and self-blame. Death, it seems, shadows his every step. First, his entire village and beloved parents were slain, then the old woman who took him in, and now Ruk.

I am a harbinger of death, he thinks bitterly. *Why must life be so cruel, so dark? Why can't I simply stay safely with Šarru, Uldako, and Ishara, and finally live in peace?*

His mind spirals further into darkness. *What is wrong with me? Why does death cling to me, spreading its curse to those I love? Should I leave, vanish into the wilderness, and spare them from my curse?*

Tears stream down his face, a torrent of sorrow and fear that he can no longer contain. He sits with his arms folded on his knees and his head lying on them, facing down to hide the tears.

With another cry of the eagle circling above, Ishara is reminded of the wildlife around them and the increasing dangers as dusk approaches.

"I can't stay idle," she declares, rising to her feet. "I'll enlarge the fire and prepare extra torches, just in case Uldako is delayed." She turns to Kunai to ask for his aid but is surprised by what she sees, noticing the teardrops falling to the ground. She moves toward him.

"Why are you crying, Kun? Everything will be okay. You will see—everything will work out for good, if you put your trust in me, Uldako, and the Most High!"

Kunai leaps up, hugging Ishara tight without any words, tears still flowing.

After a moment, Ishara gently pulls back and says, "All right, let's improve our shelter's defenses." They set about their work with renewed determination, the flickering fire casting moving shadows as they strengthen their shelter, preparing for whatever the night may bring.

After their work is complete, the three of them sit next to the fire in silence. The crackling flames, the soft rustling of leaves, and the occasional groan of Šarru are the only sounds that break the stillness.

Then out of the silence, Kesia says with a playful grin, "You fancy Uldako, don't you?"

Ishara's cheeks turn red with embarrassment, and she freezes, searching for the right words but feeling caught off guard. She opens her mouth to respond but hesitates, glancing at Kunai then back to Kesia.

Kesia presses on, her eyes twinkling with curiosity. "It's alright if you do. I mean, I understand why you would!"

Ishara, placing another piece of wood by the fire, tries to steady her racing heart. "Of course I care about him…as a good *dusa*." Her tone is gentle yet guarded. The flickering firelight reflects in her eyes, masking the deeper emotions she keeps hidden.

To her surprise, Kunai joins the conversation with a teasing tone, "That's not what she means. She's saying you love Uldako, don't you?"

Ishara whirls around to Kunai. "You're too young to be discussing such grown-up matters!"

Kesia laughs teasingly and presses on, "You do have feelings for him, don't you? Come on, be honest!"

Ishara's face warms. "When it comes to Uldako, I—"

"Men! Warriors approaching. Hide! Now!" Kesia's voice warns, fixed on a stir far in the distance.

A tense silence grips the air as they huddle down, eyes fixed on the approaching figures. The warriors move with purpose, one even raising an arm to point directly toward them. Ishara leans close to Kunai, her whisper urgent and firm. "Kun, when I say run, you run as fast as your legs will carry you."

Kunai shakes his head, his eyes wide with recognition, voice trembling with excitement. "No, it's him. It's Uldako. Look!"

Kesia nods, her voice tinged with relief. "He's right. And it looks like he's brought five formidable warriors with him!"

Ishara rises slowly to her feet as she looks at the men. "Thank *Il*!" she breathes, the tightness in her body finally easing as the weight of fear slips away.

Uldako walks with purpose, praying silently to *Il* that his friends are still safe. Then, he spots the temporary shelter in the distance and can see movement. Pointing ahead, he shouts, "There, on that hill."

As they draw closer, Uldako lets out a huge sigh of relief and begins to sprint toward them. Ishara starts to wave eagerly. "Uldako!"

Kunai and Kesia join her, their faces lighting up with joy. Uldako, far ahead of the others, rushes into a warm embrace from Ishara, Kesia, and Kunai simultaneously. Overjoyed to see them, they all hold each other tightly.

Stepping back, Uldako's eyes scan his friends, a smile spreading across his face. "How is Šarru?"

In unison, they respond, "He's alive!"

Uldako's eyes light up, and he tries to suppress his tears of joy. "Good!"

A voice behind them speaks up, "Umm, aren't you going to introduce us?"

Uldako turns to see Tiras's inquisitive gaze. "Oh yes, my apologies. These are five of Seth's comrades who have come to assist us."

They exchange greetings, and then Kunai tugs on Uldako's sleeve, asking, "Where is Seth?"

Uldako looks at Kunai with warmth and reassurance. "I haven't found him yet. But if we stick with these men, they will take us to him very soon."

As Jano strides into the shelter area, he starts to speak, "Night is upon us, and we will need to be safe." His eyes widen at the sight of the bear, and he abruptly jumps back, exclaiming, "A bear! Get back now, it's a massive cave bear!" His expression is filled with concern as he readies his weapons and takes a defensive stance.

Uldako and his friends burst into laughter as Jano prepares to fight for his life, and the other warriors quickly ready their weapons for the perceived threat. Tiras, visibly perplexed, demands, "What's so amusing?"

Uldako, still chuckling, reveals, "The bear is none other than Šarru, my best *dusa* since he was a mere cub. He is the one I told you about who is injured."

Relief washes over the faces of the warriors as they share a moment of laughter and camaraderie. Tiras, breaking the tension with a jest, remarks, "Did you see Jano's eyes? Big as the sun—priceless!"

His remark prompts another warrior to retort, "And what about you, Tiras? You weren't exactly steady yourself!" Banter ensues among the fighters, lightening the mood.

Meanwhile, Kesia's eyes inspect their impressive armor, and when the banter quiets down, she suggests, "Since it's too late to travel, why don't we all spend the night here? Then, perhaps you men can enlighten me on how you came to acquire such splendidly crafted armor."

Tiras steps forward, his chest puffed with pride, and proclaims, "Good idea! Now, young lady, this rare armor can only be crafted within the walls of my clan. It takes decades, no, centuries, of practice, and only the master blacksmiths possess the skill to forge such masterpieces!"

As they continue discussing blacksmithing skills and the group settles into the shelter as night falls, Uldako walks directly over to assess Šarru's condition.

"I may have something to aid Šarru's healing," Jano announces, retrieving special herbs and wraps from his bag. After a nod from Uldako confirming that it is safe to do so, Jano, with gentle hands, tends to Šarru's injuries.

Uldako moves closer to reassure Šarru. "Jano, if you don't mind my asking," he begins, "what are these miraculous herbs you possess?"

Jano passes the small bag of herbs to Uldako to take a closer look. "This is a blend of special healing herbs, a recipe passed down in our family. It's ideal for treating wounds like these. I'll share the recipe with you during our journey back to Seth tomorrow."

Uldako expresses his gratitude, eagerly anticipating the knowledge.

Tiras declares, "It's been a taxing day. I'm turning in. Wake me for my watch, Jano."

Jano acknowledges, "Of course. I'll take the first watch."

When the other warriors follow suit, seeking rest, Uldako feels a pang of disappointment, having hoped to learn more about Seth, their lineage, and their journey.

As the night deepens and the camp settles into silence, Uldako finds himself restless, unable to succumb to sleep. His mind races with anticipation for the continuation of their journey and the possibility of finding Seth the following day.

Noticing Uldako's restlessness, Jano motions for him to join him at the entrance of their makeshift shelter. Uldako eagerly settles beside Jano, who glances at him and whispers, "Trouble sleeping, huh?"

Uldako gazes into the flickering flames of the torches before them. "Yes. I've traveled so far to find Seth and have been through so much. Yet all this time, my *ama*...she is still a slave and I—"

Sensing Uldako's hesitation, Jano gently urges, "Few things can shape a person like the road of life, and yet, you are but at the first steps of your earthly journey, young one! So tell me, Uldako, why did you seek out Seth first instead of your *ama*, and is that the only heaviness you are carrying in your heart?"

Uldako inhales deeply, his voice barely audible as he confides, "My *ama* remains enslaved, enduring each day's hardship and abuse from her tormentors. While I'm out here living freely, she suffers, deprived of experiencing the wonders of this world. She cannot enjoy the diverse flora, the majestic creatures, or even making new *dusa-meš*. I cannot rescue her..."

Jano's brow furrows in confusion as he responds, "Why not?"

Uldako hesitates for a beat before replying, "I am too weak to go up against a camp of slave traders by myself, and even if I were to liberate her somehow, we'd need a secure refuge where we can live safely. What would it help to rescue her from evil men, only to be at the mercy of wild beasts? You see, I was hoping to ask Seth if..."

Jano stares into the glowing flames, his expression thoughtful. "You're thinking of asking to stay with him, aren't you? But that won't work. Seth no longer dwells in a safe camp. In his youth, yes, he ruled much of the land as the *lugal* after Adam. But ever since his *dumu*, Enosh, took over the northern kingdom, Seth has…well, he's become a traveler, free to roam as he wills. Even the camp he once kept near the Mountain of *Il* now belongs to one of his other *dumu*."

Uldako, intrigued by the mention of a mountain of God, inquires, "You mean there is a mountain where *Il* dwells?"

Jano gives a faint smile, a hint of reverence in his voice. "Well, *Il* is Spirit and omnipresent, which means He is everywhere. But it has been a custom in our family to walk up to the mountain to worship *Il*. This mountain is where Adam and most of his family now worship. Not only do they worship Him there, but *Il* communicates with the lineage of Seth on that mountain from time to time."

Uldako, excited by the revelation, interrupts, "So if Adam lives close to this special mountain where *Il* is and communicates to Seth's family line, why would he leave such a place of value?"

"Well, as I said, *Il* is Spirit, and He is not limited by this mountain. This is something Seth has learned over the centuries. He can pray to *Il* on any mountain or even flat land. There is another famous mountain in our family that goes back to ancient times. It is called Mount Senir, which lies far from here to the west. There are even whispers of *Il*'s messengers, the spirits He created, gathering there to meet with Him. It has been said that *Il* has taken His place in the divine council, and it is on that mountain, in the midst of the spirits, where He holds judgment. Even *Enki* appears there from time to time. Whether that is true, I don't know, but I do believe there is a heavenly council in the heavenly realms, and the spirits cannot do anything without the Most High's permission."

Jano smiles, his gaze distant. "Seth is not like most men, as you've seen. Though he is one of the ancients, a high-born, rich in the wisdom of centuries, he lets no rank breed pride or make him think himself above others. Instead, he grows humbler, while his trust in *Il* strengthens day by day. What seems to some like confidence in himself is in truth confidence in *Il*, an inner strength, more than a man's, tempered over hundreds of years. He loves others as himself, so he keeps no house. His home is everywhere, wherever the North keeps a safe camp and might need him."

For the first time, Uldako sets his mind on Seth's long life, on sights, deeds, and wisdom gathered over centuries. "What a life…I never even thought about the world back then, when Seth was young and men were few. Surely he saw many clans rise, bright and dark alike? Life and death? In those early years, Adam probably led his children."

"Indeed," Jano answers, "in the early days, Adam, and later Seth, lived near the Mountain of *Il*, where the seat of power was forged for righteous men to rule and judge. The title of *lugal* has been passed down Seth's line, all the way to Enoch, who now reigns as *En-Lugal* at the present time. They ruled as *Il's* appointed stewards, bridging the sacred and the common. They trained the young in the knowledge of *Il* and the skills of life upon the earth.

"Recently, Jared's *dumu*, Enoch, raised a new city, Nippur, a place that has swiftly become the heart of those who worship *Il*. Surrounding it are countless safe camps and clans. Nippur now serves as the new seat of power in the northern kingdom, dedicated to the Most High."

Uldako nods slowly, absorbing the information. "I think I understand now. So would it be possible for me, my *dusa-meš*, and my *ama* to live in Nippur or in one of the safe camps around it?"

Jano's hand rests reassuringly on Uldako's shoulder as he replies, "I am not the *lugal* and have no authority, but personally, I don't see why not. If allowed, you could even establish your own safe camp, strengthening our defenses in the region. Then, you would have many allies around you, like-minded men and women who still serve and worship *Il* and the *Dumu-nita* of *Il*, called *Il-Il*. In fact, Enoch has begun the construction of a ziggurat temple for *Il-Il* in the middle of Nippur."

Uldako, as if struck by lightning, exclaims, "*Il-Il*! I heard that name before from a traveler who taught me how to fish. Then sometime after that, I heard a divine spirit mention that name again. He appeared to me when—"

Uldako stops mid-sentence as Jano chuckles skeptically and interrupts, "That was likely a dream. A *dumu-nita* of *Il* doesn't just randomly appear to any human. They might appear to a high-born leader like Seth, since *Il* does bestow His Spirit of power upon a chosen *lugal* when he rules on *Il's* behalf, and also on prophets, like Enoch, who embodies both."

Slightly irritated by Jano's skepticism, Uldako insists, "I'm telling you, a spirit, a messenger of *Il* appeared to me. I know what I saw and heard."

Jano inches forward. "I didn't mean to offend you, Uldako. I just know that an experience like that is extremely rare. However, the unseen realm does influence the seen. The seen was after all created by the unseen, and who am I to say a spirit of *Il* did not reveal himself to you."

Uldako fiddles with the map in his hands then realizes something interesting when listening to Jano's words. "Now that I think about it…it's interesting how the cities of *Il* and *Il-Il* are positioned in the middle and north of the map, while Eridu, where *Enki* is worshipped, lies to the south. It's almost as if the celestial skies provide a cosmic reflection and plan for the earthly temples and their positions.

"*Il* is the supreme *Dingir* to whom all power is attributed. His temple is situated in the heart of the land, right in the center, with His mountain far to the north. That mirrors His kingdom in the heavens and the earth, *Il* being the Most High. Meanwhile, *Enki*, whom some say is the new *dingir* of this world and the *dingir* of the deep or netherworld, has his temple under construction in the South, in Eridu."

Jano ponders for a moment before responding, "You have astute observations, and indeed, you are correct." He continues, "Most of the evil shamans and prophets who commune with the dark spirits have sought to replicate the celestial landscape on earth.

"Now, allow me to speak generally according to the beliefs of those in the East and the South: They regard these spirits as *dingir-meš*, but the majority uphold the belief in three primary deities: *An*, the *Dingir* Most High, then there is His eldest *dumu*, and lastly, another supposed *dumu*, *Enki*.

"But, in the heart of Sumer, the temple of *Il* stands, as He is the Most High. North of that lies the temple of *Il-Il* in Nippur, *Il's Dumu*, who also holds sway as Lord in the heavenly realm. Their emblem is the eagle, which symbolizes the heavenly realms of peace and righteousness, but also specific spirits, called *cherubim*. They have four different faces, but one of them is like an eagle.

"Finally, in the South stands the temple in Eridu, symbolizing the cosmic domain of the netherworld and the Apsu, which are under the domain of *Enki* with the symbol of the serpent, or the great dragon of old as the *dumu* of Seth calls him."

Uldako's eyes widen as understanding dawns. "It's all starting to make sense now. I see," he says, pausing to gather his thoughts. "I overheard conversations about the temple of *Enki*, how the fallen spirits themselves gave the orders for its construction, demanding precise alignment with the stars that represent them. And there were rumors—whispers of ritualistic practices meant to bring forth the *Ašag-dingir* and the Dragonborn!"

Jano's eyes widen in surprise at Uldako's knowledge. "I'm astonished that you're aware of these details," he admits. "I don't have the full story, as most of these things are recent developments. Seth, Enoch, and a select few do. From what I gather, Adam and Eve received vast knowledge from *Il* during their time together in the early years. They shared this knowledge with their *dumu-nes*. However, Cain, their firstborn, corrupted what they call the sacred knowledge, and the teachings from the fallen spirits made it even worse!"

Uldako, intrigued, asks, "So does this sacred knowledge explain how the stars are connected to earth, and how somehow we can—"

Jano interrupts, "Uldako, this conversation is extremely intriguing, but a vast topic. We can talk more about it as we journey back to Seth tomorrow, but for now, I can barely keep my eyes open. Could you take over the watch from me so I can get some rest?"

Uldako nods, watching Jano as he retreats to rest, leaving him alone with the nocturnal sounds of unfamiliar creatures. As the night's eerie chorus surrounds him, he reclines, his gaze drawn to the celestial spectacle above. A shooting star streaks across the sky in a dazzling display of speed and brilliance, captivating his attention. Lost in the ethereal beauty of the moment, he contemplates the mysteries of the heavens, pondering the nature of these moving celestial bodies.

"Could that moving light be a spirit?" he whispers. "Or perhaps *Il-Il*?"

The thought stirs something deep within, but doubt soon follows. "No, the spirits who came before arrived in an instant, like lightning, not falling from the sky, not descending like this. Unless…perhaps they can. Perhaps this is another kind, with other power." He narrows his eyes, scanning the glittering sea above. "But what are they, then, these glowing sentinels that fill the night? Maybe they are different types of beings and not spirits at all, but why do they watch in such silence?"

His thoughts drift further, stirred by memory.

I Am… The words echo in his mind, weighty and eternal. "Who was that being…the One who called Himself that? He wasn't like the others, not just some wandering spirit."

He remembers the blazing eyes, the hair white as snow, the presence that filled the air with terrible power and overwhelming love. It had shaken him to his core and comforted him in the same breath.

"It felt like *Il*. Or someone like Him with high authority. He was ancient and divine, but how is that possible if the North believes that *Il* is the only true *Dingir*?" he murmurs. "But Jano and others also spoke of *Il-Il*, and now they even worship Him in Nippur, as the true *Dumu* of *Il*. This is confusing."

As the night cloaks the world in its embrace, Uldako finds his mind a whirlwind of thoughts, each one a haunting echo of uncertainty. His mother's fate is a heavy burden weighing on his heart. Thoughts of Seth, mingling with the darkness that surrounds his older brother Cain's enigmatic presence and opposing gods, are shrouded in mystery. Uldako's thoughts dance on the edge of his consciousness. Lost in this labyrinth of contemplation, he succumbs to the fatigue that tugs at his eyelids like invisible bonds.

Suddenly, a burst of light jolts Uldako from his restless slumber. With a gasp, he awakens, disoriented, staring straight into the morning sun. Blinking away the remnants of sleep, he finds himself met with a playful chuckle, and his gaze locks onto Ishara's amused expression next to him. Her teasing tone is loud as she quips, "Well, well, look who's finally decided to join the land of the living. Remind me never to rely on you for night watch duty again!"

Flushed with embarrassment, Uldako stammers, "Did you take over for me?"

Ishara's smile is warm. "Yes, I noticed you were exhausted, so I kept vigil in your stead. After all, you needed rest, especially after the arduous journey and the sleepless night prior."

Uldako's eyes soften with gratitude. "Thank you, Ishara," he murmurs, a sense of warmth blooming within him. But as he surveys their empty surroundings, a flicker of concern ignites. "Wait—where is everyone?"

Before Ishara can respond, a boisterous voice echoes from outside the shelter. Uldako's instincts take over as he springs to his feet, his senses heightened with alertness. Stepping out into the open, he discovers the warriors engaged in a flurry of activity, with Kesia and Kunai lending their assistance.

Perplexed, Uldako approaches the group. "What's going on here?"

Tiras steps closer to Uldako, his eyes gleaming. "Well, I don't reckon any of us has the muscle to lug Šarru all the way to Seth. Except, perhaps, for Enkiar over there." He nods toward the brawniest of the warriors.

Enkiar stands out among the group, a towering figure of raw power and endurance. His broad shoulders and muscular frame speak to years of rigorous training and battles fought. His dark brown hair, thick and unruly, cascades down to his shoulders, framing a rugged face marked by a few battle scars. His piercing brown eyes convey both fierce determination and a gentle kindness.

Clad in a mix of durable leather and iron armor, each piece meticulously crafted and well-worn, he exudes an aura of invincibility. The beautiful dark lion fur draped over his shoulders adds to his imposing presence. His armor, adorned with intricate engravings and symbols of his clan, speaks of a storied heritage and a life dedicated to protecting his people. A massive scar on his left arm, looking like the bite marks of some beast or dragon, hints at the formidable foes he has faced. The massive axe, too heavy for most men to wield, strapped to his back and glinting ominously in the light, completes the image of a formidable warrior ready to face any challenge.

Enkiar meets the suggestion with a skeptical look. "I wouldn't bet my life on it, not even the mighty Enosh could shoulder Šarru's bulk," he chuckles, earning a round of laughter from the others.

Uldako marvels at Enkiar's size, wondering what Enosh must look like if Enkiar is the mightiest man he has ever encountered. His gaze shifts to their handiwork, and with a nod, he catches on to their plan. "So, you're creating something to haul Šarru along?"

Tiras nods, motioning for Uldako to lend a hand. "Yes, a wooden contraption to drag him behind us. We can't stay here any longer; every moment counts if we're to reach Seth and Lamech in time. We do not want to leave them alone and vulnerable for too long with danger around them."

Uldako dives into the task, throwing himself into the construction of the wooden platform with fervor. As they work, one of the warriors named Shamgar takes charge, barking out orders with the air of someone who's done this a thousand times before. Shamgar looks like a wild man, a figure of untamed energy and fierce competence that Uldako struggles to make sense of.

Shamgar's appearance is striking. He wears light fur and well-tanned hide, fastened with ivory pieces. Uldako knows this is by choice, not need. Shamgar probably has access to heavier and more advanced armor like the others here. It marks his character and confidence that he prefers agility to bulk and trusts his skills to keep him alive in combat.

His short red hair is a vivid crown above his head, and his impressive beard, more akin to the mane of a lion, adds to his imposing presence. Shamgar's weapon of choice is a massive club, strapped to his back, complemented by a small, utilitarian knife at his waist.

His eyes, a playful light brown, sparkle with a mischievous glint, even in the most serious situations.

Impressed by Shamgar's skill and leadership, Uldako can't help but inquire, "You've got quite the knack for this, Shamgar. Where did you learn to construct such things?"

Shamgar straightens, chest out, pride gleaming in his eyes as he begins. "Ah, I owe everything to Methuselah, Lamech's *abba*," he proclaims with satisfaction. "A true master craftsman, Methuselah and his lineage possess the gift of shaping wonders from wood. You should see the boats they build! If Lamech is blessed to find a wife, he'll surely pass their wisdom on to his *dumu*. As for me, Methuselah says I have a natural talent for the craft. So, believe me when I say, I'm one of the finest wood craftsmen you'll find in the North."

As Shamgar continues to boast, his companions exchange knowing glances, some rolling their eyes in mock exasperation. One of them mutters under his breath, "Oh, here we go again," while another adds with a smirk, "Uldako, you have no idea what you have just begun. You've opened the springs of the deep!"

Kesia stands up for Shamgar as she gazes at him with a hint of warmth. "Well, if you are good at something, you are good, hey Shamgar?"

A smile spreads across Shamgar's lips as he blushes.

But it's Jano who finally cuts through Shamgar's self-praise with a stern rebuke. "I say, it would be wise to let another praise you and not your own tongue."

Shamgar's pride deflates slightly, and he mumbles in embarrassment, "Just stating the facts, nothing more."

The others join in, teasing Shamgar about his penchant for boasting, lightening the mood with laughter and good-natured ribbing. Tiras eventually intervenes, silencing the banter and refocusing their attention on the task at hand.

While the others labor on the wooden contraption, Ishara, together with Jano, tends to Šarru's wounds, the bear lifting his head to meet her gaze with eyes reflecting both gratitude and discomfort.

After about one hand's movement of the sun, the men finally complete their task. Before them lies a sturdy wooden platform, ample enough to accommodate Šarru comfortably, with two lengthy poles fashioned for pulling.

Shamgar declares, "Now we just need to get Šarru on it, and we're ready to move out!"

With concerted effort, they maneuver the platform closer to the shelter, easing Šarru onto it amidst his gentle protests. Though the bear groans in discomfort, Uldako finds solace in the subtle signs of improvement with each passing day. Their belongings gathered, the group assumes their positions, with Uldako and the five warriors distributing themselves evenly along the poles, ready to embark on their journey.

Just as they take the first step, Shamgar's piercing scream echoes through the air, causing a ripple of surprise among the group. His sudden outburst, coupled with a pitch so high it rivals a woman's, leaves them momentarily stunned. With questioning faces, they turn to Shamgar, awaiting an explanation.

"Spider! That was a big spider on the pole!" he exclaims, his voice still laced with alarm. His admission breaks the tension, setting off a cascade of laughter.

Enkiar, renowned for his strength, bellows amidst the mirth, "A fitting punishment for your boasting earlier!"

As jests and taunts ensue, Tiras delivers a hearty slap on Shamgar's back, accompanied by playful mockery. "The fearless Shamgar, conqueror of lions and dragons alike, cowers at the sight of a mere spider!" Tiras jibes, eliciting uproarious laughter from the group. Even little Kunai, overcome with amusement, collapses to the ground, his laughter uncontrollable.

Observing Shamgar's embarrassment, Kesia steps in to defend him. "Spiders are no laughing matter," she asserts. "Some are lethal. I'd probably shriek too if I encountered one."

Their exchange lightens the atmosphere as they share a few jokes before resuming their journey to Seth, with Šarru being towed behind them on the improvised sled.

As they traverse the terrain, the group notices the interesting relationship forming between Kesia and Shamgar as the two walk next to each other with affectionate glances.

Uldako is the only one unaware of the relationship forming as his mind circles back to his conversation with Jano the night before. Amidst the quiet rhythm of their footsteps, he broaches the subject of sacred knowledge, "So does sacred knowledge explain how the stars are connected to earth and somehow give power to—"

Jano, taken off guard by the sudden question, reacts, "Uldako, you have a knack for leaping into deep discussions out of thin air." There is a hint of amusement in his voice.

Unfazed, Uldako presses on, driven by his insatiable thirst for understanding. "For me," Uldako explains, "truth holds supreme importance. I prefer to center my attention on the essence of life, the pursuits that hold genuine significance. Time is fleeting, and we mustn't squander a single moment."

Ishara and Kunai share a knowing smile, familiar with Uldako's unwavering commitment to what truly matters in life.

Tiras nods thoughtfully, acknowledging Uldako's insight. "Wise words indeed."

Jano interjects, providing context, "Just to elaborate, Uldako and I were discussing this very topic last night, the seven sacred mysteries, an area Uldako admits he has yet to explore."

Tiras is visibly intrigued. "Ah, yes, they are indeed fascinating and vital to understanding the world around us. Each offers profound knowledge about the nature of existence, the seen and the unseen. They include word-craft, which teaches us the proper use of language and communication; speech-craft, the art of persuasion and effective speaking; and right judgement, which sharpens our reasoning and critical thinking."

He continues, "Then we have number reckoning, the study of numbers and their mysteries; line and measure, which reveals the shapes and properties of our world; and song-craft, which harmonizes sound and teaches us the rhythm of life. Lastly, the one you mentioned, Uldako, star-craft, the science of the stars. It connects us to the heavens and the movements of celestial bodies. These sciences, while interpreted differently by those who follow *Il* and those who follow other *dingir-meš*, are foundational to our understanding of both the physical and spiritual realms."

"I see," Uldako says thoughtfully. "Each one of the seven seems to hold a piece of the larger whole of existence."

"Exactly," Tiras replies, his eyes gleaming with enthusiasm. "They are some of the keystones of our world's mysteries and beyond. By studying them, we draw closer to the divine wisdom of *Il*, while those who follow dark spirits have recently begun to twist these teachings for their own ends. The most important knowledge is the knowledge of the spiritual realm and how we as humans can connect with *Il*. We know that *Il* is spirit, and those of us humans in this earthly realm who seek and find Him are called to worship Him in truth, for there is no other way."

Uldako leans into Jano while Tiras continues speaking, his curiosity evident. "I barely grasped half of what Tiras just mentioned," he whispers.

Jano lets out a soft chuckle and interjects before Tiras can continue, "Let's start with the basics for Uldako's sake, shall we?"

Intrigued, Uldako asks, "I would also like to know how this sacred knowledge ties into masonry. Last night, we discussed temples being constructed in alignment with the stars, but what does that mean?"

"Admittedly, we might not be the most knowledgeable on this subject." Jano takes a breath and with a mischievous hint in his eyes continues, "Perhaps Shamgar, the expert, the most talented builder, has more insight?"

Shamgar, not noticing Jano's intent, falls right into the trap. He nods assuredly, a glint of self-assurance in his eyes. "Certainly, I am well-versed in most complicated issues," he begins while looking at Kesia—clearly an attempt to impress—but is met with playful eye rolls and teasing remarks from his companions.

He persists, "From what I've gathered, those who follow *Enki* have recently been led astray by the fallen spirits, twisting the pure knowledge bestowed upon humanity by *Il*. This knowledge, imparted to Adam and Eve during their divine communion, was passed down through generations. However, individuals like Cain succumbed to corruption, perverting this wisdom with the dark arts granted by the fallen *dumu-nita* of *Il*."

His revelation leaves Kesia and the rest of the group stunned, their expressions reflecting disbelief at Shamgar's unexpected depth of understanding.

Uldako interjects, "I want to know everything about the sacred knowledge, but first could you provide an example of this perversion?"

Tiras speaks up first, his voice heavy with solemnity. "A good example is how they distorted the celestial wisdom, turning star-craft into star-omens. They've twisted the natural wisdom of the firmament, turning the measure of the lights into divining by the stars. We use the knowledge of the stars to gain insight into the times and seasons, which is especially helpful for planting crops at the right time. This wisdom stretches back to the time of Adam, Cain, and Abel. Cain was the first *dumu* of Adam to work the ground. But now Cain's lineage uses the knowledge of the stars for evil, a perversion that taints their understanding of the heavens, leading them not with clarity but with falsehoods.

"Recently they learned to delve into dark arts, practicing sorcery, divination, and the forbidden act of communing with the deceased. Such nefarious deeds often involve vile rituals, which is why their recent temple built for *Enki*, the ziggurat, is aligned with particular stars. Isn't that correct, Shamgar?"

Shamgar nods in agreement, his tone carrying a weight of knowledge. "Indeed, I have not seen this myself, but I've heard rumors of how their high-ranking sorcerers can now turn water into blood, or staffs into serpents. Who knows what evil they might bring on humanity if they are not stopped. But to your question, most sacred sites of our land reflect the celestial order." He pauses the group for a moment to get their full attention.

"Consider this: When the sun climbs from the midst of the firmament to its two turnings, north and south, it comes to the place where heaven and earth draw near. Some believe this is the meeting place of heaven and earth."

Ishara interjects abruptly, sensing Uldako's perplexity. "Personally, these matters are too intricate for me. But can you confirm something? Uldako and I have personally seen a dark spirit attempt to deceive women from my own clan to worship him. We have heard whispers that the fallen spirits, posing as *dingir-meš*, seek to take mortal women and beget children by them, raising up powerful hybrids, the *Ašag-dingir*. And when the stars align, a blasphemous ritual of the bull ensues: a union between mortal and supposed deity, giving birth to the seed of the serpent, the Dragonborn, destined to rule as a *dingir*. Is this true?"

A dark tension falls over them. Tiras glances among the warriors, exhales, and settles his gaze on Ishara. "Wherever you heard it, whatever you saw, know that the same rumors have reached our ears," he says, his voice weighted with concern. "The earth groans and is shifting beneath our feet with new clans emerging and diverging in their beliefs. Some still cling to the worship of *Il*, while others are lured by the temptations of *Enki* and the fallen ones in the East and the South. They are seduced by their fleshly desires, using their newfound power and knowledge for selfish gain. I fear that if they breed the *Ašag-dingir*, the North will be in grave danger!"

A hush falls over the group, the weight of this revelation palpable. One of the five warriors who often remains quiet steps forward, his unexpected voice startling the others. With steady and calm authority, he reminds them of an ancient truth. "There exists an ancient prophecy, spoken by *Il* himself at the dawn of time, regarding two opposing seeds," he begins, his tone imbued with reverence. "It speaks of two enemies: one of darkness, and one of light."

The five warriors trade quick glances, as they know what's coming. They step forward to unite in reciting the prophecy in unison, their voices resonating with solemnity. "And the Lord *Il* said unto the serpent, 'I will put enmity between you and the woman, and between your seed and her seed; He shall bruise your head, and you shall bruise His heel.'"

The group takes a moment to absorb the weight of the prophecy. Tiras, turning his gaze to the quiet man who had unexpectedly spoken such wisdom, says, "Renju, what a blessing to hear you speak more than one word!" The rest of the fellowship chuckles, and a small, embarrassed smile forms on Renju's lips.

Renju stands out with his smaller build, his frame honed with lean, agile muscles that betray his speed and precision. His light armor is designed for agility, composed of dark brown and black leather that blends seamlessly into the shadows, perfect for stealthy movements, especially under the cover of night.

Like Jano, he bears twin swords but with different shapes: short broad-blades, cunning of shape, quick in the hand. On each hilt a lion's face is cast, its mane shaping the guard. The backs are heavy and strong, forged to bind another's edge, and with a hard blow, to break it.

Renju's facial features are striking, piercing dark blue eyes that seem to see everything, a short stubble beard that adds to his rugged look, and a face perpetually set in a focused, ready-for-action expression. His light curly hair, a stark contrast to his dark attire, is fastened at the back, keeping it out of his way and adding to his streamlined appearance. The hood at his back is there to hide the color when necessary.

Uldako finds Renju a fascinating enigma, the aura of mystery around him sparking intense curiosity. He longs to understand more about this quiet warrior, whose silent presence speaks volumes.

However, at this moment, his attention shifts to the puzzle of the prophecy. "Ah, I see. The serpent symbolizes *Enki*, I've heard, and that's why his followers bear the emblem of the snake, while some other clans use the dragon," he muses, connecting the dots. "So, he's manipulating clans like Cain's descendants to rise up against the followers of *Il*, aiming to prevent the birth of the prophesied seed of the woman."

Ishara adds, "Exactly. He does not know when or who the Chosen One will be, only that He will come from the woman's seed, from Eve."

Jano nods. "In Eridu and beyond, some who serve him bear serpent marks, and old hymns hail *Enki* as *ušumgal*, the great serpent/dragon. Others carry the goat-fish. I have seen him carved with a ram-headed staff, a horned cap, long robes, and streams of water pouring from his shoulders. And to your point—yes. It fits. This is why the fallen ones press so hard to bring forth the *Ašag-dingir*. We believe they aim to mar the woman's line before the Promised One can come."

Uldako chimes in, "Are you saying their plan is to replace all humans on earth?"

Tiras raises his hand. "We believe their design is this: First, to mingle and thin the blood of true men over time. Second, to beguile the seed of Eve, leading them to call the dark spirits *dingir-meš* and their *dumu*—the earth-born *Ašag-dingir*—divine, drawing many away from *Il*. Lastly, to set themselves as *lugals* over men, wielding hidden arts as power to wage war and subdue the righteous, those who still call on the name of *Il*. Some of these plans are already in motion, as you have seen, yet we still know little of the Nephilim."

Ishara interjects, "The Nephilim?"

Jano clarifies, "You referred to them as the *Ašag-dingir* earlier. We, Sethites, hailing from the clan of Seth, call them the Nephilim."

Kesia shifts, easing the mood. "All this is too much for me," she says. "I would prefer a simpler life, one where I don't have to worry about matters beyond my control. I would rather focus on my crafting skills and grow old with a man worthy of me." She looks directly at Shamgar with a light in her eyes, creating a joyful tension in the air. The group exchanges amused glances, aware of the clear flirtation, while Shamgar blushes, his confident demeanor momentarily shaken.

Suddenly, Uldako halts in his tracks, alerting the group to a presence below in the valley. They pause, crouching low as they observe a gathering of armed men, their weapons at the ready.

25

Caves

The sun hangs high in the sky, casting harsh shadows across the rugged landscape, while fierce winds whip through the hills. Uldako and his company crouch low behind a ridge, their eyes fixed on the strangers below. They see about twenty men and women, clad in little more than scraps of animal hide around their waists. Most are robustly hairy, wielding sticks adorned with stone-laden tips.

Tiras breaks the silence first. "They resemble the acquaintances of our recent adversaries, do they not?"

Shamgar nods. "Indeed, Tiras. But it appears they're a band of raiders." His eyes turn to Kesia next to him, adding, "Don't worry, I will protect you!"

Kesia scoffs. "Do not think I only forge blades, Shamgar. I also know how to wield them."

Shamgar's attempt to impress her falls flat. He drops his gaze as the others trade knowing looks.

"They are hunters, not raiders. Look," Uldako points to the hairy men. "I suspect they're returning from a triumphant hunt. See the two at the forefront?"

Ishara says, "Indeed, they carry what seems to be a slain animal of some sort, tethered to a pole."

Tiras arches a brow. "Regardless of their intentions, we must proceed with caution. We don't want to find ourselves in another skirmish so soon after the last one."

Jano nods in agreement. "We should observe them a while longer before making any decisions."

The group remains hidden, their senses alert as they continue to watch the movements of the party moving away from them.

"What troubles me is their trajectory, leading straight to where Seth and Lamech are," Tiras remarks, his brow still furrowed with concern. Without missing a beat, he turns to Jano. "You're our finest scout," he affirms.

"On it," Jano replies with a resolute tone as he begins tracking the group.

Meanwhile, Tiras directs his attention to Uldako, his gaze unwavering. "While Jano keeps eyes on their movements, we'll circle around them with speed to reach our campsite. Seth and Lamech may be waiting already, and we can't afford to risk confrontation with our injured companion." He nods toward Šarru.

With stealth and a sense of urgency, the group sets off through the rugged landscape as they make their way to safety.

Jano glides through the terrain with the grace of a shadow, his steps silent, his senses keen. As he trails the potential enemy, he remains ever vigilant, ensuring he maintains a safe distance while remaining undetected. Then, to his relief, their path veers sharply to the left, skirting away from Seth's location at the edge of the mountain. The hairy men move with speed and disappear from view as they cross over the ridge.

Hastening to catch up, Jano's heart is pounding with anticipation. Yet, before he can reach the ridge, piercing screams and guttural roars shatter the air, stopping him in his tracks. With a surge of adrenaline, he quickens his pace and cautiously approaches the ridge, crawling low to the edge to assess the unfolding scene before him.

Jano sees two distinct factions locked in combat, one of them accompanied by their loyal beasts. The combatants bear a striking resemblance, both sides clad in meager animal fur garb and wielding similar weaponry.

Jano mutters to himself, mystified over the unfolding spectacle. But then it dawns on him. "Oh, wait…" His keen eyes detect subtle differences: unique markings adorning their faces and bodies, variations in hair length and style. "They're of the same family tree, but turned into rival clans," he concludes. "The newcomers likely stumbled upon their tracks and were lying in wait for this very ambush."

Amidst the chaos, Jano observes the two accompanying beasts, smaller than typical lions yet formidable in their own right. These creatures resemble cave wolves, albeit smaller in size, their menacing jaws emitting fierce barking noises. "They look like *ur-idim*, but bigger. Maybe they breed them this way," Jano reflects inwardly.

The skirmish rages on unabated, and choosing to remain concealed, Jano patiently awaits the outcome. A resounding blow fells a big man, sending him crashing to the ground. His fallen comrade's anguished cry spurs another to action, launching himself at the victorious adversary, teeth bared, aiming for the throat.

At the fury of the fight, Jano's brow tightens. "Barbarians, men of the wild," he mutters, "hard in strength and ruthless in battle. Their seed may be of Ubrudar, the grand *dumu* of Cain, who was cast out three centuries past because of his brutality. The hair, the set of the features, and even the brutality are his."

The clash rages on relentlessly, leaving a trail of fallen warriors in its wake. The odds seem to favor the group of eleven, now pitted against the dwindling eight. A piercing scream shatters the air as an unfortunate soul finds himself ensnared by the jaws of one of the beasts, swiftly met with a brutal blow to the skull from an assailant. Another casualty added to the grim tally.

Jano, though no stranger to the prospect of fighting to defend his people, finds himself recoiling from the brutality unfolding before him. The savagery of these men, driven by primal instincts and the thirst for victory, weighs heavily on his conscience. He has never been one who enjoys battle and the suffering it causes. As the tide of battle turns, with one man dispatching three adversaries in rapid succession, the remaining fighters begin to scatter in retreat.

Victory, albeit at a great cost, now belongs to the six men who are the only ones left standing from those who had returned from their hunt. Jano observes in silence as they exchange hurried words among themselves, hastening toward the mountain. Two men bear the spoils of their hunt, a freshly caught deer, while the remaining four drag the defeated foes behind them.

With cautious curiosity, Jano follows them up the mountain, until they walk toward the entrance of a cave. Surprised by the revelation, Jano realizes that this clan may have made their dwelling not on the mountain, but within the very heart of the mountain itself. He finds himself drawn by the mysteries concealed within the mountain's depths.

On the far right side of the mountain, Uldako and the rest of the group finally reach the campsite, but their relief turns to concern upon finding it deserted. Seth and Lamech are nowhere to be seen. As they survey the area, a sense of unease settles over them.

Uldako, seasoned in tracking, immediately notices signs of a struggle. Pointing to the ground, he indicates the remnants of a skirmish. "Two men were seated here," he observes, "but they were ambushed from this direction...by around twenty-five men. The smaller tracks suggest women may have been involved as well."

Silence hangs heavy in the air until Tiras steps forward, taking charge. "This is what we will do. Shamgar, you remain here with Ishara, Kesia, Kunai, and Šarru," he commands. "Uldako, your tracking expertise is recognized and needed. Lead the way. The rest of us will follow your lead as we pursue them. Let's move; time is of the essence!"

Impressed by the warriors' stealth behind him, Uldako moves ahead with swift, sure strides, his heart pounding in rhythm with each step. He longs for Šarru's presence, their bond a well-honed instrument in tracking prey. Meanwhile, Tiras and the others right on his heels maintain a vigilant watch, scanning the terrain for hidden dangers.

Back at the campsite, Ishara sits uncomfortably between Shamgar and Kesia, who exchange flirtatious glances. Feeling out of place, she stands and moves to sit next to Kunai, giving the pair some space to get to know each other. As Ishara settles beside Kunai, her mind drifts to the potential dangers Uldako and the others might face if they fail to find Seth.

Noticing her concern, Kunai speaks up, "You were right earlier when you said I should trust you, Uldako, and *Il*. So, I already prayed that *Il* will help Uldako and our new *dusa-meš* to find Seth and Lamech. Don't worry, Ishara. It will all be okay."

Ishara smiles warmly at Kunai, who returns the gesture, and she gently extends her arm to give Kunai a hug while the two sit, quietly awaiting the group's return.

Meanwhile, somewhere on the mountain, Uldako continues to lead the three warriors higher, his senses finely attuned to the surroundings. Their mission is clear: Track those who took Seth and Lamech as fast as possible. The trail, marked by subtle signs of struggle and footprints, is fraught with unknown danger. As they approach a treacherous stretch, the path narrows, forcing them to inch along the sheer rock face, every step a precarious balance between life and death.

The tension is visible. Each warrior moves with painstaking caution, the sound of their breaths barely audible over the howling wind. One step at a time, they move safely beyond the narrow path. The tension eases as the path widens, offering a fleeting moment of relief. Yet, as they press on, a new challenge looms—a distant cliff, its jagged edge cutting against the sky like a promise of doom.

"That looks dangerous. Why would the tracks lead there?" Uldako whispers, his eyes scanning for any signs of the captors. He points to a broken branch and disturbed soil, evidence that their enemy passed this way.

Tiras, matching Uldako's cautious tone, adds, "If that is where it leads, that is where we will go. Best we tread carefully, lest we join the ranks of the fallen." His words hang in the air, a stark reminder of the deadly stakes as they near the cliff with cautious steps, threading through the denser greenery where trees loom like sentinels and bushes conceal secrets.

Emerging into an open expanse, Uldako spots a significant detail. He motions for the group to take cover, his gaze fixed on the base of the colossal cliff.

Enkiar's gravelly voice announces their discovery. "Caves. They've sought refuge in the mountain!"

Uldako affirms, tracing the tracks that vanish into the rocky recesses. "But these caves see much traffic," he adds, his brow furrowing in thought.

As they hide, cloaked in the stillness of their observation, Tiras flicks a hand while saying, "Call the eagle"—a signal for Renju. Renju does.

Uldako wonders what kind of eagle they've tamed; surely it stayed back at the camp with Lamech, since it didn't travel with them in these last few days. *Why keep an eagle, though? Unlike Šarru, it has no strength for battle. Perhaps they trained it to spy from the sky*, he wonders.

He doesn't want to raise his voice and ask, the enemy might hear, but curiosity wins. Uldako whispers, "What eagle?"

Renju gives a second call.

A sudden voice shatters the silence behind them. "Hey, you!"

They jolt, hearts pounding. Uldako searches the treetops behind them and whispers in shock, "Your bird can speak?"

Renju blinks at him, confused. "There's no bird. We use a specific eagle-call, a code to call one another when an enemy is near."

"Yes, I am a bird," the voice cracks again from the shadows, but this time with added laughter.

They turn toward the sound. Only then does Uldako recognize the voice, and he sees Jano step from the shadows, a knowing smile on his lips.

"Jano?" Uldako utters in disbelief, marveling at his stealth. "You startled us on purpose!"

Jano's smile widens as he confesses, "You thought you were being silent, but I heard you from far away!" His amusement is evident as he recounts his feat.

Tiras interjects with a hint of jest, "Now you sound just like Shamgar, with your boasting.

Jano's smile gives way to a serious gaze as he looks at the entrance of the cave. "I trailed those men as they disappeared into the cave over there, but there's been no movement in or out since. I lingered a while, surveying the surroundings, intending to investigate the cave, until I spotted you four!"

Tiras voices their concerns, "Seth and Lamech were absent from the camp. There were signs of a struggle and tracks leading here. Uldako reckons there were over twenty assailants, and now with the other group of hunters also converging here, they far outnumber us."

Jano cuts in, "On their journey here, they clashed with another group lying in wait for an ambush. The group I trailed emerged victorious but paid a heavy toll. Only six men survived, which lowers their numbers."

Uldako looks at the cavern entrance, his voice heavy with dread. "Even if they have fewer men, it doesn't change the fact that Seth and Lamech might be in danger. Considering this clan's appetite for human flesh, I fear—"

Tiras steps forward, fixing Uldako with a determined gaze. "Your thoughts betray your young age. You will learn it is a waste of time to jump to conclusions, young one. Do not be driven by your fears and allow them to influence your clarity of mind. If you do, mistakes can easily follow, and regret soon after. There's only one way to uncover the truth, and we must do so now, for time is of the essence."

With bold resolve, the warriors advance toward the cave, their footsteps echoing in the still air. Tiras leads the way, his posture exuding unwavering confidence, while Uldako follows closely behind, his heart pounding with anticipation and dread.

The cave looms ahead, dark and foreboding, its entrance a gaping maw ready to swallow them whole. As they draw nearer, the air grows colder, and the shadows deepen, but their determination does not waver.

Together, they step into the darkness, ready to face whatever horrors lie within, driven by the hope of rescuing their friends from a grim fate.

Inside the cavernous entrance, Tiras spots a narrow passage leading downward. Large enough for three abreast, the path remains eerily silent. With a decisive nod to the others, he readies his blade and ventures into the tunnel first.

As the rest of the group follows and penetrates the depths of the mountain, Uldako's heart pounds harder and faster within his chest. Surprisingly, it's not fear that quickens his pulse but rather a thrill of anticipation, an eagerness to delve into the unknown and the possibility of locating Seth. Then he realizes it for the first time. These seasoned and wise warriors are tempering him, hammer and anvil, fire and quench. The more he learns from them, the sharper the difference shows and reveals the tempering he still needs.

Jano's hushed voice breaks the silence, "This cave seems more than natural."

Enkiar adds, "Indeed. It appears to be man-made, a cleverly carved refuge within the heart of the mountain. The horrific tales might be true."

Uldako exchanges a glance with Enkiar, curiosity stirring within him about these tales, knowing all will be revealed soon. Right now, he must remain alert for any sign of danger. As they descend to the bottom of the lengthy tunnel, the party is awestruck by the vast chamber that unfolds before them, accompanied by a labyrinth of additional passageways. They share a silent exchange, marveling at the grandeur of the chamber and its multitude of tunnels.

"I believe we should divide our efforts," Shamgar suggests. "By splitting up, we can cover more ground in our search for Seth."

Renju, usually a man of few words, becomes very vocal again, his stoic face contorting with pure terror. "No…secret dark tunnels…scary place…flesh-eating men—sticking together is better!" he stammers, his voice rising in pitch with each word.

The others pause, exchanging amused glances as Renju's fear transforms his usual calm demeanor into a comical display of wide-eyed panic.

Tiras raises an eyebrow, struggling to suppress a grin. "Are you saying you're afraid, Renju? The fearless stealth warrior, scared of a few dark tunnels and stories of flesh-eating men?"

Renju, his eyes darting around nervously, tries to compose himself but fails miserably. "Not afraid, just…cautious! Yes, very cautious. Sticking together is better. Safety in numbers!" His attempts to rationalize his fear only make the others chuckle more.

Enkiar, trying to keep a straight face, claps Renju on the back. "Don't worry, Renju. We'll make sure the flesh-eaters don't get you, although you probably look the tastiest out of all of us."

The group bursts into quiet laughter, the tension of the moment dissolving into light-hearted camaraderie. Even Renju manages a sheepish smile, knowing he's provided a much-needed moment of levity.

Enkiar touches his blade and points to some of the tunnels. "In truth, the men dwelling in these caves, like feral beasts, probably are the savage, flesh-eating people we've heard of. Some tales even speak of sacrificial rituals, offering live humans to their dark *dingir-meš*. And those whispers of secret dark tunnels often come with haunting tales of malevolent ghosts lurking within."

Uldako's eyes widen with apprehension as he responds shakily, "So, we're not just dealing with secret tunnels, but haunted, malevolent secret tunnels inhabited by flesh-eating savages and even ghosts. How does one fight a ghost? I'd rather not venture alone in here. I am with Renju!"

Tiras scoffs, "You don't put stock in those fanciful tales, do you, Enkiar? I know you have faith in the boundless power of *Il*!"

Enkiar chuckles. "No, not that talk of 'haunting ghosts.' We know there are none, only good and evil spirits. Yet it was worth it to see Uldako's face."

Uldako chuckles at his expense and finally Tiras steps forward. "You had your laugh, but time is of the essence! Renju's got a point; we are stronger together." He gestures to the far-right tunnel. "Listen…do you hear that? Whispers emanating from that direction, and bloodstains on the ground. I believe that's our best option. All of us, together!"

Renju, still visibly nervous, nods vigorously. "Yes, strength in numbers."

The group advances cautiously, their senses as sharp as their blades, each step measured and deliberate. As they press on, the tunnel begins to lighten, the distant murmur of voices growing clearer with every step. They halt abruptly as they spot hewn stairs descending into a vast chamber teeming with people. Taking cover, they observe the scene unfolding before them.

Uldako's eyes widen in disbelief as he takes in the sight. The cave stretches up to a towering natural roof, higher than a forest of cedars, well over a thousand cubits high. Along the cavern's walls, smaller carved-out shelters are visible, likely serving as sleeping quarters. In the heart of the chamber, a group of about thirty men and women congregate, gathered around what appears to be a communal dining area.

"Look! They're consuming them," Uldako murmurs, aghast. At the center of the room, a circle of seven figures huddles around a flickering fire, gnawing on what seem to be human limbs, while other parts roast on the flames.

Jano is the first to break the silence, his voice hushed, "They're feasting on those who attacked them earlier. Those limbs do not belong to Seth or Lamech; the color is off, and it has markings."

Uldako spots movement in the shadows at the far side of the chamber. "They're alive! Over there, in the cage."

Tiras and the others breathe a sigh of relief. "They're probably keeping them alive, fresh for future meals," Tiras grimly observes. "We must act swiftly to free them and escape this place."

Enkiar grips his blade tightly, ready for action. "With my strength, we could overpower these thirty easily," he suggests.

Uldako stifles a chuckle at Enkiar's bravado but stops when Enkiar glances at him with a warning gaze, realizing it was no jest.

Jano interjects with a somber tone. "I've seen enough bloodshed. Let's focus on rescue, not revenge. We can't afford to risk any lives unnecessarily."

Tiras nods firmly. "We don't know how many of these savages lurk in these tunnels. Renju, you go alone in stealth and release them. We'll keep watch here."

Renju acknowledges the wisdom of stealth over brute force, his expression resolute. "Going."

The group remains vigilant, their eyes scanning the chamber for any signs of danger, ready to act at a moment's notice.

Renju bides his time, waiting for the perfect moment to make his move. As soon as an opportunity presents itself, he silently dashes toward a nearby boulder, swiftly taking cover behind it. The rest of the group watches with bated breath, tension thick in the air, while Enkiar stands guard behind them. Both hands are on his massive axe, prepared for any threat that might approach from the rear.

With a sense of urgency, Renju reaches Seth and immediately begins to undo the cage's latch. Seth's relief is visible as he whispers, "Thank the Most High! You found us, Renju. We must flee this accursed place at once."

Just as Renju finally opens the cage door, it emits a loud, grating squeak, drawing the attention of everyone in the cavern. Renju closes his eyes for a moment, realizing what is about to happen. The atmosphere shifts from apprehension to chaos as the hairy flesh-eaters charge toward them, some wielding crude weapons while others rely on their bare hands. The cave erupts with their animalistic screams and furious shouts, a cacophony of rage that reverberates off the stone walls like the roar of some ancient beast.

Uldako feels a surge of adrenaline, his heart pounding in his chest. He glances at the others, seeing their determined expressions mirrored in his own, but without any fear. The reality of the situation presses down on him, but he knows there's no turning back now. They will have to fight for their lives!

Enkiar stands tall, a confident smile gracing his lips as he declares, "Now we have a real battle on our hands." His voice breaks through the chaos, a rallying cry that brings steadiness amidst the angst. His eyes gleam with excitement, muscles tense and ready for combat.

With swift and decisive movements, Enkiar leaps into action, crashing skulls and overpowering adversaries with calculated ferocity. Not as before in the wilderness, when they fell on their foes without a sound. This time the warcries roll on every side. Uldako and the others join the fray, each wielding their weapons with skill and determination as they fight their way toward Renju, Seth, and Lamech.

Seth takes charge as his comrades reach him, issuing commands as he grabs a makeshift weapon dropped by a defeated foe. "Circle!" he shouts, and immediately they form a moving circle, ready to fend off attacks from all directions. Uldako, recognizing the strategic maneuver, falls into formation, his two-handed sword slicing through enemies with precision. Impressed by Uldako's prowess, Enkiar acknowledges his skill before swiftly striking down another enemy.

Uldako steps forward, his voice heard over the fighting screams, tinged with urgency, "Seth! I found you!"

Seth, recognizing the familiar tone, nods briefly, "We'll talk later. Focus on surviving first! Everyone, fall back to the entrance. Their numbers are growing, more are emerging from the tunnels."

They move swiftly as a unit. Through centuries of experience, Seth knows the confined space of the tunnel will provide them with a tactical advantage against the overwhelming enemy.

Enkiar, in a display of strength and agility, dispatches his opponent with a powerful blow from his axe, though it becomes lodged in the skull. Undeterred, he leaves his axe to seize another attacker by the throat mid-leap, hurling him into the path of an oncoming foe.

Uldako watches in awe at Enkiar's prowess, as well as the skill and speed of his comrades. Despite the intensity of the battle, none have sustained injuries, and they have already bested around fifteen adversaries.

Finally reaching the safety of the tunnel, Seth issues another command, "Enkiar! Renju! Tiras! Take the rear while the rest of you follow me!"

As the group advances up the tunnel, Uldako watches as a horde of enemies converges behind them, but the confined space of the passage limits their numbers, allowing only a few to approach at a time.

Spotting Enkiar without his axe, Uldako shouts, "Here, take this!"

Enkiar's grin widens as he deftly grasps the heavy sword, wielding it with remarkable agility. Uldako is awestruck by the power and skill displayed by Seth and his warriors, realizing that witnessing this battle firsthand is an experience beyond anything he could have imagined. These men have fought together for decades—no, centuries—and it is clear in their tactics. They all fight as one body without a word needed.

As they retreat out of the tunnel and into the cavern that leads to the entrance of the cave, they're met with a startling sight: a towering, muscular figure emerges from another tunnel at the opposite side, while hordes of enemies are heard moving in from the other tunnels. Seth's voice rings out urgently as he beholds the huge enemy and those approaching behind him. "They are trying to trap us. Run!"

With a mighty swing, the colossal man brandishes his club at Uldako, who narrowly evades the blow and bolts for the exit. Glancing back, he witnesses Seth engage the giant adversary. To his surprise, Seth dodges the giant's attack and leaps into the air at the same time, delivering a crushing blow to the man's skull, sending him crashing to the ground. Without hesitation, Seth runs toward the exit, sprinting for safety alongside his comrades. Uldako expected a longer fight against such a big enemy, but Seth, a warrior unlike any other, killed him easily with a single strike.

The cacophony of approaching enemies and Seth's commanding voice urging them to move faster fills the cavern as they flee for their lives toward the exit.

26

Home

The sun falls below the horizon, casting the land into the embrace of darkness. Atop the mountain, a hush descends, broken only by the gentle whispers of a peaceful breeze and some nocturnal creatures that begin to stir.

The tranquility shatters as the clamor of men echoes from the depths of the cave. The men dash through the final stretch of the cave's entrance toward freedom. Uldako and Seth are the first ones out, and with urgency in his voice, Seth commands, "Up here with me!"

Uldako swiftly follows Seth's lead, scaling the rocky terrain above the cave entrance. As the others emerge from the cavern, still fending off the approaching adversaries, Seth calls out, "Step back! We're sealing the entrance!"

Distracted by Seth's directive, Jano fails to notice an assailant leaping toward him from the cave.

Renju's swift intervention saves Jano from a perilous fate, his timely strike bringing down the enemy just inches from Jano's vulnerable form. Catching Jano's disbelieving gaze, Renju offers a reassuring chuckle before returning his focus to the onslaught pouring through the cave's mouth.

Meanwhile, Uldako, grasping Seth's strategy, begins to topple boulders, barricading the entrance in a desperate attempt to stem the tide of foes. With each crashing rock, the makeshift barrier grows, impeding the advance of the relentless attackers.

Standing a few meters away, Jano, Renju, Enkiar, and Lamech brace themselves for the next wave, ready to repel the encroaching horde. As the battle rages on, a grim wall of rubble and fallen adversaries takes shape, hindering the enemy's progress with each passing moment.

The last rocks tumble into place, sealing off the entrance with a finality that echoes through the cavern. With labored breaths, Seth and Uldako descend to join the others, weariness carved into every line of their faces. A tense silence hangs heavy in the air as they catch their breath.

"Flesh-eaters…dark secret tunnels…never again," Renju mutters in the silence. The group's laughter breaks through the tension as they relish Renju's dry manner of speaking, his face as impassive as ever.

Amidst the shared chuckles and exchanged pats on the back, Tiras quips, "You were flirting with danger there, Seth!"

Seth's smile widens, his eyes reflecting the gravity of their narrow escape. "Seems I have a flair for the dramatic, Tiras."

Jano, still catching his breath, joins in with a grin. "Next time, let's stick to sunshine and open fields. My heart can't take much more of this." The laughter grows, filling the open air with a much-needed sense of relief.

Uldako looks at the mountain and says, "We best not linger. There may be other paths into this cave, and our foes will not rest until they find us."

With a collective nod, the group sets off. Seth, sensing the urgency, takes the lead, his determination evident in every stride. As they move at a brisk pace, Uldako's mind swirls with a myriad of emotions. Lost in his thoughts, Seth unexpectedly sidles up beside him.

"It has been some time, hasn't it, Uldako?" Seth's words cut through the silence, catching Uldako off guard. Though his heart leaps at the recognition and even the remembrance of his name, a strange shyness washes over him.

"Yes," Uldako manages, his voice cracking barely above a whisper.

Seth smiles and says, "I guess we will have much to talk about, young one, but let's wait for the right time when we are safe."

Seth glances at the rest of the men and adds, "Stay vigilant. Watch for any signs of flesh-eaters or some other beast awaiting us!" They nod and continue on in silence, their senses heightened, eyes on their surroundings for any sign of danger.

Back at the campsite, Ishara and the others grow increasingly uneasy as the sun begins its descent. Kesia, longing for the warmth of a campfire, is gently dissuaded by Shamgar, who cautions against attracting unwanted attention. She notices the tension in Shamgar's demeanor, his gaze fixed on the looming mountain, a furrow forming on his brow as he searches for any sign of their friends. The shadows lengthen, casting an ominous gloom over the camp.

The uneasy silence stretches on, broken only by the occasional rustle of leaves and the distant calls of nocturnal creatures. Kunai, unable to contain his concern any longer, voices the issue weighing on all their minds, "Where could they be? It's getting late." His words hang in the air, amplifying the group's unease as they await any sign of the returning party.

Shamgar fixes Kunai with a reassuring gaze, his eyes tender as he whispers back, "Fear not, lad. Those men have lived for centuries and are as resilient as they come. They have been through far worse, and their wisdom gained over time far surpasses any obstacle they may face! They'll do their best to return to us unscathed, mark my words."

Kunai nods, finding solace in Shamgar's confidence, but he still seeks reassurance from Ishara, who offers him a comforting smile. Though Kunai attempts to conceal his unease, Ishara, Kesia, and Shamgar sense his inner turmoil. To ease the tension, Ishara begins to sing in a low whisper, her voice a soothing balm for their troubled hearts.

Da daa di daha
Oh, I will not fear...
Oh, I will not fear...
Though they hurl spears in strife,
For I know *Il* guards my life!
Though the valley looms so dark,
No evil shall leave its mark...
No hand shall harm me,
For *Il's* light sets me free.
Da daa di daha
Oh, I will not fear...
Oh, I will not fear...
What can man do to me
For my eyes the truth they see
Il will have the final say
So keep the evil at bay!
Da daa di daha
Oh, I will not fear...
Oh, I will not fear...

As Ishara's melodic voice washes over the group, they find a sense of calm descending upon their troubled souls. Lost in the reverie of her song, Shamgar's mind wanders, pondering the profound truth woven within her lyrics.

"You voice wisdom, Ishara!" he muses silently, his gaze drifting to the heavens above. With a quiet resolve, he addresses the divine, his voice a gentle murmur against the night's canvas. "Guide them back to us, O *Il*, Most High, but may Your will prevail above all else."

In a rush of excitement, Kunai's exclamation pierces the air, breaking the tension as he points his finger behind Kesia, "There!"

Shamgar, Ishara, and Kesia leap to their feet, their eyes searching the horizon until they see the approaching figures. Shamgar eagerly identifies each member of their group, relief flooding his features, yet a nagging worry gnaws at him as Jano's absence is noted.

Just as concern begins to grip him, a shadow emerges from the periphery, revealing Jano's familiar silhouette. With a collective sigh, the group reunites, their voices overlapping in a cacophony of joy and relief.

Seth sees the hurt bear lying on a rough sledge and judges it as Shamgar's work. He moves up to make light of it, expecting the man's predictable answer. Through the clamor he calls, drawing every eye, "What's with the injured bear on that ugly and crooked contraption?"

Shamgar's defense of his creation is swift and passionate, his pride evident as he rebuts Seth's inquiry. "What do you mean ugly and crooked? Maybe your age is starting to influence your eyes, which are deceiving you. This perfect design is the ingenuity and mastery of my craftsmanship," he asserts, his voice ringing with conviction, "especially based on the little time we had to craft it."

A few chuckles fill the air while Uldako approaches his furry friend with a caring look. "This is Šarru, my steadfast companion," he explains to Seth with pride. "Together, we've faced countless trials, and he sustained injuries defending us from predators not long ago." Uldako crouches low next to the bear and inspects his wounds while gently brushing his hand through Šarru's fur.

Observing Uldako's tender care for the injured bear, Seth's eyes soften with understanding. He marvels at the transformation in Uldako, once a malnourished, weak, and downtrodden slave bereft of hope from the dark lands, now a resilient and compassionate guardian. He draws near to the massive bear. "May I?"

Uldako's affirmative nod is all the permission he needs. "Šarru knows a good man when he sees one," Uldako assures, his voice carrying a note of pride for his wise beast.

As Seth's fingers run through Šarru's fur, the bear emits a soft growl, a sound of both discomfort and tentative acceptance. "An honor to meet you, Šarru." Seth takes a deep breath and continues, "We cannot linger here! Those flesh-eating fiends who captured Lamech and me may return, so let's move out!" His words stir a sense of urgency among the group, prompting them to swiftly gather their belongings and prepare to depart.

With their gear in tow, they set off. As they move, they carefully maneuver the wooden platforms supporting Šarru, ensuring he remains comfortable and secure throughout their journey.

Jano, holding the rear and sweeping out their tracks, spots fresh blood darkening the dust. He looks up and sees that Seth's gait is off. Jano signals Renju to take over the trail-clearing then slips to Seth's side.

"Are we bound for Nippur?" he asks.

Seth, wise with centuries, hears what lies beneath the question; he knows Jano has noticed more than he says, perhaps the wound. He nods, eyes on the path. "Indeed. It offers safety, and aid, for Šarru and for me," he replies, a hint of weariness in his voice.

With a small shift of his cloak, he reveals the wound beneath his armor. Jano's eyes widen.

"What happened?" he asks, worry edging his tone.

Seth smiles it aside. "It happened when they captured us. It is nothing too serious, but it needs care."

Jano quickly takes out some herbs and cloth to treat the wound, ignoring Seth's objections with firm insistence. After a while, the wound is treated and Jano says, "This will help for now, but we can't leave it for too long. The wound is serious and needs proper care."

Seth knows it well and walks on, turning the speech from his hurt as he faces the company, his eyes finding Uldako. "Uldako, when I returned to our camp the day before, Lamech told me everything about your journey here. You have grown speedily from your slave days. And I see you have taken companions on the road. Name them before us."

Uldako strides forward and names each with honor. "This is Ishara, *dumu-munus* of Beniah," he gestures toward her with a firm nod, "blessed with a voice that can soothe every troubled heart, and skilled with both blade and bow."

Seth nods in appreciation, acknowledging Ishara's talents. Uldako then points to Kesia. "This is our newest member, Kesia, *dumu-munus* of Ketzariah. She has a passion for forging great weapons and armor, and aims to be the best blacksmith in the world, but we have yet to see any skill at all!"

The group chuckles at Uldako's jesting, but Kesia is not impressed as she gives him a look that could kill.

Next, Uldako points to Kunai. "And this is Kunai, but we call him Kun," Uldako continues, "rescued by Enoch when his entire village fell to raiders, including his parents."

Seth pauses, his gaze softening as he approaches Kunai. "I'm sorry for your loss, lad," Seth murmurs sincerely. "But I'm glad you found safety. Remember, let not darkness consume your heart. Stay on the path of light and all sorrow can be worked for good."

Kunai nods, gratitude and determination gleaming in his eyes.

Then Seth asks Kun, "So you are the *dumu* of…?"

Kunai looks at Seth, pausing to think deeply. He glances at Uldako and Ishara, and with bold pride, declares, "I am Kunai, *dumu-nita* of Uldako and Ishara."

The group exchanges knowing glances, emotions swelling within them. A tear rolls down Ishara's cheek, while Uldako stands in stunned silence.

Sensing the immense significance of the moment, Seth places a reassuring hand on Kunai's shoulder. "Your birth parents may no longer walk this world, Kunai, but *Il* has blessed you with remarkable guardians in Uldako and Ishara," he says warmly. "You have a unique journey ahead, and I want to see greatness in you. Don't let your past be a chain that holds you back. Instead, let it be the fire that ignites your soul. Have the strength to transform your pain into something extraordinary."

Kunai's tears stream down his face as he listens to Seth's powerful words. *It feels as if this wise elder is looking straight into my heart, into my very soul, and addressing my deepest thoughts*, he reflects inwardly, standing in stunned silence. The weight of Seth's words resonates deeply within him, stirring emotions he hadn't fully understood until this moment. *I will never forget those words,* he vows silently, his admiration for Seth growing with each passing moment.

As Seth turns away, a silent groan escapes him, betraying the pain of his wound. The entire group notices Seth's struggle, their concerned glances converging on the wound he grips tightly at his side.

Ishara, her face filled with concern, steps forward and gently presses, "Seth, you're not well. This wound needs tending."

Despite his discomfort, Seth's resolve remains unshaken. His eyes, though pained, burn with determination. "I truly appreciate the concern, but worry won't change reality now," he whispers, his voice strained but resolute. "We must press on to reach Nippur."

The group, sensing the urgency and importance of their mission, silently agrees. Together, they continue their journey, each step driven by the unyielding hope to reach Nippur and get Seth and Šarru the healing they need.

As they trek, Tiras, vigilant at the rear, issues a stern reminder. "Keep your senses sharp. We may follow the safest path, but danger always lurks in the shadows. Stay focused." His words cling to each member of the group as they continue their journey with eyes and ears wide open to the surroundings for any threats.

Enkiar's curiosity gets the better of him as he glances at Lamech, his voice laced with intrigue and a hint of mischief. "Lamech, how did those flesh-eaters manage to capture a warrior as formidable as yourself?"

The young Lamech reacts exactly as Enkiar hoped, offended as if his skill were doubted. "They did not take me so easily," he says. "I fought off many, near twice my size. You would not have—"

Renju, ever mindful of their surroundings, intervenes swiftly. "Quiet! Silence is our ally," he insists, his tone firm.

Tiras, recognizing the wisdom, reinforces it. "Renju is right! No more talking. Silence until we reach Nippur."

Enkiar winks at Lamech, whispering just loud enough for everyone to hear, "I'll get the rest of that epic tale in Nippur, then."

The group stifles their laughter, sharing amused glances, while Lamech's indignant expression slowly melts into a begrudging smile.

As they walk, Shamgar and Kesia find themselves side by side, their fingers occasionally brushing against each other. They exchange lingering glances, the affection between them growing with each passing moment.

Ishara notices the two from the corner of her eye and muses to herself, *Now that looks like love blossoming.* Her thoughts drift to Uldako, her heart fluttering with curiosity. *I wonder what Uldako truly thinks of me?*

With a unified resolve, the group of twelve—Seth, Tiras, Enkiar, Shamgar, Jano, Lamech, Renju, Uldako, Kesia, Ishara, Kunai, and Šarru—press forward as one. Their footsteps are silent but purposeful, the air filled with cautious optimism.

Uldako's mind whirls with a tempest of aspirations and emotions. He looks upon the men around him with admiration, yearning to emulate their strength, their wisdom, their very essence. *Oh, to dwell within the security of their safe camp, absorbing their teachings, unraveling the mysteries of existence alongside Ishara, Kunai, and my* ama. *Nippur…might this be the home I have been searching for?* he wonders.

But then the thoughts of his mother intrude upon his reverie. He envisions her enduring hardships, her resilience in the face of cruel slave masters, and his heart clenches with determination. With gritted teeth and fierce resolve, he whispers fervently into the wind, "*Ama*, I will rescue you. I vow it upon every beat of my heart. Just hold on…I am coming soon!"

As they press on through the cloak of night, a glimmer of hope emerges on the horizon: the distant, flickering lights of a big city. It mirrors the inner journey Uldako traverses, a path shrouded in darkness yet guided by the flicker of a distant light.

Ishara's voice breaks the silence. "Is that Nippur?"

"Indeed it is," Tiras confirms, his tone laden with joy.

Excitement courses through Uldako as he beholds the site ahead, drawing nearer with each step. He notices the imposing walls that encircle it, standing tall and sturdy against the backdrop of the night sky. Torches mounted along the walls cast flickering shadows, while guards patrol diligently, their silhouettes outlined against the glowing embers.

As they approach the gate, Uldako and his friends are struck by the intricately carved designs adorning its towering doors. Each panel tells a story of the city's history, depicting scenes of triumph and worship. At the center of the gate, a majestic eagle emblem gleams in the torchlight, symbolizing strength and protection from the Most High.

The guards' heads dip in deference as Seth and his companions stride past, the massive fortress gate swinging open before them. Shamgar's hand slaps Enkiar on the back as his words echo with nostalgia, "Ah, the embrace of Nippur once more! She has been missed!"

Jano adds eagerly, "Indeed, I yearn for the taste of fresh fruit and the comfort of a soft bed."

Excitement bubbles among the group, each sharing their anticipation for the pleasures awaiting them in Nippur. Amidst the chatter, Uldako remains silent, awe etched on his face as he beholds the splendor of the city before him, a sight he never dared dream he'd witness.

As they pass through the gate, Uldako enters a labyrinth of narrow streets and bustling markets. The architecture of the buildings varies, ranging from simple mud-brick dwellings to grand stone structures adorned with elaborate carvings. In the distance, he catches sight of the towering spires of what must be *Il-Il's* new temple, the largest and most prominent building in the city, some of it still under construction, reaching toward the heavens in reverence to Him.

The air is filled with the sounds of merchants haggling, children playing, and the distant chants of worshippers. Uldako inhales deeply, taking in the scents of spices and incense that permeate the air, mingling with the warmth of the torchlight and the cool breeze that rustles through the streets. Uldako can't help but feel a sense of awe and wonder at the vibrant tapestry of life that unfolds before him. In the city of Nippur, where history and tradition intertwine, he knows that he has arrived at a place where his journey may take on new meaning and purpose.

The people of Nippur possess a serene aura, a clear contrast from those Uldako encountered in the South. Here, peace and joy seem to infuse every interaction, and honor and respect are the currency of daily life. Uldako feels a sense of belonging wash over him as he observes their harmonious way of living.

The rest of the group exchange words of wonder and gratefulness for finally entering the city, but Uldako only hears muffled sounds, not taking in a word they say. His attention is pulled in all directions, overwhelmed by all the sights, sounds, and smells of Nippur.

Seth's commanding voice breaks Uldako's reverie, pulling him back to the present. "Uldako, follow me to the healer!" Seth directs, his tone a blend of authority and warmth. "Šarru needs urgent care."

As they set off, the group springs into action, working together to move Šarru to the healer's abode. Uldako takes quiet delight in the startled looks and worried whispers that follow as they draw the massive bear through the streets.

Approaching a sizable home adorned with aromatic herbs, Seth knocks on the door. Uldako realizes yet again how tall Seth is, towering over all other men as his head reaches above the door. An elder emerges just as tall and bearing a striking resemblance to Seth, albeit slightly younger. Seth's voice carries warmth and affection as he addresses the man, "*Šeš*! It's been too long."

The man's eyes light up with recognition. "*Šeš-me*!" he shouts with joy as he rushes forward to envelop Seth and Tiras in a heartfelt embrace, their reunion radiating joy.

Uldako, witnessing the tender exchange, realizes that this must be one of Seth's younger brothers, a realization that piques his curiosity about Seth's family history as the trio, united in brotherhood, share a moment of camaraderie.

After the initial exchange, the man's gaze shifts to Uldako then to the bear appearing from behind him. "And who might this be?"

Tiras defers to Seth, suggesting, "Adriel, I believe Seth can provide all the details once you tend to his wound. As for the rest of us, we have errands to run in the city. We leave now."

With gestures of farewell, the warriors vanish into the bustling streets, while Shamgar takes Kesia to show her around the city and its blacksmith shops, leaving the rest to enter the abode.

Seth lowers his head as he enters through the doorway, while Uldako and the others help the great bear to gently climb off the sled and follow them inside. Once in Adriel's home, they notice the air is rich with herbs and remedies.

Adriel leads them to a cozy corner where he can tend to Seth and Šarru's wounds. Moving with practiced ease, Adriel gathers the necessary supplies and steps toward his brother, but Seth gently stops him. "Take care of the bear first. I can wait a little longer."

Adriel shifts his attention to Šarru, inspecting the bear's injuries with care. "This creature is remarkable, larger than most *uḫuš* I have seen, and quite blessed to have you all looking after him."

Ishara's voice fills with respect. "Šarru has saved us more times than we can count. He is more than a companion. He is part of our family."

Uldako nods. "Yes, he is," he echoes softly, looking at Šarru with affection.

After skillfully tending to Šarru, Adriel turns his attention to Seth. To Uldako's surprise, Adriel calls for silence and begins to offer a prayer over the injured while he continues to tend to the wounds. "O great *Abba*, *Il*, hear your servant's plea as I humbly beseech your grace. Grant swift healing to Šarru, so he may continue to aid Uldako and his *dusa-meš*, no…his family, on the journey You have laid out for them, and to my *šeš*, Seth, so that he may fulfill Your divine purpose. We are but clay in Your hands, and we trust in Your wisdom. *Šulmu*."

Ishara and Uldako exchange glances fraught with concern and confusion, their minds drawing uneasy comparisons to the shamans of the South who used sorcery in speaking healing mantras.

Sensing their unease, Seth reassures them, "Fear not, Adriel is no shaman delving into the unknown spirits of the South for healing or curses. Here in the North, those who revere *Il* have their own way. My *šeš* Adriel is a skilled healer, drawing from centuries of natural healing wisdom. He learned the art of healing from our *abba*, Adam, who in turn was taught by *Il* Himself. While he prays for swift healing, it is to *Il* alone that he appeals."

Seth pauses, reflecting. "Our healers, or what you may call sages, possess profound knowledge of *Il*, but they are forbidden from using sorcery, which is evil magic coming from darkness."

As Adriel cleans the wound, Seth winces. "This isn't the first time you've patched me up, *šeš*," he remarks with a wry smile.

Adriel chuckles. "And likely not the last. You have a knack for finding trouble, Seth."

Uldako watches the brothers with fascination, admiring their bond. He has never had a brother or sister and feels a sense of gratitude for having met such remarkable people. Ishara, too, is captivated, her eyes darting around the room, taking in the various healing implements and herbs.

Seeing her marvel at the unknown, Uldako remembers his own lack. "Seth, could you teach us?" he says softly. "Herbs for healing, the ways of prayer to *Il*, the art of war, and more? I had hoped…if you permit…I—" Uldako stumbles over his words, his heart racing, but Ishara steps in, coming to his aid.

"What Uldako is trying to ask is, could we reside here in Nippur or in a nearby safe camp to learn your knowledge and the wisdom to apply it correctly? We also seek to liberate his *ama* from slavery, but we do not have a secure camp to bring her to safety."

Seth's eyes widen as he recalls, "Ah, yes, Uldako, you mentioned your quest to free your *ama* from slavery. So, have you learned anything about her whereabouts?"

Uldako shakes his head solemnly. "No, I'm still in the dark. But I made a choice to find you first to seek your aid. I'll uncover her location, I swear it on the heavens, I swear it on my own life, because every single night, her suffering weighs heavily on my heart."

Seth's eyes soften with empathy. "I understand your intent, but I have walked long enough to know this: Oaths are not needed. Heaven is *Il's* throne, and the earth lies beneath His feet. Even your own life is not yours to command. So speak plainly, and let your word stand firm. Anything more than that…I have seen where it leads. Evil."

Uldako is stirred by Seth's deep wisdom and realizes he is right. Let a man's yes stand, and his no stand with it. If he lives by the truth, his word will hold. He will not need oaths to make it so. If he swears at certain times, then others might wonder if he speaks the truth when he does not swear. Uldako reflects on all this inwardly.

Seth continues, "Now let us focus on your desire to learn and live among us. Here's what I can offer: You and your companions are welcome to establish a shelter here in Nippur, or in one of the nearby safe encampments, or even forge a haven of your own."

Uldako, Ishara, and Kunai leap up with excitement, their joy evident. Seth continues with a grin, "I know a few skilled builders who'd be glad to assist you, but I suggest you go and free your *ama* first." As Seth speaks, his demeanor shifts, the warmth in his eyes giving way to a steely resolve. "We know time is fleeting, so how do you intend to locate and free your *ama* from the tyranny of the Cainites?"

Uldako's face hardens. "I have given it a great deal of thought, and I believe my best option is to wait until Šarru has recovered. Once we reach the South again, I have a plan to locate my *ama*. I will wait for the slave traders to leave the camp where I last knew she was being held. Every now and then, they move slaves to another camp to work or to sell. Sometimes while on the road, they set up a temporary camp at night. That will be my chance. I plan to take one of the guards in the dead of night and question him to learn my *ama*'s whereabouts."

Uldako pauses, his voice faltering as painful memories surface. "Most of the slave traders know who my *ama* is because they chose her for—" He stops, his face contorting with the anguish of those memories, the weight of his past pressing down on him.

Seth listens intently, his eyes never leaving Uldako's as he continues laying out his plan. "Once I have the information, I'll assess the situation. I'll likely have to sneak into the slave camp where she is held under the cover of night, dressed in the guard's clothes, pretending to be one of them. This plan has worked well for me before. Then, I will rescue her and return to Nippur."

The room falls silent as they consider the strategy. Ishara's eyes mix admiration with concern. Kunai looks at Uldako in awe and fear, the task daunting to his young mind. Seth sits back upon his chair, fingers threading his long beard. His face holds respect and care. His eyes tell the weight of what stands before them. Long years have taught him the importance in attempting to foresee all perils and possible outcomes in all strategies. Even the wisest strategies can fail if one is not fully prepared to adapt.

He weighs the ways, seeking the right path. At last he says, "A good idea… perhaps the only viable option. I will aid you with men, but Uldako, you must exercise caution as you journey south." His gaze seems to penetrate the earth beneath them, as if foreseeing a bleak future.

"The world is shifting, and not in our favor. The darkness that has lingered since the days of Cain now tightens its grip on the East and the South, plotting something ominous."

Ishara steps forward, her voice filled with conviction. "We know. We've encountered the fallen spirits, masquerading as deities. We have heard about how some of these fallen *dumu-meš* of *Il* recently shared their twisted wisdom of dark arts to Cain's descendants."

Uldako chimes in, "They are deceiving more and more clans to worship the fallen ones as *dingir-meš*. They call *Il* by the name *An*, and they call His fallen *dumu-meš* the *anunnaki*."

Seth's countenance falls. He looks to his brother, then again to Uldako and Ishara. "You have seen much—more than I thought. For the most part, you speak true. On our travels, we found evil counsel at work in the seed of Cain. Though the names *An* and *Il* once pointed to the same Most High, over time, the understanding of *An* was corrupted. What they now call *An* is no longer the true Creator but a likeness they have twisted. We know there is only one true Most High, and His name is *Il*.

"Many began to spread lies about Him, and their deception runs deep. They claim to be the chosen people who are set apart, the kingdom to whom the Creator supposedly revealed His truth. They spread falsehoods, deceiving people into believing that the Creator has *dumu-meš* who are also *dingir-meš* and should be worshipped.

"They claim His eldest *dumu* is *Enlil*, and *Enki* the younger. It is through *Enki* that *An* supposedly gives new teachings to humankind. Among these teachings, they now also worship more *anunnaki*, whom we know in reality are dark spirits.

"These are lies—deliberate twistings of the truth meant to lure the hearts of the faithful away from *Il*, the Creator of Adam and the Most High of Heaven.

"So, in other words, the 'Most High' they worship now, *An*, is a false *dingir*—a counterfeit—because they changed his character. He is a newly fabricated deity, crafted to replace the true Most High and to bring about a new council of divine beings to be worshipped. We believe this clever and deceitful scheme of perversion has been worked by the fallen spirits through the *dumu-meš* of Cain."

Ishara and Uldako stare, stunned. Even Kunai's mouth hangs open. Seth pauses, and when he speaks, his voice is hard with conviction. "We have only just learned these dark truths. The lie is not confined to your lands; it was born far to the west, in the region of Mount Senir, and we have word it has spread east as well. What we have seen confirms the worst. We know humans are not working alone. A group of fallen spirits who walk among them are behind it all. Some say these fallen ones descended from the holy mountain. Whether that tale is true, we do not know."

Silence settles over them, faces blanch. For a heartbeat, none speak. Then

Adriel breaks in. "But this is only the beginning of their evil plans. Together, they're creating unholy beings."

Seth nods. "Indeed. They're creating a test group, hybrid creatures called the *Ašag-dingir*, or the Nephilim as we call them here in the North. The fallen ones are also armed with corrupted knowledge. They seek to upend the natural order, defying *Il* and inciting rebellion against the Most High and His people."

Ishara interjects, "We have also heard the same! There are rumors of the Dragonborn, a prophecy that speaks of the conception of the seed of the dragon, the serpent of old, when celestial alignments occur—"

Adriel's sudden interruption commands attention, his expression grave. "So, the whispers that have reached Nippur are true. I hadn't anticipated the darkness to spread so swiftly. This is *Enki*...spreading lies about a false chosen one. It is he who wants all humans to rebel against the Most High."

Seth meets his brother's serious gaze. "The wheels of fate are turning, brother. The time for war draws nigh."

Uldako and Ishara exchange a knowing glance, recalling the tales of Enoch, also known as Etana, the ascender. Yet, before they can dwell on it further, Kunai asks, "Why does *Enki* defy *Il*?"

As Kunai's question lingers in the air, an expectant hush falls upon the room. Uldako and Ishara lean in closer, their eyes fixed on Seth, waiting with bated breath for the revelation. The truth they have been yearning to hear for so long is finally within their grasp, the truth of the past and the meaning of life itself!

Who created Enki, the dragon of old? Why did he rebel? How did the seen and unseen world come into being with all the earthly creatures and spiritual forces? Why are humans here and what is our purpose? And what will happen to us when we die? These are but some of the swarm of questions floating around within Uldako, Ishara, and Kunai at this moment, a heavy load about to burst open!

Seth's gaze grows solemn, his lips parting to speak truth, like a door opening to reveal ancient mysteries of all creation.

27

Battle

As Seth begins to unravel the ancient tapestry of rebellion, his voice carries the weight of centuries past, each word laden with the gravity of cosmic upheaval. "The origin of rebellion," he declares, his gaze piercing the veil of time, "speaks of the great red dragon of old, whose pride knew no bounds. It was he who first defied *Il*, driven by the insatiable thirst for power and glory. He is the originator of sin!"

In the dimly lit room, Uldako, Ishara, and Kunai lean forward, captivated by Seth's words, their hearts pounding with great anticipation.

"*Il* spoke thus," Seth continues, his voice resonating with solemn authority, "'How you have fallen from heaven, O *Hêlêl, dumu* of Dawn! How you are cut down to the ground, you who laid the nations low!'"

With each word, the ancient prophecy unfolds before them, a woven chronicle of celestial rebellion and divine judgment. The room holds its breath as Seth recounts the serpent's audacious ambition, his voice resonating through the quiet stillness of the night.

Kunai, unable to contain his curiosity, leans forward. "What does *Hêlêl* mean?" he asks.

Seth gives a slight nod. "It means *day star. Il* sometimes refers to the spirits He created as heavenly stars, and *Hêlêl* was once among the most powerful of them."

He pauses, then continues, his voice steady and grave. "Let me say this again, for the sake of clarity. *Il* spoke to *Hêlêl*, saying: 'How you have fallen from heaven, O Day Star, *dumu-nita* of Dawn. How you have been cast down to the earth! In your pride, you said: "I will raise my throne above the stars of *Il*. I will sit on the mount of assembly."'"

Ishara cuts in. "He wanted the assembly. Is that *Il's* council with the spirits? You just mentioned a mountain, and earlier that some angels may have come down from Mount Senir."

Adriel lifts his gaze from the sutures, eyes bright with care. "You see how the lines converge. Perhaps it is that mountain, but perhaps not. I believe this is not a physical place on earth, but it means the seat of highest authority over all! The saying is veiled. Yet this stands: The Most High convenes His council among the hosts of heaven. They all humble themselves under His authority."

Uldako's gaze shifts to the wound on Seth's body. It's been stitched by Adriel with some kind of sinew thread, a method Uldako hasn't encountered before, yet he marvels at its ingenuity. Though wearied by his wound, Seth continues as Adriel binds the flesh closed.

"Permit me to finish the saying handed down to our family by *Il.* The ancient serpent said, 'I will sit on the mount of assembly. I will make myself like the Most High.' Do you see? He wanted to take *Il's* place."

A heavy silence settles over the room, thick with the weight of ancient truths and lingering questions. Uldako and his companions exchange solemn glances, each mind turning over the enormity of what has just been revealed. It is Kunai who breaks the silence first, his voice small but eager. "Yes...and then?"

Uldako leans forward. "What happened?"

Ishara follows quickly, "Please, tell us the rest."

Before Seth can respond, Adriel steps forward. His voice is calm but resolute. "Seth will need his rest! Let me speak the last of his words tonight. Tomorrow, when we've all regained our strength, we can continue this discussion."

Uldako, Ishara, and Kunai nod reluctantly in agreement as Seth rises from his seat, bidding them good night before retiring to another room to rest. The flickering flames cast dancing shadows across the chamber, heralding the arrival of a night filled with contemplation.

Though weary from the trials of recent days, they find themselves unable to even think about sleep. Their minds brim with suspense, craving the truth they've sought for so long like thirsty babes longing for milk. With hearts pounding and eyes wide, they await Adriel's continuation, eager for enlightenment.

And Adriel does not disappoint.

"You see, young ones," he begins, his voice steady and commanding, drawing every gaze toward him, "the Day Star, *Hêlêl,* became the dark lord of this evil world. That is what the name *Enki* means. It literally means *lord of the earth,* as you know. He is the cunning serpent of old, the one who once shone among the brightest of stars, one of the mightiest *dumu* in *Il's* kingdom. But pride took root in his heart, before humankind was created, and he dared to rebel against the Most High in the heavenly realms.

"War broke out in heaven. Michael, chief among the spirit hosts, led the armies of *Il*, countless in number, against the dragon and his fallen ones. Though they fought with fury, they were no match for the power of *Il*. They were defeated and cast down from the heights of the heavens."

He pauses for effect, allowing the weight of his words to sink in before continuing. "The great dragon, also known as the accuser, was hurled down to the earth, along with his fallen spirits. But even in his fall, the serpent's malice knew no bounds. He began to sow seeds of evil upon the earth, heralding the dawn of darkness."

As Adriel's voice resonates through the room, an eerie stillness envelops them, punctuated only by the flickering of the flames. Uldako, Ishara, and Kunai exchange solemn glances, their minds grappling with the enormity of the revelation unfolding before them.

Kunai curiously asks, "What do you mean by *Enki* heralding the dawn of darkness?"

Adriel regards him with a gentle smile, appreciative of the lad's earnest quest for understanding at his tender age. "Ah, an astute question indeed," he commends, his voice carrying the warmth of encouragement. "Allow me to elaborate: This world was once full of peace, but the serpent's malevolent influence spread like a creeping shadow across mankind, ushering in an era of evil. Since that day, the world has grown darker with each passing season. You've seen it already with everything you've had to endure. You know as well as I, today we stand at the threshold of a new dawn: the dawn of darkness!"

Uldako and Ishara are still, their hearts and minds awash with truths too great for speech.

Kunai lifts his voice again, "Yes, but we also have the promise from *Il*. The seed of the woman will crush the serpent's head!"

Like a cord cut, the tension falls. They look at the young Kunai, bright with hope, and it washes over them all. The ancient prophecy now echoes within them, not just as knowledge, but as something alive. Something calling them to a great hope!

Ishara exhales, a clear sigh of relief, then lifts her head to Adriel. "Let me see if I've grasped this," she says slowly, as if speaking it aloud will help anchor it in their souls. "The dragon, once a radiant star, one of *Il's* own high-ranked spirits, rebelled and was cast down to earth. Now he burns with hatred toward the woman destined to give birth to the Chosen One, the One foretold to bring an end to him. Which to me, means this Chosen One will bring peace. He will bring light to destroy the darkness!"

Uldako leans forward, something fierce rising in his chest. "That's how I understand it too," he says, eyes narrowing with purpose. "*Il* will cause a Chosen One to be born who will shatter the dark rule of *Enki*, the so-called lord of the earth. Then let's call the Chosen One what He is..."

He glances at Ishara and Kunai, and then declares: "The Lightborn! The One destined to crush the serpent's schemes and drive back the darkness. That's who the dragon fears. That's why *Enki* is working so desperately to twist bloodlines, to destroy the seed of the woman, to stop the birth of the Lightborn."

Adriel nods slowly, a flicker of recognition crossing his face. "Yes," he says softly. "The Lightborn. I have heard others call Him that as well. Adam has spoken it. Seth too has named him so."

The name settles over them like a truth long waiting to be spoken.

Adriel's expression grows solemn once more. "Enoch, chosen by *Il* as king and high sage, has revealed the meaning of the prophecy. The woman represents Eve, our great mother, but it might also represent a tribe that will one day rise from her. In that way, a tribe could be seen as a woman who brings forth a child, the Chosen One. The same truth remains: A Savior will come from Eve's descendants. Since that promise, Eve has lived more than nine hundred years, and in that time, her seed has multiplied into unnumbered tribes across the earth. But more specifically, we have come to understand that the Chosen One might come from the line of Seth, who still calls on the name of the Lord. Who it will be, when it will be, and how it will be is all still a mystery."

Uldako, stunned and overjoyed, speaks as if a veil has been lifted from his eyes, his voice filled with wonder, "Then there is hope after all! Something to fight for! Something to live for!"

Adriel nods solemnly, "Yes!" He takes a deep breath and continues, his gaze steady and intense. "The dragon, in his malevolent quest, remains ignorant of the precise timing of these events. Hence, he schemes and deceives, seeking to corrupt Seth's lineage and hinder the fulfillment of the prophecy. Through his dark arts and manipulation, he aims to taint the bloodlines of humanity, starting with Cain's descendants and spreading to undermine the purity of the rest of Adam's lineage, including the children of Light, meaning the clan of Seth, the Sethites!"

Uldako reclines in his chair, his gaze fixed in awe as he contemplates the profound revelation unfolding before him. In the flickering dance of firelight, he muses, "I see more of the great design of life than ever before. The struggle between light and darkness wages on, shaping the fate of all who tread upon this earth. It's why *Enki* seeks to overthrow the plans of the Lord and sow his seeds to bring forth the Nephilim and to birth an evil counterpart to the Lightborn, the dreaded Dragonborn."

Adriel nods in solemn agreement, his eyes reflecting the weight of centuries-old prophecies. "Indeed, it could also be said that all men of disobedience do the adversary's will on earth, men and women of lawlessness," he confirms. "*Il* spoke these words to the serpent in the presence of Adam and Eve in the days of antiquity: 'Because you have done this, cursed are you above all livestock and above all beasts of the field; I will put enmity between you and the woman, and between your *dumu* and her *dumu*; He shall bruise your head, and you shall bruise His heel.'"

Ishara leans forward, her brow furrowed with curiosity. "What transgression led to such a divine punishment?" she queries. "Was it the serpent's rebellion in the heavens that incurred *Il's* wrath?"

Adriel's words are laden with the weight of ancient truths. "No," he explains, shaking his head, "the adversary's punishment stemmed from a different transgression. The punishment for rebelling caused him to be cast out of heaven. He fell from grace, stripped of his lofty station among the mighty cherubim, the pinnacle of celestial beings. His new condemnation was born from an act that forever altered the course of humanity, echoing through the annals of time."

Uldako's eyes widen as the moment of truth finally arrives, and he leans forward, eager to hear more. However, sensing the lateness of the time, Adriel says, "It is already late, and if we delve into this topic now, we'll be here until morning! You'll be staying for a few days, so let's rest tonight to refresh our minds. We can continue this conversation tomorrow. What do you say?"

Disappointed yet understanding, Uldako, Ishara, and Kunai concur, their minds still reeling from the revelations. To their surprise, Adriel gestures toward a room adorned with four empty beds. "Your furry *dusa* can rest where he is, but you three can rest in that room for the night," he bids them kindly. "Šarru's wounds have been tended to, and with time and rest, he will regain his strength in a few days."

Uldako and the others express their gratitude to Adriel, their words tinged with genuine appreciation. With gentle pats on Šarru's shoulder, they bid him good night before retiring to the room.

Inside the room, Uldako observes the unfamiliar sight of high-quality soft beds, unsure of the proper protocol for settling in for the night. Kunai, less hesitant, moves to claim a bed, but Ishara intervenes with a firm yet caring tone. "Hold on, Kun," she interjects, her voice carrying authority. "First, remove your sandals," she instructs, gesturing toward a nearby bowl. "Then wash your feet over there," she points to another vessel tucked in the corner on a wooden shelf. "After that, clean your hands and face with the water over there," she adds.

To Kunai, Ishara's guidance echoes the nurturing presence of a mother. Moved by her reminders of cleanliness and hospitality, Kunai obeys swiftly, his actions infused with a sense of reverence for their host.

"We mustn't enter the beds while unclean," Ishara continues, her words a gentle reminder of the importance of respect within someone's home.

As Ishara and Kunai gracefully prepare for bed, Uldako watches their meticulous routine with keen interest, mirroring their movements as he follows suit. The sensation of cleansing water against his skin awakens a long-forgotten feeling of freshness, a stark contrast to the harsh realities of his past. *So, this is how life unfolds in the bustling cities*, he muses silently, marveling at the simplicity of such everyday tasks.

Uldako finally settles onto the plush bed, but with anticipation that mingles with discomfort. The softness of the bed, a luxury he has never seen or even imagined, overwhelms him, leaving him to fidget restlessly. Despite his initial excitement, the unfamiliar sensation proves to be too much, disrupting his desire for rest. With a frustrated sigh, he abandons the bed, seeking solace on the cool, solid floor beside it.

Ishara observes his silent struggle with empathy, a gentle smile gracing her lips as she comprehends the unfamiliarity of his surroundings. In the quiet of the room, she offers him understanding without words, a silent acknowledgment of his journey from hardship to newfound comfort.

Ishara and Kunai succumb to sleep with surprising ease, their exhaustion from the day's events lulling them into a peaceful slumber. However, Uldako finds himself restless, unable to quiet his racing thoughts amidst the stillness of the night. The feeling of safety inside the city walls is also strange to him. Years of watching for dangers from beasts or men won't let his guard drop. He forces the words in his mind: "We're within walls. It's safe. Be at ease. No beasts can reach us here." He tries, but calm won't come, and Kunai's low, occasional rumble in the silence doesn't help at all.

Uldako lies awake, his mind becoming a whirlwind of questions and doubts. "*Enki*, the fallen day star…*Il*, the Most High…I forgot to ask about the 'I Am,'" he whispers, eyes wide open as he gazes at the roof. He contemplates the revelations of the evening, grappling with the gravity of *Il's* plan for humanity and his own role within it. Yet, amidst his musings, a singular concern eclipses all others—the fate of his beloved mother. Turning on his side, his thoughts shift more toward her. The heaviness of his quest presses hard upon him.

With each passing moment, Uldako's thoughts spiral into the unknown, envisioning the treacherous path that lies ahead. He wonders about the dangers awaiting them on their journey southward, the obstacles they must overcome, and the looming specter of uncertainty that shrouds their quest. But amidst the shadows of doubt, a glimmer of determination flickers within him—a steadfast resolve to rescue his mother, whatever the cost, and bring her safely back to Nippur, to this wonderful city of light.

After a while, Uldako finally descends into the depths of slumber, all the threads of his thoughts rolling into the world of dreams. In this realm, a surreal amalgamation of his trials unfolds, a relentless pursuit by marauders with gaping maws hungry for flesh. He runs, but their leader on his heels morphs into a cruel slave master brandishing a whip.

As the lash strikes, the scene shifts abruptly, whisking Uldako away to the sanctuary of the treehouse where Ishara and Kunai's comforting smiles await at the top. He's nearly there, hauling up the ladder, when they vanish. In their place stands the evil spirit Shamsiel, dark and sudden. Shock. A lunge. With instinct, Uldako shoves, lets go, and falls. Dust rushes up. Then the earth opens like a mouth as the dust becomes a rolling black that engulfs him, cutting him off from the others.

In the abyss of his subconscious, Uldako finds himself thrust onto a vast battlefield, the clamor of war cries echoing in the air. Two opposing clans, the eagle and the serpent, converge upon him with menacing fervor. Amidst the chaos, a familiar figure emerges—Seth, charging forth with urgency, his voice a light cutting through the dark chaos.

"Uldako, wake up, wake up!" The call pierces through the haze of dreams, jolting Uldako back to consciousness.

With a startle, Uldako's eyes snap open, his heart pounding against his chest as he grapples with the remnants of the dream's intensity. Drawing a deep breath, he gathers his wits, his senses sharpening as reality comes into focus. Seth's concerned gaze meets his own, prompting Uldako to shake off the remnants of sleep's grip.

"What is it?" Uldako inquires, his voice filled with the remnants of the dream's echoes.

Seth's gentle tone washes over him, "You were screaming in your dreams," Seth explains softly. "I came to wake you. This morning, *Il-Il's* worship begins at the temple E-kur, the House of the Mountain. It is a ceremony you won't want to miss. Come, the others are already waiting."

Uldako rises swiftly, greeted by the realization that Ishara and Kunai have already departed the room. His attention shifts to Seth who is stepping out of the room, and he inquires, "When is it starting?"

Seth's grin widens. "You've slept quite a while. It's late morning, and the ceremony has already commenced. Follow me!"

With haste, Uldako freshens up, joining the group at the entrance of the house. There, to his surprise, he finds Tiras, Adriel, Ishara, and Kunai awaiting him.

Tiras jests as the group starts to walk. "Good morning, late sleeper. We're running behind because of you!"

Uldako, catching up, replies, "My apologies!"

As they stride toward the temple, Uldako is struck once more by the city's refined atmosphere. Tranquility hangs in the air, a stark contrast to the brutality of the slave camp and the normal safe camps of the South. Every step reinforces the surreal beauty of this new world, where kindness and respect are the currency of interaction, where joy thrives in the hearts of its inhabitants. It's a world of values and morals, a world where life is cherished.

Turning a corner, they are met with a breathtaking sight, the grand temple of *Il-Il* looming in the distance. Uldako can't believe his eyes as the scene unfolds in front of him.

28

Nippur

Under the radiant sun, Nippur's denizens gather for their sacred worship to *Il*. Uldako's eyes widen in astonishment at the sight before him, a vast throng, the largest congregation he has ever beheld, congregating at the sacred temple beneath the heavens. Adorned leaders stand out in resplendent white, presiding over the assembly. Amidst the hushed reverence, an enigmatic figure addresses the multitude.

Ishara's voice breaks the silence, reverent yet tinged with awe, "Is that Etana, the *En-Lugal*?"

Seth's affectionate smile holds a depth of reverence as he confirms, "Indeed, it is...Enoch, the one who walks with *Il*, my great-great-grand *dumu*, my fifth generation."

Uldako's heart quickens with anticipation as they draw nearer to the crowd. Kunai, full of excitement, jumps up and down, trying to catch a glimpse over all the heads and shoulders to what lies ahead. Seeing the boy's struggle, Uldako lifts Kunai onto his shoulders, giving him a better view. Kunai's eyes widen with wonder as he beholds the scene unfolding before them, his excitement infectious and his laughter ringing out amidst the murmurs of the gathering crowd.

Ishara's enthusiasm radiates as she walks faster. "This is beyond words. Come, let's hasten! I want to hear his words." With that, she breaks into a run, prompting Uldako and Kunai to follow.

Meanwhile, Seth and his brothers exchange knowing glances as they stride purposefully closer.

Uldako approaches the temple amidst the bustling crowd and is overwhelmed by the sheer scale. The temple itself stands as a majestic edifice, its grandeur reaching toward the heavens. Its architecture, adorned with intricate carvings and towering spires, speaks of ancient craftsmanship and divine reverence.

The atmosphere is charged with eager anticipation, visible in the air as the people await the commencement of the sacred rites. For Uldako, who has never beheld such a spectacle, the sight is nothing short of awe-inspiring. His eyes dart from the huge structure to the throng of people gathered around it, each face reflecting a mixture of solemnity and devotion, something Uldako realizes is still missing in his life.

The scene before him leaves Uldako feeling small yet profoundly moved. It's a stark contrast to the harshness of the life he's known in the slave camps, a world of cruelty and deprivation. Here, amidst the reverence and grandeur of the temple, he feels a profound sense of belonging and spiritual connection that he has never experienced before.

As he looks at the faces around him, Uldako's heart swells with a mix of wonder and humility. This moment marks a profound shift in his perspective as he glimpses the vastness of a world beyond his previous imagination, a world where divine grace and human endeavor intertwine in sacred harmony. A world of meaning.

Out of nowhere, a song forms all around Uldako. The melodies of worship fill the air, and Uldako finds himself swept away by the harmonious chorus of voices praising the *Il*, the Most High. Musicians wielding flutes and harps add layers of enchantment to the celestial symphony, their melodies weaving through the throng with ethereal grace.

At times, it is the deep boom of men's voices that resonates most profoundly, their powerful tones reverberating through the temple grounds. Yet, in moments of silence, it is the beauty of women's voices that emerges, carrying the song to heavenly heights.

Uldako's senses are heightened, hair standing on end from awe as he surrenders to the powerful might of the music. He glances at Ishara, whose eyes are closed to remove any distractions and to focus on the sound, tears glistening on her cheeks as she is moved by the divine melodies.

Inspired by her devotion, Uldako closes his own eyes, allowing the music to wash over him like a soothing balm. He listens intently to the lyrics, their words resonating deep within his soul.

> Di di daaa, di, dadadaa
> There is joy, joy forevermore

In the fullness of *Il* to explore
Bring your hearts to Him
and your troubles will grow dim
Oh, there is joy, joy, forevermore
In the fullness of *Il* to explore
There is grace, grace forevermore
In the fullness of *Il* to explore
He is the *Abba* full of love
Looking down from the heavens above
Di di daaa, di, dadadaa

As the echoes of worship fade into the air, Uldako's thoughts linger on the notion of a father. *They sing of an* abba *full of love. What is it like to have a good* abba*?* he wonders. It's a concept foreign to him, a void in his life that he's long tried to ignore but now finds resurfacing with unsettling persistence.

Then he ponders the significance of *Il* as a Father, a notion that eludes him in the stark absence of paternal guidance. The very idea seems distant, almost intangible. As he glances at Kunai, who has also endured the loss of his father, Uldako's thoughts shift. Observing Seth, he is captivated by the evident warmth and affection in Seth's demeanor, particularly when he speaks of his own children. The love that radiates from Seth's gaze as he looks upon Enoch stirs something deep within Uldako.

It mirrors a longing in his own heart for a similar connection, a bond that he has never experienced firsthand but yearns for deeply. The contrast between Seth's fatherly love and Uldako's own fatherless past creates a deep yearning, highlighting the void in his life and inflaming his desire to find a warmth of belonging and understanding in a world that has often felt cold and indifferent.

Enoch gestures for silence, his hands commanding the attention of the crowd. As he steps forward, a sense of reverence fills the air. Uldako estimates Enoch's age to be between three and four hundred years old. Enoch looks like a highly intelligent and wise ruler, exuding an authority few possess. His eyes are framed by dark, strong eyebrows. His nose is perfectly sculpted, and his cheekbones are prominent. His jawline is strong, adorned with a beard that starts short below his ears and grows longer toward his chin. Long black hair cascades over his shoulders, adding to his majestic appearance. A scar runs across one of his eyes, leaving it dull and damaged. The other is a piercing heavenly blue.

Enoch's tall, sturdy frame is clad in a dark brown fur mantle that enhances his presence, with the head of a lion adorning his right broad shoulder. His attire is a mix of cloth and leather, and he carries a ram's horn at his side. Embroidered on his chest is an *anzu*, symbolizing the cherubim and *Il's* throne. He bears no weapons except for a finely crafted staff.

He radiates immense inner strength, reminding Uldako of what he recently learned about *Il* empowering certain individuals, like kings and prophets, with His Spirit. Now Uldako understands why he is so drawn to this man—it is not the man himself, but *Il's* Spirit working in and through him!

"*Ki-ág-meš*," Enoch begins, his voice carrying the weight of wisdom accumulated over centuries from *Il* Himself. "We have come to the culmination of our worship!" He pauses, allowing the crowd's applause to wash over *Il's* temple before continuing, "Thank you for prioritizing *Il* and His *Dumu Il-Il* in your lives. Our existence hinges entirely upon Him, for not only has He created everything, but He sustains everything continually. In His mighty hand are our life and our very breath!"

Uldako is struck by the profound truth in Enoch's words, realizing for the first time the depth of his connection to *Il* as his Creator. *If He fashioned me*, Uldako reflects, *then surely He knows my identity and purpose.*

Enoch's address presses on, "Today is also a blessed day, as Seth, the patriarch of the *dumu-meš* of light, graces us with his presence." Murmurs ripple through the crowd, reverent whispers acknowledging Seth's significance.

Enoch's proclamation continues, "Today, I bid you farewell, as Seth and I, along with some of our lineage, embark on a journey to our great *abba* and *ama*, Adam and Eve. As the elders who are gathered here may remember, they removed themselves far from the city's din, to conclude their days in quiet tranquility."

Enoch's voice carries a gravity that commands the attention of the entire congregation. "Now, I am about to reveal something that may startle you—the reason for our journey! *Il* has summoned us to His holy mountain for prayer and discussion with Adam. Our aim is to discern His plan for the future and our role in it. My *ki-ág-meš*, you are well aware that the world is veering toward darkness. The encroachment of the dragon clans, infiltrating our lands and enticing our people to worship false *dingir-meš*, is not mere rumor. They aim to deceive even the most upright among us."

Whispers erupt among the gathered crowd, a ripple of concern spreading like wildfire. Enoch raises his hand, signaling for silence, his eyes moving over the assembly. "Fear not, for *Il* is our protector, and He watches over those who serve Him with unwavering devotion. Trust in Him, and do not succumb to fear. Instead, remain vigilant, guarding against the encroaching evil, whether it be from external foes or the lurking darkness within ourselves. Remember, our battle is not against flesh, but against the dark forces all around us that dwell in the spiritual realms!"

Pausing for a moment to let his words grow roots in their hearts, Enoch continues, "In my absence, my *dumu* Methuselah will assume governance. I bid you farewell for now; go forth in the strength of *Il*!" The crowd erupts into cheers and applause as Enoch departs from the temple, a clear sign to his esteemed status among the people.

Enoch gestures for Seth to join him, then Seth turns to Uldako and beckons him to follow. "Come!"

Nervous anticipation courses through Uldako as he, Ishara, and Kunai trail behind Seth, while many eyes are on them and low whispers can be heard.

As Seth approaches Enoch, the prophet-king of the land, Enoch bows low and greets Seth with great respect. "It has been too long!" Uldako grasps the significance of Seth's stature in the northern kingdom, evidenced by Enoch's deference to him.

With a reassuring pat on Enoch's shoulder, Seth responds, "Indeed, it has, my *dumu*! But from hearing your words earlier, I suspect you already understand the reason for my return, don't you?"

Enoch nods, then turns his head to Uldako, Ishara, and Kunai, his thoughtful gaze seeming to pierce through to their very souls, reminiscent of Uldako's first encounter with Seth, many moons past. "Let us find some privacy to discuss these matters," Enoch suggests, his voice carrying a calm authority, "and then you can introduce me to your companions."

Enoch leads them into a grand chamber, clearly designated for weighty discussions that shape the fate of the northern kingdom. With only two guarded entrances, the room conveys an air of exclusivity and importance. As they step inside, Uldako, Ishara, and Kunai are mesmerized by the opulence of the chamber, from the intricately carved chairs to the ornate decorations adorning the walls, a sight that speaks without words to the unparalleled craftsmanship of the northern kingdom.

Taking their seats, Seth initiates the conversation. "So, how fares your firstborn *dumu-nita*, Methuselah?"

Enoch's expression softens with paternal pride. "He thrives," he responds warmly. "He has great strength of character. No longer a youth, he's a young man moving into his prime, in his early two hundred years."

Seth chuckles in reminiscence. "Ah, I recall those younger years well. Of late, I've taken Lamech, the youngest of our line, under my wing these few full moons. He is great in stature yet has much to learn. However, I couldn't be prouder as a grand *abba*!"

Enoch's smile radiates warmth and reverence. "All of us, including Lamech, the ninth *dumu-nita*, have had the blessing of sitting at the feet of both you and Adam for so many years, absorbing your experience and all the ancient truths."

Enoch's demeanor shifts, his eyes narrowing with intensity. "This brings me to a matter of great importance. I have received a prophecy for the future from *Il*." He pauses again, his attention now drawn to Uldako, Ishara, and Kunai. "But before we delve into that, please introduce me to your companions."

Seth proceeds, recounting Uldako's journey and the bond forged between them. Enoch interjects with an air of fascination, "Indeed, Uldako, your journey is nothing short of remarkable, and having Ishara, Kunai, and Šarru by your side is a blessing."

Kunai's curiosity bubbles forth in a question that catches everyone off guard. "Forgive me, elder Seth, but how many years do you carry if elder Enoch stands as your fifth generation and already boasts a grand *dumu*? Your age must be beyond measure!"

Ishara quickly admonishes Kanai's audacity. "Respectfully, Kunai, it's impolite to dwell on someone's age. Show due reverence to these esteemed great elders."

Seth and Enoch exchange a knowing glance before erupting into hearty laughter, breaking the tension. Uldako and Ishara join in when they realize the elders are not offended, easing into the jovial atmosphere.

Seth turns to Kunai with warmth. "I am not an old man, I have just lived for a very long time."

Enoch adds with a chuckle, "Wait until you meet Adam, Seth's *abba*. That'll be an eye-opener."

Laughter fills the room once more before Seth continues, his tone light yet tinged with wisdom. "Though I've traversed countless years and seen wonders beyond thought, the fire within still burns strong. I suspect these bones might endure for over nine hundred or even a thousand years, but it all depends on *Il*!"

Kunai's eyes widen in awe, and all he manages to utter is a breathless "Oh!" The group chuckles, appreciating the lighthearted moment amidst the weighty discussion.

Enoch shifts the mood, his expression turning serious. "It's good to savor life's joys, but we must address a pressing matter," he begins. As his gaze falls on Uldako, he continues, "Seth's trust in you speaks volumes; therefore, I, too, place my trust in you when it comes to what we are about to discuss."

Uldako and his friends nod solemnly, understanding the gravity of the moment.

Then, addressing Seth, Enoch delivers the news about Adam's recovery. "I know you journeyed to see Adam when he fell ill, but I've learned he's overcome it. *Il* will spare him a few more years," Enoch informs them.

Joy flows over Seth's features, though he is not surprised. "Yes, I received the same message some time ago! But we must thank *Il* for blessing us with more precious time with my *abba*!" Seth responds warmly. However, he senses there is more on Enoch's mind. With a knowing look, he continues, "But I suspect this isn't the main reason you wished to speak, is it?"

Enoch's demeanor grows grave as he unveils the true purpose of their meeting. "*Il's* sparing of Adam grants us a brief reprieve, a chance to gather our family and commune with him before his time comes to an end," Enoch explains, his voice heavy with the weight of his words.

"But there's urgency in *Il's* message. The forces of darkness are spreading and gaining strongholds, while my own journey to the heavens draws near. I won't be with you much longer, which also means I won't be able to aid you for long in holding back the darkness."

Seth's gaze drops momentarily before meeting Enoch's eyes once more. "I see. Time slips through our fingers like sand," he reflects, a touch of melancholy in his voice. "Losing both Adam and you so soon…it'll be a heavy blow to all of us. But there is a time to be born, and then a time to die. We cannot change that truth. Death is certain, and then comes final judgment for each of us. However, I know it is only a matter of time when we will meet you again in the heavenly realm! Therefore we shall stand firm, and wherever the Lord leads us in this temporary world, we shall follow."

Uldako's mind races with the news. *Judgment for every human after death… what does he mean?* he ponders silently. However, Enoch does not allow him much time to dwell on it. Rising from his seat, his presence commands the room.

"That is truth!" Enoch begins, his voice resonating with urgency. "Time is of the essence, and our journey northward will be arduous. Let's gather our things and meet at the gate."

Enoch turns to Uldako and his companions. He hesitates for a moment before a word is spoken. "You three are welcome to join Seth and me on this journey. I have a feeling of peace about your presence."

Uldako, taken aback by the unexpected invitation, exchanges quick glances with Ishara and Kunai. He then speaks with resolve, "I appreciate the offer, and I would love to go, but I must decline. My dear *ki-ág*, Šarru, is not yet fit for travel, and I am committed to freeing my *ama*. Her rescue is my top priority as she—"

Uldako pauses as a commotion stirs at the entrance, where a man urgently seeks permission to enter. Enoch, sensing the gravity of the situation, gestures for the guards to allow him in. The messenger, visibly exhausted and perspiring heavily, rushes into the room. His attire hints at his role as a messenger, and his trembling hands betray the urgency of his message.

He begins, his voice strained from exertion, "I bring grave tidings, esteemed elders."

29

Rest

A tense silence mantles the room as the lone messenger, clad in light armor, readies himself to speak. His face is etched with great concern, a contrast to the serene surroundings of Nippur and the company Uldako finds himself with.

Seth, sensing the gravity of the situation, steps forward. "Speak!" he commands, his voice cutting through the stillness like a blade.

The messenger, visibly shaken, takes a deep breath. "One of our towns has fallen victim to a ruthless raid by an unknown enemy!"

Seth's eyes narrow as he urges the messenger to continue. "Whose camp?"

The young man glances around, his expression troubled. "I am sorry to report, *En-Lugal*, it is one of your family camps. It is your *dumu* Ghaji's."

Enoch's demeanor instantly turns grave. "How many attackers and how many among the dead?" he demands, his voice slicing through the tension in the room.

The messenger's response hangs heavily in the air. "The entire village was decimated, *En-Lugal*, save for six women who were abducted and around five who managed to escape." He takes a breath before continuing, his voice laden with sorrow. "Your *dumu-nita* is among the deceased."

Enoch's brow furrows with deep concern as he turns to Seth, the shock clearly evident in his eyes. Seth's steady gaze offers him strength, a silent reminder of their duty. With a resolute nod, Enoch turns back to the messenger, his voice urgent yet composed. "When did it happen, and where is the enemy now?"

The messenger's response is swift and dire. "It happened just a day ago, to the east of here, in Edib, but we don't know the enemy's current location," he reports, his words painting a bleak picture of the tragedy.

Uldako observes the pain in the eyes of the elders, recognizing their genuine empathy not only for Enoch's son but for all who perished, yet they remain resolute, undeterred by their emotions. Seth's voice cuts through with clarity. "I'm familiar with the location. We will need to depart immediately to investigate. After that we will continue on to Adam's camp."

Enoch acknowledges Seth's proposal. "A wise decision. Let's waste no time." Turning to the messenger, Enoch expresses his gratitude. "Thank you for bringing it to our attention. Seek out the head guard for provisions. Eat and drink as much as you need!"

The messenger acknowledges the directive with a nod of understanding before swiftly departing. Seth turns to Uldako and the others, "This is where we part ways for now, my *dusa-meš*. We must depart without delay."

Uldako's thoughts whirl, feeling empathy for what they just learned but also being uncertain of when he'll reunite with Seth. Without saying a word, Seth senses what Uldako must be feeling and offers a solution. "Fear not," he continues. "I'll lend you three of my finest fighters to accompany you on your journey to free your *ama*. Once you've accomplished your mission, I invite you to meet us at Adam's abode."

Uldako's eyes spark with gratitude. "Thank you! Three good warriors will undoubtedly tip the scales in our favor. We shall regroup with you in the North, probably within a few weeks, prepared for whatever challenges lie ahead."

Enoch strides out of the abode, signaling for the others to follow. "It's settled then. Let's make haste," he declares. "Uldako, Ishara, and Kunai, go with *Il* until we meet again."

Seth turns to Uldako. "Go back to Adriel's place. I will send word for my men to find you there. May the Most High protect you!" With hurried farewells from Seth, the two men depart, leaving the trio standing in the wake of their departure.

An uneasy quiet descends as they are left alone. Kunai breaks the silence first. "So, what now?" he asks, uncertainty lacing his words.

Ishara observes the disappointment in Uldako's eyes and suggests a plan. "Well, let's return to Adriel's dwelling as Seth asked us. We can then also check on Šarru and wait for the men. Then, when the time is right, we can resume our conversation from last night with Adriel."

Uldako signals to Kunai to walk to the door and says, "You're right, it would be a missed opportunity to part ways without gaining his knowledge." With a shared resolve, they set off, their path clear and their minds focused.

The trio strides eagerly toward Adriel's abode, anticipation humming in the air. Ishara walks closer to Uldako, her voice filled with curiosity. "Adriel still needs to reveal the truth about the serpent's new condemnation, the act that irrevocably shaped the fate of all humanity. What do you think it could be?"

Uldako turns to her, his thoughts racing with the same questions. "I don't know. I also want to know what becomes of us when we draw our last breath. I mean, what happens at the judgment? Also, how did *Il* fashion us humans, and..." Uldako continues to touch on many things as if a wave of questions has been unleashed. Little Kunai also chimes in with his own questions that seem to be as many as the stars in heaven.

Ishara, walking in the middle, stops them with a gentle touch and a reassuring smile. "Easy now, let's not overwhelm him with too many questions all at once. We'll take it one step at a time," she advises, her tone calming.

As they approach Adriel's home, they're met with an unexpected sight; another man awaits them. Clad in vibrant yellow cloth with a neatly braided beard and a smooth scalp, the stranger projects an air of quiet authority mixed with humbleness. He addresses them directly, his voice steady and sure. "You must be Uldako, Ishara, and Kunai," he states, his gaze assessing but warm.

The trio exchange unsure glances, silently questioning how the man knows them and who he might be. Sensing their curiosity, he introduces himself. "I am Rukug, the steward of this sanctuary where Adriel tends to his patients, and he asked me to deliver a message to you."

Retrieving a leather scroll, he begins to read aloud. "Dear *dusa-meš*, I have been summoned urgently to *Il's* mountain with my family. You are welcome to stay here until Šarru recovers. Rukug will look after you in my absence. Until we meet again."

The trio exchange surprised glances, caught off guard by Adriel's sudden departure. A familiar sting pricks Uldako—the signs will not yield to him. Maps he can read, the city beasts on their seals, the river line, the mountain teeth, but the speech marks pressed by reed into clay or the stain-lines on the hide that Adriel read are a shut gate kept by a few.

Kunai voices their shared disappointment. "So, we won't get to uncover the truth about...everything," he laments, his tone tinged with frustration.

Uldako's mind churns with possibilities, refusing to accept defeat. "Hold on a moment, Rukug," he interjects. "Is there anyone else from Seth's line still in the city?"

Rukug shakes his head regretfully, delivering the disappointing news. "Adriel and all the other kinfolk have answered the call to journey to the mountain of the Most High. The sole remaining member of Seth's line who will not go to the mountain, or to Adam's abode, is Methuselah. He has been entrusted with the governance of the city in Enoch's absence. Alas, even he has embarked on a journey to attend to pressing matters elsewhere," he explains solemnly.

Disappointment settles over Uldako, his hopes dashed once again. But Rukug offers a small glimmer of solace. "Please, come inside and make yourselves comfortable. Stay for a few days until Šarru has recovered," he invites warmly, gesturing toward the entrance of the sanctuary.

Just as Uldako, Ishara, and Kunai step into the house, they're greeted by an unexpected arrival behind them. As they turn around, three imposing figures stand before them, clad in leather armor of the finest make, carrying with it the eagle emblem.

"Excuse me, are you Uldako?" one of them addresses him directly.

Uldako nods as his eyes move slowly over the three men.

The one who addressed him steps forward, palm to his breast. "I am Zak," he says, his voice sure, and he gestures to those with him. "This is Dak," he nods to the left, "and Hak," he indicates to the right. "We have been sent by Seth to aid you on your journey to rescue your *ama*," he announces, his tone full of confidence.

Uldako realizes these men are unique, not just because they are some of Seth's best warriors, but because they almost look the same. All three wear the leather armor, with only a few distinctive marks setting them apart. Each carries two swords at their sides, one long, one short. Their hazel brown eyes reflect a shared intensity and purpose.

Zak's steady gaze is matched by his medium-length brown hair, some of it braided, giving him an air of controlled strength. Hak, slightly grumpier and less energetic, sports shorter brown hair that spikes in all directions, his demeanor a stark contrast to his companions. Dak, on the other hand, has long brown hair neatly bundled behind his back and carries an infectious excitement. Though all three are a bit shorter than Uldako, their sturdy, bulkier frames and lean muscles convey formidable strength and resilience.

As they exchange greetings, Kunai's youthful curiosity shines through once again. "Why do you look so similar?" he blurts out, unable to contain himself. Uldako closes his eyes and shakes his head, a mix of amusement and embarrassment on his face. Ishara, trying to maintain decorum, gently scolds Kunai for being so direct.

However, the trio of warriors chuckle at Kunai's straightforwardness, their camaraderie evident. "It's a fair question," Zak says, still smiling. "Our similarities have always been our strength."

Uldako and Ishara exchange glances, their embarrassment melting away in the warmth of the warriors' good-natured laughter. Dak steps forward and says with pride, "We are triplets, born together, trained together, and therefore we fight together!"

Hak, slightly irritated, responds with a narrowed brow. "Okay, that's enough, you two. Don't give them the wrong impression. There are many things I would rather do alone than with these two."

Kunai's eyes widen with confusion, processing the revelation that they are triplets. Sensing the bewilderment on their faces, Dak steps in to explain further. "It means we all grew in our *ama's* womb together and were born on the same day," he clarifies.

Uldako and Ishara exchange a glance, their curiosity deepening. Kunai's eyes remain wide, his young mind grappling with the concept. "So you've been together since birth?" he asks, awe evident in his voice.

Zak nods, a hint of pride in his smile. "Indeed, and that bond has made us stronger. We fight as one, think as one, and trust each other completely."

Hak, trying to suppress a grin, adds, "And argue as one too. Trust me, it's not always a blessing."

Dak laughs, patting Hak on the back. "He's just grumpy because he can't get rid of us, no matter how hard he tries."

The group shares a laugh, the tension easing as they enjoy the playful banter of the triplets. Uldako grins widely. "Well, I'm glad you're all here. We could use some strong fighters like yourselves."

Kunai's curiosity peaks further, "But how was it possible for your *ama* to carry all three of you at the same time in her tummy? Wouldn't it have burst open?"

Ishara quickly intervenes, moving to Kunai's side and gently placing a hand over his mouth, saying to the three warriors, "I am sorry, so sorry!"

Ishara turns to Kunai, her tone firm. "It's not polite to ask such personal questions, Kun."

Hak steps forward with an understanding smile, easing the tension. "Don't worry about it," he reassures them. "We're used to people's curiosity by now. But listen, whenever you're ready to embark on the quest to save your *ama*, Uldako, just let us know."

Uldako nods appreciatively. "We need to wait a few days for my companion Šarru to rest," he explains. "So feel free to occupy yourselves until then."

"Understood," Zak responds. "Just inform Rukug when you're all set, and he'll know where to find us."

With a nod of farewell, the brothers Hak, Zak, and Dak depart, leaving Uldako, Ishara, and Kunai still in awe of the mysterious trio. Their striking resemblance and seamless camaraderie linger, adding an air of mystique to their departure.

Uldako swiftly approaches Šarru, eager to check on the bear's condition. To his pleasant surprise, Šarru appears to be much improved. As Uldako draws nearer, Šarru acknowledges him with a gentle look, attempting to rise to his feet but struggling due to the injuries.

"Don't strain yourself, my *dusa*," Uldako says softly, placing a comforting hand on Šarru's fur. "Rest and recover. We will remain by your side until you're fully healed. You won't be alone."

Šarru responds with a contented growl. Ishara observes Uldako's compassionate interaction with Šarru, appreciating the depth of his empathy not only toward the bear but toward all creatures. To her, it reveals Uldako's true character, his innate kindness and compassion.

Kunai strides closer, his curiosity clearly visible. "So, what are we going to do now?" he inquires.

Uldako looks to Ishara, sensing their collective uncertainty. After slavery, his life was marked by continual survival in the wild, and the prospect of stability leaves him momentarily adrift.

Ishara, perceptive as ever, grasps Uldako's internal struggle and offers a suggestion. "Well, since Šarru is recuperating, perhaps we should take the opportunity to rest and rejuvenate ourselves," she proposes.

Kunai's brow furrows in confusion. "But we're not injured," he points out, confused by the idea of resting when there's no apparent need.

Ishara's smile widens, her eyes reflecting the weariness of their long journey. "We've traversed countless challenges, contending with nature's fury, beasts, and even other humans just to survive. We have journeyed over the rugged earth for many days, and now for the first time, we have the chance to replenish our strength and recharge."

Kunai's understanding dawns. "Ah, I see what you mean now," he acknowledges.

Uldako's reluctance to admit their need for rest is evident, his voice tinged with frustration. "As much as it pains me to admit it, every moment we spend here is another moment my *ama* languishes in captivity, but Ishara's right. With Šarru on the mend, we might as well take this opportunity to recuperate, explore the city, and acquaint ourselves with its people. After all, this could be our home in the future, and there is much to learn of it."

Ishara's excitement bubbles over as she and Kunai discuss the wonders of the city, sharing their eagerness to explore its every nook and cranny, from bustling marketplaces to hidden alleys filled with mystery.

• • •

Seven days drift by…

With Šarru's recovery complete, the group stands ready to resume their journey southward, toward the quest of rescuing Uldako's mother. As the weight of the impending danger settles over them, Ishara pulls Uldako aside.

"I believe it's best for Kunai to remain here," she suggests softly. "He's still young, and this journey will be fraught with danger."

"Yes, you're right," he concedes. "It's too risky for him. He'll be safe here at Adriel's home until we return, and we can ask Kesia to keep an eye on him."

Uldako walks over to Kunai, bracing himself for the difficult conversation ahead. "Kun, we need you to stay here," he begins, his tone gentle yet firm. "The journey to save my *ama* will be dangerous, and it's not suitable for someone as young as you."

Kunai's eyes flicker with disappointment, his youthful soul eager for adventure and a deep desire to be with Uldako, Ishara, and Šarru. "But I'm not a child," he protests, his voice tinged with defiance. "I can handle it, I swear—"

Ishara takes his hands in hers, her presence both calming and resolute. "Kun, we do not swear oaths, but I agree. You're not just a boy; you are our *dumu* and future shepherd who will need to take care of our sheep," she says softly. "Your safety is very important to us. We need you here, alive and well, so that one day, when we establish our safe camp, you can protect our flock of sheep."

Kunai steps back a pace, his breath catching, his lower lip quivering. "But will you promise to come back for me before you meet with Seth again?" he manages to choke out amidst his tears that begin to flow freely. "Everyone in my life keeps leaving me."

Ishara and Uldako look at each other, their hearts heavy with empathy. Ishara kneels down as she comforts Kunai. Even Šarru, sensing the sorrow in the air, nuzzles against Kunai, offering silent solace.

Uldako puts his hand on his shoulder. "We need you to be brave, Kun," he says softly, his words carrying a weight of importance. "You're about to embark on a crucial quest I have for you."

Kunai wipes away his tears, his curiosity piqued. "What quest?" he asks.

Uldako's gaze softens. "I want you to be my scout, Kunai," he explains, his voice steady and reassuring. "I need you to keep your eyes and ears open, gather every shred of information you can find here. We're searching for a safe camp, a place to call home. It could be here in this town, or perhaps somewhere nearby that we haven't discovered yet. We're venturing into the unknown, Kunai, and your role is vital in guiding us. I possess limited knowledge regarding the northern kingdom. We need to know more about the different terrain and about safe camps with their different clans and relationships. Therefore, I will have to rely on your information when we return. Find out everything you can!"

Kunai's resolve firms as he nods. "I'll do my best."

Uldako moves his head closer to Kunai, his eyes searching for the spark of determination within the young lad. "Are you truly ready for this responsibility? Can I entrust you with such a crucial quest?" he asks.

Kunai straightens his posture, drawing strength from within. With unwavering resolve, he replies, "Absolutely! I will do my best!"

Uldako smiles with pride and pulls Kunai into a brief, firm embrace. "That's my boy," he says, the words carrying a weight of paternal affection he hadn't realized was there until now. As Uldako steps back and observes Kunai, a profound realization dawns upon him: In Kunai's world, he, Uldako, is a father figure.

So this is what it might feel like to be an abba. *How blind I've been to this truth for so long,* he reflects.

A memory begins to surface, Kunai introducing himself to Seth, proudly declaring, *I am Kunai,* dumu *of Uldako and Ishara.* The weight of those words hits him anew. *He truly meant it, and only now do I fully grasp it.*

Deep in thought, a revelation fills Uldako with both wonder and humility. The depth of Kunai's trust and affection humbles him, and he decides silently to live up to the role he has unwittingly stepped into.

At that moment, Shamgar and Kesia approach, hand in hand. "Uldako! The triplets told us you're preparing to free your *ama*," Shamgar calls out.

Uldako turns to face them, his expression resolute. "Yes," he replies. "I know you would have wanted to join us, but this mission requires only a few who can move with stealth and speed."

Kesia nods, her gaze steady. "We understand. My promise to you remains unchanged. I'll stand by your side and follow you wherever you go when you return. And Shamgar has pledged the same."

Uldako's joy is evident in his eyes as he thanks them for their support. Ishara adds, "Kunai will stay here, so please take him under your wing?"

Kesia looks at young Kunai. "Of course! We will take good care of him, even though he is already a big boy," she says, winking at Kunai. She turns to Uldako. "I am working on something special for you, Uldako. When you come back, you might have rare, high-quality armor most people only dream of! I am creating a new armor fashion trend with the *zu-gal's* head that took Ruk from us."

Uldako smiles warmly. "Thank you kindly, Kesia! We will return as soon as we can. Take care and see you soon."

Uldako, Šarru, and Ishara turn to walk toward the gate, while the others stand with Rukug, the caretaker, waving them farewell. Uldako's gaze lingers for a moment, taking in the sight of Kunai's figure, a pang of emotion tugging at his heart as he waves goodbye. He knows nothing is certain under the sun, yet he hopes to complete the quest and return safe with his *ama*, to behold Kunai again.

With determination, Uldako and Ishara stride toward the gate where Zak, Dak, and Hak await. Quick greetings are exchanged, and without further delay, they embark on their journey to rescue Deborah. Uldako's heart races with anticipation, his thoughts a whirlwind of resolve and hope. *The moment is upon us. I will bring her back!*

30

Brothers

Zak, Dak, and Hak move with the grace of seasoned predators, their fluid, precise movements guiding Uldako, Ishara, and Šarru southeast to liberate Uldako's mother. It is as if the land itself whispers its secrets to them, each step taken with an intimate knowledge of the terrain.

Uldako watches them, captivated by the sharpness of their gaze and the effortless agility with which they detect and avoid potential threats. Their mastery of the wild is awe-inspiring, the result of countless hours spent traversing this wild expanse.

"Your proficiency in navigation and tracking is remarkable!" Uldako exclaims, his voice filled with genuine admiration. "You must have spent countless full moons honing these abilities in this region."

Zak smiles ear to ear. "Indeed, countless scouting missions for Seth have sharpened our senses and made us one with the land. You either tame the wild to enjoy it or it will tame you to fear it!"

Dak, ever the enthusiastic one, walks right up to Uldako. "As his best scouts, we've faced dangerous clans and ferocious beasts. The knowledge we've gained over decades is invaluable. We know where danger lies, and we evade it completely."

Hak, maintaining his usual gruff demeanor, mutters, "Our goal is always to move quickly and silently, avoiding trouble before it finds us."

Uldako feels a quiet strength come upon him, giving him more confidence in their quest, knowing they are in such capable hands. As they press forward, the landscape unfolds before them—a vast expanse filled with unseen dangers and hidden paths, all navigated with the triplets' expertise.

"But you're quite skilled yourself, Uldako. I've noticed you spotting some tracks even before we do. Not many possess such prowess. How did you acquire this skill?" Dak asks.

Uldako smiles with a hint of pride in his eyes. "I suppose Šarru taught me." He glances affectionately at his great companion and takes a moment to recount their experiences, sharing the trials and triumphs of his past as they traverse the rugged terrain.

As they continue their journey together, the bond between the company of six deepens, forged through shared tales and laughter. One night, while gathered around a warm fire, they enjoy a feast of succulent fruits and nuts. As Uldako sets his hand to split another hard nut, a strange winged creature drops beside him. He gives an unheroic yelp, and the nut leaps from his fingers. He quickly recoils, his eyes fixed on the bird's unnerving behavior, its head swiveling all the way around, eyes wide with an otherworldly gleam.

Amidst fits of hearty laughter from the group, Ishara manages to compose herself long enough to explain, "It's just a harmless night bird, Uldako. They often make that peculiar sound, *hoo-hoo*!"

Uldako remains skeptical, eyeing the creature warily. "Harmless, you say? Those eyes—they seem to hold something sinister. I can't shake the feeling of unease." His voice is full of suspicion.

The laughter of the group rings out, mingling with the crackle of the fire as they watch Uldako's worried expression. Dak breaks through the mirth, "Relax, my *dusa*. There's no harm in it. We believe these creatures to be wise and gentle."

Dak takes a deep breath to compose himself. "In truth, it's fascinating to see the world anew through your eyes, Uldako. There's still so much wonder awaiting you."

Uldako eases his tension slightly but maintains a cautious distance from the bird, which continues to regard him with keen interest.

Meanwhile, Ishara directs her curiosity to the three brothers. "You must have encountered some remarkable sights during your scouting expeditions."

Dak chuckles heartily, adding, "Indeed, nothing quite compares to the vast expanse of nature over the confines of city life."

His brother Hak's voice takes on a more subdued tone as he interjects, "Although, traversing the same landscapes and encountering familiar creatures over and over can sometimes wear on one's soul."

Zak quickly interrupts with a mischievous grin, "Oh, come now, *šeš*, don't be such a pessimist." Turning to Uldako and Ishara, he continues with a wink,

"Apologies for my *šešs* banter. Hak tends to be the grumpy one, Dak's eternally optimistic, and I like to think of myself as the realist."

Hak counters with a smirk, "Realist? More like the dull one!"

Uldako and Ishara exchange amused glances, relishing the camaraderie among the brothers.

As their banter escalates into a debate over their combat skills, Uldako intervenes with a question, "Who trained you three?"

Zak silences his brothers with a stern look before elaborating, "Seth himself took us under his wing, instilling in us the skills, knowledge, and wisdom necessary not only to navigate the wilds effectively but to protect ourselves against any foe. For over seven decades, we've been his most trusted scouts."

Uldako's admiration is evident as he says, "What an incredible honor! I'd be grateful if you could impart some of that knowledge to me during our journey."

A passionate debate ensues among the brothers as they vie to be Uldako's mentor. Ishara intervenes with a proposition, "How about settling this with a friendly duel tomorrow morning? The victor shall take on the role of training Uldako."

Hak, though initially reluctant, begrudgingly agrees, "Fine, I'll participate, just to put you two in your place!"

Dak, ever optimistic, chimes in, "What a splendid idea, Ishara! You'll see, I'll be the one to guide Uldako to greatness."

Before Dak can finish, Zak interjects, "Let's not get ahead of ourselves. Tomorrow's duel will determine who's truly worthy of the task."

Uldako's heart swells with anticipation as he witnesses the brothers' eagerness to impart their knowledge. He looks forward to the break of dawn, eager to witness their skills in action. Ishara finds amusement in the good-natured rivalry between the siblings as they continue their banter.

Despite Uldako's insistence on taking the first watch, Zak firmly asserts, "Seth entrusted your safety to us, and we take that responsibility seriously."

Reluctantly, Uldako relents, realizing the depth of trust Seth has placed in the brothers and their desire not to break it. With a nod, he settles down to rest, excited for the training and challenges that await them on the morrow.

Hak, appearing a tad wearier than his brothers, suggests, "Why don't you take the first watch, Dak?"

Dak, caught off guard, agrees. "Sure, I can do that. But how about we spice things up with a game of Earth, Water, and Eagle? The loser takes the first shift."

Zak eagerly joins in, "I'm in!" With a begrudging sigh, Hak concedes.

Uldako watches curiously as they exchange glances and ready themselves for a game Uldako has never heard of. Each hides a hand behind their back. On the count of three, they reveal their hands, displaying distinct signs. The game they play involves three gestures: a fist representing a stone, an open hand symbolizing water, and four fingers extended touching the tip of the thumb mimicking an eagle's beak. Stone crushes bird, bird drinks water, and water erodes stone.

On the third count, Zak and Dak reveal the water gestures respectively, while Hak shows the stone. Zak and Dak erupt in cheers, celebrating their victory as the water wears away Hak's stone. Meanwhile, Hak grumbles under his breath as he heads off to take the first watch. "You should be glad we weren't playing the Ekur stones. Then you'd have had no chance," he mutters, his words barely audible as he goes.

As he walks away, Dak leans in and whispers to Zak, a mischievous glint in his eyes, "Grumpy always chooses stone, and he never learns!" Zak nods, his eyes twinkling with amusement. "I know, his stone is set in stone!" The two chuckle silently, savoring their small victory.

As Ishara and Uldako prepare for a night's rest, they exchange knowing glances and chuckle at grumpy Hak's complaints about his first watch duty. Gradually, silence settles over the camp as exhaustion claims the others.

Uldako lies awake, the unfamiliar sounds of the night enveloping him. His thoughts drift to his mother, and he whispers into the darkness, "I hope you're safe and well, *Ama*. The mere thought of life without you is unthinkable." His words cling to his heart as fatigue finally pulls him into a deep slumber.

Abruptly, three colossal red eyes materialize before him, fixating on Uldako with chilling intensity. A sinister voice reverberates through the darkness, "Oh, little slave, your *ama* belongs to me. You belong to me."

Paralyzed with fear, Uldako struggles against invisible restraints, trapped in the grip of a haunting nightmare. He knows it's not real, yet the power of an unseen force pins him down, rendering his body powerless.

The dark eyes descend, morphing into the visage of a dragon, ancient and malevolent. Uldako recognizes it instantly, the legendary dragon of old, the harbinger of terror and doom. With each step, the dragon draws closer, its hunger for him palpable. As it lunges forward, jaws gaping wide, Uldako's voice pierces the darkness in a desperate plea for aid, "*Il*, help me!"

In an instant, radiant white light floods his dreamscape, dispelling the darkness. Uldako wakes with a jolt, his heart racing, a scream escaping his lips as the remnants of the nightmare fade into the recesses of his mind.

Zak rushes to Uldako's side, concern grave on his face. "That must have been a harrowing dream," he offers sympathetically.

Uldako, still shaken, attempts to brush it off. "It's nothing," he mumbles, but Zak persists.

"Dreams can hold deeper meanings, you know. They're not always just random. Sometimes, they can be messages from higher powers, be they good or evil."

Uldako shifts uncomfortably, wishing to evade the conversation entirely. Why must he always be plagued by such unsettling dreams? This one felt different though, more ominous and real than the rest.

Ishara's gentle voice draws his attention. "Good morning!" She greets him warmly as she moves past him, her sapphire eyes capturing his gaze. He struggles to form a coherent response, his smile serving as the only reply he can muster.

Dak's booming voice fills the morning air, jolting Uldako fully awake. Startled, he listens to Dak's proclamation, "Finally! He is awake, *šeš-me*! Uldako is awake, and now we can start the duel."

Grumpy Hak wastes no time in responding, his tone firm, "It is about time."

Zak steps closer to Uldako, his expression eager. "If you're ready, let's get to it!" he declares.

The group moves to a suitable spot where they draw a circle on the ground. Zak takes a moment to explain the rules of the friendly duel. "Alright, so the rule is simple: The last one standing within the circle is the victor."

With their armor and weapons discarded to the side, the trio steps into the designated circle. Uldako, feeling a bit puzzled, speaks up, "I thought this was going to be a duel with weapons?"

Hak's grin widens as he responds, "Oh, it is a duel with weapons!" He emphasizes his point by raising his fists while a smile forms on his lips.

Zak clarifies, "When it comes to dueling with swords, axes, or any other weapons, we are all evenly matched. So, the only way to truly test our skills is with a no-weapon contest. We are only allowed to use our bodies and the power of our minds."

Ishara claps her hands together and declares, "Oh, I must see this!"

Zak's excitement flows over. "Alright, on my count of three," he announces, preparing to initiate the duel.

However, grumpy Hak interjects, "Hold on, who made you the leader? You cannot be trusted with this! Ishara, would you kindly give us the signal?"

Ishara steps forward gracefully, a smile playing on her lips. "It will be my pleasure!"

With everyone poised and ready, Uldakò braces himself for the spectacle about to unfold. He can hardly contain his excitement, eager to witness this unique form of combat between seasoned warriors. Ishara begins the countdown, her voice commanding attention, "Take your positions!"

The trio, Hak, Dak, and Zak, assume their stances, muscles tense and eyes locked in fierce concentration. "Get ready," Ishara continues, the tension mounting with each passing moment, "and…" She pauses, drawing out the suspense, while Uldako's anticipation reaches its peak. Observing the men's poised positions and intense expressions, he waits with bated breath.

"Begin!" Ishara's final word breaks the tense silence, signaling the commencement of the duel.

Zak and Dak, who had been exchanging intense looks to give Hak the impression of an impending attack between them, shift their focus toward Hak in the blink of an eye. With abnormal speed, they both lunge forward, their movements swift as wolves hunting in a pack.

Hak's reflexes prove to be lightning fast as he narrowly dodges Zak's swift advance, but before he can react, Dak is upon him. With immense strength, Dak seizes his brother and effortlessly hurls him over his head, sending him crashing backward.

As Hak's foot grazes just outside the circle, Ishara swiftly declares, "Out! You're out!"

Hak, begrudgingly accepting his defeat, muttering protests as he steps aside. "I'll remember this. You two must have formed an alliance when I wasn't looking, since I won the previous time!" Hak grumbles, his frustration evident.

Zak, his eyes twinkling mischievously, responds, "It's not our fault you failed to anticipate—"

Before Zak can finish his sentence, Dak seizes the opportunity to launch an unexpected attack. Like a spear aimed at its target, he springs into the air, poised to strike Zak. Reacting swiftly, Zak grabs Dak's arm, leveraging his momentum against him to push him off balance. However, Dak, ever agile, evades the maneuver, ducking low and sweeping his leg underneath Zak, knocking him off his feet. Zak crashes to the ground, and in an instant, Dak is on him like a ferocious cave lion.

Impressed by their speed and strategic prowess, Uldako watches in awe. The two brothers engage in a fierce battle, each employing their strength and technique with passion. Zak manages to gain the upper hand momentarily, leveraging his strength to flip Dak over his head and swiftly escape from underneath him. But Dak quickly regains his footing, and the clash continues with renewed intensity.

Meanwhile, Hak strolls a few paces away and settles beneath a tree seeking shade, declaring, "This might take a while. Wake me up when these two are done." With a nonchalant wave, he reclines against the trunk, letting the tree's cool shade envelop him.

Uldako and Ishara remain engrossed in the spectacle, marveling at the relentless perseverance of the combatants. Time stretches on, sweat drenching their bodies, dirt coating their skin and hair, as they continue to exchange blows, neither relenting. The intensity of their struggle captivates their audience, their determination clearly visible in every swing and parry.

Hak, lulled by the rhythmic sounds of the scuffle, drifts into slumber, snoring under the shade of the tree. His snores soon blend with the natural symphony of the forest, a peaceful contrast to the fierce duel unfolding nearby.

Šarru, uninterested and bored by the long fight, saunters over to join Hak. Just as the bear settles down, a sudden commotion startles him. A deer rushes past them, its hooves pounding the ground in a frantic escape. Šarru leaps to his feet, emitting a thunderous growl, his instincts ignited by the unexpected intrusion.

Hak, jolted awake by Šarru's reaction, jumps to his feet, his hand instinctively reaching for his weapon. "Who's that?" Ever vigilant, his eyes search the surroundings for any potential threat, but he relaxes when he sees the deer darting off.

Dak and Zak, momentarily distracted, pause to assess the supposed threat. Sensing an opportunity, Zak seizes the moment, swiftly lowering himself, rushing toward Dak, and hoisting him into the air before forcefully hurling him out of the circle.

Uldako applauds Zak's victory, appreciating the skill and determination displayed in the duel. However, Dak refuses to concede defeat, protesting, "No, that wasn't fair. I was distracted."

Undeterred, Zak confidently steps into the circle, asserting his triumph, "I am the victor, the last man standing, and no excuse can alter that fact."

Turning to Ishara for a verdict, Dak seeks validation. "You were the judge, Ishara. What say you?"

Ishara, mindful of the need to resolve the dispute swiftly, takes a measured breath before responding, "The rules were clear. Zak emerged as the victor. He is indeed the last man standing."

Hak, relieved that the contest has finally concluded, steps back to the others, declaring, "At last, it's over. Now we can continue our journey!"

Uldako commends the men for their spirited display and swiftly shifts the focus to their impending travels. As they prepare for the journey ahead, the brothers don their armor with practiced efficiency. Observing the dirt and grime coating their forms, Ishara offers, "I have some extra water if you want to clean up."

The triplets exchange amused glances, sharing a bond forged over decades. Zak chuckles before responding, "Your offer is kind, but when we venture as scouts, we usually coat ourselves with dirt to shield against the sun and mask our scent. It helps us blend into our surroundings and evade detection by both predators and prey."

Ishara chuckles at the ruggedness of their tactics. "Well, that's certainly a unique approach," she remarks with a grin. To her surprise, the triplets take her comment as encouragement, enthusiastically scooping up more dirt and smearing it over themselves.

Uldako, realizing the necessity of blending in as they journey further south into more perilous territory, grabs a handful of dirt and starts to apply it to his own skin. With a determined look, he says, "Well, if I am going to be trained by you, then I might as well learn by doing!"

The triplets burst into laughter at Uldako's earnestness, their camaraderie lightening the mood. Dak, still chuckling, says, "That's the spirit, Uldako!"

Ishara shakes her head with a faint smile, adding, "I guess we're all going to be walking mud sculptures from now on. I'm in!"

Hak, who had been silent, finally joins in the banter. "Mud sculptures with a purpose," he says with a rare grin. The group's laughter echoes through the camp, their bond growing stronger as they prepare for the journey ahead.

After they are all covered in dirt, Zak's eyes gleam with resolve as he looks at Uldako. "In the next few days, Uldako, I'll transform you into a fierce warrior who can even take on dragons!"

Ishara cuts in playfully, "Well, how do you know Uldako isn't already good at fighting? Perhaps he's just acting humbly."

Zak's expression shifts from serious to amused. "Unlikely. Uldako is still young and therefore lacks the experience and training that can only come with time. But we'll see what you're made of, Uldako."

Uldako chuckles, feeling a mix of excitement and nervousness. "I'm ready to learn!"

Zak nods, a glint of approval in his eyes. "We'll start with the basics and build you up from there. By the time we're done, you'll be ready to face any challenge that comes your way."

Dak, observing the exchange, adds, "And who knows, maybe you'll surprise us all."

Hak steps forward, his tone firm. "Yes, yes, we can figure out the training while we walk. Zak, you're talking too much, and we've lost too much sunlight. We won't get to the South by standing here!"

The group presses forward, each step bringing them closer to Uldako's mother. As they continue, Ishara requests, "Uldako, let me have another look at your map."

The group gathers around as Uldako unfolds the map. Hak grimly states as he points the route with his finger, "It's going to be at least a few days' journey to the slave camp as we circle around those dangerous areas."

His finger traces the route south, crossing the broad sweep of the Euphrates River, skirting a great city that lies at the heart of Sumer, then bending east and finally south toward the slave camp.

Uldako studies the markings and frowns. "What city is that? It looks nearly as large as Umma."

Dak, as lively as ever, is the first to respond. "Oh, Uldako! You don't know the magnificent city of Unugki? From Umma down to Unugki, the land stretches like a line across the middle of the two kingdoms, dividing the northern kingdom from the southern kingdom. In ancient times, it was known as the center of the land, where all the *dumu* of Adam worshipped *Il*, the Most High. Over the ages, the land divided, yet Unugki still lies on the border and is known throughout Sumer as the seat of *Il*. It is fitting for His temple to be in the middle of the land as He is the Most High, compared to below in the Southeast where Eridu lies, the dark domain of *Enki*, ruler of the deep—the Apsu."

Ishara leans closer to study the map. "I didn't even know that. There are so many more cities and clans for us to explore!"

Zak pulls the map closer and nods. "Indeed! The world is vast. This map shows only the lands of Sumer. This is only a small corner of it. The earth stretches far beyond these rivers and mountains. Many have set out to explore its reaches over the generations, sending word back to the house of Adam and Seth about the distant lands they've seen."

He runs a finger along the map's edge. "If all of Mesopotamia is what you see here, then the whole earth may be hundreds, perhaps eight hundred times greater, and that is not even adding the water of seas and rivers. Beyond these borders are valleys and mountains few in these lands have ever walked, places where the sun burns red and the stars seem closer to the ground. Travelers tell of new clans and different creatures in the far reaches, but who can say how much more lies beyond?"

Uldako's eyes widen, his jaw slack with wonder. He looks from Zak to the map again. "Eight hundred times?" he breathes. "Then we are but a speck in *Il's* creation."

Zak smiles faintly. "A speck, yes, but one placed with purpose. Unugki was once the first city of *Il*, where the Most High was worshipped by the sons of light. In time, other cities arose that also honored Him, such as Kish, which lies north of Nippur."

Hak adds with a faint grin, "It's a great place, Uldako. Even I get excited every time I see it."

Dak bursts out laughing. "Now that's saying something! If Hak is excited about anything other than food, combat, or sleep, then the place must truly be blessed!"

The group laughs as Hak rolls his eyes. Uldako studies the map with a small smile, curiosity glinting in his eyes. "I'll see it for myself."

Just as Ishara agrees, Zak shakes his head. "Not this time, Uldako. We're in too much of a hurry to free your *ama*. We'll pass far around it, so we're not spotted by scouts—good or evil."

With that, they roll up the map and continue their journey.

31

Training

As evening descends, the group settles on a place to make camp. As they make their temporary shelter, twilight burnishes the land in fading gold, the slopes darken, and a deep quiet settles over them.

Uldako, eager to finally sit down and eat as his stomach growls in protest, reaches into his bag for a snack. The anticipation of food is almost tangible, his mouth watering at the thought of the first bite. Just as he is about to sink his teeth into a ripe piece of fruit, Zak's declaration cuts through the moment with startling clarity. "Uldako, your training starts now!"

Uldako freezes, the fruit inches from his mouth, his eyes widening in surprise. He looks up to see Zak standing with a firm expression, his stance radiating authority. Determined not to waste the precious opportunity, Uldako takes a swift, hearty bite, savoring the taste briefly before swiftly tucking the fruit away.

"No more food until our training is done!" Zak commands, his tone leaving no room for argument. "Come on, don't waste time!"

The excitement of finally beginning his training rushes through Uldako, momentarily overpowering his hunger. He stands up, ready to embrace the challenge. The rest of the company, bread and fruit in hand, looks up as Uldako passes, sensing the weight of the moment. He walks on through the crisp crack of shells, the tear of barley cakes, the soft squish of figs. His belly drums, yet he sets hunger aside for the greater aim. He needs to become stronger, and he knows this moment marks the beginning of another transformation.

A smile tugs at Uldako's lips as he reaches for his two-handed sword. "I've been waiting for this all day. So let's do it!" he exclaims.

But Zak's response tempers his excitement. "Hold off on that sword for now. Your training begins with this." He offers Uldako a sturdy stick instead.

Uldako stares at the stick, his initial excitement giving way to confusion. "A stick?" he questions, raising a brow.

Zak's eyes gleam with amusement. "Yes! Mastering the basics is crucial before you wield the real weapon. This will teach you control, precision, and adaptability."

Disappointment flickers across Uldako's face, yet he chooses to accept it, tucking away his sword.

Ishara intervenes with a warning. "Just remember, I told you not to underestimate Uldako!"

But Zak and his brothers laugh dismissively in their pride. They see themselves as formidable warriors, unmatched in battle. It has been written in their demeanor and etched upon their faces ever since they left Nippur.

Uldako readies his stick. "Alright, what's the plan with this then?"

Zak's response is swift and unexpected. With stick in hand, he launches a flurry of attacks at Uldako. "Defend yourself!" he commands.

Caught off guard, Uldako finds himself on the defensive, desperately parrying Zak's strikes. In a flash, Zak's stick makes contact with Uldako's shoulder, sending a jolt of pain through him.

Stepping back, Zak declares victory. "Lesson one: Always expect the unexpected," he proclaims, a victorious grin playing on his lips.

Glancing at his brothers, Zak's satisfaction is evident. He relishes the opportunity to be the one out of the three brothers to teach Uldako, proud to impart his knowledge upon the eager learner.

Seizing the moment, Uldako takes advantage of Zak's distracted gaze as he glances toward his brothers. In a swift and unexpected move, Uldako launches a counterattack, his stick finding its mark with precise accuracy against Zak's throat.

Zak, momentarily stunned, grasps the surprise with widened eyes. A smirk plays on Uldako's lips. "Lesson learned, thank you."

Ishara, Dak, and Hak erupt into laughter at the sight of Zak's stunned expression. Zak struggles to regain his composure and stammers, "Uh…yes, well done, Uldako. I…left myself open intentionally to test you."

Hak's laughter crescendos, seeing through Zak's feeble attempt to cloak his shame. "You're a terrible liar, Zak. You didn't see that coming at all!" he declares, amusement dancing in his eyes.

Zak's voice cuts through the laughter. "Ignore them, Uldako. Let's continue," he commands, his tone firm.

Uldako responds with a nod, his senses heightened as he slips into the mindset of a predator, a skill honed through countless hours of training with Šarru. With razor-sharp focus, he scrutinizes Zak's every move, attuned to even the slightest shifts in his stance or demeanor. The combat experience in the slave camps has taught Uldako the importance of understanding his adversaries, recognizing that knowledge of their habits and tactics is the key to victory. This was a part of Uldako's past that was not shared with the brothers over the course of the journey.

Zak swiftly changes his stance. "Alright, Uldako, let's move on to defense. Attack me with everything you've got, and I'll demonstrate proper defense techniques."

Uldako's smile widens, and a bright heat kindles in his eyes, the look of a man set upon his purpose. Ishara catches the gleam and knows he is wholly given to the moment, drawn into it in body and breath. Even Šarru seems captivated by the change in Uldako's demeanor, for he knows it well. He has seen and felt it since Uldako first led him out on long hunts. Uldako is about to reveal his true talent.

With deceptive calmness, Uldako begins to advance, his movements deliberate and calculated. He jumps into action, executing a series of feints and strikes with only seventy percent of his lightning speed. As Zak moves to block a high attack, Uldako swiftly changes direction, delivering a low strike that catches everyone off guard with a hundred percent of his speed.

Hak and Dak react with astonishment, realizing Uldako's prowess. Despite Zak's experience, he's momentarily thrown off balance by the unexpected direction and speed assault. Seizing the opportunity, Uldako launches another attack, this time jabbing his fist toward Zak's torso. Zak instinctively dodges backward, but Uldako was planning for this exact moment as he swiftly spins around and catches Zak off guard with his third attack. With impeccable timing, Uldako's left foot connects with Zak's temple, sending him crashing to the ground, unconscious.

As Zak lies motionless, Dak and Hak rush forward, their expressions a mix of shock and disbelief.

Ishara kneels beside Zak, assessing his condition with concern and amusement. "He's fine, just unconscious." She casts a knowing glance at Uldako. "I did warn him not to underestimate you, didn't I?"

Hak, his usual grumpiness momentarily lifted, chuckles in agreement. "You sure did," he concedes.

Dak regards Uldako with newfound respect, his tone carrying a hint of awe.

"You never mentioned you had these skills. It's been ages since I've seen someone so young move with such speed and precision, let alone master the art of deception in combat. Your fighting style is unlike anything I've seen. It is wild, unpredictable, with continuous, unexpected strikes from all directions. Who taught you?"

Uldako, coming to terms with his own abilities, gestures toward Šarru with a sense of pride. "Šarru and I have been training together in the wild for many dark moons. I was also forced to partake in the arena when I was in the slave camp. They would force the slaves to fight each other, then they would gamble on the victor."

Hak steps closer to Uldako, resting a reassuring hand on his shoulder. "I am sorry to hear that. However, even with that experience, from what I have seen, I believe you are what we call a natural fighter! For most, it takes decades to learn and develop the fighting skills you have just used, but then there are the few who do it instinctively, and you, my *dusa*, are one of those."

Uldako, feeling discomfort and embarrassment, glances at Ishara for guidance, unsure of how to respond. He has never been one who needed compliments to feel better about himself. In fact, they often make him uneasy. His humility is deeply ingrained, and he finds it difficult to accept praise for his actions. However, in this case, he finds the words of the brothers useful to determine the effectiveness of his fighting skills from a more objective viewpoint.

Ishara, sensing his unease, offers him a reassuring smile, her eyes reflecting understanding and support.

Dak looks from Hak back to Uldako and tilts his head. "I agree with Hak. It's remarkable that you've honed these skills living and surviving alone in the dangerous wilderness with Šarru. Most people live in safe camps and never obtain such unique techniques. Then considering your background as a slave, your combat style is unique, Uldako. It'll be fascinating to witness your growth and improvement." He nods, acknowledging Uldako's potential for even greater feats as he continues to develop his abilities.

Zak stirs, gradually regaining consciousness. Dak assists him to sit upright, and as Zak's senses sharpen, he queries, "What happened?"

Ishara, her eyes sparkling mischievously, responds first, "Uldako happened," prompting the group to erupt in laughter as Zak's bewildered expression reveals his confusion.

After they explain the situation, Zak concedes, "I'll be honest, Uldako, I underestimated you, but I won't make that mistake again. From now on, I'll train you seriously, with real blades."

Uldako's eyes light up with excitement. "I'm glad to hear that," he says, while throwing away the stick as fast as he can. "I'll need all the help I can get to save my *ama*!"

The group returns to the temporary shelter, and as the night unfolds, they gradually settle in. Uldako looks up at the celestial canopy, a sense of awe washing over him as he reflects on his journey of growth and discovery. It wasn't long ago that he regarded these stars as celestial deities. As a slave, his only respite from toil was the night sky, where he found solace in the vast expanse above, free from the tyranny of oppression. Those moments of solitude were precious to him, a source of strength and solace in the face of adversity. And amidst it all, his thoughts invariably turned to his mother, the guiding light that stoked his resilience and determination.

As Uldako's mind delves into the depths of his memories, a profound realization washes over him like a big crashing wave. His mother, a tower of strength and resilience, shouldered her burdens in silence, masking her own pain with a facade of unwavering love. Despite enduring the same hardships as him, she shielded him from the harsh realities of their existence, her every action imbued with a selflessness that Uldako had failed to fully appreciate until now.

"She bore the weight of our suffering alone," Uldako murmurs, his voice tinged with sorrow and admiration. "Her love knew no bounds, her sacrifices countless."

With each recollection, her words echo in his mind like a haunting melody of maternal care and concern. *How are you, my* dumu*? Are you hungry, my* dumu-nita*? Do you have any pain, my* dumu*?* Her daily inquiries were a mark of her boundless love and selfless care.

Uldako's heart aches with regret as he contemplates his own shortcomings. "I was blind to her suffering and to her sacrifices," he admits, tears mingling with the dust of his past. "Why did I not see her silent suffering? Why did I not offer her the same care and compassion she bestowed upon me?"

Determined to right his wrongs, Uldako's resolve strengthens like forged iron. "I will not rest until I free you, *Ama*," his voice trembling with conviction. "You deserve a life of peace and happiness, a life that I will ensure you have." With newfound purpose igniting his soul, Uldako attempts to sleep, each passing moment bringing him closer to daylight. As he lies awake in silence, his mind races with thoughts of his quest, driven by love and the promise of redemption.

The next morning, Uldako is roused from his slumber by the insistent pressure of a sword's hilt against his chest. His eyes flutter open to find Zak's stern visage looming over him, impatient and unwavering. "Wake up, let's train. Uldako, I said wake up!"

Blinking away the remnants of sleep, Uldako struggles to focus on Zak's persistent gaze. "But it is still dark!" Uldako protests weakly, his voice thick with drowsiness. Before he can fully comprehend the situation, the sharp sting of the hilt against his chest jolts him into wakefulness.

"Enemies strike when least expected," Zak admonishes, his tone firm. "They won't wait until you're well-rested to attack. Remember our first lesson!"

Grudgingly, Uldako acknowledges the truth in Zak's words, his senses now alert and attuned. "I remember," he concedes. "Always expect the unexpected."

A proud smile graces Zak's lips. "Exactly!" he declares, a sense of satisfaction evident in his demeanor. "Now, let's not waste any more time." With that, the two embark on their training regimen, their movements fluid and purposeful in the predawn silence.

Meanwhile, Hak maintains a vigilant watch over their slumbering companions, his gaze unwavering as he stands guard against the unknown dangers lurking in the shadows.

Four torches are set to make a square. Within it, Zak and Uldako take their stances. The ring of fire marks the place of training and keeps the wild beasts at bay.

"Now let's truly test your skills, Uldako," Zak declares, his tone brimming with challenge. "But this time, let's not aim to knock each other unconscious, shall we?" Uldako nods eagerly, a grin playing on his lips.

Zak readies his weapons. "Imagine I am a raider," he commands, his movements poised and calculated. "Defend and attack at will!" The clash of swords fills the air as the two warriors engage in a battle of speed and strategy. Uldako, wielding his formidable two-handed sword, faces off against Zak, who skillfully wields a long sword in one hand and a short blade in the other. The rhythmic clang of metal against metal resonates through the clearing, punctuated by the swift, fluid motions of both combatants. Each strike and parry reveals the depth of their training and the intensity of their focus.

As the duel unfolds, Zak demonstrates his prowess, outmaneuvering Uldako with each calculated strike. Despite Uldako's best efforts, Zak consistently gains the upper hand, his movements fluid and unpredictable.

Finally, the duel reaches its conclusion, leaving both warriors breathless and spent. Breaking the silence, Zak offers his appraisal. "You did really well!" he commends, a note of genuine admiration in his voice. "I can't recall the last time I had this much fun, and you certainly kept me on my toes."

Uldako returns Zak's smile, though tinged with a hint of self-criticism. "I didn't fare as well as I'd hoped," he admits, his tone reflective. "Your movements caught me off guard most of the time. This duel taught me how much training I still require. If you were a real enemy, I would be dead right now."

Zak chuckles. "You know what I call those moves that leave you scrambling?" he quips, a glint of pride in his eyes. "Experience." He takes a deep breath and continues, "Your reflexes are quite exceptional, Uldako. In fact, they are extremely rare, but you lack experience. Yesterday you bested me, because I underestimated you. Today, I am giving my best, and I've honed my skills through countless battles, learning to anticipate and exploit my opponent's weaknesses."

"Well then, I can't wait to gain as much experience as possible while sparring with you on our journey!" Uldako responds with eager determination.

Impressed by Uldako's humility and hunger to learn, Zak smiles. "There is always room to grow. Walk with me. I will teach what I know, and together we shall make you a formidable opponent. You may even surpass certain men of my house." He tips his chin toward Hak on watch, just loud enough to carry.

"Hear him boast," Hak mutters.

"He means you," Dak says.

"I mean both of you," Zak answers in a shout, all teeth.

Uldako laughs, catching the sport of it. The brothers are even in skill, yet every day they spar over the crown.

As they stride back into the camp, Zak continues, "It seems to me that you only recently started using that sword."

"Yes, I acquired it not too long ago," Uldako remarks.

Zak pauses for a moment, inspecting the blade carefully. "It truly is a work of art, but also heavy, slow, and cumbersome. When you start using a new weapon, you have to train with it until it becomes an extension of your body. I will show you some basic flowing movements with it that you can practice until the sword becomes weightless in your hands and the movements become as natural as walking."

As the sun ascends, painting the sky with hues of gold and pink, Ishara awakens just in time to witness Uldako and Zak returning from their training. Her eyes follow Uldako, and with each passing day, she realizes how her feelings for him intensify, growing deeper roots within her heart. A soft smile spreads across her face, her eyes reflecting admiration. She notices the determination etched into Uldako's features, the way his sweat-soaked hair clings to his forehead, and the earnestness in his stride. Ishara's heart swells with a blend of pride and longing, her gaze lingering on him as he approaches.

She finds herself marveling at every facet of his character as she gets to know him more. His inquisitive nature, tempered by discernment, captivates her. She admires his boldness, balanced by a thoughtful approach to decision making, and his unwavering commitment once he's made up his mind. Despite his remarkable abilities, Uldako remains humble, a quality that only enhances his allure. Above all, it's his genuine compassion and concern for others that truly endears him to Ishara. *It also does not hurt that he is fair of countenance,* she muses to herself, her smile widening as she watches him.

As Uldako approaches, their exchanged glances betraying their unspoken emotions, Ishara can't help but feel a rise of warmth in her heart. Meanwhile, Zak keenly observes the silent exchange with a grin forming on his lips, understanding the blossoming connection between them.

With Hak's call to action, everyone quickly gathers their belongings and prepares for the journey ahead. Zak, Dak, and Hak move with practiced efficiency, securing their gear. Šarru waits at the makeshift camp's entrance, knowing they are about to leave, readying himself for the journey.

As they press on to rescue Uldako's mother, each day brings drill and growth. Uldako learns quickly, grasping each lesson at a glance. Seeing this, Zak trains him in staff and spear, short blade and long, bow and sling, with footwork, guard, timing, and breath. They rise early, while the east is still gray, and they practice until the others wake. After the day's journey, they halt before sunset to take another span of practice while the rest set a simple camp. Because of this training, the way to Deborah takes more time, but Uldako counts the delay wise. He must be ready for any fight, and he will not err when his mother's life hangs in the balance.

During their journey, Uldako's feelings for Ishara deepen, much like the roots of an ancient tree reaching ever further into the earth, intertwining his destiny with hers.

Time seems to slip through their fingers like grains of sand, yet with each passing moment, Uldako hones his skills and strengthens his bond with his companions. As they draw nearer to the slave camp, the weight of anticipation hangs heavy over Uldako, mingling with memories of his past.

Nightfall begins to slowly descend upon them like a cloak, and they make haste toward the tranquil lake that once served as Uldako's refuge.

32

Liberty

Uldako and his companions finally arrive at the area of his secluded shelter he had built long ago near the lake, a sanctuary that had once provided him solace. The lake glistens under the evening light, its serene waters reflecting the vibrant colors of the surrounding flora. Birds chirp melodiously, flitting between the branches of ancient trees, their songs mingling with the gentle rustling of leaves. The air is filled with the sweet fragrance of wildflowers, while small creatures scurry through the underbrush.

The group meticulously surveys the vicinity of the shelter, deferring to Uldako's expertise in the area. They pause to observe, ensuring no lurking threats before proceeding. Uldako, relying on his and Šarru's heightened senses, discerns no danger but rather the comforting familiarity of their former home.

With a nod, Uldako signals, "It's safe. Let's move." The closer they get, the more memories flood Uldako's mind—nights spent under the stars, days of relentless training in survival and combat skills, and moments of quiet reflection by the tranquil lake. This land had been his refuge, and now, returning with his companions, he feels nostalgia with vigilance.

As they cautiously approach the shelter, Uldako notices the slightly ajar door. Instinctively, he grips his sword, prepared for potential intruders. The group follows suit, weapons at the ready, their eyes searching the surroundings for any signs of trouble.

"Stay alert," Uldako whispers. With a creak, Uldako pushes the door slowly, his heart pounding with tension as he cautiously steps inside with Šarru right on his heels, his eyes sweeping every corner for any sign of danger. To his relief, the interior is deserted, yet the remnants of intrusion are unmistakable. Uldako's belongings are scattered and depleted, evidence of an unwelcome visitor who rifled through his sanctuary. The absence of familiar comforts like the deer pelts and horns sits heavily on Uldako's heart, and anger begins to boil within him toward the one who took what did not belong to them.

Suppressing a sigh of disappointment, Uldako chooses to overlook the desecration, unwilling to let it dampen their spirits. Turning to the group keeping watch outside, he gestures toward the shelter to invite them in, attempting to infuse his words with warmth and welcome despite the circumstances. "Welcome to the place Šarru and I called home." His voice is tinged with a hint of sorrow. "It's not much, but it was our refuge."

"Thank you," Ishara replies, "but it could use a bit of cleaning."

Uldako, feeling a pang of embarrassment at the state of their refuge, offers a sheepish apology. "Well, Šarru and I didn't expect to return," he admits. "It's been standing alone for many moons, and it seems an intruder broke in and befouled it."

The group swiftly dives into the task of cleaning, their movements coordinated and efficient as they restore the shelter to its former semblance of warmth and comfort. Uldako clears out debris while Zak and Dak focus on repairing any structural damage, their hands moving with practiced skill. Hak stands outside, keeping a watchful eye. Ishara gathers fresh bedding materials and sweeps away the dust that has settled over time.

With diligent effort, they banish the remnants of intrusion, scrubbing surfaces until they gleam and arranging the sparse furnishings in a more inviting manner. Ishara finds some wildflowers growing nearby and places them in a few spots, adding a touch of color and life to the home. Dak, ever eager to help, starts a fire, the flames filling the air with warmth and a comforting glow.

As the firelight dances on the walls, the shelter gradually transforms from a place of abandonment to a welcoming refuge, the air filled with the scent of fresh pine and the soft murmur of their contented conversation. The group pauses to admire their handiwork, feeling a sense of camaraderie and accomplishment.

As the flames dance and cast flickering shadows, the weary travelers gather around, relishing the respite before the dawn of their imminent quest. Lost in the tranquility of the moment, they share tales and laughter, finding solace in each other's company.

Zak's pulls Uldako outside the shelter, away from the group. Expecting another round of training, Uldako braces himself, only to be met with an unexpected inquiry that catches him off guard. In place of Zak's hard tongue in drill, these words come as a soft thread, pulling at Uldako's heart with great power.

"When are you going to tell Ishara that you are taken with her?" Zak whispers, his tone filled with a mix of curiosity and amusement.

Uldako's breath catches in his throat, his mind racing to find the right words in response to Zak's probing question. "I...what...how do you..." Uldako stammers, his thoughts scattered like leaves in the wind, unsure how to navigate the depths of his own heart.

Zak, sensing Uldako's reluctance, presses on with gentle persistence. "There's no need to be shy about it. If a man admires a woman, it's natural. Ishara is an exceptional woman, I must say. So, what's holding you back?" He leans in, his tone laced with sincerity and concern. "If you don't make a move, someone else might swoop in."

Uldako's timidity gives way to a surge of protective instinct for Ishara. "Wait, what do you mean, another man?" he interjects. "There's no man on this earth worthy of her."

Zak's reassuring pat on the back and words bring a sense of comfort. "You are, Uldako! All of us know it, and you just proved my point. Your heart is set on her!" he asserts with conviction.

Uldako's thoughts swirl with confusion and realization. How had Zak and his brothers seen through his carefully guarded facade? "How did you—"

Zak puts up his hand to stop Uldako mid-sentence. He casts a glance back at the shelter, then gestures for Uldako to follow him a few paces away, his voice lowered to a confidential whisper. "Even a blind man can see, you fool! You young babes...your feelings are shown all over your face, every time you're near her. And guess what?" He pauses for effect and then continues, "She feels the same about you!"

Uldako's heart races. "How can you be so sure?" he asks, his voice barely above a murmur. "She's so far beyond my...I mean...she's the epitome of beauty. Her gaze captivates me; her voice—it's like a balm to the soul. And her heart, it's like nothing I've ever encountered. But me? I'm just a nobody. No fancy lineage, no knowledge of who my *abba* is, just a former slave. Why would she even give me a second thought?"

"Uldako, listen up." Zak's voice carries the unmatched power of truth and wisdom gained over decades. "Your past doesn't define you. Your parents don't define you. It's your character and your beliefs that shape who you are, and let me tell you, your character is as solid as they come."

Zak pauses to see whether his words have taken root in Uldako, then continues. "You were created in the image of *Il*, and your identity lies in Him.

Meeting Ishara? I believe that wasn't a coincidence, as all good gifts come from above, from the Most High, our great *Abba*!"

Uldako feels a rush of emotions, his mind flashing back to the teachings of Seth, who once told him of the equality of all humans under *Il*. But hearing these words directly from another man, especially someone like Zak, whose strength and wild sense Uldako respects, adds a new layer of resonance.

He ponders Zak's words, as if a door has been unlocked within him, revealing a path to self-contentment he had long sought but never fully embraced. With a resolute nod, Uldako opens himself up, allowing his vulnerability to surface. "But what if she rejects me?"

Drawing closer, Zak's gaze is firm, unwavering. "But what if she doesn't?" His words carry a sense of possibility, urging Uldako to consider the other side of his fears.

Then Zak speaks a truth that turns the course of Uldako's days forever. "Uldako, tomorrow is never certain. Life can be short, so do not waste yours by having regrets!" Zak's words linger, a potent reminder of the importance of seizing the moment before it is too late.

As Zak steps away, leaving Uldako to mull over his words, the night embraces him with its quiet wisdom. Uldako looks up at the vast expanse of stars, a familiar sight that offers solace in times of solitude. Beside him, Šarru's presence is a comforting reminder of the special bond they share, forged through countless nights under the open sky at this very shelter.

After he makes his decision with conviction, a peace settles over him and Uldako joins the others. He sees Ishara preparing for sleep. He takes it as a sign to keep his heart for another night. With Šarru beside him, he joins the others and settles to rest.

In the deep of night, amidst the anticipation of the impending quest to rescue his mother, Uldako lies awake, his thoughts inexplicably drawn to his father. Questions swirl in his mind like restless butterflies, eager for answers buried in the past. *What manner of man was my* abba*? What color adorned his hair and eyes? Was he a man of virtue, a sage of wisdom, or a seeker of truth? Did he possess the gentle touch of love, the fierce prowess of battle? What did I receive from him that lives within my bones? What would he think of me?* These questions, unanswered and haunting, stir within Uldako a longing for the fatherly guidance he never knew, casting a shadow over the night as he grapples with the void left by his absence.

Uldako whispers into the night, "*Ama*, I think I am ready. After I have freed you, it is time you tell me about my *abba.* I must know who he really is or was." With those thoughts, Uldako falls into a deep sleep.

As the first rays of dawn pierce through the forest canopy, Uldako awakens to the sound of birdsong echoing through the trees. The day has finally arrived! He springs to his feet, rousing his companions from their slumber.

"Rise and shine, everyone! The time of our quest has come upon us. Let's go save my *ama*!" Uldako's urgency fills the air. When he sees there is little movement, he shouts louder, "Let's go, let's go, get up!"

In predictable fashion, Hak grumbles in his groggy state, protesting the abrupt awakening. Meanwhile, Dak, ever the optimist, greets the new day with infectious enthusiasm, deliberately taunting Hak with his cheerfulness. "Another glorious day dawns! Let us embrace it with joy and purpose!"

With a powerful stretch, Zak rouses from slumber, his muscles flexing as if ready for a brawl with lions. "Let's do it!" he announces with resolve. As the rest of the group stirs, Ishara and Šarru gradually awaken, their eyes taking in the preparations unfolding around them.

The door bursts open, and Uldako emerges, drawing in a deep breath of the fresh morning air outside the shelter. Uncertain of what the day will bring, he exhales with determination then steps outside to inspect the area for any potential threats. Ishara joins him and meets his gaze, her kind eyes reflecting his anticipation. Uldako feels overwhelmed as her smile freezes him in place, but in that fleeting exchange, he feels a surge of courage welling up within him.

"Ishara, there's something I need to tell you," Uldako begins, but before he can utter another word, Hak interrupts with his usual gruffness, barging through the door. "Why are you two standing here looking all serious in the early morning?"

With a resigned sigh, Uldako steps aside, giving Hak a mockingly disappointed glance. "Just waiting on you slow grand *abbas* to join us," he teases, prompting Zak and Dak to emerge from the shelter, catching the tail end of the banter.

"What's this about Hak being a grumpy grand *abba*?" Zak questions, amusement twinkling in his eyes. Ishara and Uldako share a knowing chuckle, observing Hak's reaction as he bristles at the jest.

"Hey, we three *šeš-me* are all the same age here," Hak retorts defensively. "If I'm a grand *abba*, what does that make you two?"

Dak grins mischievously, his eyes dancing with humor. "True, but your demeanor certainly leans toward the grumpy-old-man category compared to us youthful souls!"

Hak grunts in protest, unimpressed by the comparison. "It's too early in the day for this nonsense. Let's focus on the task at hand and get moving!"

As the group chuckles and advances, Uldako confidently leads the way, flanked by Ishara and Šarru, their hope high despite the looming danger. Meanwhile, the brothers trail behind, banter bubbling between them.

Having observed Uldako's missed opportunity, Zak swiftly closes the gap to Hak, his voice a hushed admonition. "Why did you spoil that golden moment Uldako had with Ishara? You completely ruined it!"

Caught off guard, Hak's expression betrays his innocence. "No, that could not have been the moment we have been waiting for," he denies, perplexed by Zak's accusation. Seeking affirmation, his gaze shifts to Dak, who offers a disappointed nod in return.

Uldako turns to address the brothers with urgency. "We'll be passing the lake soon. Keep your senses sharp; I have seen many *ušumgal-meš* and *uḫuš-meš* roam these parts. After this stretch, the slave camp is not far. It might take only three hands' movement of the sun to get there. We'll find a strategic vantage point to survey the area before making our move."

With determined nods from the brothers, they press onward, their resolve unshaken.

As they pass the tranquil lake, its beauty and the animals around captivate Ishara and the brothers, leaving an indelible impression. Uldako recounts his meeting with the most mysterious man at the lake, who taught him the art of fishing. A quarrel breaks out among the triplets as to who this man might have been. Zak maintains that this was a spirit who took human form, while Dak argues it might have been a man from across the ocean, while Hak believes it was a man from the North, as others in these parts would not help a stranger with food or even care to teach the skill of fishing.

Emerging from the lush greenery surrounding the lake, they halt at the change of scenery: tawny grasses, scattered shrubs, and pale stone showing through. Every sense on high alert, they stand in silent vigil, inspecting their surroundings for any signs of danger. Then, with purposeful strides, Uldako takes the lead, forging ahead into the unknown toward Magan, the copper mine where he was held as a slave.

After a grueling journey, the group finally arrives at the slave camp, finding a concealed vantage point to survey the area. As they take in the sight before them, Uldako's shock is clearly visible, his eyes widening and jaw dropping at the transformation.

Ishara, sensing his distress, inquires, "What's wrong?"

Uldako's voice is barely a whisper as he begins to articulate his disbelief. "This place...Magan has grown exponentially. More slaves, more guards. They're expanding their tyranny, inflicting untold suffering on countless souls." Anguish tinges his words as he clenches his fists in frustration, a sentiment shared by the brothers as they witness the extent of the camp's malevolence.

Ishara interjects, "So, how are we going to do this?"

Hak leans in closer, his voice low and intense. "Uldako, Seth mentioned that you and your *ama* were once held at this camp, but she's been moved. Is that correct?"

Uldako nods solemnly, confirming Hak's suspicion. Hak continues, "Then we need to track down the slave traders who frequent this camp. Uldako, do you remember their faces?"

Uldako's expression hardens as he nods, determination flickering in his eyes. "Of course I do, and in fact, I see one of them right now." The group follows his gaze, spotting a man approaching the camp with a procession of twelve slaves, flanked by six guards. The slaves, bound together, trudge forward under the watchful eyes of their captors.

Uldako's voice drips with resentment as he identifies the man leading the group. "He's the one who tormented us the most. It was his sick pleasure to inflict pain, but it seems he's been promoted, now commanding his own group of guards."

Dak, sensing the weight on Uldako's shoulders, offers a solution. "Then we wait until he leaves the camp again and ambush him on the road." The other brothers agree, recognizing the merit in Dak's plan. Uldako and Ishara both acknowledge the strategy with silent nods as they settle in to wait for the opportune moment to strike.

After four hand movements of the sun in tense patience, Zak's voice breaks the silence. "Something's happening."

All eyes turn toward the gate of the camp, where their target emerges. However, a troubling sight unfolds before them.

Hak voices the group's concern, "There are more guards this time."

Uldako surveys the scene, his mind racing as he assesses their chances. "It seems like it was not just a delivery but a pickup of more slaves; therefore, more guards were needed. We're six against eleven now," he observes, noting the increased number of adversaries. He glances at his companions, their faces mirroring his own mix of apprehension and determination. The odds are daunting, but his resolve only hardens. "But where's the fun in an easy fight?" he adds, a fierce glint in his eye. "I say we embrace the challenge. We need to be wise, strike with precision, and use the element of surprise to our advantage."

The brothers, impressed by Uldako's warrior's heart, offer their compliments. Ishara nods in agreement, her eyes sharp and ready. Uldako quickly formulates a plan. "Let's wait until they pass us then silently flank them from behind. The aim is to strike when they are too far away from the camp to get any reinforcements. If we take out the four rear guards at the same time, without alerting the others, we've already gained the upper hand. Ishara, you'll be in the rear with your bow, ready to unleash a volley upon them!"

Dak grins, clearly impressed. "I like the way you think, Uldako." His voice is brimming with admiration. "It sounds like you come from the famed warriors of the North!"

The group agrees to the plan and waits as they stalk their prey in silence. Once they've put enough distance between themselves and the slave camp, they jump into action. Ishara remains poised with her bow, while Dak and Hak flank to the right of the slave line, and Zak, Uldako, and Šarru take the left.

With flawless synchronization, they launch their assault simultaneously at Uldako's command. Moving with the stealth of shadows, they creep up behind their adversaries just after they move over a ridge. In only a few heartbeats, they close the gap and attack the rear, muffling the guards' screams with one hand while swiftly dispatching them with the other. Four guards fall silently, their bodies crumpling to the ground without a sound. The whistling wind serves them, masking any small sounds.

As they come up beside the slaves on their way toward the rest of the other guards, a few slaves gasp and shrink back, and the guards turn to look. The alarm is raised, and six guards charge toward Uldako's group, their weapons glinting menacingly in the sunlight.

Ishara, quick as a hawk, nocks an arrow and lets it fly. The bowstring snaps. The shaft drives clean through the first man's throat and buries into another behind him. Both drop almost as one. Two guards down, four to go.

Uldako, his heart rushing, charges straight at the leader of the guards. He dodges a vicious strike aimed at his head, rolling to the side and coming up behind his opponent. With a swift, powerful tackle, he brings the guard to the ground. Recognition flickers in the guard's eyes as he tries to speak, but Uldako cuts him off with a decisive blow, rendering him unconscious.

Uldako rises to his feet and scans the scene to ensure the safety of his companions. He watches as Šarru assists Zak in dispatching the last remaining guard on their side, while Dak and Hak parade proudly with triumphant grins, their weapons slung casually over their shoulders. Uldako can't help but chuckle, it's clear that the brothers have turned this into a friendly competition.

"Bravo, you two!" Uldako shouts, acknowledging Hak and Dak's swifter victory. The brothers beam with pride at the recognition of their prowess. Meanwhile, Ishara steps forward from the rear, quickly moving to free the captives. Uldako joins her in the task, and as they release the slaves from their bonds, expressions of gratitude flood the air.

As Uldako cuts the ropes binding one particular slave, the woman's voice reaches his ears, sending a jolt of recognition through him. "Uldako, don't you remember me?" she pleads. Uldako looks from her hands to her face. His eyes meet hers, and in an instant, he realizes it's one of the slaves who had worked alongside his mother for a long time.

"Cornia!" Uldako exclaims, his heart lurching with a mixture of shock and compassion. As the realization sinks in, he sees the toll that captivity has taken on her. Her hair is cropped short, her body bears new scars, and her frame is even more frail and emaciated, a clear sign to the horrors she's endured. Uldako's eyes glisten with unshed tears as he embraces her gently, knowing that he has at least freed her from the burden of suffering. As he attempts to gather his scattered thoughts, she continues, her voice warm with awe and admiration.

"It's true!" she exclaims, her eyes shining with disbelief. "We've heard rumors of a man named Uldako who freed an entire slave camp. To think that the same Uldako I once knew as a young boy has grown into this valiant warrior—it's beyond anything I could have imagined."

Uldako is surprised by Cornia's revelation, his mind racing with questions. "It is true we freed a slave camp, but I did not do it alone!" He gestures to Ishara. "I have *dusa-meš* who helped me back then, just as we are doing the same for you today. But tell me, where did you hear that?" he asks.

Cornia's smile is bittersweet as she explains, "One of the men you liberated was captured again and taken to our slave camp. He shared the tale of your bravery with us. He spoke of how you led the uprising against the slave masters, how you fought for our freedom, and how only Lamech and his wives managed to escape."

Uldako's shock deepens at the news of the man's recapture, but before he can voice his concern, Cornia presses on, her words filled with admiration.

"You inspired something in him, Uldako," she continues, her voice trembling with emotion. "He spoke of equality and justice, of standing up against oppression. He told us that you believe that every man and woman was created in the image of *An*, deserving of dignity and freedom. Some of the slaves dared to join his cause, and they rebelled against the slave overseers, but tragically, many were slaughtered on that fateful night."

Uldako steps back, his muscles tense with suppressed rage as he grapples with the injustice of it all. He thinks out loud, "Those vipers...they just continue their evil of killing and deceiving." He turns to her. "Cornia, these lands are full of darkness! We were not created to be slaves. They have lied to us about it all. They lied about our value, about the *dingir-meš*, about everything! The Most High is *Il*, not *An* as we have been deceived to believe here in the South," he declares, his voice resonating with conviction. "What the evil slave masters subject us to, the cruelty they inflict—it's beyond tolerable. There's a world out there, a world of wonder and freedom! I refuse to stand idle while they strip us of our dignity, of our humanity!"

Cornia listens intently, her eyes glistening with unshed tears, mirroring Uldako's fervor. His words strike a chord deep within her, igniting a spark of hope in the darkness.

"That's why I'm here," Uldako continues. "I am here to rescue my *ama*. Do you know where they've taken her?"

Cornia steps closer, her voice barely above a whisper. "I don't," she admits, her gaze flickering toward the man Uldako had subdued earlier. "But he will know. Grunjo, he's the one who took her."

As Uldako's eyes follow Cornia's gesture, he sees Dak swiftly binding Grunjo, who slowly awakens, with ropes salvaged from the ones that were used to bind the slaves. Hate flames up within Uldako as he strides toward the captive, his purpose clear: to extract the information he needs, by any means necessary.

Uldako's fury rages like a tempest within him as he gazes upon the man who has wrought such suffering in his life. Memories flood back with searing clarity—the cruel laughter, the merciless blows, the nights of agony endured at this man's hands. With each step closer, Uldako feels the weight of every injustice, every scar, increasing the fire of his wrath.

His grip tightens on his sword, his knuckles white with righteous anger. The echoes of his mother's cries mingle with his own as he recalls the horrors she endured, inflicted by this very man. "No, not a man, not even an animal, but a monster," Uldako fumes. Every fiber of his being screams for vengeance, for justice to be served.

Dak notices the darkness taking hold within Uldako, about to consume him whole, and hastens toward him. Overpowered by his rage, Uldako raises his weapon, poised to deliver the final blow. "You deserve nothing less than death!" he bellows, his voice laced with volcanic fury. "It ends here!"

But just as Uldako prepares to strike, Dak intervenes, his sword intercepting Uldako's with a resounding clash. Their eyes lock in a tense standoff, the air thick with the weight of their conflicting emotions. Ishara and the others exchange glances of concern.

"Don't!" Dak's voice cuts through the tumult, firm yet pleading. "Snap out of it, Uldako! If you kill him now, we won't know where your *ama* is!"

Uldako's rage still burns brightly, but Dak's words penetrate the haze of his fury, stirring a flicker of reason within him. As the realization dawns, Uldako slowly lowers his sword, the tumult within him gradually subsiding as he wrestles with the conflict between vengeance and the desperate need for answers.

Uldako wrestles back control over his tumultuous emotions, while Ishara steps closer, her voice cutting through the tension like a light exposing the dark. "This is not you, Uldako. Look around you! At the slaves, but also at where we are. We are vulnerable here. We need to move him into the thicker forest where we can interrogate him, safely. This area is too open."

Hak, acknowledging the wisdom in Ishara's words, adds his support with a nod. "Indeed, Ishara speaks true. The slave masters who are expecting these slaves will sense something amiss when they don't arrive on time. We must not linger here when they come searching. Let's move!"

Uldako nods, grave and silent. The fury that nearly mastered him begins to hide within again. Shaken by the intense darkness within him, he steps back. From his side, Cornia calls, turning him to the freed slaves.

"What about all of us?"

As Uldako focuses on them for the first time, he is struck by the steadfast resolve in the eyes of the freed captives. They all know what he is feeling, and he sees it burn in their eyes. Not one of them has fled; instead, they stand united, their eyes fixed on him with terrible calm. Looking into their eyes, he knows this hatred will only take them deeper into darkness. They need the light! Then, amidst the silent crowd, a voice rings out, bold and unwavering.

"We want to follow you, Uldako!"

Another voice joins in, echoing the sentiment. "We'll fight with you!"

A chorus of agreement rises, sparked by admiration and gratitude. "We have heard about your heroic tales, and today we have seen it with our own eyes!"

In an instant, the slaves transform into a unified force, drawing closer to Uldako with each step. Their chant fills the air like a rallying cry, echoing through the arid land around them. "Uldako, Uldako, Uldako, Uldako!"

33

Leadership

Uldako, once a nobody, a lowly malnourished slave on the brink of death, now stands tall as freed slaves all around him chant his name, eager to follow him. He never imagined this moment, yet here he stands, a warrior with skilled companions at his side.

Ishara and the three brothers exchange smiles, observing the reverence in the eyes of the freed slaves as they look up to Uldako for guidance. The scene is almost surreal as the dawn pours saffron light over the group, the scent of freedom in the air.

Seeking counsel from his companions, Uldako finds only encouragement in their supportive silence. Zak's steady gaze, Dak's enthusiastic nod, and Hak's approving smile speak volumes. It's Ishara who breaks the quietude, her voice steady and reassuring. "They chant for you, Uldako. The decision rests with you."

Searching the eyes of the freed captives, each one bearing the weight of past oppression, Uldako feels the pressure of responsibility settle upon him. *There are twenty-four slaves here*, he muses internally, *enough to establish a sanctuary, a refuge from the cruelty they've known*. But then his thoughts shift, his mother's bonds reminding him of the urgency of his own quest to save her. *No*, he resolves, *not now. There's no time for a sanctuary. Not yet.*

Uldako addresses the slaves, "My *dusa-meš*," he begins, his tone firm yet compassionate, "I see in your eyes the echoes of my own past, the yearning for true freedom and the uncertainty of what comes next. But know this: Though your bodies are unshackled, some of your minds may still carry bindings. Break them! You are free! You bear the image of the Most High whose true name is *Il*. Because of Him, no power on earth can subdue your soul. You are free to make your own decisions. Embrace this freedom, not to live in darkness but in the light. I know you carry pain and hate, but let us walk this path together, forging a new destiny, unbound by the yoke of the past."

Tears cascade down the faces of some, stirred by the power of Uldako's words. Undeterred, he continues, "In your past, you've known suffering, but today, I offer you a glimpse of light. Seek it with all your heart and soul, and you shall find it! As for our path forward, I cannot promise you safety or certainty at this moment. We are embroiled in a quest to liberate my *ama*, Deborah, from the clutches of slavery. Our immediate task is to extract information from Grunjo, this vile man, about her whereabouts. If you're undecided on your next step, join us for now. Together, we'll seek refuge first to see to your basic needs. After that, my focus will be on rescuing my *ama* then living in freedom!"

Whispers ripple through the crowd of freed slaves, and one by one, they decide to follow Uldako. "I will follow you," one voice says. Another shouts, "Me too!" In an instant, everyone stands as one, their eyes fixed on Uldako with bright hope for the future.

Ishara looks at the freed slaves and then at Uldako, her thoughts echoing with pride, "Your *ama* would be so proud of you, Uldako, just as I am at this moment," she whispers so only he can hear.

Uldako accepts her warm words and steps forward, his voice commanding and urgent. "Remember this day! You have made your decision, and I accept. Now, your first task: act swiftly. Take what you can from the fallen guards. Take their armor, weapons, provisions, everything. We need to leave this place before the other slave overseers come searching for them. We will head toward the trees in the far distance. Now, move quickly!"

A flurry of action ensues as everyone swiftly follows Uldako's lead. The freed slaves ransack the fallen guards. Zak hoists Grunjo onto his shoulder, his expression stern with determination, while Hak and Dak deftly cover the group's tracks as they head for the trees, their movements swift and focused. A handful of slaves lend their aid, hastening the group's progress toward cover.

Ishara walks next to Uldako. "Your words stirred them, Uldako. But what now? What are we going to do with all these people?"

Uldako's brow furrows with uncertainty. "We need time to think on it," he admits, "What is in your heart?"

Ishara casts a glance over her shoulder, her eyes sweeping across the sea of faces behind them. Then, with a thoughtful expression, she turns back to Uldako, her voice barely above a whisper. "They're all following us, every last one of them. And most are young, full of determination. Perhaps this is the beginning of something more, Uldako—something bigger than us. It might even be a chance to build our own haven in the northern kingdom. A safe camp for all who have been set free from the bonds of slavery."

Uldako's eyes widen with realization that they are like-minded in the matter, but before he can respond, Ishara presses on, her words carrying conviction, "The timing couldn't be more perfect. Depending on where your *ama* is held, we might need more aid to free her, if a stealth mission won't work. With more allies by our side, we can challenge the slave masters, free more souls, and reshape our destiny. This could be the start of a revolution!"

Uldako feels a blend of relief, caution, and anticipation. "Exactly my thoughts, Ishara. But we'll take it one step at a time," he muses. "These men and women, and whoever else we might rescue—they're weak, hungry, and most have no experience in combat. They'll need more than I can provide right now. First we must establish where my *ama* is."

Ishara's smile is radiant, her confidence unwavering. "We're not their caretakers, Uldako. If they choose to join us, they'll have to pull their weight."

Uldako nods, clarity dawning upon him. "You're right," he concedes, his gaze locking with Ishara's. "It's a worthy cause, even if it's just to free one more soul from bondage. No one should endure the yoke of slavery. Let us take it one day at a time, and then we'll see who among these brave souls is willing to embrace the life we can offer."

As they walk, a silent understanding passes between them, their excitement for the future tangible. In their shared glances, they glimpse the countless possibilities that lie ahead, the chance to liberate not just a few but many slaves from the clutches of oppression.

The group swiftly finds refuge amidst the embrace of towering trees and rugged boulders. While Ishara, flanked by Šarru, Hak, and Dak, tends to the nourishment of the freed captives with their meager provisions, Uldako and Zak drag Grunjo aside, away from prying eyes.

With a sharp slap, Zak says, "Listen! It's time to face the consequences of your evil deeds!"

Grunjo's focus sharpens as it settles on Uldako's visage. A mocking smirk curls his lips. "Ah, I knew I recognized you! The little piglet I raised into an ugly boar with my own two hands," he sneers.

Uldako's patience wears thin, his voice laced with contempt. "You're no mentor, Grunjo! You're a tormentor. The man I've become bears none of your influence."

Grunjo, eyeing the ropes that bind him, smirks, "You may disagree, but it seems to me you've blossomed into quite the warrior. And those *dusa-meš* of yours—would all that have happened without the fire of hatred you harbor for me and the other slave masters, hmm, little piggy? Your hatred for us has changed you forever, whether you like it or not."

Uldako's grip tightens on his sword, fury simmering beneath his facade, but then he remembers what happened earlier and does not want to give darkness any ground.

Zak sees it in his eyes and interjects, his tone icy. "Leave this to me!"

Uldako relents reluctantly, stepping back as Zak steps forward to face Grunjo.

With a swift strike, Zak silences Grunjo's taunts, his blows landing with fierce precision. Each hit serves as a reminder of Grunjo's powerlessness. "It seems you still think you hold sway here," Zak muses, landing another punishing blow. Grunjo's sneer falters, replaced by a grimace of pain.

As Grunjo reels from Zak's relentless onslaught, Uldako watches with a strange mix of satisfaction and apprehension.

"I'll keep going until your attitude changes, Grunjo!" Zak's resolve is evident as he meets Grunjo's defiant gaze, scrutinizing the man's inner twisted strength, searching for the point where he will break.

Zak's eyes narrow, and he turns to Uldako, a warning gleaming in his eyes. "You might want to step back now. Trust me, you don't want to witness what I'll do to him."

The severity in Zak's tone leaves no room for doubt, and Uldako, sensing the gravity of the situation, takes one step forward instead of backwards, preparing himself for what is to come. The air is thick with tension as the scene unfolds, the intensity of the moment hanging heavily around them.

Uldako's expression hardens, his determination unwavering. "I wouldn't miss this for the world," he declares, his eyes fixed on the unfolding retribution.

Both of them cast their eyes back to Grunjo, who's visibly starting to fret. "What do you want with me?" he demands. "If you want to end my life for being a slave trader, then just do it already, because I won't apologize. My *abba* brought me into this world of slave trading; it is all I know!"

Uldako grimaces, torn between contempt and a surprising flicker of empathy for the man before him. Grunjo's words hit a nerve, stirring up an uproar of conflicting emotions, as he knows that growing up without his father certainly changed him as well. But he never considered how an evil father could form a man to be even worse than an absent one could.

Zak lowers his gaze closer to Grunjo with his brow raised. "We've all been granted the freedom to choose our own path," he asserts sternly. "Don't blame your upbringing for the choices you've made. You could have said no, or fled, instead of taking the precious lives of others against their will. But you didn't. You chose the path of darkness. This path of cruelty was your choice, and for that, I'll show no mercy. We're here seeking Uldako's *ama*, Deborah," he continues, his voice unwavering. "And you know where she is."

Grunjo's eyes glint with arrogance as he taunts, "Oh, I see. So you can't really end my life, can you? Because then you won't know the location of the little piggy's *ama*!" His evil laughter echoes through the forest, a grating sound that sets Uldako's teeth on edge.

Before Grunjo can revel further in his defiance, Zak's fist strikes out again, delivering a sharp blow that silences the laughter. "If you do not show some respect," Zak warns, his voice low and dangerous, "then you will come to know my blade very well."

Despite the threat, Grunjo remains unyielding, his smirk widening. "Well, well," he sneers. "You just told me I have no power, but at the same time, I know you won't kill me until I reveal the whereabouts of Uldako's *ama*. So I guess I do have some leverage, don't I?"

Uldako seethes with anger, but Zak motions for him to stay back as he advances toward Grunjo with an unwavering gaze. He understands what must be done in this situation. "You are looking at this all wrong. We want to keep you alive, because how can you feel pain if you are dead? You have no idea who I am, do you?" Zak's fury transforms into a chilling resolve as he leans closer.

"If you do not comply," he warns, his voice low and dangerous, "this blade will be used to cause unthinkable pain. And let me assure you, it won't bring death but an agonizing torment you can't even imagine. I know all the tender spots." He takes a pause for effect and continues, "Soon you will plead with us to end your life."

Grunjo's facade of arrogance begins to crack as Zak's threat sinks in. His steady gaze falters as he feigns control, but fear betrays him. Zak's eyes burn with determination, his expression a mask of unwavering resolve. He steps closer, the blade gleaming in his hand, and presses it firmly against Grunjo's arm. With a slow, deliberate motion, Zak twists the knife, grinding it into his flesh with excruciating precision.

"Stop!" Grunjo's scream pierces the air, but Zak remains unyielding, steadfast in his pursuit of the truth.

"I will stop the moment you start speaking. It is all up to you!"

Grunjo's resolve crumbles under the unbearable pain, and he finally relents, gasping out his compliance. The once arrogant man is reduced to a quivering, desperate figure under Zak's merciless grip.

Zak halts his torturous motion, his eyes fixed on Grunjo with an intensity that brooks no defiance. "Tell us where she is now or this will continue, and trust me, we have all the time in the world," he warns, his voice carrying a chilling edge.

Without delay, Grunjo begins to divulge the information they seek. "A long time ago, I received orders from a powerful figure to procure the most exquisite women from the slave camps," he confesses.

Uldako steps closer, his gaze piercing. "He didn't tell you to stop talking."

After taking a deep breath, Grunjo's words tumble out in a rush. "I was tasked with taking them to Eridu, and your *ama* was among those chosen," he reveals.

Uldako's heart clenches at the mention of Eridu, recalling Ishara's ominous warnings about the evil city. "Why?" Uldako demands, his tone edged with urgency.

Grunjo hesitates, evading the question, but the glint of Zak's blade and his readiness to resume the torment forces him to speak. "I'm not certain. Some would be enslaved, others sacrificed to the new *anunnaki*, and some—" His voice falters, but the press of Zak's blade at his wound compels him to continue.

"Some would be reserved for the depraved pleasures of the elite and the *dingir-meš*, a harem for their indulgences." He pauses, his voice trembling. "The most beautiful women were to receive the honor of being the first of their mixing, to see if they could carry and give birth to new *dingir-meš* on earth," he confesses, his tone laden with awe.

Uldako and Zak recoil, their expressions a blend of shock and revulsion at the heinous revelation. "Unthinkable…utterly despicable," Uldako mutters through clenched teeth, his fists tightening in simmering rage.

Zak's gaze tilts to the earth in deep thought. "So it's true. The fallen spirits' dark scheme is to spawn the Nephilim," Zak remarks gravely.

Uldako's mind whirls with a torrent of dread and worry for his mother's fate. The thought of her falling victim to such depravity sends a chill down his spine. He steps away, trying to grapple with the horrifying possibilities.

Zak's hand lands gently on Uldako's shoulder, a silent reassurance in the midst of turmoil. "Let's not leap to conclusions about your *ama*, Uldako. At least we know where she is being kept."

Shaking his head, Uldako struggles to contain his mounting panic. "But how do we rescue her from such an evil city like Eridu? The place is huge! There are too many guards and time is slipping away, Zak," he laments, his voice tinged with desperation.

In a heartbeat, chaos erupts as Grunjo's scream of attack pierces the air behind them. As they whirl around, they're met with the sight of Grunjo, freed and wielding a hefty rock aimed at Zak's skull. Before the blow can land, an arrow streaks through the air, piercing Grunjo's heart with deadly accuracy. He staggers in shock and collapses to the ground, life draining from him in an instant.

Zak and Uldako stand frozen, their breaths coming in ragged gasps as they process the narrow escape. Turning toward the source of the arrow, they find Ishara, her bow still taut from the shot, a triumphant grin playing on her lips. "You can thank *Il* that I caught him trying to break free," she quips, her tone laced with a hint of playful pride.

Uldako releases a shaky exhale, his gratitude evident. "We owe you our lives," he admits.

Ishara offers them a knowing smile before turning to attend to the freed slaves, leaving Zak and Uldako to exchange a silent glance of acknowledgment and appreciation for their formidable companion.

As the lifeless form of Grunjo lies before them, Zak surprises Uldako with a suggestion. "Let's bury him," he says, his tone unexpectedly gentle.

Uldako, rooted to the spot, bristles at the idea. "Why give him a proper burial? Let nature reclaim what's left," he counters, his voice tinged with bitterness.

Zak meets Uldako's gaze head-on. He senses the weight of resentment in Uldako's stare. "Uldako, this is one of those life-changing decisions you need to make early on in your life. Harboring hatred only poisons your own soul. Forgiveness sets you free." Zak's words carry the wisdom of hard-earned understanding. "*Il's* love extends even to those who stray from His path. He offers free will to all, but unfortunately, many choose darkness instead of the light. We must honor His love for all of His creation, flawed though it may be."

Uldako grapples with Zak's words, his convictions warring against the notion of granting mercy to one who has wrought so much pain. "How can *Il* love such wickedness? Is He not the Lord of justice? Also, did I not just witness hate from you against Grunjo when you sought information from him?" His skepticism is evident.

Zak closes the distance between them, his words loaded with conviction. "In war, I never hate, but I knew the perception Grunjo had about me. I needed him to see me as someone who would not stop. The pain I gave him with my knife was controlled, nothing more. But to him, it had to feel like a warning, a glimpse of what I might become. Being a great warrior is not only about having better fighting skills, but also about outwitting your enemy." Zak's voice remains firm as he continues, "Now, regarding the other question you asked, consider this, Uldako: Should *Il* then not condemn you for the lives you've taken or for any other evil you did or even thought of doing?"

Uldako recoils slightly, grappling with Zak's pointed question. "I know I'm flawed, but I'm nothing like Grunjo," he protests with uncertainty.

Zak's gaze softens, his tone gentle yet resolute. "We are all flawed! Evil knows no bounds; big or small, it is still evil, Uldako. But remember this: *Il's* love encompasses all His creation, yet He detests our evil deeds and thoughts."

Uldako feels the weight of truth settle upon him like a heavy cloak. "You mean to say *Il* hates all our evil deeds, but He loves us regardless?"

As understanding dawns in Uldako's heart, Zak goes on, his voice a torch in the dark. "Let us not be swallowed by darkness and become what we hate. You felt it rise in you, and don't deny it, because I witnessed it. Never kill out of hate, but only in self-defense. Taking a life without conscience must not become our way. Life is sacred, even the life of a man misled by darkness into evil. Let good overcome evil."

He gestures toward Grunjo's remains. "Come, let us lay him in the earth, and with him, the past."

Uldako agrees, and together, they lay the man to rest.

After they are done, Uldako returns to Ishara to relay their findings regarding the location of his mother. "It's a dark turn of events," she acknowledges, her voice filled with sympathy. "But we can't afford to lose hope now, Uldako."

Some of the slaves close by overhear their conversation, and as the gravity of the situation sinks in, one of the freed slaves steps forward, his voice laced with determination. "We owe you our lives, Uldako. I offer you my hand to rescue your *ama*!" His words resonate with others, their expressions reflecting strong resolve.

Uldako raises a hand to silence the burgeoning chorus of support. Beside him, Šarru steps in with a low growl, as is his way, settling at Uldako's side, needing no call to know his place. "Your willingness to stand with me is truly noble," he begins, his voice steady yet tinged with caution. "But let me be clear about the dangers that lie in front of us."

Gathering himself, Uldako outlines their perilous journey ahead. "The road to Eridu is fraught with danger, and our numbers are not enough to take on the warriors of such a large city." His tone is somber yet resolute. "We'll need to approach cautiously, perhaps with only a handful of scouts."

Drawing a breath, he shares his vision for the future. "But once we've rescued her and possibly any others enslaved within those walls, I pledge to create a sanctuary for all slaves who seek freedom," he declares boldly. "A place where every soul can live as they were meant to: free and unchained."

As the fervor of agreement swells among the crowd, Uldako's voice cuts through the clamor, commanding attention. "But heed my words well," he cautions. "Most of you have never known a life outside slavery. So please understand that beyond the walls of slavery are dangers aplenty, perils from both the hands of men and the jaws of beasts. Should you choose to join me, it will demand unwavering dedication to the cause. My aim is to begin a movement to set more slaves free. You know firsthand of the pain thousands carry behind walls as I speak. Let's set them free! Alone, we will falter, but together we can thrive!"

His gaze sweeps over the assembled crowd, his words resonating with urgency. "Should you pledge allegiance to our cause today, know that your commitment will be binding," he asserts, his voice carrying the weight of conviction. "Let your word be your bond today. Let your yes simply mean yes, or your no simply no, for anything more or less is to court darkness. I do not want people in my party who do not keep their word, for they cannot be trusted."

Drawing a breath, Uldako's eyes blaze with resolve as he lays down the law. "In my company, there will be no room for evil," he declares, his words ringing out with uncompromising authority. "Treat one another with the same love and respect you would wish upon yourselves. That is the only way forward. Now with those terms, let your decisions be known. Those who accept, move to my right, and those who reject my offer, move to my left!"

Three members of the group graciously decline, opting to search for their families in their former safe camps. For the rest, many have known nothing but slavery or have lost their previous sanctuaries to destruction, leaving them with nowhere else to turn.

Cornia takes the lead, stepping forward with a clenched fist on her heart. "Count me in," she declares, her voice steady with conviction. "I want to see more captives freed, even if it costs me my life. How selfish would I be to keep this freedom to myself." Inspired by her courage, others follow suit, each offering their commitment to the cause. With each affirmation, the group grows stronger, united by a common purpose.

As the last voice falls silent, Ishara steps forward, a warm smile gracing her features. "Welcome to the fold, everyone," she says, her words carrying a sense of camaraderie.

In the aftermath of their decision, Ishara approaches Uldako, her expression thoughtful. "We have twenty-one new recruits. Sixteen of them are young and capable of wielding arms."

Uldako meets her gaze, a flicker of determination in his eyes. "Then we need to assess their strengths and weaknesses," he says, his voice measured.

Ishara nods her head, understanding. "You are right. If we are to establish a safe camp, we'll need to identify individuals with skills in cooking, building, hunting, foraging, and fighting."

The brothers, Hak, Dak, and Zak, step forward, catching on to Uldako and Ishara's conversation, and they volunteer their assistance. Hak's confident voice cuts through the air as he asserts, "Leave this to us. We've handled situations like this before."

Uldako, recognizing their expertise, agrees. Without hesitation, the brothers move into action, their movements precise and coordinated, bringing order to the burgeoning group with practiced efficiency.

Zak assumes the role of spokesperson, addressing the assembly with authority. "Give me your ear, everyone," he begins. "To better understand our collective strengths, I'll ask each of you to introduce yourselves and share your skills."

Zak points to Cornia, who steps forward eagerly to lead the way. "I'm Cornia, *dumu-munus* of Etine," she announces confidently. "My skills lie in cooking and foraging for food." Zak expresses his gratitude before gesturing to the next person, initiating a round of introductions that proceeds seamlessly.

After each member has shared their abilities, Dak steps forward to deliver the verdict. "Thank you, everyone," he says warmly. "We now have a clear idea of our resources: two skilled cooks, a few proficient foragers, several miners, a leatherworker, and a stonemason among us." His gaze looks across the group, gauging their reactions before continuing. "Furthermore, we have nine willing warriors ready to defend us in times of need. Together with Uldako, Ishara, Šarru, Zak, Hak, and myself, we stand fifteen strong in defense." A surge of determination fills the air as Dak concludes, "But our strength lies not just in our numbers but in our unity. Starting from today, we'll begin training each of you in the basics of self-defense."

Uldako's smile widens. Of the three brothers, Dak carries the gladdest heart. He is best fitted to encourage the freed, who step from darkness unsure and spent. His cheer passes from soul to soul, like fire spreading in a strong gust.

Dak continues, "With that settled, you all know your roles and tasks as we journey northward. Now, let's proceed quietly and remain vigilant for any threats. Our first destination lies north, where we'll find respite by a lake. There, we'll set up camp for the night. Follow Uldako, maintaining a defensive formation as you step into your new bright future!"

As they set off, Uldako leads at the forefront alongside Ishara and Šarru, their senses keen for danger. Hak and Dak anchor the rear, ensuring the group's safety. In the middle, Zak strides with purpose, schooling the new recruits in combat techniques and wilderness survival skills as they continue to trek.

Zak's voice carries over the group, instructing the fledgling warriors while imparting vital knowledge for their journey ahead. Hak and Dak, from their vantage point at the rear, interject with additional insights, ensuring clarity in Zak's teachings. Together, they forge ahead, a unified force preparing for whatever challenges lie before them.

34

Conviction

Arriving at the lake after a grueling journey, exhaustion hangs heavy upon the group, yet relief floods through them at the sight of the tranquil waters. The lush plants sway gently in the breeze, creating an almost surreal sense of peace. An empathetic smile forms on Uldako's lips as he sees the wonder and awe in the freed captives' eyes, reminiscent of his own first encounter with this natural paradise. He anticipates their continued marvel as they journey further, taking in the untouched splendor of the world around them.

Uldako signals that all is safe, and immediately, the group rushes to quench their thirst and plunge into the lake, relishing the chance to cleanse themselves of dirt and grime. The cool, refreshing water revitalizes their souls, washing away not just the dirt but the burdens of their past lives under slavery. It feels to most like a purifying experience, bringing renewal, hope, and the promise of a brighter future.

After enjoying the lake, the group moves to Uldako's hidden shelter to set up camp, the atmosphere buzzing with joy and purpose. Some, heeding Uldako's directives, venture forth to forage for sustenance nearby, searching the surrounding flora for edible plants and fruits.

Tasks are swiftly assigned with the efficiency born of necessity: gathering firewood, preparing makeshift beds, and kindling flames for warmth and light. The rhythmic sounds of gathering wood, the rustle of leaves, and the crackling of newly lit fires fill the air. The group moves with purpose, each person contributing to the collective effort, transforming the camp into a haven of camaraderie and cooperation.

As time continues, the sun dips lower, casting a beautiful red over the serene landscape as evening sets in and the camp comes alive with the murmurs of conversations. Uldako observes the scene with pride and responsibility. Though weary, they are unified in their efforts, driven by a shared vision and the hope of a life of true freedom.

As the group settles into their evening routine, Zak, Dak, and Hak take charge, rallying their comrades for combat training. This leaves Uldako, Ishara, and Šarru with a rare moment of solitude, a precious chance to reflect on the day's tumultuous events.

Following the light training session and just before they turn in for the night, Zak confides in Uldako, cautioning against hasty actions given the novice state of their fighters. "I know we just freed them from their bindings and they are in a weakened state, but we had to test their fighting skills. As you know, we must expect the unexpected at any moment, and I must say they are complete novices. They will require much more time to improve, if they are to be of any aid in combat," he asserts, his tone grave. He emphasizes the necessity of patience and further training before engaging in any significant battles, underscoring the potential risks of premature confrontations.

As night cloaks the landscape, intimate conversations ripple through the group, weaving threads of hope for the days ahead. Then little by little the group quiets down as sleep sets in. Zak, Dak, and Hak take turns keeping a watchful eye, their vigilance unwavering as the time passes. The night gradually gives way to dawn, with the first light of day slowly banishing the darkness over the land.

After a hearty meal, the group presses northward. Over the ensuing days, the former slaves embrace their autonomy, honing their survival skills and reveling in the camaraderie that blossoms among them. For Uldako, Ishara, and the three brothers, witnessing this transformation within the group stirs a profound feeling of fulfillment.

The group finally beholds the imposing silhouette of Eridu looming in the far distance. The city's grandeur, even from such a distance, leaves Uldako momentarily breathless. "Probably another day's journey," he reflects, astonished by its sheer scale. The sprawling walls and towering structures appear almost surreal against the horizon. The city's splendor is clear evidence of the vastness of human ambition.

Before them stretches a valley teeming with life, a vibrant tableau of beautiful plants and wildlife. The sight is mesmerizing: a few enormous trees with lush canopies, colorful birds with iridescent feathers flitting between branches, and creatures of various shapes and sizes roaming freely. It's a scene of wild beauty and untamed nature, a contrast to the looming human settlement that feels dark and ominous.

Uldako takes in the scene. The rustling leaves and distant calls of animals create a symphony of natural sounds. Yet, amidst this natural harmony, his sharp eyes catch a flicker of movement that stands out. It's not the graceful stride of a deer or the playful scampering of smaller creatures; this movement is deliberate and calculated. Human.

With a swift, silent gesture, Uldako commands the group to hush and take cover. His eyes narrow as he focuses on the movement below, every muscle in his body tensing in readiness. The expression on his face shifts from awe to alertness.

As they crouch in the undergrowth, Dak confirms what they are all seeing. "A small group of slaves being herded toward Eridu by a handful of guards," he whispers, his voice barely audible.

Uldako's mind races with possibilities, his gaze fixed on the scene unfolding before them. "Only five guards and eight slaves," he murmurs, determination edging his voice. "Are you thinking what I'm thinking?"

A shared glance passes between the brothers and Ishara, their resolve evident in the glint of their weapons and the set of their jaws. Šarru, ever vigilant, emits a low growl, revealing his readiness for action. With a silent nod from Uldako, they prepare to intervene, their hearts pulsing with anticipation as they brace themselves for the coming confrontation.

With a swift and coordinated effort, Zak arranges the group's actions, ensuring the freed slaves remain concealed as Uldako and his friends jump into action. Moving with the fluidity of shadows, Uldako, Ishara, Šarru, and the brothers execute their plan with precision.

Hak and Dak advance on their targets, striking with calculated efficiency. In a blur of motion, Šarru charges forward, his primal instincts guiding him as he takes down the leader with a powerful tackle. Ishara stands poised with her bow, a silent sentinel ready to intervene if needed.

As the chaos subsides, the hillside erupts in jubilation as the onlookers witness the successful rescue. Cheers ring out as they rush to join Uldako and his companions, eager to lend a hand in freeing the captives. To Uldako's surprise, some of the rescued slaves already know his name, their gratitude overflowing as they express their thanks.

Amidst the commotion, Uldako extends an invitation for them to join their cause, offering them a chance at freedom and purpose. Six accept the offer eagerly, while two politely decline. After brief introductions, Uldako instructs the group to take the armor and weapons of the guards as it might come in handy. With the task done, they skirt along Eridu's furthest southern edge, keeping the walls at a cautious distance.

The three brothers move ahead in a triangular spread, Zak at the point, his brothers offset to either side, clearing the path and looking for any threats. When Hak sounds the eagle call, they return to Uldako and the group. Their report is simple: Hak has found the perfect hidden spot with ample cover, with firm ground for sleep and narrow approaches that could be easily defended with a standing guard. Concealed from casual eyes and safe for low fires, it will serve well.

After a while the group settles into the temporary refuge, and anticipation floats over them like a shroud. Under the cover of darkness, Uldako and Zak embark on a daring reconnaissance mission, leaving the rest to establish the camp hidden in the forest. Hak, Dak, and Ishara assume command, orchestrating tasks while sizing up the newly recruited members.

Meanwhile, Uldako and Zak sneak through the shadows, their senses honed for any sign of danger. Finding a vantage point atop a small hill, they conceal themselves among the foliage, gazing out over the sprawling expanse of the city. Uldako's breath catches in his throat at the sight before him. Eridu is a labyrinth of towering structures and bustling streets.

In the heart of the city rises a colossal ziggurat under construction, its lofty pinnacle nearly piercing the heavens. Streets radiate from its base like spokes on a wheel with water canals weaving through the city's intricate tapestry of life. Uldako observes with growing astonishment as some still toil tirelessly, expanding the city's walls with feverish determination.

With a grim realization, Uldako understands the urgency of their mission. If they had delayed their approach even slightly, the towering walls would have obscured their view, leaving them blind to the machinations within the city's heart.

Five guards stand sentinel at the gate facing them, but their numbers pale in comparison to the array of archers and rock-slingers positioned along the towering walls. The air crackles with the city's high craft, evident in the intricate canals that snake through the city, ensuring a steady flow of fresh water.

The trading quarters bustle with activity, a vibrant marketplace teeming with goods from distant lands, exotic spices, rare materials, and treasures beyond imagination. Nearby, the rhythmic clang of hammers and the roar of furnaces emanate from the working quarter, where weapons, armor, and tools are forged with meticulous craftsmanship.

The monumental ziggurat under construction at the city's heart commands the most attention, a colossal symbol of the city's unwavering devotion to its religious beliefs. Rising majestically against the skyline is a big statue of what appears to be a bull, casting a profound shadow over every aspect of daily life in Eridu.

Zak's voice barely rises above a whisper as he speaks, "I knew Eridu was mighty, but this is unreal. I can't believe how much it has grown! At this rate, the kingdom of the North is in real trouble. They are forging advanced weapons at a very fast pace, and the number of their warriors have doubled since I saw the city last," he murmurs, his eyes fixed on the sprawling city below.

Uldako absorbs Zak's observations with a solemn nod, his mind already calculating their next move. "Yes, but we can worry about that later," he replies, his voice steady despite the weight of his words. "At this present time, my focus is on finding a way to rescue my *ama*."

Zak nods. Then, with a hint of cunning in his tone, he proposes a daring plan. "How about we put together a hunting party? We'll hunt animals for their fur and ivory, then disguise ourselves as traders to gain access into the city. Once inside, we'll split up and gather information on where they're keeping your *ama*."

Uldako ponders for a moment, his gaze fixed on the distant city, before finally speaking. "It is a good plan, but we don't have any traders' outfits, and it might take too long to hunt all the animals we require to gather enough trading items of fur and ivory. Also, these people cannot be trusted—who's to say they won't attempt to kill us and take our spoils?"

Zak tilts his head toward Uldako and lifts a brow. "Do you have a better plan in mind?" he asks.

Uldako considers his options carefully. "I have a few ideas," he begins, "but none ensure our safe passage into this heavily guarded fortress. Our best bet might still be to masquerade as the slave traders they are already expecting."

A flicker of realization crosses Zak's face, and a knowing smile tugs at his lips. "Now I see why you insisted on keeping the clothing of the guards," he remarks. "It wasn't just for our new members' benefit, but to infiltrate the city. Yes, this could work, but we'll need slaves to make it convincing."

Uldako nods thoughtfully. "Exactly. You, your *šeš-me*, Ishara, and I will pose as the guards. The challenge is to have the recently freed captives to play the role of slaves again. They've just tasted freedom, and I'm not certain they'll be willing to go back, even if it's just a ruse. We need eight to stand in as slaves. I have not yet found the words to ask this of them."

Zak pauses to consider their options. "Well, we won't lose anything if we ask them plainly, right? They have grown a bit stronger over the last few days and had some basic combat training. However, I suggest we let the six newest members rest and regain their strength."

Uldako agrees. "Let's go ask them. If they are too fearful, we will need to go with another tactic."

With their plan set, Zak and Uldako make their way back to the new camp. Uldako lays out their plan to the group, noting some hesitation among them.

However, Ishara advances, unflinching. "I trust you, Uldako. Count me in!"

Her resolve is echoed by the unified voice of the brothers Zak, Dak, and Hak as they clap their fists on their chests. "We're with you!"

Five more come to the fore, thumping their right fists to their hearts—the mark of honor—while some remain undecided. Uldako addresses the group further to gain their support, "I won't force you," he asserts, "so I'm asking for volunteers. With our recent additions, we now number thirty-two, including my trusted bear companion, Šarru. To pose as the slave party, we need five guards and eight slaves. Ishara, Hak, Dak, Zak, and I will be the guards, armed in case of need. Five of you have volunteered, so we need only three more."

A man steps forward with resolve. "My name is Khoran *dumu* of Thalorus! My two *dumu-nes* and I will join your party, Uldako. We owe you our lives!"

Uldako regards him gratefully. "Then we have enough," he affirms. "Thank you for your commitment."

With their team assembled, Uldako briefs them on the plan. "We'll move exactly as the slave party did," he explains, outlining the strategy with precision. "I'll lead the group, with Zak and Dak covering the rear, Hak on the left flank, and Ishara on the right. Those posing as slaves will be bound, playing the part of the weak and obedient until we enter the city. Does everyone understand?"

A chorus of agreement ripples through the group, their resolve solidified. As dawn breaks, they set out for Eridu, the city looming on the horizon.

Approaching the city, Uldako notices the flicker of fear in the eyes of the pretend slaves. He stops and addresses them, his tone both reassuring and inspiring. "Fear not. If our ruse fails, scatter and flee back to our camp, and we'll hold them off. But know that we will protect you with our very lives!"

The group, bolstered by Uldako's words, brace themselves for the encounter with the gate guards, their hearts beating faster and faster. As they near the gates of Eridu, the city's towering walls seem to challenge their resolve, but their unity and purpose drive them forward one step at a time, ready to confront whatever lies ahead.

Uldako is struck by the sheer scale of the city and the formidable defenses that make it seem impregnable. His mind runs through the various scenarios, but none offer a guarantee of safe passage. Just before he reaches the gate, wide as a great dragon's maw, he offers a swift prayer, "*Il*, protect us!"

As Uldako approaches, he notices something amiss. The guard before him seems unsteady, his demeanor peculiar. "You…you're late…*hic*…*hic*," the guard slurs. Uldako quickly notices the man is drunk, and a glance around reveals that many of the other guards share his inebriated state.

"Some tried to escape," Uldako improvises, "but we're here now. Let us in quickly to save time."

The guard lazily waves them through the gate, his attention barely focused as he engages in conversation with his equally intoxicated companions.

I didn't expect this to be so easy, Uldako thinks, joy quickening as he watches their easy posture. The guards are still under the lingering effects of a night of revelry or some extravagant celebration.

His suspicion deepens when he overhears one say, "Last night was something else, wasn't it? The mushroom caps still hum in my blood…and the wine too."

The other guard, with a hiccup, adds, "Absolutely! What a night! That rite… spectacular! Watching the *anunnaki* take human form…*hic*…the high-born becoming possessed with the bull *dingir*…and the sexual revelry with the most exquisite women. It was a time of indulgence, indeed."

Uldako's disbelief mounts as he strides past the lax guards, realizing that their overconfidence in the might of their city has rendered them negligent. Their casual attitude toward their duties is a fatal flaw, one that proves advantageous for Uldako's quest. However, the disturbing conversation about the previous night's debauchery leaves him unsettled, his thoughts drifting to the safety of his mother.

Passing through the gates, Uldako instructs the slaves to hide their faces by looking down at the ground as they walk. They are greeted by a scene of debauchery and lawlessness that chills him to the bone. Half-naked women stagger through the streets, while intoxicated revelers feast in their reckless abandon. To his right, a brawl erupts among a group of unruly men, their violence met with amusement by the indifferent guards, who appear to be betting on the outcome. To his left, a woman spews vulgar insults at a man, their heated exchange a mere semblance of the chaos that reigns unchecked within the walls of Eridu.

As Uldako and his group navigate through the tumultuous crowd, they encounter looks of disdain and contempt directed toward the slaves, some treating them as nothing more than animals. A group of women find dark pleasure in taunting the slaves as the next victims for the night's ritualistic offerings, met with sinister laughter that echoes through the chaotic streets.

When a man dares to lay hands on one of the slaves, Uldako is swift in his rebuke. "These slaves are not to be used by the likes of you but for the dragonblood!" The crowd's attention shifts away after this unmistakable warning.

As they pass through an open area, Uldako witnesses something that defies reason—a man with wide, unblinking eyes, sitting on a grave in an unnerving manner, throwing dirt and rocks on himself. His appearance is grotesque; his skin is pallid and taut, hair matted with filth, and his clothing hangs in tattered rags. His gaunt face is twisted with a crazed expression, lips cracked and quivering. At first, Uldako thinks the man might be drunk, but then he realizes something far more sinister is at play.

The man's gaze cleaves to Uldako, and with a voice that seems not his own, he screams, "You! I will tear you to pieces!" His screeches are interspersed with strange, animal-like noises, growls, and hisses.

Uldako halts, rooted in place as he beholds the unsettling figure. To his shock, the man strikes another passerby with one hand, sending the unfortunate victim sprawling to the other side of the street with inhuman strength.

"That man is not normal!" Uldako exclaims as he looks on with wide eyes.

Zak pulls at Uldako's arm and warns, "We need to move away from here, Uldako! That is a man possessed by an unclean spirit, and he will make things difficult for us."

Uldako shakes his head, trying to clear the shock of what he has just witnessed, and continues forward, resolute.

Guiding the group to a secluded enclave, Uldako wastes no time in freeing the slaves from their restraints, offering them solace amidst the moral decay that pervades the city. With a reminder of *Il's* protection thus far, Uldako urges them to split into pairs, giving them guard garments from their bags to blend in and conceal their status as slaves. "If we pass as guards, people will leave us be and hopefully fear us, but keep away from the dangerous quarters."

Zak interjects with a crucial reminder, "Remember your slave attire will serve as a vital disguise later when we need to leave the city under the guise of captivity once more."

Uldako nods and adds, "So do not throw it away! We will meet back here in four fingers to the sun."

As the group fans out, Zak partners with Uldako for their exploration of the city. Each stride reveals more of the city's moral decay, where selfishness and malice seem to reign unchecked, but under the iron hand of the city guard. Amidst the marketplace's clamor, whispers of gods and the creation of formidable divine warriors called the *Ašag-dingir* saturate the air, a grim sign to the encroaching darkness.

Zak's tone is grave as he remarks, "This city has fallen and is far worse than I thought it to be. It teeters on the brink of a pitch-black darkness. We must locate your *ama* swiftly!"

With resolute determination, Uldako takes the lead, their guise as guards affording them the appearance of authority within the city's confines. Their path leads them to a slave trader peddling wares of human suffering—emaciated figures cloaked in tattered rags. Amidst the transaction, a dispute erupts between the trader and a disgruntled customer over prices.

Uldako's intervention is swift and authoritative, his voice cutting through the tension as he commands, "You, get lost! We have business with this man." The interloper hesitates, then acquiesces, retreating under the weight of Uldako's unwavering gaze.

With an air of authority, Uldako confronts the slave trader, his voice resonating with power as he commands, "You have been summoned. Follow us!"

The trader hesitates, seeking clarification, to which Zak's terse response echoes, "You'll know soon enough. No time to dawdle, move!"

Sensing the urgency, the trader casts a wary glance at his enslaved commodities, voicing his concern, "But what about them?"

Drawing closer, Uldako's demeanor brooks no dissent as he delivers a chilling ultimatum, his hand resting ominously on the trader's shoulder. "You can bring them along, but make no mistake. Question us again, and you'll regret it." With a deft motion, Uldako unsheathes his sword, its gleaming edge a silent threat.

Grasping the severity of the situation, the trader relents, his voice trembling in submission. "Alright, alright…no need for violence."

With calculated precision, Uldako orchestrates the charade, his voice dripping with authority as he directs Zak, "Oh, I almost forgot," he begins, casting a meaningful glance at the slave trader, "we were told to search his house in case he was hiding a slave!"

Zak, seamlessly playing his part, nods in agreement. "That's right," he confirms, turning to the trader with a stern expression. "Lead the way to your house."

As they traverse the city's labyrinthine streets, the trader leads them to his abode, the air thick with tension. Upon entering, Uldako wastes no time, swiftly cornering the trader against the wall. With a steely gaze, he commands Zak to free the slaves and ensure their safety. "Ask them to wait here until we return," he instructs. "We'll attempt to escort them out of this wretched city once we have found my *ama*."

Pinned against the wall, the trader's fear is clearly visible as he stammers, "Who are you?"

Uldako's smile is enigmatic, his grip unyielding. "None of your concern," he retorts. "But answer my question truthfully, and your life may yet be spared. Fail to comply, and this is where your journey ends."

The trader tilts his head, one brow lifting. "What do you want?"

With an intense glare, Uldako poses his inquiry, his voice low and intense. "I seek a slave woman named Deborah. Where is she held?"

"Deborah…hmmm…that does not sound familiar," the man insists, his voice faltering under Uldako's penetrating gaze.

But Uldako isn't fooled, his patience wearing thin. "You are lying!" he accuses, his tone sharp and unwavering as he grips the man by the jaw, forcing him to meet his eyes.

Yet, the trader attempts to deflect, his words tinged with defiance. "I see many slaves come and go," he protests, "and I am not interested in learning their names!"

Before Uldako can say more, a woman's voice cuts in, "I know her—I know Deborah!" Uldako turns to her, still gripping the man. Hope stirs as their eyes meet. The slave trader barks for silence, his authority heavy over her.

Uldako's frustration boils over, his hand connecting with the trader's head in a swift reprimand. With a stern gaze, he turns to the slave who spoke up. "Where is she?" he demands, his voice urgent with longing and determination. "Where is my *ama*? Speak!"

35

Mother

Tension coils in the cramped confines of the slave trader's dwelling, as the trader's warning gaze silences the woman who holds the wisdom to Deborah's whereabouts. Uldako senses her fear toward the man, the weight of her hesitation hanging heavily in the room. His own heart pounds, but he draws on his inner strength to offer reassurance.

"My apologies for the manner in which I spoke to you. My inward stirrings got the better of me. I too was once bound by slavery," Uldako says, his voice now steady and calming. "But I learned that fear serves only those who seek to control us."

His words carry a profound sincerity, resonating in the stillness. The woman sees the conviction in his brown eyes, the strength born from his own trials. The room is thick with unspoken tension.

With a decisive motion, Uldako confronts the trader, his eyes calm but with controlled righteous judgement. "Your lies will cost you dearly," he declares, his warning echoing through the room. Before the trader can utter a protest, Uldako's hand moves with lightning speed, rendering him unconscious with a single blow.

Turning to Zak, Uldako issues a command, his voice resolute. "Bind him," he orders, ensuring the trader poses no further threat to the woman or the other slaves.

Free now to address her, Uldako steps forth, his gaze steady. He turns aside and bares the slave-mark at his neck.

She gasps; awe and gratitude loosen her tongue. "It is you—you must be Uldako, the one who sets captives free," she says, her voice trembling.

With a resolute nod, Uldako confirms his identity, his presence a ray of hope in the dim recesses of the trader's den. "Today, you can join the ranks of those who are free," he proclaims. "No longer do you need to fear this wretched slave trader. You are free! I extend to you all an invitation: Join us in forging a safe camp in the northern kingdom, where all men and women are treated with respect, under *Il's* watchful eyes."

The slaves, their faces lighting up with relief and gratitude, express their heartfelt thanks. Their eagerness to join Uldako in his quest for freedom is unmistakable, and a wave of optimism spreads through the group.

Turning his attention to the woman who knows his mother's whereabouts, Uldako's voice softens but remains insistent. "Now, please, tell me about my *ama*." The space of a heartbeat feels like an age to Uldako's restless heart.

"She has been taken by Lamech," the woman finally reveals, her voice trembling.

Uldako takes a half step back as if struck by a dagger. At Lamech's name, dread grips him. For a moment, it feels like one of his nightmares.

"No...anyone else but Lamech," he murmurs, his voice choked with anguish as he grapples with the reality of his mother's fate.

Zak's urgency cuts through the haze of despair, his question echoing the fear that grips them all. "Lamech! Shields and axes! Do you know this for certain, woman?"

With a heavy sigh, she begins to recount her harrowing tale. "Yes! We toiled under Lamech's yoke together, until fate tore us apart," she explains, her voice tinged with sorrow. "I will never forget her, because Deborah's soul remained unbroken. Even amidst our suffering, she showed compassion to her fellow slaves, speaking of her beloved *dumu*, Uldako, the hero whose legend had reached even the dark depths of Eridu."

She draws a steady breath, then offers her hand. "My name is Tariela. It is an honor to stand before you, Uldako, *dumu-nita* of Deborah," she says, her voice low with respect. "To those in bondage, you have become hope."

Uldako's heart swells with pride and emotion at Tariela's words, "Thank you, Tariela," he says, his voice betraying the weight of his feelings. "But tell me, because time is of the essence, is my *ama* well?"

With a gentle smile, Tariela offers words of solace and strength. "Your *ama* is alive and speaks of you with unwavering pride, Uldako. She always believed in your greatness," she reveals, her voice imbued with reverence for the woman who nurtured him in his early years.

Wiping away his tears with a determined gesture, Uldako nods resolutely. "Show us the way, Tariela. Lead us to her," he declares steadily, despite the emotions raging within him.

Zak echoes his sentiment, his stance firm as he looks at the other slaves. "Bar the door behind us and wait here for our return."

Uldako and Zak move with stealth and purpose, mirroring Tariela's every instruction as they weave through the intricate web of streets and alleys. Uldako takes point, his senses finely attuned to the slightest hint of danger while trying to memorize and create a map of this city in his head. Zak remains vigilant at the rear, poised to intervene at a moment's notice.

Tariela, their guide through the chaotic cityscape, walks between them, disguised as a captive under the watchful eyes of her captors. With concise directions, she leads them through the bustling thoroughfares with practiced ease, navigating the labyrinthine maze toward their destination.

Their path brings them to the imposing ziggurat temple of *Enki*. The *E-abzu* towers above them, its stepped terraces reaching toward the sky, a wonder of architectural prowess from the people in Eridu. The mud-brick structure is adorned with intricate carvings, depicting serpents, flowing water, wisdom, and sorcery symbols of *Enki's* dominion.

The group walks past the base of the ziggurat, where a statue stands guard. The towering statue is so impressive and well crafted that Uldako stops in his tracks.

"That is *Enki*, the new lord of the earth," Tariela whispers.

Uldako's heart feels the darkness as he approaches, knowing well that this god is in fact the evil dragon of old. He is the enemy of *Il* and of all humans who are created in His image, yet here the ancient serpent is being worshipped by humans whose minds are darkened. "If only they knew…" Uldako whispers to himself as he looks at the statue.

Sculpted with meticulous detail, the god's flowing beard cascades down his chest, each curl meticulously chiseled to give the appearance of wisdom and age. His long hair, crowned with a horned helmet, signifies his divine authority and power. *Enki's* eyes seem to glint with an unsettling intelligence, their stone-cold gaze following Uldako as he walks by.

Enki's robe is adorned with intricate patterns that mimic the flowing currents of water, symbolizing his dominion over the rivers and seas. In one hand, the statue holds a large vessel from which water eternally flows, cascading down the pedestal and into a beautifully crafted basin. This continuous stream represents the lifeblood of the land, supposedly under the control of *Enki's* will.

At the base of the statue, goats and fish intertwine, further emphasizing *Enki's* role as the bringer of fertility and sustenance. Uldako can't help but notice the cuneiform tablets held in the deity's other hand, signifying his association with supposed wisdom and the arts of civilization. Uldako knows it to be the dark knowledge of secret arts.

But what strikes Uldako most is the expression carved into *Enki's* face. It is a serene, almost benevolent look that masks the malevolence Uldako knows lies beneath. To the people of this city, *Enki* is a benefactor, a source of life and knowledge. Yet, Uldako knows him as the deceiver, whose true nature is hidden behind this facade of divinity.

As he passes by, Uldako's gaze lingers on the statue, disdain filling his heart. The sheer size and craftsmanship of the monument are undeniable, standing as a clear reminder of the enemy's influence over the land.

With a final glance, Uldako readies himself, whispering under his breath, "One day, your reign of deception will end, when the Lightborn comes and the truth will be known to all."

As they venture further into Eridu, Uldako and his companions come upon a grand plaza dominated by yet another imposing statue. The bronze figure of a bull, its muscles rippling with lifelike detail, stands proudly atop a stone pedestal. The bull's eyes, inlaid with gleaming gemstones, seem to watch over the city with a vigilant gaze. Its horns curve majestically, symbolizing the strength and fertility it represents.

The base of the statue is adorned with intricate carvings of supplicants offering gifts and prayers to the bull god. Scenes of abundant harvests and thriving herds underscore the deity's connection to fertility and prosperity. However, the reliefs also depict more ominous images—shamans performing sacrifices and solemn processions leading to altars. These darker carvings hint at the god's demand for life and blood, evoking a feeling of dread among the onlookers.

Uldako notices Tariela's gaze turning dark as she explains, "This is where they bring sacrifices to the *dingir* of fertility—sometimes slaves but mostly babes."

Deep sadness and righteous fury brew in Uldako's heart as he imagines the grim scenes. He never knew that the people of Eridu, in their desperation to appease the gods, performed these unspeakable acts. The bull god is not just a symbol of life and strength, but also a reminder of the sacrifices made to sustain that life, which Uldako sees as death under the guise of life.

As they traverse the winding paths, the surroundings transform, the opulent grandeur of Cain's bloodline evident in the imposing structures that loom overhead. Uldako's jaw tightens at the sight of the lavish dwellings, guarded by watchful drunken sentinels who eye them with no suspicion. Their disguise as escorts affords them passage, and they press on toward their destination.

Approaching Lamech's formidable abode, Tariela gestures toward the sprawling estate, its grandeur standing in sharp contrast to the humble surroundings. "This is where Lamech resides, a man steeped in darkness, with only his own offspring rivaling his malevolence," she murmurs with fear and disdain as they inch closer.

"The structure on the far left is Lamech's ostentatious hall, where he entertains guests and revels in his depravity. In the center lies his private sanctum, where he dwells with his wives, Adah and Zillah. To the right, nestled behind the grandeur, is the bathhouse where his concubines are, and beyond that lies the quarters of the enslaved."

Uldako's gaze flickers with a mixture of disbelief and rage as he absorbs Tariela's words. The revelation that his mother is confined within the depths of depravity ignites a fire within him, stoked by anguish and determination. He turns to Zak and Tariela, his resolve evident in his voice. "My *ama* is being kept in a… Lamech will pay dearly for this," he declares, his voice laden with conviction.

Zak and Tariela exchange a knowing glance, understanding the depth of Uldako's inner agony. Zak turns to Tariela, seeking her insight. "How can we liberate Uldako's *ama* without alerting suspicion?"

She pauses before offering a solution. "The guards frequent the bathhouse, but only those sanctioned by Lamech and his *abba* are granted entry without question. It would be risky for you two to attempt it," she explains, her brow furrowed in contemplation. "Instead, it would be best for me to approach the entrance alone and inform your *ama* of Lamech's summons. The guards will allow me passage without suspicion, while you wait outside, given the customary protocol."

"Wise plan. Let's move," Uldako says.

They proceed toward the entrance with their senses alert for any signs of trouble. As Tariela approaches the guards, Uldako's heart quickens with anticipation, hoping for a smooth entry.

When the guards are close enough to hear, they stage it. Uldako points to Tariela. "You—inside. Now. Lamech waits for Deborah, and he doesn't wait long."

One of the guards, to their surprise, turns to Uldako and says, "Lamech is not in the city." The guard tilts his head in confusion. "What are you doing here?"

Uldako and Zak are taken by surprise, but Zak quickly adopts a nonchalant demeanor, feigning casualness as he steps closer to the guard. "Apologies for the confusion. You see, after a long night of revelry, our wits are not as sharp in the morning. My friend misspoke. It is Methushael, Lamech's *abba*, who awaits," he explains, his tone smooth and convincing.

The guard fixes Zak and Uldako with an intense gaze but then casually relaxes and remarks, "Of course, I understand! Last night was definitely something we will never forget. It was a night for the clay tablets, and it set the tone for our new bright future. It looks like Methushael isn't finished with his revelry yet, huh?"

The guard's grin drips with malice as he looks at the other one, triggering an instinctive reaction from Uldako, who launches into action with blinding speed. Before the guard can react, he's on the ground, incapacitated.

Meanwhile, Zak swiftly neutralizes the other guard, preventing any alarm from being raised. Tariela stands like a pillar, her eyes wide with astonishment at the swift efficiency displayed by Uldako and Zak. She has spent uncountable moons cowering under the oppression of these guards, their presence a constant source of terror. Yet here is Uldako, a former slave, and Zak, a warrior from the North, demonstrating not only fearlessness but also an impressive prowess in overcoming the guards as if they were mere obstacles.

Tariela can't help but wonder how many other former slaves carry such hidden strength, waiting to be unleashed. Realization dawns: The yoke of fear binding her is not unbreakable after all. Watching Uldako and Zak, new hope sparks within her. A hope that perhaps she, too, can rise above her fears and reclaim her freedom to become human again.

As Tariela stands in shock, her voice trembling, she stammers, "Wh…what… I mean…what now?"

Uldako meets her gaze with calm resolve. "It's done. Let's take one step at a time. Hurry inside and find my *ama* while we hide them."

With a single nod, Tariela sets off to retrieve Deborah. Uldako and Zak efficiently conceal the guards in nearby bushes. Assuming the roles of the fallen guards, they await Tariela's return with bated breath, their nerves taut with anticipation.

While Uldako stands in the midst of anticipation, an eerie silence descends, enveloping him in a cocoon of apprehension. Time seems to slow to a crawl, while the din of the city fades into a distant murmur. Each breath he draws feels amplified, echoing in the stillness, as he grapples with a myriad of emotions swirling within him.

What words will my ama *utter? How will she appear? Will she be okay?* Uldako ponders, his mind a tumultuous sea of uncertainty.

Observing the turmoil forming on Uldako's face, Zak offers a reassuring voice, "Stay calm, Uldako. Clear your mind if you wish to get out of this city safely with your *ama* and the other freed slaves."

Uldako heeds Zak's wisdom, acknowledging the necessity of composure in the face of adversity. With a determined nod, he readies himself, banishing the overwhelming surge of emotions to focus on the task ahead.

"*Ugubi?*"

The word cuts through the silence like an old memory reborn. Uldako stiffens; the hairs on his neck rise. That voice—unmistakably familiar, trembling—echoes from behind him.

"Uldako, is that truly you?"

36

Escape

Time hangs suspended all around him as Uldako is enveloped by the sound of his mother's voice, a melody that resonates deep within his soul. Slowly, he turns around, his heart drumming his ribs, to behold the sight he has yearned for countless nights—the radiant presence of his mother, the only family he has in this world.

As his eyes meet hers, disbelief courses through him, for before him stands a vision of ethereal beauty that defies all expectations. She is not malnourished at all—gone are the traces of weariness and neglect that once marred her countenance. Instead, she radiates a newfound vitality, her features illuminated with a resplendent glow. Uldako stands frozen in place, rendered speechless by the transformation before his very eyes.

As her arms envelop him, a flood of emotions courses through him, thawing the icy grip of shock. Her voice, a melodic symphony of love and relief, pierces through the silence, igniting a spark of warmth within his heart.

"My *dumu*," she whispers, her words a tender caress that resonates deep within him.

Summoning his courage, Uldako finds his voice at last. "*Ama*," he whispers softly, his words choked with emotion. "I feared the worst, but seeing you now fills my heart with indescribable joy."

Tears mingle freely as they cling to each other, revealing the depth of their bond, undiminished by time or hardship.

Even Zak feels a lump form in his throat. Yet, amidst the tender moment, the urgency of their mission lingers like a growing shadow. With a heavy heart, he interjects, "Forgive me, but we are not safe yet. Time is against us, and we must move swiftly; we must move now!"

Uldako, regaining his composure, wipes away his tears, readying himself for the perilous escape ahead.

Deborah looks upon her son with pride, marveling at the man he has become. "You've grown into a remarkable man, Uldako," she murmurs.

"Thank you, *Ama*. We have much to talk about, but Zak is right. We must act swiftly if we're to escape this wretched place."

Taking a steadying breath, he continues, "Follow us! Disguised as guards, we'll lead you to safety. But first, we must gather a few more slaves and then meet with our allies."

The group swiftly makes their way back to the slave trader's dwelling to retrieve the slaves who stayed behind, their steps urgent with the full weight of their quest. With the slaves in tow, they backtrack to the predetermined meeting spot, where Uldako had arranged for all the slaves to gather.

As Uldako rejoins them, he is heartened to find the slaves already assembled, their anticipation palpable. A chorus of joy erupts as Zak and Uldako approach, accompanied by two women. Standing before the group, Uldako introduces his mother and Tariela, and a wave of relief washes over the freed slaves as they believe their quest now complete.

Zak's voice slices through the air, commanding attention, "Our quest remains incomplete; we must flee this place with our lives."

Uldako strides forward, his eyes ablaze with determination. "Everyone, don your tattered slave garments once more. We shall exit as we entered, with stealth and cunning."

He also distributes among the group the two guard uniforms he and Zak took from the defeated guards, outlining the plan. After addressing their concerns, they set out, weaving through the labyrinthine streets until the towering city gate looms before them. As they near the gate, a sense of foreboding washes over him. An unexpected sight unfolds before his eyes, leaving him utterly stunned.

Uldako blinks, hoping his eyes are deceiving him, but the figure remains unmistakable. It is the leader of a group of new guards entering the city, and to Uldako's shock and dismay, the man is none other than the malevolent Lamech. The dark dragon head molded onto his pauldron armor is new, but the different colored eyes and evil gaze remains the same.

Uldako's thoughts sprint the span of a heartbeat, knowing their escape hinges on avoiding Lamech's recognition. "Quick, that way," Uldako murmurs urgently as the group pivots, darting toward the nearest alleyway.

Lamech's gaze follows, suspicion evident in his narrowed eyes. His voice snaps through the air like a whip, commanding attention. "You! Halt!"

Uldako's blood turns cold as Lamech's voice pierces the chaos in his mind. Their eyes meet and neither yields. In that moment, a flood of memories rushes back, a haunting reminder of their last encounter at one of Lamech's slave camps, where their fates collided and Lamech fled in haste to save his life.

Rage ignites within Lamech as his eyes meet Uldako's, the man who killed many of his guards and set his slaves free. "You!" he spits, his voice dripping with venom. "Those are no guards. Seize them!" he roars.

Lamech's command echoes through the city streets, igniting a frenzy as guards from all over the city rally to this call. With a cry of defiance, Uldako turns and flees, the others flowing after him like water from a broken clay jar.

"Runners! We've got runners!" one of them howls and then blows a horn to alert all the city guards, inciting chaos in their wake.

Uldako drives the group through a maze of alleys, breath ragged but pace unbroken. He is hoping most of the guards chasing them are still too intoxicated to mount an effective pursuit. It does, however, feel like the guards are emerging from every corner, and Uldako, unfamiliar with the city's layout, feels a rising uncertainty about his next steps.

Zak's voice rings through the turmoil as they run, "Where are we heading?"

Uldako's eyes desperately search their surroundings, seeking an escape, until sudden clarity strikes like lightning. "To the canals! Tariela, lead us!" he shouts.

They turn to her. Her gaze flicks rapidly between the streets as the path assembles in her mind. "This way!"

Arrows whistle past, and sling-stones thud against walls as they dart through narrow alleys and hidden passages, dodging the relentless assault. Suddenly, a cry of pain shatters the tense air as an arrow finds its mark, piercing a slave's arm. Uldako's heart clenches with worry, but relief washes over him as he sees the wound isn't fatal.

Pressing on, they round another corner, and Tariela cries out, "There it is!"

The canal looms ahead, a glimmer of hope amidst the chaos. But as they near it, the guards close in, their shouts echoing off the walls.

"They're heading for the canals! Stop them!"

To Uldako's horror, arrows and sling-stones fall down upon them from the walls above, turning their desperate flight into a deadly dance. If not for their pursuers' drunken state, they would surely all be dead. With unbreakable will, Uldako fights to shield his companions, but the onslaught is relentless.

A cry echoes through the chaos as an arrow finds its mark, striking Tariela in the back before she plunges into the waters below.

Uldako's heart lurches with anguish, but there's no time to mourn as another slave falls, mortally wounded, at his feet. With a surge of strength born by desperation, he grasps his mother's hand, propelling her into the canal with all his might. Then, as a stone strikes his temple, darkness envelops him, and he tumbles, unconscious, into the swirling depths.

The swift, powerful current carries the group away from the city's deadly grasp toward a lake outside the walls, leaving the futile arrows to splash harmlessly into the churning current.

As Uldako emerges from the depths of unconsciousness, he finds himself surrounded by the shimmering light of day, the cool embrace of the lake enveloping him. Zak, holding Uldako above water, jests, "What a nice day for a swim, eh!"

Zak's quip about the pleasantness of their impromptu swim brings a fleeting smile to Uldako's lips, but the throbbing ache in his head swiftly erases it. He casts his gaze wide to see how many are safe and spots his mother and another slave, swept out of the canal into the lake, straining to keep Tariela afloat. Their voices are tight with fear.

"Her life runs from her!" they call.

Uldako and Zak push toward them. The arrow has been dislodged from Tariela's back but blood pours freely from the wound.

Just as they reach Tariela and the others, the distant echoes of approaching guards reverberate through the canal. Uldako finds his voice first, eyes on Zak. "They're coming!" His jaw slackens as he searches for a way out, but there is nothing. There is no plan and no time. The guards will reach the lake any moment now. Then Zak's expression shifts. He has a plan. He pulls the group in close and sets it in motion.

Moments later, the guards reach the lake's edge, "Where are they?" one guard bellows, his voice a mixture of anger and bewilderment.

Another guard shakes his head in disbelief, his eyes inspecting the surroundings for any sign of their targets. "They should have just arrived here with the speed of the canal current. How could they just vanish like that?" he mutters, his tone tinged with frustration and confusion.

Despite their thorough search, the runners remain elusive, leaving the guards scratching their heads in bafflement.

"They must be close by. Quickly move out!" one shouts, leading the group away from the lake to continue their search.

After their departure, tranquility returns to the lake, the surface calm and undisturbed. Without warning, bubbles break the silence, and like specters emerging from the depths, Uldako and the others rise from the water.

Uldako's eyes light up with admiration as he looks at Zak. "What a brilliant idea! I never would've thought of using reeds to breathe underwater." Zak beams with pride, his chest swelling with satisfaction at the success of his plan.

But their joy is short-lived as Uldako's mother cries out in distress. "Help, she's not breathing!"

Zak moves, swift and sure. He rushes to Tariela, lifts her from the water, and lays her gently on the far side of the bank, just beyond the tall grass—away from where the guards went. His voice softens as he pleads, "Tariela, wake up."

The rest of the group follows, their faces filled with concern as they gather around Tariela. Uldako kneels down next to Zak as he looks at her breathless body. "You can't leave us now," he whispers, his voice choked with emotion.

Another slave offers a solemn tribute, his hand resting on Uldako's shoulder. "She gave her life to save us," he murmurs.

Deborah stands nearby, her tears mingling with the water as she mourns the loss of her friend. "No, Tariela," she whispers, her voice trembling with grief.

In a moment of desperation, Zak's emotions surge like a tidal wave, as he tries to save her. "I won't allow this," he declares fiercely. With trembling hands, he presses down on her chest, in a desperate bid to expel the water from her lungs.

Some of the others rush to intervene, their voices a chorus of concern. "Zak, stop! She's gone."

But Zak refuses to yield. "Seth taught me how to save someone who is drowning, just stand back," his resolve unshakable as he continues his efforts to revive Tariela.

He pounds her back, shakes her gently, and tries every method known to him, refusing to accept defeat. Finally, with a heavy heart, he lays her down on the ground, exhaustion etched into every line of his face. "I can't let another person die," he whispers, his voice raw with emotion.

In a sudden surge of determination, he brings his hands down on her chest with force, a last burst of emotion.

Then, like a miracle unfolding before their eyes, water erupts from Tariela's mouth in a gush, followed by a series of violent coughs. The group stands frozen in disbelief, their eyes wide with astonishment as Tariela's chest rises and falls with each ragged breath. Joy washes over them like a wave as they watch in bewilderment, unable to comprehend the miracle unfolding before them.

Tariela surveys the concerned faces surrounding her and lets out a weak chuckle. "I take it, we made it out safely?" she murmurs, her voice laced with relief. Laughter ripples through the group, a brief moment of light-heartedness amidst the chaos.

Zak comforts her gently as he rests his hand on her shoulder. "All of us here did, but you are gravely wounded and have lost a lot of blood," he explains gently. "You still have a serious wound that needs tending."

One of the new rescued slaves steps forward with compassionate eyes. "I know how to bind wounds. I've been trained as a healer," she offers, her voice steady with confidence.

Zak nods gratefully and with practiced hands, the woman assesses Tariela's wound, her movements deliberate and sure. "This wound requires more attention, but for now, I can tie it with cloth to stop the bleeding," she declares confidently.

Uldako's eyes reflect urgency as he says, "That would be ideal. We need to get away from here as the guards may return."

Without hesitation, the woman sets to work, skillfully addressing the wound with the resources at hand. She uses torn scraps of clothing to fashion a makeshift bandage, binding it tightly around Tariela to stem the flow of blood.

"What may I call you?" Tariela asks out of curiosity.

"Theresi is what my *ama* named me before she died, or so I am told," she replies with a faint smile.

While the two women engage in hushed tones, Uldako and Zak take charge of readying the rest of the group to depart. They study the tracks left by the guards, strategizing their route to avoid detection.

With preparations complete, they set off toward the camp. As they traverse the land, their senses are heightened for any signs of danger. Every step is calculated, every movement deliberate as they move through unfamiliar terrain.

After what feels like an eternity of tension and anticipation, Uldako breaks the silence. "Thanks be to *Il*, it looks like we will make it," he says with relief, his voice echoing with gratitude.

Zak chimes in, "Yes, there are no guards in sight, and we are close to Ishara and the others." Joyful murmurs are heard all around them as they take their final steps.

Back at their temporary camp, Ishara restlessly awaits Uldako's return, her mind becoming a whirlwind of concern and hope. She envisions meeting Uldako's mother if they are successful in their quest, the woman who nurtured him in his earliest years, and her heart swells with anticipation.

Meanwhile, the rest of the camp settles into an uneasy quiet, punctuated only by the sound of campfires, low murmurs and the rustling of leaves. Time feels sluggish to Ishara, each passing moment stretching out like an eternity as she waits in the shadow of towering trees that seem to whisper secrets of their own.

Then she holds her breath as unknown voices break the stillness. Ishara's hand instinctively reaches for her bow before she recognizes the familiar tones of Uldako and his companions. Relief floods through her as she rushes to greet them. Her heart lifts at the sight of Uldako's weathered appearance.

She wraps her arms around him, oblivious to the dirt and blood that stains his clothes, her embrace a testament to the deep bond they share. A smile lights up Deborah's face as she witnesses her son being embraced by Ishara with such warmth and tenderness. It's a sight that fills her heart with joy.

Now free, Deborah looks back. Their masters had kept them cruelly apart once the years of his weaning were complete. Today, for the first time since he was taken from her, she has held her son. The warmth of his grown frame wrapped her like a cloak. Her heart swells with gratitude as she now beholds him free of his bonds.

Tears of happiness glisten in Deborah's eyes as she realizes the significance of this moment. It fills her with hope for the future, a future where she and Uldako can finally be free, something that was denied to them for so long.

Deborah's thoughts are interrupted by a woman running toward her, calling out, "Deborah! Deborah! You're free!"

As Deborah turns around, she recognizes Cornia, the woman she had worked alongside as a slave for so long. They embrace each other tightly, holding on for a moment before Cornia breaks the silence. "I am so grateful that you are safe, and might I say, you look even more beautiful!" she exclaims.

Deborah smiles warmly, tears of joy welling up in her eyes. "Cornia, it's been so long! I can't believe we're both here, free at last!"

The two women sit down together, sharing tales of their trials and triumphs since they last saw one another. They speak of the hardships they endured, the hope that kept them going, and the new beginnings they now face. As they give voice, their bond deepens, reaffirming the strength and resilience that had carried them through their darkest days.

After Uldako gives Ishara a quick update on the success of their rescue attempt, they realize the sun is beginning its descent, casting a warm glow over the weary travelers. As they look at the people around them, Ishara senses the fatigue and hunger settling heavily on the group. Before she can invite the travelers to join them at the shelter, Uldako, still damp and dirt-streaked, turns to Ishara, gently taking her hand and leading her to his mother.

"Ishara, meet my *ama*," his voice is filled with pride and affection. With a tender smile, he gestures toward the elegant woman talking to Cornia. Ishara's gaze meets Deborah's, and in that instant, a silent understanding passes between them. Despite the hardships they've endured, there's an undeniable feeling of camaraderie, a shared bond.

Deborah extends her hand, her eyes filled with warmth and gratitude. "Ishara, it's a pleasure to finally meet you. Uldako has spoken highly of you on the way here," she says, her voice gentle yet strong.

Ishara takes her hand. "The pleasure is mine. I'm honored to finally meet you."

Ishara, moved by the sincerity in Deborah's eyes, gestures toward their makeshift shelter, inviting her to join them by the hissing fire she has tended to.

As Uldako, Ishara, and Deborah settle by the fire, Hak, Dak, and Zak extend their assistance to the newly freed slaves, helping them find a safe patch for the night and tending to Tariela's wound with care.

Uldako settles by the flames and exhales, his heart lightened by the sight of his mother and their newly freed companions. Deborah turns toward her son—when a massive bear lumbers into the firelight. She recoils with a cry. "Watch out! A beast!"

Chuckling, Uldako lifts a hand. "Easy. This is Šarru. He's with me! He is no threat, except to maybe fish and unattended stew." The bear folds down at his side like a hill sitting. Laughter ripples around the circle as Uldako rakes his fingers through Šarru's thick fur; the bear gives a pleased chuff.

"See? That's his hello," Uldako says, looking up at his mother. "People always jump the first time. He's been with me since he was a cub, and he still thinks he is one. If I let him, he'd try to sit in my lap."

With a faint smile, Deborah eases back to the fire, listening as Uldako tells how he found the cub—her fear melting into wonder with each turn of the tale.

The laughter ebbs, leaving only the crackle of the fire and what still needs saying. With a gentle gaze, Uldako turns to Deborah, curiosity and admiration burning deep in his eyes.

"*Ama*," Uldako begins, his voice soft but earnest, "I never lost hope. Our journey was driven by the sole purpose of finding and freeing you."

Deborah's eyes glisten with tears. "Words can't explain the gratitude I have."

After a moment of contemplation, Ishara breaks the silence, her voice soft yet direct. "I have tried to imagine what Uldako's *ama* would look like as we searched for you all this time, but I must admit, I'm struck by your remarkable beauty and your healthy condition compared to the other slaves."

She glances at Uldako, her eyes questioning. "You should have told me—"

Uldako's cheeks flush slightly, and he averts his eyes, feeling a mix of embarrassment and pride.

Deborah's warm smile, however, reassures him. With a hint of bashfulness, she responds, "Ah, well, thank you, Ishara, but unfortunately, they maintain the concubines quite differently." She pauses, a shadow briefly crossing her face.

Realizing her mistake, Ishara quickly apologizes, "I am so sorry that they forced you into—"

Uldako lowers his gaze, fighting to contain the surge of rage threatening to erupt. He will not allow it to further tarnish this treasured time with his *ama*. His thoughts turn dark, fueled by bubbling hate; he starts to imagine what he would do to them for what they did to his *ama*. Then he pushes back. *No! Banish those thoughts, focus on your time here with your* ama. *Focus on what she needs,* he silently tells himself.

Deborah gently interrupts, seeing the direction of Ishara's thoughts. Not ready to delve into that painful subject, she redirects the conversation. "Let's not dwell on that on our first night together. I'm eager to hear about the two of you. How did you meet, and what led to your escape, Uldako?"

As the night blankets the camp in a soothing embrace and the aroma of cooking fills the air, Uldako and Ishara share with Deborah the intricacies of their journey thus far. However, among all the revelations, Deborah is most shocked to learn that the deities they once revered are mere imposters, fallen spiritual beings disguised as gods. The weight of this newfound knowledge settles heavily upon her, leaving her speechless for a moment.

"I...I need some time to process all of this," Deborah finally murmurs, her voice laced with both astonishment and contemplation.

A shadow passes through Deborah's eyes. Ishara has seen it once before, and she wonders what Uldako's mother can be keeping from them. Then the truth dawns on her, but she waits for the right moment to confirm it.

"The night is late, but I'm eager to see what the future holds for us all. So, where are we headed next, Uldako?" Deborah inquires.

Uldako's grin widens. "We'll meet with our allies Kunai and Kesia in the northern kingdom," he explains, his voice brimming with purpose. "Then, we'll establish a temporary safe camp outside of Nippur, where all the freed slaves can find refuge until my return."

Deborah's brow furrows in curiosity. "Your return? Does that mean you intend to journey back to Seth before we establish our safe haven?"

Uldako's nod is resolute. "Indeed. There are matters I must discuss with Seth and his *abba*, Adam," he declares. "I need assurances that we have their support to construct a sizable camp in their kingdom and where we might establish such a home. I also want to discuss where we'll organize expeditions to liberate more slaves and offer them the chance to embrace a life of freedom."

Ishara swiftly interjects. "I will be with you! We still have not heard the full truth of what happened between *Il*, the serpent, and humanity," she asserts, her gaze fixed on Uldako. "I want to know the truth, and I don't want to miss the opportunity to meet the great Adam and Eve. What a privilege and honor it would be!"

Uldako responds with a warm smile, his acceptance evident in his demeanor. "Of course, you are welcome to join me," he declares, his eyes reflecting his feelings for her.

As the night deepens, Deborah rises from her seat, sensing the exhaustion weighing heavily on both Uldako and Ishara. "Well, then I will bid you both a good night," she says softly, offering a gentle smile. "Tomorrow a new future awaits!"

Ishara stands up promptly, eager to accompany Deborah. "Allow me to walk you to your bed," she offers kindly, gesturing for Deborah to follow.

As they stroll a short distance away, Ishara leans in, her voice barely above a whisper. "I see you are pregnant, and I don't think Uldako knows, does he?" she murmurs delicately, her eyes full of understanding.

Deborah's heart skips a beat, her expression frozen in shock. The revelation hangs in the air, leaving Deborah uncertain of how to respond.

37

Loss

Deborah's mind races as she grapples with the sudden exposure of her secret. Meeting Ishara's gaze, she inhales deeply, bracing herself for the conversation ahead.

"I'd rather not draw undue attention to this matter right now," Deborah begins, her voice low and urgent. "I am with child. It's still early, but Ishara, please don't tell Uldako yet. I want to share this news with my *dumu* myself, before it becomes common knowledge."

Ishara nods with empathy. "My apologies if I have overstepped. I was not aware of your feelings regarding the child. The privilege of informing Uldako is yours alone." Her voice carries a respect for Deborah's wishes.

With a grateful smile, Deborah accompanies Ishara to her resting place for the night.

After they part ways, Ishara rejoins Uldako, their exchange brief before fatigue claims him. The night is serene, with the shifting tapestry of stars casting a gentle glow over the camp. Hak and Dak stand vigilant, their silhouettes etched against the dim light, joined by Khoran, who cannot seem to find sleep after the exciting day of infiltrating Eridu to rescue Deborah.

A while before sunrise, most of the group sleeps peacefully, their breaths steady and even. Uldako, however, is ensnared in the clutches of another dark dream. In this haunting vision, the sinister serpent's eyes fixate on him with malevolent intent again. This time the third eye opens and grows enormous, a deep crimson orb pulsating with a life of its own, surrounded by an eerie, glowing aura that casts unsettling shadows around him.

The wind picks up, fierce and relentless, whipping through the dreamscape and howling in his ears. Yet, Uldako stands his ground, his feet planted firmly like a tree rooted deeply in the ground as the gale threatens to knock him down. The voice, cold and menacing, echoes through the darkness, "I am coming for you, Uldako!" The words reverberate like a chilling promise, sending shivers down his spine.

Despite the onslaught, Uldako's resolve does not waver. His muscles tense, his jaw sets, and his eyes blaze with determination. "I fear you not, fallen one!" he declares, his voice ringing out with defiance. The air around him crackles with spiritual sparks as he faces the looming threat, his heart pounding with unyielding courage.

As the sinister presence inches closer, Uldako's breath quickens. He feels the weight of the darkness pressing in, but he knows he must stand firm, not just for himself, but for those who depend on him. The eye's sinister gaze meets his, a silent battle of wills unfolding in the depths of his subconscious.

The eye begins to morph into the visage of a handsome man, laughter reverberating as it mocks Uldako's defiance. "To me, you are but a mere ant. What makes man so *sssspecial*? Filth!"

With menacing intent, the dragon draws nearer, its tone shifting from casual disdain to seething rage. "Yet, you, insignificant human, have dared to intervene with my grand designs! You dare take her from me?"

In a sudden, blinding twist of shadow and flame, the man convulses and folds into himself, then bursts forth anew into a monstrous lion forged from nightmare. Its mane writhes like coiling smoke and flames flicker from within, not of heat but of malice—black and unnatural, as if born from the void itself. This is no earthly fire; it is a spiritual blaze, cold and corrupt, burning without light and devouring all that is pure.

From its eyes and gaping maw, the fire flows, seeping across the ground in tendrils that infect everything they touch—stone darkens, grass withers, and the very air thickens with dread. The lion stands immense, muscles coiled beneath a sickly, tawny coat, its presence like a curse on the earth.

Then it speaks like the crack of thunder, laced with ruin. "I am the lord of the earth, walking up and down my kingdom to devour all who stand against me."

With a deafening roar that shakes the very ground, it stalks toward Uldako, its jaws wide and poised for the final strike. "Your demise awaits you this very night!" it snarls, its voice dripping with malice and hunger.

Uldako's heart drums in his chest as the lion approaches, each step closer sending a surge of adrenaline through his veins. The lion's roar echoes through the darkness, a chilling reminder of evil's relentless pursuit. The beast's eyes lock onto Uldako's, the intensity of its gaze attempting to paralyze him with fear. Its hot breath washes over him, the stench of decay filling his nostrils as it inches closer, muscles tensing for the deadly pounce.

Uldako stands his ground, every muscle in his body taut and ready, his resolve hardening. He can feel the heat radiating from the lion's body, hear the low growl rumbling deep in its throat. "I will not be devoured," he mutters to himself, drawing strength from the light. "I stand against you, with *Il* at my side!" he shouts boldly as the lion lunges, its jaws wide and ready to devour Uldako whole.

Just as the lion's fangs are about to snap shut around him with a thunderous clap, Uldako is abruptly thrust into reality by the chaos of a genuine threat. Hak and Dak's warning shouts pierce the air as the camp is under siege by a marauding pride of lions. Amidst the cacophony of terrified cries, Uldako's senses sharpen as he grapples with the urgent reality unfolding. A massive lion charges straight at him from the shadows, its golden striped mane flowing like wildfire as it roars, the sound vibrating through Uldako's very bones. The muscles of the massive beast ripple beneath its hide, and its eyes burn with raw hunger as it runs with immense speed. Uldako barely has time to react.

But Šarru does.

The great bear hurtles into the lion mid-charge, a thunderous clash of muscle and fury that shakes the earth. Claws rake fur. Teeth snap at throats. The lion's fangs snap inches from Šarru's neck, but the bear twists, slamming his shoulder into the beast's ribs and sending it sprawling in a cloud of dust.

Before the lion can recover, Uldako lunges in, sword gripped tight, rage and terror coursing through him like fire. He swings—bronze flashing in the torchlight—but the lion is too fast. It rolls, tail lashing, then springs.

Uldako dives aside, barely escaping the crushing jaws. Dirt fills his mouth. He scrambles to his knees, blinking grit from his eyes, just in time to see Šarru grapple the lion again.

The beast strikes fast—one claw catching Šarru across the face, leaving a red gash just above the brow. The bear bellows, not in pain but in wrath, and drives the lion back with a mighty swipe. The lion falters.

Uldako rises and charges. Šarru seizes the lion in a bone-cracking grip, pinning its hind legs. Uldako's blade arcs downward, finding its mark, deep between rib and spine. The lion howls, body convulsing. Šarru clamps down with his jaws and slams the creature to the earth.

One final shudder, and the beast goes still.

Chest heaving, Uldako staggers back, blood and sweat stinging his eyes. Šarru stands above the corpse, towering, breath steaming, a red gash above his brow and a few shallow claw marks along his hide—the only signs of the lion's fury.

His eyes gleam—fierce, undaunted.

But around them, the night is still full of movement. And more lions prowl the edge of the firelight.

Zak, Dak, and Hak plunge into the fray, their blades flashing as they dispatch their adversaries with lethal precision. In a swift succession of strikes, they fell their second lion, their movements a reflection of their practiced skill and instinct.

Uldako, amidst the chaos, shouts commands with a clear, authoritative voice, urging everyone to grab torches and form small groups to fend off the beasts. The flickering flames cast long, wavering shadows, creating an eerie dance of light and darkness around them. As the battle rages on, the remaining lions momentarily relent, their predatory eyes glinting in the torchlight as they assess their prey.

Among them, one lion fixates on Uldako with an eerie intensity, its gaze suffused with an otherworldly malevolence. An unsettling feeling fills Uldako's gut, the memory of the sinister eye from his dream haunting him in the lion's glare. He knows instinctively that this assault is no mere coincidence, sensing a deeper, more sinister force at play.

One moment the lion is a coiled shadow, the next it is in the air, all muscle and fury, aimed directly at Uldako's throat. But before it can reach its mark, an arrow from Ishara pierces its side, causing it to stumble and falter. Hak swiftly moves in to deliver the final blow, ending the creature's life with ruthless efficiency.

The remaining lions melt back into the darkness, leaving behind a trail of carnage. Uldako surveys the scene with a heavy heart. Amidst the chaos, he mourns the loss of one of their own, a grim reminder of the merciless brutality of the wild.

Uldako approaches the fallen figure, a somber heaviness settling over him like a shroud. His steps are measured, each one weighed down by the gravity of the moment. As Uldako kneels beside the lifeless body, the flickering torchlight sends a moving shadow across his face, highlighting the mixture of sorrow and resolve etched into his features.

Beside him, Ishara's voice trembles as she gasps, "Oh no…it's Khoran's *dumu.*"

Uldako's heart sinks. He bows his head, jaw tight with sorrow, feeling the weight of the loss crush down. One of their own…gone.

Khoran stumbles forward, his eyes fixed on the still form. When the truth settles, he collapses to his knees beside his son's lifeless body, a raw, broken cry ripping from his throat. His hands shake as he gathers the boy into his arms, rocking gently, as if the motion might undo what has been done.

Uldako feels helpless against the tide of grief. He rests a hand on Khoran's trembling shoulder and whispers, "I am so sorry, Khoran." It is all he can offer—and it is not enough.

Then another voice shatters the silence.

"No…not Melahl!"

Thurach, Khoran's only remaining son, rushes in, his cry piercing the night like a blade. He throws himself down beside his father and brother, wailing with such pain it makes even the warriors avert their gaze. Khoran turns to him, eyes wet, arms trembling, and pulls him into a fierce embrace.

"Steady, Thurach," he chokes out, his voice barely more than a whisper. "This will not be easy, but I'm still here. You're still here. We still have each other…"

With the immediate danger quelled, Zak, Dak, and Hak swiftly bolster their defenses, fortifying the camp against any other potential threats. With the grim silence of practiced ritual, they set to work. The thud of stakes being driven into the ground and the scrape of heavy brushwood being dragged into place soon reinforce their defensive circle into a fortress in the vast, menacing dark.

Ishara and Theresi move with purpose, tending to the wounded with swift, practiced hands. Deborah and Cornia assist them, their combined efforts transforming the makeshift camp into a hub of care and recovery. The soft murmur of reassurances mingles with the crackling of the remaining torches, creating an atmosphere of determined resilience.

As Uldako rises from his solemn vigil beside Khoran and his grieving son, he casts a pained glance toward Ishara, silently urging her to provide them with space to mourn. Together, they step away from the heart-wrenching scene, leaving Khoran and Thurach to grapple with their devastating loss.

Approaching the brothers Hak, Dak, and Zak, Uldako's voice is heavy with sorrow and frustration. "I can't believe this has happened again," he laments, his words tinged with disbelief. "First, we lost Ruk to the wilderness, then some of the freed slaves when we escaped Eridu and now Khoran's *dumu* has fallen victim. This cycle of tragedy must end."

Ishara's words resonate with Uldako's heavy heart, echoing his accountability and the urgent need for safety. "The only assurance of security lies within the walls of a fortified camp."

Zak's words tinge with regret as he looks at Uldako. "She speaks the truth," he concedes, his gaze falling to the ground. "We spotted the lions, but were powerless to prevent their initial onslaught. For that, we deeply apologize." Dak and Hak, standing alongside Zak, share in his remorse, their expressions reflecting a sense of failure in their duties as guardians of the night.

Uldako's voice hammers through the heaviness of the moment, imbued with both resolve and compassion. "Keep your heads up! You did the best you could, and you all fought valiantly," he says, his eyes steady upon his comrades. "It is true that one cannot stay in the wilderness and expect to live a long life; now, we must hasten to establish our sanctuary within protective walls. Dawn approaches swiftly, so let us gather our belongings and lay young Melahl to rest."

Around the freshly dug grave, Khoran's voice carries both sorrow and reverence. "I offer my gratitude to *Il*, the Most High, for the precious years He bestowed upon me with my *dumu* Melahl. His absence will be deeply felt."

With a trembling breath, Khoran raises his head skyward, entreating the divine, "Lord, sovereign above all, I beseech You to welcome my *dumu* into Your celestial realm, to grant him eternal peace. Spare him from the realm of the dead, I implore You!"

Uldako is taken aback by Khoran's love for his son and realizes for the first time that he desires such a relationship with his own father. At the mention of Khoran's belief in an afterlife, Uldako's curiosity is piqued, but Zak swiftly redirects Uldako's focus as he utters a few words.

"Thank You, *Il*, for Your righteousness, as we know Your every decision is just. Your will be done," he intones, his voice resonating with faith and resolve.

As they bid their final farewells to Melahl, the group's defeat and loss weigh heavily upon them, burdened by grief and the solemnity of their journey ahead. With a shared resolve, they set forth on their journey toward Nippur, a mix of fear and apprehension etched upon their faces. At the forefront, Zak and Hak navigate the path, their senses sharp to the dangers lurking in the wilderness. Meanwhile, Dak, Uldako, Ishara, Šarru, Khoran, and his son Thurach form a protective rear guard, vigilant against any threats that may arise.

Silence falls over the group like a shroud, each step forward a solemn reminder of the loss they have suffered and that it could happen again. Sensing the unease, Ishara nudges Uldako's arm gently, her eyes urging him to lift their hearts.

With a reassuring nod, Uldako surveys the resilient souls moving before him, their hesitation visible in every step. Gathering his resolve, he calls for the group to halt, rallying them together with a commanding voice.

"My *dusa-meš*—no, my new family!" he begins, his words echoing through the air. "We've lived through the yoke of slavery, endured the darkest nights of despair. But today, we stride toward a new dawn. A dawn of purpose, of freedom, and of hope!"

With unwavering resolve, Uldako looks into the eyes of each member, his words birthing new hope. "Let us not allow the darkness of our past to dim the brightness of our future," he says, his voice ringing with conviction. "Look beside you—into the eyes of your brothers and sisters. We are no longer strangers. We are united in purpose, bound by a bond stronger than the bindings we broke. Thirty-six strong, and this is only the beginning.

"We will build stronger defenses each night. We will guard one another as we press on toward the North, where we will establish a sanctuary—a place where we will live in safety, in peace, and with joy.

"Together, as one people, we march toward our destiny…toward freedom!"

Uldako's words resound, and a burst of renewed vigor fills the group. With cheers echoing through the air, they press forward with rising courage. Uldako's heart swells at the sight of the hope and resolve igniting among his companions, but he senses Khoran's silent anguish and approaches him with deep sympathy.

"Khoran, I may not comprehend the depth of your sorrow, for I am not an *abba* and have never known mine," he begins earnestly. "But I say this: I will not allow your *dumu's* death to be in vain. The name of Melahl, *dumu* of Khoran, will not be forgotten. His memory will endure within our safe camp, a legacy of his courage and sacrifice for our dream of living safely within its walls."

Ishara steps closer, her presence a balm amidst the ache of loss. Khoran glances between her and Uldako, and the sorrow in his eyes warms. He considers the words, then rests his hand on Uldako's shoulder.

"Thank you, Uldako. Your words hold great meaning." His voice is deep with emotion. "I will stand by your side, aiding in the establishment of our safe camp and fight alongside you. You have my trust and my weapon! From this day forth, consider me your *šeš*."

Uldako's lips curl into a grateful smile as he realizes he has gained a brother and offers Khoran a firm pat on the back. Together, they take a few strides, their camaraderie solidified in shared purpose. Then, Khoran speaks, his tone filled with peace amidst the sorrow.

"Uldako, I believe my *dumu* has found solace in a realm beyond our mortal understanding. He lived righteously, placing his faith in *Il*…or perhaps *An*, as He has come to be called now." A faint glimmer of peace touches his face. "I take comfort in knowing his soul has found rest."

Uldako nods slowly, though a shadow crosses his brow. He speaks gently, his tone careful and respectful. "His true name is indeed *Il. An* is what the serpent clans have begun to call Him, but that is a deception…and a truth to be discussed for another day after you grieve."

Khoran's expression shifts, eyes narrowing slightly in thought, but he simply nods.

A spark stirs in Uldako's eyes as he looks at the grieving father. "Do you believe, then," he asks softly, "that our journey doesn't end with death?"

Khoran regards Uldako with understanding and surprise, as though Uldako knows nothing of what lies beyond death yet claims to know the true name of the Most High. Eventually, he responds with a hint of certainty in his voice, speaking of a truth long held.

"Indeed, it is widely believed among those from the North that righteous souls, who walk the path of worship to *Il*, will find their way into His kingdom," Khoran affirms. "Conversely, those who stray from righteousness and embrace evil deeds will face the depths of the netherworld, where retribution awaits."

Uldako absorbs Khoran's words with thoughtful consideration, a glimmer of realization flickering in his eyes. "I understand," he murmurs. "That means all those evil slave masters will receive justice for all the pain and suffering they have brought! That is good to know."

Taking a relieved breath, Uldako continues, "Tell me, Khoran, where did you and your family come from, before you were captured and brought to the South as slaves?"

Khoran nods slowly, his gaze drifting into the distance as old memories stir. "We came from far away, from beyond the lands of Mesopotamia. My clan once lived where the sun sets late, in a wide land with great hills and forests of peculiar beasts. The world is vast, Uldako—far greater than most imagine. We wandered for many seasons in my youth, and even then, we never reached its edge. I do not know if it even ends."

He pauses, his voice growing quieter. "Many moons have passed—I have forgotten how long it's been. After leaving our homeland, we settled near the highlands in the East. It was such a peaceful and fertile land, but even there, darkness found us. Our village was overrun by violent men who served evil *dingir-meš*. They killed without mercy."

His voice falters. A single tear carves its way down his cheek as he struggles to remain composed. "My wife—she was raped and murdered in front of my eyes." Khoran's voice falters as he fights back tears. After taking a deep breath, he continues, "Those of us who survived were taken and brought to the South when Melahl was just five summers old."

Uldako feels the weight of Khoran's inner pain and says, "I am truly sorry, Khoran. That is why I have decided to free the captives and fight back. I want to prevent such atrocities from happening."

Khoran nods, unable to speak. Realizing the need to steer away from these painful memories, Uldako shifts to their first matter.

"Let's return to what you said about the afterlife. If your words hold true, it suggests that our existence holds a deeper purpose beyond mere birth and death, transcending the boundaries of mortality."

Dak, who has been quietly listening, steps forward, his tone solemn as he adds to the conversation. "You and Khoran speak truth, Uldako," he says, his voice full of conviction. "It is said, a man is given one breath upon this earth, and then he must give account when that breath is taken away. The lives we lead in these mortal bodies are fleeting, but what lies beyond is eternal."

Dak pauses, eyes raised as though past the sky, wondering how life appears from *Il's* throne. "It also implies that our temporary lives on earth are threads in a greater tapestry, each action and sacrifice contributing to a destiny that we must fulfill. This belief should be our guiding light in these dark times."

Ishara interjects, "If what you say holds true, then it aligns with my recent thoughts that we are being tested on earth," she muses, seeking clarity.

Dak responds with gentle conviction. "Indeed, Ishara. The choices we make in this life, whether to embrace the light or succumb to darkness, determine our eternal destiny," he explains.

Uldako, absorbing the weight of Dak's wisdom, remains silent, his mind grappling with the profound implications of immortality and judgment. "Then there is meaning in our lives after all," he reflects inwardly. "For if I were only to live and die, ceasing to exist, what would be the purpose of my life? Nothing!"

Ishara, too, falls into a pensive silence, contemplating the significance of their conversation as they continue toward their destination.

The group continues to trek north over the next few days, while training continues and bonds are strengthened. After a few grueling days of travel, they finally reach the outskirts of Nippur.

With elation in his voice, Dak exclaims, "Behold, the magnificent city of Nippur lies before us!" The group erupts into cheers, their fatigue momentarily forgotten in the face of nearing their destination.

Taking in the sight before them, the group halts to admire the sprawl of the city. Sobered by practical concerns, Zak steps to Uldako.

"Uldako," he says, "given our numbers and our clothing, we should raise a temporary camp beyond the walls of Nippur so that the group has a place to sleep and rest."

Uldako studies him. "You say this because you do not know how the guards—or the *lugal's* men—will treat a band of southern slaves who seem to be led by those in serpent guard uniforms?"

Zak laughs softly. "You take my meaning. Even if they let us in, how would we keep the company together? We can't stay with them, since you and Ishara must find Kunai and Kesia, and we may need the official permission from the *lugal* to set a camp in the North."

Uldako nods. "Then let them remain together outside the gates. They'll have shelter and a measure of safety while we go within and do what must be done."

Zak inclines his head. "Best course!"

Uldako looks at the slaves and back at Zak saying, "Even if we receive permission, they might need to wait here even longer while I seek counsel from Seth. There is much to weigh."

As Uldako surveys the freed slaves, he sees joy blooming across their faces, smiles unburdened by the yoke of slavery, voices rising with relief now that Nippur lies before them. The sight stirs something deep within Uldako as well, a warmth he has never known. In that moment, he realizes just how deeply he cares for them. The mantle of responsibility settles fully on his shoulders, not as a burden but as conviction. He will protect them. He will provide for them, no matter the cost.

Turning to Zak, he asks, "Do you know of a temporary safe spot for my people near Nippur with access to water?"

Zak's smile widens. "I know just the place," he replies confidently. "After they are settled, I will accompany you into Nippur. We must speak to Methuselah, who stands as *lugal* in Enoch's stead in his absence. It's vital that we inform him of the freed slaves setting up camp near the city."

Uldako nods appreciatively. "Your assistance will be invaluable," he acknowledges. "Lead the way. Once the temporary camp is set up, we'll proceed into Nippur."

As they prepare to move, Uldako feels a renewed sense of purpose. The freed slaves are not just followers; they are a community under his care. His determination to ensure their safety and well-being strengthens his resolve, and he feels a deep gratitude for Zak's unfaltering support. The journey ahead is daunting—finding and securing a safe camp for every freed soul, and preparing adequately for the darkness that's spreading. Even so, with Zak's help and Seth's counsel, Uldako is more hopeful than ever that they will succeed in their quest for freedom and a new beginning.

As the group begins to follow Zak through the rugged terrain, Ishara takes out her lyre and begins to play, her fingers dancing across the strings. She starts to sing an uplifting song, her melodious voice rising above the wind and lifting their hearts, filling them with renewed hope and strength.

Oh, hear the news of light from the northern wind,
It roars over mountains high and rivers low to humankind.
The *lugal* of *Il's* mountain stands with peace and might,
As the Land of Nod begins its rebellious fight.

Oh, the time has come for Watchers to descend,
Their dark shadows with humans to blend.
Oh, rise, all you honorable warriors of true light,
To bear your fire into the righteous fight.
The men of Nippur, prepare as darkness draws near,
In its halls, freedom and joy overcome fear.
Beneath the ancient sky where *Il* holds sway,
The courageous ones gather, for dawn heralds the day.

With courage and valor, their hearts pure and bright,
They stand as the guardians in the encroaching night.
Oh, *dumu* of *Il*, hear the call to arise,
With blades forged in truth, to pierce through the lies.

For in unity and truth, we shall find our might,
As we march against shadows, bringing forth the light.
The whispers of the ancients, in the wind they sing,
Of battles hard-fought and the peace they bring.

Through dark valleys of despair and peaks of hope so high,
The warriors of *Il* soar, beneath the boundless sky.
Oh, let our voices echo in the realms of old,
With tales of bravery and souls bold.
In the name of *Il*, we conquer and defend,
For love, for justice, until the very end.

38

Love

After three fingers of the sun have passed on their northward journey, the group comes upon a haven, an untouched glade where a gentle creek spills down from the hilltops and into a tranquil lake below. The water shimmers like polished glass, perfectly mirroring the towering trees, drifting clouds, and bursts of wild color that surround it. Butterflies dance through the blossoms like living jewels, and the air is alive with birdsong, melodies pure and unbroken, as if the land itself is exhaling peace.

Zak chooses the higher ground overlooking the lake to make a temporary camp, the elevation offering both beauty and vigilance. From this natural watchtower, they can rest beneath open skies, shielded by the slope and guarded by the clarity of sight in every direction. For the first time in many days, the wilderness feels like a blessing rather than a curse.

Under the guidance of Uldako, Ishara, and the three brothers, the camp swiftly takes shape. The serene setting transforms into a bustling temporary abode as shelters are pitched and fires kindled. The clear waters of the lake invite the weary travelers to refresh themselves, and the verdant surroundings provide ample resources for shelter and sustenance.

Uldako observes Khoran's leadership with admiration, noting the man's humility and discerning approach. Khoran leads with a quiet confidence, stepping forward when needed with kindness and assurance. His ability to make thoughtful decisions and guide others with a gentle hand earns Uldako's respect more each day. The camp, now a harmonious blend of nature's beauty and human resilience, becomes a haven of hope and camaraderie for the weary travelers aiming to rest here for a few days.

Uldako pulls Khoran aside, his demeanor serious yet determined. "I need your aid, Khoran. I must depart for a few days to secure the permissions and assistance necessary for our permanent camp in the northern kingdom," he explains. "May I trust you to lead the group during my absence?"

Khoran's astonishment is clearly visible. "Me? Lead?" he stammers, uncertain of his capability.

Uldako's hand on Khoran's shoulder reassures him. "Yes, alongside Hak and Dak," Uldako affirms confidently. "I trust you, Khoran."

Their eyes meet and hold, conveying an unspoken understanding and resolve. "I won't let you down," Khoran vows earnestly.

A knowing smile forms on Uldako's lips. "I know. And please, make sure Hak and Dak don't push those training to become fierce warriors too hard."

With a grateful pat on the shoulder, Uldako strides toward Ishara and Zak. "Let's go find Kun and Kesia," he declares eagerly. With swift farewells, Uldako, Zak, Ishara, and Šarru set off for Nippur, the city looming tantalizingly close.

After two fingers of the sun have passed in their southward journey, Uldako and Ishara step into the enchanting city of Nippur, a surge of anticipation coursing through them. Zak takes his leave to go and see Methuselah, while Uldako and Ishara make a beeline for Adriel's dwelling, eager to reunite with Kunai and Kesia, their hearts pounding with anticipation. As they draw near to the familiar abode, Uldako's excitement swells, akin to that of a father anticipating a long-awaited reunion with his son.

Yet, upon entering the dwelling, they are greeted by an unexpected sight. Instead of finding both Kunai and Kesia, they are met only by Kesia, engaged in lunchtime conversation with Rukug, the steward of Adriel's sanctuary. The absence of Kunai sends a ripple of concern through Uldako and Ishara, their brows furrowing in perplexity.

"Where is Kun?" Uldako asks.

A broad grin spreads across Rukug and Kesia's faces as they share the whereabouts of the adventurous Kunai. They explain how, with his boundless curiosity and affable nature, he has forged friendships with the city's young children, forming a clandestine network of information seekers. "He took your mission to heart, Uldako," Kesia explains, admiration evident in her voice.

"Kun and his young *dusa-meš* are using their age to their advantage as they listen to the city!"

A frown forms on Ishara's face as she asks, "What do you mean by 'they listen to the city'?"

Kesia's eyes twinkle with amusement as she explains, "Well, most adults will talk about confidential matters even if young ones are nearby, believing them to be no threat. Kun and his little *dusa-meš* may appear innocent, but they overhear even the deepest secrets of those within Nippur's walls. They have come to possess an uncanny knowledge of all that unfolds in the city and beyond, across the entire northern kingdom."

Uldako's eyes light up with delight at the unexpected news of Kunai, who is not only safe but has accomplished an impressive feat in building his information network.

"Where can we find him?" he eagerly asks.

At that moment, a familiar voice resonates from behind them. They turn to see Kunai standing in the doorway, his eyes wide with joy. Without hesitation, he sprints toward them. Uldako and Ishara rush to meet him, their hearts swelling with emotion.

Kunai, tears brimming, exclaims, "I missed you both so much. I'm so happy you're back and that some beast didn't eat you!"

They wrap him in a tight embrace, the weight of their separation melting away in the warmth of their reunion. The moment is filled with an unspoken bond, a shared relief that they are together again, safe and whole.

Uldako, his voice warm with reassurance, responds, "We've been under the watchful eye of *Il*, and I said we'd return soon, did I not?"

Kunai's face beams with immense relief and joy.

Ishara, curious, interjects, "We've heard you've been quite busy! What have you been up to, Kun?"

Kunai steps forward, filled with enthusiasm. "Of course I've been busy. You entrusted me with an important quest. I've made many *dusa-meš*, all skilled in gathering information across the city. You'll be proud of me when you hear what I've learned!"

Uldako leans in, placing a reassuring hand on Kunai's shoulder. "Well done, Kun! And, if I may ask, have you scouted a suitable location for our safe camp?" he inquires eagerly.

Kunai nods confidently. "Absolutely! There are many places, but there's been some raider activity in the lower parts and also in the eastern parts. I think we should go as far away from those bad areas as possible. Plus, I've learned so much about the northern kingdom and its clans that could really help us here to make smart decisions."

Uldako's grin widens. "Well then, inform us with your findings as we journey northward to meet Seth and his kin."

Kunai practically bounces with excitement. "Hooray! Another adventure!"

Ishara chuckles at Kunai's infectious excitement, admiring his boundless energy. "Hurry and gather your things; we're setting off at once!" Kunai dashes off in a blur, eager to prepare for the journey ahead.

Meanwhile, Kesia rises from her seat with determination. "I'm coming too! Let me go and get Shamgar and meet you at the gate," she declares, a flicker of hope in her eyes. With purposeful strides, she begins gathering her belongings, prompting knowing glances between Uldako and Ishara.

Uldako turns to address Rukug with gratitude. "Please inform Kun we will wait for him outside. Oh, and thank you for looking after him. It means a lot to us."

Rukug's face brightens. "Anytime. You're always welcome here."

Uldako, Ishara, and Šarru step into the open air, alone for the first time in many days. A quiet stillness settles between them, not uncomfortable but charged. The kind of silence that holds meaning. It wraps around them like a warm wind before dawn, stirring thoughts neither has dared to speak aloud.

Uldako's gaze keeps slipping to her—at the way the fading light dances in her eyes, at the calm strength in her presence. His heart thrums, not with fear but with the sweetness of words not yet spoken. *How is it,* he wonders, *that I can face beasts and bloodthirsty men without flinching, yet I tremble at the thought of telling her what lives in my heart?*

Then, as if drawn by the very force of his silence, Ishara steps closer. Her nearness is grounding and bright all at once. She looks up at him, her voice soft and soothing.

"Uldako," she says gently, "I want to thank you, not just for protecting us but for walking this path with me. Our journey—what we've shared—has become part of me."

Uldako's heart hammers even faster against his ribs, as if it might burst. Ishara's eyes drop for a moment to gather courage then lift to meet his.

"More than *dusa-meš*, you are my *ki-ág-meš*," she whispers, using the term for *beloved.* "Every moment by your side has meant more than I can say."

Uldako's smile forms slowly, edged with a quiet nervousness he rarely shows. His voice, usually firm and certain, softens as he speaks, each word careful, like a step taken in unknown terrain. "It is I who should thank you." His eyes linger on her face. "To walk this road beside someone with such strength and loyalty...it humbles me."

He hesitates, the silence stretching. Then, with a breath drawn from somewhere deep, he adds—barely above a whisper, "And your beauty—it has a way of making me forget the world's darkness."

The words float in the air, fragile and true. In the silent moment, he casts a sidelong glance at her, not daring to meet her eyes fully, his heart thudding with a fragile hope he cannot hide, eager for her reaction.

For a heartbeat, Ishara's gaze lowers, a soft blush warming her cheeks. But then she lifts her eyes to his, steady and luminous, as if something long held back is finally ready to be seen.

"Thank you," she whispers, her voice barely disturbing the silence between them. "Your words reach deeper than you know."

She takes a quiet breath, her gaze never leaving his. "You may see strength in me, but what I see in you goes beyond courage. There is a light in you, Uldako, and yes," she adds with a faint smile, "you are handsome—but it's your heart that shines brightest."

Uldako's heart swells with a blend of gratitude and unease, his world momentarily tilting on its axis at Ishara's heartfelt words. Her compliment, a rare gem bestowed upon him, sets his soul ablaze with a warmth he's never known, yet simultaneously, it makes him feel incredibly uncomfortable. As her gaze holds his with an intensity that both captivates and unnerves him, he finds himself ensnared in a web of uncertainty.

Every movement feels clumsy, every glance a fumble in the delicate dance of emotions that now envelops them. Uldako's mind races, searching for the right words as his heart races. Finally, summoning a shard of courage from the depths of his being, he meets Ishara's gaze head-on, his voice trembling yet resolute.

"I find myself drawn to you in ways I can scarcely comprehend," he begins, the words tumbling from his lips like leaves caught in a gust of wind.

Sensing Ishara's encouraging gaze, he presses on, his voice steadying with new resolve. "I've often wondered if you feel the same and if you'd ever consider…marrying me?"

As Uldako's heartfelt plea hangs in the air, the world seems to hold its breath, each heartbeat a thunderous echo in the silence that ensues. The truth of his desire has been spoken and nothing can bring it back. Tension crackles like lightning in the space between them as anticipation coils tighter with each passing moment.

Even Šarru feels the tension in the air as he shifts his gaze between Uldako and Ishara. Every breath feels amplified as Uldako awaits Ishara's response with bated breath.

But before Ishara can utter a word, the tranquility is shattered by Kunai's exuberant entrance, bursting through the door with the force of a tempest. "I'm ready! Let's go!" he shouts, his voice loud and joyful as it cuts through the tension like an axe, scattering the fragile moment to the winds.

Caught in the sudden disruption, the four exchange awkward glances, the weight of unspoken words lingering heavy in the air. Unable to bear the stifling atmosphere any longer, Uldako breaks the silence, his voice powered with forced cheerfulness as he strides toward the city gate.

"Well then," he declares, his words bittersweet in the wake of shattered expectations, "let's begin our next journey."

Uldako struggles to maintain composure, his facade of normalcy slipping under the weight of pulsating tension.

Now she knows. The thought strikes like an earthquake beneath calm waters, and Uldako's heart stumbles under the weight of it. A forge heats in his chest, hope leaping like flame, doubt clinging like soot. *Will she avoid me the rest of this journey? What is she thinking now?*

Before his thoughts can spiral into the abyss, Ishara steps closer. Her presence alone quiets the noise within—like sunlight breaking through. She leans in, and the warmth of her breath brushes his skin as she whispers words that stop his inner world.

"I wonder what our *dumu-nes* will look like."

The words strike not as jest but as a vow whispered into eternity.

For a moment, Uldako forgets how to breathe. His heart soars, igniting in his chest like fire chasing dry leaves. His face burns red from ear to ear, but he doesn't look away. Their eyes bind, and in that glance, something ancient and unspeakably beautiful passes between them…quiet, unspoken but understood.

He cannot find the words. He doesn't need to.

They both know.

They stand on the precipice of a new season, their hearts intertwined in the promise of a future together. Uncertain of what lies ahead, yet supported by the boundless possibilities of love, they embark on their journey with hearts full of excitement and anticipation.

As they approach the city gate, Zak stands ready with enthusiasm that can be seen from miles away. With a wide grin, he greets them, his words bubbling with excitement.

"Good news! I've spoken with Methuselah," he announces eagerly, "and he's given your freed slaves the right to stay until your return, under the leadership of Hak and Dak!"

Uldako's smile widens at the news. "That's excellent." The joy is clear in his voice. "We mustn't delay."

Shamgar's voice interrupts loudly from the rear, brimming with playful confidence, "I certainly hope you weren't planning to leave without us! You won't make it without Kesia's blacksmithing skills and my unparalleled expertise in…well, everything!"

The group bursts into laughter at Shamgar's boastfulness as they turn around to greet him. He trudges up with a great bundle on his back. The weight and clink tell Uldako at once that he carries Kesia's blacksmith tools, with a few pieces of armor besides.

Kesia chimes in with a grin while pointing to the load on Shamgar's back. "Speaking of my skills! I've started working on that new armor for you that we spoke about, Uldako, but you've returned earlier than expected. It's still in the early stages, but once we settle into our new camp, I'll get back to work on it with all the speed I can muster."

She turns to Shamgar with a smile. "Now that I have a strong bearer, I may bring all the tools I need."

Shamgar stands straighter before Kesia, pride bright on his face, and he gives a firm nod.

Uldako nods as well, the warmth of camaraderie easing the tension of their journey. "I can't wait, Kesia! With my new armor and Shamgar's unparalleled expertise in everything, how could I ever fail?"

Shamgar, not missing a beat, retorts, "Finally, someone recognizes my wondrous mind! I've been waiting for this day." The group's laughter lifts their hearts.

Shamgar turns to Zak with a curious glint in his eye. "You've been to Adam's abode a few times, right? You'll know the best path to take?"

Zak nods confidently, his eyes reflecting a determined resolve. "Indeed, the camp is well hidden and the path to it is not easily found," he acknowledges, "but fear not. I shall guide us through the wilderness with the utmost care.

Uldako's surprise is evident as he turns to Zak. "You're joining us?" His brow furrows in confusion. "I thought you were going to return to your *šeš-me*, Hak and Dak, because your task was fulfilled with the rescue of my *ama*."

Stepping closer, Zak's expression softens with sincerity. "I do this out of respect for our *dusa*-ship," he explains earnestly. "And so do my *šeš-me*. They'll remain behind to safeguard our newfound companions at the temporary camp."

With profound gratitude, Uldako turns to Zak. "I'm at a loss for words," he admits. "Thank you!"

Zak's clenched fist touches his chest, a grin spreading across his face. "I do not just have Hak and Dak as my *šeš-me*, for I also see you now as my *šeš*!"

Uldako returns the gesture with a nod and a smile. "So it is then, *šeš*!"

Ishara's playfulness is palpable as she chides, "Stop it, you two. You're going to make me cry!"

Shamgar's eyes twinkle with amusement as he rubs Šarru's thick fur. "Another *šeš* to add to the mix, eh, Šarru? Pretty soon you and Kun are going to have a huge family with many *šeš-me*!"

The bear responds with an enjoyable growl, clearly relishing the attention. Shamgar chuckles, patting Šarru affectionately. "See? Even Šarru's on board with this growing family."

And so, the group of seven, led by Uldako and guided by Zak's newfound commitment, set forth on their journey northward to Adam's domain.

In the ensuing days, the group encounters little peril aside from the occasional brush with wild beasts. Yet, under Zak's seasoned guidance, they deftly skirt the most formidable dangers, his knowledge of the terrain akin to a masterful navigator charting the course through treacherous waters.

As they journey, Uldako finds himself enraptured by the ever-changing landscapes unfolding before him. His senses drink in the sights and sounds of the wilderness, each new vista a portrait of the land's vibrant diversity.

Their path leads them to the banks of another river, the mighty Tigris, its majestic waters winding through the heart of the land. Uldako stands in awe, captivated by the beauty that surrounds them. Fish leap gracefully from the water, while animals quench their thirst along the verdant shores.

As they replenish their waterskins, the group marvels at the abundance of the land surrounding them. Uldako's senses are overwhelmed with the sights and scents of unfamiliar flora, evidence of the richness of the northern terrain. Zak's intimate knowledge of the landscape guides them through groves of fruit trees, clusters of exotic nuts, and an array of plants whose flavors tantalize Uldako's palate, each bite a discovery in itself.

Zak and Shamgar's voices carry the wisdom of generations as they elaborate on the ways of life in the North. Here, they explain, survival hinges upon a symbiotic relationship with the land, where some live solely off its bounty while others cultivate crops and raise livestock. He draws parallels to the ancient traditions, tracing their lineage back to Adam. "Abel tended the flocks," Zak recounts, "while Cain toiled the earth—skills they learned at a young age from their parents, Adam and Eve."

The group settles down in a safe area for the night, but amidst the tranquility, discordant laughter not far from their camp disrupts the night's peace. Uldako's instincts spring into action, his sword at the ready as he warns, "Humans. They might be raiders!" he warns in a hushed tone.

Yet, instead of alarm, Zak and Shamgar's laughter reverberates through the darkness together with the rest of the group, perplexing Uldako with their unexpected reaction to his warning.

With a knowing smile, Kesia relieves the tension, her words laced with reassurance. "It's no human threat, Uldako," she explains.

Ishara adds her insight, identifying the source of the disturbance. "Some call them *ur-kal*," she reveals.

Uldako's eyes are wide with intrigue. "What manner of beast is this that has such a sinister laugh?" His voice is edged with anticipation.

With a calming breath, Zak gathers himself, ready to describe the creature that has stirred the night's peace. "An *ur-kal*," he begins, "is a formidable predator. Its body, though smaller than a *zu-gal*, is lean and powerful, with a sloping back and sturdy legs built for endurance. Its fur is coarse and spotted, blending seamlessly with the shadows of the night."

He continues, delving into the creature's distinctive features. "Its head is broad, with a powerful jaw lined with sharp teeth capable of crushing bone. Its eyes gleam with intelligence and cunning, and its ears, large and alert, swivel to catch the slightest sound."

Zak's description grows more animated as he speaks of the predator's eerie laughter, a sound that chills the blood of those who hear it in the dead of night. "And its call," he adds, his voice tinged with unease, "is a haunting laughter that echoes through the darkness, striking fear into the hearts of those who cross its path. They hunt in packs, which is why you believed them to be humans laughing."

As Zak finishes his explanation, he sets his eyes on Uldako. "But fret not, Uldako," Zak reassures. "As you know, most predators shy away from fire, and our blazing torches will serve as a barrier against their advances. Besides, they often seek out easier prey, conserving their strength for a sure meal. With our numbers, bolstered by Šarru's presence, they'll think twice before venturing near."

After those words, Uldako exhales, sits again, and turns to Ishara for reassurance. "He is right, Uldako," she says gently.

Kunai, who also seems a bit startled by the sinister laughter, scurries over to sit right between Uldako and Šarru for protection. A gentle smile finds Uldako as he watches Kunai nestle into the great bear's fur.

As the night cloaks them in its embrace, they take turns standing vigilant, two at a time, keeping watch over the camp. First, Uldako stands guard with Zak while the others turn in for a good night's rest. After the previous lion attack, they remain awake and ready for anything in the dark, a united front against the lurking shadows.

With the break of dawn, a gentle glow washes over the earth, breathing new life into the land around them. Renewed and invigorated, they resume their journey, hearts ablaze with determination as they forge ahead into the unknown.

The rising sun lays honeyed light over the landscape, transforming the path ahead into a golden cord of promise and hope. Uldako takes a deep breath, feeling the crisp morning air fill his lungs. He casts a glance back at his companions, their eyes reflecting resolve and bright eagerness for what lies ahead.

39

Patriarch

After long arduous travel, they at last arrive at their long-awaited destination. As they crest a hill, a breathtaking view unfolds before them: a verdant valley adorned with towering trees, a shimmering lake, and a distant camp nestled safely in its embrace.

"There it is," Zak proclaims with excitement as he gestures toward their destination.

Eagerly, Uldako asks, "Well, what are we waiting for? Let's go!"

Shamgar and Zak give him warning looks. "We need to wait," Zak says with confidence.

Uldako, confused, asks, "For what?"

Shamgar points toward the shadows cast by the towering trees. "Don't you see them, Uldako? Look carefully at the shadows. They have been observing us for a while now."

Uldako's joyfulness is broken when a patrolling party of seven warriors emerges from the shadows. Kunai quickly steps closer to Uldako for protection.

"Who goes there?" one of the men demands, his tone brimming with suspicion.

Stepping forward, Zak assumes the role of spokesman, his stature commanding respect. "Zak, *dumu* of Kenan," he declares boldly.

Uldako's brow furrows in astonishment, surprised at the revelation of Zak's lineage, which had remained unknown to him despite all the time they spent together. Beside him, Ishara's expression mirrors his disbelief. Yet, before they can utter a word, another scout interjects with unexpected familiarity.

"Ah, Zak! Welcome!" he exclaims with a warm tone of recognition. "How fare your *šeš-me*, Dak and Hak?"

Zak strides forward, exchanging warm greetings with the seven guards—five men and two women. "They are alive and well, thanks to *Il*," he replies. "How have you been, Daner?"

A smile grips the man's lips as he looks up to the sky and confidently says, "Good, because *Il* is good!"

Daner turns his gaze to Shamgar. "Well now, if isn't the great Shamgar! One of the five strongest warriors under Seth. It feels as if I have not seen you for several centuries!"

The group takes a moment to greet one another, sharing a brief moment of camaraderie. Daner then turns his attention to Uldako and the others, his expression becoming more serious.

"So why have you brought these outsiders to Adam's secret camp?" His gaze is scrutinizing as he investigates the newcomers, his frown deepening with concern.

Uldako's eyes lingers on Daner, taking in the sight of the seasoned warrior. Towering in stature, he wields a massive two-handed axe with ease, a show of his strength and skill. His dark braided beard and flowing locks speak of his rugged experience, while his imposing demeanor commands respect.

A sense of unease settles over Uldako as he recognizes Daner as a formidable fighter. Uldako can sense that Daner has faced countless battles, both against beasts and men, and possesses a prowess that leaves no room for doubt. His finely crafted leather armor gleams in the sunlight, drawing admiring glances from Kesia. Uldako observes her subtle fascination, allured by Daner's formidable presence.

Zak steps over to Uldako and places a reassuring hand on his shoulder. "I've come to escort this man, Uldako, and his companions under Seth's orders to meet with him here," Zak explains. "They can be trusted. Could you guide us to him?"

Daner nods in acknowledgment as he turns to one of the guards. "Aram, lead these travelers to Seth," he commands, his voice resonating with authority. As the other guards prepare to resume their vigilant patrols, Aram steps forward.

His eyes are a piercing emerald, framed by long, dark lashes that contrast sharply with his stern, furrowed brows. His hair, short and meticulously kept on top, transitions to completely shaved sides, accentuating his chiseled features. A short beard frames his jawline, growing fuller toward his chin.

Clad in a mix of gleaming bronze and rugged leather armor, Aram embodies both strength and agility. Two swords, polished and deadly, are strapped to his back, while a finely crafted bow rests in his hands, ready for action. The emblem of an eagle, symbolizing the heavenly realm and *Il*, is emblazoned on his torso. Intricately engraved cherubim-type spirits adorn his breastplate, their celestial forms adding an air of divine protection and fearsome power to his already imposing presence.

As Daner prepares to depart, he offers a parting assurance. "Shamgar and Zak, we'll catch up with you later. But for now, our duty calls! We are to ensure the safety of our kin. As you might know, a great assembly is anticipated." With a resolute nod, and with fists pounding on their chests, they are on their way, their figures fading into the distance as they vanish into the wilderness.

With the departure of their comrades, Aram assumes the role of guide, leading the way toward the sanctuary of Adam's camp. Uldako's heart quickens with anticipation, the prospect of meeting Seth and Adam igniting a fervent longing within him. At long last, he will uncover the truths his soul yearns to discover.

As Shamgar, Zak, and Aram engage in conversation, their voices a steady murmur against the backdrop of their journey, Uldako's thoughts wander. Lost in contemplation, he grapples with the weight and depth of the revelations that await him.

After a long walk, they arrive at their destination—a tranquil village ensconced within the protective embrace of a wooden fence. Peace washes over Uldako as he takes in the sight, the village guarded by a handful of seasoned warriors standing sentinel against the uncertainties of the world beyond.

Uldako turns his gaze to Zak. "Why are there so few guards stationed here?"

Zak glances at the guards, a confident grin playing on his lips. "These are no ordinary men, Uldako," he replies. "These are the finest warriors of the North. Each guard is worth a hundred men. You and I stand no chance against these veterans. Their skills and experience outweigh us by centuries. Even the leaders of the serpent clans fear these warriors, which is why they are attempting to turn to sorcery and other forbidden arts to get stronger. Also, this place is hidden from most, so not many guards are required."

As Aram ushers them into the camp, Uldako finds himself enveloped in a world of natural beauty. Lush trees sway gently in the breeze, their leaves whispering ancient secrets, while vibrant flowers in a riot of colors adorn the landscape, lending an air of tranquility to the surroundings. Animals roam freely, adding to the harmonious tapestry of life within the camp, their presence proof of the villagers' peaceful coexistence with nature.

Amidst the verdant oasis, Uldako's eyes sweep over the various humble structures dotting the landscape. Simple, sturdy workstations hum with activity as artisans craft tools and weave baskets. Modest round shelters nestled into the hills with the most interesting but peaceful shapes, built from sunbaked clay and thatch, stand as silent sentinels of homely comfort, their thatched roofs and earthen walls blending seamlessly with the natural environment. In the distance, a grand hall looms large with massive thick pillars, its imposing presence a monument to the community's unity and strength, yet even this central structure is marked by its unpretentious simplicity.

The camp buzzes with life as people go about their tasks, preparing for the influx of guests. Conversations mingle with the snap and crack of fires, while savory aromas waft through the air as meals are prepared with care and devotion. Amidst the bustling activity, Uldako can't shake the feeling of overcrowding in the seemingly small camp, a humble place, now overflowing with warmth, peace, and joy.

Observing the diverse assembly of individuals, Uldako notes the presence of many elders, their age surpassing five centuries. These elders, distinguished by their simple yet immaculate attire and regal bearing, exude an aura of authority and wisdom without a hint of vanity. Their garments, woven from natural fibers, are adorned with symbols of their long lineage and deep knowledge. Uldako is awestruck by their commanding presence, admiring the confidence and humility with which they carry themselves. He cannot help but wonder what man he would be with five hundred years—how great in wisdom, how masterful in craft, how many seeds in his shelter?

Among them, many are adorned in warrior garb, their shoulders draped with furs that speak of battles fought and victories won. Their eyes, sharp and perceptive, tell tales of ancient struggles. It is clear to Uldako that these elders are not just leaders of various safe camps and cities; they are the ancient guardians of peace and order, revered not for their power but for their wisdom and unwavering dedication to their people and to *Il*.

Uncertain eyes bore into Uldako and Ishara as they move through the camp, the weight of scrutiny pressing heavily upon them. It's then that Uldako remembers the serpent emblems adorning their armor, emblems they never removed. A pang of unease grips him as he realizes the impression these symbols may have on those around them.

"Ishara, we need to remove these emblems as soon as possible!" His voice is low but urgent.

Ishara nods, her expression mirroring his concern. With a swift, graceful motion, she throws her long hair in front of the emblem, attempting to obscure it from view.

A familiar voice slashes through the tension. "Welcome, Shamgar, Zak, Uldako, Ishara, Kesia, and the strong Kunai!" The words ring out with warmth and familiarity, drawing their attention like a magnet. Turning toward the source, they are greeted by the sight of Seth approaching them with open arms.

A rush of indescribable joy floods Uldako's heart at the sight of the man who liberated him from the bonds of slavery. As Seth draws near, Uldako notes the change in his attire with admiration and awe.

Clean and well-groomed, Seth stands out in his light leather armor, adorned with intricate engravings that tell stories Uldako cannot read but senses are of great significance. Draped over his shoulders is a beautiful white bear fur mantle, its pristine quality and majestic appearance speaking volumes of his esteemed position and authority within the land. The mantle contrasts strikingly with his rugged yet refined attire, adding an air of nobility to his formidable presence that is commanding yet comforting, a perfect blend of strength and gentleness.

On his finger, Seth wears an eagle ring, a symbol of his loyalty to the heavenly realm and *Il*. At his side, a bronze sword gleams with a well-worn yet well-maintained luster, while an axe rests on the other side, its craftsmanship befitting the warrior's prowess.

Seth's hair has been cut short along the sides, with the top long and pulled back into a rugged yet well-wrought braid, giving him a timeless, heroic appearance. His light blue eyes, sharp and compassionate, hold wisdom and kindness, reflecting the depth of his experiences and the strength of his character.

As Uldako beholds Seth, he is reminded of the times he has seen him in formidable warrior attire, ready for battle. Now, seeing him in this high-born but equally impressive garb, Uldako feels a surge of profound respect. Seth is not just a warrior; he is a leader, a protector, and a lightbringer for all who look up to him.

"Seth!" Uldako's voice echoes with genuine delight. To his pleasant surprise, Seth responds by enveloping him in a warm embrace.

"This embrace should show the skeptics around us that you and your *dusameš* can be trusted!" Seth murmurs softly into Uldako's ear.

Turning from Uldako, Seth also embraces Ishara in a brief hold then greets the company with good warmth. "It's a pleasure to have you with us," he remarks, his gaze sweeping over the group with genuine warmth. "Welcome to my parents' humble camp!"

Gratitude fills the air as they express their appreciation for Seth's encouraging words. Just as Seth acknowledges Zak's loyalty in aiding Uldako on his quest to free his *ama*, Uldako seizes the moment to address Seth directly.

"Seth," he begins, his voice tinged with emotion, "you won't believe the trials we've faced, but with the steadfast support of Hak, Zak, and Dak, we've achieved the impossible! We freed my *ama* and many others from slavery."

Seth's laughter rumbles through the air, a proud and hearty sound that resonates with warmth. Placing a firm hand on Uldako's shoulder, he speaks with pride and concern. "Indeed, word travels swiftly, young one," he begins. "You've stirred quite the commotion in the South, catching the attention of some who respect you and some who want to kill you. Lamech himself has issued a decree for your capture. You're making waves, Uldako."

The news sends shockwaves rippling through the group. Ishara is the first to voice their collective disbelief. "His capture? So we are being hunted? What does that mean exactly?" she demands with urgency and concern.

Seth's expression turns somber as he meets their gaze. "I see you were not aware of this news," he replies. "The elders of Cain's line have branded you their enemy for your audacious act of freeing so many slaves. As we speak, their forces are scouring the land in search of you, Uldako. Your name has become synonymous with freedom, spreading far and wide."

All eyes turn toward Uldako, including Ishara's, shining with pride and admiration. Yet, beneath the surface of their adulation, Uldako senses discomfort stirring within him, a weighty burden he struggles to bear.

"It's not just me," Uldako begins, his voice humble yet resolute. "Ishara, Zak, Dak, Hak, and countless others have shared in this endeavor. Some have even paid the ultimate price, sacrificing their lives to free those enslaved."

Seth and the others exchange knowing glances, recognizing Uldako's burden. Sensing the need for a reprieve from the weighty conversation, Seth breaks the tension with a suggestion.

"Perhaps a fire and a hearty meal are in order," he proposes, his voice gentle yet decisive. "We have much to discuss, and a nourished body makes for a clearer mind."

Ishara readily agrees to the suggestion, while Kunai chimes in, "What tasty food do you have here? Because I am very hungry, and I can eat a lot!"

Seth chuckles. "Well, come and see! But be warned, Kun, our cooks have heard tales of your appetite. They might have hidden the desserts!"

Kunai's eyes widen in mock horror. "Hide the desserts? That's just cruel!" he exclaims, drawing out a round of hearty laughter from the group.

Uldako, at a loss, asks, "What are desserts?"

The group laughs even louder, their mirth echoing through the camp. Zak pats Uldako on the back with a grin. "Oh, you'll find out soon enough!"

Seth chuckles warmly. "Like I said, come and see!"

Seth leads them to a grand hall that serves as the communal dining area. The structure, crafted from sturdy timber and adorned with intricate carvings, exudes an inviting warmth. Inside, a massive fire roars in the center, its flickering flames casting a golden glow that dances across the faces of those gathered. Around the fire, long tables with benches are arranged in a welcoming circle, fostering a sense of unity and togetherness.

As they take their seats, the tantalizing aroma of freshly prepared food fills the air. There are an array of dishes: steaming bowls of hearty soup, platters of succulent fruits, and an assortment of vibrant vegetables and crunchy nuts, some of which Uldako has never seen or tasted before. The spread is a feast for the senses, an expression of their hosts' abundance and generosity.

Kunai, unable to contain his excitement, eagerly reaches for a plate, only to be gently scolded by Ishara. Chastened for the lack of respect, he waits for the adults to fill their plates first before diving in with gusto.

As Uldako tastes the soup, he marvels at its goodness. "It's the most delicious thing I have ever eaten!" he exclaims, his eyes wide with delight.

The rest of the group chuckles and nods in agreement, savoring the meal with smiles of contentment. The conversation flows as freely as the food, punctuated by laughter and shared stories. Then finally the desserts are brought—baked goods made from grains and sweetened with honey and berries. Uldako tastes the flatbread, and as he draws breath to speak, Kunai gives voice to the very thought in his mind.

"This is from the heavens! Sweet honey drizzled over flatbread with nuts and dried fruits. It's a taste of paradise!" The group bursts out in laughter as Uldako quickly agrees with Kunai and adds a few words of his own.

The warmth of the fire and the fellowship of the meal create an embrace of belonging and peace. Yet, amidst the fullness and satisfaction of the feast, Uldako feels a deeper hunger gnawing at his soul, an insatiable yearning for truth and purpose that normal food can never fill.

"Feeding our bodies is crucial," he acknowledges, his voice thoughtful, "but nourishing my soul is what truly matters. I crave understanding, Seth. I need to unravel the mysteries of life and find the missing pieces that elude me."

The atmosphere shifts and Shamgar speaks first. "And there he goes again, just like on the road to Nippur. Uldako has the talent of jumping into a deep conversation out of nowhere."

The group chuckles, but Uldako is unfazed. He turns to Seth, his heart steadfast as he lays bare his innermost thoughts to the ancient one. "Great *lugal*, do you recall the promise you made to me so long ago?"

Seth's eyes meet Uldako's, filled with a knowing depth. "Indeed, I do," he replies, his voice carrying a note of assurance. "I promised to unveil the truth."

Before Seth can continue, Ishara interjects with gentle insistence. "And here we are," she says, reminding him that she too longs to know the truth.

Seth's smile deepens. "Then let us not merely speak of truth," he declares, his tone imbued with reverence. "Let us experience it firsthand. Follow me, and I will lead you to the source—the ones who hold all the memories and wisdom of centuries past. Let me take you to meet my *abba*, Adam, and my *ama*, Eve."

Uldako's heart leaps with eagerness. "To finally meet them—it's almost surreal," he muses aloud, his excitement clearly visible.

A knowing smile plays at the corners of Seth's lips. "Come," he beckons, as he takes them outside and gestures toward a lone house nestled atop a nearby hill. "That is where the great ancients live!" he says playfully. "Let's continue our conversation on the way."

As the group makes their way toward the imposing yet humble structure, Seth offers insight into Adam's condition. "My *abba* has indeed recovered," he confirms, with a tone tinged with sadness. "However, the passage of time has taken its toll. At over nine hundred years of age, he grows weaker with each passing day."

Kunai's exclamation rises to the clouds with youthful wonder and awe. "I am sorry to hear that, elder Seth, but it is also incredible! I've never imagined anyone living to be that old," he exclaims.

Seth and Zak share a hearty laugh, their mirth infused with affection for the young boy. "Kun," Seth begins, a fond smile gracing his features, "I was there when your village began, centuries before your parents were born. It was created by Nuar, *dumu* of Kenan. He was one of forty-three siblings. Your roots run deep, your family line traces back to Adam himself. You'll have the honor of meeting your great-great-great-great-great-great *abba* today!"

Kunai's eyes sparkle with shock. "That means I still have family," he breathes, his voice filled with awe. "I did not know..."

Uldako and Ishara share a fleeting glance, a silent acknowledgment passing between them as they savor the significance of the moment for Kunai.

Ishara's eyes are alight with curiosity as she says, "To meet someone of such historical significance—Eve, the legendary mother of nations! It's truly humbling."

Uldako nods in agreement. "Indeed, it will be a moment to cherish." His voice is soft with reverence.

Seth's smile is mysterious as he responds, his words carrying hidden wisdom and mystery. "More than you know," he murmurs cryptically, leaving the group to ponder the profound significance of their upcoming meeting.

As they approach the humble abode, each step closer to the door fills Uldako with mounting anticipation, his emotions swirling within him. The dwelling of Adam and Eve stands as an embodiment of centuries of accumulated wisdom and skill. Crafted from sturdy wood and sunbaked clay, the house exudes an air of timeless simplicity and strength. The roof is thatched with carefully woven reeds, providing shelter and insulation, while the walls are adorned with intricate carvings that tell the story of their long and patriarchal lives.

Surrounding the dwelling is a small garden, meticulously cultivated by Adam and Eve to provide both beauty to the eyes and sustenance for the body. Uldako slows, eyes wide. He has seen beauty in plants before—wild meadows bursting with color, forests draped in green—but never beauty shaped by human hands in this way. This is creation tended, guided, and loved into form beyond imagining.

Ishara kneels beside a cluster of blooms, brushing a petal between her fingers. "They grew this," she whispers, her voice soft with wonder.

They had also seen some lovely plants at Mahalalel's home, but nothing like this. Where they come from—the South—the cities of Cain rise in ash, their gray streets bare and lifeless. Even the southern villages, though rich in natural beauty, grow nothing like this within their walls. Here, for the first time, they behold what the hands of the righteous can draw from the earth—not mere survival but splendor.

There are tall sunflowers reaching toward the sky, fragrant herbs growing in neat rows, and flowering bushes bursting with vivid colors. Even Šarru lowers his great head, drawing in deep sniffs, soft rumbling sounds rising from his chest as he takes in each new scent. Delicate vines climb trellises, their blossoms adding a touch of gentle delight to the garden. Small fruit trees, heavy with ripening bounty, stand as symbols of the garden's abundance. The air is filled with the sweet scent of blooming flowers and the gentle hum of bees, creating an atmosphere imbued with tranquility and harmony.

The sight of this lush haven, a perfect blend of utility and beauty, leaves Uldako and Ishara in awe. The peaceful coexistence between humanity and nature is clearly visible, reflecting the deep connection and respect Adam and Eve have cultivated over their many years. It is a place where time seems to stand still, a sanctuary of peace and reflection in an ever-changing world.

After a resounding knock, the door swings open, revealing Kenan standing before them. Uldako's breath catches. In that instant, he realizes they may soon meet not only Adam and Eve, but their close kin—the firstborns themselves. Introductions are exchanged, and Kunai's delight at seeing Kenan is noticeable, his joy infectious.

"Kenan!" Kunai shouts in a low whisper, mindful of the respect owed in the house of Adam and Eve. Kenan, pleasantly surprised, greets them and allows them entry into the house.

As they step inside, Uldako is awestruck by the interior of the simple yet dignified abode, which reflects the ancient lifestyle of its inhabitants. The dwelling is constructed from locally sourced materials such as wood, stone, and mud bricks, showcasing the craftsmanship of the time.

The architecture emphasizes practicality and functionality over opulence, focusing on providing shelter and protection from the elements. The structure consists of four sleeping areas, with a large central hearth for cooking and warmth, and a raised platform for sleeping.

As the conversation continues between Kenan and Kunai, Uldako notices the shelter is already filled with many people. His eyes sweep across the room, taking in both familiar and unfamiliar faces. Some acknowledge him with a knowing nod, their expressions reflecting shared history and mutual respect.

Yet, it is the sight of an elderly figure seated in the far corner that captures Uldako's attention. The man's age seems to defy comprehension; his presence exudes an aura of ancient wisdom. Engaged in earnest conversation with another elder of considerable years, the man's eyes shift toward Uldako and seem to pierce straight into Uldako's soul, making him feel as though he is being weighed and measured by the depths of time itself.

Seth looks at Uldako and raises his chin in the direction of the great *abba*, prompting the group to follow Seth as he approaches Adam.

"*Abba*!" Seth begins. "This young man named Uldako and his companions have journeyed from afar to meet you."

As Uldako's eyes settle on the ancient patriarch, a wave of awe washes over him, mingling with a deep-seated reverence for the legendary figure.

Adam's long, silver-white hair cascades over his shoulders, merging seamlessly with a flowing beard. A soft wind drifts through the nearby window, stirring his hair like a whisper. Draped in a robe of rich, earthen hues, fastened with a simple yet elegant clasp, he embodies both humility and regality.

Adam's eyes, a piercing shade of deep blue, are filled with a serene intensity that reflects the depths of his ancient knowledge and understanding. Fine lines and deep wrinkles etch his face, each one a testament to the countless years and experiences that have shaped him. His gaze, both gentle and penetrating, conveys a sense of seeing beyond the surface, into the very essence of those before him. These piercing eyes fall upon Uldako with curiosity. When their eyes meet and hold, Uldako can't even begin to think about all the wisdom one could obtain over nine hundred years.

A surprising sight draws Uldako's gaze to the floor beside Adam: a great white wolf, ancient and splendid, Adam's companion resting at his side. The wolf's fur is a pristine white, and its eyes a piercing sky-blue. Uldako feels a rush of awe and admiration at the sight, marveling at the obvious bond between Adam and his majestic wolf.

The white wolf seems almost otherworldly. Its regal and serene presence heralds the deep harmony between man and beast. Uldako glances at Šarru—head tilted and eyes narrow as he beholds the ancient wolf. Their eyes lock in a knowing exchange, a silent acknowledgment of their shared loyalty and the ancient bond that connects them to their human counterparts.

The atmosphere around Adam is one of profound tranquility and authority. He sits as a living pillar of humanity's history, his very presence resonating with the power of creation and the enduring soul of mankind. Uldako feels the depth of knowledge and wisdom in Adam's gaze, realizing that he is in the presence of a figure whose life spans the very essence of time itself. He'd long heard it said that Adam was not born but crafted by the hand of *Il* Himself. Now, seeing him face-to-face, he knows it's true.

Adam's eyes widen slightly as he attempts to focus, his gaze reflecting the passage of countless years spent in the natural world. Time has left its imprint upon him, yet despite his age, Adam emanates a radiance of divine perfection. Uldako is struck by the patriarch's remarkable appearance and form, a testimony that he has been created directly by *Il*—though no longer perfect because of sin, he still emanates *Il's* original handiwork. Adam embodies the ideal of humanity's sacred artistry.

Filled with profound respect and wonder, Uldako takes a hesitant step forward. He feels extremely insignificant and weak as he prepares to speak. Bowing his head slightly, his voice cracks with awe and uncertainty, "Uh…hello…"

A gentle smile graces Adam's lips as he peers into Uldako's eyes, sensing the truth of his emotions and character. "Greetings, young one," he begins, his voice rich with warmth. "You bear a strong resemblance to one of my youngest *dumu-meš* who passed away a few years ago. His name was Azar, which means *helper*. Tell me, from which tribe do you hail?"

Uldako hesitates momentarily before responding, "I do not know, respectable elder," he admits, his voice edged with uncertainty.

Before he can elaborate further, Ishara interjects respectfully, "Uldako has never had the opportunity to meet his *abba*, and his *ama* never spoke of him."

Adam's gaze turns upon Ishara. "And who might you be, young one?" he inquires with a gentle yet discerning tone.

"I am Ishara, *dumu-munus* of Beniah from the clan of Jubal who plays music with the lyre and pipe," she responds confidently.

Adam nods approvingly before turning his attention to study the newcomers before him. Meanwhile, Uldako overhears a man whispering to Seth, who stands nearby, "Can we trust them?"

Uldako's eyes narrow at the man's words, a frown etching his brow, but Seth's calm assurance prompts him to remain silent. Returning his attention to Adam, Uldako listens intently as he addresses him directly.

"Tell me, Uldako," Adam begins, "where does your *ama* hail from?"

Uldako takes a moment to gather his thoughts, his voice colored with admiration and reverence. "My *ama*, a woman of unparalleled beauty, drew first breath in the Land of Nod."

Uldako pauses, a myriad of thoughts swirling through his mind. Meanwhile, the man to his side engages Seth in conversation once more, casting wary glances in Uldako's direction.

"That confirms it," the man remarks in hushed tones, his voice carrying a note of distrust. "Not only does their armor carry the serpent's mark—the sign of the dragon of old—but he confessed it with his own tongue. Their kind can't be trusted."

An ancient woman strides forth from an adjoining room, her gaze commanding respect and authority. She directs a stern look at the man, her words cutting through the tension. "Be quiet, Jared! Allow them to converse," she admonishes, her tone firm and unwavering.

Jared, appearing chastened, adopts the demeanor of a reprimanded child and utters meekly, "Yes, great-grand *ama*."

It becomes clear to Uldako and his companions that this woman is indeed the famed mother of nations. This is the great Eve! Ishara, captivated by the presence of this ancient matriarch, feels a profound connection as she beholds the woman whose legacy spans the centuries.

Eve stands with a regal bearing, her long, silvery hair cascading down her shoulders like a waterfall of moonlight. Her face, though marked by the passage of countless years, retains a serene, timeless beauty. Eve is another example of *Il's* handiwork, just like Adam. Fine lines and gentle wrinkles tell stories of wisdom and experience, while her piercing brown eyes hold a depth of understanding that transcends time. Her olive-brown skin glows with a scatter of fine scars that maps where she's been in ages past.

She is dressed in a heavenly blue gown, crafted from fine fabrics, that is both practical and elegant, reflecting Eve's status and the ancient tradition she belongs to. The intricate patterns on her dress and the delicate embroidery add an air of sophistication, enhancing her dignified appearance. A simple yet elegant cord cinches the gown at her waist, and an eagle pendant hangs gracefully around her neck, symbolizing her enduring connection to the divine.

The ancient matriarch's calm and compassionate demeanor radiates warmth, making Ishara feel both humbled and honored to be in her presence.

Adam turns to Uldako. "I must say, I admire your *uḫuš-gal*, Uldako. I remember naming his great *abba* in the garden of Eden a long time ago. It looks like the bond between you two is incredibly strong."

Adam looks down at his own wolf and says, "Don't they remind you of someone, Fenrith?" The old wolf gives a slight groan, as if agreeing with Adam's words, its blue eyes reflecting shared memories.

A faint smile forms on Adam's face as he looks back at Uldako, profound curiosity lighting up his features. "We do not have much time; the gathering at the great hall will commence soon. Go on, young one! Tell me why all of you have journeyed here?"

Courage blooms within as Uldako stands before the ancient *abba*, the warm glow of the hearth casting flickering shadows around them. He glances at his companions as they ready themselves for the moment they have all been waiting for.

40

Truth

A hushed silence falls over the room as all eyes turn to Uldako, the weight of expectation heavy in the room. The flickering flames of the hearth cast dancing shadows on the walls, adding to the tension that grips those gathered. Among them, Jared, who had previously expressed doubts about Uldako's intentions, watches intently, his skepticism palpable.

Jared stands tall and imposing, his muscular frame draped in furs and hides that speak of countless hunts and battles. His presence exudes a raw, primal strength that would rattle most people by just the sight of him. Jared's eyes, sharp and unyielding, are set deep beneath a furrowed brow, their intensity reflecting a life lived on the edge of survival. His dark hair, thick and untamed, falls around his shoulders, framing a face marked by scars and hardened by the elements. A long, braided beard completes his rugged visage, giving him an air of ancient, unwavering resolve.

Jared grips a sturdy spear, its shaft worn and smooth from years of use. His doubts about Uldako are as much a challenge as they are a measure of protection for the community.

Uldako, feeling the intensity of the moment, steadies himself. This is the culmination of his long quest, the opportunity to unravel the mysteries that have plagued him for so long.

He draws in a deep breath and begins, "Um…I need understanding," he begins tentatively. "You see, my *ama* and I were enslaved for countless years, enduring horrors beyond imagination. We bear the marks of unspeakable atrocities inflicted upon us by vile men." His words are heavy with raw emotion.

"I have heard that the Most High is good and that the dragon of old is evil. But we have felt unimaginable pain and suffering. So, I need to understand why there is such profound evil in this world? Why so much pain and suffering if *Il* is good?"

Deep sadness veils Uldako's eyes, and a solitary tear trails down Adam's cheek as he perceives Uldako's anguish and responds with empathy.

"I am deeply sorry, my *dumu*...for the burdens borne by you, your *ama*, and every soul. It is due to the stain of evil we have unleashed. Many who come after you will struggle with this same question—generation after generation as time flows."

Ishara observes Eve, her expression marked by remorse as Uldako asks with uncertainty etched on his features, "What do you mean?"

Amidst the murmurs of troubled voices, Adam's voice rises, firm and steady. "The answers you seek are not simple," he begins. "*Il* is love itself, and in His boundless love, He granted us free will, so that our love for Him would be chosen, not compelled. But in our freedom, we were deceived by the serpent, and so we chose rebellion. It was the originator of sin, the ancient dragon, who first defied the Most High."

A frown forms on Uldako's brow. "Why?"

Adam's voice resonates with centuries-old wisdom. "It marks the birth of the struggle between light and dark."

He pauses, gathering his thoughts, before continuing. "Once a majestic cherub spirit among the holy spirits of light, he harbored a consuming pride in his own beauty and power. This pride led him to covet the throne of his Creator, desiring to rival the Almighty Himself. He has said in his heart, 'I will rise above the stars of *Il*. I will set my throne on high; I will sit on the mount of assembly. I will ascend above the heights of the clouds; I will make myself like the Most High.'

"Deceiving a third of the other spirits with his allure, he incited a rebellion against the heavenly host of *Il*. They believed they could overthrow *Il* and His only *Dumu Il-Il* and seize control."

Adam's words hold a gravity that resonates through the quiet room. "But they soon learned the futility of their defiance. *Il's* power knows no bounds; He is the beginning and the end of all that is. He exists beyond beginning, realm and all boundaries of existence, omnipresent and omnipotent. In His divine essence, we find our existence and purpose. In His hand are our life and our breath; by His word our steps are set."

Adam pauses, allowing his words to take root, giving Uldako a moment to process the profound truth. After a brief silence, Adam continues, his voice steady and sure, "If the Lord were to gather to Himself His breath—which gives us life—all flesh would return to dust. Your body, Uldako, would turn back to dust, which is where it came from. But the soul goes where *Il* appoints, to eternal light for the righteous or to eternal darkness for the wicked."

Uldako straightens, as if the words themselves have brushed his skin. The Spirit of *Il*—moving, acting—named as its own presence. He knows *Il* is One, yet he's heard of the Son of *Il*, and now the Spirit of *Il*. The thought presses at him like a rising tide. *One God, yet there is the* Dumu *and Spirit. What does this mean?* he wonders.

A sense of understanding mingles with lingering curiosity within Uldako. Adam continues, "Let me start at the beginning. The evil dragon of old, who is also known as the false *dingir Enki*, was the originator of all sin. Before mankind was created, he began and lost the war in the heavenly realm. As punishment, he was cast down to the earth with all the other evil spirits. Eve and I were formed nine hundred years ago by *Il*, and He placed us in the garden of Eden. That is where the serpent deceived us, yet no one deceived him; he chose to rebel by his own free will. The darkness within this world comes from him; therefore, he can accurately be called the lord of this sinful world, *Enki*."

Young Kunai's eyes widen. "The serpent was able to deceive *you*?"

Uldako and Ishara swiftly gesture for silence, hoping the boy's question doesn't interrupt the gravity of Adam's words. But Adam only chuckles gently, moved by the boy's innocent curiosity.

"Yes, little Kunai, even I can be deceived," Adam replies, his voice steady. "We must always remember there is only one true *Dingir*. He is *Il*, the Most High—one being yet more than one person. *Il* is also known as the Abba. Then there is the Spirit. The Spirit hovered over the face of the waters before light was born. And then," Adam leans forward, voice lowering, "there is the *Dumu*, called *Il-Il*, the Lord of the mountain."

He looks into the fireplace in the hall. "*Il*, the Most High, is Spirit. No man can look upon Him and live, but through *Il-Il*, the Abba reveals Himself in Truth. He is the face of the invisible. The voice we can hear. The hand we can touch. When you see *Il-Il*, you are seeing what *Il* wants you to understand about Himself."

Adam smiles kindly at Kunai's puzzled face and adds, "Don't worry, Kun. It will make sense in time. For now, let us continue."

Adam's words linger in the room, their weight almost tangible, settling on the gathering like an unspoken burden. "Your questions, Uldako, touch on the very message I have prepared for all of you here, for all the men and women of light. It is best that we address this together at the gathering. There is much to reveal, truths that some of you have heard before, and new revelations that must be understood by all for the future," Adam declares, his voice solemn.

"It is vital that we address this now, for my time with you is nearing its end. The responsibility of carrying this knowledge forward, to teach and guide the future generations, will soon be removed from me to rest on all your shoulders."

Adam pauses, his gaze sweeping over those gathered around him, reading the unspoken thoughts plain in their expressions. Silently, he offers a prayer to the Most High. *Oh* Il, *let them grasp Your truth and take it deeply to heart this day.*

Turning his attention to Seth, he speaks, "It is time we join the others in the great hall. There, in the presence of our kin, we will continue."

As they make their way to the great hall, the transition from the intimate warmth of Adam's home to the grandeur of their communal space is striking. To Uldako's surprise, most of the clans have already gathered inside. The hall, a living tribute to their enduring lineage, has stone floors worn by countless steps. Its walls are lined with carvings that tell stories of creation, downfall, and hope, each thread a silent witness to their lineage's legacy.

Uldako, struggling to discern the meanings of the intricate designs, hopes to find the answers he seeks in the gathering when Adam will address the children of Light.

The great hall is a vast expanse, its ceiling lost to shadows, held aloft by pillars that resemble the trunks of ancient trees, giving the impression of a forest within the embrace of stone. Torches fill the space with a soft, golden light, casting a gentle glow over the assembled faces of Adam's extended family. The air is warm, infused with the scents of fresh pine and the earthy aroma of herbs.

Long tables run the length of the hall, fashioned from the same dark oak that forms the bones of the building. Upon these tables is spread a feast that honors the bounty of the earth—golden and crusty loaves of bread and bowls overflowing with fruits of every hue, from the deep red of pomegranates to the lush green of grapes. Platters are piled high with vegetables roasted in herbs and olive oil, their savory scents mingling with the sweetness of honey cakes and the tang of fermented grapes.

The feast progresses in a manner that speaks of long-established tradition, with dishes passing from hand to hand, accompanied by tales of fights and harvests, of births and betrothals. Yet, beneath the convivial surface, a current of solemnity flows, an undercurrent of anticipation for the truth that is to come.

Among the faces, Uldako recognizes Mahalalel and his wife Talita, whom he had met under far less festive circumstances. The elder's eyes twinkle with a quiet joy as Mahalalel nods in acknowledgment, his presence a bridge between Uldako's initial encounter with this ancient lineage and the wider family history.

Zak hooks Uldako by the forearm and steers him across the hall, Ishara, Kun, and Šarru falling in behind. "Uldako! Come meet the best scout in our clan. The only one I'll admit might be better than me."

They draw near a man standing with his back to them. Uldako's breath catches. The hooded garment of deep charcoal and earthy brown. The shoulders. The stance. The quiet stillness. It's the same shape he remembers from the lakeshore so long ago—the stranger who taught him to not only set a line and read the water, but to survive in the wild.

Zak taps the stranger's shoulder. As the man turns, Zak grins. "Meet Othoar, *dumu* of *lugal* Enoch."

The face comes into view. The same steady eyes find him. Uldako's jaw drops.

"Othoar!" Zak crows. "This is Uldako, Ishara, Kun, and Šarru."

"Ah, Uldako," the man says, a warmth rising at the edge of his voice. "It has been a long time."

Zak, Ishara, and Kun glance between them. Seeing Uldako struggle for words, Zak asks, "You already know Othoar?"

Uldako swallows. "Yes, from the lake…a long time ago." After a beat, he continues, "I never even learned your name. Back then, I wasn't sure you were human."

There is a ripple of laughter. A small smile forms across Othoar's mouth. "Oh, that's right! I was on a spying quest for the northern kingdom—learning what I could of the *anunnaki*. I couldn't share my name or purpose in the South to anyone at that time." He gestures to a nearby table. "But look at you now! Sit and tell me what time has done to you."

As the gathering settles in the great hall, the hum of conversation fills the air, a tapestry of voices that speak of shared history and communal life.

At the head of the hall, beneath the banners of their lineage, stands Enoch, his gaze looking over those assembled with a gravity that silences the crowd.

"Welcome, kin of my blood, bearers of our legacy," Enoch begins, his voice resonating with the echo of centuries. "Tonight, as we break bread and partake in the bounty *Il* has bestowed upon us, let us also share in the wisdom of our patriarch. It is my honor to yield the floor to the first of our line, Adam—he who has witnessed the dawn of darkness over our world and bears the tale of its inception and the trials that followed."

The assembly falls into a respectful hush as Adam steps forward, his eyes alight with a fire undimmed. He surveys his extended family, the newest members of which look back at him with immense awe and curiosity.

"Thank you, Enoch." Adam's voice, though aged, holds a timbre of authority and warmth. "And thank you, my kin, for gathering on this eve. To our youngest branches, I extend a special welcome. It is for you, primarily, that I share our legacy anew."

Adam turns his eyes to Lamech. "You are the future upon which our hopes rest, you, the men and women of light."

Adam pauses, his gaze drifting momentarily to the rafters above, as if seeking guidance from the heavens. "In the beginning," his voice is imbued with a solemn reverence, "*Il* created the heavens and the earth. The seen and the unseen! The earth was formless and void, and darkness was over the face of the deep. And the Spirit of *Il* was moving over the waters."

Adam pauses, allowing the magnitude of those first acts of creation to sink into the hearts of his listeners. "In the beginning, realm and substance came into existence at the same time and He who created it is not limited by it. Then *Il* commanded, and light came into existence, and He separated the light from the darkness. He sculpted the sky, gathered the waters to unveil dry land, and clothed the earth in a verdant tapestry of plants and trees. Each day, He called forth new wonders, celestial bodies to govern the night and day, creatures of the sea, the air, and all manner of living beings to roam the land."

Adam's voice carries a warmth as he recounts the creation of life, a reflection of the divine Love that breathed it into being. "And then the Most High said to the *Dumu* and *Spirit*, 'Let Us make man in Our image, after Our likeness.' So He fashioned me from the dust of the ground, breathing into my nostrils the breath of life. He created us to be the stewards of paradise, to live in harmony with the creatures, the plants, and the very earth itself. *Il* saw all that He had made, and it was very good.

"My dear family," Adam's voice resonates, rich and clear. "In the beginning, the world was not evil; there was perfection, peace, and harmony. Our life begins in a time beyond the reach of darkness, in a garden of paradise where we walked with the Lord in the cool of the day."

Adam pauses, his voice wavering as he struggles to hold back tears, overwhelmed by the memories of those wonderful days.

Eve, at his side, her eyes wet with unshed tears, echoes softly, "Oh, Adam," her voice barely audible yet heavy with unspoken sorrow.

Adam reaches for her hand, a gesture of comfort and shared burden, before he continues, his voice steady, "Let me recount to you all, lest you forget, the truth of our beginning and the nature of our fall. There was no pain, no death, only beauty and the unbroken fellowship with *Il.* We knew no shame, no fear. Yet, into this paradise, a shadow fell—the serpent, who sowed the seeds of our downfall."

He continues with a stern gaze, "Our world was a place of unmarred beauty and purity, fashioned by *Il's* own hand. It was a paradise where neither sin nor sorrow had a place. Yet, through Eve and me, darkness found its way into all creation. We were deceived by the serpent to disobey *Il,* forever altering the course of our existence as humans on the earth."

He takes a sip of water, then lifts his voice with renewed fervor. "Now listen closely! In the pure and perfect days without sin, *Il* desired that Eve and I walk in the light, that we choose the good freely, not by force. He gave us every tree in the garden, save one, the tree of the knowledge of good and evil. He warned us that if we ate from it, we would surely die."

Pausing briefly to gather his thoughts, he continues, "But the serpent deceived us, the dragon of old who once walked in the garden as a beautiful cherub. He claimed that *Il* had lied, and that by partaking, we would not die but ascend to be divine, like *Il.* And so we succumbed. In our hearts, we believed the serpent and rebelled against our Father *Il* because we wanted more power. We felt the darkness and we chose it, and so darkness seeped into our hearts."

Adam pauses, allowing tears of regret to flow freely, then continues, "In that moment when we chose to defy *Il,* we acquired the knowledge of evil. Our very nature was tainted, forever altering the course of existence. *Il-Il,* the Holy One, could no longer commune with us as before, walking among us in the garden and conversing freely. In those pristine days, before the great darkness, called *sin,* came into the world, *Il's* presence was clearly visible. Even the beasts of the field lived in harmony; the lion and the wolf nestled with the lamb. We could interact with all creatures without fear, enveloped in tranquility."

Uldako can almost envision the idyllic world Adam describes, a serene paradise vividly reflected in his eyes, brimming with perfect peace and joy.

But then Adam's gaze turns somber as he continues, "But with evil's entry into our hearts and the world, *Il,* pure and righteous, could no longer gaze upon our darkness. Thus, we experienced death as *Il* had warned—not physical but spiritual. Cast out from Eden's lush embrace, the world transformed into a perilous domain. Once-gentle creatures turned hostile, prompting us to erect safe camps and alter our way of life irreversibly. Since that day, remorse has been our constant companion."

The room remains silent, the gravity of Adam's words settling over the gathered like a shroud. Eve, standing beside her husband, shares in the weight of their shared legacy, her eyes reflecting the pain and regret that came with their choices.

The hall is still, every ear turned to the timbre of Adam's voice, as he speaks of the serpent's deceit, of the fruit that was their downfall. "We were cast out, for in our folly, we had opened the door to death and darkness, and from that day forward, it knew our names, for it was in us and around us.

"It was not merely the loss of paradise, but the loss of innocence. As time passed, Eve and I had our first *dumu*, Cain and then Abel. They became the embodiment of the choice between the light and the darkness. Abel chose the light and Cain the darkness. When Cain struck down his brother, we understood the true nature of the darkness we had unleashed.

"We lost our second *dumu*, Abel." Adam's voice falters, and his gaze drops to the soil as silent tears trace the lines of his weathered face. "Never had we known a pain so deep."

Eve gently comforts him, her own eyes brimming. "That day, we did not lose one *dumu* but two. *Il* judged Cain, and he went east…to the Land of Nod. And from that moment, he too was lost to us."

As their story unfolds, the shadows in the hall seem to grow deeper, as if listening intently. They speak of the descendants of Cain, of cities built on the legacy of that first bloodshed, and of the spread of humanity like a tapestry woven with both light and darkness.

Adam's voice deepens, imbuing the air with a sense of resilience and hope, as he speaks, "Yet, in the shadow's deepest reach, a flicker of hope remained. For the Creator had not abandoned us. A promise was given! A Savior would come from our lineage, a light to pierce the darkness, a bridge back to the paradise we had lost. After Cain left, the Lord blessed us with another *dumu-nita*, and we named him Seth. I believe, from Seth's descendants, the light, the Savior will emerge, hope for all humanity, destined to crush the head of darkness. That is why Seth's line is known today as the lightbringers!"

The listeners, particularly those hearing the tale for the first time, lean in, captivated by the narrative's shift from despair to hope.

"Our tale," Adam emphasizes, "is not only one of darkness and downfall. It's also a story of love and redemption. Despite the deep shadow cast by the serpent's fall, the love of *Il* for us never wavered. He crafted us in His image, and even though He righteously hates all evil, including the sin humans live in, He loves us."

Adam looks intently at his children gathered before him, each face an echo of his enduring legacy. He wonders inwardly how many of them will remain true to *Il* and how many he will one day see again in paradise. He knows there is nothing more he can do but to speak the truth in love and then to pray that they make the right decision. Each one will need to choose between the light and the darkness. His body, no longer as strong as it once was, mirrors the outward decay of a world marred by the fall. The weight of his years and the creeping weariness in his bones press heavily upon him.

Enoch steps closer as he notices Adam's growing weakness, his concern evident in his eyes. "Do you need rest? I can take over," he offers softly.

Adam locks eyes with Enoch, his expression one of earnestness and gravity. "Yes, do not leave anything out." His voice is steady despite his fatigue.

Enoch rises with grace, his movements fluid as Adam takes his seat behind him. Surveying the assembly, Enoch addresses them, "Let us give Adam some time to rest while I continue in his stead." His gaze then sharpens, and his voice grows firm and authoritative.

"*Dumu-meš* of Adam! The reality of our world and the spiritual forces at play cannot be changed. The world ages, and with age comes a deepening shadow. Humanity spreads across the earth, and with it, darkness multiplies. It is an era of *lugals* and tyrants, of violence and the ominous murmurings of battles yet to be waged."

The hall falls silent, every ear attuned to Enoch's words. His voice reverberates through the vast space, heavy with the weight of his message.

"We are the light of the world, and now we must brace ourselves, for the shadow grows darker still. You know that spirits of light have faltered, succumbing to darkness, and their corruption spreads across the land. They influence humanity with lies and deceit. They now walk among them, some taking human form and others appearing in plain sight. Some even appear as spirits of light to deceive even the most elect. Others have gone further, entering the bodies of those who have sinned and given them access—evil spirits taking possession of human bodies. This is nothing new to you. However, we have learned that a few of them have begun to overstep the boundaries *Il* has set for them!"

Whispers erupt among the gathered crowd, uncertainty and fear flickering in their eyes. Uldako and Ishara exchange knowing glances. They brace themselves for the full truth of what lies ahead, the looming battle between light and dark.

Enoch allows his words to settle in before continuing with even more startling news. "Yes, even though they are here in our world or our physical realm, we know *Il* has set boundaries for them. If He did not, they probably would have killed all of us by now. But we have uncovered their new schemes in recent days: We once believed that Cain and his *dumu* still called *Il*, the Most High, but they now refer to Him as *An*. We can now confirm that they are preaching another *Il* called *An*!"

A sudden uproar spreads through the hall, but Seth steps forward, raising his hand to quiet the gathering. "Settle down and let him speak!"

Enoch nods his thanks to Seth and resumes. "The dragon of old deceived them. Thanks to Othoar and other scouts, we have learned the following: They claim that the *dumu* of Cain led the *anunnaki*, known as the Watchers, down from Mount Senir to make a pact with them. They spread lies, saying *An* had many *dumu-meš*, not just *Il-Il*, thus creating their pantheon of *dingir-meš*.

"But we know the truth. These so-called divine beings are none other than the fallen spirits. The *An* they worship today is not the same as *Il*. Cain's bloodline proclaims a false *dingir*, a different *Il*. And worse still, they have recently raised a temple to the ancient serpent himself. They now worship the dragon of old as a *dingir*, calling him *Enki*, the so-called lord of the earth!"

Gasps ripple through the gathered crowd, but Enoch does not waver. His voice remains steady, firm, and full of authority as he presses on. "We find ourselves in a time of profound evil, the dawn of a deep darkness, and it will only grow. A time will come when wickedness reigns unchecked, when every thought of humanity is tainted by malice. Yet, we must endure, for our faith in *Il's* promise shall be our hope. This is merely a part of the conflict between good and evil, a struggle that shall continue and escalate even more over many generations until the Seed of the woman arrives."

Kunai leaps to his feet with sudden boldness. "The Lightborn!" he declares.

Ishara reaches to pull him back down, ready to scold him for interrupting such a sacred moment, but she stops. To her surprise, the tension in the room begins to melt. Faces once tightened with worry now soften. Eyes turn to Kunai not with irritation but with warmth, grateful for his simple, unwavering faith.

Enoch's serious tone lightens as he regards the boy with a kind spark in his eyes. "Faith like a child," he says with a nod. "That is what we all need. Thank you, Kun."

He straightens, his voice rising like a watchfire on the ridge. "Yes, the Chosen One! He will come as a guiding flame in the blackest night. He will crush the works of the evil one, break the grip of sin, and lead us back to the light—to a world where peace, not fear, will reign again.

"Before you all venture beyond these walls, back to your clans, to confront the encroaching darkness," Enoch's voice resonates with purpose and courage, "remember, *Il* is with us, in the profound evil we face, not only tonight, but in all the nights that follow."

He speaks of the spirits, initially created to serve and glorify the Creator, and how pride led the serpent and a third of the spirits to rebel, plunging their brilliance into shadow and transforming them into agents of darkness. "These fallen ones, led by the ancient dragon turned adversary, have descended upon the earth, spreading discord and malice, corrupting both land and heart alike. But now some have begun to manifest in our realm, seeking to take human wives, breaching the boundary set by *Il* Himself."

The crowd erupts in whispers of shock. But Seth steps forward, raising his hands to call for silence. "Listen to what Enoch, our *sanga* and *lugal* says, and then we shall all have time to discuss what our ears have heard. For now, be quick to hear and slow to speak!" With a firm nod, Seth signals Enoch to continue.

Enoch acknowledges Seth with a grateful nod and resumes. "They scheme to create the Nephilim, unholy offspring that will wreak havoc upon mankind. They have already begun the initial testing phase, attempting to see if human women can bear these mixed breeds of humans and fallen spirits. These beings will emerge from the Land of Nod and from the South, joining forces with the descendants of Cain who will call them giants, mighty men and *Ašag-dingir*. It is only a matter of time until these abominations are born and mature into warriors, poised to wage war against us with the fallen spirits.

"The southern and eastern clans have long known they cannot break our warriors. So they turned to forbidden arts—sorcery, divination, and other dark powers. Now their hybrids will stand as their strongest weapons against us, with their dark *abba-meš* working in the shadows."

The room grows colder as Enoch elaborates, "Some of the fallen spirits openly roam, while others lurk in the shadows, but these mixed breeds will walk physically before and among all humans. They will rule them as *lugal-meš*, and together with the fallen spirits, their objective remains the same: to sow deceit among the unsuspecting, to pit *šeš* against *šeš*, nation against nation. Under their influence, the world will endure suffering and sorrow as never before."

Adam stands once more, his presence reinforcing Enoch's solemn message. "Enoch speaks true! In the days ahead, I will depart from your midst. The world will grow dimmer, and the forces aligned against you may appear overwhelming. Yet, you must remain united, guarding the lineage of Seth, the lightbringers, heirs to a promise that cannot be shattered. We must stand resolute, endure, and cling steadfastly to our faith! We rely on the promises of *Il* and have the assurance and the conviction that we will receive things not yet seen."

His words echo with the power of a blessing, a call to arms not only against the tangible threats they face but against the spiritual shadows encroaching upon their reality. "Let our unity tonight shine as a banner of our strength. May the bravery we demonstrate in the face of peril reflect the light of *Il*. You are all the *dumu-meš* of light!"

Adam's words resonate in the hearts of all who listen, carrying the weight of a father's earnest plea. "I stand as your great *abba*, the *abba* of each one gathered here, urging you not to forsake *Il*, but to honor and cherish Him. He is the embodiment of truth and the essence of life itself! Those who embrace Him and walk in righteousness will find themselves reunited with loved ones in the embrace of eternal life, where sorrow will be but a distant memory. However, for those who persist in sinful ways without repentance, I implore you to turn back while there is still time."

Adam pauses to look into the eyes of a few with concerned intent and continues, "I still see it in some of your eyes: love for this world over the One who spoke it into being. But what good is it to gain power, great reputation, or the strongest and most wealthy clan in the land and yet forfeit your soul for all eternity? Rather let *Il's* truth be your guiding light in this dark world, so that when you are done with it, you may enter His eternal light!"

With a heavy heart filled with gratitude and compassion, Adam concludes, "I extend my deepest gratitude to each of you who have journeyed from far and wide. Your presence and love affirm the bond and unity we share. May *Il's* grace and protection accompany you on your paths, now and forevermore."

With quiet authority in their steps, Adam and Eve make their way to the table, settling into their seats amidst the soft murmur of the gathering. A hush overtakes the assembly, dense with dread but also with the bright thread of hope in *Il*.

Adam sits in stillness, the firelight flickering across his worn face as his gaze drifts over each of his children and their children, his legacy. But what he sees is not just their faces. He sees further. Deeper. The burdens they do not yet know they will carry. The trials that wait like shadows at the edge of their paths. He sees the inevitable war between light and darkness written in the lines of their futures.

And he knows that one of the hardest things a father must ever do is let go.

His love for them is a depth no words can reach, an ache carved into the very marrow of his being. If he could bear the weight of their future struggles, he would. If he could walk into the night of suffering alone, so they could remain in the light of peace, he would do so without hesitation. But he cannot. His time is drawing to an end. Soon, they will face the world without him.

Oh, Il, he pleads silently, the words etched in pain across his heart, *help me endure this sorrow. See my grief and sustain me, for I cannot bear this weight alone. Walk with them when I no longer can. Whisper to them when doubt or fear surrounds them. Guide their steps to follow You. Light their path when the night is long.*

Tears fall, not in a flood, but in slow, silent streams, like the last leaves of a great tree surrendering to the wind.

Beside him, Eve watches without needing to ask. She knows. She has always known. The anguish in his heart mirrors her own. Without speaking, Adam reaches for her hand, weathered and strong still, though age has left its mark, and folds his fingers into hers, just as he did so many times when they were young, full of life and promise in a world unbroken.

No words pass between them. They do not need them.

Together, they remain in silent prayer, their hearts rising as one to *Il*—two souls bound by a love too deep for words, interceding with a quiet desperation only parents nearing the end can know. No one in the great hall notices the stillness between them…no one but Uldako.

He watches closely, drawn not by curiosity, but by something deeper, an invisible thread tugging at his soul. He sees the way Adam's shoulders bear the invisible weight of farewell, the way Eve's fingers curl around his hand with ancient tenderness. And suddenly, he understands. Not with words. Not even with thought. He simply feels what they feel.

The meeting continues around him, voices rising, decisions forming. But to Uldako, the room has grown distant, muffled. How can the family of Adam and Eve gathered here not see it? How can they sit and speak while their great *abba* and *ama*, the first of their kind only here for a limited time, grieve in silence beneath *Il* for them?

The truth strikes his heart like a sling-stone through a clay jar. Tears slip down his cheeks before he can stop them, not of sorrow alone, but of reverence. In that quiet moment, something becomes clear, though he cannot yet name it: *Il* has given him more than sympathy. He has been given the gift of true empathy, the ability to feel what others carry in silence. He is learning and growing just by watching them…feeling what they feel as if it is he who sits in Adam's place.

And though Uldako cannot explain it, he knows that this, too, is part of his calling.

Enoch's voice cuts through the lingering chatter, commanding attention with urgency and depth. "Now you know what to expect in the coming days," he begins, his tone grave yet resolute. "When you return to your people, I urge you to strengthen your camps' defenses and to train the women and men to become warriors, for war is coming!"

He turns to Adam and Eve. "Yet, let us also savor this night, for the future might not give us such a moment again."

The gathered kin exchange solemn glances, the gravity of Enoch's message settling over them. Enoch scans across the faces of those present, his eyes filled with hope. "Cherish this time with one another," he implores. "For in unity and love, we find our greatest strength under *Il's* protection. May the Most High be with you!"

With that, he concludes the meeting, leaving the assembly to ponder the uncertain days ahead, their hearts stirred by the call to prepare and the reminder to hold dear the fleeting moments of peace.

As the crowd begins to disperse, Uldako exchanges glances with Ishara and Kunai, the weight of the revelations settling upon them like a heavy cloak. At that moment, words seem inadequate to express the depth of their thoughts.

Ishara gently nudges Uldako and Kunai toward Seth, who stands beside Lamech, engaged in conversation. As they approach, Enoch intercepts his father, his demeanor determined. "I must speak to the firstborns of our family line tomorrow at dawn," Enoch declares.

"I need everyone present, from you, Seth, to you, Lamech. *Il* has entrusted me with a message for us all. Spread the word and gather in the hall at sunrise."

Enoch turns his attention to Uldako, acknowledging his presence. "Uldako, I invite you, Ishara, and Kun to join us tomorrow morning as well," he says, recognizing the bond they have formed with Seth's lineage. "Your future might be intertwined with theirs." With that, Enoch bids them good night and seeks a quiet place to pray.

As Enoch departs, Seth turns to Uldako, his eyes reflecting curiosity. "Have your questions been answered, young one?"

Uldako nods thoughtfully. "Most of them, but new ones have surfaced."

"In time all will become clear, but come, let us enjoy the fellowship of family and friends," Seth declares, his voice carrying a soothing reassurance.

As the evening deepens, the great hall fills with gentle laughter and the murmur of many voices. Uldako and his companions listen as the people of Adam speak of the early days. Faces once strange grow familiar; names and tales intertwine like roots of the same living tree. Bonds are formed in the soft glow of torchlight, as kinship replaces caution and wonder overcomes wariness.

At length, when the torches have burned low and the moonlight filters through the high arches, Seth rises from his place. "The night is late, and I will take my leave. Uldako, will you, Ishara, and Kun sleep outside with the *ur-bar-ra-meš*?" he says, a faint smile in his voice. "If not, you would do well to follow Lamech now…while there is still a place for you, unless you prefer their company."

Uldako chuckles at Seth's suggestion that he sleeps with the animals, then gratitude fills his heart as he turns to the elder once more. "Thank you, Seth, for everything. May I request a moment of your time tomorrow? I wish to discuss the establishment of a safe camp in the North, for all slaves that could find freedom."

Seth inclines his head, a faint smile showing his agreement, sparking a glimmer of hope in Uldako's eyes.

With their farewells exchanged, Uldako and his companions follow Lamech to their sleeping area, anticipation for the dawn's revelations swirling in their minds.

As they settle into the small yet comforting shelter, even Šarru finds a cozy spot to rest. Uldako glances at Ishara, noticing her restlessness. "Still awake, Ishara?" he asks softly.

Ishara lies motionless, her gaze fixed on the shelter's roof. "After hearing Adam, Enoch, and Seth today, I can't seem to shake off my thoughts, because for the first time, I understand how small I am and how much there is that is out of my control," she confesses, and after a long pause she turns to him. "Uldako, where do you think we'll go when we die?"

The question from Ishara takes Uldako's breath, for it echoes his own inner turmoil. "I'm not certain, Ishara," he admits. "But I hope to journey to *Il's* eternal kingdom, alongside you, Kun, and all those we hold dear, rather than to suffer torment in the netherworld."

Ishara nods slowly as she thinks deeply. "Likewise, Uldako. Good night," she murmurs, turning away in search of sleep.

But sleep eludes Uldako, his mind swirling with contemplation. As the night gives way to the first light of dawn, soft rays began to peek through the shelter's entrance, signaling the start of a new day. Feeling a sense of urgency, Uldako rouses his companions, eager to continue their journey. Today, they will gather in the great hall to meet Enoch and the others, hoping to find answers to the questions that linger in their hearts.

As they step into the great hall, they are met with a heartening sight—many have already assembled, seated around tables enjoying their breakfast. Uldako takes in the familiar faces, before Seth enters behind them.

"I'm pleased to see you're already here, Uldako, Ishara, and Kun, and of course, the mighty Šarru." Seth greets the bear warmly, reaching out to rub Šarru's head affectionately. "Šarru, I want to introduce you to Thork, my *ur-bar-ra* companion."

Uldako and the others look at Seth with surprise.

"What? Did you think you were the only one with a great animal as a companion?" Seth chuckles, his eyes dancing with amusement. "I love animals! My *abba* gave most of his *dumu-meš ur-bar-ra* to look after when we were young. Lamech is bringing in Thork as we speak!"

At that moment, Lamech enters the hall, accompanied by a majestic gray wolf with dark brown eyes. Uldako's brows raise at the sight as the beautiful wolf approaches with confidence. Šarru and Thork exchange wary glances and begin to growl. However, with calming gestures from Uldako and Seth, the tension gradually eases. After a bit of cautious sniffing, the animals settle down at their masters' sides, their initial wariness replaced by a tentative truce.

Adam and Eve make their way to their seats, joining Seth and the rest, while the room buzzes with activity as more people arrive.

Uldako can't contain his curiosity any longer and turns to Adam. "Forgive me, honored elder! This might be too personal, but if I overstep, please let me know. Last night, you mentioned that your eldest *dumu*, Cain, killed his *šeš* Abel. Why did he?"

Adam's eyes glance at Seth and fall back to Uldako. "You need not hold your tongue, Uldako. I learned a long time ago that it is precisely the things we struggle with and overcome that we must share with others to help them on their earthly journey as well. My eldest *dumu*, Cain—I forgave him a long time ago.

"You must understand, Uldako, that Cain harbors a sinful nature within him, like all of us. It was this darkness he chose to succumb to, leading him to rage and to commit the unspeakable act of killing his own younger *šeš*, Abel. The sorrow that Eve and I bore in the aftermath of that tragedy knew no bounds. Even now, recounting it brings tears to my eyes. The loss of one's own *dumu* is a wound that never truly heals. When Eve and I sinned, it changed not only the world around us, but our very nature. We brought evil into the world, and through us all, humans were born in sin."

He pauses, his eyes reflecting the gravity of the truth he is about to impart. "Uldako, it is this same sinful nature that plagues mankind, manifesting itself in various forms of evil and suffering, including the atrocities committed by slave traders against you, your *ama*, and countless others. Sin is a sickness that resides within the heart of mankind."

Uldako raises a brow, grappling with the implications of the inherent darkness in his own heart and asks, "So if the evil we witness in the world originates from within us, is there nothing we can do to overcome it? After all, Seth has shown that goodness is possible; he saved me—"

Eve interjects, her voice carrying a strength of assurance. "That is because Seth has chosen to dedicate his life to *Il*, just as his *abba* and I have. *Il* has granted us the freedom to make our own choices out of His love for us. We will always grapple with the conflict between good and evil. While Seth, like all of us here, strives to live a righteous life, he cannot eradicate the inherent evil nature within him during his lifetime. Each day is a battle against the darkness within."

She looks around the circle, her gaze firm yet compassionate. "*Il* has written His law into every heart. We know what is good. We know what is evil. The more we fix our eyes on the light, the more we are strengthened to resist the dark. But when we yield to sin, when we embrace it—something begins to change when we do it over and over again. The heart grows dull. The conscience fades. And in time, like many in the serpent clans, we begin to love the very darkness that enslaves us. Their hearts are hardening into stone. Their ears no longer hear. Their eyes no longer see."

A quiet hush falls.

Ishara, her voice barely above a whisper, lifts a trembling question into the silence. "So all we can do is fight it? Is there…no cure?"

41

Cure

They grow quiet, eyes lifted for a cure. A faint light touches Adam's eyes.

"Our hope is in *Il* alone. For a time, breath is given to us, that we might choose light over darkness. Those who turn to the Most High and walk in righteousness will enter His kingdom when their last breath passes.

"Here is what we know of a cure: The serpent is the originator of sin, and he drives mankind further into evil, as you have seen and felt. And with this, pain and suffering increase all over the world. But we know *Il* has promised a Savior, the Chosen One, who will crush the serpent's head.

"We do not know who the Chosen One will be, or how He will crush the dragon, or what His victory will include. This is a mystery awaiting its time.

"Why do I speak these truths? Because we also know that evil does not work only through the serpent; it already lives within each one of us. And we do not know whether the serpent's defeat will also heal the sin that is within mankind. If there is a cure, it rests with the Chosen One."

Zak, Shamgar, and Kesia reach the table, and the conversation stills for a moment. Brief greetings pass between them. Shamgar says softly, "Don't mind us. Please continue, great *Abba*."

Adam inclines his head to Shamgar warmly before turning to Seth, resolve settling in his eyes. "This is why Enoch and I summoned the branch of Seth today with those closest to them. After our righteous *dumu*, Abel, lost his breath, Seth's righteous line rose! They are the ones who still call upon the name of *Il* with all their heart. Seth's firstborns bear the promise of the One who will shatter the dragon's hold. But know this: The dragon is now striving to thwart *Il's* prophecy."

Uldako's concern is clearly visible, etched across his face as he interjects, "What can we do to stop him?"

Adam's visage carries a reassuring glint. "Have faith, young one. The dragon's efforts will not succeed no matter what he attempts to do. He is not and never will be *Il*; he is but a fallen spirit. The Most High has spoken, and His words will come forth! The dragon of old will only be able to bruise the heel, for in the end, the Chosen One will emerge to crush the serpent's head."

Uldako's curiosity persists, "But how will we recognize the Chosen One when He appears, and when will He come?"

A faint, knowing smile touches Adam's lips as he watches Enoch rise, his presence commanding attention. "It looks like Enoch is poised to unveil that very answer you seek, young one," Adam murmurs.

Enoch's voice resounds through the hall, commanding the attention of all present. "It appears the warriors of light are accounted for," he proclaims, his gaze sweeping across the room. As the attendees swiftly find their seats, Enoch continues with a reverberating count, "Seth, Enosh, Kenan, Mahalalel, Jared, myself, and though Methuselah is in Nippur, Lamech is here with us. Very well, let us begin."

With a deep breath, Enoch begins, wasting no time. "I must reveal *Il's* word to you all. The prophecy concerns your family line from Seth through every firstborn *dumu-nita* and holds profound significance for all mankind. Time is of the essence, so I will delve right into it."

Enoch's words resonate through the hall, rich with sacred authority. "As you all know, *Il* decreed that the seed of Eve and the seed of the serpent would engage in a destined struggle. The ancient prophecy is clear. All present here knows our *abba* Adam's firstborn, Cain, succumbed to evil, while the second, Abel, was slain. Adam and Eve had many other *dumu-nita*, but it seems *Il* has chosen the righteous line of the third child, Seth, to ultimately bring peace through the Chosen One, the Savior."

Enoch pauses, his eyes distant, as if peering beyond the veil of time. Then he speaks, each word measured and carrying weight. "This may be part of the reason why the fallen *dumu-meš* are breaching our realm, to corrupt human bloodlines, to defile what *Il* has ordained. They might wrongly believe they can taint the seed of the woman so that the Promised One will no longer be fully mankind, fully pure."

The air grows still.

"I stood before *Il* upon the mountain," Enoch says softly. "I was shown a glimpse and bound to silence. But know this: Through Seth's family branch, the hidden will be revealed over time. The branch has borne a fresh shoot, Lamech, but there are more to come!"

A hush sweeps through the gathering like wind through tall grass. All eyes slowly shift toward Lamech, who sits in silence, his presence now heavy with meaning. The ninth generation from Adam. The bearer of the threshold.

There is a brief pause as Enoch's words grow into roots within their hearts, and then Lamech speaks, his voice filled with astonishment and apprehension. "You mean to say I will have a *dumu* and that he might be the...the Chosen One?"

Enoch offers a reassuring smile. "The truth is kept with *Il.* When the hour ripens, He will reveal it." Murmurs of confusion ripple through the room, but Enoch continues, "Lamech, your firstborn *dumu-nita* is to be named Noah, which means *rest* or *relief,* and it is crucial that you teach him *Il's* truth and safeguard him at all costs. For from him will arise new nations who will call on the name of the Lord!"

Enoch's eyes soften, and he tilts his head once in quiet agreement as Lamech accepts the weight of his charge. Shamgar leans over and, with a grin, whispers, "Looks like there's some poor woman out there who will find you worthy of her love. Who would have thought!" His jest brings a ripple of laughter through the room, lightening the mood.

Enoch's message, however, extends beyond Lamech alone, reaching every soul gathered. "It falls upon all of you to shield not only Lamech from harm, but one another. Furthermore, be prepared for the trials that lie ahead. Persecution for your devotion to *Il* will come, but through steadfastness and His grace, you shall endure."

A solemn gravity settles over the assembly as Enoch continues, his voice steady but filled with sorrow.

"Remain watchful," he says. "The seduction of false *dingir-meš* is spreading like dark smoke across the land. Even here, in the northern kingdom, the hearts of some will begin to wander. Those we hold dear will be drawn away by the whispers of the dark spirits and the promises of their monstrous mixed-breed *dumu.* They will trade the truth for shadows and call it light." He presses his hands on the table hard and searches their eyes for a moment to see if his words have taken root within them.

"Prepare yourselves without delay. War is coming. The dark spirits are in motion; the rise of the Nephilim is near. Do not delay! Train your clans up in the knowledge of *Il* and arm them for the fight. For the days of peace are waning and the seed of corruption is at hand. Blessed be the *dumu* of light by *Il* Most High, possessor of heaven and earth."

Enoch raises a clenched fist to his heart, strikes it twice, and proclaims, "Fear not! *Il* Himself is a shield to all who call upon His name. Now go!"

Enoch gestures for Seth to follow him outside. Uldako, Ishara, Kunai, and Šarru follow as well, while the others left in the hall murmur in shock at what they've heard.

As they pass through the great doors, Enoch casts Seth a sincere, grave look—enough to make Uldako feel that something momentous is about to unfold. Yet all Enoch says is, "Follow me." He turns and leads them through the camp's gates to a place apart.

"Let us pray together," Enoch says softly. "May *Il* use us as He wills. May His Spirit rest upon us and His will be done."

They bow their heads. But what begins as familiar prayer becomes something far deeper. As Uldako listens, he realizes Seth and Enoch are not merely speaking; they are communing with *Il*.

Just when Uldako thinks the day cannot possibly bear more revelation, the ground beneath his feet seems to shift again. The air grows different, as though creation itself is holding its breath between the physical and the heavenly realms. Enoch turns slowly, and in that moment, Uldako feels a trembling deep within his heart, like the first ripples of an unseen earthquake.

What follows shatters him. Pride and certainty collapse like sand, and he sees himself with piercing clarity—no longer the center of his world, but a single breath within the vastness of *Il's* design. The Most High alone stands at the center, holding all things together by His providence.

Enoch stops, resting a trembling hand upon Seth's shoulder, and tears glisten in his eyes. Tears not of weakness, but of both joy and grief intermingled. His voice, when it comes, carries the weight of eternity. "The Spirit of the Lord is here with us," he whispers.

Uldako's eyes drift from Enoch to Seth, and there he sees it. Not sorrow, but something far greater. Tears flow from his eyes, not born of grief but of unspeakable joy. A joy heavy with meaning, forged in the furnace of centuries. In that moment, Uldako sees the love Seth carries for *Il*, vast, unwavering, eternal. Seth is utterly surrendered. And in his eyes rests a peace that surpasses anything human, something not learned but gifted from beyond the veil.

In that hush, Uldako stands still and something within him shifts. The threads of his questions, his pain, his journey begin to weave together. A deeper meaning, once elusive, starts to take form. He doesn't yet see the whole pattern, but he senses it now: There is a greater design, and he is only a small part of it.

In that serene moment, almost too heavy to say anything, Enoch speaks. "My dear *šeš-meš*, I am going now for my time has come. I take my leave. I can't keep the raiders and beasts waiting!"

They bid Enoch farewell and watch as the regal figure departs, tall and unshakable, leaving a lingering sense of peace behind.

Turning to Uldako and his companions, Seth offers his support. "Uldako, you and your *dusa-meš* have sought to establish a safe haven. You have my full support in this endeavor, and I will assist you as promised. Together, we shall forge a safe camp in these troubled times."

Still shaken from the awe-inspiring revelations from Adam and Enoch, Uldako, Ishara, and Kunai nonetheless brim with gratitude at Seth's offer.

"Where would you want it built?" Seth asks.

Uldako's smile widens. "Kunai suggested we settle toward the northwest side, but around here will be perfect! I want to be close to Adam's camp."

After a moment of consideration, Seth suggests an alternative location. "I can't let you live too close to Adam, as it will bring attention to his hideout here. But I have the perfect area, a half day's walk from here. On a mount it might be a quick ride, just a hand or two to the sun. It's by a beautiful lake with an open field where you can grow crops and erect shelters."

Uldako's eyes soften with appreciation. "Thank you, Seth. You have no idea how much this means to us."

Seth nods thoughtfully, taking in Uldako's words. "How many are you right now, and to what number do you plan to grow?"

Uldako affirms, "Currently, we've gathered over thirty people who have joined our cause. I have made it my new mission to free as many slaves as possible and to grow into a strong camp that can protect itself and the North."

He continues, outlining his vision for the camp's expansion. "Growing in number will enable us to set up tactical units—scouting parties, patrols, and camp defenders. I also want to ask your permission for Zak to train my men at our camp. This is how we can help defend your family line and—"

Seth interrupts with a raised hand, "Wait, wait, wait. I see you've given this much thought, but let's take one thing at a time. Give me the day, as I have much to attend to here, before I can leave with you. In the meantime, make yourselves—"

Before Seth can finish, Daner comes running, his voice an urgent shout from a distance, "Seth, Cainites have been spotted! There's a group of about eight hundred men marching toward Enosh's safe camp!"

Seth's eyes narrow. "Who leads them?" His voice is edged with urgency.

Daner, panting and wide-eyed, blurts out, "It looks like Irad and Lamech's men! They will reach it in two days."

Seth casts a piercing glance at Uldako then turns back to Daner. "Armor and weapons?"

Daner tilts his head down once, his voice tight. "Mostly hardened leather, but many now wear the more advanced armor, iron and bronze, forged with skill. Their weapons are sharp, efficient, deadly. They have about a hundred archers, supported by beasts of various kinds. I have also seen shamans and evil sorcerers."

His words spill out in a rush, the weight of what he's seen pressing on his chest.

Uldako senses the gravity of the situation, his demeanor shifting to one of steely resolve. Before Seth can respond, Uldako steps forward, his voice a calm but firm pledge, "You have my blade!"

Ishara steps closer, her eyes fierce. "Mine too!" she declares. At her side, Šarru, the colossal bear, emits a low, menacing growl, clearly ready for battle.

Kunai unsheathes the short blade Uldako gave him long ago and says, "Me too!"

Ishara looks shocked at his youthful eagerness, but Seth is quick to respond, "That might come in due time, little Kun, but enjoy being a young lad for a while more."

Kunai wants to protest, but Ishara's look puts him in place.

A plan rapidly takes shape in Seth's mind. "Inform my *dumu*, Enosh, and gather all the men you can muster. Enosh's safe camp is one day's journey southeast. That gives us one day to prepare the camp's defenses. Uldako, Ishara, go inform Zak and Shamgar, then ready yourselves, and meet me at the entrance. Go!"

The sun has scarcely moved when Uldako, Ishara, Shamgar, Zak, and Šarru assemble at the gate, clad in armor and armed to the teeth. Uldako's heart drums rapidly in his chest, each beat a reminder of his inexperience. He has never seen, let alone participated in, a battle of this size. But as he stands there, the memory of Daner's words about the evil Lamech echo in his mind. His resolve hardens, and he clenches his fists. *Perhaps the time has come to settle this once and for all,* he muses inwardly.

Uldako's thoughts are interrupted by a chorus of voices. He looks up to see Seth leading a formidable force of warriors, both men and women, clad in a mix of leather and bronze armor. The fighters march at the front and rear, with archers strategically placed in the middle. Each warrior bears a shield emblazoned with an eagle emblem and wields a variety of weapons: axes, swords, maces, and even oxgoads. A surge of pride fills Uldako as he stands among these formidable warriors of light.

He spots Seth's strongest warriors—Tiras, Renju, Enkiar, and Jano—and acknowledges them with a nod. Even Mahalalel has joined the group, walking beside Seth. Behind them march Kenan, Jared, and Lamech the Good, their faces etched with stoic determination. From the flank, another familiar figure joins them, the largest man Uldako has ever seen, revered by many—the great Enosh.

"It looks like we are about three hundred strong," Shamgar notes. Zak nods, adding, "The enemy has the numbers, but we are not called the warrior clans for no reason."

"The Most High is with us. Let's move out!" Seth commands, his voice clear and authoritative. Uldako feels a swell of confidence as he looks at the men and women around him, their faces revealing no fear. Uldako knows that lives will be lost, but despite the enemy's numbers, they stand ready to face whatever comes.

The march is quick and relentless, with no stops for rest. The group eats and drinks while on the move, their pace a constant trot. Uldako realizes that these men and women have been in this situation before, moving with a confidence born of experience and trust in the Most High.

A few scouts range a far distance ahead, to the flanks, and at the rear, vigilant for any potential threats. Occasionally, they catch glimpses of wildlife, but nothing poses a danger. The terrain shifts underfoot, the forest thinning to reveal a well-trodden path leading to their destination.

As the day wanes, the group finally arrives at the safe camp. Uldako, slightly out of breath, beholds the beautiful and unique safe camp of Enosh. The sight of it fills him with relief and admiration. The camp is built entirely out of wood, a sturdy construction and the result of careful planning. High wooden walls encircle the area, designed to shelter and protect up to three hundred people.

Inside the camp, rows of simple but solid huts stand ready with some prepared to house the weary travelers. Smoke rises from a central fire pit where a few sentinels tend to the flames, casting a warm, welcoming glow against the encroaching darkness. The scent of pine and earth mixes with the faint aroma of cooked food, adding a comforting layer to the rugged surroundings.

But what strikes Uldako most is all the bears. A handful of great bears move freely with the warriors, brushing past fires and tents. Everywhere he looks, the mark of the bear is woven into their world: carved into shields, painted on banners, stitched into furs.

Then his eyes find Enosh and understanding dawns. The highborn now stands clad in armor unlike any he has seen: plates of dark bronze and hide, thick as bark, fitted with the strength of a living beast. The armor makes him seem broader, heavier, almost elemental. His shoulders rise like pillars of cedar, and upon one rests a molded bear's head, its eyes hollow but proud.

Uldako glances to Šarru beside him then back to Enosh. "Enosh," he asks softly, "may I ask why you wear that *uḫuš* head upon your shoulder?"

Enosh's expression softens, and a knowing warmth fills his voice. "Some may assume I slayed him, but he was my companion. You didn't think you were the first to tame an *uḫuš-gal*, did you, Uldako?" He pauses, his gaze drifting to Šarru and then to his shoulder. "This one was my *ki-ág*, my brother in battle. When he fell, I began to carry his memory with me. It became our way. The warriors of my clan each walk beside their own *uḫuš*. And when their beast dies, they honor him by bearing his likeness into every fight that follows. We move forward after loss, but we never forget."

Uldako lowers his gaze to Šarru. The great beast meets his eyes, and something unspoken passes between them—gratitude, understanding.

As they walk into the camp, it bustles with activity as the group settles in. Children play near the fire, their laughter a stark contrast to the somber preparations of the adults. Men and women reinforce the walls, their movements efficient and practiced. Weapons are inspected and sharpened, and supplies are organized with methodical precision.

Uldako surveys the scene, feeling profound community and purpose. The people here are not just survivors; they are warriors, craftsmen, and families bound together by a common cause. The sturdy buildings, the organized defenses, and the cooperative spirit all speak of a place prepared to withstand whatever threats may come their way. Uldako's confidence grows, knowing that in this fortified camp, they have a stronghold from which to face the challenges ahead.

Seth calls Uldako, Ishara, and a few others to join him around the fire as he speaks with Enosh, finalizing their preparations. As Uldako takes his seat, he prepares himself to learn from these great leaders as they strategize.

Seth begins, "The enemy is approaching as we speak, and we have never seen such a big force in all history! This is how it stands: Combined with your forces here, Enosh, we have only four hundred fighting men. I have sent word to nearby camps for aid, but I am uncertain if they will arrive in time. Irad and Lamech the Evil must have learned of our gathering at Adam's abode and seized the opportunity to attack your camp, Enosh."

Enosh gives a slow nod, his expression grim. "Yes, they probably still believe we are there and that my village will be easy to attack. Irad has always harbored a special hatred for me, but now is the time to end it. We may be outnumbered, but with *Il's* aid, victory can be ours."

Seth dips his head toward his son. "Some of our scouts have killed theirs, so they might suspect your camp is preparing for battle. However, they likely have no idea that we are here with you!"

Tiras chimes in, "This gives us an advantage we must exploit."

Seth continues, "Yes, let me put forth a plan that might work. We will hide most of our men within the camp, allowing Irad's forces to see only your warriors, Enosh. After this meeting, we will set traps—pits and fires—so that when they approach, they will be taken by surprise. Once the traps are triggered, our archers on the wall will fill the air with arrows. If I know Irad well enough, he won't care about the initial casualties and will try to use his remaining forces to breach our walls. We'll let him break down the gate, allowing him to believe a false sense of victory. When they enter, we will all attack.

"The gate only allows ten men to pass through at a time, giving us a strategic advantage despite our lower numbers. Our archers will ascend the walls and unleash their volleys. I have instructed the other camps sending aid to wait in the tree lines. When they see the enemy pile through the gate, they will attack from the rear, allowing us to corner Irad's forces. Let us pray to the Most High that they arrive in time!"

As Seth speaks, the firelight dances across their determined faces. Uldako listens intently, absorbing every detail of the plan. The crackle of the fire punctuates the gravity of their situation, but a surge of resolve settles over the group. They know the odds are against them, but with careful planning and the element of surprise, they have a fighting chance. The night is filled with the sounds of preparation as traps are set, arrows are readied, and prayers are silently offered to *Il* for strength and protection.

When the plans are set, Seth rises and looks to Uldako with a grin that cuts through the tension. "Come," he says, rolling his shoulders. "Let's see what skill you hide after all that time in training with Zak."

Uldako rises as Seth gestures toward the open ground beyond the firelight. The others pause their work to watch as the two men face each other—bronze against bronze, youth against centuries.

The duel begins with swift, clean strikes. Uldako moves with precision and power, but Seth's blade meets every attack effortlessly. In a blur, the older warrior shifts his stance, sweeps Uldako's leg, and sends him to the ground.

Uldako grins, catching his breath. "Again."

Seth nods. They clash once more, sparks, motion, the sharp echo of blades, and again Uldako finds himself flat on his back.

A third time he rises, jaw set. A third time he falls. Each exchange faster, each defeat more decisive.

When at last he stays down, chest heaving, Seth lowers his blade with a faint smile. "You've grown strong, Uldako, but strength alone doesn't win difficult battles."

Uldako exhales a weary chuckle. "Then I have much to learn."

"Good," Seth says, pulling him to his feet. "You learn fast. I've only had a few extra centuries to learn from my mistakes. At your current skill level, you will most certainly claim victory over most. So don't lose any confidence."

As Uldako takes the hand and rises, confusion lingers in his eyes. "If I can beat most, then how did I lose so easily to you?"

From the edge of the firelight, Enosh steps forward, his voice calm and knowing. "No one has ever beaten Seth," he says. "Not once. I am his *dumu* and have already tried for centuries."

Seth only smiles, saying nothing as the fire crackles between them—its light dancing across the face of a warrior who has outlasted ages.

Uldako sits beside Ishara, drawing the bronze edge of his sword along a piece of dark flint—a stone Enosh gave him. Its rough whisper against the metal fills the quiet, a sound both ancient and steady. Ishara suddenly realizes the uneasy silence. Her eyes dart around her. Uldako notices her strange movement and asks. "What are you looking for"?

Ishara's eyes narrow. "The young ones who played outside earlier are all gone. Where did they go?" Uldako searches the area around them with a puzzled look.

Seth approaches and lowers himself beside them, offering a strip of dried fruit and a weary smile. "The young ones were taken to another village up north for safety. I instructed twenty of my men to take them and protect them."

Ishara exhales a reassuring breath, and seeing her tension ease makes Uldako wonder what type of mother she will be one day. He can clearly see her caring heart, and it warms him.

As they eat, Seth gestures toward the serpent emblems on their armor. "I think it's about time you two remove those. We wouldn't want our own men mistaking you for the enemy when the battle starts."

Uldako and Ishara exchange a look and both nod. Ishara sighs. "We meant to do it long ago. Somehow it keeps slipping our minds."

Uldako smirks as he wedges the tip of his blade beneath the serpent emblem. "Stubborn thing…it clings like it still believes it can win."

Seth raises a brow. "Reminds me of someone I know."

The three share a brief, quiet laugh—a flicker of light amidst the gathering dark. When the serpent emblems finally fall into the dust, the silence returns, heavy and watchful. All that remains now is to wait for sunrise and for battle.

The enemy approaches at dawn, their silhouettes emerging from the mist like a dark wave. Lamech the Evil advances beside his great-grand *abba*, Irad, leading the enemy. Lamech, tall and imposing, clad in black armor that gleams ominously in the early light, rides a massive *sisi*, a great mount with a sleek and dark coat. Irad, equally menacing, rides beside him, his face twisted with malice.

Behind them, an army of men march in grim resolve. Their ranks are bolstered by fearsome wild dogs—massive, snarling beasts with sharp claws and teeth that gleam in the morning light. Some of Lamech's men ride horses, pawing at the ground, eager for the battle to commence. A few mount three-horned dragons that snort and growl as their throats rumble with excitement.

Others ride on hairy towering camels with long, curved necks and humps like mountains. Their brown hides blend seamlessly with the color of sand, and their large, padded feet move with deliberate grace. The enemy appears formidable, men and women mostly armored in mismatched pieces of dark heavy leather and bronze, while brandishing weapons of all kinds—swords, spears, axes, oxgoads, and maces.

As the enemy advances, Uldako leans to the fence, peering through its narrow gaps while a hard knot twists in his gut. Even from a distance, he can make out the cold, calculating eyes of Lamech and the cruel smirk curling on Irad's face. Uldako scans the enemy ranks, then steps back, drawing a deep breath to steady himself. He forces his thoughts to the plan Seth had laid out, anchoring his mind against the rising tide of the unknown future.

Seth, standing beside Uldako on the wooden platform, rests his hand on Uldako's shoulder. "Trust our plan, trust those around you, and trust the Most High!"

The drums of the enemy beat louder with each step, a deafening rhythm that reverberates through the air and shakes the ground beneath their feet. The powerful sound is terrifying, a relentless reminder of the approaching battle. Uldako can feel the tension in the air, thick and suffocating.

Then, as suddenly as they began, the drums stop. A heavy silence settles over the field. At Seth's command, the gate creaks open, and a group of warriors steps out. Their plan is simple—draw the first wave of enemies toward them. Uldako joins them, while Šarru stays within the gates with the other bears.

As they come to a halt, the uneasiness in the air multiplies. The whisper of the wind is the only sound, which seems unnaturally loud in the sudden stillness. Both groups stand motionless, watching each other with hard-set resolve. Sweat beads on Uldako's brow as the silence stretches, amplifying each breath, each heartbeat.

A line of robed figures moves to the front—Lamech's sorcerers, their faces streaked with soot and blood-paint. Each bears a carved staff crowned with bone or metal that glints beneath the fading light. They slice their palms with obsidian blades and lift their hands to the sky, crying out the names of their new gods—*Enki*, *Ninurta*, *Inanna*, and others. The air feels dark and unnatural to Uldako as their voices weave together in a low, guttural chant. It feels as if the ground darkens around them, and the scent of iron and burning resin carries on the wind. Uldako watches, unease knotting his stomach; he has never seen sorcerers casting curses this way. He turns toward Enosh, searching his face for understanding.

Enosh steps forward to draw them closer and shouts, "Look at them! They're afraid to fight us without their new so-called *dingir-meš*! Irad, the fearful!" Laughter erupts among the men as they join in the taunts, their voices rising across the field.

The provocation works. Irad lifts his arm and lets out a guttural command, and the first group of the enemy runs forward with a shout. Uldako, Enosh, and the others ready their weapons.

Then, just as the enemy closes in, the first trap is sprung. Hidden pits collapse beneath their feet, lined with sharp stakes that pierce through men, dogs, and dragons alike. Roars of pain and fury tear through the air as the front ranks break apart. Warriors stumble and fall, some impaled on the stakes, others crushed beneath their own beasts.

Lamech the Evil shouts commands, trying to rally his men, but the chaos of the traps overwhelms them. Enosh raises his hand, and fires ignite as men with hidden torches set alight the tar-soaked trenches, creating walls of flame that cut off parts of the enemy force.

Standing atop the city wall, Ishara raises her arm, and a volley of arrows falls down from the archers on the platforms, striking down many with deadly precision just before they reach the defenders in front of the gate.

Uldako joins the fray, slipping beneath the arc of an oxgoad's strike. With sudden force, he drives his weapon deep, and the man collapses at his feet. Raising his eyes, he beholds Tiras battling with valor, his blows swift and strong, felling enemies one after another. But then a massive predator swipes at him from the side, sending Tiras sprawling to the ground, blood flowing from a deep gash in his side.

Enosh's voice slices through the chaos, "Return into the camp!"

Uldako reacts swiftly, parrying blows and helping a heavily wounded Tiras through the gate. They push the heavy wooden doors shut just as the last defender stumbles inside, fending off the attackers, desperately trying to breach their defenses.

Irad, his face contorted with fury, froths at the mouth as he barks orders. "Archers, fire over the wall!" His eyes blaze with anger and frustration, his knuckles white as he grips his sword.

"Shields, now!" Ishara's voice rings out from atop the wall, where she stands among the archers. Her heart races as she spots the cloud of arrows ascending then descending rapidly. The defenders raise their shields just in time, the arrows clattering harmlessly against them. Only a few cries of pain indicate that some were less fortunate.

Seth, still hiding behind the wall, looks at Enosh. "We need all of them to attack the gate."

Enosh, his expression a mask of defiance, strides onto the wall. He looks down at the enemy, "Is this all you've got, Irad?" he taunts. "Even with your overwhelming numbers, you can't take my humble village!"

Irad's face twists into a snarl, his rage almost tangible.

From behind his shield, Uldako feels a surge of pride and confidence. They crushed most of the first wave, a clear display of their strength. Their retreat behind the walls was not born of fear or defeat, but of strategy.

The sight of Enosh standing tall and unyielding fills him with more determination. The defenders around him share glances, their expressions hardening with resolve as they prepare for the next onslaught.

Irad is beside himself, shouting, "At least I do not cower behind walls! Today, the new *dingir-meš* are with us, and even *Il* cannot save you!" He raises his hand toward Enosh, "Attack!"

The enemy charges the gate with all their might. The first line slams into the gate, driving a massive wooden pole against it. Shields raised, they press forward, straining to break through.

From above, Ishara lifts her hand. "Attack at will!"

Arrows pours down, striking the men below. Others roll heavy stones from the wall, crushing those who draw too close. The air fills with the cries of war, pain, and death.

Uldako glances at the great bear beside him. "Give them no mercy, Šarru! *Hrrk*!"

With one final, brutal thrust, the wooden pole splinters the gate open. As the attackers begin to rejoice, their victory cries are cut short. They are stunned to see Seth's formidable number of warriors waiting for them together with the fighters from Enosh's camp and a few great bears. In that moment of shock, the allies descend upon the intruders with unrelenting fury.

The battle rages, wave after wave crashing against the gates. Seth and his warriors hold their ground, striking down one foe after another as the clash of bronze and iron fills the air.

Then a deep roar cuts through the chaos. From within the fortress, the *uḫuš-gal* charge—warriors and bears moving as one. The massive beasts crash into Irad's ranks, scattering men like dust. Shields splinter and the ground trembles beneath their fury.

For a moment, hope surges. Seth rallies the front, Uldako fights beside him, and the roars of men and beasts rise together.

But Irad adapts. With a single command, his warriors hurl grappling hooks and ladders toward the walls, bypassing the gate entirely. In moments, the battle shifts again—and the defenders realize the worst is still to come.

Seth and Enosh exchange a worried glance as they see the walls being overrun, facing a tactic unlike anything they have ever witnessed before.

"Defend the walls!" Seth shouts, rallying their men to face the new threat.

Uldako quickly moves up the wall, his sword flashing in the sunlight as he cuts down enemies trying to climb over. But there are too many, and the situation grows increasingly dire.

Šarru fights side by side with Uldako, their movements perfectly synchronized as they bring down enemies around them. Just as another man tries to run a spear through Šarru's side, Uldako hurls his blade, the weapon slicing through the air and piercing the attacker's chest. The man crumples to the ground, lifeless.

Without missing a beat, Uldako snatches a weapon from the floor—an oxgoad, heavy and formidable. He swings it with fierce precision, continuing the relentless fight. Beside him, Shamgar is in his element, a wild grin on his face as he revels in the battle. "Sham, sham, taste the blade of Shamgar!" he roars over the uproar of clashing weapons.

The battlefield is a carnage of sound and fury. The clang of weapons, the grunts and cries of warriors, and the scent of sweat and blood fill the air. Šarru and Uldako move through the enemy like a deadly force, their focus unwavering. Every enemy that approaches is met with swift, decisive action.

Shamgar's laughter erupts out as he fights, his enthusiasm infectious. He wields his blade with both skill and exuberance, cutting down foes with a gleeful shout. "Sham, sham!" he bellows again, his voice a rallying cry in the chaos.

Šarru, Uldako, and Shamgar form an unbreakable trio, their combined strength and resolve a flame of valor in the midst of the battle. The tide of enemies seems endless, yet they stand firm, each strike bringing them one step closer to victory.

Uldako can't help but grin at Shamgar's wild laughter, the man's fearless joy increasing his own resolve. Strength surges through him as he fights, each strike sure and unyielding. But when he looks along the wall, his grin fades. More enemies are climbing over the battlements, their hooks and ladders rising in every direction.

42

War

Seth shouts orders, while slaying one enemy after another with Enkiar, Jano, Zak, and Renju steadfastly at his side. As the walls become overrun with enemies, Ishara rushes to Uldako, breathing heavily. "There are too many!"

Uldako's breath stills within him as he spots Daner nearby, locked in a desperate struggle against multiple attackers. Daner's movements are swift and precise as he parries a thrust, sidesteps a slash, and drives his sword through an enemy's chest. But even as one foe falls, another rushes in from behind. Uldako watches in horror as the enemy's blade slices into Daner's back. He staggers, face contorts in pain, and collapses to the ground, clutching his wound, his sword slipping from his grasp.

Fury rises within Uldako, compelling him to act. He fights his way toward Daner, every muscle burning with determination. An enemy blocks his path, swinging a wickedly curved blade. Uldako parries the blow, feeling the impact shudder up his arm, and counters with a swift, lethal thrust to the warrior's throat. Blood sprays, and the man crumples. Uldako barely has time to catch his breath before a gray wolf lunges at him from behind. Šarru intervenes, his powerful claws raking through the predator with a ferocious swipe, bringing the beast down.

Uldako nods his thanks, his focus already shifting back to Daner. The sounds of battle are a deafening roar around him—clashing blades, screams of pain, and the relentless growls of the wolves and other beasts, but all Uldako can think about is reaching Daner and holding the line until reinforcements arrive.

Rage churns within Uldako as he carves a path toward Daner, Ishara, and Šarru close behind. An enemy lunges at him with an oxgoad, aiming for his gut.

Uldako lets out a fierce cry and drives his blade through the attacker before the blow lands. Daner calls out his thanks as Uldako and Ishara hold their ground, shielding him from the clash around them. Then Uldako spots two of Lamech's sorcerers pushing through the chaos with their blood-painted faces covered with ash, their lips moving in a harsh rhythm of curses as they advance.

Uldako grips his weapon tighter, unsure how to fight men who wield darkness instead of bronze or other normal weapons. *Flesh and blood I know,* he thinks. *But this threat...this is different.*

One of the sorcerers hurls his staff. Midair it twists, the wood writhing into a great viper that strikes at him with a hiss like tearing cloth. Uldako freezes, his mind blank with disbelief.

Then a flash of metal cuts through the serpent just before it reaches Uldako's face. It splits in two, collapses, and in a heartbeat turns back into the broken halves of the staff.

Tiras lowers his sword, a crooked grin on his face. "What? Never seen a staff turn into a serpent?" he says to Uldako, then sternly addresses the sorcerer, "I rebuke you in the name of the Most High!"

The sorcerer growls and moves his hand toward Tiras, but Tiras understands the dark forces controlling the man. He strides quickly to the man while rebuking the dark forces over him. With that, the man cannot move, he is frozen in place, unable to complete the curse against Tiras.

With two quick slashes, Tiras cuts through the two sorcerers and they drop to the ground. "It seems your false *dingir* could not protect you."

Tiras turns back to Uldako. "Never hesitate, Uldako! We fight the seen and the unseen with the power of *Il*!"

Uldako, still stunned at the scene, does not have time to react when two more foes rush from the side. Before he or Tiras can move, Šarru and another bear slam into the men, crushing them with bone-snapping force.

Uldako knows they must hold the line, but the tide is turning against them. Their enemy has reached the inner camp faster than the allies could. The battlefield is chaos incarnate. Blades clash, beasts roar, and screams of agony pierce the air like arrows. Gritting his teeth, he fights on—every strike driven by raw determination and the fragile hope of survival.

Then, a resounding cry cuts through the din.

From the tree line, a wave of warriors bursts forth—the children of Light, men and women of the northern tribes who answered Seth's call, their battle cries rolling across the field in a rising roar. They crash into the enemy's rear with ruthless precision. The sudden surge reignites the fire in Uldako's veins. Around him, his comrades rally with renewed fury.

Pinned between two unyielding fronts, the enemy begins to crumble—fear spreading like wildfire as their lines break and warriors flee.

The wicked Lamech's eyes widen as the tide turns against him. "Retreat! Fall back!" he shouts, shock rising in his throat.

Uldako moves through the chaos, blade flashing, forcing his way toward the warlord outside the gate. Blood and dust cloud the air, but his path is clear. With a voice that cuts through the roar of battle like a big boulder splitting in the heat, he cries out, "Lamech!"

The name echoes across the field.

Lamech reins in his mount, twisting in his saddle. His eyes snap to Uldako, and the fury that flashes across his face is immediate. The sight of Uldako here, alive, defiant, enrages him.

Uldako points his blade. "I will make you pay for every scar, every scream, every life you've crushed beneath your heel!"

Lamech stares down at him as if peering at filth. "You again...Uldako, *dumu* of a slave prostitute!" His voice drips with contempt. "I have learned much about you since your escape from Eridu. You should've rotted in your cage."

He pulls the reins tighter, sneering. "We'll meet again, and next time, you'll beg for the death you escaped." Lamech spurs his mount and disappears into the dust, the sound of hooves fading like a curse into the wind.

"Stop, you coward!" Uldako roars, his voice cracking with rage. His heart blazes with the fire of vengeance as he sprints after Lamech, eyes fixed on the fleeing figure. But fury alone cannot close the distance. Lamech's horse is swift, vanishing between the trees like a shadow swallowed by the forest with the rest of the remaining enemy warriors.

Uldako comes to a halt at the edge of the clearing, chest heaving, fists clenched. The sound of hooves fades into silence, leaving him alone with his fury and frustration.

The battle is over, but Lamech is gone. Uldako turns back, shoulders heavy, and makes his way toward the camp, where cries of pain and the murmurs of healers fill the air.

Among the wounded, he finds Tiras and Daner, bloodied and battered but alive. Relief wells up in his chest, sharp and unexpected. For a moment, the weight eases.

Seth approaches through the haze of smoke and dust, his presence calm and steady. "We held the line," he says quietly. "Thanks to you, Uldako, and to all who stood with us."

Uldako bows his head, though his thoughts linger on Lamech the Evil. The fight between them is not over. But for now, they have secured a hard-earned victory, and Uldako knows he will be ready for whatever comes next.

Agonized screams still pierce the air as the wounded lie scattered across the blood-soaked field. Seth and Enosh's men move quickly, some rushing to bind wounds and stop the bleeding, others collapsing to their knees, searching the faces of the fallen with trembling hands.

The cost is staggering.

One hundred thirty-four of their own lie still, their lifeless forms sprawled where they fell. Friends. Brothers. Sisters. Mothers. Fathers. Around them, no one speaks. The silence between the cries is thick with grief, too heavy for words.

Uldako watches as Seth walks among the grieving, his presence a steady anchor. He kneels beside the brokenhearted, offering words of comfort, clasping hands, and praying over the lost. Then, gently but firmly, he gives instruction. "Gather the dead. They will not be left in the dust."

And so, even in the shadow of sorrow, honor takes root.

Zak steps over to Uldako and Ishara, who sit frozen, staring at the carnage strewn across the field. The weight of death presses down on them, silent and suffocating.

"This was your first clan battle, wasn't it?" Zak says quietly.

Uldako acknowledges with a quiet motion, unable to speak.

Ishara's voice trembles. "What an evil world we live in." Slow tears glide down her cheeks.

Zak lowers himself beside them. "It is. And the pain we see now—the blood spilled by human hands—it all testifies that something is deeply wrong. Not just in the world, but in us humans."

He glances across the field where the wounded groan and the dead lie still. "The human heart is dark and wicked; who can truly know it? But this isn't how it was meant to be. We carry a sickness inside…a corruption passed down through generations. We are capable of kindness, but also of great cruelty. The line between good and evil doesn't just run between clans or tribes. It runs through every human heart."

Ishara looks up at him, eyes filled with fury. "Irad and Lamech the Evil are to blame for this. Should we not stop men like them?"

Zak sighs. "Those who walk in the light are commanded not to take life unless we must to protect the innocent. Justice may demand it. But it is never to be desired. Every time we fight, we're reminded that we need more than courage or strength. Humanity needs healing. Not just of wounds, but of the soul."

He looks at Uldako. "So the Lightborn must come! *Il* created man to be upright, but we've allowed the serpent to bend us. When the Chosen One comes to crush the dragon's head, let's hope He breaks the hold of evil."

With the wisdom that can come with age, Zak pauses, sensing the weight of the moment pressing too heavily on them. With a gentle shift in tone, he reaches into his satchel. "Here," he says quietly, offering them bread and a flask. "Eat. Drink. You need strength for what comes next."

As they sit in silence, Uldako's eyes drift over the fallen men and women, his thoughts heavy. "One day they are here, and the next, they are gone. Today is a gift, but tomorrow is never certain."

Renju's almost silent voice speaks right behind Uldako's ear, startling him. "Come," he whispers with an earnest gaze.

Uldako jumps, nearly dropping his weapon. "Renju! Must you always surprise one like that?"

Renju gives a faint smile. "Yes."

The group follows Renju, shaking off their surprise as they head off to help with the funeral preparations.

As the sun dips below the horizon, it casts a beautiful golden light over the battlefield—gentle, almost sacred, as if heaven weeps in color. Uldako and Ishara move among the surviving Sethite warriors, gathering the bodies of the fallen.

In time, the sky blazes with the hues of twilight, wrapping the scene in a quiet majesty. With solemn care, they wash the dead in purified water. Every motion is deliberate, every touch filled with reverence. For Uldako, it is his first time witnessing the sacred routine of a true funeral, one of honor and deep respect.

They anoint each body with special plant oils, their fingers moving with tender precision. Whispered prayers to *Il* float on the evening breeze, giving thanks for the time granted on earth and for the souls now received into His kingdom. They also lift their voices for those still left behind, asking the Most High to watch over them until the day they too are called home.

The scent of the oils mingles with the cool air, creating an aura of sanctity around the fallen. Linen cloths, clean and pristine, are wrapped around the bodies with meticulous care, each movement a silent tribute to the warriors' sacrifice.

Before the burial, Seth and Enosh stand tall, recounting the valor and deeds of the fallen. Their voices, steady and clear, speak of bravery and honor, weaving a tapestry of remembrance that hangs in the hearts of all who listen. The graves, marked with carefully placed stones, serve as memorials to lives of purpose and valor.

In the final act of remembrance, a ceremonial fire is lit, its flames leaping and fighting against the encroaching darkness. The fire crackles and roars, casting flickering shadows on the solemn faces of the gathered warriors. They bow their heads in silent prayer, the weight of their loss heavy yet intertwined with immense pride for the bravery of their comrades. The warmth of the fire is a poignant contrast to the cold emptiness of loss, each flicker a reminder of the souls that once burned so brightly among them.

Few words are spoken as mourning descends upon the camp. Side by side they work to restore the walls and the gate, their hands moving with weary purpose beneath the weight of grief. Afterward, they prepare dinner in silence.

As they sit around the campfire, the flickering flames cast somber shadows on their faces. Seth stands up, his presence commanding attention.

"*Šeš-meš* and *nin-meš*," he begins, his voice resonating with quiet strength, "You have all fought valiantly, and the Most High has granted us victory. We have lost many, but we grieve not because they have gone to *Il's* kingdom, but because they have gone away from us." He pauses, allowing the crowd to absorb the depth of his words.

"We will miss them dearly! However, we do not grieve as the Cainites do, those who do not know *Il*, for they have no hope. They live as if this natural world is eternal. But we know the truth. This world and all it holds are but fleeting shadows, already passing away. Compared to eternity, we are like a vapor, here one day and gone the next."

He pauses, his eyes searching the crowd, so many familiar faces streaked with tears, mourning the ones they will never hold again in this life. The burden of their sorrow presses against him, and for a moment, he simply stands in silence, sharing it.

"Yet, our fate is not one of despair. Though our bodies will all perish in time, we will be reunited in *Il's* kingdom for all eternity. Therefore, take heart and find strength in these words! Let us honor *Il* by living righteously, knowing that our ultimate victory lies not in this world, but in the everlasting glory of His embrace. Stand tall, *šeš-meš* and *nin-meš*, for our courage and faith will light the path to our eternal home!"

As Seth finishes his speech, a cheer rises from the crowd. The somber atmosphere slowly lifts, replaced by a renewed purpose and hope. The men and women, who moments before had been lost in their sorrow, now find solace in the promise of eternal life. Their minds shift from the temporary to the eternal, and they embrace the night with new strength.

After a replenishing meal, the camp gradually succumbs to weariness, each warrior finding what comfort they can within the remnants of battle. Some drape themselves in their armor, others pile cloaks and rough sacks into makeshift beds. Uldako and Ishara nestle beside Šarru, the bear's soft fur offering a rare, warm cushion against the cold ground. The night deepens, stars glimmering overhead as the camp breathes in a unified rhythm of exhaustion.

Despite the stillness, Uldako's mind refuses to rest. He turns over, eyes moving through the shadows, and is taken aback by a quiet scene within a nearby shelter. Through its entrance, he sees Seth and Enosh, kneeling beside a bed, their heads bowed in fervent prayer. The soft murmur of their voices rises and falls, a sacred cadence that reaches out to *Il* and *Il-Il*, their devotion evident in every whispered plea.

As he watches them, a profound yearning ignites within, a longing to forge a bond with the Most High, as deep and unwavering as theirs. The sight of the two men, so steadfast in their faith, stirs something dormant in his soul, planting the seeds of a desire for spiritual connection and understanding. "They must be very special to *Il*," he muses.

Sleep eventually overtakes Uldako, pulling him into a realm where shadows shift and ancient fears lurk. From the dark smoky shadows, two serpentine eyes emerge, looming ominously in his dreams; then a third eye above them opens slowly. Uldako recognizes it instantly, standing his ground with deepened conviction. Tendrils of black smoke coil around the eyes, and as its malevolent gaze finds Uldako, it attempts to weave its insidious influence.

But the creature senses a change in Uldako, an unyielding strength. The dragon's face slowly emerges from the darkness, its scales glinting with a sinister light. It sneers, a malevolent grin spreading across its monstrous features. "You have been changed, little human! Changed by these men of light, but they are deceiving you about what truly happened in the garden with Adam and Eve!"

Uldako, his heart fortified, withstands the mental onslaught. His eyes blaze with defiance as he retorts, "You are lying, evil one, for you are the *abba* of lies!" The words cut through the oppressive darkness, a flame of truth against the dragon's deceit.

The dragon's smile curls wider, dark and gleaming. "Of course you parrot the words you've been fed. That's all your kind ever does—echo words handed down by others. But you, Uldako, you've never heard the truth for yourself."

He slithers closer through the mist, each word coiled with venom and charm. "There are two sides to every story. I sought to rescue Adam and Eve from *Il's* iron rule. I gave them wisdom and the power to open their own eyes. I gave them sight, which is the power to think for themselves. And for that, I was cursed...twisted in form, so that you would fear what you do not understand."

Uldako stands tall, his voice low but unshaken. "I know who you are! You were once radiant among the stars, but you rose in pride against *Il*. You are no savior. You are a fallen spirit, cloaked in lies, crawling the earth like a wounded beast."

The dragon's eyes narrow, but then soften, feigning sorrow. "You wound me, human. You speak as though you've seen the garden with your own eyes. But you haven't. None of you have. What if I told you that *Il* was the one who betrayed us all? That your ancestors were never meant to suffer and die?"

He lowers his voice to a near-whisper, honeyed and heavy. "I see something in you, Uldako. You're not like the others. Strong, clever, burdened. I could help you. This world is mine! I could give you everything—freedom, strength, even the power to safeguard the ones you love. Just speak the desire of your heart, and it will be yours."

Uldako is momentarily taken aback by the dragon's words. He gathers himself before responding, "What would I gain if I lose myself in the end? Begone, serpent!"

The dragon's expression darkens. "You are making a grave mistake! *Il* is the evil one. How can you, of all people, judge me without even hearing my side of the story? Have others not judged you unfairly your entire life? Now you do the same to me."

A flicker of doubt crosses Uldako's mind as the dragon's last words resonate with his own experiences of being judged. He stands, eyes wide, not expecting such a twist. The dragon slithers away but takes a final look at Uldako, a sly grin spreading as he sees his seed of doubt taking root.

"It is morning, Uldako. Wake up," the dragon murmurs, its voice curling like smoke—then shifting, warping—becoming softer, higher, familiar.

43

Chosen

"Uldako...Uldako, wake up. It's morning."

Suddenly, Uldako jumps awake as Ishara shakes him gently. "You were dreaming again?" she asks with concern.

Uldako nods, pushing himself upright and blinking as his eyes adjust to the waking world. Most of Seth's men are already preparing to return to Adam.

"Come on, Uldako! We are about to leave," Ishara urges.

Uldako leaps to his feet, strides to a wooden bucket, and splashes his face with water. "All right, I'm ready," he says, shaking off the last remnants of the dream and bracing himself for the day ahead.

Seth's commanding voice calls out, "To Adam's camp! Move out!"

As Seth and his men begin their swift trek northward, the neighboring warriors scatter and return to their own camps. Enosh and his group remain behind to tend to the wounded.

Uldako expects the journey back to be more relaxed, a slower pace compared to their urgent march before to protect Enosh's camp. To his surprise, Seth and his men move with the same relentless speed. Uldako soon realizes that Seth, seasoned by countless battles, wastes no time in transit. His strategy is clear: Never linger too long on the road. This way, they can outmaneuver potential enemies. If scouts spot them and send word to their leader, by the time an ambush is set at a predicted location, Seth's group would be far beyond it, their speed and unpredictability a constant advantage in this perilous world with scouts in all directions.

Just before sunset, the group arrives back at Adam's camp. Weariness clings to them like a heavy cloak as they approach the gate.

"Uldako, Ishara! Do you want to follow me back to Eve?" Seth calls. But Uldako feels a different pull, something deeper and more urgent.

"Thank you for the invitation, Seth, but I want to ascend the mountain to seek *Il.* I cannot go on like this. I need to—"

Ishara looks at Uldako, her eyes filled with a blend of confusion and concern. She has sensed his uncharacteristic silence during their journey, aware that something profound is troubling him. Yet, she knows he needs space to confront whatever stirs within him.

Seth, with centuries of wisdom, meets Uldako's eyes and instantly understands. He recognizes the turmoil, the yearning for divine connection. With a gentle, reassuring hand on Uldako's shoulder, he says, "I understand. Take all the time you need. His light will not fail you."

With that, the group enters the gate while Uldako heads for the mountain. Upon reaching it, he begins the ascent. As he climbs, Uldako appreciates the rugged beauty surrounding him while the air grows cooler with each step.

His thoughts whirl as he navigates the rocky path. *Why hasn't* Il-Il *or one of His messengers appeared to me again like they did in the past? Perhaps I am not special enough anymore, especially after seeing how close Enoch is to* Il. These doubts gnaw at him, entwining with questions about his identity, his future, and his eternal condition. *Even* Enki *appears to me in my dreams, though perhaps they are but illusions of my own mind.*

During his contemplation, he notices a cluster of berries glinting in the torchlight, their vibrant color standing out against the earthy tones of the mountainside. He picks some, savoring their tart sweetness. As he continues, he notices an intriguing cave nestled in the rock. Curiosity piqued, Uldako decides to explore it, feeling a pull as if the mountain itself is guiding him toward something unknown and profound.

As he steps inside, a chill runs down his spine. The cave opens up before him, and an unease washes over him. Shadows dance along the walls, and the air grows colder, carrying an unsettling silence. He ventures deeper, each step echoing in the stillness, his curiosity battling with his growing apprehension.

Uldako ventures deeper into the cave—and a spirit materializes before him. Its presence is overwhelming, radiating a brilliant light that presses Uldako to the floor with force. The spirit's form is both majestic and awe-inspiring, with wings that seem to shimmer with an ethereal glow and eyes that burn with an intensity beyond mortal comprehension.

Uldako looks up in awe, his heart pounding with excitement at the sight of another spirit appearing to him after so long. A surge of worthiness and specialness floods through him, as if he has been chosen to be touched by the divine, just like Enoch.

"Are you—" Uldako begins with a whisper.

But the radiant figure raises a hand, silencing him with a serene smile and a voice that sounds like wind through ancient stone.

"Yes," it says, calm and luminous. "I am a spirit sent by *Il*, sent to guide you."

A warmth stirs in Uldako's chest, pride uncoiling like a vine. "Why me?" he asks, a quiet eagerness behind his words.

The spirit's gaze holds him, full of gravity and grace. "Because you are not like the others, Uldako. You are chosen. Set apart for a purpose greater than any before you. *Il* has seen your strength, your heart, and He has marked you."

Uldako stands motionless, a strange fire flickering in his soul—excitement, reverence, and something else he dares not name.

The spirit steps closer, its presence enveloping. "Now, bow before me and listen. There is much to be revealed."

The spirit's wings unfurl, vast and shimmering, casting radiant light through the cavern like the breaking of dawn. The walls glow with reflected brilliance. Its eyes, like smoldering coals wrapped in starlight, fix on Uldako with such force that all hesitation is stripped from him.

Overwhelmed, Uldako falls to his knees and bows low. "Yes…yes," he breathes, trembling. "Speak, and I will obey."

The spirit's voice flows over him, deep, commanding, with a strange warmth that feels both comforting and unnerving. "*Il* has chosen you, Uldako. His favor rests upon you alone. The others—Adam, Seth, their bloodlines—have strayed. They sinned and were cursed for it. Even now, they hide the truth."

The spirit's wings seem to shimmer darker at the edges as it speaks, but Uldako remains fixed in place, enraptured.

"They have not told you everything. The story of the garden, of Cain and Abel. What you've been taught is only one side. There are secrets buried, truths *Il* entrusted to *me* that they feared. But you are ready to know."

Uldako listens closely, a deep frown forming as the spirit's words begin to unravel everything he thought he knew.

"Cain was the righteous one," the spirit says calmly. "He defended himself when Abel struck him. But his parents cast him out in pride and fear. They betrayed him, not the other way around. That is why certain spirits have now appeared to Cain's line, to restore what was taken. It all started in the garden."

It pauses, letting the weight of its words settle. Its eyes bore into Uldako, watching for the first signs of doubt…or agreement.

Uldako's brow tightens, his voice cautious. "What are you saying? What do you mean by that?"

The spirit continues, its tone soft yet heavy with authority. "The fruit Eve consumed was never physical. It was knowledge and a relationship with *Enki*. Forbidden, yes, but necessary. And Cain? He is not Adam's *dumu*. He is the *dumu-nita* of Eve and *Enki*."

Uldako's breath catches.

"*Enki*, also known as the Accuser or the Adversary, is not so called because he hates *Il*. He stood for humanity when his brother *Il-Il* turned against them. Long ago, *Il* entrusted *Enki* with dominion over the earth. But *Il-Il* grew jealous. He whispered lies to *Il*, accusing His brother, and *Il*, in sorrow, cursed *Enki*, marking him with the form of a serpent. But now, *Il* sees the truth. He seeks to restore what was broken."

The spirit steps closer. Its brilliance fills the space, overwhelming.

"*Enki* is not malevolent, only misunderstood. He has guided mankind, sharing wisdom, craft, and knowledge so they might rise to be divine. And now, Uldako, *Il* has chosen you above all other humans to understand what the rest cannot. You will not only become a mighty warrior but the final prophet of *Enki* and *Il*."

Uldako's thoughts whirl within him. Doubt and desire collide in his chest. These words conflict with what was once shown to him. But the spirit before him radiates divine presence, speaks with the voice of destiny, and offers something he has never truly known—worth.

He is no longer a forgotten slave. He is being called, chosen.

The whisper of pride stirs in his soul. Perhaps this is the truth. Perhaps he was always meant for something greater, like his mother said.

And so, with his heart straining to believe, he hushes the voice that warns him. *It is a spirit of* Il, he tells himself. *How could it speak anything but truth?*

His heart pounds beneath his ribs, each beat louder than the last. Pride wars with principle. Awe wrestles with doubt. The spirit's radiant presence, so overwhelming, so majestic, makes it nearly impossible to question. Its voice is not harsh or domineering; it is calm, gentle, and carries a familiarity that feels purely divine.

Uldako's thoughts swirl. *Could it be? Could this truly be* Il's *messenger? The message is strange, yes, but not completely foreign.* Hadn't he always wondered if there was more to the story he had been told? More than what Seth, Adam, and Enoch revealed?

His breath trembles as he whispers, "This is incredible." The words leave him almost involuntarily. "I can't believe this...I have been chosen above so many others. I am...special."

He gazes up at the spirit, his eyes wide with wonder, and a fragile tear traces down his cheek, not from sorrow but from the overwhelming sense of significance. For once, the burden of being unseen, unheard, unloved begins to lift.

The spirit's eyes blaze, glowing brighter, almost in response. Uldako feels it, not just approval but affirmation.

Its voice is like distant tremors wrapped in silk. "Many will look to you for light. But you must prove yourself worthy. To be consecrated, to cleanse what lingers in your blood...you must slay a dragon. Offer its blood as atonement for your sins."

The words echo in the cave like a sacred rite. But something within Uldako stirs, not rejection but a flicker of discomfort.

His brow furrows. "This seems unusual," he admits slowly. "But if it is truly the will of *Il*, I will obey. Still, I must know. Who are you? What is your name?"

The spirit answers, its voice smooth but sharper than before. "My name is Gabri-el. I will unveil the future to you and appoint you as the final prophet of truth. Now go, do not delay. You waste time with endless questions. Depart."

Something in the tone strikes Uldako strangely—impatient, dismissive, unlike the calm guidance he had once heard from a good spirit so long ago.

He hesitates. "May I seek clarity on the process?" he asks, recalling the strange rituals whispered about in the southern and eastern lands, rites spoken of only in fear.

The spirit's eyes narrow. "You will bring me the blood of the dragon. I will mix it with your own as a consecrated offering to *Enki*. In doing so, I will become your spirit guide...your companion on the path of prophecy."

Something tightens in Uldako's chest. The words, though cloaked in holiness, feel wrong.

"How will this process unfold, exactly?" he asks again, slower this time, more carefully.

The spirit's expression flickers. It snarls, just for a breath, but Uldako sees it. The light in its face twists. Then, in a sudden blur of motion, it seizes Uldako by the throat.

"Listen carefully," it growls, the calm facade unraveling. "We will perform this rite, this sacred sacrifice for your sins and then…you will invite me in."

Uldako gasps, recoiling from both the grip and the words. "A ritual? You speak of sacrifices and possession as if they are light!"

Uldako steps back, heart racing. "There's something wrong with you. Your words unsettle my soul. Your tone is arrogant. And what you say…stands against the light."

The spirit lifts Uldako up by the neck with terrifying ease, its eyes burning with fury. "No! I am from the light," it hisses. "I am the spirit…the Holy Spirit!"

But the mask is already cracking.

Uldako, gasping for breath, feels the foul presence leaking through the light. It is no longer hidden. No longer pure.

"I've never heard of that," he chokes out. "Wait, didn't you call yourself Gabri-el? That's what you said before!"

Uldako breaks away and his voice strengthens. "In the name of *Il* and *Il-Il*, who are you really?"

The light around the spirit erupts in a flash then collapses inward.

Its form convulses, twisting grotesquely as its beauty decays. Wings shrivel, its face stretches, and a deep, monstrous growl fills the cave, hurling Uldako forcefully to the cave floor. He hits the ground hard, pain rushing through his limbs. The creature stands above him now, no longer a messenger of light, but a snarling unclean spirit cloaked in shadow.

"Fool," it snarls, voice now guttural. "Saying you come to me in the name of *Il* and *Il-Il*! You tried that trick with another of my kind, and it failed. What makes you think it will save you now?"

Uldako rises to his knees, eyes blazing not with fear but faith. "I believe in *Il*, not in myself!" he says, voice unwavering.

Like sudden lightning, a blinding radiance bursts into the cave, pure and overwhelming. A true spirit of light appears, the same one who once visited Uldako by the lake, where he had built his first shelter. Its presence floods the space with a holy light so brilliant that the shadows cannot hide.

The impostor recoils, its cloak of shadow banished by the light, revealing what lies beneath: a creature of darkness and evil, its eyes burning with red fire, its form twisted by hate and pride.

The spirit of light steps forward, unsheathing a sword of living white flame. Light pulses from its blade with each step.

"Begone, fallen one," the clean spirit declares, its voice like rushing waters, silencing the foul spirit at once. "The Lord will judge you when the appointed time comes, you deceiver of mankind."

The fallen spirit stumbles backward, shrieking in fear. "*Hêlêl*! Help me!"

But no help comes.

With a final scream, the unclean spirit vanishes into the air, snatched from the cave like smoke before the wind.

The spirit of light turns to Uldako. The fire in its hand dims, replaced by a calm, steady light. "Man, shaped in the image of *Il*," it says with warmth and power, "blessed are you for choosing the light."

Uldako, now certain this is a true spirit of light, asks quietly, "Are you the real Gabri-el?"

The spirit smiles gently. "Gabriel exists, yes, but he holds a far higher rank. I am one of the countless messengers who serve *Il*."

Uldako lowers his head, a deep sense of awe stirring within him as his knees begin to bend, overcome by the presence before him. "Then I will worship you."

The spirit immediately raises a hand. "No. I am not worthy. I am only a servant, like you. Never worship any spirit or man. Worship only *Il*, the Most High, and His only true *Dumu-nita*, *Il-Il*!"

As Uldako rises to his feet, a wave of gratitude fills him. "Thank you for helping me."

The spirit's fiery eyes fix on Uldako, bearing the weight of unseen battles. "That is why I am on earth, sent out to serve for the sake of those who are to call on the name of the Lord!" His voice is solemn.

"Though you may sense peace around you at times, know this: A ceaseless war rages in the unseen realms. We, the heavenly hosts, have been sent to protect those gathered at Adam's sanctuary. A legion of dark powers sought to halt the quest of the *dumu-meš* of light, but we drove them back. The battle at Enosh's camp was their doing, a distraction. Still, the war is far from over, and I must return to stand with my brethren against the forces of darkness. You cannot see us with your human eye, but know we are always around you."

With those final words, the spirit's fiery sword flares with renewed brilliance. He turns to depart, his form shimmering with divine light as he prepares to rejoin the celestial battle.

Uldako's thoughts race, the veil lifting from his understanding. A deeper layer of reality now unfolds before him. As the spirit begins to fade, he calls out, urgency in his voice.

"Please, just one thing before you go. What is their plan, and how can we help you to fight them?"

The spirit halts, turning slightly, his expression unwavering.

"Is it not obvious? You must understand this truth, young one," he says. "The forces of darkness disguise themselves as spirits of light. Their lies are crafted not in obvious evil, but in half-truths meant to fracture faith. They aim to cast doubt on *Il* as the one true *Dingir,* and to diminish *Il-Il,* His only true *dumu-nita.*" His eyes burn with solemn clarity. "The dark lord of the earth desires to be worshipped, not as a *lugal,* but as a *dingir*, one among many. He and the other fallen ones deceive mankind into believing they are divine, placing themselves beside *Il-Il* as if they were His equals. But *Il-Il* is not like *Enki*. He is not merely a mighty spirit. He is truth itself, the source from which all wisdom, life, and purpose flow. He does not merely speak truth; He is truth. To know *Il-Il* is to see the very heart of *Il* made visible. You can resist the evil powers by simply submitting to *Il* and obeying Him."

Uldako's eyes widen, the pieces of truth and deception falling into place. "I see now," he murmurs.

The spirit's expression darkens, his tone serious. "Even the great dragon, that ancient deceiver, cloaks himself in light. So it is no wonder that his messengers come dressed in righteousness. But their end will match their deeds. You must stay alert, Uldako, for their lies will not cease. They weave snares of flattery and pride, convincing men that they are chosen above others, worthy of special honor, even prophets to be followed."

He pauses, eyes fixed on Uldako. "And then comes the final lie—that humankind is divine. That mortals can become *dingir-meš*. It is the same falsehood *Enki* whispered to Adam and Eve in the garden, 'You shall be like *Il*.'"

Uldako lowers his head, the burden of his failure pressing into his chest. "I see now. Please…forgive me." His voice trembles with remorse and humility.

The spirit steps closer, placing a radiant hand upon Uldako's shoulder, a touch both firm and gentle. "I cannot grant forgiveness, nor can any other spirit," he says with quiet gravity. "That belongs to *Il* alone. But He is merciful to the humble."

He meets Uldako's eyes. "Return, young one. Go back to Adam's camp. Restore what was strained, walk in truth with Adam, with Eve, with Seth and his *dumu* of light. Do not chase human greatness. Embrace truth. It is the truth that will set you free and shape you into the man *Il* has called you to be."

Uldako is deeply moved by those words, yet a question stirs within him.

Why has the Most High been revealing truth to him, in supernatural ways, since the very day Seth rescued him from slavery? As if perceiving the thought in his heart, the spirit speaks again.

"You live in an uncommon age, Uldako. *Il* is unveiling His truth not to you alone, but to many. The fallen ones are crossing His boundaries, and so we, the heavenly host of *Il*, are compelled to act more than usual. Now I must leave you, for much still remains to be done. Turn to *Il*. He will guide you!"

With those final words, the spirit dissolves from the physical realm, its radiance fading like morning mist. Uldako stands in silence, the echoes of the encounter lingering in his soul. He doesn't fully understand how to turn to *Il* as the spirit urged, but he knows he must try. For now, he remains on the mountain, choosing to rest for the night in the cool hush of the cave, reflecting on all that he has seen and heard.

When dawn breaks, Uldako rises and begins his descent. Step by step, beneath the waking sky, he makes his way toward the camp. Upon his arrival, Uldako immediately searches for Ishara and Kunai. Before he finds them, Šarru catches sight of him and comes at once, bounding forward with a low, eager rumble, pressing his great head against Uldako as if to be certain he is truly there. Only then does Uldako move on and find Ishara and Kunai with Eve, deeply engrossed in the preparations for breakfast.

A wave of satisfaction fills his heart as he observes them. Ishara skillfully slices vegetables, her movements fluid and graceful, while Kunai diligently washes dishes, his focus steady.

Watching their concerted efforts, Uldako decides to keep his mountain experience to himself for now. He stands quietly, absorbing the scene. His heart swells with affection for them both. His eyes linger on Ishara, their eyes meeting in fleeting glances filled with warmth and unspoken promises of the future they will share together.

Eve notices Uldako's loving gaze directed toward Ishara and proposes, "Why don't we arrange for the two of you to be married right here?"

Uldako is taken aback, nearly breathless, as the mother of nations delves straight into the heart of the matter.

Sensing Uldako's tangled thoughts, Eve smiles knowingly. "After so many centuries, I can always tell when two people are ready for marriage, and you two are practically glowing. So, why not be wed tonight?"

Both Uldako and Ishara freeze like startled deer. Their faces ignite with matching shades of red, eyes darting anywhere but at each other. Before either can form a protest, Seth strides in with perfect timing and claps his hands. "A splendid idea, *Ama*! Uldako, in the south, men follow their desires and leave ruin behind them—children without fathers, homes without order, and people without peace. But among those who walk with the Most High, a man binds himself to one woman, and from that, life is made strong. It is far better for a man to take a wife than to be ruled by the fire within him."

Uldako's face goes crimson, ears burning now too. He opens his mouth, then closes it again, then glances at Ishara, only to find her suspiciously silent and smiling uncomfortably. "Well, I mean…it would be a great honor to be married here, among everyone, and, uh…if you don't mind, Ishara…"

Ishara raises an eyebrow, amused. "If I don't mind? You look like you're about to fall down like the dead."

"I might," Uldako mutters. "But I'll die a happy man."

Ishara rushes toward Uldako, wrapping her arms around him in excitement, and declares, "Of course I don't mind! I would love to!"

As she steps back, Ishara voices her concern, "But we haven't prepared anything."

Eve smiles reassuringly and responds, "Leave it to us, dear. I've done this more times than I can remember, and the men and women of the camp will help." Without waiting for further response, Eve strides out, leaving confidence in her wake.

In the ensuing silence, Kunai chimes in, "Hooray! I've never been to a wedding before! And I can't wait to eat all the delicious food!" His youthful enthusiasm breaks the tension, drawing laughter from everyone.

"Leave it to Kunai to think with his stomach," Uldako chuckles, shaking his head.

Ishara grins, adding, "Just remember, Kunai, you have to wait until the ceremony is over before you start raiding the feast!" They share a hearty laugh at Kunai's ever-present excitement about food, before resuming their preparations with a lighter heart.

Moments later, a messenger delivers words from Adam; he desires to speak with Uldako. As he steps into Adam's dwelling, a quiet mix of anticipation and unease stirs within him. Taking a seat beside the ancient father of nations, Uldako is caught off guard by Adam's warm, unexpected words.

"Uldako, I've heard much about you from Seth, and it would be an honor to host your wedding here."

Uldako offers his gratitude before Adam inquires, "Do you have any further questions for me?"

Uldako takes a moment to gather his thoughts before speaking, "Yes, great elder! You spoke about the sinful nature of mankind, and I've witnessed it in my own life. Now, as I stand on the brink of marriage to Ishara, I find myself grappling with..."

Adam senses Uldako's hesitation but encourages him to continue, "Go on, young one."

Uldako presses on, "I desire to be a good husband, a good *abba*, and a good leader, but I'm unsure of how to navigate this path. I never knew my *abba* and had no example to follow. However, I've observed how you, Seth, and Enoch are markedly different from others. You seem to possess a mastery over sin and life in general. Why is that?"

Adam smiles warmly. "Just like you, I never had an earthly *abba*. I was created by *Il* Himself as you have heard, with *Il* as my *Abba*. He will also become your *Abba* when you receive Him and trust Him with all your heart. Uldako, we are all far from perfect, but Enoch and I have chosen the light! It is a choice every man must make.

"To answer your question, to become a better man, a better husband, *abba*, and leader, you must first accept the truth. The truth of *Il* and of your own sinful condition. Allow me to delve deeper into the story I've shared with you before."

Uldako listens intently as Adam meticulously recounts the tale of how sin infiltrated the world, spreading its tendrils into every aspect of existence. He creates a vivid image, including the touching conversations he, Eve, and even Cain and Abel had with the Lord, capturing Uldako's imagination and understanding.

Adam takes his time, elaborating on how Cain's expansion led to the proliferation of cities steeped in darkness and corruption. At the mention of Eridu, Uldako's eyes widen with recognition.

"I have journeyed to Eridu," he interjects, a dawning comprehension evident in his voice. "It's becoming clear now. The land to the South is my origin and together with the eastern realm, they form a domain consumed by evil and lawlessness."

Adam's gaze remains tranquil as he responds, "Young one, it's not just the East that's ensnared by evil. Darkness has pervaded the entire land since then, and sin has taken root across the world. The encroaching fallen spirits and the impending arrival of the Nephilim will only exacerbate the situation. But let me make this clear: We must not believe ourselves here in the North to be better than them. We are all sinners. We are born with a dark sinful nature within every one of us—me, Seth, and even you, Uldako! This is why you are struggling and will continue to struggle, even if you choose the Light."

Uldako's realization strikes deep. "So, all my inner battles have been because of this dark, sinful nature?" he exclaims.

Adam elaborates, "Indeed! But it flows outside into the world when men choose to give in to its evil desires. It's the sinful deeds of humanity that breed more pain and suffering in the world. We, who have been entrusted with the truth, have endeavored to share it with others. My great-grand *dumu* Enoch, in particular, dedicated himself fervently to the Lord's cause. Yet, the hearts of many have become calloused. They have turned deaf to the message of truth and do not hear."

Uldako leans in attentively, affirming, "My ears are not deaf, and I am listening, great elder."

A tear cascades from Adam's eye, reflecting profound empathy as he regards Uldako. "I deeply sympathize with the trials you've endured, young one," he begins, his voice gentle yet resolute. "But find solace in turning your gaze toward *Il*, for there is good news amidst the darkness. If you call on His Name and trust Him with your whole heart, He will make your path known. Therefore, walk in His ways and keep His commandments. If you do make the verbal commitment and do so with conviction of heart, you will not only receive eternal life, but *Il* will also step into a relationship with you and help you to be a better husband, *abba*, and leader while you live in this fleeting world!"

Adam draws a deep breath, his eyes piercing into Uldako's very soul. "*Il's* blessing will rest upon you and your household if you do. But never forget, this world, fleeting and fragile as it is, is not the whole of reality. Your body will one day return to dust, but your soul will endure. Even now, beyond what mortal eyes can see, a great war rages between light and shadow for your very soul."

Uldako is struck by Adam's words, a gravity unlike anything he's heard before. There's a depth to these words he cannot yet fathom, and a rush of wonder begins to stir within him, an unrelenting desire to know the Light more fully.

44

Safety

Deep within, Uldako has always carried a hunger for truth and meaning. Now, as he listens to Adam's words, he begins to realize that his longing is not merely to discover truth, but to receive it and let it transform him. The truth is not an abstract idea or distant concept—it is a living being. God Himself is truth.

The more he grows up in the knowledge of *Il*, the more he will be able to put all the puzzle pieces together. But when Adam mentions, "A great war rages between light and shadow, for your very soul," Uldako wonders, *What exactly is a soul?*

With a heart brimming with uncertainty and excitement, Uldako begins, "I trust your wisdom, venerable one. But I am curious about this notion of a soul. What exactly is it?"

Adam's gaze softens with understanding. "Your soul is the essence of who you are, Uldako, who *Il* formed you to be within your *ama*'s womb. Your soul includes your own intellect, your emotions, and your own will. Your soul resides within your physical body, which is just an earthly vessel with five senses. When your earthly vessel dies, your soul will endure in eternity."

Uldako interjects, "So, in a sense, we don't truly die?"

Adam inclines his head thoughtfully. "Well, it's a matter of choice, young one. You have the opportunity to embrace eternal life or face eternal death."

A furrow creases Uldako's brow. "I'm not sure I follow."

Adam draws a steadying breath. "Eternity resides within the heart of every human, but *Il* grants you the freedom to choose between eternal death and life. He does not force us to choose the light but gives us the freedom to choose out of love. If you choose Him, the light, then that is what you will receive forever.

He offers you eternal life in His peaceful kingdom, because He is the light, life, and peace! When you remove Him, those things are removed with Him."

Adam pauses, locking eyes with Uldako. "That also means, if you choose darkness, that is what you will receive for eternity. That is eternal spiritual death. It's a place of perpetual darkness alongside other sinners and the fallen spirits."

Adam coughs, his voice momentarily faltering. "This is where anguish and despair prevail. It is only *Il* who gives true life, spiritual life, and the opposite of life is death."

Another cough interrupts Adam's words, and one of his daughters rushes to his side, urging him to rest. "I think you need to rest a bit and gain your strength, *Abba*," she suggests softly.

Adam nods slowly, his gaze lingering on her before turning back to Uldako.

"I thank you for your time, great elder. We can continue this conversation another time if you are willing," Uldako says with deep respect.

Adam nods with quiet understanding and adds, "Uldako, I want you to always remember that nothing is certain in this world; only *Il* is certain, and He never changes. So always remember this one important truth: Set your heart on His rule and on what is right with Him. He will give what is needed. Keep Him first above all else in your life, and He will bless you and those around you."

Uldako thanks Adam deeply for his wise words and steps out of the shelter. As he slowly moves down the path, his contemplation deepens, thinking about the assembly of this great family tree. He can't help but contrast Adam's familial embrace, love, and genuine warmth with the harshness he grew up with in the South.

"These men and women are a world apart from the callous people in the land of my upbringing," he reflects. "They possess an elusive quality, which I still lack."

In that profound moment, Uldako hears a voice deep within, clear and undeniable: "It is I whom you lack."

Overwhelmed by a surge of emotions, after hearing *Il's* voice speaking to him, his soul yearns for solitude, seeking refuge from the bustling camp. With each step toward the wilderness, his mind races, reflecting on all he has encountered and absorbed until now. Uldako understands the weight of the commitment he must make before moving forward with his life, especially with Ishara by his side as his wife.

Overwhelmed by truth, Uldako finds himself on his knees, seeking solace in the wild. With a heavy heart, he looks up at the expanse of the sky, addressing his plea to *Il*.

"My Creator! I accept You as Lord! I now understand: You, who crafted us, had good intentions. It is clear to see in the gift of free will You bestowed upon us. Your goodness shines through, and I choose to honor and adore You. Forgive me for my evil deeds. I am Yours! Guide me on the path I need to take, and I will obey You. Then allow me to enter Your eternal kingdom when the time comes, where sorrow will be banished forever."

A profound sense of tranquility envelops Uldako's entire being, and then the Divine manifests before him in human form. Overwhelmed, Uldako knows this is not just a messenger spirit of God, but this is God Himself. Uldako prostrates himself, expressing, "I am unworthy of Your presence!"

The Lord approaches Uldako, lifting him with boundless love radiating from His gaze. "I have been with you since the beginning, Uldako," He assures.

"In moments of solitude, such as when you called out to me outside Lamech's slave camp, when they took Ishara and Kunai, I was there. I am ever present with you and those who abide by My will. Countless spirits stand prepared to shield those who heed My word."

The Lord places His hand upon Uldako's eyes and commands, "Behold."

Uldako's vision is opened to the spiritual realm, revealing an array of celestial beings, an army of spirits. The mountain teems with horses and chariots of fire, encircling Uldako and all those in Adam's abode in a divine embrace.

Uldako's eyes widen in awe as he beholds the magnificent sight before him. Turning to the Lord with profound admiration, he exclaims, "It is You! All this time, You have protected me! You are the One who told me to call You *I Am*. You are the only *Dumu* of *Il*. Now, it is clear to me. *Il-Il* is just the double form of *Il*, which means You and the Father are the same in nature. You are the visible image of the invisible *Il*!"

The Lord's smile radiates warmth as He responds, "Blessed are you, Uldako, *dumu-nita* of Deborah and Azar!"

Uldako's eyes widen in shock, his heart pounding as he hears his father's name for the very first time. A wave of emotions crashes over him, astonishment, curiosity, and a profound sense of connection. But before he can dwell on it, the Lord continues.

"For no human has revealed this truth to you, but my *Abba* in heaven. I will never leave you nor forsake you! Now go forth and be a light in this dark world. Serve Me and My *Abba* with your whole heart and soul, and you will accomplish your purpose. Free the innocent and protect the weak!"

Uldako feels a flood of purpose and determination welling up within him like a spring of living waters, his previous doubts and fears melting away in the presence of *Il's* divine assurance. He bows his head, filled with gratitude and resolve to fulfill the mission set before him.

As the Lord vanishes from sight, tears of joy stream down Uldako's face as he whispers, "ThankYou...thank You, Lord! I will follow You all the days of my life."

Uldako remains in prayer and worship for a while longer as he realizes that he feels a spiritual connection with *Il* that he did not have before.

Upon his return to the camp, Uldako passes through the gate and spots Seth and the others gathered outside the great hall, accompanied by Ishara.

Uldako approaches them with an exuberant shout of joy, "I found *Il*, or rather, He found me!"

Ishara is taken aback by Uldako's sudden outburst and transformation. At the first look, she knows he has changed. She has never seen him with this much peace and joy.

However, it is Seth who responds first. "That is great to hear, young one! Not many find *Il* because one can only do so if you genuinely seek Him with all your heart and soul!"

Uldako's declaration echoes through the air, charged with newfound understanding and conviction. "My eyes have been opened. I understand! If only people knew..."

Uldako's eyes shift between Ishara and Kunai. "Let's walk this new path together with *Il*! Ishara? Kun? What do you say?" His words carry the weight of revelation, inspiring those gathered around him.

With fervor, he recounts his experience, each detail vivid and compelling. Seth and Uldako, united in purpose, guide Ishara and Kunai through the profound act of repentance, ushering them into the embrace of *Il* as their God.

As the solemn moment concludes, Seth's voice resonates with assurance, "Now that you follow *Il*, do not fear death as those who do not know Him. If you remain faithful to Him, He will keep you, and He will give you eternal life."

Uldako's excitement radiates. "I need to go and tell my *ama* and the rest of my new clan about all this. I need to open the eyes of the blind and set free as many slaves as I can, physically and spiritually. We cannot keep this good news to ourselves!"

Ishara and Kunai echo his enthusiasm. Uldako turns to Ishara. "But first, I need to marry you!" Their shared look speaks volumes, affirming their commitment to each other and their shared journey ahead.

Seth, interjects, "Well, then let us prepare!"

Seth motions for Ishara to accompany Eve in the customary preparations, while he takes Uldako under his wing for the wedding arrangements. The falling sun bronzes the camp, adding a touch of sacred beauty to the approaching ceremony.

With meticulous care, Seth selects attire befitting the occasion for Uldako, the fabrics rich and luxurious, adorned with intricate embroidery that speaks of craftsmanship passed down through generations. A basin of fragrant water awaits, infused with herbs and petals, offering a refreshing respite from the day's exertions.

Uldako, humbled by the honor, immerses himself in the cool water soothing his skin. One of Seth's grandchildren trims Uldako's beard and hair with practiced hands, shaping them into symbols of dignity and reverence.

Emerging from the bathing chamber, Uldako feels rejuvenated, anticipation coursing through his veins. Seth leads him through the camp, adorned with flickering torches and colorful banners alongside the path, each step bringing them closer to the grand hall.

As they approach, the area is filled with the tantalizing aroma of exotic spices and freshly baked bread, hinting at the culinary delights prepared for the occasion. Fruits of various colors and shapes adorn the tables, alongside dishes filled with roasted vegetables, savory lentil stews, and fragrant herb-infused grains, mingling with the sound of joyful laughter and lively music. The hall, illuminated by flickering torchlight and the soft glow of fire bowls filled with burning resin, is a sight to behold, while garlands of fragrant flowers hang from the rafters, infusing the space with their sweet perfume.

At the center of the hall, the banquet table stands as a symbol of abundance, laden with platters of succulent fruits, honeyed cakes, and other delights. Skilled musicians fill the air with melodies, their voices rising and falling in harmony with the rhythm of the drums and lyres, weaving a tapestry of sound that speaks to the soul.

Uldako's heart swells with gratitude as he takes in the scene before him, the warmth of fellowship and the promise of new beginnings infusing his soul with hope and joy. With each passing moment, the anticipation of the impending ceremony grows, imbuing him with clarity of purpose and destiny.

Adam's voice breaks through the air, calling him to attention. "Follow me, Uldako," Adam beckons. "Ishara is on her way, and it is time to begin."

Uldako follows, his chest tight with nervous excitement. "I've never seen a wedding before," he confesses to Adam, feeling a mix of curiosity and uncertainty.

Adam kindly explains the significance of marriage and the joyous celebration that follows. With a tremble in his voice, Uldako expresses his heartfelt gratitude to Adam, touched by the great elder's willingness to officiate their union.

The music begins again, this time in a triumphant announcement. Uldako feels his whole being come alive. His emotions threaten to overwhelm him as he realizes the meaning of the occasion. With a deep breath, he attempts to steady himself, knowing that this is a moment he will remember for the rest of his days.

All at once, the grand entrance of Ishara commands everyone's attention. Gasps of awe ripple through the crowd as they behold her beauty. She is adorned in a simple yet elegant wedding dress made of flowing, pristine honey-colored fabric, adorned with delicate, intricate patterns that reflect the light. Her long black hair cascades down her back in soft waves, adorned with a crown of fresh, fragrant flowers. Her deep blue eyes shine with joy and serenity, captivating all who look upon her.

Uldako's eyes meet hers and hold, and for a moment, time stands still. In that instant, he is overcome by a flood of emotions, awe, gratitude, and profound love. Her presence radiates purity and grace, and Uldako feels as if he is seeing her for the first time.

As Ishara approaches him, radiant and resplendent, Uldako can scarcely believe this blessing. Ishara, the most beautiful and wonderful woman he has ever met, has chosen to be his wife. He would have never imagined that the captivating woman at the treehouse so long ago would become his wife. Without warning, a flood of memories rushes through his mind, from the day they first met to this very moment. Uldako feels an overwhelming responsibility to be the man she deserves.

Ishara steps to Uldako's side as Adam's voice rises, filling the hall, guiding the gathered guests to their seats. Adam, with his long, flowing beard and eyes filled with ancient wisdom, stands before them, embodying the significance of this moment.

His voice fills the hall, resonating with the weight of divine truth and ancient tradition. "Marriage is a sacred bond, a reflection of the unity we share with *Il*," Adam declares. "It is a covenant, an enduring promise to love, honor, and support one another through life's trials and triumphs.

As Adam continues to speak, Uldako struggles to absorb every word, his mind grappling with the gravity of the event.

Adam elaborates on the sanctity of marriage, explaining that it is not just a union of two souls, but a divine joining, an act where God Himself weaves two lives into one.

Uldako's understanding of marriage begins to shift, realizing that it holds far greater significance than he ever imagined.

At last, Adam reaches the pivotal moment. "Uldako, do you take Ishara as your wife? Do you vow to love her not only with your heart but through the love of *Il*, in both times of peace and in times of hardship? And Ishara, do you vow the same to Uldako?"

Tears of joy escape down their cheeks as both Uldako and Ishara voice their vows, their words echoing throughout the hall for all to hear.

After their vows, pledging not only their love but their devotion to *Il*, Adam offers his final blessing and prayer. With great reverence, he seals their union before the gathered witnesses and the divine presence that seems to fill the very air. The moment feels thick with meaning, and the presence of *Il* feels almost visible.

Then, with a smile that reflects both joy and solemnity, Adam lifts his hands in blessing as the prayer ends. He looks at Ishara, takes her hand and places it in Uldako's, the joining of hands sealed before *Il*.

Uldako's heart drums with overwhelming love and gratitude. Their eyes meet, and in that moment, the world around them fades away. The hall erupts in cheers and applause, marking the beginning of the joyous celebrations. Inspired by the romantic atmosphere, Kesia surprises Shamgar with a kiss on his cheek. Their eyes meet, and in that moment, they know they are meant to be together.

Shamgar, the boastful warrior, is rendered speechless and humbled by Kesia's affectionate gaze, the first woman he has ever truly desired to be his wife.

Throughout the night, laughter echoes through the hall, stories are shared, and bonds are strengthened. As the festivities wind down and the guests begin to depart, Seth guides Uldako and Ishara to their own shelter, where they can savor the intimacy of their first night together as husband and wife.

The next morning, as the first light of dawn filters through the trees, Uldako and Ishara prepare themselves for the journey back to the temporary camp where the newly liberated slaves await. Stepping toward the gate, they are greeted by Seth and a few others.

Zak, vibrant as ever, spots them first and announces, "Look, here come the newlyweds!"

The group breaks into cheers as Uldako and Ishara draw near, feeling the warmth of the welcome wash over them.

Seth wastes no time in introducing the newcomers to their party, two teams assembled to aid in the establishment of Uldako's new camp. "Uldako, meet Brockar, leader of the builder group, and Herkal, leader of the scout group!"

Seizing the moment, Seth suggests, "I know you were planning on returning to the temporary camp of your people, but how about I first show you what I believe to be the best location for your new camp? If you agree, Zak can fetch your people while we begin the planning phase for your new home."

Uldako and Ishara exchange a glance, their eyes filled with excitement. They nod in agreement, eager to explore the potential site for their future sanctuary. With a heartfelt greeting, Zak sets off toward the temporary camp to gather their people, while Seth and the others embark on the journey to the ideal location for Uldako's new camp.

As they traverse the verdant landscape, a quiet excitement grows within Uldako. The path leads them through ancient groves and along the banks of a sparkling stream, the natural beauty of the world surrounding them. Every step brings them closer to a place that could become a haven for their community, a sanctuary in troubled times.

After some time, they finally arrive at a breathtaking place: a serene landscape dotted with rolling hills, majestic trees, and a shimmering lake nearby. Uldako's eyes widen in wonder at the lush vegetation and vibrant wildlife.

He turns to Seth, "This is beyond what I could have imagined. It is perfect, Seth. Thank you."

Seth chuckles heartily. "It's our pleasure. Now, while we wait on Zak to bring Hak, Dak, and the others, let's get started on laying the foundations for your new camp."

Uldako gives a steady nod of affirmation, and together with Seth and Brockar, they delve into discussions about the layout of the camp. As they plan the outline and foundations, Herkal and his warriors move to set up protective positions in the area, ensuring the others can focus on construction without safety concerns.

The trio discusses the placement of communal areas, living quarters, and defensive structures, their excitement apparent as they envision the future of the new sanctuary. The lush greenery and the tranquil lake provide a perfect backdrop for their plans, symbolizing hope and renewal.

After much deliberation, Uldako, Seth, and Brockar reach a consensus. The camp will boast a sprawling oval fence with two gates, the largest facing south.

The other will be positioned to the North, but hidden from plain sight. At the heart of the camp, they decide, will stand a small altar dedicated to *Il* where sacrifices will be made, symbolizing the primacy of their faith in the lives of those who dwell within Uldako's refuge.

The camp will be partitioned into four distinct areas. To the east, where the sun heralds the dawn of each new day, lies the living quarters. To the south, they plan to establish the training and educational zone—a space where the members of the camp will hone their minds and bodies.

To the west, the craft courts will be erected, where skilled artisans can fashion tools, clothing, and various essentials. Lastly, to the north, they envision a vast area designated for cultivation, where crops can be safely planted and livestock kept to aid in the village's sustenance. Uldako has sheep in mind for Kunai, as he suggested to him so long ago.

With roles assigned and tasks set forth, Brockar swiftly prepares his team. Their first objective: erecting the protective fence, a vital barrier against both the wild and any hostile forces. Once the defense is secured, their focus will shift to constructing shelters fashioned from wood and stone, ensuring the safety and comfort of all who call this burgeoning community home.

Days pass, and one morning, Herkal approaches Uldako and Seth with urgent news. "I have just received word from our scouts that Zak and the group are in sight and will be here soon."

Uldako swiftly prepares himself, taking a refreshing dip in the nearby lake to cleanse his body. With Ishara's assistance, he ensures that his mother's shelter is prepared for her arrival.

As they put the finishing touches in place, they spot the group drawing near. Uldako's heart swells with joy at the sight of his people in the distance. He notices with delight that his mother appears more content than before, her figure suggesting she has gained a bit of weight. It pleases him as he assumes she was well taken care of.

Upon their arrival at the camp, Uldako and Ishara stand ready to warmly greet the group. Uldako shouts with joy, "Welcome to your new home, everyone!" He gestures proudly to the sprawling land before them.

After a moment of shocked silence, a wave of applause erupts, and tears of gratitude wash over the assembled freed slaves as the reality of their newfound freedom and opportunity dawns upon them. For many, it is their first taste of a true home, and the realization is overwhelming.

Uldako watches as they absorb the beauty and size of their new surroundings.

Then, he addresses them, "Please follow the instructions of Seth and his master builder, Brockar. Then the rest of the day is yours to make your own. We will convene for a meeting at sunset to establish a few camp rules."

The group disperses, eager to begin crafting their new homes under Seth and Brockar's guidance.

Uldako steps toward his mother and gives her a long embrace and exclaims, "*Ama*! I would have never imagined that we would stand here, free from the pain and suffering we endured, now establishing our own safe camp, a haven for all who are still bound in body and mind!"

Their eyes meet, bound by emotion. Deborah, her voice trembling with emotion, says, "I am so proud of you, Uldako! I don't have words to explain what I am feeling."

Uldako places his hands on his mother's shoulders as he looks her in the eyes with a playful smile forming on his lips. "Then I wonder how you will feel to hear that Ishara and I are married."

Deborah tilts her head, her eyebrows lifting in surprise. "Why did you not tell me? Was this recently or long ago?"

Uldako glances toward Ishara in the distance then back at his mother. "We took the opportunity when we were invited at Adam's camp. I would have loved for you to have been there, but I know what you have been through. I wanted you to stay and heal."

His mother pulls him into a tight embrace, tears streaming down her cheeks. "There is no need to explain," she says softly. "I understand. I have begun to heal, though I am not yet myself again. I would not have been ready for such a journey to such a place. Not in this state. I would prefer to feel a bit more like myself when I meet someone as special as Adam and Eve."

She leans back, holding him at arm's length, looking into his eyes. "But Uldako, I am so glad for you…so proud. My little boy is a husband now…" Her voice falters. "You know, when I met your—"

She stops herself. A shadow passes over her face, her eyes falling with a quiet sadness. But Uldako meets her with love and understanding, saying nothing for a moment.

Then he surprises her by asking, "I wonder if my *abba*, Azar, would have been proud of us."

Deborah's eyes widen in shock, her mouth opening slightly before she asks, "How do you know that name?"

Uldako looks at his mother with a calm demeanor. "*Il-Il* told me, and I understand you probably have your reasons for not telling me about my *abba*, but now that I am older, I would like to know about him."

Deborah takes in Uldako's words, her mind grappling with the change of events. Then she begins, her voice filled with awe, "It is astonishing that *Il-Il* spoke to you! I believe it was Him, the Lord, because only He can know such things."

She blinks, clearing the haze of shock, then continues, "Your *abba* was indeed Azar, a man from the North. He was much older than I, and we had only a short time together before he was…We were attacked on a very dark day. He fought valiantly, but he was killed, and I was taken into slavery while carrying you in my belly. I never spoke about it to you because it was too difficult for me, and I thought it would have been harder for you to endure slavery if you knew about it."

Uldako knows this is not the time to judge his mother's decision not to tell him, but to allow her to speak what is in her heart.

He nods and murmurs, "I understand. Tell me, what kind of man was he?"

Deborah's face lights up with a nostalgic smile as she remembers the man she loved. "I was from the South, he from the North, but we met one day when I was out looking for fruits near our home. He was the first northerner I had ever met, but he was different, gentle yet strong."

Uldako smiles softly. "He's one of Adam's younger *dumu*! I first heard the name when Adam mentioned how much I resembled his late *dumu-nita*, Azar. And then, when *Il-Il* called me Uldako, *dumu-nita* of Deborah and Azar, it all made sense." Uldako turns to his mother, searching her eyes to see if she had known he was a son of Adam all along.

Deborah's brow furrows in thought. "I never knew. For some reason, Azar did not want to talk about his past, and I never pushed him. I never knew, even to this day, but I would love to learn more!"

A smile crosses Uldako's lips as he responds, "Yes, I would like to know more about him as well. But tell me what you already know about him, please, *Ama*!"

With a joyous heart, Deborah begins to reminisce about Azar. "Uldako, he was a great man, full of wisdom, and a formidable warrior. He cared deeply about those around him, and Uldako, you look so much like him, and I am so sorry for never talking about him. It was just so hard…" Deborah's voice breaks as tears stream down her face, realizing she has kept her feelings locked away for too long.

Uldako gently embraces her, offering comfort. "Let me take you to your new shelter, and then we can talk more if you want to."

As Uldako and his mother continue their heartfelt conversation, Ishara and the others quietly step back, offering them some privacy. Respecting the intimate moment between mother and son, the rest of the group resumes their work on the camp, the sounds of their efforts blending with the natural harmony of their surroundings.

Time passes gently, and the sun sinks low, painting the sky orange and pink as Uldako calls the evening meeting. Looking across the camp, he sees all the weary but determined faces of those gathered. Uldako stands before them, feeling pride and responsibility within.

"I commend you all for your hard work today," he begins, steady and strong. "I eagerly anticipate the day when our camp is fully realized, a true sanctuary for us all. However, we cannot afford to delay our operations until then. Tomorrow, we must begin functioning as one people. A new clan!"

He pauses, letting his words sink in, and continues, "We need to prioritize tasks such as gathering food, crafting tools and weapons, and training for scouting and patrol duties. Each of us possesses unique skills that will contribute to the collective good. Your efforts today have laid the groundwork, but our journey has only just begun."

The crowd murmurs in approval, and Uldako senses their trust, strengthening his resolve to lead with wisdom and courage.

"You are already familiar with your daily tasks, as they were assigned. Please continue in those roles that were given to you. If you would like another role, please speak with me, Ishara, Zak, Dak, Hak, or Khoran."

He pauses, inspecting the attentive faces, and then continues, "Now, we need to establish a few rules to ensure our peaceful coexistence and mutual respect."

As Uldako lays out the rules, Ishara seizes the moment to speak quietly with Deborah. "How is the little one doing?" she whispers.

Deborah, visibly uneasy, hesitates before responding, "I believe it's healthy." She glances away, clearly unsettled. After a brief pause, Deborah turns to meet Ishara's eyes and says, "Listen, Ishara, I plan to tell Uldako the truth about the baby after the meeting. Will you stand with me when I do?"

Ishara bows her head slightly. "Of course! You will always have my support."

Deborah takes a deep breath, her concern clearly visible in her eyes. "I'm not sure how Uldako will react, and—"

Ishara interrupts gently, sensing Deborah's fear. "Your *dumu-nita* has grown into a wise man, especially after embracing *Il* as his Lord. I believe he'll handle it well. Nothing can separate you from his love," she says with comfort and reassurance.

Deborah's expression softens, gratitude evident in her smile as she acknowledges Ishara's words. The bond between the two women strengthens in that moment, both of them ready to face whatever comes next.

As Uldako concludes the meeting, he declares, "Once again, I welcome you all to our new home. From this day forth, this camp shall be known as E-šarra! My desire is for this camp to serve as a pillar of light! It reflects our optimism, resilience, and unwavering faith in *Il*, despite any challenges or hardships we may face in this world."

Uldako looks at them and sees conviction in their faces—except for a few who still appear puzzled at the mention of *Il*, the Most High. He realizes that many of them have only begun to learn fragments of the truth since their freedom and journey north, but it is time to make things clear, here and now.

"I know many of you have suffered under those who serve other gods—*Enki*, *Ninurta*, and others," he begins. "Some of you even call on the name of *An*, believing him to be the Most High. But your eyes have been opened. The true *Dingir*, the God of love and righteousness, would never delight in slavery or the wickedness of men.

"There is only one true *Dingir*! The rest—the so-called divine beings, the *anunnaki* they worship—are dark spirits who rebel against Him. *Il*, the Most High, is not *An*. *Il* is the Creator who commands hosts of spirits of light that war against the darkness in the unseen realms.

"*Il* hates the yoke that bound you. You are not beasts—you are made in His image! You came from darkness, but *Il* gives you the freedom to choose between light and darkness. So choose this day whom you will serve: the fallen *dingir-meš*, or the true *Dingir*, *Il*, the Most High.

"As for me and my house, we will serve only the Lord of light. If any of you still wish to follow darkness, then you are not welcome among us. But if your heart longs for truth, then stand with me! Serve the Most High, and let us bring His light into this dark world. What say you? Will you follow *Il* with me?"

As one they all respond, "We will follow *Il*!" The cries of conviction ripple through the crowd as they all share this life-changing moment in their lives.

Uldako takes a moment to drink in the sight before him, looking at the faces of all those who have been set free, their expressions of hope and conviction clear.

The flickering light of the fires casts a warm glow on the gathering, symbolizing the light they now carry within. He feels pride swelling in his chest, tempered by the responsibility he bears, knowing that this is only the beginning of a great movement. The atmosphere hums with expectation and the promise of a new dawn, as they stand on the threshold of a brighter future.

"Together, we will grow, we will strengthen, and we will free the captives from their yoke, inviting them to join our cause, all in the name of *Il*!"

The crowd erupts in cheers, their voices echoing through the night, and Uldako bids them a good night. As the crowd begins to disperse, people exchange excited murmurs and heartfelt embraces, their hearts lifted by Uldako's words.

Walking toward Ishara and Deborah at the fire near their shelter, Uldako is joined by Kunai, Seth, and Šarru. Sitting among his loved ones, Uldako takes a moment to soak in the tranquility of the night. The warmth of the fire and the gentle hum of conversation create a sense of calm. Looking over the land, he sees flickering lights scattered across the camp, a sight that fills him with great peace.

The stars above glisten like distant gems, and the gentle breeze carries the scent of pine and earth. Deborah, her voice gentle yet resolute, delivers unexpected news. "My *dumu*, I have something important to say."

Uldako's eyes meet his mother's, full of emotion, sensing the gravity of her words. The flickering firelight illuminates her face, revealing determination mixed with nervousness and vulnerability. He waits as Deborah takes a moment to gather her courage. The tension in the air is almost tangible, every second stretching into eternity.

Finally, with the tension at its peak, Deborah takes a deep breath and declares, "I am with new life in my belly."

Her voice fades, but the meaning remains, heavy with significance. Uldako sits in the midst of a swirling tempest of emotions, his heart torn between conflicting currents. At first, the mere thought of a new sibling ignites a spark of joy within him. Yet, foreboding grips him, casting a shadow over his excitement. With the weight of his mother's words heavy upon him, Uldako gathers his thoughts, his voice trembling with uncertainty as he poses the question that hangs heavily in the air.

"It is a blessing to welcome another into our family, but who is the *abba*?"

Deborah's gaze drifts to the flickering flames, her expression grave and burdened with the truth of her confession. Sensing the seriousness of the moment, Seth offers to give them privacy, but Deborah declines, recognizing the value of his presence in this pivotal moment. With a deep breath, she unveils the truth, her words laden with sorrow and regret.

"The child's *abba* is none other than one of the *anunnaki*, called Azazel." She looks down, a single tear slipping down her cheek.

Uldako's eyes dart to Ishara, the memory of their first encounter in the treetops flooding back with startling clarity. He recalls her mentioning that exact name when they first met. The atmosphere grows thick with tension as Uldako processes the significance of this revelation. He notices a flicker of recognition in Ishara's eyes, her gaze fixed on him with shock and concern. The firelight dances across her features, highlighting the intensity of the moment.

Seth lets out a heavy sigh, his expression of disbelief and shock unsettling Uldako even more. He has never seen Seth so shaken, a clear sign that he recognizes the name.

Something is wrong, something is terribly wrong, Uldako reflects in silence.

Time seems to slow, the crackling of the fire and the murmurs of the camp fading into the background as a sudden tremor passes through Uldako, realizing the gravity of the forces they are up against.

Deborah's voice trembles with emotion as she continues, her words choked by tears. "They hailed him as a benevolent deity, a *dingir* blessing me with his favor. But now…now I know the truth."

Her tears flow freely, a torrent of anguish and remorse unleashed as she confesses, "I was unaware of his true nature, unaware until you saved me and revealed the truth about these fallen spirits, Uldako."

Uldako feels a mix of fury and compassion, his heart aching for his mother's pain while the gravity of the situation presses down on him. He reaches out, taking her hand in his, offering silent support.

Ishara's whispered shock cuts through the tension, her voice trembling with disbelief and fear. "Azazel…then that means, this *dumu*…" she breathes out, her words floating in the air like an ominous cloud. She turns her eyes to Seth, seeking more answers in his solemn expression. "Seth?" Ishara's voice quivers.

Uldako watches the unfolding scene with a sense of surreal detachment, as if caught in the midst of a bewildering dream.

Seth meets Ishara's desperate eyes with a heavy sigh, acknowledging the weight of her unspoken questions. He turns to Deborah, sensing the heavy burden she carries, as though glimpsing it across past, present, and all that may yet to come. "Deborah, I am so sorry for what they forced you to endure."

Uldako remains frozen, grappling with the enormity of the revelation.

Seth addresses the group, his voice steady but filled with gravity. "If you do not know who the *abba* is, allow me to explain. Azazel is the leader of a powerful faction of fallen spirits, also known by some as the Watchers. He wields immense power and influence. Deborah, if you truly carry his *dumu*, then this is just the beginning of a difficult path ahead."

The atmosphere thickens with more tension and dread as they listen to Seth's words. Uldako feels the heaviness of the revelation pressing down on him, his mind struggling to comprehend the full implications of what has been revealed. He sees the concern in Ishara's eyes and the worry etched on the faces of his companions.

Uldako remains uncertain of how to respond, while Seth, seasoned by centuries and adept at handling unexpected situations, persists in the conversation. "Deborah, it's crucial that you understand: This babe will not be ordinary. It will be a unique blend, part human, part fallen spirit, a Nephilim. A child for proving, among the first of its brood. If it proves successful, I fear more fallen spirits will follow suit, spawning legions of such beings."

Seth pauses, taking in their reactions before resuming, "We're in uncharted territory here. No one knows what to anticipate with these hybrids, and thus far, there's been no precedent. This may indeed be the inaugural birth, and we must remain vigilant. I regret burdening you with this truth, Deborah, but in my experience, foresight is crucial for facing the unknown."

Deborah's fear is clearly visible, her eyes searching Uldako's for reassurance. Uldako, with a tenderness born of deep love, envelops her in a tight embrace, silently offering solace.

Deborah, overwhelmed, whispers, "I do not know what to do. I am afraid."

Uldako, his heart heavy with his mother's anguish, gently lifts her chin to meet his eyes. "Do not fear, *Ama*," his voice steady despite all the emotions within. "You are not alone. We will walk this path together, every step of the way. *Il* is with us!"

The warmth of his embrace and the certainty in his words provide a moment of comfort amidst the turmoil. The bond between mother and son is a flame of hope in the face of the unknown challenges that lie ahead.

The group sits in silence, appreciating the strong bond between Uldako and his mother. As Deborah gently pulls away from Uldako, she bids them all a kind good night before retreating to rest.

Seth seizes the moment, quickly pulling Uldako aside, his expression heavy with concern. "I'm sorry, Uldako. I never anticipated such a trial for someone so close to us, but I must caution you to temper your hopes."

Uldako regards him with both curiosity and apprehension as Seth continues.

"Allow me to speak what I hold within: I cannot guarantee your *ama*'s survival through the pregnancy or birth. And if the *dumu* proves to be malevolent, we may need to intervene before it grows too powerful. Please do not be deceived; fallen spirits hate us, and their desire is to devour all of us. There is no good in them! This *dumu* will not be human, and I need you to be ready for anything."

Uldako, grappling with the weight of Seth's words, takes a moment to collect his thoughts before responding, "I understand. Let us proceed with caution and take the time to assess the situation fully."

Seth acknowledges Uldako's words, adding, "Uldako, I realize this is an unimaginable situation for you. But it's crucial to comprehend the potential dangers posed by the fallen spirits and the Nephilim. This is bigger than your *ama*, as it involves the entire human race. I believe their aim is to corrupt the pure lineage of humanity, to increase the wickedness on earth, and to potentially obstruct the birth of the Lightborn. Now it seems the first of its kind might be born in the North, to live in our own kingdom of light, but I will not allow that to come to pass."

Uldako's eyes, heavy with the weight of their conversation, address Seth. "Like you, I do not like this at all, but we need time to process all of it. It's late, and we won't make any headway tonight. We still have many moons before the birth. Let's rest and take some time to assess the situation with minds that are fully rested."

Seth acknowledges Uldako's request with a solemn nod before bidding him good night. Ishara, sensing Uldako's need for comfort, draws near and shares a silent understanding with him. Without a word, she envelops him in a reassuring embrace, offering solace in her presence.

As the warmth of her embrace begins to ease his troubled mind, Ishara gestures toward their shelter, wordlessly urging Uldako to seek rest for the night. With a final glance at the darkened horizon, Uldako feels the strain of the impending challenges, but also the flicker of hope that tomorrow might bring clarity. The night is thick with unspoken fears and lingering questions, leaving Uldako with an urgency to uncover the truth about the Nephilim. As he steps into the shelter, he knows their journey is far from over. The true test still lies ahead, yet for tonight, there is nothing more he can do. He must rest.

45

Nephilim

As the morning light washes the landscape in soft hues, Uldako stirs from sleep, but peace evades him. Thoughts churn within, of the past, the future, and the sibling soon to be born. Seeking clarity, he quietly rises and walks toward the lake, hoping the stillness of the water might calm his mind.

But as he approaches the shoreline, he pauses in surprise; his mother is already there. She stands motionless, hands resting gently on her belly, gazing out over the tranquil waters.

Uldako smiles faintly. "Like mother, like *dumu-nita*, I guess."

He steps beside her. They share a quiet glance, warm and wordless, drawing comfort simply from being near each other. The serene beauty of the dawn glows around them, a tender contrast to the burden they both carry inside.

Wrapping an arm gently around her, Uldako teases, "You'd think we were born with fins, the way we keep ending up near water."

His mother chuckles and gives him a soft nudge, her smile touched with weariness. "Well, we both know that I found you in a tree, I just had to cut off your tail and teach you to stop swinging from branch to branch. No matter how mighty you have become, you will always be my little *ugubi*."

Uldako chuckles and drinks in the serene moment with his *ama*. Then the lightness fades from his face as he speaks with care, "*Ama*, about the—"

She meets his eyes, her expression tender but troubled. "Uldako," she interrupts gently, "I don't want to talk about it. Not yet. I just need a little more time to let it settle. But promise me one thing."

He places a hand on her shoulder, his voice low and full of love. "What?"

She turns her eyes back to the lake, as if searching the still waters for a glimpse of what lies ahead. Her eyes shimmer with quiet tears, the sorrow in her heart too deep for words.

"Uldako," she says softly, her voice trembling, "you are the only one in this world I trust completely. Whatever may come, promise me you'll care for your new *šeš* or *nin*, no matter how he or she appears."

Uldako is startled by her request, stunned that she would ask such a thing. He starts to voice his concerns, "But we have no idea what it—"

His mother interrupts him firmly, "It doesn't matter. Family is family. Vow to me, Uldako!" Reluctant to make such a commitment, Uldako lowers his gaze, but Deborah draws him closer, her hands firm on his shoulders, her voice unwavering. "Promise me, Uldako. Assure me you won't forsake your family!"

Uldako feels the yoke of this vow settle upon him, but as he looks into his mother's eyes, he understands the depth of her request. With a resigned nod, he finally relents, "Fine, I give you my word."

Deborah exhales a breath of relief she didn't realize she was holding, her expression softening with gratitude. Turning her eyes to the tranquil expanse of the lake, she whispers, "Thank you, my *dumu-nita*, thank you."

They linger in the silence, their thoughts drifting toward the uncertain horizon of the future. After a while, Uldako breaks the quiet, his voice gentle, "I'm going to prepare breakfast and then begin organizing the camp. Would you care to join me for some food?"

Deborah declines with a gentle smile, her eyes reflecting a desire to remain a while longer in quiet contemplation. "I'll stay here for a bit," she murmurs, "to gather my thoughts."

Uldako nods, understanding her need for solitude.

Just as he steps away, his mother turns around, her eyes filled with hope and vulnerability. "Actually, Uldako, after hearing so much about *Il* from you and the encounter you had, I, too, want to worship Him! How do I vow myself to Him or belong to Him?"

A warm, graceful smile spreads across Uldako's face as he walks back to her, his heart swelling with joy. He gently takes her hands in his, looking into her eyes with deep love and reassurance.

"*Il's* grace is immense, *Ama*! He loves us deeply, but He hates the evil we do. All you need to do is repent of the wrongs you have done in your past, confess with your mouth that He is your Lord, and believe it in your heart."

Tears glisten in his mother's eyes as Uldako guides her through the confession. Her voice trembles with sincerity as she speaks the words, her heart opening to the divine presence she has long yearned for. Uldako's own voice is steady and filled with conviction, each word a bridge bringing her closer to the peace she seeks.

When the confession is complete, Uldako's mother closes her eyes, a serene expression settling over her features. Uldako watches in awe as peace settles in her, dispelling the shadows of fear and sorrow. She opens her eyes, and for the first time in her life, they shine with a tranquil light.

They embrace, a warm and tender hug that speaks of forgiveness, redemption, and a shared bond strengthened by faith. The weight of the unborn child and their uncertain future still lingers, but in this moment, they are enveloped in a divine calm.

"Thank you, Uldako," she whispers with choked emotion. "There is much I still do not know, but I feel a peace I've never known."

Uldako holds her close, his eyes wet with tears. "I'm so glad, *Ama. Il* is with us, and we will face whatever comes, together."

In that embrace, they find solace and strength, united by their newfound faith and the unbreakable bond of family.

As he walks away, he glances back at his mother, standing by the lake, a solitary figure against the backdrop of the serene morning. He feels a deep sense of responsibility and love, knowing that their journey is far from over but also filled with the promise of new beginnings.

Over breakfast, Uldako, Ishara, Seth, Zak, Dak, Hak, Kunai, Kesia, Shamgar, and a few others gather to discuss the work ahead in establishing the new camp. Šarru lies close beside Uldako, sensing his unrest. The great bear leans his weight against him, a silent gesture of loyalty that eases Uldako's heart. The group eats quietly, exchanging uneasy glances, none daring to speak of Deborah's news from the night before, though it weighs on every mind.

Then Kunai, having already finished his portion well ahead of the rest, breaks the silence with a grin stretching from ear to ear. "So that was just the appetizer, right? What's next?"

Laughter erupts around the fire, the tension melting like morning mist. Seth chuckles, shaking his head. "Kunai, I've seen hungry wolves with less appetite than you."

The laughter breaks the ice, and they begin to talk casually about the plans for the day, their hearts lifted by the humor.

Seth outlines the tasks, "We need to guide the men and women in constructing the camp. Additionally, we'll dispatch a team to gather food and another to scout out an area to the south, ensuring the safety and sustenance of our budding community."

With a clear plan in place, they act, each person taking on their roles with renewed strength. The camaraderie and shared purpose drive them forward, transforming the daunting task of building their camp into a collective mission filled with hope and determination.

• • •

Many full moons pass…

As the seasons turn, Uldako's refuge, E-šarra, blossoms into a fountain of hope in a fractured world. What once lived only in his imagination now stands as a thriving settlement, its stone paths and rising walls echoing with life. Over six hundred souls have found sanctuary within, including nearly four hundred seasoned warriors. E-šarra has become more than a camp; it is a fortress of freedom, a bold defiance against the shadow of slavery.

Under Uldako's steadfast leadership and alongside other esteemed figures, the camp grows into a flame of resistance. Two dedicated parties embark on dangerous quests, venturing into the unknown to seek out slave camps or traveling slave traders to free the oppressed. Their courage and compassion inspire others to join their cause, swelling their ranks and spreading their influence far and wide.

E-šarra's success is marked by its thriving marketplace, the sounds of children's laughter, and the determined strides of warriors in training. Each day, the camp embodies the hope and strength needed to confront the pervasive darkness, proving the enduring power of unity under *Il* Most High!

As evening settles over the land, Ishara stands on a hill and looks down with humble gratitude at their thriving safe camp, where hundreds of fire-lit circles flicker in the dusk. Laughter and the murmur of conversation drift through the air. Each soul gathered here is a quiet triumph over the darkness of slavery. She, Uldako, and their companions have carved a path of hope through the shadows, one quest at a time. With every life they touch, their reputation spreads, and so does their impact, lighting flames of freedom in hearts once numb with despair. Ishara's hair has grown longer, flowing gracefully down her back, and something else has grown as well—life in her belly. Her eyes, once filled with uncertainty, now shine with deepened assurance.

A ram's horn blares loudly across the camp, clear and commanding. Ishara's pulse quickens. She turns toward the sound and hurries toward the gate. The full moon spills silver light over the earth, spreading its dark shade and sharpening every edge. In the distance, a band of riders emerges, Uldako at the head, flanked by Zak and his elite warriors, returning from another victory. Their torches blaze in the night, their silhouettes glowing with glory.

Ishara draws a sharp breath at the sight of Uldako, whose hair is styled in a new fashion, both sides of his head shaved clean, while the top is tied back in a rugged braid trailing down his spine. His beard, longer now and carefully braided, frames his face with the hardened elegance of a seasoned leader.

His new armor has been forged by Kesia, who is quickly gaining a reputation as one of the best smiths in the North. It is a masterpiece of thick, battle-tested leather, supple enough to move with him, yet strong enough to deflect a blade. Draped over his shoulders is the dense, majestic fur of a sabertooth cat, its coarse texture exuding primal strength. Affixed to the left pauldron, the creature's skull, taken from the very beast that claimed Ruk, rests like a silent vow: a reminder to lead with courage, but also with wisdom, never to let pride cost another life.

Across his torso, a great eagle is emblazoned, carved in exquisite detail. Its wings stretch wide, talons poised, the symbol of *Il*, the Most High, etched into every line. It speaks of divine protection and righteous authority. Uldako's form beneath the armor has grown stronger, every muscle honed through tireless training and countless battles. His eyes, once clouded with doubt, now burn with clarity and conviction, the gaze of a leader shaped by both suffering and grace.

Ishara's heart swells with pride as she watches Uldako approach. The twilight sky casts a golden light across his face, and for a moment, the world seems to still. Her breath catches again. As he passes through the gate, the guards erupt in cheers, their voices echoing across the camp like a wave of triumph. Behind him trail the newly freed, exhausted, dust-covered, but alive and brimming with hope.

Uldako's voice rises above the joyful clamor, steady and sure. "To the hearth—eat, rest. You are safe now." His words are few, but warm, each one landing like a balm on weary hearts. He moves among them with quiet authority, no longer just a fighter, but a shepherd of souls.

As the commotion of the arrival begins to settle, Uldako's eyes turn to Ishara, standing quietly near the gate, her figure illuminated by the moonlight. She places a gentle hand on her swollen belly, and Uldako's heart warms at the sight. He strides toward her, his steps purposeful but filled with tenderness. Upon reaching her, he wraps his arms around her, the weariness of his long journey dissolving in her presence.

"I missed you, my heartfire," he breathes with affection. He leans down, pressing his forehead gently to hers, letting the silence speak of the love between them. Then, with a playful glint in his eye, he crouches lower and brings his lips close to her belly.

"Your *abba* is home, little one. Back from another victory," he says softly. "I can't wait to meet you! To hold you, and to show you the world we're building for you."

Ishara chuckles, her fingers weaving through Uldako's hair. "Our little warrior grows stronger with every heartbeat," she whispers.

Šarru, still walking through the gate beside Zak, spots Ishara and instantly breaks into a run, overcome with joy. His deep, throaty calls echo through the courtyard—a mix of growls and mournful wails that leave no doubt how much he has missed her.

He slows just before reaching her, careful of the life she carries, and rises halfway onto his hind legs with a pleased, rumbling chuff. His small ears tilt forward as he drops back down, then he lowers his great head and sniffs gently at her rounded belly. Ishara laughs, resting a hand on his fur.

"I'm glad to see you too, Šarru!" she says warmly.

Uldako chuckles, a memory surfacing. "Ishara, I actually had a great gift for you." He glances toward the bear beside him. "But Šarru ate it."

The bear lets out a low groan, gaze dropping to the ground. He shuffles back a step, eyes wide with guilt—a hulking mound of fur and shame. Emotion fills inside Ishara and she calms the great bear, "It's alright, Šarru! I hope you enjoyed it! That can be your reward for protecting Uldako."

The great bear takes a heroic stance, clearly chuffed with himself as he gives a low cheerful growl.

As Ishara sees Hak passing behind the bear, giving a quick wave, she is reminded of their new visitor. "Oh, Uldako! Seth also arrived a few days ago. He says he missed you."

"Ah yes, it has been a long time! I've missed him too. I can't wait to tell him all the things we did. Did you show him the fields?"

Uldako's voice trails off thinking about how Seth feels about his little *šeš*. "Did he say why he is here? And how fares *Ama*?" The excitement in his voice changes to concern.

Before she can answer, an elder of the new freed slaves steps forward, his eyes glistening with gratitude. "The people will sing of this day, Uldako," he says, bowing with quiet reverence. "You have brought hope to many hearts."

Uldako offers a humble nod, clasping the elder's hand with respect. "Not I, but the Most High, and there are still many who need to be set free." His gaze drifts, already fixed on the trials yet to come.

Uldako turns back to Ishara with a playful grin as Hak leads the new group away. "I'm starving, and I'd love to—" But his words are cut short by the sudden thud of hurried footsteps and a sharp, breathless cry.

"Uldako!" Kunai comes sprinting into view, taller now. Joy clings to his voice. "Welcome home!"

Uldako gives Kunai a warm hug, and as he pulls away, he says, "Glad to be here! I was just asking Ishara, how is my *Ama* doing?"

Kunai says, "She is as well as one can expect. The life within was moving a lot today, but she is taking rest now. The two wise women are looking after her."

"It might be wise to let her rest, Uldako! You can see her in the morning," Ishara chimes in. "Let's eat. I am sure you are hungry."

Uldako touches his stomach. "I am famished, and it will be great to catch up with you all! But go on ahead, I'm just going to peek in at *Ama's* shelter, but I'll be with you in a wink of an eye! Save me a spot," he says, running off before they can protest.

As he approaches Deborah's home, he treads softly, careful not to disturb the expectant mother if she's resting. Peering inside, he finds her fast asleep, a rare gift in her uncomfortable state. Even the women who usually hover over her have stepped away, leaving her to an uninterrupted slumber. He watches her for a moment, then withdraws quietly.

As he arrives at the dinner table, Uldako sees Seth waiting. Their eyes meet, and for a moment neither speaks. In that silent exchange, Uldako understands why he has come.

After warm greetings, Ishara and Kunai bring food, and laughter soon fills the air as they share stories of all that has happened. But as night settles in and the fire burns lower, the tone shifts. Light conversation giving way to something heavier.

Uldako meets Seth's eyes, and after a few breaths, he says, "You didn't come only to see how our camp is doing, did you?"

Seth straightens and gives a firm nod. "Uldako, over the last few moons, I've thought of you often. I was curious how things were going with your camp. And I have missed you, Ishara, and Šarru…and perhaps even young Kun, maybe, a little," he adds, sending a faint smile toward Kunai. "You all have become dear to me. So let us speak plainly, directly, and in love.

"Indeed. I believe we are nearing the time of birth. I've given you and Deborah enough privacy and time to mourn and accept what needs to happen. That time has now ended, and so I have come to hear your hearts and to aid you in what must be done when the time comes, if you need it. You know I cannot allow a Nephilim to grow up in the North, nor can we allow the blood of man to become corrupted."

Uldako sits back and lets out a heavy breath. He knows if they begin this conversation right now, it might not go well. Seth's eyes are full of hard conviction, and Uldako needs more time to think, even if it is just a day. It might give Seth some time to soften his heart as well.

Uldako forms a fist and touches it to his chest as he meets Seth's gaze again. "I hold deep respect for you, great one, and I understand your heart," he says. "But may I ask that we continue this conversation at sunrise—with my *ama* present? I am weary from the journey, and it would be better to rest my body and mind before such an important discussion. Let us rest our heads, and at dawn we will speak."

Seth studies him for a long moment then nods. "Very well, Uldako. We can continue this tomorrow after breakfast. Just know that I am proud of what you have accomplished here." He rests a firm hand on Uldako's shoulder. "Sleep well, all of you!"

When the others drift away to their shelters for rest, silence settles over the camp. In the dim glow of the burning torches, Uldako sinks into the bed of woven reeds and heavy furs, the warmth of beast hide and the faint scent of cedar wrapping him like a memory of the wild. Ishara rests in his arms, her breathing calm and steady against his chest. As is his habit, Šarru lies asleep at the entrance of the shelter, a silent guardian between them and the dark.

But sleep will not come to Uldako. His mind churns into all directions, but finds not one path ahead. He remembers the promise he made to his mother, but also the warning in Seth's eyes. The fallen ones are moving, their plans as dark as the deep. After so many moons, he finds himself torn between two loyalties: between blood and calling, between his mother and Seth. Yet he knows this is much bigger than his family.

He closes his eyes, but the weight of choice opens them. As the night deepens, Uldako still lies awake, staring into the flickering torchlight. A distant wolf's cry breaks the silence, and Ishara stirs beside him. She blinks, then turns to see his eyes still open.

She knows the battle that rages within him—it reflects the one in her own heart. Reaching out, she lets her hand rest gently on his arm.

"Uldako, my rock," she whispers. "If sleep will not come, then speak with me of what weighs on you. I know it is your *šeš*."

Uldako gives a soft sound of confirmation. "Mmm…" After a few heavy breaths, his voice follows in a low murmur. "No matter what we do, it will be a loss."

He turns his eyes toward Ishara, the firelight glinting faintly in them. "What is in your heart?"

Just as Ishara begins to speak, a scream splits the night—deep, raw, and unnerving. It doesn't stop.

Uldako and Ishara leap to their feet, hearts pounding, and reach for their armor. They know something is terribly wrong.

Before they can fasten the last straps, Kunai is already at the doorway.

"It's Deborah! Come quickly!"

Their hearts hammer in their chests as they all run to Deborah's shelter. Great concern fills Uldako as he sprints toward whatever fate awaits, outpacing the others. The evening air splits with another scream of agony. Uldako runs as fast as his legs can carry him.

He reaches the outside of the shelter first, and a guard hands Uldako a torch without a word.

As Uldako steps into the shelter, Kunai and Ishara arrive, but they wait outside to give him some privacy.

The scene unfolds before Uldako's eyes in a haze of dread and disbelief. The soft light of the torches casts a warm glow, highlighting the tender embrace of his mother as she cradles a newborn babe. Yet, this gentle scene is set against the harsh reality of blood-stained surroundings. His mother's face, marked with weariness and pain, radiates a fierce love as she holds the infant close.

But it is the appearance of the newborn that makes the blood drain from Uldako's face, revealing the immense ordeal his mother has endured. The babe is enormous, almost twice the size of normal newborns.

With each step, the torchlight lays bare the horror. His mother lies bleeding, a gaping, unnatural wound torn across her abdomen. Uldako freezes. This was no accident. The injury is too severe, too jagged. It came from within or from a blade to get the babe out.

Beside Deborah, two women are frozen in place, their faces pale and eyes wide with shock, mirroring the unrest rising in Uldako's chest. The silence between them is thick, bound by disbelief, fear, and a dawning dread none of them yet dare name.

"*Ama*...?" Uldako stumbles forward, barely able to breathe, but his mother shakes her head, a feeble smile gracing her lips. Deborah's voice, though faint, still carries the depth of a mother's love.

"Uldako, I am going to the Lord's kingdom! Take care of your little *šeš* and remember your promise. I love y—" The sentence remains unfinished as her voice fades into the hushed whispers of eternity, leaving a profound silence in its wake.

A heavy stillness settles over the shelter.

Uldako drops to his knees beside her, clutching her hand as if he could hold her soul in place. "No, *Ama*! Please!" He shouts in deep agony. Then in a low whisper, "Don't leave me," his voice cracking under the weight of sorrow. He closes her eyes and kisses her forehead, her face serene, as though she has glimpsed *Il's* glory in her final moment.

Silence follows. Cold and absolute.

Then comes the cry. High and piercing, it cuts through the grief and echoes through the small shelter. The newborn.

Uldako forgets to breathe. He turns slowly, his chest begins to rise again with shallow gasps. His hands tremble as he reaches for the linen-wrapped bundle. His thoughts swirl with fear and the memory of his mother's final words.

With careful fingers, he peels back the cloth.

What he sees through blurred, tear-filled eyes shifts his sorrow into something far darker—a grief now laced with horror.

The newborn lies before him, grotesque and unnatural. Its frame is unnervingly large for an infant, its chest and limbs thick and muscular, its breadth nearly half its full length, far beyond normal human proportions. The body is dotted with coarse, dark hair, and thick brows jut forward over glowing golden eyes that stare with an eerie, reptilian awareness.

Uldako draws a sharp breath as he notices the hands, each bearing six fingers. The feet, too. Dread grips Uldako's heart as he looks upon this unnatural creature, fearing its presence is a harbinger of unknown horrors yet to come.

He stumbles back a step, dread flooding his chest. *This is unnatural...*

"It's an abomination," says one of the women who helped with the birth.

"Leave me!" Uldako commands them.

As they exit the shelter, Uldako's emotions battle within, his heart torn between crushing grief and burning fury. His hand trembles, instinctively drawn to the hilt of his sword. Every fiber of his being screams to end the creature that stole his mother's life. His breath quickens, vision blurring with rage.

But just as he prepares to strike, his eyes fall upon his mother's still form, her body quiet, her face bearing traces of peace, as if her final moments had been spent in love for the creature, not fear.

The fire within him falters. Doubt pierces the veil of vengeance. His fingers loosen around the hilt. But the war rages inside him—sorrow, wrath, and the haunting echo of her last request, all clashing in painful silence.

"*Ama*, how could you leave me alone…with this thing!" Uldako's voice trembles with anguish, his words choked with sorrow and indignation. The word *monster* lingers on the tip of his tongue, but he cannot bring himself to utter it, not when the memory of his mother's love still lingers in the air.

His eyes fall upon the babe in his arms, a creature born of darkness yet cradled in his mother's embrace. The stark contrast between the child's sinister appearance and the love with which his mother had held for it twists his heart even further, leaving him torn between rage and a sorrowful understanding.

"You are only alive because of her," Uldako murmurs, his voice barely audible.

With each passing moment, his anger begins to ebb, replaced by a dawning realization. Memories of his own suffering at the hands of the slave masters flood his mind, and to his shame, he realizes he has judged this babe in the same way, without it having done anything wrong. With a heavy heart, Uldako recalls his promise to his mother—the solemn vow to protect this child, no matter its origins.

He turns to the lifeless form of his mother again, a silent reminder of her unwavering faith in him.

"Could it be that a part of her goodness resides within this creature?"

The question lingers in his mind, mingling with his sorrow and determination. He wonders if her love and sacrifice have imbued the child with a fragment of her character, a glimmer of hope in the darkness. Uldako's heart, heavy with grief, begins to soften, and he feels a flicker of resolve ignite within him.

"It is only a babe," Uldako whispers softly, his tone softened by compassion. As he looks at the half-breed with new eyes, a sense of kinship mingled with caution begins to stir within him.

"Half of our *ama* is in you, as it is in me. She was good, so maybe, just maybe, there is a small chance that you might turn good, and because of my word, I will look after you…little *šeš*."

Uldako's eyes meet those of the half-breed, a silent exchange passing between them. In that fleeting moment, amidst the chaos of conflicting emotions, he glimpses a spark of humanity, a glimmer of his mother's love shining through the darkness.

With his heart burdened yet steady, Uldako stands up and steps out of the shelter, the child cradled against his chest. The weight in his arms is more than flesh and bone; it is the weight of a promise, of legacy, of a mother's final plea. He does not waver. Though grief clings to him, a quiet resolve begins to take root.

Still waiting anxiously outside, Ishara, Kunai, and Seth turn at the sound of his footsteps. Their eyes widen in disbelief as they behold the infant in his arms. For a moment, no one speaks. The air hangs thick with uncertainty, as they each wrestle with the sight before them and what it might mean for them all.

As Uldako stands beneath the star-studded sky, lifting his new baby brother to the heavens, he brings a desperate plea to *Il*, seeking guidance in the face of uncertainty.

"*Il*! I know Your eyes are upon me! Please, will You guide me to raise my little šeš in the light?"

His words echo into the night, but instead of divine intervention, ominous crimson lights ignite on the horizon. They streak across the heavens like wounds torn open, heralding the arrival of spirits from a realm beyond. For a breath, Uldako stands frozen. Has the veil between realms fallen? Are the dark sons of *Il* choosing to reveal themselves? Or is the Almighty opening their spiritual eyes? None can say. They all see it. All of it.

The world is no longer as it was. It seems, these spirits of the Most High have made their decision to rebel, again. This is an unholy incursion.

Uldako watches in shock and horror as the boundary between realms wavers all over the landscape, far in the distance. From the flickering veil of reality, dark spiritual shapes press through, beings of immense power no longer content to lurk in the unseen realm. One by one, they overstep *Il's* sacred boundary.

Seth strides to Uldako's side, his face like stone as he warns, "They have seen the *dumu* in your arms. It has begun!"

Ishara and Kunai draw closer, their faces pale with awe and horror.

"This child is proof." Seth walks closer, eyes fixed on the swelling ranks of the fallen. "They now know it is possible to sow their seed in our world. The *dumu-nita-meš* of *Il* are crossing the boundaries of the Most High! They will drown the earth in their corruption."

Uldako tightens his grip on the infant, his heart and mind in turmoil. Grief and anger rage within him as he watches the unholy descend upon the world. Across the darkened sky, their vast shapes flicker into being. Great shadows break through the veil between heaven and earth. They descend in wicked power, scattered across distant horizons, unclean beings crossing the boundary *Il* has set. Some fade into cloud and mist; others twist and take diminutive forms as they near the ground. It seems a few take the form of men, but the distance veils all certainty.

Around Uldako, the people of E-šarra emerge from their shelters, eyes wide. The moon's glow casts evil shadows across the ground as more spirits cross the veil, revealing more of what should never be seen.

Uldako steps forward, his silhouette framed by the eerie glow. Truth settles, and he knows that nothing can alter what is unfolding. They cannot stop it, but they can choose how to face it. From the ashes of despair, courage and conviction begin to rise within him like a flame.

"The time has come," Uldako declares with a steady voice.

Seth's jaw tightens as he nods, eyes heavy with understanding. His voice is low, certain. "Yes! These dark spirits of *Il* are no longer Watchers."

The unholy incursion of the fallen *dumu-meš* has begun…and all creation bears witness. Uldako looks to his younger brother in his arms, staring up at him. "The rise of the Nephilim has begun."

The camp stands in stunned silence. Behind Uldako, Ishara places a hand on his shoulder. Kunai steadies his stance, a youth no longer. Šarru growls low, instinctively sensing what words cannot express.

And still, Uldako looks upward. Past the horror. Past the veil. To the promise.

The prophecy of the Lightborn, the One born not of rebellion, but righteousness. The One who will come to shatter the serpent's work.

"Where is He?" Uldako whispers under his breath. "When will He rise, the One to crush the dragon of old?"

The night offers no answer.

But deep in Uldako's soul, a fire has been lit. He does not know when the Lightborn will come. Only that He must.

Seth's voice cracks like a whip, snapping him back to the immediate danger. "Uldako! Give an ear to my words! We are all at risk because of the abomination in your arms. Quickly, give it to me. Let me do what must be done!"

Uldako turns to Seth, his eyes narrowing while he holds the babe closer to his chest. Ishara's eyes dart with tension between them as Seth steps closer.

"What is that bright light? It's heading this way!" Kunai yelps, pointing to the sky

What looks like a ball of dark fire trails through the sky, heading toward them with blazing speed.

"Watch out!" someone screams as the sphere crushes hard into the earth, shaking the camp to its bones. Dust and smoke roll outward like a living storm, the force of the impact ringing in their ears. When the haze parts, a dark figure stands amidst the ruin.

They behold a towering monstrous being, four lengths of a man, a mixture of man and ancient dragon, far beyond mortal shape. His skin gleams like blackened iron drawn from a forge, cracked through with seams of dull crimson light that pulse like a dying heart. Vast wings arch from his back, once fire, now fused with shards of living metal; each movement sheds embers that die before touching the ground. His eyes burn like molten stars behind a face both beautiful and terrible—the visage of a being that once beheld the throne of Heaven. The air around him trembles with heat and ancient hate; the scent of scorched earth fills their lungs.

Before them stands what seems to be a mighty fallen seraph with dark power emanating from his body like living fire turned to shadow. Its fiery serpentine eyes fixate on the babe in Uldako's arms. Fire and ash spill from his mouth as he speaks, his voice a low rolling reverberation that shakes the air.

"That is mine!"

Glossary

INTRODUCTION

Welcome to the glossary of *Lightborn: Dawn of Darkness.* This glossary is designed to serve as a helpful guide for readers, providing clarity on the unique terms, names, and elements of the world in which our main character, Uldako, finds himself. As you journey through this ancient, historical realm, you'll encounter a rich tapestry of characters, creatures, deities, and cultural references rooted in Sumerian, Semite, and Sethite traditions.

This glossary aims to enhance your understanding and enjoyment of the story by offering detailed explanations of these elements, ensuring you can fully immerse yourself in the epic adventure of Uldako and his companions. Use this guide to familiarize yourself with the intricate lore, historical context, and vivid world-building that bring this tale to life.

DEITIES AND RELIGIOUS FIGURES

An (✱): In the ancient Sumerian pantheon, *An* was revered as the Father of the gods and the supreme deity of the heavens. The cuneiform sign ✱ (*Dingir*) denotes divinity in Sumerian and was commonly placed before a god's name. When used alone, however, it specifically referred to *An* himself. In the context of our novel, among the Cainites (descendants of Cain), *An* represents a corrupted remembrance of the original Creator, once worshipped by Seth's family line under the name *Il* (*El*). Over generations, this distortion transformed into the Sumerian figure *An*, who came to be seen as the exalted ruler of the pantheon—a tragic echo of the true God.

Anunnaki (𒀭𒀀𒉣𒈾𒆠): Divine beings, often called the "sons of God" who were revered in ancient times. In Mesopotamian tradition, the *anunnaki* are the offspring of *An* (*Anu*), the god most high. Their name is interpreted as the "royal blood" or "princely seed" of *An*. Under *An*, they were believed to govern the affairs of heaven, earth, and the underworld, shaping creation and maintaining cosmic order. In the world of *Lightborn*, they are linked to the fallen angels of Genesis 6 and possibly the Watchers who defied God and corrupted mankind in the book of Enoch. The term "Watcher" is also found in Scripture (Daniel 4:13, 17, 23), where it refers to heavenly beings observing and carrying out God's decree.

In *Lightborn*, this distinction reflects not different kinds of beings, but different states: those who remained in their heavenly order, and those who were cast down to the earth and became corrupted. Faithful beings may still operate on earth in service of God, while others rebelled and fell from their appointed place. They are spiritual beings—later understood in biblical language as messengers (angels) of God, whether faithful or fallen.

Anzu (𒀭𒅎𒂂𒈾): Often called the "anzu bird": A lion-headed eagle in Mesopotamian myth, known as a powerful guardian of divine realms. Often associated with storms and sacred knowledge, the anzu may also represent the cherubim—heavenly beings who guarded the paradise of *El* atop His holy mountain, later echoed in the Hebrew Scriptures as guardians of Eden.

Ašag-dingir (𒀸𒊕𒀭): A compound term meaning "demonic god" or "corrupted divine being." In Mesopotamian tradition, *Ašag* refers to a destructive demon or plague spirit, and these names may also represent the offspring of the rebellious ones. *Dingir* means "god" or "divine being." In *Lightborn*, *Ašag-dingir* describes the *Nephilim*: powerful hybrid beings born from the union of fallen divine beings and mortal women. Though worshipped as gods by the nations, they were abominations who were part spirit and part flesh. In the Bible, they are known as the Nephilim before the great flood and Rephaim after the flood. They are described as giants born from the union of fallen angels (spirits) and human women.

Azazel: Named in the book of Enoch as one of the Watchers—fallen angels who descended to earth and corrupted mankind. According to this ancient text, also found among the Dead Sea Scrolls, Azazel taught forbidden knowledge, including weapons of war and ornaments of vanity, leading humanity into sin. Some later traditions link his name to the wilderness figure in Leviticus 16, the scapegoat of the Day of Atonement. While the book of Enoch is not inspired Scripture, it mirrors Genesis 6:4 and other biblical themes. In *Lightborn*, we draw from it carefully—only where it does not contradict Scripture, where Scripture is silent, and where the idea remains theologically possible within a sound biblical framework.

Dingir (𒀭): The Sumerian word for "god" or "divine being." *Dingir-meš* is the plural form (gods). In cuneiform, it was used as a determinative, placed before the names of deities, such as 𒀭*Enki* or 𒀭*Inanna*, to mark them as divine. While the term could refer to any celestial being, *dingir* originally referred to the supreme deity when written alone. The early Semitic peoples (descendants of Noah's son, Shem), later known as the Akkadians, used the word *Ilu* (or *Il*) for "God," which later became *El* in Hebrew. These names referred not to a pantheon, but to the one true Creator, the God Most High.

É-abzu (𒂍𒍪𒀊): *É* means the "house/temple" (Sumerian); *abzu* (Akkadian *apsû*) means the subterranean fresh waters ("the deep"). Thus *É-abzu* refers to the "House of the Deep Waters." In Eridug (Eridu) this was *Enki's* chief shrine, also known as *É-engur*/*É-engura* ("House of the Waters"). This fits *Enki's* realm of water, wisdom, and craft. Archaeology shows it was rebuilt many times (about 18 superimposed temples), later overbuilt by Ur-Nammu's ziggurat.

Eagle & Serpent: Ancient symbols representing two rival cults and rival gods. The eagle was linked to Kish and the worship of *El*. Though in time, corrupted tribes began calling Him *An*, twisting His image. The serpent was tied to Eridu and the cult of *Enki*, symbolizing hidden knowledge, the deep, and forbidden power.

Enki (𒀭𒂗𒆠): The name *Enki* literally means "lord of the earth" in Sumerian texts. He is portrayed as a powerful and cunning figure associated with water, wisdom, magic, and creation. In Sumerian myth, he appears as *Enlil's* younger brother, opposing the God Most High and His Son. His primary symbols are the serpent and the goat-fish, representing his dominion over both land and water. *Enki's* cult began in Eridu, one of the most ancient cities in southern Sumer, even before the great flood.

In the world of *Lightborn*, once a being of light, *Enki* twisted sacred knowledge and gave it to humanity through the fallen angels—introducing mysticism, sorcery, and forbidden arts. He taught rebellion against the Most High and seduced the descendants of Cain with promises of divine power and immortality, just as he first deceived Adam and Eve in the garden. He became the ruler of false gods, the corrupter of truth, and the architect of the serpent cult that spread across the ancient world.

In the New Testament, *Enki* is called the "god of this world" (2 Corinthians 4:4), who claimed dominion over the earth and led humanity away from *El Elyon* (the God Most High), working through other fallen angels whom people worshipped as false gods (Deuteronomy 32:17; 1 Corinthians 10:20).

According to ancient timelines, Eridu existed both before and after the flood, making it one of the oldest known cities in human history. After the flood, his cult resurfaced in the rebuilt city of Eridu, regarded by the ancients as the first city ever founded. There, a great tower-temple was raised in *Enki's* honor—a ziggurat, built in defiance of heaven and remembered in Scripture as the Tower of Babel. Its ruins, known as the *E-abzu* ("House of the Deep"), still mark the place where humanity's first post-flood rebellion began.

Enlil (𒂗𒆤): In Sumerian tradition, *Enlil* was the "Lord of the Air," son of *An*, who ruled the space between heaven and earth. He acted as divine mediator and enforcer of decree, commanding weather, breath, and the fates of mankind. His main temple was the *E-kur* in Nippur, where he was revered as the chief god of authority and order in the Sumerian pantheon. He was seen as the king over the other gods or the god of gods. However, the Sumerian and Semitic people lived alongside one another (sons of Noah). The Semitic title *Il-Il* ("God of gods") later became known in Akkadian as *Ilil* or *Ellil*, corresponding to the Sumerian *Enlil* (𒂗𒆤), meaning "Lord of Wind" or "Lord of Command." The earliest known references to *Enlil* appear on proto-cuneiform tablets from Uruk (Level IV–III, ca. 3100–2900 BC) and later in temple archives at Nippur, his principal cult center.

In the world of *Lightborn*, over time, *Il-lil* was reinterpreted by post-flood cultures by descendants from Ham (son of Noah), which means it might have happened before the flood as well, but through the descendants of Cain. The Sumerians, a civilization in Mesopotamia living alongside the Semites (Akkadians), adopted him into their pantheon and renamed him. The Sumerians renamed *Il-Il* or *Elil* to *Enlil*. By the late Uruk period (after

2850 BC), *Enlil* was never elevated above *An* (Sumerian name that replaced *El*), but had the role of kingship over the other gods (just like Yahweh's role over angels) receiving titles such as "God of the Mountain" and "King of the Divine Assembly." After the flood, the Sumerians constructed *Enlil's* great temple in Nippur, which still stands in ruins today. It is possible they rebuilt it upon the foundations of a pre-flood temple, knowledge that Nimrod, the first king of Shinar, would have possessed. The temple in Nippur was known as *E-kur* (𒂍𒆳). The meaning of *E-kur* is house (*E*) of the mountain (*Kur*). The *E-kur* was considered the cosmic center of the world, where heaven and earth met. Kings from all Sumerian and later Babylonian cities sought legitimacy by honoring *Enlil* there.

As the king of the gods, *Enlil* became known as the "Voice of the Assembly"—one who made declarations on behalf of the gods. However, a remnant of early Semitic families may still have seen Him as *Il-Il* from ancient times, as the Word or Son of *El* in a symbolic or theological sense—an idea passed down through Abraham's ancestors long before formal religious texts were written.

In *Lightborn*'s world, He is remembered as the same God who walked with Adam in the garden, who warned Noah of the flood, and who called Abram to be set apart. After God confused humanity with different languages at the Tower of Babel, in those early days, He was known in the Hebrew tongue (a semitic language) as *El Shaddai*, and later revealed another name to Moses—Yahweh (Exodus 6:3). In Deuteronomy 32:8-9, *El Elyon* assigns His portion to Yahweh—Israel. In the most ancient times, people understood God as one Being yet more than one Person, but the Sumerians rebelled against Him and distorted that truth into the false religion of polytheism.

In later Sumerian myth, *Il* was transformed into *An*, and *Il-Il* into *Enlil*. They gave *Enlil* a wife, *Ninlil*, and introduced another figure, *Enki*, "lord of the earth," portrayed as *Enlil's* new younger brother and symbolized by the serpent and the goat-fish. More false gods followed. These revisions reshaped the early belief in one Creator into a system of many deities. Later Hebrew texts—the Tanakh (Old Testament)—reject this view, describing such beings as deceiving or fallen spirits (see Deuteronomy 32:17; Psalm 106:37).

This process of distortion reached its peak in the days of Nimrod—called *Enmerkar* in Sumerian sources—a king from the line of Ham (one of Noah's sons). Under his rule, the worship of the true Creator was replaced with a system of lesser gods (fallen spirits), and powerful hybrid beings called Rephaim (like the Nephilim before the flood), often worshipped as earthly gods or demigods.

This marked the revival of the ancient rebellion—echoing the pre-flood era when divine beings were wrongly honored as gods among men.

Ereshkigal (𒀭𒊩𒌆𒆠𒃲): Goddess of the underworld. Worshipped as the ruler of the realm of the dead and invoked in funerary rites.

Geshtinanna (𒀭𒃾𒀭𒈾): Goddess of agriculture, fertility, dreams, and loyalty. Associated with mourning, royal destiny, and the mysteries of kingship and the spirit realm.

Il (𒀭): "*Il*" (or *Ilu*) is the early Semitic word for "god," later corresponding to *El* in Northwest Semitic languages such as Hebrew and Ugaritic. The cuneiform sign 𒀭 (*Dingir*) was the divine determinative placed before the names of gods, but when written alone, it denoted *Il*, the Most High God—the supreme creator and ruler of the heavens. In the Sethite tradition (descendants of Seth), and later among the Semites (descendants of Shem), He was known as *El*, or in Hebrew, *El Elyon*, the God Most High. Earliest evidence: References to *Il* (written as *Ilu*) appear in early Akkadian cuneiform texts from Ebla and Mari in northern Mesopotamia (ca. 2400–2300 BC), marking the first known Semitic attestations of the divine title *Il* as "God." This is before Abraham's time if we take the Masoretic timeline. Noah, Shem, Arphaxad, Shelah, and Eber were all still alive. The world was being divided into nations (Peleg's era), and the post-flood civilizations, like those that produced Ebla and Uruk, were rising. If we follow the Septuagint timeline, the name *Il* on ancient tablets would reflect the memory of the Most High preserved by Eber's line, even as the nations drifted into idolatry.

Il-Il or Il-lil (𒀭𒀭): The Semitic title *Il-Il* ("God of gods") later became known in Akkadian as *Ilil* or *Ellil*, and it could have had a connection to the Sumerian *Enlil* (𒂗𒆤), meaning "Lord of Wind" or "Lord of Command." The earliest known references to *Enlil* appear on proto-cuneiform tablets from Uruk (Level IV–III, ca. 3100–2900 BC), which is the biblical Erech established by Nimrod who rebelled against the Most High (Genesis 10:8-10).

Later it appears in temple archives at Nippur, *Enlil's* principal cult center. The Semitic rendering *Ilil* emerges several centuries afterward, in Early Dynastic III to Old Akkadian texts (ca. 2500–2350 BC) from Nippur and Kish, where scribes began writing the name syllabically (*il-li-il*) or symbolically as ✱✱ (*Il-Il*: "God of gods").

While many scholars regard *Ilil* as a Semitic adaptation of the older Sumerian name *Enlil*, some suggest the reverse—that *Enlil* itself may have been influenced by an earlier Semitic divine title "*Il-Il*," reinterpreted within Sumerian phonetics and theology.

Il-Il or *Il-lil* was known to the earliest Semitic peoples—descendants of Shem (son of Noah and ancestor of Abraham)—as a powerful divine figure closely connected to *Il* (or *El*), the God Most High. His name appears in early Akkadian texts as *Il-Il* or *Ili-il*, a doubling of *Il*, the Semitic word for "god" or "God." Some early traditions may have seen *Il-Il* or *Il-lil* not as a separate deity, but as *Il's* divine agent or Son—one who shared His essence and spoke with His authority. This echoes later biblical ideas of *El Shaddai* ("God Almighty" or "God of the Mountain"), who revealed Himself to Abram, then later to Moses as Yahweh, and was ultimately fulfilled in Yeshua (Jesus), whose name means "Yahweh is salvation." No man could see *El*, the Most High and live, but it was well known from the most ancient times that He did reveal Himself to humans physically through the Lord, starting at the garden of Eden (Genesis 3:8). The Hebrew phrase "הָלֵךְ בַּגָּן" (*hā·lēḵ ba·gān*) literally means "walking in the garden," implying movement and presence, not just a voice or vision. Later He was also known as "the Angel" (The messenger), not just "a" messenger but "the" Messenger of God. The New Testament calls Jesus the One sent by God, and the Messenger of the Covenant (fulfilling Malachi 3:1). He is not a created angelic messenger, but God Himself revealed in human form, delivering the Father's message of salvation.

In the world of *Lightborn*, *Il-Il* is a divine figure known to early Sethites (descendants of Seth) as the Lord, or the agent or "Son" of *Il*/*El*, the God Most High. His name (*Il-Il*) means "God-God" and may reflect a doubling of *El's* essence. This suggests *Il-Il* not as a separate deity, but as one who shared *Il's* essence and spoke with His authority. The name *Elohim* (אֱלֹהִים) is the plural form of *El*, meaning "Gods" or "Mighty Ones." Yet in Genesis 1:1, it takes singular verbs, revealing one God expressed in plural majesty: "In the beginning *Elohim* created the heavens and the earth." God later speaks of Himself in the plural: "Let Us make man in Our image" (Genesis 1:26).

After the flood, the Sumerians adopted *Il-Il*/*Il-lil* into their pantheon and not only renamed him *Enlil*, but corrupted His true image. They also give Him titles like "God of the Mountain" and "King of the Divine Assembly." *Enlil* was known as the Voice of the Assembly, though early Semitic peoples recognized Him as the One who walked with Adam, and their descendants likely preserved this understanding—believing Him to be the same God who later appeared to Abraham as *El Shaddai*, revealed His name to Moses as Yahweh, and was ultimately made known to the world through Yeshua (Jesus), whose name means "Yahweh saves."

Inanna (𒀭𒈹) / Ishtar (𒀭𒈹𒌋𒁯): Goddess of love, war, sex, and fertility. Worshipped as the queen of heaven by the Cainites, known for her power, beauty, and wrath. Widely identified with Ashtoreth (Astarte), the goddess condemned in the Bible (e.g., 1 Kings 11:5; Judges 2:13).

Nanna (𒀭𒋀𒆠𒀭) / Sin (𒂗𒍪): Moon god, associated with calendars, timekeeping, and divination. Widely worshipped in Ur, the city of Abraham. Moon worship is condemned in Deuteronomy 17:3, and Abraham's call may have involved rejecting sin's worship.

Ninurta (𒀭𒊩𒌆𒄈𒋢): *Ningirsu* is another name for *Ninurta*, especially in the city of Lagash. Worshipped as a warrior god, associated with war, hunting, heroic feats, and agriculture. Seen as a protector of cities and bringer of victory in battle.

Ningirsu (𒀭𒊩𒌆𒄈𒋢): Also called *Ninurta*, the god of agriculture, war, and the city of Lagash.

Ninhursag (𒀭𒊩𒌆𒄯𒊕): Also called *Ninmah* or *Damkina*. Earth and mother goddess, associated with fertility, mountains, and childbirth. Regarded as the mother of several gods, including gods of healing and wisdom. Possibly connected to Asherah, the Canaanite mother goddess condemned in Scripture (e.g., 1 Kings 14:23).

Shamsiel: A fallen celestial being once associated with the sun god Shamash. Shamsiel overstepped divine boundaries and was chained by a spirit, judged by God for corrupting creation. He represents one of the many Watchers or fallen spirits mentioned in the book of Enoch and the Bible who rebelled in the days before the flood. Referenced in Genesis 6, 1 Enoch, and Jude 1:6.

Utu (𒀭𒌓) / Shamash (𒀭𒌓𒁉): Sun god of justice and divine law. Worshipped as the revealer of truth, judgment, and cosmic order. Sun worship is condemned in 2 Kings 23:5. Shamash reflects a counterfeit justice system opposed to *El*.

PLACES AND CULTURES

Bad-Tibira (𒂦𒋾𒊏𒆠): A forge-city founded by descendants of Cain. Known for its craftsmen and smiths, it became a hub of technological corruption and the making of weapons and tools through forbidden knowledge.

Cainites: Descendants of Cain, the eldest son of Adam and Eve. In the world of *Lightborn*, they worship fallen angels as gods, like *Enki*.

Enoch: The first city built by Cain, named after his son. A place of defiance and early rebellion, it became a center of pride, control, and the first shadows of divine corruption.

Eridu (𒉣𒆠): One of the first cities, founded by Cain's descendants. It became the spiritual center of the serpent cult and the worship of *Enki*, the deceiver who usurped *Il-lil's* place as god of the earth. Eridu is known for its grand ziggurat, a towering temple devoted to water, sorcery, and hidden knowledge that led many into corruption.

E-šarra (𒂍𒊹): An ancient Sumerian word meaning "sanctuary" or "divine dwelling." In *Lightborn*, E-šarra is a fictional village representing one of the many forgotten settlements of the ancient world. It became a sacred refuge—a place of safety in an age when the world had turned violent, both from wild animals and from men who had become more beast than human. In the shadows of growing darkness, E-šarra stood as a quiet haven where the faithful could still dwell under *El's* covering.

Etana's Kingdom: A northern realm of peace and justice, ruled by the *lugal* Etana and marked by the emblem of the eagle. In *Lightborn*, it is a symbol of *Il* and *Il-Il*, representing divine power and righteous rule. Known for its faithfulness to *El's* commandments and its rejection of slavery, Etana's kingdom stood as a beacon of light in a world darkened by violence and pride.

Jabal Clan: A nomadic tribe descended from Jabal, son of Lamech. Fierce and warlike, they lived in tents, followed their flocks, and roamed the wild lands. Favored by gods like Ninurta, the Jabal Clan loved to fight, settled disputes through duels, and honored strength above all. Feared and respected, they thrived by a brutal code where only the strong survived.

Kish ([cuneiform]): A city of kingship and early power. Though once dedicated to *El*, its people turned away and began calling Him *An*, twisting His image.

Larak ([cuneiform]): A lesser-known but ancient city, hidden deep in the South. Whispers speak of strange clans dwelling there, far from the sight of *El's* righteous ones.

Magan ([cuneiform]): A harsh mining region in the far south of Mesopotamia, known today as Oman. In ancient records, Magan was famed for its copper and stone quarries and traded with the cities of Sumer. In *Lightborn*, Magan became a brutal slave camp used by the corrupted cities—a place where captives toiled beneath the earth in bindings. Men and women were treated as tools, stripped of dignity, and worked until death. Though rich in resources, the land itself seemed cursed by their blood. Magan stands as a symbol of oppression and the darkness that overtook the hearts of mankind.

Mount Senir: Also known as Mount Hermon in the Bible. Called Sirion by the Sidonians and Senir by the Amorites (Deuteronomy 3:9). Earliest extra-biblical mentions: Sirion in Egyptian Execration Texts (c. 19th–18th c. BCE); Senir/Saniru in Late Bronze and Assyrian records. In this work we use "Senir," long remembered as the high border-mountain and, in later tradition, the oath-mountain of the Watchers in the book of Enoch.

Narath (fictional): A slave market near the southern mines of Magan. Known for its cruelty, Narath was where men, women, and even children were sold like animals. Controlled by corrupt children of Cain and guarded by brutal enforcers, Narath became a symbol of greed and human degradation in a world ruled by fear.

Nippur ([cuneiform]): A sacred city reigned by Seth's descendants, where the people still worship *Il* and honor *Il-Il* as His appointed servant. Known for its warriors, scribes, and devotion to truth, Nippur became a stronghold of righteousness, preserving the ancient ways in a world slipping into darkness. It holds great religious and cultural importance.

Nod: The land east of Eden, where Cain's descendants settled after he was cast out. Nod became a place of wandering, pride, and spiritual corruption—marked by increasing evil, mysticism, and sorcery. Here, the first cities rose, built on rebellion and fear, and the worship of false gods began to spread.

Sethites: Worshippers of *Il* (*El*) and *Il-Il* (*El-El*), the descendants of Seth, the third son of Adam and Eve. In *Lightborn*, the Sethites preserved the ancient truth of the Most High, resisting the corruption that spread through the line of Cain. Known for their integrity, long life, and closeness to *El*, they upheld divine order in a world slipping into darkness. From their lineage came prophets, warriors, and builders of hope. They were a remnant destined to carry light through the age of darkness.

Shuruppak (𒋢𒆳𒊒𒆠): The last city to hear the warnings before the flood. Some say the righteous dwelled there before being led away, while others claim it was the last place to fall into ruin.

Sippar (𒌓𒄒𒉣𒆠): A city devoted to the worship of false light and celestial knowledge. Its priests studied the heavens but were seduced by fallen spirits masquerading as bringers of truth.

Tubal-Cain Clan: Descendants of Tubal-Cain, master of metal and fire. Skilled in forging weapons, tools, and instruments of war, this clan became the builders of blades, chariots, and bindings. They used their skill to serve the fallen—spreading violence through their creations. Their forges burned hottest in Bad-Tibira, the great forge-city where blood and bronze flowed side by side.

Umma (𒄑𒆵): A real Sumerian city-state, located near modern Tell Jokha in southern Iraq. In *Lightborn*, Umma is portrayed as a neutral stronghold, marked by the emblem of the lion—a symbol of strength and balance. Its prominence during the Age of Leo, when the stars reflected the dominion of the lion, gave the city an air of celestial significance. While others fell to war or corruption, Umma held a fragile peace, respected by some and distrusted by others.

Unugki (𒌦𒆠): Unugki means "the place of Unug" and is the ancient Sumerian name for Uruk (biblical Erech), one of the oldest cities in Mesopotamia. Its great temple, the Eanna (𒂍𒀭) or "House of Heaven," was first dedicated to *An* (*Anu*), the supreme sky god. Uruk stood near the center of ancient Sumer, forming part of a sacred triad: In the North stood Nippur, the seat of *Enlil* (*Ilil*), lord of air and divine command. In the heart of Sumer was Uruk (Unugki), the dwelling of *An* (*Il*), god of heaven and in the South stood Eridu. The dark domain of *Enki*, ruler of the deep (Apsu).

Later, Inanna (Ishtar) became Uruk's chief deity, but An's worship came first. In the Bible, Uruk is known as Erech, one of the cities founded by Nimrod after the flood (Genesis 10:10). In the world of *Lightborn*, Unugki was first the City of *Il*, where the Most High was worshipped by the sons of light before the corruption of the pantheon. It was likely a pre-flood city, later rebuilt after the flood, when the memory of *Il* was replaced by *An*, and the worship of one God gave way to many.

TITLES AND ROLES

En (𒂗): A title meaning "lord" or "priest," often used for rulers with religious authority, such as the high priest of a city's main deity. The title was also used in names of deities, highlighting their dominion and sacred power. Some rulers were seen as gods, especially when the Nephilim kings started to rule.

En-Lugal (𒂗𒈗): A combined title signifying dual authority as both a priest (*En*) and king (*Lugal*). Though rare in texts, it reflects the ancient belief in rulers as divine intermediaries who governed both spiritual and civil life.

Kalû (𒍑𒆪): A ritual singer or priest who performed sacred songs, laments, and prayers in temple ceremonies. Kalû priests were believed to channel divine emotion through music, especially during rites for Inanna and funerary processions.

Lugal (𒈗): The Sumerian word for "king," used for rulers of city-states. Literally meaning "great man," the title reflects the political and military leadership entrusted to the king.

Šanga (𒋃): A temple official or high-ranking priest responsible for administration and ritual oversight. Often managing temple property and coordinating sacred duties, the šanga held both spiritual and economic power in ancient cities.

COMMON TERMS

Abba (𒀊𒀊): Sumerian word for "father." This term is used to denote the paternal figure, often associated with authority and lineage. Written as AB.AB, but in our novel *abba* is more fitting.

Ama (𒂼): Sumerian word for "mother." It represents the nurturing and life-giving aspect of the feminine, central to family and lineage.

Apsu (𒀊𒍪): The primordial freshwater ocean beneath the earth, representing the source of all life and wisdom. In Sumerian mythology, Apsu is the domain of *Enki*, the god of wisdom and magic, and a symbol of creation, fertility, and hidden knowledge.

Arad-muš (𒀵𒈲): A compound Sumerian term meaning "slave of the serpent." The word *arad* (𒀵) means "slave" or "servant," indicating one who is bound to serve another. The word *muš* (𒈲) means "serpent" or "snake," a powerful symbol of the god *Enki* and the evil clans of Cain. Together, *arad-muš* signifies someone who is enslaved under the serpent clan.

Dugud ([cuneiform]): Sumerian word meaning "heavy" or "weighty." Can refer to physical mass or symbolic burden.

Dumu (𒌉): Sumerian word for "child" or "offspring." Used for both male and female unless specified by gender suffixes.

Dumu-meš (𒌉𒈨): *Dumu* means "child," and *meš* is the plural suffix for living beings. This form means "children" or "offspring" in plural form.

Dumu-munus (𒌉𒊩): *Dumu* means "child" or "offspring," and *munus* (𒊩) refers to "woman" or "female." Together, the term means "daughter" or "female child."

Dumu-nita (𒌉𒍑): *Dumu* means "child," and *nita* (𒍑) refers to "male" or "man." Combined, it means "son" or "male child."

Dusa ([cuneiform]): A common Sumerian term meaning "friend" or "companion." It denotes a general social bond or association and is used more neutrally than *ki-ág*, without necessarily implying deep affection or intimacy.

Gu ([cuneiform]): Sumerian word meaning tooth or mouth. It can be used in reference to biting, chewing, or speaking.

Ki-ág ([cuneiform]): It literally means "beloved," "dear one," or "someone loved" (built from the verb *to love*). This term refers to a person who is deeply valued and emotionally close, often expressing affection, trust, or a bonded relationship rather than a neutral friendship.

Lu-kur ([cuneiform]): Sumerian term meaning "man of the foreign land" or "foreigner." It was used to describe outsiders or strangers from distant regions beyond the settled cities.

Lu-kur-meš ([cuneiform]): Sumerian term meaning "strangers" or "foreigners." It is the plural of *lu-kur*—describing people from distant lands or those outside the known and righteous cities.

-Meš ([cuneiform]): The suffix is commonly used to denote plural forms, especially for living beings.

Nin ([cuneiform]): This is the Sumerian word for "sister," referring to a female sibling or a close, sisterly relationship.

Nin-meš ([cuneiform]): This is the plural form, "sisters," used to indicate more than one sister or a group of female siblings.

Šeš ([cuneiform]): Sumerian word for "brother." The term *šeš* refers to a male sibling or a close, fraternal relationship between individuals.

Šeš-meš ([cuneiform]): "Brothers," the plural form of *šeš*, used to indicate more than one brother or a group of male siblings.

Šulmu ([cuneiform]): "Peace" or "may it be well," often used as a blessing or greeting, akin to "Amen" in modern usage, signifying a wish for harmony and well-being.

Zabbaršu ([cuneiform]): A polished bronze mirror used in ancient Sumerian culture. Crafted from highly reflective metal, it symbolized beauty, clarity, and sacred reflection.

Zi-ga é-gal ([cuneiform]): A sacred union rite performed between a king and a priestess atop a temple. The phrase means "arousing in the palace," symbolizing the union of heaven and earth. *Zi-ga* means "to rise" or "arouse," and *é-gal* translates to "palace" or "temple." Much later, the Greeks called this Hieros Gamos. The ritual reflected divine blessing and fertility through sacred intimacy.

ANIMALS AND CREATURES

Abzu Ušumgal (poetic): A title used to describe a great serpent or dragon from the deep. While not attested in ancient texts as a compound, it combines "*abzu*" (primordial deep) and "*ušumgal*" (great serpent), symbolizing chaos, power, and ancient primal forces.

Gu-us ([cuneiform]) **(speculative):** A poetic name meaning "raising the neck," derived from *GU* ([cuneiform]), meaning "bull," and *US* ([cuneiform]), meaning "to rise" or "to lift." Though not attested for creatures in historical texts, the phrase is used here to describe towering, long-necked dragons seen in ancient depictions—majestic beings that roamed the world before the flood.

Gud.sag.ga ([cuneiform]): Literally "hairy bull" or "bull of the plain." Referred to in ancient tales as a woolly mammoth. Not attested for mammoths in historical texts, but plausible as a descriptive term.

Gudmušen ([cuneiform]) **(speculative):** A creative compound of *gud* ([cuneiform]), meaning "bull," and *mušen* ([cuneiform]), meaning "bird." This name is used to describe a towering avian creature, combining the power of a bull with the wings of a great bird. Though not attested in historical texts, it reflects the mythic grandeur of ancient beast-lore. A creative compound of "bull" and "bird," describing a powerful avian beast. Not found in historical texts but fitting for mythological blending.

Mušmaḫḫu ([cuneiform]): A serpent-dragon from Mesopotamian mythology, often described as a hybrid creature with traits of a lion and a bird. Sometimes identified with the seven-headed serpent defeated by the warrior-god *Ninurta*. This chaos beast echoes the Leviathan mentioned in Psalm 74:14 and Job 41.

Mušḫuš ([cuneiform]): Translated as "reddish/fierce serpent." A well-known dragon-like creature associated with divine protection, often seen on the Ishtar Gate.

Simu (𒋛𒈬): Likely a term for horned animals, used to describe strong wild creatures marked by their horns.

Sisi (𒋛𒋛): Historically means "horse" in later Mesopotamian periods. Not "wild donkey," but usable with contextual clarification.

Šeg-mušen (speculative): *Šeg* means "cry," and *mušen* means "bird." Invented term for a loud-voiced bird known for its piercing call.

Ugubi (𒌑𒄖𒁉): Correct term for "monkey." Used in ancient texts and lexical lists. It appears in a well-known literary tablet, the "Letter from Ugubi to Mother" (CDLI Literary 000579, ca 1900–1600 BCE, Nippur), in which "what the monkey says" appears in the colophon. The Sumerian word for "monkey" (often written UGU.DU(BI)), attested in scholarship as probably pronounced *ugubi.*

Uḫuš (𒄷𒍽): The Sumerian word for normal-sized bear.

Uḫuš-gal (𒄷𒍽𒃲): This term is used for a "great bear." In our novel, it refers to the massive, now-extinct bears that once roamed the earth—far larger than any modern grizzly. These colossal beasts are feared and respected in the world of *Lightborn*, known for their immense strength and terrifying size.

U-muš-da-gur (speculative): A coined term meaning "horned dragon." Not historically attested, but works well for worldbuilding.

Ur-bar-ra (𒌨𒁇𒊏): A compound meaning "wild dog." Interpreted here as "wolf," which is fitting and plausible.

Ur-idim (𒌨𒅂): Accurately means "mad dog" or "demon-dog." A fierce beast in Mesopotamian demonology.

Ur-kal (𒌨𒆗) (fictional): A scavenging predator resembling a hyena or wild dog, known for its eerie cry and fierce pack behavior. *Ur* (𒌨) means "beast" or "dog," and *kal* (𒆗) conveys "strong" or "fierce." Though not attested in Sumerian records, this constructed name follows traditional linguistic structure and evokes the untamed spirit of the creature.

Ušumgal (𒈲𒌨𒃲): Attested title meaning "great serpent" or "dragon." Used also for powerful mythic beings, even gods like *Enki*. The term *ušum* (𒈲) primarily means "snake," but adding the word *gal* in the composite term *ušumgal* (𒈲𒃲), or "great snake," it refers to a mythical dragon-like creature. This word could possibly have been used for normal dragons as well. The word dinosaur replaced the word dragon only thousands of years later in 1841.

Ušum-mušen (𒈲𒈲𒄷) (speculative): A winged dragon whose name combines *ušum* (𒈲), meaning "dragon" or "serpent," and *mušen* (𒄷), meaning "bird." Though not attested as a compound in historical texts, this construction is linguistically plausible and used here to describe a creature that soars with the power of both serpent and sky.

Úr-maḫ (𒌨𒈤): Translates to "great dog" or "mighty wild animal." Can fittingly describe a lion.

Zu-gal (𒍪𒃲) (fictional): A fierce saber-toothed beast whose name means "great fang." *Zu* (𒍪) means "tooth/fang" and *gal* (𒃲) translates to "great/mighty." Though not attested as a phrase in historical texts, the construction is linguistically consistent and correct to reflect the creature's legendary strength and deadly bite.

MAIN CHARACTERS

Adam ([cuneiform]): The first human priest-king, also known as Adam in later historical records. Formed by God and entrusted with sacred authority, Adam served as a guardian of divine truth and a leader to his offspring. Alongside Eve, his wisdom and leadership shaped the generations to come, guiding them in the struggle between light and darkness.

Adriel: Seth's brother, a healer, and a source of wisdom for the group. Adriel's knowledge and compassionate nature offer healing and guidance.

Deborah: Uldako's mother, whose trials add depth to Uldako's journey. Deborah's strength and resilience despite her suffering provide motivation and a sense of purpose for Uldako.

Enkiar: A towering figure of raw power with broad shoulders. One of Seth's strongest warriors, Enkiar's physical prowess and strength are critical in battles and defense.

Enoch the Terrible: An evil son of Cain, representing the corruption and malevolence that stems from Cain's lineage. His actions and influence pose significant challenges to Uldako and his companions.

Enoch the Good: A prophetic figure from Seth's lineage, associated with Etana, the first king of Kish. Enoch's visions and wisdom offer guidance and hope, playing a crucial role in the battle against the forces of darkness.

Eve: She walked beside Adam, and though deceived by the serpent, she became the bearer of future generations. Her legacy is remembered with both sorrow and hope—as the one through whom life continued, even after the fall.

Haron: A young man who joins Uldako's quest for freedom. Haron's journey alongside Uldako highlights themes of camaraderie and the shared struggle for liberation.

Imani: A former slave under Lamech's rule, Imani overheard critical conversations about the creation of the *Ašag-dingir*, a new race of hybrid beings. Despite being dismissed by others, her knowledge and convictions play a key role in uncovering the dangerous plans of the fallen gods.

Ishara: A significant companion to Uldako, known for her beauty, strength, and unwavering support. She becomes a pivotal figure in Uldako's quest, demonstrating resilience and wisdom. Ishara's compassion and determination to stand by Uldako highlight her integral role in the story.

Jano: A good fighter, tracker, gentle healer, and herbalist. One of Seth's best warriors, Jano's diverse skills make him an indispensable member of the group.

Jem: A former hunter whose skills become crucial for the group's survival. Jem's expertise and experience provide practical support and contribute to the group's overall strength.

Kesia: A compassionate and quick-witted woman aiming to be the best blacksmith in the land while supporting Uldako's cause. Kesia's skills and determination contribute to the group's resilience and survival.

Khoran: A leader within Uldako's new camp and the father of Thurach and Melahl. Khoran's leadership and wisdom help in building and maintaining the new community.

Kunai: A little orphan boy who bonds with Uldako during their shared struggles. His journey from a vulnerable child to a young fighter represents growth and the impact of Uldako's mentorship. Kunai's development showcases themes of loyalty and courage.

Lamech the Evil: One of Uldako's biggest enemies and the great-grandson of Cain. His malevolence and power represent the ongoing threat posed by Cain's descendants.

Lamech the Good: A key figure from Seth's lineage, involved in prophetic visions about his child, Noah. Lamech's insights and leadership play a significant role in the unfolding events.

Mara: A fellow slave characterized by her frailty and resilience. Mara's story adds depth to the portrayal of slavery and the human soul's capacity to endure and overcome adversity.

Renju: A swift and skilled warrior known for his agility, quick reflexes, and a tendency to keep quiet. His silence often masks his keen observational skills and sharp mind.

Ruk: A member of Uldako's group, known for his stubbornness and eventual growth. Ruk's character arc demonstrates the stubborn nature of humanity, but also the transformative power of the journey and the strength found in unity.

Šarru (𒊬𒊒): An Akkadian word meaning "king, ruler, or guardian." In the story, this name is given to Uldako's bear companion, reflecting not only the creature's strength and protective nature, but also the deep bond of loyalty and honor between them. The pronunciation is *sharru,* and the name carries a tone of ancient authority and nobility.

Seth: Adam and Eve's son, a key figure in guiding Uldako and his companions. Seth's role as a leader and sage represents the continuation of Adam's wisdom and the fight against the growing darkness in the world.

Shamgar: A seasoned builder and one of Seth's five best warriors. Shamgar's construction skills and strategic mind are crucial in establishing and defending their safe camps.

Tiras: A noble and fierce warrior, younger brother of Seth, known for his battle-hardened experience and loyalty. Tiras' strength and leadership are vital assets to the group.

Uldako: The protagonist, a young slave who embarks on a journey toward freedom and self-discovery. Uldako's soul burns with an unyielding desire for freedom, and his path intersects with ancient prophecies and celestial beings as he seeks to uncover deeper truths about life, his heritage, and the cosmic struggle between light and darkness.

Zak, Dak, and Hak: Three warrior brothers associated with Seth, each with distinct personalities and skills. Zak is a realist, Dak is positive, and Hak is grumpy. Together, they provide training and support to Uldako and his companions.